Absolutely Truly

ALSO BY HEATHER VOGEL FREDERICK

The Mother-Daughter Book Club
Much Ado About Anne
Dear Pen Pal
Pies & Prejudice
Home for the Holidays
Wish You Were Eyre
Once Upon a Toad
The Voyage of Patience Goodspeed
The Education of Patience Goodspeed
Spy Mice: The Black Paw
Spy Mice: For Your Paws Only
Spy Mice: Goldwhiskers

Absolutely Truly

A Pumpkin Falls Mystery

HEATHER VOGEL FREDERICK

Simon & Schuster Books for Young Readers
NEW YORK • LONDON • TORONTO • SYDNEY • NEW DELHI

SIMON & SCHUSTER BOOKS FOR YOUNG READERS
An imprint of Simon & Schuster Children's Publishing Division
1230 Avenue of the Americas, New York, New York 10020
This book is a work of fiction. Any references to historical events, real people, or real places are used fictitiously. Other names, characters, places, and events are products of the author's imagination, and any resemblance to actual events or places or persons, living or dead, is entirely coincidental.
Text copyright © 2014 by Heather Vogel Frederick
Jacket illustration and hand-lettering copyright © 2014 by Charles Santoso
All rights reserved, including the right of reproduction in whole or in part in any form.
SIMON & SCHUSTER BOOKS FOR YOUNG READERS is a trademark of Simon & Schuster, Inc.
For information about special discounts for bulk purchases, please contact Simon & Schuster Special Sales at 1-866-506-1949 or business@simonandschuster.com.
The Simon & Schuster Speakers Bureau can bring authors to your live event.
For more information or to book an event, contact the Simon & Schuster Speakers Bureau at 1-866-248-3049 or visit our website at www.simonspeakers.com.
Jacket design by Krista Vossen
Interior design by Hilary Zarycky
The text for this book is set in Fournier.
Manufactured in the United States of America
0621 SKY
8 10 9 7
Library of Congress Cataloging-in-Publication Data
Frederick, Heather Vogel.
Absolutely Truly / Heather Vogel Frederick.—First edition.
pages cm.—(A Pumpkin Falls mystery)
Summary: Twelve-year-old Truly Lovejoy's family moves to a small town to take over a bookstore. Soon, she has to solve two mysteries involving a missing book and an undelivered letter.
ISBN 978-1-4424-2972-7 (hardcover)
ISBN 978-1-4424-2974-1 (eBook)
[1. Mystery and detective stories. 2. Families—Fiction. 3. Moving, Household—Fiction. 4. Community life—New Hampshire—Fiction. 5. New Hampshire—Fiction.] I. Title.
PZ7.F87217Ab 2014
[Fic]—dc23
2013046926

For my grandfathers

PROLOGUE

A week before the January thaw finally arrived in February, I found myself hanging like a bat from a rafter inside a church steeple, face-to-face with a bell made by Paul Revere.

If you'd have told me a month ago that I'd find myself in this position, I would have said you were crazy.

But then, a month ago my life was completely different. A month ago, my career as a middle-school private eye hadn't begun.

And by the way, it didn't begin inside a steeple. Absolutely truly not.

It began the day my report card made it home before I did.

CHAPTER 1

"What is THIS supposed to mean?" my father demanded as I followed my brother through the front door, our arms full of boxes. My father stalked across the entry hall, waving a slip of paper at me with his good hand.

Hatcher flashed me a sympathetic look and vanished upstairs. I didn't blame him; I'd have done the same thing in his place. No one wants to face the wrath of Lieutenant Colonel Jericho T. Lovejoy.

"An F plus in pre-algebra?" The chill in my father's voice could have single-handledly reversed global warming. "F *plus*, Truly?"

Yes, that's really my name. It's a family thing.

"Does that mean you almost passed, or that you failed spectacularly?" My father pinned me with one of his signature glares.

I hadn't counted on this—I thought it would take at least a week for mail from Texas to reach the East Coast. And I'd counted on being able to snag this particular envelope from the mailbox before anyone else spotted it.

"Um," I said.

"This is unacceptable, young lady."

Silence is the best strategy when my father gets like this.

"I don't understand it," he continued, pacing back and forth. "Not one bit. Lovejoys can do anything! We're naturally good at math."

Actually, there's a whole long list of things I can't do and that I'm not good at. Usually, though, math isn't one of them. It's one of my favorite subjects, in fact. But how was I supposed to concentrate on stupid pre-algebra when my world had been turned upside down? The F plus wasn't my fault; it was his, and I said so under my breath.

My father stopped midpace. "What was that?"

"Nothing, sir," I mumbled.

My father isn't one of those hypermilitary dads—when we lived on the base in Colorado, I had a friend whose father used to do actual room inspections for her and her brother every Saturday morning in full dress uniform, white gloves and all; still, all of us Lovejoy kids have been trained to add "sir" to the end of our sentences when we're talking to our dad, especially when we want to be on his good side.

And with a math grade like mine, that was definitely the side I wanted to be on.

My father grabbed his coat from off the banister. I resisted the urge to offer some help as he swung it awkwardly around his shoulders. No point adding fuel to the fire. "Wait until your mother hears about this."

That wasn't a conversation I was looking forward to. When my father's mad, at least everything's out in the open and you know where you stand. With my mother, whenever one of us messes up, she just looks at us sorrowfully and shakes her head, like we're the biggest disappointment in the history of the world. Which I probably am.

"Finish unpacking the car," my father said. "I'm heading back to the bookstore. And don't forget, you and Hatcher have Kitchen Patrol tonight."

And with that he left, slamming the door behind him.

I slumped down on the hall bench and banged my forehead against one of the boxes I was holding. It was so unfair! The math grade, the move—everything! Why couldn't we have just stayed in Texas?

This time, there wasn't even the prospect of moving someplace decent again in a year or two either. This time, I was stuck. Forever. In population you've-got-to-be-kidding-me Pumpkin Falls, New Hampshire.

CHAPTER 2

Bumpkin Falls would be a better name for it, I thought bitterly. I still couldn't believe we'd traded Austin for this peanut-sized blip on a map. And a very cold blip too. Winter lasts six months out of the year in Pumpkin Falls, and the likelihood of anything interesting ever happening was about the same as that of me sprouting wings. The nearest mall was an hour away. The town didn't even have a movie theater. It did have a swimming pool, at least. That was some consolation.

I stacked the boxes on the bench, carrying the one labeled TRULY'S BIRD BOOKS over to the bottom of the stairs. I'd take it up to my room later. "Hatcher!" I yelled. "Get yourself down here on the double! Dad wants us to finish unloading!"

I could hear my brother rattling around up there, and wondered what he was doing. Usually, the first thing that happens when we move into a new house, which is often since Dad is in the army, is that Hatcher and Danny run inside to stake out

ABSOLUTELY TRULY

their territory. Mom always lets them, because they're the oldest, I guess. This time, though, there was no territory to stake out. We all knew this particular house like the backs of our hands, and Mom and Dad had decided our room assignments back in Texas.

I opened the front door and was struck by a blast of icy wind. Shivering, I ran to the minivan for another armload of boxes. Dropping two of them on the sofa in the living room, I took the third into the dining room. We were traveling light this time, most of our furniture headed for storage since we wouldn't be needing it. The stuff here was much nicer than ours, anyway.

I rummaged in the box for place mats. I wouldn't win any brownie points with Dad if I shirked Kitchen Patrol—better known as "KP," Lovejoy shorthand for setting the table, helping with dinner, and doing the dishes.

"Where've you been?" I snapped as my brother finally galumphed down the stairs.

"Didn't go so well with Dad, huh?"

"Nope."

"Want to talk about it?"

"Nope."

If there's one good thing about Hatcher, it's that he knows when to leave me alone. He shrugged and vanished out the front door.

Counting out seven place mats and seven napkins, I

arranged them around the table. One set for each of my parents, a set each for my two older brothers and my two younger sisters, and a final set for me, smack-dab in the center of the Lovejoy lineup.

"Truly-in-the-Middle," Dad used to call me, back before he turned into Silent Man. He had a nickname for our family back then too—the Magnificent Seven. The theme song from the old movie used to be the ringtone on his cell phone.

The war changed all that.

Since he came home from Afghanistan, Silent Man doesn't joke around anymore, and there's no fun ringtone, and he hasn't once called me "Truly-in-the-Middle" or referred to our family as the Magnificent Seven. I don't know if we'll ever be that family again. "Magnificent" isn't exactly the word I'd use for us these days.

Six months ago, though, things were different. Six months ago, my life was perfect.

We were living in Texas, for one thing, instead of Nowheresville, New Hampshire. We'd moved to Austin after school got out in Fort Carson, Colorado, at the end of June, so that we could get everything ready for Dad's homecoming. He was set to return from his final tour of duty after Labor Day.

We were giddy the day we moved into the new house. My brothers and sisters and I could hardly believe it—a real, permanent home of our own, at last! And a nice one too, with a swimming pool out back and a big family room with a fireplace, and enough bathrooms so that us girls didn't have to share with Hatcher and Danny. No more rentals or temporary base housing, no more barely-unpacked-before-we-had-to-pack-everything-up-again lifestyle, no more switching schools every two years, along with teachers and coaches and neighbors and friends.

For the first time in my life I had a bedroom all to myself, and best of all, I was living in the same zip code as my cousin Mackenzie. Mom found us a house just down the street from Aunt Louise and Uncle Teddy's, which was the most awesome thing about moving to Texas as far as I was concerned.

Mackenzie and I were born a week apart, and the two of us have been best friends since we were in diapers. When we were little, we actually used to pretend we were twins. Not that anyone would ever mistake us for them. Mackenzie totally has the Gifford genes. She's just over five feet tall and cute as a button, with curly strawberry blond hair just like Uncle Teddy's, and just like my mom's and my little sister Pippa's.

I, on the other hand, have straight brown Lovejoy hair and am not even remotely petite. I've always been the tallest one in my class, but this past year, shortly after I turned twelve, I shot up to just under six feet. I felt like the scene in *Alice in Wonderland* after she eats the cake and grows that weird long neck and says good-bye to her feet, which she can hardly see anymore because she's such a giant.

HEATHER VOGEL FREDERICK

I wish I could say good-bye to my feet. They grew right along with me, unfortunately. I wear size ten and a half now, and my shoes look like something a clown would wear. Especially next to Mackenzie's.

My cousin is a really good best friend. She knows how much it bothers me to be so tall. My father calls me an Amazon. They were warrior women a zillion years ago, and I guess it makes sense for him to call me that, being a soldier and all, but still, that's a nickname I don't want to get stuck with. Anyway, Mackenzie promised to take me under her wing and introduce me to everyone when school started, so for once I'd be ahead of the curve. I'd be the cousin of cute, perky Mackenzie Gifford, instead of just the freakishly tall new girl.

After our family's move to Texas, Mackenzie and I had the best summer ever. I talked her into trying out with me for the summer swim team, and we rode our bikes to the pool every morning for practice, then hung out for the rest of the day at my house or hers. We had sleepovers and backyard barbecues, and she helped me pick out paint for my new room—a really pretty shade of aqua called "Mermaid." We went to the movies and shopping and to Amy's for ice cream at least once a week. July and August were heaven.

Then came Black Monday.

That's what Mom called it, afterward.

I was practicing the piano that morning while I waited for Mackenzie to finish breakfast and come over. Hatcher and

ABSOLUTELY TRULY

Danny had gone fishing, and Mom was paying bills and keeping an eye on my younger sisters, who had made a fort under the dining room table and were playing zoo with Lauren's hamster, Nibbles, and Thumper, her rabbit.

I didn't pay much attention at first when my mother's cell phone rang.

"J. T.!" she cried happily.

I looked up. She was talking to Dad! As I watched, though, her smile faded and the color drained from her face, until she was as white as the sheet music in front of me. My fingers stumbled on the piano keys, leaving a jangle of sour notes hanging in the air. Something was wrong.

My mother listened for a minute, then stood up abruptly, sending her chair toppling backward onto the floor. She pressed her cell phone against her chest and turned to us. "Go upstairs, girls."

My sisters poked their heads out from underneath the table.

"But, Mom—" Lauren protested.

"Now."

"Yes, ma'am," my sisters chorused. Wide-eyed, they scrambled out of hiding.

"Make sure y'all take those animals with you." My mother turned her back on us and raised the cell phone to her ear again.

Automatic pilot kicked in, the kind that obeyed without

question when given an order. I crossed the room, scooping up an armload of critters and hustling my protesting sisters up to the room they shared.

"What's happening?" Lauren asked me. "Is everything okay?"

I wasn't sure, and I didn't want to scare her. She's only nine. "It's probably nothing," I said, and steered her and Pippa over to Pippa's Barbie house.

I waited until they were busy building a new zoo, then slipped out of the room. I heard the front door open, and tiptoed over to crouch at the top of the stairs. I didn't care if it was bad news—I needed to know what was going on.

"Dinah, I'm so sorry." It was Aunt Louise. Uncle Teddy was with her, and he had his arms around Mom. She must have called and asked them to come over.

I squeezed my eyes shut tight. *Please, Dad, still be alive! Please, please, please!*

"He only had a few days left!" my mother sobbed. "Just a few days!"

My heart nearly stopped.

"He's just wounded, Dinah," Uncle Teddy murmured. "He'll be safe at home again soon."

My heart started again. Wounded was better than dead.

"What happened?" asked Aunt Louise. "Was it a helicopter accident?"

My father was an army pilot.

ABSOLUTELY TRULY

Mom shook her head. She drew a shaky breath. "IED," she replied.

My stomach lurched. I knew what that meant. Every military kid with a parent serving in a war zone knew what that meant: "Improvised Explosive Device"—a homemade enemy bomb.

I saw Aunt Louise and Uncle Teddy exchange a glance.

"How did he sound when you talked to him?" Uncle Teddy asked gently, and my mother let out a soft sound, halfway between a sigh and a moan.

"Not like himself!" She started to cry again, and Aunt Louise patted her shoulder. After a few moments, my mother drew another shaky breath, then added, "He's in the hospital in Kabul, but he's being transferred soon to Germany. I want to book a flight just as soon as possible."

"You leave that to me," my uncle told her.

Everything was a bit of a blur after that. As the news of my father's injury spread, the rest of Mom's family started to gather. My mother has six brothers scattered all over Texas, so there were a lot of aunts and uncles and cousins underfoot for a couple of days.

In the end, while Mom flew to Germany to be with Dad, Aunt Louise, Uncle Teddy, and Mackenzie came to stay with Danny and Hatcher and my little sisters and me. Over the next few weeks there were lots of phone calls at odd hours, and whispered conversations between the adults, and then, finally, a videoconference with Dad. He didn't say much, but I was relieved to see that he looked like himself. Well, mostly. If you didn't count the fact that where his right arm should have been there was a whole lot of nothing.

"Upper extremity loss," the military calls it.

"He's alive," Mom reminded us every time she called to talk to us, first from Germany and later from the military hospital in Maryland. "We need to be grateful for that. Not every family is as fortunate as we are."

She meant the Larsons. Dad's best friend, Tom Larson, had been in the same transport hit by the IED, and he wasn't coming home. I couldn't even imagine how his family must be feeling. We'd spent lots of time with them over the years—we'd even gone to Disney World together last spring break.

"Your father's going to get through this, and so will we," Mom told us.

I didn't see how, though, and I couldn't stop worrying about it.

Not that anyone noticed. You wouldn't think I'd be that hard to overlook, given the fact that I'm now the family Clydesdale. Somehow, though, I still tend to get lost in the shuffle.

My cousin Mackenzie is an only child, and after just a few days of looking after the five of us Lovejoys, I could tell that Uncle Teddy's and Aunt Louise's heads were spinning. I guess they decided that divide and conquer was their only hope of survival, because pretty soon my uncle was busy having lots of man-to-man talks with my brothers, while my aunt turned her attention to us girls. Which mostly meant Pippa.

My baby sister is a Drama Queen with a capital *DQ*. Pippa may just be a kindergartner, but she knows how to grab the spotlight. She can turn on the waterworks at the drop of a hat. And with her halo of blonde curls, two missing front teeth, and pink sparkly glasses—well, hardly anybody stands a chance. Pippa had Aunt Louise wrapped around her pinkie finger in nothing flat.

Mackenzie and I were assigned to keep an eye on Lauren, meanwhile, which pretty much left me to fend for myself. I didn't say anything, though, because I knew everybody was doing the best they could.

By mid-September, my father was deep into physical therapy, learning how to use his new temporary prosthesis—the fake arm he'll have to wear—and adjusting to life as a lefty. I could only imagine how that was going. My father is not the world's most patient person.

"He's a real trouper" was all my mother ever said, but from the tone of her voice I could tell that wasn't the whole story.

Somewhere in the middle of all this, school started. Before Black Monday, I'd actually been looking forward to it, which is kind of unusual for me. Since military families move every couple of years, you'd think I'd be used to changing schools. This is our normal. For me, though, I'd always dreaded that first day, especially since I turned into Truly the Amazon. Austin had felt different, thanks to Mackenzie, and for once I didn't have butterflies stomping around in my stomach during the weeks leading up to it.

After Dad was injured, though, I didn't think about school at all one way or the other. It just kind of snuck up on me. I was pretty dazed that first week, even though Mackenzie took me under her wing just like she said she would. Her friends were all really nice to me and everything, but somehow it all felt wrong, like I was sleepwalking or something.

I tried to act normal, and I tried to focus on my classes, and I made an effort to get involved, the way my mother's always urging me to do whenever she catches me moping after one of our moves. I continued swimming, and I even joined a bird-watching club, ignoring Mackenzie's snarky little comments about my bird obsession.

Which isn't an obsession. Not really. Well, okay, maybe a little bit.

It didn't help that Mackenzie had suddenly become interested in boys. And not just boys in general, but one boy in particular: Cameron McAllister, seventh-grade star of Austin's Nitro Swim Club. All my cousin wanted to talk about was how cute he was, how funny he was, and how she was pretty sure that he liked her back.

Crushes were the furthest thing from my mind. It was all I could do just to get through each day. In spite of my efforts

ABSOLUTELY TRULY

to blend in and be normal, underneath I was anything but. Underneath, I was "Hi-my-name-is-Truly-and-my-father-just-lost-his-arm-in-the-war." I thought about Dad all the time. I couldn't help it. I wondered if he was scared when the bomb exploded. I wondered how he felt about losing his best friend. And I wondered if he'd ever be able to fly again.

The one thing my father loves more than anything else in the world, except maybe us, is flying. Being a pilot was his life. Would he still be able to fly, with just one arm? I had so many questions.

And then he finally came home, and my life turned upside down again.

CHAPTER 3

"J. T., what are you thinking?" I overheard Mom ask as my father hung up the phone in the kitchen. He'd been back in Texas less than a week. "They made it very clear they want you, despite—you know, everything."

"A one-armed wrestling coach?" Dad scoffed. "That's about as useful as a one-armed pilot. It wouldn't be fair to the team in the long run, and I don't need their pity."

"That's just pride talking and you know it. You have plenty to offer."

My brother and I, who were doing our homework at the dining room table, looked at each other wide-eyed. We probably weren't supposed to be hearing this conversation.

"Did Dad just turn down UT?" Hatcher whispered.

"Um, I think so," I whispered back.

"That can't be good."

The whole reason my parents had decided to settle in

ABSOLUTELY TRULY

Texas—besides the fact that my mom's family was there—was because my father had two job offers lined up. The airline he was going to fly for was based out of Austin, and on top of that, the University of Texas had offered him a part-time job as an assistant wrestling coach. Dad had been an all-star wrestler for the Longhorns, recruited out of high school on a scholarship, and UT was where he'd met Mom. After college, he'd joined the army, but he and his former coach had stayed in touch, and when UT heard he was retiring, they'd jumped at the chance to add him to their coaching staff.

All of this was before Black Monday, of course. Since the injury, my father's plans for flying had been dashed. Apparently commercial airlines aren't exactly lining up to hire one-armed pilots.

And now it looked like his wrestling days were over too.

Dad wouldn't reconsider, despite Mom's pleas. Lieutenant Colonel Jericho T. Lovejoy has a stubborn streak.

After that, he turned into Silent Man. He barely went out, and none of us kids quite knew how to act around him. We're used to Dad either barking orders or joking around, but while the barking continued, the joking did not. Our fun-loving father seemed to have vanished into thin air. He still got up every morning, still shaved, still got dressed in khaki pants and a white shirt, his usual off-duty uniform. But he rarely wore his prosthesis—the hook at the end of it scared Pippa—so one shirtsleeve was usually empty, and there was an emptiness to the rest of him too. Mom tried to make up for it by being extra cheerful, but by Halloween, her upbeat attitude had wilted, and she was looking strained and pale.

And then Gramps and Lola showed up.

The two of them arrived unannounced in early November, a taxi having deposited them on our doorstep one evening just as we were finishing dinner.

"We thought it would be fun to surprise you!" Lola told Dad, giving him a hug. She stepped back and looked him up and down, then patted his good arm. "You're looking well, J. T. Much better than when we saw you in Maryland."

My grandmother turned and spotted me. "Truly!" she cried, flinging out her arms.

"Lola!" I cried back, flinging myself into them. We've always called her Lola instead of Nana or Grandma or anything like that. Mom says it's because her name is catnip to kids, the way it rolls off the tongue, like "lullaby" or "lollipop."

"How's my most beautiful eldest granddaughter?"

I laughed. "You mean your *only* eldest granddaughter, right?"

"You're still beautiful," she replied, kissing me on the cheek.

When Lola says something like that, I almost believe her.

Lola and Gramps are two of my favorite people in the whole world. They live in New Hampshire, where Dad grew

ABSOLUTELY TRULY

up, and where they own a bookshop. We usually go to see them every summer, but this summer, because of the move and because of Dad's injury, we didn't make it there. Having them turn up in Texas was a nice surprise.

The real surprise came the next morning, though, when they sprang the true reason for their visit on us.

"We've joined the Peace Corps!" Lola announced at breakfast.

We all looked at her like she'd said she was planning to take up belly dancing.

"You're kidding, right?" said my father.

"It's something we've always wanted to do," Gramps explained.

"Since when?"

"There's a lot about your mother and me that you don't know, son," Gramps said loftily.

My dad's hippie-dippie sister is usually the one to drop bombshells like this. Aunt True—who's named after the original Truly Lovejoy, just like me—is always heading off to go trekking in Nepal or sea kayaking in Patagonia or volunteering in some third-world orphanage. She sends us postcards from all over. Our fridge looks like the United Nations made a house call.

I looked at my grandparents, trying to imagine them in the Peace Corps. If they were birds, Lola would be a dove, small and serene. Gramps, on the other hand, with his piercing gaze, bushy eyebrows, and prominent nose—he calls it "the Lovejoy proboscis"—was more of a great horned owl. He was quiet like an owl too. Quiet like me. Gramps was the one who'd gotten me hooked on birding. Whenever we get together for a visit, he takes me on walks and tells me the names of all the birds we see. He sends me bird books every Christmas and every birthday, and he's the one who got me started keeping a life list, which birders do to record all the different species they've spotted. His is about the size of a dictionary, though, while mine is just a few pages.

Lola cleared her throat. "The thing is," she continued, "we've decided it's time to turn the bookstore over to the next generation. You'd be doing us a big favor if you'd consider taking the reins, J. T."

Gramps nodded. "Things haven't been going so well, and we think the business needs a fresh approach. Your sister says if you're in, she's in."

Dad looked stunned. "Run Lovejoy's Books? With True? In *Pumpkin Falls*?"

"Unless you plan to pick it up and move it, yes, in Pumpkin Falls," said Gramps, sounding a little testy. He's very proud of our family's connection to the town. There have been Lovejoys in Pumpkin Falls since before the American Revolution.

My father swiveled around, pinning my mother with one of his signature Lieutenant Colonel Jericho T. Lovejoy glares. "Did you know about this, Dinah?"

Mom bit her lip. "Well—"

"It's either turn it over to you and your sister or sell," Lola said briskly. "We've been avoiding this for a while now, but it's time to face facts. Not that selling would be the end of the world, but the bookshop has been in the family for nearly a hundred years."

Dad grimaced. "No pressure or anything, right?"

My grandfather placed his hand on top of Dad's remaining one. "Would you at least consider the possibility, son? Nothing would make your mother and me happier."

I could tell that running a bookstore with his sister wasn't exactly on my father's list of "Top Ten Things I Most Want to Do When I Grow Up." For one thing, he's not the biggest bookworm in the world, plus he and Aunt True don't always see eye to eye on things. Hardly ever, in fact.

At first, Dad flat-out refused. He said it was all a plot, hatched by Mom and his parents, and that he wouldn't be backed into a corner, even if it meant selling the bookshop. But with no pilot job, and no coaching job either, what choice did he have? By Thanksgiving, it was a done deal. Our new house went on the market a week later, and the movers came right after New Year's.

And now here we were: stuck in Pumpkin Falls, in the middle of the coldest winter on record, moving into the house my father grew up in, in the town he couldn't wait to leave.

CHAPTER 4

"Gimme a hand with the salad, Drooly?" Hatcher called from the kitchen a few minutes later.

Most of the time I don't mind it when my brother calls me that. It's been his nickname for me forever. Tonight, though, I wasn't in the mood. I barged through the door ready to let him have it, then stopped abruptly.

"What?" said Hatcher innocently, batting his big brown eyes at me. He was wearing Mom's favorite apron, the pink one with DON'T MESS WITH TEXAS on it, and he'd stuffed the top with dish towels to give himself a bust. A couple more wadded into the seat of his pants added an exaggerated bottom. He did a little dance, wiggling his rear end at me, and I couldn't help it, I laughed.

Which was the whole point, of course. Hatcher's always trying to crack me up.

Mom says that except for his hair color, he's pure

Gifford. Her whole family loves practical jokes, and telling funny stories, and they've all got these big, loud laughs just like Hatcher's. My brother is the definition of happy-go-lucky. Nothing much bothers him, and he's always looking on the bright side, just like Mom. "Cheerful as a sunflower," she calls him.

I, on the other hand—well, nobody's ever called me a sunflower. Hatcher and I look a lot alike, with our freckles and brown eyes and stick-straight brown hair (his is shorter than mine, of course, thanks to Dad's vigilance with the clippers), but that's where the resemblance ends. He's sunshine; I'm shadow. Like I said, I'm the quiet type. Except for the times when I stick my foot in my mouth, and when you wear size-ten-and-a-half shoes, that's a whole lot of foot. Unfortunately, my foot spends a lot of time there. I'm kind of famous in my family for blurting out the wrong thing at the wrong time.

Hatcher danced over and placed a colander on my head like a crown. "Duty calls, milady," he warbled. "Prepare to wash and chop."

My smile vanished. Grumbling, I crossed to the fridge and started pulling out salad fixings. KP was my least favorite chore. The plan was for Hatcher and me to alternate weeks with Danny and Lauren, to help Mom out now that she's going back to college. It's always been her dream to be an English teacher, but between juggling all of us kids and our constant moves with the military, it was pretty much an impossible one. Now that we were finally putting down roots, she had decided to finish her degree. It's really convenient for her, what with Lovejoy College being right here in Pumpkin Falls.

The college was founded in 1769 by one of our ancestors: Nathaniel Daniel Lovejoy, my great-great-great-zillion-times-great-grandfather, who built this house and who looks down his Lovejoy proboscis at us from his oil portrait hanging over the fireplace in the living room. His wife, Prudence, whose nose is a normal size, stares back at him from her portrait above the piano. There are more Lovejoys scattered over the walls in other parts of the house too, so many that I can't always keep track of their names. Nathaniel Daniel is pretty hard to forget, though. What were his parents thinking?

Even Pippa thinks it's a stupid name. "Nathaniel Daniel looks like a spaniel," she sing-songed the first time she heard it.

"When's everybody due back?" asked Hatcher.

I shrugged. "Soon, I guess. Mom said they'd be home for dinner." Lauren and Pippa had gone along for the ride while she and Danny registered for classes—my mother at Lovejoy College, and Danny at the high school over in West Hartfield. Not only is Pumpkin Falls too small to have its own movie theater, it also doesn't even have its own high school, which means Danny will have to drive himself nearly half an hour to school each day.

My brother slid the lasagna into the oven and gave me a sidelong glance. "So, what's the deal with the grade?"

I made a face and sliced into a tomato. "I don't know, Hatch. Ever since I found out we were moving again, I couldn't concentrate on anything. I tanked a couple of tests."

"Did you think Dad wouldn't find out?"

"I thought I'd beat him to the mailbox, that's for sure."

"Moron," he said, punching me in the arm. It was a friendly punch, though, and I gave him a rueful smile.

By the time dinner was ready I was feeling a whole lot happier. My mood took a nosedive again a few minutes later, though, when Dad walked through the door, scowling.

Mom was right behind him. "Mmm, that lasagna smells delicious," she said, taking off her coat and hat and hanging them on a hook in the mud room.

"Supermarket's finest," said Hatcher.

She swooped in to kiss each of us on the cheek. "Sounds good to me. I think I'm going to like this new KP arrangement."

I gave my father a speculative glance. Mom was way too upbeat for someone who knew about an F plus. Maybe he wasn't planning to tell her about my report card after all.

My mother watched, her lips pressed together, as my father struggled with the zipper on his jacket. I could tell she wanted to help, but we've all learned to wait until asked unless we want to get our heads bitten off. It takes a lot for Dad to ask for help with anything.

"Danny's all set for tomorrow, and so am I," Mom said lightly, squatting down to help Pippa with her zipper instead. "It's kind of funny to think we'll all be starting school together."

My little sister flung her arms around her. "You can come to my clathroom, Mommy," she lisped, thanks to her missing teeth. "I'll let you thit right nextht to me."

"Thanks, Pipster," my mother replied, ruffling my sister's curls. "I really wish I could—but I have to go to my school." Straightening up, she glanced around the kitchen and frowned. "Where's Lauren?"

"Out in the barn," Danny told her. Gramps and Lola's house has a really cool old barn that they use as a garage. Gramps has his woodshop out there, and they turned part of the hayloft into an art studio for Lola. "She's still in the car. She said she wanted to finish her chapter."

"For heaven's sake, it must be ten below out there!" Mom exclaimed. "Get her in here, would you?"

Danny went to do as she asked while the rest of us sat down at the table. When he and Lauren returned, we said grace and then dug in. I glanced over at my father now and then as we ate, bracing myself for the ax that I knew would eventually fall. We made it all the way to dessert without a peep about my report card.

ABSOLUTELY TRULY

"Did we get any mail?" my mother asked as Hatcher passed around a plate of the Pumpkin Falls General Store's famous maple walnut blondies.

I froze.

My father looked over at me and raised an eyebrow. "Do you want to tell her, or shall I?"

I sighed. "Go ahead."

"Excuse me?"

"Go ahead, *sir*."

He reached into his shirt pocket and pulled out the envelope, then passed it wordlessly to my mother.

"Truly," said my mother, shaking her head sorrowfully when she spotted my math grade, just as I knew she would. "I'm so disappointed in you."

Hatcher kicked me under the table. I glanced over to see him tap his two forefingers under his chin. That's our shorthand for "chin up." I sighed again. What I really wanted to tell my mother was that it was all Dad's fault, that he was the reason we'd had to leave Austin, which was why I hadn't been able to concentrate on stupid pre-algebra. But I couldn't say that, naturally.

"I know, Mom," is what I said instead. "I'm sorry. I promise I'll try harder."

"You certainly will," said my father, his voice as crisp as the creases in his starched shirt. "In fact, I've decided on a plan of attack."

Of course he had. Lieutenant Colonel Jericho T. Lovejoy is big on plans of attack.

"I'll tutor you until your grade is acceptable again," he continued. "I'll expect you at the bookstore by 1530 hours every afternoon after school."

1530 is military-speak for three thirty p.m. "But—" I began.

He ignored me. "You can stay and help your aunt and me when we're done with tutoring, then Danny can pick you up on his way home from practice."

"But—" I tried again.

"We're about to start inventory, and we could use an extra pair of hands," he continued. He glanced down at his own left hand, which was awkwardly gripping his fork, and frowned briefly. "I'd enlist your brothers, but they'll be too busy to help right now, what with wrestling season starting."

The table fell silent as he jabbed his fork into a bite of lasagna. Hatcher and I exchanged a glance. Wrestling was a sore topic these days. Before Black Monday, Dad had always helped coach Hatcher and Danny when he was home, but now—well, now he could barely even say the word.

"But—"

"No buts, young lady. That's an order."

Lieutenant Colonel Lovejoy is big on orders, too.

"What about swim team tryouts?" I burst out, unable

to contain myself any longer. I did remember to add "sir," though. Lola and Gramps had checked for me, and the tryouts were scheduled for the end of the month.

"You bring your grade up, then we'll talk swim team," my father replied coolly. "Until then, young lady, this is a done deal."

CHAPTER 5

Good-bye sunshine, hello snow, I thought glumly the following morning, staring out the window of our minivan as we pulled out of the driveway. It's not a very long walk to school from where Gramps and Lola live, but Mom had offered to drop us off on the way to her first class because of the storm.

Heaps and heaps of the white stuff had fallen overnight, at least a foot of it, and it was still coming down. Just to torture myself, I'd checked the weather in Austin this morning: sixty-two degrees and sunny. It was practically summer there. The thermometer outside Gramps and Lola's kitchen window, meanwhile? A frigid seventeen degrees.

If we were thinking maybe school would be canceled, though, we were wrong. My father snorted when Hatcher brought it up at the breakfast table.

"A snow day in Pumpkin Falls? Don't get your hopes up,"

he'd told us. "A little precipitation never stops anything here in the Granite State."

A little? Staring out at the yard, which was barely visible, I caught a flash of red by the bird feeder as a male cardinal swooped down from a nearby tree. Cardinals are already on my life list, of course—they're a really common bird—but they're still one of my favorites. I just love those bright red feathers, especially this time of year.

"How about cold, then?" Hatcher clearly wasn't going to give up. He'd tapped the newspaper lying on the table in front of Dad. Half the front page of the *Pumpkin Falls Patriot-Bugle* was devoted to a picture of the town's famous waterfall, along with a headline that screamed FALLS FREEZE FOR FIRST TIME IN A CENTURY! I couldn't believe this was what passed for news here. A frozen waterfall? Seriously?

"Nope, cold won't do it either," Dad had replied calmly. "Better get your jackets on."

A snow day would have been really nice. I wasn't feeling ready to face a new school again. After our move to Austin, I'd thought I was finally done with that.

The snow crunched beneath the minivan's tires as Mom turned off Maple onto Hill Street and headed down toward town. Tourists call Pumpkin Falls picturesque because of the waterfall and the covered bridge and the old-fashioned bandstand on the village green—village white, this morning—that anchors the center of town. They flock here like migrating geese every fall to tour the college campus, famous for its cluster of white clapboard buildings, and to take pictures of the steeple on the church, with its giant clock and the bell made by Paul Revere, and to buy maple syrup and maple sugar candy and souvenirs at the General Store. Mostly they come to gawk at the fall foliage, though. Everybody calls them leaf peepers, but I call them stupid. Who cares about a bunch of leaves?

We skirted one end of the village green, passing several big, square, Colonial-style houses, the post office, the Pumpkin Falls Bed & Breakfast, the Pumpkin Falls Savings & Loan, and, right by the iron gates and big driveway leading onto the campus, the official residence of the president of Lovejoy College. I knew this because the sign out front said so.

"The wheels on the bus go round and round . . ." From her booster seat in front of me, Pippa belted out a tuneless rendition of her favorite song. Lauren was seated next to her with her nose in a book as usual, and Hatcher was in the front passenger seat, talking to Mom. I was in the way back in my seat of choice by the right-hand window. Usually Hatcher is beside me because Danny likes to ride shotgun, but Danny was long gone. He'd gotten up at zero dark thirty this morning to drive himself to West Hartfield.

I'd noticed that Danny wasn't complaining much about the move to Pumpkin Falls. Probably because Gramps and Lola had given him their car to use while they were in Africa. He'd hardly stopped grinning since he got the keys.

ABSOLUTELY TRULY

"Round and round, round and round," droned Pippa.

My mother glanced in the rearview mirror. "Could you maybe keep it down a little, please, peanut?"

Pippa cranked it up a notch instead. "ROUND AND ROUND, ROUND AND ROUND!"

My mother sighed. We eased to a stop across from the world's teeniest public library, then turned onto Main Street, which Gramps always rather grandly refers to as "the heart of the business district." If this was the heart, I figured it must be on life support. There were only a handful of businesses besides the bookshop, and if you ask me, which nobody ever does, the only one that's the least bit interesting is the Pumpkin Falls General Store.

Dad says it's the biggest tourist trap north of Boston, but my brothers and sisters and I love it. They're not kidding about the "general" part. You can buy anything there. Need a mop? They've got it. Tulip bulbs? Those, too. From plumbing supplies and fishing tackle to printer ink, livestock feed, kitchen gadgets, snow shovels, postcards, T-shirts, underwear—if you can think of it, the general store probably has it. At Easter, they even sell baby chicks and ducklings. Plus there's a penny candy counter and an old-fashioned soda fountain with homemade ice cream that's almost as good as Amy's in Austin. One of my favorite things to do whenever we visit Gramps and Lola in the summertime is to sit out on the store's front porch in one of the rocking chairs, eating a strawberry ice-cream cone.

Mom slowed as we approached Lovejoy's Books. A big sign across the front window read CLOSED FOR INVENTORY. Someone was standing outside, and Pippa stopped singing long enough to shout, "Daddy!"

"No, honey," my mother told her. "I think it's Aunt True."

It was kind of hard to tell from the back, because whoever it was was wearing a big hooded jacket. Then I realized they were shoveling snow, which meant it probably wasn't Dad. Stuff like that is still awkward for him, even with his new prosthesis.

Aunt True spotted us and waved the shovel. We waved back. Mom pulled over to the curb and lowered her window.

"Howdy!" she said. "Working hard, I see."

My aunt grinned. "You bet. Everybody ready for school?"

Pippa and Lauren nodded happily. Hatcher and I shrugged. Kindergarten and fourth grade are still something to get excited about, but once you hit middle school, it's not as much of a thrill.

My aunt smiled at me. "Your dad says that you'll be joining us at the bookshop later, Truly."

"Yes, ma'am."

"That's way better than stupid day care," Lauren grumbled. Mom's class schedule means that my sisters have to go to after-school care, and Lauren is not happy about it.

Aunt True reached over my mom's shoulder and plucked

Lauren's book away. *"The Long Winter,* huh?" she said, reading the title. "Good choice for a day like today." She gave it back. "I love Laura Ingalls Wilder. I have all her books—maybe there's one you'd like to borrow. How about you come over for tea at my apartment one afternoon soon?"

"What about me?" said Pippa. Her lower lip trembled, poised to turn on the waterworks if the answer was no.

"You're invited too, of course," Aunt True told her.

My aunt is living above the bookstore. Gramps and Lola own the whole building, and she moved into the apartment upstairs when she came home to Pumpkin Falls to help out.

To be honest, Aunt True is a bit of a mystery. She's visited us a few times over the years, and she always remembers to send presents at Christmas and birthdays, but I don't really know her very well. Everybody says we look alike, but I think it's just because we're both tall. Well, maybe that and the freckles. She sure isn't quiet like me, though. If I had to compare Aunt True to a bird, I'd have to pick a loud one.

Mom I've always thought of as a robin. They're such cheery, dependable birds. And Dad's an eagle for sure, what with his strong jaw, piercing gaze, and prominent nose. He got stuck with the Lovejoy proboscis, just like Gramps. So far, none of us kids have shown signs of sprouting it, although I've caught Hatcher staring at his profile in the mirror a few times recently. He's worried it's going to appear out of the blue one of these days, like chest hair or zits.

My gaze settled on Aunt True's hat. Multicolored and lumpy, it had braided yarn ties dangling from the earflaps and was obviously hand-knit. It was identical to the ones she'd brought back for Danny and Hatcher and me from her trip to Peru. We were smart enough not to wear ours in public, though.

Parrot, maybe? Yeah, that fit. Aunt True was a parrot, loud and bright and squawky.

"Bye, kids! Have fun!" she called as we drove off.

Fun? I sincerely doubted it. I felt a prickle of nausea as we made a left onto School Street—how original—and pulled up in front of a brick building with the words DANIEL WEBSTER SCHOOL carved in stone above the entrance. A bunch of kids were milling around outside, trying to make a snowman, but the snow was too dry and powdery.

We went directly to the front office inside, where the principal came out to greet us.

"You must be Dinah Lovejoy," he said, shaking Mom's hand. "I'm John Burnside—J. T. and I were at school here together many moons ago. I was so sorry to hear about his injury."

That's another thing about small towns. Everybody knows everybody, and everybody knows everybody's business.

"I'm looking forward to catching up with him as soon as you're settled in," Mr. Burnside continued. "I hear he and True are going to be running the bookshop?"

ABSOLUTELY TRULY

"That's right," Mom replied.

"Excellent, excellent. Wish you could have been here for the good-bye party for Walt and Lola. It was a humdinger." He cocked his head and looked me and my siblings over. *Flamingo*, I thought. Tall and bony, with thinning red hair and a skinny neck that popped up out of his shirt collar like a periscope, Mr. Burnside reminded me of the large pink birds we saw last spring break in Florida. I half expected him to tuck one leg up under him, the way flamingos often do. "We certainly are looking forward to having Lovejoys here at our school again."

"And they're certainly looking forward to being here, aren't you, kids?" said my mother, nudging Hatcher, who nodded and gave the principal one of his big sunflower smiles.

"You'll practically double our school population!" Mr. Burnside joked.

That almost wasn't a joke, as it turned out. Daniel Webster School had fewer than a hundred students, with kindergarten through eighth grade all crammed under one roof.

"It's like the one-room schoolhouse in *Little House on the Prairie*!" said Lauren, sounding excited.

Mr. Burnside laughed. "Not quite."

After sorting out all the paperwork and locker assignments, our new principal offered to show my little sisters to their classrooms. Pippa was acting clingy, so my mother went with them.

"Got your lunch?" she called back to me over her shoulder. I nodded, and she blew me a distracted kiss.

"Daniel Webster doesn't have a real middle school, but they put the seventh and eighth graders upstairs so they can pretend like we do," said the bubbly girl who'd been assigned to escort my brother and me to our classrooms. "You're Lovejoys, right? My name is Annie Freeman and I'm in fourth grade. I live on a farm with my family up near the ski run on Lovejoy Mountain."

Not only had Nathaniel Daniel founded the college, he'd also named a mountain and a lake after himself. I guess he figured why not, since he was one of the first settlers in the Pumpkin River Valley. "Mountain" is a pretty grandiose name for the big hill on the far side of the covered bridge, though. Especially for someone like me who spent two years in Colorado, where the real mountains live.

Hatcher's classroom was at the top of the stairs. "You'll like Mr. Mazzini," Annie told him. "He's the most popular teacher in the eighth grade." She grinned. "Of course, he's the only teacher in the eighth grade, except for Mr. Bigelow, who doesn't count, because he teaches science to everybody."

"Good luck," Hatcher said to me, rolling his eyes as he went into his class.

"Thanks," I said. I was going to need it. My brother knows exactly how I feel about the first day at a new school.

"Ms. Ivey is a great teacher too," Annie continued, turning

to look at me. Her braids bounced around on her head like a bouquet of antennae. "She's young and really pretty, and she's funny, too. At least that's what my brother, Franklin, says. He's in your class. I have Mrs. Ballard, who's okay, I guess." Without pausing to take a breath, she chattered on. "So you're from Texas? They say 'howdy' there a lot, don't they? I went to Texas once, to San Antonio for the national spelling bee championship—I'm the best speller in the school, and I won first place in the Grafton County tournament, not that I'm bragging or anything." The girl gave me a sidelong glance to see if I was impressed, but didn't wait for a reply. "I guess our mountain is named after you, huh? Well, your family, I mean. And the college and the bookstore and the lake and everything?"

I nodded silently, wishing the little magpie would shut up. She didn't, of course.

"I love the lake! I go to Camp Lovejoy every summer," she continued. "Last year, I was in a cabin with this girl from Connecticut—that's spelled C-O-N-N-E-C-T-I-C-U-T—and she wet her bed almost every night."

As Annie chattered on, I tuned her out, wondering instead what Mackenzie was up to. It was two hours earlier in Texas, but I decided to send her a text anyway:

SEND HELP! TRAPPED IN HICKSVILLE, USA!

There was no reply. She was either asleep or in the shower. I sighed and slipped my cell phone back in my pocket. Ever since I'd woken up this morning, I'd been hoping this would all go away, and I'd find myself back in Austin. But it was painfully obvious that that wasn't going to happen.

It was time to go into stealth mode.

Hatcher calls this my defense mechanism. It's not that I'm shy—I'm not. Quiet, yes. Shy, no. My growth spurt has put me in the spotlight, though, which is my least favorite place to be. Stealth mode helps, but there's no way I can be completely invisible. I'm too hard to hide. There aren't too many seventh-grade girls who are almost six feet tall—it's like trying to hide a Winnebago in a parking lot full of Mini Coopers. Still, it's not impossible to fade into the wallpaper if you really try. I just stay quiet, speak when spoken to, and generally try to keep a low profile.

So far, it's worked pretty well. Of course, I've had plenty of time to perfect it. This is the sixth school I've attended so far. I went to kindergarten in Alabama, spent first and second grade at Fort Hood near Killeen, Texas, third and fourth in Germany, fifth and sixth in Fort Collins, Colorado, and half of seventh in Austin, Texas. I think it's fair to say that when it comes to stealth mode, I'm a pro.

"This is it," said Annie, her dark braids bobbing again as she skipped ahead to hold my new classroom door open for me.

"Thanks."

"You're w-e-l-c-o-m-e," she replied, smiling broadly.

ABSOLUTELY TRULY

Despite the fact that my stomach was churning and Annie was mildly annoying, I couldn't help smiling back. I'd have to remember to introduce her to Lauren. I had a feeling that the two of them would really get along.

"Welcome!" said Ms. Ivey, coming over to greet me. Annie was right; Ms. Ivey was really pretty. Her slightly upturned nose crinkled in a friendly way when she smiled. *Definitely a chickadee*, I thought as she took the enrollment form I was holding.

"Trudy Lovejoy, is it?" she said, glancing at it.

"Truly," I corrected her.

"What a pretty name! Truly original." She smiled at me again, and just like with Annie I couldn't help smiling back, even though it's kind of a dumb joke and I've heard it a zillion times before. I felt myself relax just a teeny bit. Pumpkin Falls might be a hick town, but so far the people I'd met were all really nice.

"Truly Gigantic," said someone from the back of the room in a stage whisper.

Okay, maybe not all of them, I thought, reddening.

"That's enough, Scooter," Ms. Ivey said sharply, and the ripple of snickers ceased. "Is that any way to welcome a new classmate? Where are your manners?" She scanned the room. "Let's see, Truly, why don't you take a seat next to Cha Cha Abramowitz."

She propelled me toward a petite girl who was curled up

in her chair with her legs folded gracefully under her. No bird here—Cha Cha Abramowitz was all cat. She had catlike eyes, too, large and green, and a short fluff of dark hair. Ms. Ivey introduced us, then made a beeline for the back of the room, where an argument had broken out. I was guessing the boy named Scooter was at the bottom of it.

"Truly, huh?" said the girl, who had a surprisingly deep voice for such a small person. "That's kind of unusual."

"And Cha Cha isn't?"

She grinned. "It's Charlotte, actually. My little brother couldn't pronounce it when he was a baby, and his nickname for me kind of stuck. Plus, my parents own a dance studio, so it fits. I don't mind, really."

"I don't mind my name either," I told her, which was a total lie. It's a pain to always have to explain to people that no, it's not a typo, my name isn't Trudy, it's Truly. It *should* have been Trudy, but the moron who was processing immigrants the day my great-great-great-grandmother got off the boat from Germany couldn't read. He took one look at her passport—which our family still has, framed on a wall at Gramps and Lola's house, which even I can decipher, which proves the guy really *was* a moron—and wrote down Truly instead of Trudy on her official papers. There's been a Truly in the family ever since. My Aunt True is really a Truly too, but she's always gone by True. Which is probably a good thing, now that we're both living in Pumpkin Falls. Too many

ABSOLUTELY TRULY

Trulys in this tiny town might make it explode or something.

"Looks like you could use a little help with pre-algebra," Ms. Ivey said, not unkindly, when she looked over the results from the math section of my placement tests a little while later.

"Uh, yeah. My father's going to tutor me."

She nodded. "Excellent."

Behind us, the door to the classroom flew open.

"Lucas?" trilled a blue sleeping bag. Or what I thought at first was a blue sleeping bag. On closer inspection, I saw that it was actually a slender woman in a puffy, ankle-length down coat. Her face was partially hidden by its hood, but I caught a glimpse of bright blue eyes. As they came to rest on a pale, skinny boy sitting near Cha Cha and me, I thought, *Blue jay.* Her gaze had that same intent look I'd seen on jays just about everywhere we'd lived.

"There you are!" said the woman, sounding relieved. "The weather forecast is predicting more snow, so I thought I'd better stop by on my way to work and bring you some extra mittens." She held up a pair of red ones.

"Thank you, Mrs. Winthrop," said Ms. Ivey, neatly intercepting the boy's mother as she started across the classroom toward him.

"Be sure Lucas puts them on before he leaves this afternoon!"

"I certainly will, Mrs. Winthrop," said Ms. Ivey, plucking the mittens away and gently maneuvering her back toward the door.

"I'll have hot chocolate waiting!" Mrs. Winthrop promised, waving at Lucas.

Ms. Ivey closed the door firmly behind her. But Mrs. Winthrop wasn't done yet. She tapped on the glass window and blew her son a farewell kiss.

Scarlet-faced, Lucas slunk down in his seat.

"Lucas!" mimicked someone from the back of the room, his voice going all high and squeaky. "Did you remember to put on clean underwear this morning?"

"Stuff a sock in it, Scooter," boomed Cha Cha, "or I'll remind everybody about the time you came to school wearing Jasmine's tap shoes."

"I think you just did," I blurted, the words popping out before my stealth-mode filter had a chance to activate.

The classroom erupted in laughter. Lucas shot Cha Cha and me a grateful look. I glanced over my shoulder at the boy called Scooter. He was looking directly at me, scowling. Definitely a bird of prey.

So much for stealth mode. I'd just made my first enemy in Pumpkin Falls.

CHAPTER 6

"A bunch of us are going sledding after school," Cha Cha told me a little while later, as we were heading downstairs to the cafeteria. She was as short as Mackenzie, and I could tell by the looks some of the other kids were giving us that we made a funny-looking pair. "Want to come?"

I hesitated. Stealth-mode protocol called for me to lie low until I was part of the school scenery, instead of a very tall novelty. I'd been trying that all morning, though, and Cha Cha wasn't letting me get away with it. She was determined to be friends.

"It will be fun!" she urged.

"I can't," I told her. "I have to go to the bookstore."

Cha Cha knew all about Lovejoy's Books. It turns out she and her family had been at the going-away party for Gramps and Lola. Pretty much everybody in town had been invited, I guess.

She frowned. "Can't you go later?"

You don't know my father, I thought. Lieutenant Colonel Jericho T. Lovejoy doesn't do later.

"There's this tutoring thing," I replied, and then, as Cha Cha looked at me expectantly, I caved, spilling the whole story about my math grade, and my father's reaction, and how it meant I'd be tutored every day for the foreseeable future.

"Well, if you have to be stuck someplace, the bookstore isn't such a bad spot," she said when I was done.

I looked at her in surprise. Cha Cha didn't strike me as the bookworm type.

"It's one of my favorite places in town," she continued, holding the cafeteria door open for me. "When I was little, I used to like their Story Hour better than the one at the library, because your grandmother made treats to go with whatever we were reading. You know, like cupcakes with little candy carrots on top when we read *Peter Rabbit*. Plus," she added, "my brother and I love Miss Marple."

Miss Marple is Gramps and Lola's golden retriever. Named after the elderly detective in Agatha Christie's mystery series, she's the store mascot. Her picture is on the bookmarks given out with every purchase.

"Everybody loves Miss Marple," I agreed as I followed Cha Cha to a table by the window.

"Hey, Cha Cha, can I eat with you?"

I looked over to see a tiny boy standing beside us. His face, which barely reached the tabletop, wore a hopeful expression.

"Sure, Bax, have a seat," Cha Cha told him, patting the bench beside her. "This is my brother," she told me as he clambered up. "Baxter, this is Truly."

"Hi," said Baxter shyly.

"Hi back," I replied.

"Tell Truly what grade you're in," Cha Cha said, and her little brother proudly held up one finger.

Baxter Abramowitz was kitten to Cha Cha's cat. He had the same slight build, the same curly dark hair and green eyes and dimple in his cheek. As I watched him eating his peanut-butter-and-jelly-sandwich, it struck me how different Daniel Webster was from any other school I'd ever been at. Not just because all the grades were together in one building, but because it was obvious that what my brother Hatcher calls "the universal cafeteria classification system" didn't seem to have made it as far as Pumpkin Falls. I looked around at the tables, trying to sort out who was who. Usually the jocks sit together, and the drama kids sit together, and so do the gamers, and the skateboarders, and the band kids, and so on. This was the first cafeteria I'd seen since elementary school where everybody sat together in a jumble.

Across the room, I noticed that Annie and my sister had found each other on their own. The two of them were talking a blue streak over their sandwiches. Or more accurately, Annie was talking, and Lauren was listening. What was weird, though, was that they were sitting at what I would normally have thought of as the jock table. Hatcher was beside them, and although Pippa was perched on his knee, he was talking to a bunch of guys who were clearly athletes, including Scooter Sanchez.

"Over here!" boomed Cha Cha all of a sudden, her deep voice making me jump. She waved wildly at a girl just entering the cafeteria, a girl who looked familiar, which was odd, since I was pretty sure we'd never met.

"Jasmine of the tap shoes," Cha Cha told me as she introduced us. "She and Scooter are twins."

My eyebrows shot up. "Ohhhhhh."

"Don't judge me," Jasmine replied quickly, flashing me a smile.

Raven, I thought, resisting the urge to reach out and touch her shiny dark shoulder-length hair. I smiled back. "I promise I won't."

"Where were you this morning, Jazz?" asked Cha Cha, and Jasmine bared her teeth at us.

"Orthodontist," she replied.

"Aren't you supposed to get those things off soon?"

Jasmine nodded. "One month left to go. Dr. Wilcox says I should have them off in time for Winter Festival."

"Nice," said Cha Cha, slapping her a high five.

Our table filled up quickly. Besides Cha Cha and Jasmine and Baxter and me, there was Lucas Winthrop, who hadn't spoken a word all morning, Annie Freeman's older brother, Franklin, who was just as friendly as Annie but not nearly as talkative, thank goodness, and Amy Nguyen, whose mother is my mother's academic advisor at the college, as it turned out.

"I'll tell her to make sure your mom gets straight As," Amy said with a friendly smile.

Usually on the first day at a new school, I end up either sitting by myself at lunch, or with someone who's been assigned to be nice to me. This was—different. Good different, though not different enough to make me stop wishing I was back in Austin.

I took a bite of my tuna-fish sandwich and quietly observed my new classmates. Franklin was talking about his family's farm, which from what I could gather was famous for its maple syrup. If his sister Annie was a magpie, thanks to her nonstop chatter, Franklin was definitely a wood thrush. His warm brown skin and eyes were the same shade as the thrush's cinnamon-colored contour feathers. They were also the same color as the syrup his family's farm produced.

"Who's that?" I asked Cha Cha, pointing to a boy across the room who was sitting next to Scooter. I recognized him from our homeroom.

Cha Cha turned around to see. "Oh, that's Calhoun."

"Calhoun who?"

Franklin shrugged. "He just goes by Calhoun."

"Some people call him R. J.," Jasmine added. "His dad

does, anyway. Calhoun is my brother's best friend."

"He moved to Pumpkin Falls last year, when his father took a job at Lovejoy College," Cha Cha explained. "Dr. Calhoun is the president."

Jasmine reached over and helped herself to a piece of Cha Cha's brownie. "I am so not looking forward to science class this afternoon," she said, changing the subject.

"No kidding," said Cha Cha.

"Why? What's happening?" I asked. "We have somebody else for science, right?"

Jasmine nodded. "Mr. Bigelow. It has nothing to do with him, though." She shuddered. "It's frog dissection day."

Lucas Winthrop's already pale face went about three shades paler.

"Eew," I said. We'd done that back in Austin, right before winter break. It was completely disgusting. Maybe if I asked, I'd be allowed to skip the lab and go to the library instead.

"Not going to faint just thinking about it, are you, Lucas?" teased Franklin, his dark eyes alight with amusement.

The tips of Lucas's ears grew pink. He stared down at the table.

"Of course he's not going to faint!" said Jasmine, clapping Lucas on the back. "Just remember what we told you—deep breaths, okay?"

Lucas nodded unhappily. I watched him out of the corner of my eye, trying to decide what bird he was. Lucas Winthrop

ABSOLUTELY TRULY

was even quieter than me in full stealth mode. A hummingbird, maybe?

The bell rang loudly a few minutes later and I cleared away my lunch things and followed Cha Cha and Jasmine and the others back upstairs to the science lab.

"Good news, my friends!" said the teacher, before we could even sit down. "You've been given a reprieve!" He chuckled. "Or perhaps I should say the amphibians have been given a reprieve."

Short, bald as a grape, and slightly overweight, the science teacher was definitely a duck, I thought, watching as he waddled over to greet me.

"You must be Truly Lovejoy," he said. "I'm Mr. Bigelow. You picked a fine day to join us—you're in for a treat." Turning back to the rest of the class, he clapped his hands. "Bundle up and meet me down by the front office in exactly five minutes! We're going on a field trip!"

"No frogs?" whispered Lucas.

"That's correct, Mr. Winthrop. No frogs."

Lucas looked visibly relieved.

Mr. Bigelow didn't leave us in suspense as to our destination.

"We're off to see the wizard—I mean the falls," he joked, and a collective groan went up around the room.

"Seriously, Mr. B?" said Franklin. "The waterfall?"

"Not just any waterfall, a *world-famous* waterfall," Mr.

Bigelow replied. "Don't you read the newspaper?"

Was he talking about the *Pumpkin Falls Patriot-Bugle*? I wondered. He didn't seriously expect us to take some podunk newspaper's word for it, did he? I doubted anyone outside of the Pumpkin River Valley had even heard of the falls.

"The last time the falls froze over was 1912, and they may not freeze again for another hundred years," our science teacher continued. "This is history in the making, my friends! Grab your jackets, and those of you who have cell phones with cameras, I'm setting aside my no-cell-phone rule for the afternoon. Bring them along—you're going to want pictures. I guarantee you'll tell your grandchildren about this someday!"

Fat chance, I thought as we headed for our lockers.

Outside, I was glad to see that the snow had stopped. As we followed Mr. Bigelow toward town, Scooter and Calhoun and some of the other boys started jostling each other. Ms. Ivey, who had come along to help chaperone, was keeping a close eye on them. I noticed Lucas sticking to Franklin and Jasmine like a burr. For protection from Scooter and Calhoun, probably.

"That's our family's place," Cha Cha told me proudly as we turned the corner onto Main Street. She pointed across the street to a large building that stood between a Kwik Klips hair salon (*"We cater to student budgets!"*) and Earl's Coins and Stamps, which had been there for as long as I could remember, and which I couldn't believe was still in business because really, who collects coins and stamps anymore?

ABSOLUTELY TRULY

"The Starlite Dance Studio," I replied, reading the sign. "Cool," I added politely.

I peered in the window as we passed Lovejoy's Books. My father was nowhere to be seen, but I spotted Aunt True. She had her back to us and was doing something to one of the bookshelves. Inventory, probably.

The next block contained an antiques store, a laundromat called the Suds 'n Duds, and Lou's Diner, which smelled wonderfully of fresh donuts.

"Our field trip just might include a stop here on the way back," Mr. Bigelow said, pausing to sniff the air. "If you all behave yourselves, that is."

Just then the diner door burst open and Lucas's mom appeared, looking anxious.

"Is everything all right?" Mrs. Winthrop asked breathlessly. "Are you evacuating?"

Out of the corner of my eye I saw Scooter elbow Calhoun. Poor Lucas. They'd be making hay with that one.

"Everything's fine, Amelia," said Ms. Ivey. She gave her arm a soothing pat. "Just a field trip to the falls, nothing to worry about."

"Field trip? In this weather?" Mrs. Winthrop wrapped her arms around her light blue waitress uniform and shivered. "Lucas should have an extra scarf." She dashed inside and reappeared a moment later with a bright red one, obviously hers, and obviously a match to the bright red mittens she'd dropped off earlier, which Lucas was dutifully wearing. Much to Lucas's chagrin, his mother managed to dodge Ms. Ivey this time, and in a flash he was wrapped up tight as a burrito. "There," Mrs. Winthrop said, kissing the top of his head. "That should keep you cozy." Turning to the rest of us, she added, "Be careful, kids—it's slippery with all this snow."

The minute the door to the diner closed behind her, the boys at the back of the line exploded with laughter.

"Are we *evacuating*?!" howled Scooter. "Ooh, Lucas, are you all *cozy* now?"

"Scooter!" warned Ms. Ivey, marching over to deal with him.

"Poor kid," I murmured, as Lucas drooped off after Mr. Bigelow.

Cha Cha nodded. "I know. Talk about a helicopter parent! My mother says Mrs. Winthrop really should have a bunch more kids to keep her busy. Lucas is an only child, and she hovers over him, like, well—"

"A helicopter?"

"Exactly."

We smiled at each other.

The bell in the church steeple struck a single note as we made our way past the Pumpkin Falls Savings & Loan, the library, the post office, and Town Hall.

"That's where my parents work," Jasmine told me, pointing to a white clapboard house across the village green. The sign out front said SANCHEZ & SANCHEZ. "They're both lawyers."

"So do you live upstairs?"

She shook her head. "There's an apartment upstairs, but my parents rent it out to one of the college professors. We live on Oak Street, just up the hill from your grandparents' house."

We continued on, and Jasmine and Cha Cha started talking about the Winter Festival, which apparently is a big deal this year since it's celebrating its one hundredth anniversary, plus it's scheduled for Valentine's Day weekend so it's an even bigger deal. As the two of them talked, I spotted a pair of juncos and heard the distinctive *chick-a-dee-dee-dee* that let me know there was a black-capped chickadee or two flitting through the nearby evergreens. Hearing them reminded me that I needed to put out more sunflower seed and suet in the backyard and make sure the electric heater in the birdbath was working properly. Gramps had left me full instructions on taking care of his beloved feathered backyard visitors.

A few minutes later we reached our destination.

I've always really liked the covered bridge in Pumpkin Falls. Whenever we'd come to visit Gramps and Lola, spotting the bridge was a game our family would play in the car after the long drive north from the airport in Boston. Each of us kids would jockey for position, straining for a glimpse of it as we came down the hill and around the final corner toward town. The first one to yell, "I see the bridge!" after it came into view won a dollar to spend at the General Store's penny candy counter.

Seeing the bridge used to be exciting. Now, though, all it did was remind me that I was stuck in a town tiny enough to actually *have* a covered bridge.

Still, I had to admit that its cardinal-red exterior looked pretty against the snow-covered landscape. I paused and snapped a picture of it with my cell phone to send to Mackenzie, then followed my classmates as Mr. Bigelow funneled us through the entrance.

"Stay to the right, please!" he told us. "Single file—leave plenty of room for cars."

Our footsteps echoed through the bridge's wooden interior. Overhead arched a puzzle of interlaced rafters, and to the right was a solid waist-high partition topped with a lattice of crosspieces, like a row of large *X*s.

We spread out along the partition. I leaned against it and looked down at the river, then at the falls.

Which were frozen, just as promised.

It was oddly quiet. Usually you could hear the roar of the Pumpkin River as it tumbled over the falls and rushed underneath the bridge, but now there was silence. Even Scooter didn't have any smart-alecky comments. A stone's throw from us, the frozen waterfall spanned the river from bank to bank, white as the marshmallow frosting on my favorite birthday cake.

ABSOLUTELY TRULY

"Listen up, everyone!" said Mr. Bigelow. He clapped his hands, and the sound bounced off the bridge's wooden floor and walls. "I want you to start by just observing. Feel free to take pictures if you'd like, sketch if you'd like, jot down notes if you'd like. I'll give you five minutes!"

Beside me, Lucas pulled out a small notebook and a pencil and began to draw. I glanced over his shoulder and watched him for a minute or two; he was pretty good. Then I turned my attention to the river. Most of it was frozen, and the parts that weren't were remarkably still—so still that I could see the reflection of the bridge's red paint. I took a picture of that, too. Directly below us, some water was still flowing between the clumps of ice, and I watched for a while as it swirled lazily around the stone pillars holding up the bridge. Then I glanced over Lucas Winthrop's shoulder again. He was adding a graffiti-speckled rafter above his sketch of the waterfall.

Curious, I glanced up. The rafters were decorated with names, hearts, arrows, dates—the oldest one I spotted was 1899—and interlinked initials, sure signs that Cupid had been here. Directly overhead I saw SAM LOVES BETTY; JOJO AND CARL; and E & T FOREVER drawn inside a slightly lopsided heart. I took a few more pictures.

I was so busy looking up that I didn't notice Scooter and Calhoun until they were practically on top of me.

"Whatcha looking at?" Scooter demanded.

"Nothing," I replied coolly.

He looked up, too, then nudged Calhoun. "Got a pen?"

Calhoun fished in his jacket pocket and produced one.

"Gimme a boost—I'm going to add 'Truly Gigantic loves Lucas,'" Scooter told him, and Calhoun snickered.

"Morons," I muttered.

Calhoun bent over and laced his fingers together. As Scooter placed a foot in his grip and Calhoun started to hoist him into the air, Mr. Bigelow suddenly materialized.

"Don't even think about it, boys," he said. "Besides the fact that it's incredibly dangerous, defacing the bridge is a very big no-no, and the town will charge you a very big fine."

Scooter removed his foot from Calhoun's grasp and held his hands palm up in the classic *Who, me?* gesture.

Mr. Bigelow squeezed in between us and leaned on the railing, looking out at the falls. Several of my classmates drifted over. "Drink it in, kids, drink it in," he said. "The minute the January thaw arrives, which should be any day now, this will all be water under the bridge." He waggled his eyebrows at his stupid pun, and a chorus of groans went up around me. I could tell that my classmates really liked Mr. Bigelow, though. I was beginning to, as well.

"So," he continued, "who knows why the early settlers built covered bridges in the first place?"

Franklin's hand shot up.

"Yes, Franklin?"

"To keep snow off the bridge?"

ABSOLUTELY TRULY

"Indeed!" said Mr. Bigelow. "A buildup of heavy snow could collapse a wooden bridge like this one, which would have been disastrous for a town like Pumpkin Falls, cutting it off from the outside world. Instead, the slope of the roof allows the snow to fall harmlessly into the river." He looked around. "Anyone else?" None of us rushed to answer, so he continued, "Covering a bridge also protected it from the elements, preventing rot. Our thrifty Yankee forbears liked the idea of extending a bridge's useful life by a couple of decades." He winked. "Plus, I wouldn't put it past them to have figured out that someday covered bridges would attract tourists."

"So how do waterfalls freeze, exactly?" asked Jasmine.

"Why, thank you for asking, Miss Sanchez!" said our science teacher. "Water freezes at thirty-two degrees Fahrenheit—you all know that. But for moving water, it's a little more complicated."

He went on to explain that as water cools below the freezing point, the molecules slow down and start to stick together, forming crystals. Ms. Ivey passed around a handout with diagrams showing those stuck-together bits, which were called "frazil."

"You'll note they're roughly one millimeter in diameter," Mr. Bigelow went on. "Very tiny, but small is mighty in this case. As the frazil clump together, they form snow in the air, ice in the water. Now in the case of moving water, they first accumulate against solid surfaces—like those rocks over there along the riverbank, or the bridge's supports below us." He pointed to the top of the falls. "See those icicles up there?"

We nodded.

"Those started as clumps of frazil. And so did that," he added, pointing to the broad ledge of ice that had formed at the bottom of the falls. It appeared to be holding up the entire mass of frozen water that had once been the waterfall. "Look at all the different formations! Chandeliers of icicles! Undulating folds! And all those nodules and layers and cauliflower lumps! It's like something out of a fairy tale." He sighed happily. "Isn't nature spectacular?"

I fished my binoculars out of my backpack (a birder is never without her binoculars) to inspect the waterfall more closely. Now I could see that the ledge of ice at the bottom was actually an inch or two above the river.

"Water is still getting through underneath that ledge, right?" I asked. "It's not frozen solid, I mean."

"Ah, our new student has sharp eyes," said Mr. Bigelow. "And binoculars! Extra points for bringing binoculars. You are correct, Truly. Water is still flowing through, though at a much slower speed than usual."

I panned across the face of the waterfall, then stopped. Hanging down from the top of the falls was something that looked like a large, frozen tube. With the aid of my binoculars, I could see a fine spray of mist emerging from the end of it, like clothes out of a laundry chute.

ABSOLUTELY TRULY

"What's that?" I asked, handing my binoculars to my science teacher.

"Oh my," Mr. Bigelow breathed when he spotted it. "Students, you all need to see this." He passed the binoculars down the row of my classmates. "That, my friends, is very rare! You can actually see the waterfall in the process of freezing from the outside in. At the moment, water is still flowing through it, like a pipe. Eventually, though, if this cold weather continues, it will freeze into a solid column of ice."

I stood there for a long time, gazing at the waterfall and thinking, oddly enough, of my father. Had his injury frozen him from the outside in? And was the father I'd known all my life still in there somewhere, a trickle of him at least?

CHAPTER 7

"See you tomorrow," said Cha Cha.

We were standing outside Lovejoy's Books, finishing up the donuts Mr. Bigelow had bought for us at Lou's Diner, just like he'd promised. The rest of our class had gone back to school, but our teachers had let the two of us remain behind downtown since I was headed to the bookstore anyway and Cha Cha was going to the dance studio. Their receptionist was on maternity leave, and Cha Cha's mother had texted her to see if she could fill in for half an hour while she taught a tango class.

"Have fun sledding later," I replied.

"Thanks. Have fun with pre-algebra." She laughed as I made a face, then waved good-bye and crossed the street.

I waved back, then stepped inside the bookshop—and right into the middle of an argument.

"No cat, and that's final!" said my father in his Lieutenant

ABSOLUTELY TRULY

Colonel Jericho T. Lovejoy you'd-better-not-answer-back voice.

Aunt True laughed, which startled me. Laughter is not the usual response to one of my father's orders. "Who made you boss?" she retorted.

The two of them were too wrapped up in their quarrel to notice me, so I quietly slung my jacket and backpack onto the old church pew by the door that served as a bench.

My father's face was the same color as Lucas Winthrop's mitten-and-scarf set, a sure warning sign that an explosion was imminent. This didn't seem to faze Aunt True in the least.

"We're running this place together, J. T., remember?" she continued.

"We're already saddled with a stupid dog," my dad told her. "We don't need a cat, too."

The "stupid dog" in question was curled up on her bed by the sales counter, watching this exchange anxiously.

"Memphis has been with me through thick and thin," replied Aunt True. "He'll get lonely upstairs all by himself."

Aunt True had been dog-sitting until we got settled. Miss Marple was scheduled to go home with us tonight, and Lauren could hardly contain herself. She's always wanted a dog, but our constant moves—one of them overseas—had ruled that out.

"Besides," Aunt True continued, "the two of them are already great friends."

It was possible that she was stretching the truth. Memphis

was perched on the sales counter staring balefully down at my grandparents' dog, his coal-black tail lashing back and forth. By the wary expression on Miss Marple's face as she glanced up at him, I figured it for an uneasy truce at best.

"The two of us are a package deal," Aunt True stated firmly. "If Memphis goes, I go."

Hearing her bicker with my father reminded me of Hatcher and Danny. It was weird to think that to Aunt True, my dad wasn't a lieutenant colonel in the United States Army, but just her baby brother.

The muscles in my father's jaw twitched. He swiveled on his heel. "Fine," he said, stalking off toward the office. "But one whiff of litter box and he's out of here."

Aunt True spotted me and smiled. "Truly!" She came over and gave me a hug. "Cup of tea?"

"No, thanks," I replied.

"You'd better be off to the dragon's lair, then." She nodded toward the office door. "Watch your step in there; he's a little cranky today. Bossy older sister, out of his element, too many pets. You know the drill."

She disappeared toward the back of the store and I headed into the office. "Truly Lovejoy reporting for duty," I announced with a smart salute, hoping to get a smile out of my father.

No such luck. He was too busy frowning at a piece of paper clamped in the steel pincers at the end of his prosthesis.

ABSOLUTELY TRULY

"I've got you set up over there," he said, waving his left hand at the other desk.

I slid into the beat-up leather swivel chair in front of it and stared glumly at the book that was waiting for me. *Pre-Algebra for the Clueless!* blared the familiar bright blue-and-black cover from the Clueless series.

"We'll start at the beginning and work our way through," my father said, still not looking up.

"But—" I began. It wasn't like I was a complete moron at math, after all.

"A firm foundation is the key to success," he continued, ignoring my protest. "That and review, review, review. Oh, and there are worksheets, too."

Of course there were. I sighed and opened the book. At the beginning, just like he'd ordered.

An hour later, my head was spinning. I was algebra-ed and Lieutenant-Colonel-Jericho-T.-Lovejoy-ed out. "Can I go help Aunt True now, please?" I begged, handing over my latest worksheet.

My father inspected the results, then nodded. "Dismissed."

I scuttled out before he could change his mind.

Aunt True was nowhere to be seen, but I could hear rustling in the back of the store. I found her in the room that Lola and Gramps called the Annex, where all the used books were kept. Most of the books in the store are new, but my grandparents have always had a spot where they shelved used ones.

My aunt looked up. "How'd it go?"

I made a face, and she laughed.

"Maybe this will be more fun." She passed me a handheld scanner and steered me to a back corner of the room. "If you could start on this shelf over here, that would be great. Just take one book at a time and scan the bar code, okay? The computer will do the rest. Any books without bar codes—and there are bound to be some—go in this basket. I'll deal with them later."

She walked me through the scanning procedure a couple of times to make sure I knew what I was doing, then patted me on the shoulder. "I'll leave you to it, then. Your father and I have a meeting with the accountant in a few minutes." She started to walk away. "Let me know if you find any treasures," she called back over her shoulder. "Lovejoy's Books could use all the good news it can get right now."

I took the scanner and started in on my assigned task. Half an hour later, I pulled a book off the shelf that would change everything.

CHAPTER 8

I'm not sure why I took my discovery home with me.

I probably should have just given it to Aunt True, or to Dad. By the time I found the envelope tucked inside an old copy of *Charlotte's Web*, though, they were already in the meeting with their accountant and Danny was double-parked outside, honking the horn. So I just stuffed the envelope in my backpack, grabbed Miss Marple, and left.

Dinner was the usual Magnificent Seven mayhem, as my father used to call it before Black Monday.

"Toot Soup!" cried Danny, as Hatcher ladled some into his bowl.

"Don't start," my mother warned.

Too late. My little sisters were already giggling. "Toot Soup" is what my brothers call bean soup, because of the inevitable sound effects it produces. Knowing we'd be busy with the first day of school, Aunt True had made a pot of it for us and dropped it by, along with a salad and some bread.

Eyes dancing behind her sparkly pink glasses, Pippa spooned up a bite, then made a rude noise. Lauren snickered.

"Pipster," said my mother severely. "Do you want to eat in the barn with Miss Marple?"

Pippa thought this was a great idea. Between trying to settle her down, Hatcher and Danny's instant replay of their first wrestling practices, and Lauren's glowing report on her new friend Annie, I was squeezed out of the dinner conversation as usual.

I'd brought the envelope with me to the table, but even if I'd had the opportunity to tell everybody about it, in the end something held me back. I decided to keep the secret to myself for a little while longer.

After dinner, I went directly upstairs. One of the only good things about moving to Pumpkin Falls is Gramps and Lola's house. The house Dad grew up in is so big, half the town could move in and we'd never bump into one another.

All of us kids have a bedroom of our own, and there are still a couple left over. Hatcher and Danny have taken over the entire third floor, and I even have my own bathroom, which was where I was headed. It's the warmest spot in the house.

Locking the door behind me, I sat down on the floor by the radiator. It's one of the old steam-heat kind, like all the others in the house. They hiss and rattle and clank so much it sounds like a bunch of baby dragons are on the loose. But they do the trick as far as keeping the house warm, which I guess is the main thing when you live in a climate as cold as this one. I leaned back against the claw-foot tub and pulled the envelope out of my pocket.

It was sealed shut, and as far as I could tell had never been opened. Why would someone leave a letter stuck in an old copy of *Charlotte's Web*? Had they meant to mail it, and forgotten? Or had they left it there deliberately for someone to find? There wasn't an address on the envelope, or even a real name—just the capital letter *B*. But the envelope had a stamp on it, like it was all ready to send.

So why hadn't it been?

I traced the *B* on the front with my forefinger, wondering if I should open it. I was pretty sure that was some sort of a crime, though. Mail tampering or interfering with the US Postal Service or something. I didn't want to get arrested. On the other hand, if I didn't open it, how was I supposed to figure out who it was meant for? What if it were something important?

"Truly?"

I jumped as someone hammered on the door. It was my brother.

"Hatcher!" I hollered. "You about scared me to death!"

"Quit barking at me. Someone's on the phone for you."

I scrambled to my feet and returned the envelope to my back pocket. Maybe it was Mackenzie. She'd know what to do.

It wasn't Mackenzie, though; it was Cha Cha.

"I'm calling to see if you want to sign up for a practice slot," she said. "They're going fast."

"Practice slot for what?"

"Cotillion."

I had no idea what she was talking about.

"Didn't Ms. Ivey tell you about Cotillion?" she asked as I hesitated.

"Um, maybe?" I'd come home with a stack of newsletters and sign-up sheets and flyers, all of which were still in my backpack upstairs in my room.

I, meanwhile, was now perched on a rickety old wooden chair in a tiny closet tucked under the front hall stairs. The closet contained the only landline in the house, an ancient rotary-style phone that looked like a relic from some old movie. Dad says it's the same one that was here when he was a kid, and that it's always been in the makeshift phone booth under the stairs. Gramps and Lola aren't much for change.

"So here's the deal," Cha Cha continued. "All middle schoolers at Daniel Webster are required to attend Cotillion."

"Which is?" I prodded a stack of moldy phone books with the toe of my sneaker. Above me, a bare bulb dangled from the ceiling. Not exactly the kind of place for a lingering conversation.

"Kind of a tradition in Pumpkin Falls. My mom calls it a rite of passage. Cotillion is a series of dance classes we all take

ABSOLUTELY TRULY

at school, and then the big finale is during Winter Festival, when we get to show off what we've learned at the town's annual dance."

I had no idea how to respond. A dance that the entire *town* went to? What planet was I on?

"We're lucky," Cha Cha continued. "Now that we're in middle school, we get to do ballroom instead of a stupid square dance, like the younger kids have to do. Anyway, it'll be starting up soon."

"You're telling me I have to take a *ballroom dance* class?" I could feel panic rising in me. Dancing is practically at the top of the list of things I'm not good at. "You're kidding, right?"

Cha Cha was very quiet. *Uh-oh*, I thought. Had I just insulted her?

Apparently not. "Nope, I'm not kidding," she said cheerfully. "In fact, my parents will be teaching it."

I could hear music in the background, and people talking. "Where are you?"

"At the Starlite. Anyway, in addition to the class at school, everybody's required to attend two private practice sessions here at the studio with my parents. There's no charge, of course."

"Of course," I echoed, still feeling stunned.

"So how does the Saturday after next sound?"

"Fine, I guess," I said, wondering whether I should tell Cha Cha about the letter. I pulled it out of my back pocket.

"Oops, gotta go," she said, before I could bring it up. "There's a call on the other line. I'll pencil you in for eleven thirty. Let me know if that doesn't work, okay? See you tomorrow!"

"But—"

She'd hung up.

I sighed and replaced the receiver, turned out the light, and headed back upstairs. I hesitated in front of the door leading to the third floor, but a series of random thumps from above signaled that my brothers were practicing their wrestling moves. It probably smelled like the boys' locker room up there, plus they got cranky when they were interrupted. I'd talk to Hatcher later.

"Truly!"

I poked my head into my sisters' bathroom to see my mother holding up a towel for Pippa. Pippa's old enough to get ready for bed on her own, but she likes to have Mom help her. It's part of being the baby of the family, I guess.

"How was your first day, sweetie?" my mother asked, as Pippa climbed out of the tub. "I didn't get to talk to you much at dinner."

Sometimes it feels like I'm more in stealth mode at home than anywhere else.

"It was okay," I replied.

"Make any new friends?"

I shrugged. "Maybe."

ABSOLUTELY TRULY

My mother smiled. "Good. You can tell me all about it in the morning. I need to get a start on my homework once I'm done here. Oh, and Hatcher said he has a bunch of forms for me to sign, so you probably do too. Go ahead and leave them on the kitchen table for me, okay?"

I nodded.

"Say good night to Truly." My mother gave my little sister a nudge, and she trotted obediently over, holding her arms up for a hug. I bent down and embraced her gingerly, since she was still pretty damp. She smelled good, though, and I nuzzled her hair. Pippa might be a drama queen, but I love her anyway.

"Night, Pip," I said.

"Night, Truly."

I headed down the hall to my room, pausing by Lauren's door. It was open just a crack, and a strange noise was coming from the other side. I peeked in to see her flopped on her stomach on her bed, reading. No big surprise there. That was Lauren's usual after-dinner routine. And before-dinner routine, and every-other-time-of-day routine. She was patting her pet rabbit, Thumper, with one hand while she turned the pages of her book with the other. She didn't look up. When Lauren was engrossed in a book, World War III could start and she wouldn't notice.

Thumper was curled up beside her, wearing a doll-size

nightgown and a resigned expression. My sister loves dressing up her pets. She'd put a baseball cap on Miss Marple too, who was lying on the braided rug next to the bed, keeping a wary eye on the source of the strange noise—a clear plastic hamster ball rocketing around the room and periodically crashing into the furniture. Nibbles was enthusiastic about exercise.

Miss Marple heaved herself to her feet when she spotted me. I motioned to her to stay, but she ignored me. Toenails clicking briskly across the bare wooden floor, she shook off her baseball cap and followed me down the hall to my bedroom. I paused at the door and looked down at her, frowning.

"No, Miss Marple," I told her firmly. "No dogs allowed in here."

Miss Marple sat.

"Go see Lauren," I told her.

She didn't budge.

My sister is the animal lover in the family, not me. It's not that I don't like animals—I do. From a distance. Which is maybe one reason why I like bird-watching so much. Wild birds don't shed and they don't need to be walked or have doggie breath or cages or litter boxes that need cleaning.

Miss Marple gave a tiny whine. One that I interpreted to mean, *I'm afraid of the hamster ball and I don't want to be dressed up in people clothes and I need a place where I can go into stealth mode.*

"Oh, fine," I said, relenting. "You can come in. But just this once."

ABSOLUTELY TRULY

I was still getting used to my new bedroom. It was cavernous, with high ceilings and big tall windows on two sides. During the day, light poured in from the back and side yards, which was nice, but at night it was kind of creepy, the way the tall windows stared at me blackly. Crossing the room to pull down the shades, I glanced outside to see that the sky had cleared and a full moon was casting a silvery light on the snow.

It was a perfect night for owling.

When I was little and we came to Pumpkin Falls to visit, Gramps used to make up bedtime stories for Danny and Hatcher and me about a family of owls who lived in the barn out back when he was a kid. I asked so many questions about them that he finally bought me a book—*All About Owls*. I still have it. It's on the bookcase by my bed, alongside all the other bird books Gramps has sent me over the years.

Miss Marple settled onto the rug with a wheezy sigh. I pulled down the shades and turned around, pausing for a moment to survey the room. My gaze came to rest on the tiny pottery owl on my dresser, the owl mug full of pencils and pens on my desk, and the black-and-white woodcut of a snowy owl hanging over my bed. The woodcut is my prized possession. I never get tired of looking at it. My mother found it in Germany back when we were living there, and had it framed for me for my birthday.

I guess I kind of have an owl collection.

Owls are my favorite birds. I love their beautiful faces and big round eyes. Plus, talk about stealth mode! Besides the fact that owls have awesome camouflage (their patterned feathers make them really hard to spot), they also have built-in mufflers—velvety-soft filaments on the surface of their feathers and a fringe on the edge that are designed to deaden sound. Owls fly almost completely silently, which is exactly how I'd want to fly if I were a bird.

I went over and sat down on my bed. I ran a finger over the spine of my tattered copy of *Owl Moon*, which sat between the two brass owl bookends Gramps and Lola had given me this past Christmas. *Owl Moon* was my favorite picture book when I was Pippa's age. I still take it out and read it now and then. I always wanted to be that kid in the pictures, the one whose father took him—or was it her?—out on a snowy night to look for owls. But my father was seldom home, and when he was, he was usually in bed early because like practically everybody else in the military he gets up at the crack of dawn, and anyway, we never lived where there were owls nearby.

And now that there might be, he's turned into Silent Man and I'm not a little kid anymore.

I really wished Gramps and Lola were still here. They were both so easy to talk to, and nobody in my family had much time for me lately. Plus, Gramps could have taken me owling.

Thinking about Gramps reminded me that I needed to be

sure and fill up the bird feeders tomorrow. I glanced across the room to the hook on the back of my bedroom door, where my grandfather's old barn coat and wool hat were hanging. I'd found them waiting there when we moved in, along with a bird carving that Gramps had left for me in the pocket. It was a black-capped chickadee with the words *backyard magic* carved on the bottom.

Slipping the mystery envelope out of my pocket, I went and grabbed my laptop off my desk and carried it back over to the bed. I really needed to talk to someone, and was hoping Mackenzie was online.

She was, and a minute later, her face popped up onscreen. "You got your hair cut!" I said in surprise.

She smiled the same wide Gifford smile I see daily on my mother and Hatcher. "Like it?" She swiveled around so I could check out the sides and back.

"It's really cute," I told her. Of course, everything looks cute on Mackenzie. It's easy to look cute when you come in such a small package.

"It's a lot easier for swimming."

I felt an unwelcome stab of envy. Mackenzie was only on a swim team because of me, and now I might not even be able to swim at all. I changed the subject. "How's Austin?"

My cousin quickly brought me up to speed on what was going on with her family and with everybody at school, including Mr. Perfect Cameron McAllister, of course. According to

Mackenzie, Cameron was even more amazing than ever, and he definitely liked her back because he'd teased her in social studies.

"Mom says that's how you know when a boy likes you," she told me. "So, is Pumpkin Falls as awful as you thought it would be?"

"Worse," I replied. "It's totally Sleepy Hollow here. You'd hate it." I told her about the upcoming Winter Festival, complete with its stupid dance for the entire town, and about stupid Cotillion, and the frozen waterfall that was front-page news, and how Daniel Webster practically qualified as a one-room schoolhouse.

"I think it sounds kind of cool."

"That's because you don't have to live here."

She grinned. "Your room looks nice, at least."

"Yeah."

My room is what Lola calls the Blue Room. It was Aunt True's when she was growing up—her high school yearbooks are still piled on the bottom shelf of the bookcase, right next to my stash of sudoku. Mom and Dad always stayed here before when we used to visit, but now they're in Gramps and Lola's room at the front of the house, so I asked if I could have this bedroom. Blue is my favorite color, and pretty much everything in the room is blue and white, from the braided rug to the bedspread and curtains.

"Tour?" asked Mackenzie.

ABSOLUTELY TRULY

I held up my laptop and panned slowly around. My grandparents had left all their furniture for us to use, and in addition to a desk and bookcase, I had a white four-poster bed, a rocking chair with a blue-and-white quilt folded over the back, and an old-fashioned dresser topped with a blue lamp and an antique blue-and-white china pitcher and bowl.

"Sweet!" said my cousin when I was done.

I shrugged. I still missed my aqua "Mermaid" room back in Austin. Mom says military families take their homes with them wherever they go. "A house is just a place to put your home," she'd remind us every time we moved. But we Lovejoys have been migratory birds for what feels like forever, always borrowing other people's nests. Even though Gramps and Lola's is a nice one to borrow, my family had finally had a nest of its own back in Austin. And it felt really unfair that we'd had to leave it.

"So did you try out for swim team yet?" Mackenzie asked. "Or is Pumpkin Falls too small to have one?"

I made a face. "It has one, but I'm not on it yet." I told her about the fiasco with my report card.

"Seriously?" My cousin's voice shot up about an octave. "Your dad won't let you swim unless your grade improves? That's harsh."

"Tell me about it. And even if he changes his mind, I'll be super out of shape by the time tryouts roll around."

"So when are they?"

"In a few weeks," I replied.

"Can you get your math grade up by then?"

"I don't know. I hope so." I glanced down at my bedspread and saw the envelope. I'd almost forgotten why I'd wanted to talk to Mackenzie in the first place. "Hey, this weird thing happened today at the bookstore." I explained about the letter I'd found, holding it up so she could see.

"And you haven't opened it yet?" she shrieked in excitement. "What are you waiting for?"

"You really think I should?"

"Duh! Aren't you dying to know what's inside?"

I slid a finger under the envelope's flap and ripped it open. Inside was a yellowed sheet of paper with a quote on it. I read it aloud:

> *Why, what's the matter, that you have such a February face, so full of frost, of storm and cloudiness?*

"That's it?" my cousin said.

"Yup. Except for some numbers and letters underneath." I read those aloud too: "PR2828.A2 B7."

"Weird."

"I know, right?"

"It isn't signed or anything?"

"There's a capital *B*, just like on the front of the envelope." I held the sheet of paper closer to the laptop camera so she could get a good look.

ABSOLUTELY TRULY

"It's got to be a message for somebody," said Mackenzie, her blue eyes sparkling. "Maybe it's a secret code—you know, spies or something."

I laughed out loud. "Spies? In Pumpkin Falls?"

"It could happen," she insisted.

"No, it couldn't."

"Why not?"

"Because nothing ever happens here," I told her.

"Well, something just did!" my cousin replied. "You've got a mystery on your hands, Truly!"

CHAPTER 9

I needed to talk to my mother.

Hoping that she might be able to help me solve the puzzle, I headed downstairs, passing under the gaze of several centuries of Lovejoys as I did so.

"Obadiah, Abigail, Jeremiah, Ruth," I chanted, reading the names on the brass plates embedded across the bottom of each of the frames. I slowed as I reached the last two in the lineup—Matthew Lovejoy and his wife, the original Truly. The stair tread creaked loudly as I took another step down, passing Matthew in his Civil War uniform—Union Army, of course—and coming face-to-face with my namesake's portrait. I squinted at it. Did I look like her? I guess our hair was sort of the same color, and we both had brown eyes, but if she'd had freckles like me, the painter hadn't added them.

My mother's voice drifted out from the kitchen, mingling with the clatter of dishes and silverware. "Someone's in the kitchen with Dinah, someone's in the kitchen, I know-oh-oh-oh...."

Uh-oh, I thought, suddenly struck by a pang of guilt. Hatcher and I were supposed to have taken care of the supper dishes again tonight, but I'd gotten sidetracked by the envelope.

"Someone's in the kitchen with Dinah"—my mother held the high note for a long moment, then swooped down to the final stanza—"strumming on an old banjo." Her voice was soft and sad, so different from the way Dad used to sing it. He'd always belt it out, tossing us a wink as he slipped his arm around Mom's waist and waltzed her around the room.

Singing and waltzing weren't so much on Dad's agenda these days. At all, in fact.

As I reached the bottom of the stairs, the doorbell rang.

"Could somebody get that?" Mom called. "I'll be out in a sec."

"Sure, Mom," I called back.

I crossed to the front door and opened it, letting in a blast of icy air that nearly knocked me off my feet. A tall woman, nearly as tall as me, stood on our doorstep, dressed in a long black wool coat. Her head was wound so thoroughly in a black scarf that only her eyes were visible. They gleamed behind a pair of black-rimmed glasses, darting around the hall.

Crow, I thought. Most definitely a crow.

"Um, can I help you?" I said, as the woman brushed

past me and stepped inside. I closed the door behind her.

She craned over my shoulder, peering into the living room as if she were looking for someone.

"*May* I help you," corrected my mother, emerging from the kitchen. She smiled at our visitor and held out her hand. "I'm Dinah Lovejoy, and this is my daughter Truly."

"Yes, I know." The woman shook Mom's hand, then extricated herself from her scarves, revealing a gaunt face sharply divided by a knife blade of a nose and topped with a pouf of teased hair that looked like it had been dipped in a pot of ink. She carefully patted it into place, her mouth pruning up in a thin smile. "Figured I'd drop this by on my way home," she said, holding out a stack of mail. "I'm Ella Bellow."

"Ahhh," my mother replied, as if that explained everything. "Well, thank you so much, Mrs. Bellow."

The woman looked around again. "I thought I might say hello to J. T., too, if he's in. I heard about what happened to him. We all did, of course. Such a pity. I've known him since he was just a nipper."

I'd never heard my dad called a "nipper" before. I filed this away to share with Hatcher and Mackenzie.

"He's working late at the bookstore tonight," my mother told her. "Inventory, you know."

"Yes, I heard he and his sister were taking over the business. Things haven't been going so well at the shop, from what I understand." She paused. "Not that times aren't tough everywhere—Bud Jefferson over at the coin and stamp shop is struggling too."

My mother's face flushed angrily.

"Think your family can make a go of it?" Mrs. Bellow continued. "I mean, what with J. T.'s condition and all?"

"My husband can do anything he puts his mind to," my mother replied stiffly.

Our visitor's mouth pruned up again. "Well, I suppose time will tell. Good evening to you, Mrs. Lovejoy." She nodded to both of us, then left.

My mother closed the door firmly behind her. "Well, of all the nerve!"

"Who was that?" I asked.

"Only the biggest busybody in Pumpkin Falls! Your grandmother warned me about her. She's the postmistress."

"Is the coast clear?" someone whispered.

My mother and I jumped. Turning around, I saw my father peering out from behind the kitchen door.

"I came in through the barn," he said. "Recognized her car in the driveway. I'm not up to one of Ella's interrogations. Not tonight." He shook his head wearily.

"Truly, I think it's time for you to go on upstairs and get ready for bed," my mother told me.

"What?! It's not even nine o'clock yet!"

"It's been a long day for everyone," she added, with a slight but significant nod in my father's direction.

"But—"

"No buts, honey." She gave me a gentle push toward the stairs. "Go on now."

I hesitated. I could tell my mother was worried about Dad, and I was torn between a wish to be obedient and a burning desire to enlist her help with the mystery envelope.

Obedience won out.

"Yes, ma'am," I said meekly. "See you in the morning."

"Good night, sweetheart." She stretched up to kiss my cheek, then followed my father into the kitchen.

I started upstairs, then paused, listening to the murmur of my parents' voices. Something was clearly up. I snuck back downstairs, flinching as I stepped on the squeaky stair tread. The portrait of the original Truly gave me a disapproving look.

"Yeah, I know," I whispered to her. "It's not polite to eavesdrop."

Tiptoeing down the hall, I peeked through the crack between the kitchen door and its frame.

"Did you get any dinner?" my mother asked my father. "I can fix you a plate of leftovers, if you'd like."

"True and I ordered pizza," my father replied. He shrugged his jacket off and flung it over one of the chairs at the kitchen table. "Though heaven knows we shouldn't have spent the money."

My mother leaned back against the sink. "Is everything okay?"

"Okay?" My father gave a short laugh. "It's a mess, Dinah. A real mess. I don't know how my parents kept the business afloat this last year, even with the bank loan."

I drew back, feeling guilty for listening but unable to pull myself away.

A chair scraped against the floor and I heard my father sit down. "They borrowed some money a while back to help the bookstore through what they told me was 'a dry spell,'" he went on to explain. "The note's coming due soon, and I'm not sure how we're going to pay it."

My mother murmured something I didn't catch.

"The accountant doesn't hold out much hope," my father told her, "but True seems to think we can turn things around. She wants to give it six months, but I just don't think it's worth it. Realistically, it will take every extra cent we have to keep the bank from foreclosing on the loan. We're stretched pretty thin as it is. Even with my pension and the insurance money and all, we still have college for the kids to save for, and we're dipping into savings for your tuition—"

"I'll drop out," my mother said quickly.

"You will not. Better we just admit this whole thing has been a mistake, and call it quits."

"I'll get a part-time job, then."

"On top of a full load of classes plus the kids? C'mon, Dinah."

"I'm willing to give it a go if you are," my mother told

him. "I know you, J. T.—you've never backed away from a challenge in your life. You'll have a hard time forgiving yourself if you don't give this your best shot."

My father was quiet. Seconds ticked by. Then, "Six weeks," he said finally. "I'll give it six weeks."

I turned and crept back upstairs to my room, where I lay in bed awake for a long time.

What if six weeks wasn't long enough?

CHAPTER 10

"Family meeting tonight," my mother announced at breakfast the next morning.

There were only five of us at the table. Danny was long gone, of course, and so was my father.

"What's up?" asked Hatcher, pouring himself some more orange juice.

I knew exactly what was up. The bookstore, that's what. I looked over at my mother, wondering how she'd answer.

"Nothing to worry about" was all she said, though. Checking her watch, she changed the subject. "I've got to run. Sorry I can't drive you again, but my first class starts in fifteen minutes. Hatcher, you know the way, right?"

My brother nodded. Not that it was even remotely possible to get lost in a town the size of Pumpkin Falls.

"Good," my mother continued. "Be sure and lock the house when you leave."

"What about Miss Marple?" Lauren passed a toast crust to the dog, who was lurking hopefully under the table.

My mother's face fell. "Is she still *here?* Your father was supposed to take her with him to the bookstore!"

"We can drop her off on our way to school," Hatcher told her.

"Will you have time?"

He nodded. "No worries, Mom. We've got your six."

That's military-speak for *We've got your back.*

She looked chagrined. "Guess we still have a few wrinkles to work out with this new routine."

After breakfast, I shooed my sisters upstairs to brush their teeth, then headed for the mudroom.

"Back in a sec," I told Hatcher, who was packing our lunches.

I threw on my jacket and boots, grabbed the plastic container filled with sunflower seed, and bounded out the back door. The glare from the sun on the snow-covered yard made my eyes water. Wading through the drifts over to the nearest feeder, I filled it to the brim, then quickly made the rounds to the other ones. Excited twittering and the rustle of wings in the pine trees that fringed the backyard signaled that my efforts hadn't gone unnoticed. When I was finished, I watched for a moment as chickadees and cardinals began to swoop in for their breakfast. I was tempted to linger, but I'd be late for school if I did.

ABSOLUTELY TRULY

"Time to go!" Hatcher called, as I stomped the snow off my boots back in the mudroom.

I helped him bundle my sisters into their warm things, and then we left, locking the front door behind us.

"I'm blinded!" Hatcher cried, throwing his hands up in front of his face in mock horror at the bright sunlight. "Help me, Lauren! Help me, Pip!"

He staggered down the front steps and flopped onto his back in the nearest snowbank, making my sisters giggle. I zipped my jacket all the way to the top and pulled my hat farther down around my ears. It might be sunny out this morning, but it certainly wasn't warm.

Hatcher and I swung Pippa between us while Lauren and Miss Marple trotted along behind. At the bottom of Hill Street we took a shortcut across the village green, following the narrow footpath that had been trampled in the snow.

Miss Marple broke into a trot as we reached the other side, dragging Lauren behind her down Main Street. A couple of blocks later, she stopped abruptly in front of Lou's Diner.

My sister tugged on the leash. "C'mon, Miss Marple," she said, but Miss Marple ignored her and sat down on the sidewalk instead.

A moment later the bell over the door jangled and a large balding man in a white apron poked his head out. "There you are," he said, not to us but to the dog. "You're running late this morning, aren't you?" He reached into his pocket and pulled out a donut hole. "Here you go, milady." He tossed it to Miss Marple, who caught it neatly and gulped it down.

"No fair!" cried Pippa, her pink glasses sparkling in the sun.

"You want one too, do you?" The man in the apron grinned at her. "Hang on a sec." He disappeared back inside, reappearing a minute later with a small white paper bag. "Don't expect this kind of treatment every morning," he warned, handing it to Pippa with a wink. "Gotta save some for the paying customers. I'm Lou, by the way. You must be the Lovejoy kids. Welcome to Pumpkin Falls!" He rubbed his hands together briskly. "I'd better run, it's cold out here!"

The bell over the door jangled again as he went back inside.

"I like Lou," said Pippa, helping herself to a donut. She held the bag out to Hatcher and Lauren and me, and the four of us munched on our treats as we continued down Main Street. I paused in front of the window of the *Pumpkin Falls Patriot-Bugle*.

Under a big banner proclaiming PUMPKIN FALLS THEN AND NOW! was this week's front page, alongside a front page from 1912. Old and yellowed, it sported what looked like an identical picture of the frozen waterfall, along with an equally overexcited headline.

"I can't believe what a big deal they're making out of the stupid waterfall," I said.

"It *is* a big deal," Lauren insisted. "Annie Freeman said that Ella Bellow said that a TV news crew might be coming up from Boston to film it."

"Oh, well, if *Ella Bellow* said it, then it must be true," I replied.

"Who's Ella Bellow?" asked Hatcher.

"The postmistress. She came by last night while you were upstairs doing your homework. Mom says she's the biggest busybody in town."

"Whatth a buthybody?" asked Pippa.

"Somebody who sticks their nose into other people's business," I told her.

My little sister raised a pink mitten to her own nose and pondered this as we headed for the bookstore. The door was locked, and Pippa skipped over to the window and peered in, then knocked on the glass. A minute later Dad emerged.

"You brought the dog," he said, running his hand through his hair. "I guess I forgot." He took the leash from Lauren, who bent down to scratch Miss Marple behind the ears. Then Pippa had to pat her and give her a good-bye kiss, too, of course.

"You'll be late for school," my father said, tugging on the leash. Miss Marple glanced sorrowfully back at us as the two of them disappeared inside.

"I think she'd rather stay with us," said Lauren.

"Daddy doethn't like Mith Marple," added Pippa sadly, slipping her mittened hand into mine.

Hatcher and I exchanged a glance. Silent Man didn't seem to like much of anything or anybody these days.

"He isn't used to her yet," my brother told her.

We made it to school just before the bell rang.

"Hey," said Cha Cha as I slid into my seat.

"Hey back."

"How was the tutoring session?"

I made a Toot Soup noise.

She grinned. "That bad, huh?"

Between the stuff going on with my dad, the bookstore, and the mystery envelope—now stashed in my backpack—I was practically bursting to talk to someone. A real, live in-person someone, not just an onscreen-Mackenzie-who-was two-thousand-miles-away. My mother was juggling way too much right now and didn't have time for me, I wouldn't see Hatcher again until tonight at suppertime, and Cha Cha was right here. It was time to abandon stealth mode.

"What do you know about Ella Bellow?" I asked her.

"The postmistress? Why?"

I filled her in on Ella's unexpected visit last night.

"She's always fishing for gossip," Cha Cha said, wrinkling her nose. "My mother says she has ears like a fox. Eyes, too. She doesn't exactly read the mail at the post office, but she sure keeps close tabs on the return addresses, and she watches who gets what from whom. I got a check for my birthday from my aunt Sylvia in New York last fall, and Mrs. Bellow knew about it before I did!" She gave me a sidelong glance. "So, was she right? Is the bookstore in trouble?"

I told her about the conversation I'd overheard in the kitchen between my parents.

"Six weeks, huh?" she said when I was done. "Then what happens?"

"I don't know," I replied. There'd be no reason for us to stay in Pumpkin Falls without the bookshop, but we'd sold the house in Austin, and there was no job there for my father anyway, so I doubted we'd move back to Texas. Where would we go? What would we do? I got a pit in my stomach just thinking about it. "And there's more, too," I said, thinking of the envelope. "Can you keep a secret?"

"Sure."

Before I could continue, Ms. Ivey clapped her hands. "If you'd open your social studies books to chapter seven, we'll continue our review of the Constitution and the Bill of Rights."

"We can talk more during study period," Cha Cha whispered.

Ms. Ivey crossed the room to our desks. "Truly," she said, "I've been meaning to ask you something. I coach girls' basketball here at Daniel Webster, and we'd love to have you on the team."

Why is that just because I'm tall, everybody assumes I play basketball?

"There are several other players you've probably met, including Jasmine Sanchez and Amy Nguyen," she continued. "Think you'd be interested?"

I shook my head. "Thanks, Ms. Ivey, but I'm a swimmer." At least I would be, if my father ever let me try out for the team. I didn't tell her that, though.

My teacher gave me a rueful smile. "Too bad. I know you'll have fun swimming, but we could really use a player with your height."

"Truly Gigantic," whispered Scooter as Ms. Ivey went back to her desk, careful not to let her hear him this time.

I ignored him.

"Lucas is on the swim team too," Cha Cha told me.

"Really?" I glanced over at Lucas, sizing him up. I never would have pegged him for a swimmer. Those toothpick arms didn't exactly scream, *Michael Phelps*.

The next hour couldn't pass quickly enough for me. Now that I'd decided to abandon stealth mode, I couldn't wait to spill the beans to Cha Cha. Fortunately, Ms. Ivey paired the two of us up for a research project on the First Amendment, which gave us an excuse to sit together in the library during study period.

"So what's going on?" Cha Cha whispered.

I glanced around. Jasmine and Franklin were at the table nearest to us, but they were busy talking and laughing, and from what I could tell weren't paying us the least bit of attention. "This is," I replied, pulling the envelope from my backpack and passing it to my new friend. "I found it stuck inside an old copy of *Charlotte's Web* at the store yesterday."

Cha Cha opened it and read the letter inside. "Wow! It's kind of like finding a message in a bottle."

I nodded.

Cha Cha read the note again. "Those look familiar," she said, pointing to the numbers beneath the quote.

"Really?"

"Uh-huh," she replied. "They remind me of something, but I don't know what." She picked up the envelope and inspected it. "Wouldn't you love to know who this was meant for, and who sent it? Or didn't send it, I mean. Too bad it was never mailed. A postmark would have given us a date at least."

I grabbed the envelope back. "Cha Cha, you're brilliant!" Heads swiveled in our direction, and I quickly lowered my voice. "Stamps are issued on a specific date—my brother Danny used to collect them."

Cha Cha grinned her catlike grin. "Now who's brilliant? We can stop by Earl's Coins and Stamps after school. They should be able to help us."

Ms. Ivey crossed the room toward us. I whisked the envelope and letter underneath my notebook.

"How are you girls progressing?" she asked.

"We're off to a bit of a slow start," Cha Cha admitted. Our teacher steered us to some books and websites, and the rest of the study period passed in a flurry of actual study.

Cha Cha and I didn't have a chance to talk at lunch, because there were too many people around and because Franklin Freeman, who didn't usually babble as much as his little sister, went on and on about the record cold snap, clearly worried about what it could mean for his family's maple syrup harvest.

"If the January thaw doesn't arrive soon, it's really going to affect the flow," he said.

I had no idea what he was talking about, but everybody else at the table nodded sympathetically.

This entire town is obsessed with weather, I thought. *And frozen waterfalls, and maple syrup.*

After lunch, it was time for science class again, where it turned out our frog reprieve had only been a temporary one.

"Saddle up, cowboys!" said Mr. Bigelow. "It's showtime!"

I explained to him about how I'd already dissected a frog earlier this year back in Austin, but if I was hoping that he'd let me ditch the lab and go to the library instead, no such luck.

"Terrific! You'll be the expert, then." He steered me to the table where Jasmine and Cha Cha were sitting. Franklin and Lucas were stationed on one side of us; Scooter and Calhoun on the other.

"You ladies are the roses between thorns," quipped Mr. Bigelow. He trotted off, returning a moment later to place a tray containing a dead frog on the table in front of us.

ABSOLUTELY TRULY

"Eew!" squealed Jasmine, recoiling, and Cha Cha mimed sticking her finger down her throat.

"Courage!" our science teacher told them, plopping trays with more of the limp green specimens in front of the boys.

As soon as Mr. Bigelow's back was turned, Scooter grabbed his frog by one of its hind legs, then leaned over and dangled it in his sister's face.

Jasmine shrieked and batted it away. "Scooter!"

Both the dead frog and Scooter were back in their proper places by the time Mr. Bigelow turned around.

"Is there something I need to know about?" he asked, frowning.

Scooter blinked at him innocently, his face as devoid of expression as the frog's.

"Just that—oh, forget it," said Jasmine. "Brothers," she muttered to Cha Cha and me as our teacher walked away.

"Tell me about it," I replied. "I have two of them." Picking up the lab instructions, I began to read them aloud. "Too bad there isn't an app for this," I grumbled when I was finished.

Cha Cha surreptitiously whipped out her smartphone and tapped on the screen. "Um, actually, there is."

Jasmine's dark eyes lit up. "We should totally use it!"

Mr. Bigelow materialized behind us like a genie summoned from a lamp. "No, you totally shouldn't," he said, plucking the cell phone from Cha Cha's hand. "You know the rules—you're doing this old-school, ladies."

"But why should some poor frog sacrifice his life for us?" Jasmine protested. "It's inhumane!"

"It's for a worthy cause," Mr. Bigelow countered. "Try and think of him as a little green hero, sacrificing his life for science."

"A little green hero who smells revolting," Jasmine said, making a big show of holding her nose. She picked up a scalpel with her other hand. "This is just gross."

Behind us, there was a loud thud. We turned around to see that Lucas had fallen off his lab stool onto the floor. His face was nearly as green as the frog on our tray.

Scooter and Calhoun burst out laughing.

"Shut up, you guys! It's not funny!" cried Cha Cha.

Mr. Bigelow rushed over and helped Lucas sit up. "Deep breaths, now, son," he said, bending him forward so that his head was between his knees. "You're okay—you just fainted."

While Lucas was recovering, Cha Cha rummaged in her backpack.

"Maybe this will help," she said, holding up a bottle of Sassy Lassie perfume.

Jasmine and I stared at her, puzzled.

She gave us an impish grin and tapped the lab sheet. "The directions don't say we can't." She gave our little green hero a couple of vigorous squirts, then leaned over to the neighboring lab table and sprayed Lucas's frog too.

My eyes watered. I wasn't so sure that this was an improvement.

ABSOLUTELY TRULY

Mr. Bigelow shook his head wearily. "And to think that I could have had a career in research." He flapped his hand at us. "Fine. Whatever works."

Forty-five minutes and half a bottle of Sassy Lassie later, the dismissal bell rang.

"I hope I never have to do that again," said Cha Cha, hopping down off her lab stool.

"Me too," echoed Jasmine.

"That's what I said last December," I told them, stuffing my notebook into my backpack.

Lucas Winthrop, who still looked half-wilted, trudged along ahead of us as we went back down the hall to our lockers.

"Poor kid," murmured Cha Cha. "Wait until his mother hears about this."

Jasmine nodded. "He'll probably have to start wearing a protective helmet to school or something."

I smothered a giggle. Maybe having a busy mother who didn't have a whole lot of time for me wasn't such a bad thing after all.

"Can you believe I have to go back to the orthodontist again today?" Jasmine complained, pulling on her jacket. "Stupid wire broke, and it's poking me in the lip." Her cell phone buzzed and she answered it. "I'll be right out, Mom. No, Scooter says his braces are fine." She waved to Cha Cha and me. "Gotta run. See you guys tomorrow!"

As she jogged off down the hall, Cha Cha and I joined the flow of students heading for the front door.

"Are you *kidding* me?" I said in disbelief as we emerged from the building. The sun from earlier in the day had disappeared, and it was snowing again.

"Welcome to winter in New Hampshire," said Cha Cha, sweeping an arm out in a dramatic gesture.

BLAM!

A snowball hit me squarely between my shoulder blades. I whipped around to see Scooter and Calhoun standing there laughing. Calhoun had Lucas Winthrop dangling by one of his spindly arms and was busy stuffing snow down the back of his neck.

"Welcome to winter in New Hampshire, *Truly Gigantic*!" Scooter called, mimicking Cha Cha's sweeping gesture.

"Truly big mistake, *Metal Mouth*!" I called back, furious. Two could play at this game. Scooping up a handful of snow, I took aim at Jasmine's brother.

BLAM! My snowball hit its target, exploding into a zillion bits.

My counterattack wiped the stupid grin off Scooter's face. Calhoun let go of Lucas and gaped at me, shocked.

Take that, I thought smugly.

Cha Cha darted over and grabbed Lucas by the hand. "Run!" she shouted to me.

The three of us took off down School Street. Scooter and Calhoun were hot on our heels. I paused a couple of times to fire off more snowballs for cover, then rounded the corner of Main Street behind my new friends. We dove through the door of Earl's Coins and Stamps and stood there dripping snow and panting.

"May I help you?" said the man behind the counter, just as Scooter and Calhoun charged through the door, snowballs in hand.

The store owner was pretty spry for someone his size. In a flash, he had both boys by the collar and hustled them outside.

"Sorry, Mr. Jefferson," said Cha Cha when he returned. "We got ambushed."

"I can see that," he replied, eyes twinkling beneath a pair of shaggy dark eyebrows. He was pretty much shaggy all over, from his wild tangle of curly dark hair to his rumpled sweater and corduroy pants. No bird for Mr. Jefferson—he was all bear. "So, is this just a safety zone to give you time to catch your breath, or can I actually do something for you kids?"

I looked over at Lucas, then at Cha Cha. We couldn't very well toss Lucas to the wolves. Scooter and Calhoun were no doubt waiting outside, itching for revenge. We'd have to let Lucas see the envelope.

I fished it out of my backpack and slid it across the counter. "I'm wondering if you could tell us anything about this stamp."

"Let's hope so," Mr. Jefferson said cheerfully. "Stamps are my business."

"So are you Earl?"

"Well, technically speaking, yes. But everybody calls me Bud. My father was the real Earl—this store was his baby. And you're a Lovejoy, from the looks of you."

Was it that obvious, I wondered? I nodded. "I'm Truly Lovejoy."

"There's another one?" His shaggy eyebrows shot up. "Your aunt True and I went to high school together. Well, welcome to Pumpkin Falls, Truly. Or perhaps I should say you're *truly* welcome to Pumpkin Falls." He grinned at his own joke. "We were all delighted to hear about your dad and True taking over the bookshop. Not that we won't miss Lola and Walt," he added hastily.

Picking up the envelope, he examined the stamp. "Oh, sure, I remember this one. The Battle of Gettysburg. This was from the Civil War series about twenty years ago." He spun around and ran a finger across the notebooks lining the shelves behind him. "Here it is," he said, pulling one of them out. Riffling through the plastic sleeves it contained, he pointed to a pristine horizontal strip of stamps.

Cha Cha leaned in to take a closer look while I jotted down the year. "There's President Lincoln, and Harriet Tubman, and Ulysses S. Grant," she noted. "These are actually kind of cool."

Mr. Jefferson nodded. "I like to think so."

"My father collected stamps," Lucas suddenly piped up.

ABSOLUTELY TRULY

"That's right," said Mr. Jefferson. "He used to spend a lot of time in here. The two of us were good friends."

Cha Cha had told me that Lucas's father died when he was a baby, which I guess kind of explains a lot about Mrs. Winthrop being so overprotective.

"You're welcome here anytime," Mr. Jefferson continued.

Lucas stared at the stamps. "My mother likes me to go right to the diner after school."

"I understand," the shop owner told him. "But my door is always open."

Lucas nodded.

I would have liked to stay and look at more stamps—Cha Cha was right, they were kind of cool—but I was due at my tutoring session in five minutes and my father wouldn't be happy if I was late. The three of us thanked Mr. Jefferson and left.

I looked carefully both ways to make sure Scooter and Calhoun weren't lurking behind a mailbox or something, then motioned my friends to follow me across the street.

"So did that help?" Cha Cha asked.

"I guess," I told her. "At least we've narrowed down the date range."

"Twenty years ago is a long time, though," Cha Cha said. "The person who wrote the letter and the person it was meant for might not even live here anymore."

I nodded. "Yeah, I know." It was probably going to be

impossible to track them down. But for some reason I still wanted to try.

As we approached the bookstore, I noticed a man in a dark green hooded jacket peering in the window. He stepped back, started to walk toward Lou's Diner, then hesitated. After a moment he returned to the window and peered inside again. *Odd*, I thought.

Before I could say anything, though, a snowball came sailing out from behind a parked car.

"Incoming!" I hollered, and grabbing ahold of my classmates, I pulled them into the bookstore.

CHAPTER 11

"Greetings and salutations," said Aunt True as the snowball splatted harmlessly on the glass door behind us. She glanced outside. "A skirmish, I take it?"

We nodded.

She locked the door. "It's your lucky day, then. Due to inventory, the store is officially closed. You have now entered a snowball-free zone, and on top of that, it's snack time!" She smiled as she crossed the room toward us, then drew back abruptly. The smile vanished. "Good heavens, what is that smell?"

"Um," I said. "Us, probably. We dissected frogs today in science class."

She gave me a tentative sniff. "I'm not exactly detecting Eau de Kermit."

"Cha Cha sprayed our frogs with perfume."

Aunt True laughed. "And you would be Cha Cha, I presume?" she asked, turning to my new friend.

Cha Cha held out her hand. "Charlotte Abramowitz," she said. "Nice to meet you."

"Cha Cha's parents own the Starlite Dance Studio across the street," I told my aunt, as the two of them shook hands. "And this is Lucas Winthrop. His mom works at Lou's."

"Happy to meet you both," said Aunt True. "I'm True Lovejoy, Truly's aunt."

Out of the corner of my eye, I could see my classmates giving her a discreet once-over. Aunt True was dressed parrot-style as usual, in a bright orange hand-knit sweater over jeans. Down at her ankles, purple-and-green striped socks disappeared into a pair of leopard print clogs. "I hope you kids are hungry for a snack, because I've been baking all afternoon."

My father emerged from the back office just then. "Truly? You're right on time."

"Hi, Dad." *My family, the freak show*, I thought, as Cha Cha and Lucas politely looked everywhere but the hook that protruded from the end of my father's right shirtsleeve. "This is Cha Cha Abramowitz and Lucas Winthrop. They're in my class at school."

"Nice to meet you both," he said politely. "Now say good-bye to your friends, Truly. Time's a-wasting and math's a-waiting."

I sighed. "Yes, sir."

"Not so fast," Aunt True told my father, pulling a tray out

ABSOLUTELY TRULY

from under the counter. "I promised them a snack. I've decided that as part of the bookstore's new marketing campaign, we're going to offer tea and treats every afternoon for our customers."

Miss Marple, hearing the word "treats," trotted over to join us.

"Hey, Miss Marple," said Cha Cha, giving her a pat on the head.

My father looked over at Cha Cha, clearly startled to hear such a deep voice come out of such a petite person. "What marketing campaign?" he asked my aunt. His eyebrows dove for each other as he frowned. "We don't have money in the budget for tea and treats."

"Word will soon spread," Aunt True continued, ignoring him. "Hordes of visitors will descend to sample our goodies, and stay to buy our books."

"A bunch of freeloaders will show up, you mean," muttered my father, but I noticed he reached for a cookie.

My aunt passed the tray to my friends and me. I selected a cookie too, and took a bite, which I immediately ejected back into my hand. "Um, Aunt True, what's in these?"

Beside me, Lucas started to cough. Cha Cha, who hadn't taken a bite of her cookie yet, eyed it suspiciously.

"Looks like your culinary skills haven't improved much over the years, sis," my father remarked, grimacing.

Aunt True put her hands on her hips. "I'll have you know

I've cooked to great acclaim on every continent!" she retorted. "This is a recipe inspired by my time in Tibet. I had to make a few substitutions, of course, since the General Store doesn't carry yak milk. Did I add too many hot chilies?"

"Maybe just a few," I told her, slipping the rest of my cookie to Miss Marple. She promptly spat it onto the floor, and my father gave a hoot of laughter.

"And the reviews are in!" he crowed, sounding almost like his old self. "Bad sign when the dog won't eat it, True."

"Maybe a more traditional recipe would be a better idea, Ms. Lovejoy," Cha Cha suggested, discreetly returning her cookie to the tray. "What if you did something in honor of our town, like pumpkin bread or pumpkin muffins?"

Aunt True nodded. "Pumpkin muffins. I like it. No—wait! How about pumpkin *whoopie pies*? Quintessentially New England, but with a twist." She nodded. "That's perfect! They'll be our signature treat." She gave my father a sidelong glance. "I'll make mini ones, which will be more budget-friendly," she added. "People will come from far and wide to sample the treats at Lovejoy's Books."

My father threw his cookie in the trash. "Good, because they won't come from anywhere to sample these things." His brief flash of a good mood had evaporated. He looked over at me. "I'll be in the office. Don't be long."

"No, sir."

ABSOLUTELY TRULY

Aunt True looked ruefully down at the tray. "I hate to waste these, but he's right. They're pretty awful."

"You could give them to Danny and Hatcher," I suggested. "They'll eat anything."

My aunt's eyes lit up. "Excellent strategy! Thank goodness for teenage boys."

"We should get going," Cha Cha told me. "I'm due over at the Starlite, and Lucas's mother will worry if he doesn't turn up at Lou's soon."

Hearing this, Lucas blushed.

I peered out the window. "The coast looks clear," I told them. "You should be okay."

"If you're worried about an ambush, that's a problem easily solved," said my aunt. "I have an errand to run, so why don't I just go along and make sure you both arrive at your destinations safely? I need to check on Memphis first, though—he and Miss Marple weren't getting along this afternoon, so I had to separate them."

Cha Cha turned to me as my aunt disappeared out the side door toward the stairs to her apartment. "Real quick, can you show me where you found the envelope?"

"The one with the *B* on it?" asked Lucas.

Cha Cha and I exchanged a glance. Lucas had obviously been paying attention! Cha Cha raised an eyebrow, and her unspoken question hung in the air.

"Oh, fine," I said. It wasn't as if Lucas would blab our secret to anyone—he barely spoke as it was. I explained about the mystery as I led the two of them back to the Annex.

"It was here in the used-book section," I told them, waving vaguely at the bottom shelf and handing the envelope to Lucas. He opened it and read the letter inside while I looked around for the basket of books without bar codes. There was no sign of it. "It was inside a copy of *Charlotte's Web*."

"Do you remember the pages it was stuck between?" asked Cha Cha. "That could be important."

I shook my head. "I wasn't really paying attention."

"And nothing else was in there?"

"Not that I noticed."

Just then, there was a sharp knock on the bookshop's front door.

"We're closed!" I heard my father yell from the office. "Can't you see the sign?"

The knocking escalated frantically. Grabbing the letter and envelope from Lucas, I stuffed them back into the pocket of my jeans and hurried to the front of the store to see what was going on. My friends were right behind me.

"For heaven's sake!" said Aunt True, crossing to the door and unlocking it. "What's the matter?"

"Where's that blasted January thaw when you need it?" fussed a small, plump, elderly person, barging past her into the store. She was bundled in more layers than Lucas Winthrop, but hers were considerably rattier. The two scarves wound around her neck clashed horribly with her threadbare jacket—red and blue stripes and purple plaid do not go well with green camouflage—and her boots, which looked about two sizes too big, were stuffed with crumpled newspaper. A face as wrinkled as a dried plum peeked out from beneath a bright orange hunter's hat. The earflaps were tied securely under her chin. Emerging from beneath the flaps were a few wisps of snow-white hair and the telltale wires from a pair of earbuds.

An elf owl, if ever I'd seen one.

"We're closed," my father repeated.

"Good afternoon, Miss Marple," she said, ignoring him.

Miss Marple got to her feet and trotted over expectantly.

"Don't worry, I didn't forget your treat." There was a rustling noise as the woman plunged an orange mitten into one of the many plastic bags she was carrying. "Oops, that's not it."

The five of us stared at her mittened hand. There was a kitten in it. The tiny creature let out a squeak, and at the sound another furry little head popped out of the woman's jacket pocket.

"How many kittens do you generally carry with you?" asked Aunt True, blinking in astonishment.

There was no response, so my aunt repeated her question, louder this time.

The elderly woman removed one of her earbuds. I heard

the faint, tinny strains of the Beatles' "Can't Buy Me Love." "Depends," she replied.

Tucking both kittens back into their hiding places, she rummaged in the plastic bag once again, this time pulling out what looked like toast crusts. What I hoped were toast crusts, at least. Miss Marple had had enough food surprises today, what with Aunt True's cookies.

"We're closed," my father repeated for the third time.

"It's a book emergency," said our visitor.

Seeing our blank looks, she wiped her nose on the end of one of her scarves and rooted around in another plastic bag, emerging with a battered paperback this time. "Mystery swap," she added, waving it at us. "You know, bring a book, take a book?" When that got no response either, she heaved a sigh. "Never mind, I'll do it myself."

"Who's that?" I whispered, as she trundled off toward the Annex.

"No idea," Aunt True whispered back.

"It's Belinda Winchester," said Cha Cha.

Dad's head snapped around. "*That's* Belinda Winchester?" he said, watching her walk away. "She was at least a hundred when I was a kid! I can't believe she's still living here. Or still living, period."

"She looks kind of homeless," I said.

"She wasn't when I was growing up," my father replied. "She used to live in a big old house at the end of our street."

"She still does," said Cha Cha.

"I remember her now!" said Aunt True. "A little nutty, had about twenty-seven cats—or at least she did back then—house crammed with stuff?"

"That's her," said Cha Cha.

Belinda Winchester returned a moment later with a different paperback. My father stepped over to the cash register. "How would you like to pay for that this afternoon?"

"*Pay* for it?" the older woman screeched. The furry heads popped out again, their round kitten eyes wide in alarm. "What part of 'swap' don't you understand?" She peered at my father more closely. "Say, aren't you Walt and Lola's boy?"

I'd never heard my father called a "boy" before. He hesitated for a moment, then nodded.

"You're the delinquent who broke my garage window with a slingshot!"

My father reddened. "That was a long time ago, Miss Winchester," he replied stiffly. "And as I recall, I saved up my allowance to pay for the repair."

Aunt True was smiling broadly by now. I could tell she was enjoying this.

Our visitor sniffed. "Don't know as I remember it that way." She stuffed the paperback into a plastic bag. "I'd say this makes us even." And with that she and her kittens stalked out.

Aunt True laughed so hard her knees went weak. She collapsed on the bench by the door, gasping for breath.

My father shook his head in disgust. "Whose idea was it to have a mystery swap? What are we running here, a charity?"

"Calm down, J. T." said Aunt True, wiping her eyes. "It's just a used paperback. And it was a book emergency, remember? With a side of kittens." She dissolved in laughter again.

"We're the ones with a book emergency, especially if we just let our inventory walk out of here," my father told her. "This is a business, not the public library."

Beside me, I heard Lucas suck in his breath.

"No more stalling, Truly," my father said curtly. "Say goodbye to your friends. I want you in the office on the double." He spun on his heel and left.

As Aunt True started out the door, Lucas turned to Cha Cha and me, his pale face alight with excitement. "I know what the numbers on your mystery envelope mean."

CHAPTER 12

Telling Lucas about the envelope turned out to be a good idea.

Except for the fact that I could barely concentrate on my math tutoring afterward. I stared blindly at the open book in front of me, my shoe woodpeckering against the metal base of my chair.

Across the room, my father threw down his pen. "You've got ants in your pants this afternoon, Truly!"

"Sorry."

"Try and focus, would you?"

"Yes, sir." I wondered just how well he'd be able to focus if he was on the brink of solving a mystery.

"They're library call numbers," Lucas had told Cha Cha and me. "See?" Reaching into his backpack, he'd pulled out a copy of *Your Government and You* and pointed to the sequence of numbers across the sticker on the book's spine.

Sure enough, although the numbers were completely

different from the ones on my letter, the pattern was the same.

Cha Cha had frowned. "So whoever wrote the letter was sending the person it was meant for off to find another book?"

I'd nodded. "It's like a scavenger hunt! We need to go the library."

The problem was, none of us could. My father would have been breathing fire if I hadn't shown up for my tutoring session in about thirty seconds flat, Cha Cha was due over at her parents' dance studio to fill in for the receptionist again, and Lucas's mother was probably having a cow because he wasn't there yet. So we'd agreed to meet at the library after dinner.

I chewed the end of my pencil nervously and glanced at the clock. The other problem was, my mother had scheduled that family meeting tonight. This narrowed my brief window of time even further for making it to the library before it closed. I felt like I'd explode if I had to wait until tomorrow.

I sighed and stared again at the worksheet in front of me. Math is usually something I enjoy, but word problems? *Puh-leez.*

My father pushed back from his desk a little while later and came over to check my work. "You can do better," he told me, pointing out a couple of errors.

"Yes, sir," I replied glumly.

Suddenly, there was a loud squawk from out in the store. "J. T.!" shouted Aunt True. "Come quick!"

My father bolted out the office door. I was right on his

heels, grateful for an excuse to ditch the word problems.

We found my aunt over by the travel section. "Would you look at this?" she said in amazement. She was kneeling on the floor by the basket of books I'd been looking for earlier, holding up the copy of *Charlotte's Web*. For a second I wondered if maybe she'd found another letter inside, but that wasn't what she was excited about. "It's an autographed first edition!" She showed us the inscription, which read: *To my nifty little neighbor Bee, from Andy White.*

"Who's Andy?" my father asked.

"That was E. B. White's nickname," Aunt True told him.

Dad stared at her. "And here I thought the place was on fire or something from all the fuss you were making."

Aunt True scrambled to her feet. "Don't you understand? Some autographed first editions go for thousands of dollars!"

My eyebrows shot up. There were people willing to pay that kind of money for an old book?

"Really?" Now my father sounded excited too. "We might be able to pay off the bank loan if that's the case—or at least make a serious dent in it."

Aunt True looked over at me. "Were you the one who found this book, Truly?"

I nodded. "Yeah, when I was scanning stuff in the Annex."

"You just may have saved the day." She kissed me on the cheek, then waltzed happily toward the front of the store. My father and I followed her. "I'm going to do a little research and see if I can come up with a value for it, then we'll put it in the rare books cabinet for safekeeping."

The rare books cabinet was a locked, glass-fronted bookcase by the sales counter. There wasn't much in it these days—I guess anything of value had long since been sold to help keep the store afloat.

As Aunt True disappeared into the office, there was a knock on the front door.

"Does everyone in Pumpkin Falls have a book emergency today?" my father grumbled, going to answer it.

This time it wasn't a desperate customer, though; it was my mother.

"Big news!" she announced as she came in. The rest of my family was right behind her. "I have a job!"

Pippa did a pirouette. "Mommy ith going to be a danther!"

"No, honey, I'm just *working* at a dance studio," my mother corrected. "Big difference." She turned to my father. "I saw an ad in the *Patriot-Bugle* this morning and answered it."

My mouth dropped open. "You're going to be the receptionist at the Starlite?"

My mother looked over at me, astonished. "How on earth did you know that?"

I explained about Cha Cha, and she laughed. "See? It was meant to be."

"Are you sure you're going to be able to handle it, Dinah?" my father asked.

"It's only part-time, and it's just until the dance studio's regular receptionist gets back from maternity leave," she told him. "And guess what? As one of the perks, Pippa and Lauren get free dance lessons."

Hearing this, Pippa spun around the room again.

Lauren plopped down on the floor near Miss Marple and opened her latest book—she'd moved on from Laura Ingalls Wilder to *The Borrowers*. Danny and Hatcher made a beeline for Aunt True's cookies. I watched, waiting for the fireworks, but my brothers scarfed down the cookies without so much as a peep. Their stomachs must be made of iron.

"Where's True?" my mother asked. "I can't wait to tell her."

My father gestured toward the office with his right hand. Only it wasn't his right hand any more, of course. It was a hook.

Pippa spotted it and froze. Her eyes widened, and I could see Dad's jaw muscles tighten as she ducked behind my mother and started to cry. It just kills him when Pippa does this.

My parents have tried, they really have. And so have Danny and Hatcher and Lauren and me. But no one has been able to convince Pippa that the hook isn't a big scary thing. So Dad's just given up wearing his prosthesis when he's at home. He keeps it in a gym bag and carries it to and from the bookstore every day. It's only temporary, Mom says, insisting that Pippa will get used to it. Plus, Dad is scheduled to get his new more permanent prosthetic arm soon and everyone's hoping she'll like that one better.

"What's all the commotion?" asked Aunt True, emerging from the office. "Another book emergency?"

My mother shook her head. "Not exactly. More of a Pippa emergency." Lowering her voice to a whisper that was barely audible over my little sister's wails, she explained the situation.

Aunt True crouched down beside Pippa. "Well, my goodness, and here I thought there was a hippopotamus loose in the store!"

The wails subsided into hiccups.

"I've seen a hippopotamus, you know," Aunt True continued. "Back when I lived in Tanzania. And I've seen lions and zebras and crocodiles, too."

Pippa peeked out from behind my mother.

"Speaking of crocodiles, do you know the story of Peter Pan?"

My little sister nodded, sniffling. She wiped her nose with the back of her hand.

"We went on the ride at Dithney World."

"And do you remember the crocodile?" Aunt True asked her.

Pippa nodded again. "Tick-Tock."

"That's right. And what did that crocodile do?"

Pippa's forehead puckered as she thought about it. "He thwam after Captain Hook."

ABSOLUTELY TRULY

Aunt True smiled. "Uh-huh," she said. "Tick-Tock wasn't afraid of silly old Captain Hook, was he?"

Pippa shook her head.

I could see where this was going, and so could my father. He frowned. "Really, True?"

"Come on, J. T.," Aunt True coaxed. "Where's your sense of humor?"

A corner of his mouth quirked up. I could tell he thought it was funny, even though he was trying not to.

"And you don't have to be afraid either," Aunt True told Pippa. She motioned to my father, who heaved a sigh and reluctantly waved his prosthesis. "See? You can pretend you're Tick-Tock, and that's just silly old Captain Hook."

"Thilly old Captain Hook," Pippa repeated. She didn't look entirely convinced, but she wasn't crying anymore either. A moment later, she started running around the store shouting "Tick-Tock! Tick-Tock!" as my father gamely let her chase him.

"Thanks, True," said my mother, watching them.

"Tell her about your job, Mom," I urged, and she did.

"That's fantastic, Dinah!" said my aunt, then showed her the first edition of *Charlotte's Web*. "What a red-letter day for the Lovejoys! I'd say this calls for a celebration—I'm taking us all out to dinner at Lou's."

My mother hesitated. "We have a family meeting scheduled."

"You can have it at the restaurant," said Aunt True. "Nobody's cooking tonight."

"Are you sure, True?" Mom asked. "There are rather of a lot of us."

"Really?" said Aunt True, blinking in fake surprise. "I hadn't noticed."

I was beginning to really like Aunt True.

After my aunt locked *Charlotte's Web* away in the rare books cabinet, we trooped over to Lou's and crammed in around the diner's biggest table. Lou had to bring over a couple of extra chairs to fit us all in. I took it as a good sign that Pippa asked to sit next to my father.

"Don't see big families like yours much these days," said the restaurant owner.

Like clockwork, our heads all swiveled toward Dad. This was his cue to leap in with a comment about the Magnificent Seven. But Captain Hook's smile had vanished and Silent Man was back.

Mom quickly spoke up to fill the awkward silence. "We love having a big family! I'm one of seven kids, myself." She chattered on to Lou for a couple of minutes, then Lucas's mother came over to take our order.

I looked around the crowded restaurant. I guess if you're pretty much the only restaurant in Pumpkin Falls, you're going to be busy most of the time. The tables and booths were filled with a mix of college students, older people, and local families.

ABSOLUTELY TRULY

I spotted Amy Nguyen and her brother and parents in one of the booths, and Lucas, who was sitting at the end of the counter by himself, eating a cheeseburger and doing his homework. He waved shyly, and I waved back.

Danny and Hatcher launched into a recap of their wrestling practice for Dad while Mom and Aunt True started talking about some novel they were both reading. Lauren was still buried in *The Borrowers*, so I helped Pippa color her place mat until Mrs. Winthrop returned with our food.

As she set a small plate of greens and dressing in front of my father, I waited for him to say, "Oh, a honeymoon salad!" the way he always used to. He'd grin in anticipation, waiting for the waiter or waitress to ask what he meant by that. Then he'd waggle his eyebrows Groucho Marx-style and say, "Lettuce alone!" It always got a laugh.

Now, though, he just picked up his fork and started to eat.

"You're Truly, right?" said Mrs. Winthrop, handing me my fish and chips. I nodded. "I want to thank you for helping Lucas out today after school. Those bigger boys can be a bit—rowdy."

"You're welcome."

"Lucas said something about going to the library with you later for a project you're working on?"

I nodded.

"Would you mind walking him home afterward?" his mother asked, fiddling with the salt and pepper shakers. "It's just that, you know, it's dark and the roads and sidewalks are icy."

"Don't you worry," my mother told her. "Truly will see your son safely home."

"Thanks."

I watched her walk away. I was wrong about Mrs. Winthrop being a blue jay. She was pure mother hen.

"So what was that all about?" my mother asked. I explained about the snowball fight earlier, and she smiled at me. "That was very kind of you, sweetheart."

"All hail Saint Drooly," said Hatcher in a robot voice, sticking French fries in his ears. He turned to Pippa. "Frankenfryenstein. Want. Ketchup."

Pippa giggled. Not to be outdone, Danny wedged a pair of fries between his upper lip and teeth. "Yessssss," he said, affecting a fake accent. "Fangs a lot, Truly—Count Spudula approvessss."

"Boys," warned my mother, but it was too late. Lauren was oblivious, of course—too engrossed in her book to notice—but Pippa laughed so hard that milk squirted out of her nose. This startled her and made her cry again, and when I reached for some napkins to help clean her up, I knocked over my water glass, making an even bigger mess. My father shot me a black look as some of the liquid pooled over the edge of the table and onto the leg of his pants.

"For heaven's sake, Truly!" he snapped.

"But it was Pippa's—"

"Don't answer back."

I slumped in my seat. "No, sir."

Mrs. Winthrop brought over some paper towels. As she and my mother started to mop up, the door to the diner opened and a figure in black came in.

"Oh, great," muttered my father. "Just what I need to make my evening complete."

It was Ella Bellow.

Spotting us, she made a beeline for our table. Her lips thinned in disapproval as she surveyed the lake of watery milk. "Waste of money, taking children to restaurants," she observed, shaking her head. "Especially when there are so many of them."

"It's my money, and I don't consider it a waste," Aunt True replied. "Can we help you, Ella?"

Pippa's tears instantly ceased. She looked up. "Ella Bellow?"

I felt a prickle of misgiving.

The postmistress gave my little sister a fleeting smile, but her gaze was riveted to the hook at the end of my father's shirtsleeve.

"Take a picture; it'll last longer," said Hatcher under his breath.

My mother elbowed him sharply. "It's nice to see you again, Ella," she said politely. "And now if you'll excuse us, we were about to have a family meeting."

"Of course," said the postmistress, steering herself to the

closest table. She took a seat with her back to us, but it was obvious that she was all ears.

My mother leaned forward and whispered, "I vote that we take our dessert back to the bookstore and have our meeting there."

"Mom'th whithpering becauth Ella Bellow ith a buthybody," said Pippa in a loud voice. "Right, Truly?"

The postmistress's back stiffened. The nearby tables went dead silent. Aunt True choked on a bite of cheeseburger, except her coughing fit sounded suspiciously like laughter to me.

"Truly!" my mother whispered furiously. "What did you tell your sister?"

"It's not my fault!" I whispered back. "And anyway, you were the one who said it first!"

My father glared at me. "Truly Lovejoy, don't you dare speak back to your mother."

"Truce!" said Aunt True weakly, waving her napkin like a white flag. Her eyes were watering and she was trying hard to suppress a smile. "All in favor of family harmony, especially in public places"—she tipped her head toward our neighboring eavesdropper—"raise their hands."

Hatcher and Danny raised their hands. So did I.

Mrs. Winthrop, who looked like she was trying not to smile too, finished cleaning off the table.

"Let's change the subject, shall we?" Aunt True continued. "How was your day, Dinah?"

ABSOLUTELY TRULY

"Fine up until now," my mother replied.

"Look at the bright side," my aunt told her. "It can't get any worse, right? But, seriously, any interesting classes?"

Mom nodded. "Yes, all of them. I especially like my American History for Educators class. Professor Rusty is so interesting."

Dad's eyebrows snapped to attention. He looked over at Aunt True. "I didn't know Rusty was back in town! How long's he been teaching at the college?"

Aunt True suddenly seemed very interested in rearranging her silverware. "Six months or so. Mom mentioned something about it before they left for Africa."

"Who's Rusty?" asked Danny.

"Someone your father and I went to high school with," Aunt True said lightly. "So, what do you say we all get ice-cream sundaes to go?"

I glanced anxiously at the clock, then turned to my mother. "Can I be excused to go to the library? It's going to close soon."

"*May* I," said my mother automatically. "And no, you may not."

"Mom!"

"You know our agreement."

Attendance at family meetings is mandatory. It's one of Lieutenant Colonel Jericho T. Lovejoy's rules.

"I don't need a sundae." I begged. "And it's just down the street—I'll be back at the bookstore before you guys even finish dessert. We only need to look this one thing up."

My mother frowned. "It's for your project with the Winthrop boy, right?" she asked, and I nodded. It wasn't a lie, really. Solving the mystery of the envelope counted as a project, and Lucas was helping me. My mother pressed her lips together, considering. "Well, I suppose it's okay," she said finally. "If you promise to hurry."

"I promise," I said, getting to my feet. "Absolutely truly, cross my heart and hope to fly."

I froze, aghast.

I'd said it completely without thinking, the words no sooner out of my mouth than I would have given anything to snatch them back.

My father stared down at his prosthesis, which was resting on the table. Pain creased his forehead. "I think we'll save the family meeting for another night," he said gruffly, then pushed back from the table and stood up.

Ella Bellow swiveled around in her chair and stared as he walked out of the restaurant.

"Truly, how could you!" said my mother, giving me her trademark disappointed look.

"Nice going, moron," added Danny. "You totally ruined everything."

Even Hatcher looked at me reproachfully.

"I didn't do it on purpose!" I protested. "It just came"—I caught myself before I said "flying"—"out!"

"Cross my heart and hope to fly" is this saying that Dad's

ABSOLUTELY TRULY

best friend Tom Larson made up, way back when the two of them were in flight school. We always knew when Dad was talking to Mr. Larson on the phone, because that's how they'd end their calls. It was like their own private motto, and over the years it had become our family's motto too. But now it's strictly off-limits because Mr. Larson didn't make it back from Afghanistan, and it reminds my father of that horrible day when he lost both his arm and his best friend.

Once again, I'd gone and stuck my foot in my mouth. I was Truly-in-the-Middle-of-a-Mess.

Aunt True was wrong—the evening could get worse. It just did.

CHAPTER 13

I didn't wait for Lucas; I just grabbed my jacket and ran.

"Hey!" he called, dashing through the front door of the diner after me. "Wait up!" Panting, he caught up with me as I reached the *Pumpkin Falls Patriot-Bugle* building. "What's the matter?"

"None of your business," I snapped. What was I supposed to tell him? That I desperately wished that everything could go back to the way it was before? Before Black Monday, and before Silent Man, and before we had to move here to this stupid place? That I'd give anything to hear my dad laugh again, and to hear the Magnificent Seven ringtone on his cell phone? I charged ahead down the sidewalk and didn't stop until I reached the library.

"I was worried you weren't coming," said Cha Cha, leaping up from the bench inside the lobby. "They're getting ready to close."

ABSOLUTELY TRULY

Lucas and I followed her through the main reading area, a cozy room lined with bookshelves and two big, comfortable chairs that flanked a crackling fire. Belinda Winchester was seated in one of them, still wearing her bright orange hunter's cap. Her eyes were closed; she was either napping or listening to music through her earbuds. There was no sign of kittens.

I glanced up the stairs that led to the children's room, wondering if Charlotte's Corner was still there. I'd spent a lot of summer afternoons sitting cross-legged underneath it. Gramps and Lola didn't just run a bookshop; they were book people through and through, and the Pumpkin Falls Library was at the top of their list of places to take visiting grandchildren. Story Hour was always held beneath the bronze sculpture of the doorway of Zuckerman's barn, with Charlotte the spider looking down from her web, and us kids fighting over who got to sit next to Wilbur and who got stuck beside Templeton the rat.

Cha Cha led us to a pair of computer terminals in the teeny reference area. She climbed up on a stool in front of one of them, her short legs dangling.

"Read me the numbers," she said.

I pulled the envelope out of the back pocket of my jeans and opened it. "'PR2828.A2 B7,'" I replied.

She typed this into the search field, pausing a moment and then frowning at the screen. "Again, please. Slower this time."

I did as she asked.

"It's not here."

I peered over her shoulder. "Are you sure?"

She pointed to the screen, which read ITEM NOT FOUND.

The three of us stared morosely at the computer. Our scavenger hunt was over before it started.

"We could ask the reference librarian," Lucas suggested.

"No." I clutched the letter to my chest. Maybe it was the fact that my entire family was mad at me, but I was feeling possessive all of a sudden. Three of us trying to solve the mystery was enough.

"Nobody has to actually see it, Truly," said Cha Cha, passing me a pencil and a piece of paper. "Just write down the call number."

I relented. As I started to write, the lights overhead flicked on and off.

"The library is now closing," announced a voice over the loudspeaker, and the people around us started gathering up their things.

Cha Cha grabbed the piece of paper from me and dashed across the room to the reference desk. Lucas and I followed.

"Sorry, kids, we're closed now," said the woman behind the counter.

"Please?" begged Cha Cha.

The woman shook her head. "I just shut the computer down," she explained. "Can you come back tomorrow?"

Lucas tugged on Cha Cha's sleeve. "Let's go find Mr.

Henry," he whispered, and Cha Cha dashed off again.

"Who's Mr. Henry?" I asked Lucas as we jogged after her.

"The children's librarian," he told me.

We found him upstairs by Charlotte's Corner, sorting picture books. I couldn't help staring. Except for his dreadlocks and the fact that he was African American, Mr. Henry was a dead ringer for *Where's Waldo?* He was wearing hipster glasses, jeans, a red-and-white striped shirt, and red sneakers.

"School project, huh?" he said, when Cha Cha gave him the slip of paper.

"Um, not—" Lucas started to reply. I stepped on his foot. Not correcting someone isn't exactly the same as telling a lie, right?

"It's really important," I said.

Mr. Henry smiled. "Such eagerness! Such zeal!" He rose to his feet. "Who can resist young minds intent on edification? Certainly not Henry Butterworth!"

"Thanks," said Cha Cha.

"Anything for the sister of the most awesome Baxter Abramowitz," he replied with a bow. He crossed to the computer at his desk and typed in the numbers. "Shakespeare, huh? Looks like we don't have the volume you're looking for here on our shelves, I'm afraid. But perhaps I can get it for you through interlibrary loan." He fired off a longer something on his keyboard, peering over his glasses at the screen. "Lovejoy College has a copy." He swiveled around to face us. "Shall I request it for you? It shouldn't take more than a few days, a week at most, for them to send it over."

"Thanks anyway," said Cha Cha at the same time that I said, "Yes, please."

The librarian looked from one of us to the other, bemused. "Which shall it be?"

Cha Cha elbowed me sharply. "It's a no, Mr. Henry. But thanks for your help."

"That's what I'm here for. You kids come back anytime."

"What was that all about?" I asked, once we were back outside again. My question rose like a smoke signal in the frosty air.

"That was all about the fact that I have a better idea," Cha Cha replied. "Why wait a whole week when we can just go over there ourselves?"

"How are we supposed to do that?" I protested. "They won't let middle schoolers in—you have to have a college ID and everything." I'd seen my mother's.

"They'll let us in," Cha Cha told me. "But there's a catch." She paused. "We're going to have to talk to Calhoun."

CHAPTER 14

"Can you keep the kids out of my hair this afternoon, Truly?" my mother asked. It was Saturday afternoon, and Pippa had a playdate scheduled with Baxter Abramowitz, who was due to arrive any second. Annie Freeman was already here with Lauren. "I have a pile of homework to finish before my shift at the Starlite."

I promised her I would.

"Pippa's upstairs in her room," I told Baxter a few minutes later, when I interrupted my piano practice to answer the doorbell. He and Cha Cha were waiting on the doorstep, their cheeks rosy from the cold. Cha Cha had offered to walk her brother over so that the two of us could hang out. Lucas was on his way to join us.

They came inside, and Cha Cha helped her little brother out of his jacket. He sat down and pulled his boots off impatiently, then scampered upstairs.

"Who are all these people?" asked Cha Cha, staring at the portraits on the wall as we followed him.

"Lovejoys," I told her. "That's the original Truly."

She paused. "You look a bit like her."

"You think?"

She nodded. "Yeah. Same eyes and nose."

This was good news. If I had the original Truly's nose, that meant I wasn't doomed to inherit the dreaded Nathaniel Daniel Lovejoy proboscis.

I led Cha Cha down the hall to my room. She looked around in approval. "Nice," she said. "But what's with all the owls?"

I shrugged. "I just like them, that's all."

Cha Cha plunked herself down on the braided rug in front of my bookshelf. "You have a lot of bird books."

This was an understatement.

She ran her finger across the row of titles. "Have you read all these?"

I nodded.

"Wow. So you must know a lot about birds, huh?"

I glanced at her out of the corner of my eye, trying to tell if she was really interested or just being polite. Or worse, if she was asking me out of pity. Did she think I was a bird nerd?

Well, I sort of am.

"Yeah, I guess I do," I replied, deciding she was sincere. "Would you like to see my life list?"

She nodded and I pulled a dog-eared leather notebook

from the shelf. Gramps gave it to me back when I was Lauren's age. The front was stamped with gold silhouettes of birds, but the gold had mostly worn away.

I opened it to the first page. "All real birders keep a life list," I explained. "You add to it every time you spot a new bird. See? This one here at the top, the northern cardinal? That was the very first bird I saw after I got this notebook."

I looked at my round and careful nine-year-old handwriting, remembering how thrilled I was when Gramps taught me the Latin name—*Cardinalis cardinalis*—and made me write it down. It was like a secret handshake, something that let me into his club.

I scanned a few of the pages, thinking about all the walks we'd taken together here in Pumpkin Falls, and all the birds we'd seen—from the barn swallows that came back every year to nest in the eaves over Lola's studio to the purple finch (*Carpodacus purpureus*), New Hampshire's state bird. Gramps had told me that his birding hero, Roger Tory Peterson, a naturalist who wrote a bunch of field guides, once described the purple finch as "a sparrow dipped in raspberry juice." He laughed about it, but the description stuck in my head, and I've never had any trouble spotting a purple finch since.

No owls, though. I still didn't have one of those on my life list.

Cha Cha's gaze wandered down to the bottom shelf. "Whose yearbooks are those?"

"My aunt's," I told her. "This used to be her room."

Cha Cha pulled one from the shelf at random and flipped it open. "West Hartfield Pep Squad," she read aloud. "Whoa, check out these hairstyles!"

I knelt down beside her and peered over her shoulder. "My aunt should be in there someplace," I told her. "I think this one's from the year she graduated."

Cha Cha flipped to the back to check out the senior portraits.

"Wait, you passed it," I said, and Cha Cha turned the pages until we found Aunt True. Instead of the typical headshot, my aunt had chosen a candid pose that showed her perched on the railing of the covered bridge, with the waterfall sparkling in the sunshine behind her.

"She's really pretty," said Cha Cha. "Even with the big hair."

I nodded. Looking at the picture, I realized that I had stood in the exact same spot just a few days ago on our science class field trip. I could tell because the camera had caught some of the same graffiti that Lucas had sketched: SAM LOVES BETTY; JOJO AND CARL; and that lopsided heart with E & T FOREVER inside. Things didn't change much over the years in Pumpkin Falls.

I read the list of activities beneath my aunt's picture. She'd been on the debate team, which explained how she could win so many arguments with my father, and she'd also been captain of the tennis team, editor of the school newspaper, and a member of the Thespian Club, whatever that was.

"Sweet," said Cha Cha. "She was voted 'Most Likely to See the World.'"

"They sure got that right," I replied. "Aunt True's been everywhere."

We looked for my father next, and found him lined up with the other wrestlers for the team photo. I noticed that he was already wrestling varsity, even though he was only a sophomore that year.

"He looks a little like Hatcher," said Cha Cha.

"Wait until you meet my brother Danny," I told her. "He and my dad could practically be twins." I stared at the picture. My father stared back, his jaw set and determined even then. It was weird to think he hadn't met Mom when that picture was taken, or known that he was going to join the army and have five kids.

My gaze strayed to his arms. Both of them. He certainly hadn't known about Black Monday.

"Principal Burnside was a wrestler too," said Cha Cha, pointing to a vaguely familiar face in the lineup. It was perched atop a long, skinny, flamingo neck. Our principal was a sophomore then too, just like my father, only he looked about twelve.

"Guess he hadn't hit his growth spurt yet," I remarked, and Cha Cha snickered.

She turned the page. "Check it out, Belinda Winchester used to be a lunch lady!"

"She looks exactly the same," I noted in surprise. "Well,

except for the hairnet and uniform. And her hair wasn't white back then either."

Cha Cha nodded. "I'll bet she's got kittens in her pockets, though," she said, and we both snickered this time.

I read the caption under the photo: *West Hartfield High welcomed Down-Easter Belinda Winchester to the cafeteria staff this year. Everyone's hoping she'll add lobster to the menu!*

We flipped around in the yearbook a bit more, poking fun at the stupid hairstyles and clothes.

"Hey, there's the guy from the stamp store," I said, pointing to another senior portrait. "See? Earl 'Bud' Jefferson Jr."

"Nice mullet, Bud," said Cha Cha.

"Business in the front, party in the back," I intoned, and she grinned.

"Not a good look," she scolded, wagging her finger at the picture. "Especially for a 'Future Business Leader of America.'" She turned the page again.

"Who names their kid Erastus?" I said, pointing to a photo of a boy with bushy dark hair and glasses. "Sheesh."

Cha Cha gave me a sly look. "Um, pot calling the kettle black much?"

My mouth fell open. I swatted her on the shoulder with the mystery envelope. "You're one to talk, *Cha Cha*."

Her dimple flashed again, and I had to laugh. It felt good to be joking around. I hadn't done much of that since leaving Austin, and Mackenzie.

ABSOLUTELY TRULY

I looked back at the yearbook. Erastus Peckinpaugh had been on the National Honor Society and was voted "Most Likely to Get a PhD." He also proudly listed his membership in "The Fighting Fifth"—a living history group that portrayed the Fifth New Hampshire Regiment Volunteers.

"Civil War reenactors," I told Cha Cha. My father had lots of army buddies who did that for a hobby. "In other words, total geek."

Cha Cha turned the page. "Hey, there's Calhoun's parents." I leaned in for a closer look. James Calhoun had been class president, captain of the soccer team, and, like Aunt True, a member of the yearbook staff and the Thespian Club. He had the same sandy hair and dark eyes as his son but he looked a whole lot friendlier. Mostly because he was smiling. I didn't think I'd seen Calhoun smile yet. A real smile, that was, not just a stupid smirk.

"That's Calhoun's mom," said Cha Cha, pointing to a picture of a pretty brunette on the opposite page. Jennifer Upton had played in the school orchestra, was president of the National Honor Society, and had starred in a whole bunch of plays while she was at West Hartfield.

"I overheard Ella Bellow and Lou talking about them once at the diner," Cha Cha said. "Calhoun's parents were high school sweethearts. Everybody figured they'd be famous one day, because they were really awesome actors."

"So what happened?"

"They got married after college and moved to New York."

"To be actors?"

She nodded. "After their parents retired and moved away, though, they stopped coming to Pumpkin Falls. And then one day out of the blue last year, the *Patriot-Bugle* announces that Dr. Calhoun has been hired as president of Lovejoy College, and he turns up with Calhoun and his sister, but no Mrs. Calhoun. I guess they got divorced right before the move."

As I was digesting this information, there was a knock on my door. Hatcher poked his head in. "Drooly?" he said. "Your friend Lucas is here."

"*Hatcher!*" My face flamed. The last thing I needed was for that stupid nickname to get out. I could only imagine what would happen if Scooter and Calhoun got ahold of it.

"Drooly, huh?" boomed Cha Cha, and my brother looked a bit taken aback. I was used to it by now, but Cha Cha's deep voice seemed to surprise people the first time they heard it. "You and Erastus are definitely tied, Truly."

"Shut up!" I swatted her with the envelope again.

Cha Cha laughed. "Don't worry—your secret's safe with us. Right, Lucas?"

Lucas stood in the doorway, looking like he might bolt at any second. His face was even redder than mine. He'd probably never been in a girl's room before.

"It's okay, Lucas," I told him. "You can come in. We won't bite."

ABSOLUTELY TRULY

Behind him, Hatcher bared his teeth and pretended to chomp down on the top of Lucas's head. I ignored him, but Cha Cha let out a raspy giggle.

Lucas shuffled timidly forward. He gazed around my room. "Nice owl," he said, spotting the woodcut over my bed.

"Thanks."

"What are you guys up to, anyway?" asked Hatcher, lounging against the doorjamb.

I hesitated, tempted to tell him about the mystery we were trying to solve. Between school, tutoring sessions, and his endless wrestling practices, I felt like I'd hardly seen him since we'd moved to Pumpkin Falls. I was used to not seeing much of Danny—he was three years older and busy with high school—but I really missed spending time with Hatcher.

"Homework," Cha Cha told him before I could open my mouth.

My brother made a face. "Too bad. Danny and I are heading to the General Store. Tell Mom we'll be home in time for dinner, okay?"

He'd barely left before Lauren and Annie Freeman wandered in with Miss Marple. Annie had quickly established herself as Lauren's new best friend.

"Want to meet my turtle?" Lauren asked. She loves showing off her pets.

"Sure," said Cha Cha, taking it gingerly from her. "What's his name?"

"Methuselah," Lauren replied.

"I can spell that," Annie told us, and promptly did. "Methuselah lived to be nine hundred and sixty-nine years old. Do you think your turtle will live to be that old, Lauren? I'll bet your hamster won't. I had a hamster named Nantucket, because that's where we got her. We called her Nan for short. She was only two when she died."

Lauren shot me a worried look. Nibbles had turned two just before we left Austin. We'd had a birthday party for him and everything.

"You have pets, don't you, Cha Cha?" I said hastily, and she nodded. "Tell Lauren about them."

"We have two cats—Fred and Ginger. They're named after Fred Astaire and Ginger Rogers."

Seeing our blank looks, Cha Cha added, "Guess you guys don't watch old movies. They were famous dancers. My father thought it would be funny, since we own the Starlite and everything."

She passed Methuselah back to Lauren, who offered to let Lucas hold him too.

"No, thanks," he said, taking a step back.

"He doesn't bite," Lauren assured him. "Don't you have any pets?"

Lucas shook his head. Big surprise there. His helicopter mom was probably too worried he'd get fleas.

Pippa and Baxter must have heard us all talking, because

ABSOLUTELY TRULY

they barged into my room next. Baxter ran over to Cha Cha and gave her a big hug.

"I can tap danth," my little sister announced. Without waiting for a response, she launched into a shuffle-step routine. When she was done, she went over and plunked herself down next to Baxter and Cha Cha. I rolled my eyes, and Cha Cha grinned.

"Ooh!" said Annie, pouncing on a brochure I'd left on my desk. On the cover, beneath the words PUMPKIN FALLS COTILLION!, was a picture of Mr. and Mrs. Abramowitz and a bunch of kids, twirling across a dance floor with huge smiles on their faces. Annie sighed. "I can't wait until I'm in middle school. My sister Sarah says Cotillion is totally awesome. You should have seen her at the Winter Festival the year she was in it. She had on this really pretty dress with sparkles and everything. There was a live band and decorations and snacks too. Everybody said she was the best dancer."

Did Annie ever shut up?

"Go find something else to do," I told my sisters and their friends, shooing them out of my room. I shut the door firmly behind them.

They left, but just barely. I could hear whispering out in the hall. The four of them were trying to spy on us.

"Baxter does the same thing when I have friends over," Cha Cha assured me.

I racked my brain, trying to think of someplace more

private that we could go. Danny and Hatcher were gone, but if we went up to the third floor the younger kids would simply follow us. And the basement—which my brothers had dubbed "The Spider Farm"—was too creepy.

Then I had a bright idea. But I was going to have to be sly.

"Snack time!" I announced loudly, shoving the envelope in my backpack. I shouldered it and crossed the room, motioning for Cha Cha and Lucas to follow me. Lauren and Annie and Pippa and Baxter fell in behind us as we headed down the hall. Miss Marple took up the rear.

Downstairs, my mother was still sitting at the dining room table, her homework spread out in front of her.

"Can we make popcorn?" I asked.

"Sure," she replied absently. "Bring me some, would you?"

"I want popcorn too," Pippa whined.

"You bet, Pipster," I told her. "Why don't you and Bax go help Lauren and Annie pick out a movie to watch while I make it."

The four of them vanished through the door to the ell. Most really old houses in New England have an "ell," a room that used to connect the house to the barn. That way the farmers and their families could easily get from one to the other without having to go outside in the cold. Back when Dad and Aunt True were teenagers, Gramps and Lola had turned their ell into a family room.

ABSOLUTELY TRULY

"Thanks, honey," my mother said a few minutes later, when I brought her a bowl of popcorn. "I'm so glad to see you having fun with your new friends."

I was a little surprised to realize that I was having fun. Maybe not quite Mackenzie-level fun, but still, fun.

Cha Cha and Lucas and I lingered for a few minutes, waiting until the younger kids were engrossed in the movie. Then I picked up our popcorn bowl and motioned to my friends to follow me as I slipped through the door to the garage. We tiptoed up the stairs to Lola's art studio. Nobody would think to look for us there.

Fortunately, the key was still by the door, tucked behind my grandmother's painting of Lovejoy Mountain. I slipped it from its hook, unlocked the door, and led Cha Cha and Lucas inside.

Shivering, I switched on the heat and crossed the room to the sofa. Afternoon sun flooded through the wall of windows behind it. Technically, we probably weren't supposed to be up here, but nobody had exactly told me that it was off-limits, and there wasn't anyplace else I could think of for us to go.

"The first meeting of the Pumpkin Falls Private Eyes is called to order," I said, taking a seat.

"Seriously?" Cha Cha's dimple flashed.

"What's wrong with that?" I replied, stung.

Cha Cha wrinkled her nose. "It's kind of dorky."

"You come up with something better, then."

She shook her head. "No, that's okay. You can call us the Pumpkin Falls Private Eyes if you want to."

"I don't have to," I said stiffly.

"No, really. It's fine."

Somewhat mollified, I pulled the envelope out of my backpack, along with a pad of yellow lined paper and a pen, and placed them on the coffee table.

Lucas circled the spacious room, looking at Lola's paintings. My grandmother loved flowers, and a bright spill of them lit up the canvases on the walls.

"These are really good," he said.

"I know," I told him. "Can you pay attention, please? Our top order of business today—review the evidence." Drawing a line down the center of the yellow lined pad, I wrote two categories across the top: *What We Know* and *What We Don't Know*.

"So, what do we know?" I asked, scooping up a handful of popcorn.

Cha Cha took the letter out of the envelope and looked at it again. "We know it's from B to B."

I wrote that down.

Lucas raised his hand.

"Spit it out, Lucas," I told him. "It's just us, not school."

"We know the stamp is twenty years old," he said.

I wrote that down too. "And thanks to you," I told him, "we know that the numbers at the bottom of the letter aren't code, but call numbers for a book. Anything else?"

"The letter is part of a scavenger hunt, we think," said Cha Cha, reaching for more popcorn.

I wrote down *scavenger hunt*.

"We don't know who B and B are," said Lucas.

I wrote down *Who are B and B?* in the *What We Don't Know* column, then tapped my pencil on the notepad. "Let's make a list of everyone we know whose names have a *B* in them," I said, flipping over to the next page. "Like Principal Burnside."

"And Mr. Bigelow, our science teacher," said Lucas.

"Right." I jotted down both of their names.

"How about Mr. Jefferson?" said Cha Cha. "He told us that everyone calls him Bud, and it said so in the yearbook, too."

"What yearbook?" asked Lucas.

"The one back in Truly's room," Cha Cha told him. "It belonged to her aunt."

"Good catch," I said. "Oh, and we can't forget Belinda Winchester. Don't you think she looks like exactly the kind of person who would stick a letter in a book and forget about it?"

"Maybe," said Cha Cha. "But it seems like kind of a strange letter for a lunch lady to write."

"She was a lunch lady?" said Lucas, surprised.

"Yeah," I told him, adding Belinda Winchester to the list anyway.

"How about Ella Bellow?" said Cha Cha.

"Got it," I said, jotting her name down. "And there's Mr. Henry, too."

"That's an *H*," Cha Cha objected.

"He introduced himself as Henry *Butter*worth," I reminded her. "He's definitely a *B*." I shot her a mischievous look. "And of course we can't forget Baxter."

"He wasn't even born back then!"

"I'm *joking*, Cha Cha. Anyway, there are way too many *B*s in this town." I threw down my pen. We were getting nowhere. "So what's the deal with Calhoun?" I asked. "Did you talk to him about getting us into the library?"

"Not yet," Cha Cha replied. "I want to catch him at just the right moment. I think I have an angle, though." She gave us a sly smile. "I've seen the Cotillion list. We might have an in with his dance partner."

CHAPTER 15

"Places, everyone!" Ms. Ivey clapped her hands.

Reluctantly, I took a step closer to Scooter Sanchez, who was trying his best to ignore me. It was Monday afternoon and we were in the Daniel Webster School gym with the rest of our classmates, gearing up for our first ballroom dance practice.

I still couldn't believe I'd gotten stuck with Scooter as my partner. I thought it was a joke at first, when Cha Cha told me. I know Ms. Ivey only did it because we're both tall. It's not fun being a seventh grader and my height, since most guys my age come up to my armpit, but Scooter Sanchez? I'd rather dance with Lucas Winthrop's mother.

Who'd managed to humiliate Lucas yet again about ten minutes ago, when she showed up with a video camera. Ms. Ivey had to ask her to leave.

"I promise there'll be plenty of photo opportunities later

on, Amelia, after the kids are feeling more confident," Ms. Ivey told her as she escorted her out.

Scooter was all over that, of course. "Smile for the camera, Pookey!" he warbled, doing a little leap in front of Lucas. "Mommy wants a picture for your baby book!"

"That's enough, Scooter," said Ms. Ivey wearily, closing the door behind Mrs. Winthrop. I figured she must get really tired of saying that. Scooter only picks on Lucas about a hundred times a day.

Ms. Ivey introduced Cha Cha's parents, and we all clapped politely when she asked us to thank them for contributing their time. Well, all of us except Scooter.

"This is stupid," he muttered.

I looked at him, startled. "Mr. and Mrs. Abramowitz?"

"No, dork—Cotillion."

Privately, I agreed with him. Dancing is so not my thing. Especially not dancing with Scooter Sanchez.

Ms. Ivey had paired Cha Cha with Lucas, probably because they were the two shortest kids in the class. Jasmine had asked to be partners with Franklin, of course—she's as obsessed with him as Mackenzie is with Mr. Perfect Cameron McAllister—but Ms. Ivey had put him with Amy Nguyen and assigned Jasmine to Calhoun instead.

Which Cha Cha and Lucas and I are hoping will work in our favor.

Cha Cha's plan meant telling Jasmine about the mystery

letter, so now a total of four people know about it. Five, counting Mackenzie.

Ms. Ivey clapped her hands again. She was wearing white gloves, which were identical to mine. I'd picked them up at the General Store—naturally, they carried them—just like the brochure had instructed me to.

"How come you have to wear glovth?" Pippa had asked this morning, when she saw me putting them in my backpack. "Becauth of cootieth?"

I had to smile at that logic. I'd forgotten what a big deal cooties are when you're in kindergarten.

On the other hand, now that I was actually here in the gym, I was grateful for the gloves. I definitely didn't want Scooter cooties.

Scooties? The word popped into my mind, and I stifled a giggle.

He shot me a look. "What?"

"Nothing."

The music started, and Mr. and Mrs. Abramowitz demonstrated how we should position ourselves properly. Scooter watched, then reached into his back pocket and pulled something out. A moment later, he plopped a hand covered with a giant ski glove on my shoulder. I gave him a withering look. He was trying to get a laugh from his buddies, as usual.

It worked. A ripple of laughter flowed across the gym.

"Really, Mr. Sanchez?" said Mr. Abramowitz, when he

spotted the source of the hilarity. He crossed the gym and held out his hand. Scooter grinned and dropped the ski glove in it. He was unrepentant, however, and still on the hunt for laughs. We were supposed to be learning how to fox-trot ("Slow, slow, quick, quick," Mr. Abramowitz called out over and over again, as he and Cha Cha's mother led us through the steps), but Scooter turned it into a Truly-trot instead. He spent most of his time "accidentally" stepping on my feet. By the time Mr. Abramowitz caught on and told him to knock it off, my toes were numb.

Things went downhill from there. Next, Scooter thought it would be fun to sing "Truly Gigantic" under his breath in time to the music and steer me around the cafeteria like a bumper car.

"Oops!" he said, as we crashed into Cha Cha and Lucas, sending Lucas sprawling onto the floor. "Pardon me!"

Ms. Ivey clapped her hands once more, signaling a break, and I limped over to one of the chairs that lined the wall to sit down. After helping Lucas to his feet, Cha Cha joined me.

"Having fun yet?" I asked sourly.

She smiled. "You'll get the hang of it."

"Easy for you to say," I grumbled. "You're not stuck with Scooter." Plus, Cha Cha was an old hand at this. She was even managing to make a pipsqueak like Lucas, who'd probably never danced a step in his life, look like a pro. I, on the other hand—well, let's just say that I was not looking forward to making a fool of myself in front of the entire town.

ABSOLUTELY TRULY

Jasmine flopped onto a seat beside us. "This would be *so* much more fun if Ms. Ivey had let me dance with Franklin," she said with a sigh. "Calhoun never even cracks a smile."

"It's probably because you have cooties," I told her.

She laughed. "Or because he has two left feet."

That was an understatement. Calhoun was an even worse dancer than Scooter, as it turned out. He went left when he was supposed to go right, and right when he was supposed to go left, and he tripped over Jasmine's feet as well as his own. I looked across the room to where he was lounging against the wall, scowling.

"I think he's gotten worse since last year," Jasmine said.

"That's what I'm counting on," said Cha Cha. "That and the fact that he hates to lose. Especially to Scooter."

The music started again and Scooter and I stumbled and bumbled our way—slow, slow, quick, quick—across the floor. My big feet just weren't meant for this. My whole self just wasn't meant for this. Sometimes I wonder if I'm even meant to be a land animal. Life would be a lot easier if I were a bird—especially an owl, swooping silently through the sky. A fish would be good too.

Thinking of fish made me think of swim team tryouts. They were still a couple of weeks away, but I hadn't made any headway with my father.

At least my family was talking to me again. The whole "cross my heart and hope to fly" mess seemed to have blown over. There hadn't even been a big showdown that night when I'd gotten home from the library. My father had still been at the bookstore, finishing up inventory with Aunt True, and my mother was on the couch in the family room nodding off over her homework, too tired to do more than simply remind me of my promise to be more thoughtful of Dad.

"This move has been good for him," she'd said to me. "I see it already, even if he doesn't. But he still has a long road to recovery, sweetheart. Physically and mentally. And anything we can do as a family to help smooth that road will really help him. Even the little things that might not seem important, okay?"

I nodded. "I know, Mom. I'm really, really sorry. I didn't do it on purpose."

"I know you didn't, Little O."

I hadn't heard that nickname in a long time. It was short for "Little Owl," which seems kind of silly now that I tower over my mother by nearly a foot. She's called me that ever since I was a baby and refused to sleep through the night. There's even a picture of us wearing matching sweaters that she knitted with owls on the front and the initials "L. O." for me and "M. O."—that stands for Mama Owl—for her on the back.

The thing is, there are advantages to being a night owl. With five of us kids to take care of and Dad deployed most of the time, there hadn't always been enough of my mother to go around. And ever since I could remember, when I'd wake up in the middle of the night and go to get a drink of water or whatever, she'd still be awake. Sometimes she'd be waiting for a call from Dad—when your husband is stationed halfway around the world, you can't be picky about when to schedule a call—and sometimes she'd be reading or knitting or watching a movie, or just drinking tea and staring into the dark. It was the perfect opportunity to get some alone time with her.

I loved those nighttime visits. Sometimes my mother would make me tea or cocoa too, and sometimes we'd talk or she'd read aloud to me, but mostly I'd just curl up beside her on the sofa, content to be breathing the same air.

Since Black Monday, though, the initials in my nickname might as well have stood for "Largely Overlooked." Between the move, worries over my father and the bookstore, going back to college, and now a part-time job, my mother had reformed her night-owl ways. These days, she was in bed, sound asleep, well before I was.

"Ouch!" Scooter squawked, springing back indignantly. "Quit daydreaming! You stepped on my foot!"

"Like you haven't stepped on mine a million times already!" I retorted.

The music came to a stop, and Ms. Ivey clapped her hands one last time. "Excellent work, everyone!"

"Before you go," added Mr. Abramowitz, "we have an announcement to make."

Cha Cha and I exchanged a glance. This was it—the worm we were hoping would bait the hook for Calhoun.

"This year, for the very first time, the Starlite Dance Studio will be offering cash prizes at Cotillion!"

There was an audible buzz of excitement in the gym at this news. Scooter brightened, and I glanced over at Calhoun to see if it had piqued his interest too, but the expression on his face was unreadable.

"They'll be awarded in a number of categories, including best dance partners, of course, but also best dressed and most improved." Mr. Abramowitz slipped an arm around Cha Cha's mother's waist. "Mrs. Abramowitz and I are hoping that this will give you all an incentive to work especially hard this year, since it's the one hundredth anniversary of our town's Winter Festival. We're expecting media coverage!"

Media other than the *Pumpkin Falls Patriot-Bugle*? Fat chance.

"Remember," added Cha Cha's mother, "you all need to sign up for two complimentary practice sessions at the Starlite."

"Attendance will be taken!" noted Ms. Ivey. "Be sure and show up on time, and bring your best Pumpkin Falls manners!"

I smothered a grin. I'd have to add "Pumpkin Falls manners" to my list of things to tell Mackenzie next time we talked. My cousin is completely fascinated with my new hometown.

"It's like you stepped through a wormhole or something,"

ABSOLUTELY TRULY

she told me the other night. Mackenzie is a big fan of sci-fi movies. "*Pumpkin Falls: The Town That Time Forgot!*" she added in a fake radio announcer's voice. "I can't believe there's a place that has a dance for the entire town."

"Tell me about it."

"Earth to Truly!" said Cha Cha, yanking me back to reality. "Come on—we're going to be late for math."

CHAPTER 16

"So, did you talk to him?" Cha Cha asked Jasmine, as the three of us headed back upstairs to our classroom. Lucas trailed a few feet behind.

"Franklin?" said Jasmine dreamily.

"No! Calhoun, duh," said Cha Cha. She looked over at me and rolled her eyes. Jasmine's case of Franklin-on-the-brain was starting to drive us both nuts.

"Oh, right," Jasmine replied, tucking a strand of her dark hair behind an ear. "Yeah."

"So what did he say?"

"He's interested. Especially when I told him that my brother was sure to try for one of the prizes too."

Jasmine had told us that even though they're best friends, her brother and Calhoun are super competitive.

"The worm is on the hook!" crowed Cha Cha.

Now all we had to do was get the worm to the bookstore,

where we'd unleash the second part of our plan.

The four of us were hoping to cut a deal with Calhoun. Private dance lessons with Cha Cha—and a shot at winning one of the prizes—in exchange for getting us into the college library.

Would he go for it? Would he even stay put long enough to listen to our offer? Calhoun was bound to be mad when he found out we'd tricked him.

Lucas had bravely volunteered as bait for our trap. Jasmine's job was to cut Calhoun out of the herd after school, which mostly meant separating him from Scooter. Cha Cha and Lucas and I would run on ahead to Main Street, where I'd make sure the coast was clear at the bookstore while Cha Cha covered the door. Lucas would wait outside, hiding behind the mailbox in front of Lou's Diner with an arsenal of snowballs. Calhoun always walked down Main Street to get home, and we figured once Lucas stepped out and fired off a snowball at him, Calhoun wouldn't be able to resist chasing him down.

It was like dangling a red scarf in front of a bull.

At least we hoped so.

If everything went as planned, Lucas would duck inside the bookstore, Calhoun would come after him just like he and Scooter did before, and bingo, we'd have him cornered. Easy peasy lemon squeezie, right? Of course, there was the risk that Calhoun would break Lucas into tiny pieces when he found out we'd tricked him, but probably not with Aunt True onsite as backup.

First, though, I had to get through math.

"Pop quiz!" Ms. Ivey announced as we took our seats, and everybody groaned.

I glanced down at the sheet of paper she set in front of me. Word problems! My nemesis.

"When you're finished, I'd like you to swap your test with the person next to you, and then we'll all grade them together," said Ms. Ivey.

Ten minutes later, our time was up. I handed my quiz to Cha Cha and she gave me hers. Our teacher put the answer to the first problem on the board. Dang! Cha Cha had gotten it right, but I hadn't. A lot of my other answers were correct, though, which gave me hope that the end result would be enough to convince my father to let me try out for swim team.

Final score: 76 percent.

"Much better, Truly," said Ms. Ivey, patting me on the shoulder as she came by to collect our papers. "Looks like that tutoring is paying off."

I smiled at her. Out of the corner of my eye, I saw Scooter slouched down in his seat at the back of the room. He didn't look so happy with his grade. *That's what you get for stomping on your dancing partner's feet*, I thought smugly.

After class, as I went to my locker to get my jacket, I texted the quiz results to my father.

ONLY 24% MORE TO 100%! he texted back.

I looked at his message, deflated. Lieutenant Colonel Jericho T. Lovejoy was not easy to please.

"Are you ready?" Cha Cha whispered, nodding toward Jasmine and Scooter, who were over by their lockers arguing.

"Mom didn't say anything this morning about another orthodontist appointment!" Scooter protested.

"You weren't listening, that's all," Jasmine told him. "She's meeting you in the parking lot in ten minutes. She won't be happy if you're a no-show."

Scooter's shoulders slumped. "Sorry, dude," he muttered to Calhoun, who was waiting for him. "Maybe we can hang out later."

Jasmine slipped a hand behind her back. She made a shooing motion at Cha Cha and Lucas and me, and the three of us hurried past her. Mrs. Sanchez was nowhere near School Street, but Scooter didn't know that, and by the time he found out, we'd be long gone.

Outside, it was snowing yet again. My friends and I jogged through the flurries toward town, and five minutes later we were in place.

"Don't let your mother see you," I warned Lucas, who was crouched down between the mailbox and the curb outside the diner. "Cha Cha is right over there by the door, in case anything goes wrong. She's got your six."

"My what?"

"Sorry—military-speak. Your back." I trotted over to Cha Cha. "Any sign of Calhoun?"

"Nope."

"Okay. Keep your eyes peeled."

I doubled back and made a brief stop at the diner, then ducked into the bookstore. Now that inventory was finished, Lovejoy's Books was officially open again, but business wasn't exactly bustling. The only one inside the bookshop was Aunt True.

"Truly! What are you doing here?" she said, looking at me in surprise. "You're early for tutoring. Your dad's not back from his physical therapy session yet."

"I know. I brought you a Winter Elixir." My aunt's eyes lit up, and I felt a pang of guilt. The steaming cup came with a side of ulterior motive. I was buttering Aunt True up.

"How thoughtful of you," she said. "Thanks."

"You're welcome."

Aunt True had gotten hooked on Lou's Winter Elixirs. They're the diner's most popular seasonal drink, a piping-hot blend of ginger tea, apple cider, and cranberry juice. I waited until she took a sip, then said, "Remember Lucas and Cha Cha?"

She nodded.

"They're here again today."

She looked around, frowning. "Where?"

"Outside," I replied. "Waiting."

"Waiting for what?"

I had to get this next bit just right. "Um, for a boy."

"Ohhhhhhh," said Aunt True, her eyebrows arching skyward. "A *boy*." She said the word like it had half a dozen syllables.

"You know the Winter Festival dance? Well, Cha Cha wants to—"

Aunt True held up her hand. "Say no more! I've got the picture. I'll make myself scarce when they come in, shall I?"

I nodded. "Thanks, Aunt True."

She was quickly becoming my favorite aunt.

Two minutes later, the front door flew open and Cha Cha and Lucas ran in. Our plan had gone off like clockwork, and Calhoun was right on their heels with a snowball.

"Excuse me, young man," called Aunt True. "This is a snowball-free zone."

Calhoun froze.

"Don't make me sic Miss Marple on you!"

Over on her dog bed, Miss Marple heard her name. The snoring whuffled to a stop and she cracked open an eye, sizing up the situation. Fortunately, Calhoun wasn't familiar with my aunt's sense of humor or with Miss Marple. He eyed the dog warily, then dropped his arm.

"That's more like it," said Aunt True briskly. She held out her hand for the snowball. Calhoun gave it to her, and she opened the door and tossed it in the gutter. Closing the door again, my aunt regarded us thoughtfully. "If I leave the four of you alone while I go rustle up some snacks, will you promise not to kill each other?"

Cha Cha and Lucas and I nodded. Calhoun hesitated, then he shrugged and nodded too.

"Good," said Aunt True, and she disappeared into the office.

We stood there awkwardly for a couple of moments. Then the bell over the door jangled and Jasmine came in, breathless from running. She broke into a big grin when she saw Calhoun. "Hey, it really worked!"

"What worked?" Calhoun glanced from her over to Cha Cha and Lucas and me. His eyes narrowed. "Wait a minute, you did this on *purpose?*"

Jasmine crossed her arms over her chest. "You're the world's worst dance partner," she told him. "People are making fun of us behind our backs."

Calhoun's face went from angry red to embarrassed red.

"But we can fix that for you," Cha Cha added. "And we can make it so you have a shot at beating Scooter for a prize."

Calhoun snorted.

"Really, we can." Cha Cha explained what we wanted from him.

Calhoun looked baffled. "You want me to get you into the college *library?*"

We all nodded.

ABSOLUTELY TRULY

"What's the catch?"

"There isn't one," I told him.

"So what's so important about the library?"

"None of your business," said Cha Cha. "Are you in?"

He hesitated. "I'll think about it."

Aunt True returned just then with a tray of pumpkin whoopie pies. "You've multiplied!" she said, looking over at Jasmine.

"Oh hey, Aunt True, this is my friend Jasmine Sanchez," I told her. "And you've already met Calhoun."

"Greetings and salutations!" said Aunt True. "Welcome one and all to Lovejoy's Books. Would you like one of our signature treats?" She held out the tray and we each took one of the silver-dollar-size whoopie pies.

"Take more than that," she urged. "Please. Unless we get a rush of customers"—she looked around at the empty store and sighed—"these will just go to waste."

"I'm going to walk my friends down to Lou's," I told her. "If Dad gets here before I get back, tell him I'll only be a minute, okay?"

"You bet." She winked at me as I walked past her. "Cute guy," she whispered.

My mouth fell open.

Aunt True was supposed to think that *Cha Cha* had a crush on Calhoun, not me!

CHAPTER 17

"So," said my mother, cutting up Pippa's sausages. Wednesday was breakfast-for-dinner night, everybody's favorite. "Do you think you'll be able to join us at the meet tonight?" Her tone was neutral, and she gave my father the briefest of glances.

"Let him find his way back into the family again in his own way and his own time," the therapists at the military hospital in Maryland had counseled my mother. She'd shared their advice with Danny and Hatcher and me, and we were all trying to help her follow it. It wasn't easy, though, especially since progress seemed glacial.

Before, whenever he was home on leave, Dad had always come to as many of our practices and meets as he could, but now, even though he's technically around, we hardly see him outside of the bookstore.

My father chewed his waffle, swallowed, then washed it

down with a sip of coffee. "Maybe," he said, and my mother left it at that.

I glanced at the clock on the wall. "I'm due at the library in five minutes," I said. Calhoun had thought our offer over and said yes, and my classmates and I were scheduled to meet him tonight at six. "If it's okay with you, ma'am," I finished politely.

"Sure, honey," she replied. "Just be back by seven, okay? I don't want to be late for Danny's first meet."

I practically sprinted down Hill Street into town, the freshly fallen snow crunching under my feet at every step. Passing under Lovejoy College's arched iron gates, I jogged on toward the library.

I'd been to the campus plenty of times before. My brothers and I used to play hide-and-seek here in the summertime when we'd visit Gramps and Lola. I'd never seen it in winter, though, and I looked around with curiosity as I crossed the quad. The old buildings and tall, sturdy trees were shawled in white, and the snow falling in the soft glow of the old-fashioned streetlights lining the paths was like something out of a postcard. In fact, I was fairly sure I'd seen this very scene on a postcard at the General Store. Students scurried along, bundled up in hats and mittens and scarves, and out in the middle of the quad, a group of them was building a snowman. I didn't linger to watch, though. It was too cold, and I didn't want to be late.

Calhoun was the only one on the library steps so far.

"Um, hi," I said.

He grunted a hello back. I stood beside him, squirming a little inside when I recalled how Aunt True thought I had a crush on him. Crushes are right up there on the list of things I'm not good at. The last time I'd had one I was Pippa's age. Growing up with two older brothers didn't leave much room for crushes—in my experience, boys were mostly loud, smelly creatures who liked to tease me and make Toot Soup noises and play practical jokes. I liked boys just fine—but as friends and brothers, not crushes.

Mom and I had talked about it once last summer, after we'd moved into our Austin house and Mackenzie started talking nonstop about Mr. Perfect Cameron McAllister, the guy on our swim team.

"I just don't get it, Mom," I'd said. "He's not that interesting. Or cute, whatever that means. Really, he's not."

She'd laughed. "You'll get it one of these days, honey. No rush, though. And I know exactly how you feel—you think you've got it bad with two brothers? I have six of them!"

My mother told me she didn't date much at all until she got to college, and I guess I just figure it'll be the same for me.

My feet were cold, and I stamped them, wishing Cha Cha and Jasmine and Lucas would hurry up.

A few minutes later they finally showed, and Calhoun led us inside. "Hey, Chester," he said, waving to the security guard.

"Calhoun, my man! What's up?"

"Is it okay if I show my friends around?"

The guard looked past him at Cha Cha and Jasmine and me and grinned. "Way to impress the ladies, dude!"

Calhoun blushed to the roots of his sandy hair. The security guard laughed. "I'm just pulling your leg. Sure, go on in, buddy. Anybody asks, you tell them Chester okayed it." He waved us through the metal detector.

From the outside, the library looked like just another traditional New England building, all white clapboard and sashed windows. Inside, however, was another story. I couldn't help gawking as we entered the soaring lobby. To the right a broad marble staircase curved toward the upper stories. Overhead were rows and rows of skylights, and straight ahead the lobby opened onto a huge glassed-in courtyard.

"Wow," I said. "It's like being inside a snow globe."

Calhoun gave a half smile. It made him look almost human. "Yeah, it's pretty cool," he replied. Then the smile vanished, and the gruff mask slid back into place. "For a library, I mean."

As we started to pass a bronze statue in the middle of the lobby, I did a double take. I'd recognize that nose anywhere! I drew closer and read the plaque on it—sure enough, it was Nathaniel Daniel himself. FOUNDER OF LOVEJOY COLLEGE AND FRIEND TO ALL, the plaque proclaimed.

"Hey, that's the guy in the picture over your fireplace," Cha Cha said, and I nodded.

"How come his nose is so shiny, compared to the rest of him?" I asked Calhoun.

"Chester says students rub it for good luck at exam time," he told me.

I gave it a swipe too. It felt a little weird, rubbing my ancestor's nose, but the Pumpkin Falls Private Eyes could use all the luck they could get.

"So how do we find what we're looking for?" asked Cha Cha.

Calhoun led us over to a bank of computers. I pulled the envelope from my backpack, took the letter out, and read the call number aloud.

He typed it in, then gave me a funny look. "You didn't tell me you were looking for a Shakespeare book," he said as the search results flashed onscreen.

"You didn't need to know," I replied.

"It's upstairs," he said, and led us to an elevator behind the marble staircase. We emerged on the fourth floor.

"How come he knows so much about this place?" I whispered to my friends as we followed Calhoun down a long central aisle.

"Scooter says he spends a lot of time here," Jasmine whispered back. "His father's office is in the building next door."

Calhoun stopped and pointed down one of the rows of bookcases. "It should be on one of those shelves at the end."

"We can take it from here," I told him.

Calhoun turned to Cha Cha. "What time is our first practice?"

"Saturday at eleven," she replied. "See you there."

ABSOLUTELY TRULY

He nodded and left.

The four of us walked slowly down the row, scanning the stickers on the books.

"Got it!" I said, plucking a thin volume from between two larger ones on one of the bottom shelves. I read the title aloud: "*Much Ado About Nothing* by William Shakespeare."

"Careful, it looks old," said Cha Cha.

"Is there another letter inside?" Jasmine asked eagerly, craning to see over my shoulder.

I riffled through the brittle, mottled brown pages. "Doesn't look like it," I replied. I went through the book again, then turned it upside down and gave it a gentle shake. "Nothing."

We looked at each other. Was this another dead end?

"There has to be something!" said Cha Cha.

"There isn't." I couldn't hide my disappointment.

"Check the book pocket," said Lucas.

"Huh?"

He tugged the book from my hand. Turning to the very back, he pointed to the cardboard pocket still glued in place. "Lots of old books have them," he explained. "Mr. Henry showed me. Before computers, it's where they used to put the book card that kept track of borrowers and due dates. It would make a good hiding place."

"Lucas! You're a genius!" I poked a finger inside, and sure enough, there was something there. I fished it out. It was a piece of paper with two words written on it: *Check shelf.*

We did, dropping to our knees and searching thoroughly. Nothing but books and more books.

"If I were an envelope, where would I be?" mused Jasmine.

"Hang on a sec," I said. "I've got an idea. Move over, you guys."

Lying down on the floor, I inspected the underside of the shelf directly above where we'd found the book. Sure enough, something was stuck to it: an envelope. "Got it!" I said triumphantly, peeling off the duct tape that held it in place.

I scrambled back to my feet. Like the other envelope, this one simply had the letter *B* written on the outside. Unlike the other envelope, though, there was no stamp.

"Open it," urged Jasmine, and as I did, my friends crowded around to read over my shoulder.

Just as before, this letter also contained a quote:

I see, lady, the gentleman is not in your books.

It, too, was signed simply with a *B*. I read what was written below: "Wednesday the third, B-4."

"So who do you think the *B*s are?" asked Jasmine. "And what the heck does that quote mean?"

I shook my head. "I have absolutely no idea."

"I do," said Calhoun from the other side of the stacks. He smirked at us through a gap in the books. "But it's going to cost you."

CHAPTER 18

"It's a quote from *Much Ado About Nothing*," Calhoun told us, after we'd coughed up all the money we had in our wallets.

"Well, duh," snapped Jasmine. "We didn't need to pay you almost twenty bucks for that."

Calhoun smirked again. "Not my fault you don't know your Shakespeare," he said. "The main characters in the play are Beatrice and Benedick." He pointed to the initials on the envelope and the letter. "There's your B and B."

I stared at him. "How'd you figure that out so fast?"

Calhoun shrugged. "My father is a Shakespeare scholar," he told us. "He teaches classes on the Bard."

"Who's the Bard?" asked Jasmine.

"Well, duh," said Calhoun softly, repeating Jasmine's earlier words. "Shakespeare, of course. Everybody knows that."

Jasmine flushed.

"This quote here," Calhoun continued, tapping a finger

against the letter, "'I see, lady, the gentleman is not in your books'? That means Benedick is on Beatrice's blacklist—he's not in her 'good books.' Get it? She's mad at him." Looking around at our stunned expressions, he grabbed the book away from Cha Cha. "Here, check it out, Act I, Scene 1: 'There is a kind of merry war betwixt Signior Benedick and her: they never meet but there's a skirmish of wit between them.'"

"And that is supposed to mean what, exactly?" I asked.

Calhoun sighed, clearly disgusted by my ignorance. "The two of them spend most of the play bickering with each other. They argue all the time, but it turns out that they're really in love."

My mouth fell open. "Are you telling us that this is a *love letter*?"

"Duh," Calhoun said again.

I gave him the stink eye.

Calhoun was smart. Why did he take such pains to hide it, I wondered? I looked over at Cha Cha. "Should we show him the other letter too?"

She shrugged. "Might as well."

"Sorry, kids, I'd like to stay and play but I have to go," Calhoun told us, before I could fish it out and hand it over. "My sister's cheering for some wrestling meet tonight, and my father wants me to go along and watch."

"Shoot," I said, glancing at my cell phone. "My family's going too. I was supposed to be home five minutes ago,"

"Me too," said Cha Cha. Her cousin Noah is on Danny's team.

"How about you all come over to my house tomorrow after school?" I suggested. "You're invited too," I told Calhoun.

I could tell he was curious. "We'll see" was all he said, though, playing it cool.

I ran all the way home. Fortunately, my family was running late, so nobody noticed I'd blown my deadline. Dad had gone back to the bookstore, and my mother tried not to sound disappointed as we all piled into the car.

"Danny's first meet of the season!" she said in an overly enthusiastic tone. "Won't this be fun?"

I was surprised at how full the gym was at West Hartfield High. I guess there aren't a whole heck of a lot of other things to do in the heart of maple syrup country on a weeknight in the dead of winter. I spotted Belinda Winchester up in the stands, and Ella Bellow was there too, talking to Bud Jefferson from the stamp store.

"Truly! Up here!" Cha Cha called. She and her mother and Baxter were saving seats for us.

Pippa and Baxter were so excited to see each other they nearly fell off the bleachers and had to be corralled into a coloring project. Lauren made a beeline for Belinda Winchester, who was sitting a couple of rows in front of us. Belinda reached into her pocket and handed Lauren something—a kitten, most likely. The two of them have bonded over their mutual love of animals. Mom was a little worried at first, since Belinda is, well, kind of odd. In fact, odd is putting it mildly if you ask me, which nobody ever does.

"She's nuts, but not *nuts* nuts, you know?" Aunt True assured my mother, after Belinda invited Lauren over to view the latest litter. Lauren's dying to have a kitten, but my mother says she has enough pets. "Unless you consider someone who doesn't own a TV and doesn't read the newspaper nuts, Belinda's just your garden-variety cat lady. I've spent a lot of time with her over the past few weeks—she's practically a fixture at the bookshop these days. Lauren will be perfectly safe."

"Lauren!" my mother called a few minutes later, motioning her back. "Honey, you've got homework to do. You can visit after you're done."

Lauren slumped down on the bench beside me with a sigh of resignation. Reaching into her backpack, she pulled out her book report on *Charlotte's Web*.

"Will you read what I've written so far?" she asked me.

"Sure."

"Aunt True says that if the first edition hasn't sold by the time I give my report, she'll bring it to school so I can show everybody," Lauren told me.

"Cool." I started to read.

Elwyn Brooks White, known to his friends as Andy, was born on July 11, 1899, in Mount Vernon, New York.

ABSOLUTELY TRULY

I only got as far as the part where Mr. White and his wife bought a saltwater farm in Maine, when the lights in the gym dimmed and loud rock music blared. A moment later, Danny and his team came running out in their maroon-and-white warm-up suits. The West Hartfield fans clapped and cheered.

Of all of us, my brother Danny is the most like our father. Same strong jaw, same wiry build. When he's in his wrestling singlet, he looks almost exactly the way Dad did in his yearbook pictures.

I waved to Hatcher, who was standing on the sidelines. Scooter Sanchez was there too, along with several other guys I recognized from school. In Pumpkin Falls, the middle school wrestlers attend all the high school meets and tournaments. They help set up and tear down the mats, warm up the team, and watch and learn.

Danny and Cha Cha's cousin Noah both wrestle in the 152-pound weight class, so they wouldn't be up for a while. As Cha Cha and I settled in for the long wait, I noticed that our mothers had somehow gotten onto the topic of how they met their husbands.

"Harry and I were rivals in a dance competition," Mrs. Abramowitz said as the music faded and two guys even skinnier than Lucas Winthrop stepped onto the mat for the first match. Watching 106-pounders wrestle always makes me anxious. Their twiggy arms and legs look like rubber bands that might snap at any moment as they flail around trying to pin each other. "I lost the competition but gained a husband."

My mother laughed. "J. T. and I sat next to each other in freshman English at the University of Texas," she said. "When he told me he was from a place called Pumpkin Falls, New Hampshire. I thought he was making it up!"

"Wasn't he there on a wrestling scholarship?" asked Cha Cha's mother. "I seem to remember Ella Bellow saying something about that."

"I'll bet she did," my mother replied, and she and Mrs. Abramowitz exchanged wry smiles. It's no secret that our postmistress loves to gossip.

"So wrestling runs in the family, then?" said Cha Cha's mother.

Mom nodded. "My family too. J. T. was the first guy I dated who was willing to take on my brothers." My mother loves telling this story, and we all love hearing it. It's practically a legend in our family.

"I have six of them," she continued, her Texas twang deepening as she warmed to her tale.

"You have *six* brothers?" said Mrs. Abramowitz. Her eyes, which were the same green as Cha Cha's and Baxter's, widened.

My mother smiled her sunflower smile. "A boy for every day of the week and a girl for Sunday, my grandmother used to say. Anyway, my brothers made J. T. arm wrestle each one of them before he was allowed to take me out on a date."

Cha Cha's mother laughed.

"I'm serious!" said my mother, grinning. "He must have really wanted to ask me out, because he beat every single one of them."

"That's quite an accomplishment," said Mrs. Abramowitz, glancing over my mother's shoulder. I looked up and saw my father making his way through the crowded bleachers toward us. Aunt True was with him, bundled up in a sheepskin jacket and another hat from her seemingly bottomless collection of embarrassments—a rainbow knitted number this time, with a spray of tassels on top that looked kind of like Annie Freeman's braids.

My mother gave my knee a squeeze, which I knew meant, *Don't make a big deal about your father coming along; just act normal.*

"J. T., True, this is Rachel Abramowitz," she said. "My boss at the Starlite."

"And more importantly, Cha Cha and Baxter's mother," said Mrs. Abramowitz. She smiled up at my father. "I hear you're quite the arm wrestler, J. T. Dinah was just telling me about your exploits back in college."

He gave her a brief, polite nod. "Yes, ma'am."

We all fell silent as he took his seat. I couldn't help but notice as Cha Cha's mother's gaze wandered to the hook at the end of his shirtsleeve.

My father's arm-wrestling days were over.

CHAPTER 19

"I can't believe Hatcher did that to you!" Mackenzie's shocked face looked out at me from my laptop screen.

Disaster had struck after the wrestling meet.

As we were heading to the lobby, Hatcher came bounding over and slung a sweaty arm around my shoulders. He knows I hate this, which of course makes him do it even more.

"Eew, get off!" I cried, shoving him away. "Go take a shower!"

"What's the matter?" he teased. "Just trying to share the love." He hoisted his elbow in the air and fanned his armpit in my direction.

"Mom, make him stop!" I protested.

My mother shot him a look.

Hatcher dropped his arm. "Jeez, Drooly, can't you take a joke?"

I froze. Scooter Sanchez was standing directly behind

him. At first I thought maybe I was in the clear, but then I saw a slow smile slide across Scooter's face, and I knew he'd heard my brother, and that I'd be hearing about it too, for as long as I lived in Pumpkin Falls.

I ran up to my room when we got home and slammed the door. Miss Marple whined to be let in, but I ignored her. Flinging myself on the bed, I shoved my head under my pillow to muffle the noise as I let out a howl of rage and humiliation. Angry tears spilled over, and I let them.

"Go away!" I hollered a little while later when someone knocked on my door. It was probably Hatcher. He'd tried to apologize in the car on the way home, but I wouldn't listen. I didn't plan on ever speaking to him again. Scooter would never let this go.

"I don't know what to do," I wailed to Mackenzie.

"Maybe your parents will let you come live here with us," she replied. "You know, like the witness protection program or something."

"Fat chance."

"Well, you're going to have to deal with it, then."

She was right. I needed a plan. The problem was, I couldn't think of one.

The next day at school I tried to keep my distance from Scooter, but, of course, that didn't work. Somehow he managed to pop up at every turn, with the same stupid grin on his face that had been there at the gym last night.

"Truly Drooly," he sang to me softly in math class.

"Could you pass me that beaker, Truly Drooly?" he asked in science class.

"Pardon me, Truly Drooly," he said when he bumped into me on purpose in the lunch line.

Things took a turn for the worse during our ballroom dance class, when he started calling me "Drooly Gigantic."

I stomped on his foot then, hard. Unfortunately, Cha Cha's father saw me. He frowned. "Miss Lovejoy? Pumpkin Falls manners, please."

The heck with Pumpkin Falls manners, I thought bitterly and stomped again the second Mr. Abramowitz's back was turned.

"What's your problem?" Scooter whispered angrily.

"You know exactly what my problem is!" I whispered back.

Somehow, I managed to make it through the day. At least I had the Pumpkin Falls Private Eyes to look forward to.

Nearly twenty-four hours had passed since we'd all met at the college library. My parents had left for Boston early this morning, so my tutoring sessions had been canceled for the rest of the week. My father was finally ready to get fitted for a more permanent prosthetic arm, and Aunt True was going to look after my brothers and sisters and me while he and my mother were away.

Dad would actually be coming home with two new prostheses: a flesh-colored silicone one that's strictly for show, and

ABSOLUTELY TRULY

a high-tech one made of black titanium and polymer that's controlled by electrical impulses sent from his brain. It's the latest technology, and unlike the one he's been wearing, there's no harness; it's held on by suction and is supposed to be much more comfortable. Mom showed us a video of it online, and it looked pretty awesome. Hatcher and Danny have already dubbed it "The Terminator."

Ever since that day in the bookshop, all of us had been calling his temporary prosthesis "Captain Hook." Dad rolls his eyes when we do, but Pippa thinks it's funny, so he puts up with it. We can tell he's relieved he doesn't have to hide it in a gym bag anymore.

I had the house to myself until dinnertime. Hatcher and Danny were at their wrestling practices, Lauren had gone up the street to visit Belinda Winchester and her menagerie, and Pippa had a playdate with Baxter over at the Abramowitzes'.

Even so, my friends and I still wound up in Lola's art studio. It was beginning to feel like a clubhouse of sorts. Calhoun came too, tagging along behind us on the walk home from school. Even though curiosity won out in the end, he was careful not to get too close so people wouldn't think we were together. He wanted to make it clear that we were the dorks and he was still the cool one.

"You are not seriously calling yourselves the Pumpkin Falls Private Eyes, are you?" Calhoun said when I called the meeting to order.

I could feel my face flush. Calhoun was almost as infuriating as Scooter Sanchez. "So do you want to see the first letter we found or not?" I snapped.

"You don't have to bite my head off," he said. "And, yeah, I do. I wouldn't have come otherwise."

I passed the envelope to him, explaining how I had found it at the bookstore.

He scanned the letter. "This is from *Much Ado* too," he told us. "'February face'—cold and stormy, get it? Whoever is writing the letters is trying to get someone not to be mad at them. They're trying to say they're sorry."

My friends and I looked at each other. Who was this guy, and what had he done with Calhoun?

"So why make up some elaborate scavenger hunt? Why not just pick up the phone and call, or send flowers?" asked Cha Cha.

Calhoun shrugged. "Don't look at me. I didn't write the letters."

"Um, so B and B are nicknames, then, right?" said Lucas, who was sitting scrunched up on the floor, as far away as possible from Calhoun.

We all nodded.

"That means they could be just about anybody."

My friends and I looked at each other. Lucas was right. Making a list of people with B names hadn't narrowed down the field at all.

ABSOLUTELY TRULY

"We don't stand a chance of solving this," I said glumly.

"Don't give up yet," said Cha Cha. "We still know what year the stamp was issued. That makes a difference, doesn't it?"

"And figuring out this clue's gotta help too," added Jasmine. "What did it say again?"

I recited it from memory. "'Wednesday the third, B-4.' Anybody have any ideas?" I glanced around the room. Nobody raised a hand, not even Calhoun this time.

So much for the Pumpkin Falls Private Eyes. We were back to square one: completely clueless.

CHAPTER 20

"Hatcher Lovejoy, that's your fifth piece of pizza!" exclaimed Aunt True, looking at my brother in disbelief.

He grinned at her.

"Sixth for me," said Danny smugly, taking a big bite out of the slice he was holding. Danny loves Friday nights. Pizza is his favorite food, and Friday nights have always been pizza night in our family.

My aunt shook her head. "I don't know how your parents do it—it's like raising goats."

Lauren and Pippa thought this was hilarious, especially when Hatcher and Danny stuck their forefingers up on top of their heads like horns and started bleating.

No one seemed to notice that I was on my fifth piece too. Invisible as usual—that's me.

Someone kicked me under the table. I looked up. Hatcher

passed me another piece of pizza, then held up six fingers. I smiled. Not so invisible after all.

My brother and I were speaking again. He'd barged into my room before school this morning to apologize. Well, sort of.

"I hate it when you're mad at me," he'd said, standing in the doorway in his bathrobe with his arms crossed.

"Like it's my fault!" I'd retorted, sitting up in bed.

"You know I didn't mean for it to slip out."

"Yeah, well, it's a little late for that!"

"C'mon, Drooly—please?"

"Don't call me that anymore," I'd snapped, but Hatcher looked so droopy and hangdog that after a minute I added, "Fine. Whatever."

"I'll tell Scooter to keep it quiet, okay?"

I'd nodded, knowing it wouldn't do any good. And it didn't. A nickname like mine was far too irresistible for someone like Scooter.

I was doomed to be Truly Drooly forever.

I sighed and took a bite of pizza. We were at Aunt True's apartment. It was a pretty cool place, I thought, looking around. She'd painted the dining area and living room a warm color she described as "halfway between Golden Retriever and sunset," and the walls were crowded with interesting stuff from her travels: wooden masks, tribal rugs, sculptures, bright beadwork, and art from just about everyplace imaginable, plus photographs. Tons of photographs—Aunt True teaching school in Kenya; Aunt True in a dugout canoe in the Amazon rain forest; Aunt True beside a reindeer in Lapland and planting trees in Nepal and standing in front of the Taj Mahal in India. She had stories to go along with every picture too.

Glancing at the mantel, I noticed that she'd framed our family Christmas card. This year's was particularly awkward. It wasn't just the matching sweaters my mother always forces us to wear—a Gifford tradition we keep begging her to ditch—it was me. I was smack-dab in the middle of the lineup as usual, only this year I towered over everyone else.

"I thought we'd go downstairs to the bookstore after dessert," Aunt True said, pulling my attention back to the table. "I need your help with something."

"Can we have dethert now?" asked Pippa, eyeing the cupcakes on the sideboard. No Tibetan spices or yak milk lurking in those puppies—they were in a box that said LOU'S on it. Memphis was seated beside it, a great big black lump of furry fury. His tail lashed back and forth as he glared down at Miss Marple. Memphis didn't think much of the fact that a dog had been invited home for dinner.

"Of course," said Aunt True. She reached for the box and passed it around the table. We each took a cupcake. As Danny started to take another, Aunt True snatched them out

ABSOLUTELY TRULY

of his reach. "Not so fast!" she said. "Follow me if you want seconds."

We trailed downstairs after her, Miss Marple bringing up the rear. A circle of folding chairs was waiting for us and we each took a seat, along with another cupcake. Miss Marple settled onto the floor nearby, keeping a hopeful eye on us, and our dessert.

"Here's the thing," said Aunt True, wiping some pink frosting from her lips. It matched her outfit, which Pippa had helped her choose this morning—pink leggings, a pink-and-white striped sweater, and pink clogs. "Two weeks ago, your father set a six-week deadline for turning this business around before we throw in the towel."

This was news to my siblings, and while it sailed right over Pippa's and Lauren's heads—especially Lauren, who was surreptitiously reading *A Little Princess*—my brothers looked shocked.

"I posted an ad for the first edition of *Charlotte's Web* on our website," Aunt True continued, "and we've had some nibbles, which could make all the difference in being able to pay back the bank loan. Meanwhile, though, I think there's more we can do to make this next month count."

Hatcher and I exchanged a glance. Aunt True had something up her sleeve.

"What I'm talking about"—she paused dramatically—"is a makeover!"

We looked at her blankly. Aunt True didn't wear makeup. Was she planning to start? I didn't see how that was going to boost sales. But it turned out she had something much bigger in mind.

"This is where you all come in," she explained. "You know how your father always says that Lovejoys can do anything? I want us to prove that to him this weekend! He won't recognize this place by the time we're done with it."

She was talking about a *bookshop* makeover.

"This is a family business, and the only way it's going to work is if the whole family is involved," she continued, pacing back and forth in front of us. "First, I think we should list the store's strengths and weaknesses. You kids have a different perspective, you might zero in on things I've missed." She paused and looked at us expectantly.

"Um, I'm not sure what you mean?" said Danny.

"You know, like for instance the fact that the store has great windows," she explained, with a sweeping gesture toward the front of the store. We all swiveled around and stared. The display windows looked pretty ordinary, if you asked me, which nobody ever did. "What other things does it have going for it?"

We glanced around, then looked at each other, then shrugged.

"There'th a lot of bookth," offered Pippa, and Danny snorted.

ABSOLUTELY TRULY

Aunt True ignored him. "Excellent observation, Miss Pippa."

"The ceilings are really high," said Hatcher, craning his head back. "Maybe you could use the wall space above the bookshelves for artwork and stuff." He was thinking of her apartment, I suspected, nearly every inch of which was covered with something.

"Interesting," said Aunt True. "I hadn't thought of that. See what I mean about a different perspective?"

I raised my hand.

"Truly?"

"This isn't a strength, Aunt True," I said, "but it's dark in here."

"That's because it's nighttime, you moron!" scoffed Danny.

"Daniel," Aunt True chided. "I've noticed the same thing, Truly. The place needs brightening up." She stared thoughtfully at the ceiling. "We should probably invest in better light fixtures eventually, but these still work, and they have a nice retro flair. We can certainly wash the glass globes on them for starters."

Crossing to one of the windows, she grabbed a handful of the dark green material that was hanging beside it and gave it a shake. A big cloud of dust flew up. "These drapes have got to go, don't you think?" she said, as we all started waving our arms and coughing. "Your father claims they protect the merchandise from fading, but I say they block the light. The more we can open this place up, the better. Who votes for taking them down?"

I raised my hand. So did Hatcher and Pippa. Danny and Lauren looked uncertain.

"Can Mith Marple vote?" asked Pippa, slipping the dog a bite of cupcake.

"Technically, she's family, so yes, she gets a vote," said Aunt True, and my little sister hoisted Miss Marple's paw into the air.

"So that makes four in favor—five if we count Miss Marple—and two against," my aunt continued. "Or maybe more on the fence than against. The ayes have it!"

"Um, Aunt True," Danny began, "don't you think you should wait and ask—"

Aunt True flapped a hand dismissively. "Don't worry. Your father and I don't always see eye to eye on everything, but he'll love it. So, any other comments?"

"The walls could probably use a new coat of paint," said Hatcher.

"Can we paint it pink?" Pippa looked hopeful.

"No way!" Danny and Hatcher burst out simultaneously. I shook my head too.

"Pink's probably not going to work, Pip," Aunt True told her. "But the walls definitely need painting, and they definitely need to be a cheerful color. You can help me pick one out, okay? Now, what else?"

"How about this?" said Hatcher, scuffing his foot against the carpet on the floor. "It's gross." He was right. The carpet was dark green like the drapes, and had been there for as long as I could remember.

My aunt made a face. "Hideous, isn't it? Replacing it isn't in my tiny remodeling budget, though."

I poked my toe under a loose corner by the nearest bookcase. "Do we have to have carpet? Maybe we could just get rid of it instead of replacing it."

Aunt True came over to where I was sitting and knelt down. Peeling back the loose corner, she inspected the floor underneath. "You may be on to something, Truly," she said, her voice rising in excitement. "This is wide-plank pine, if I'm not mistaken, and it looks to be in pretty good shape." She stood up again, brushing off her pink leggings. "I doubt it's something the six of us could tackle this weekend, though. It's a big demolition job."

My brothers perked up at this. "Demolition" is one of their favorite words.

"I thought you said Lovejoys could do anything," Danny reminded her.

"Point taken," said Aunt True.

My brother grinned. "What if we got some of our wrestling buddies to help?"

"Do you think they would?"

Danny and Hatcher both nodded.

"Well, then, why not? Let's take the plunge!" Aunt True put her hands on her hips and looked around. "I think that about covers it, although I'd also like to make better use of our existing space. Rearrange some of the bookcases, freshen the children's room, add a display table or two for new arrivals and sidelines—"

"What are thidelineth?" asked Pippa.

"All the stuff we sell that isn't books, honey," Aunt True told her.

Aunt True might call them "sidelines," but my father calls them a word I could get into big trouble for repeating.

"I want a gift-wrapping station behind the counter too," my aunt continued, "and maybe we could bring in some armchairs and lamps and set up a few cozy reading nooks."

Hearing this, Lauren looked up from her book. "I like that idea."

"You can be the reading-nook consultant, then." Aunt True smiled at us. "It's going to look like a brand-new store by the time we're done!"

Her enthusiasm was contagious. I liked the idea of surprising our parents, and I could tell that my brothers and sisters did too.

"Do you really think we can pull this off?" I asked.

"We're going to need some help," Aunt True admitted.

ABSOLUTELY TRULY

"But if there's one good thing about small towns, it's the fact that word travels fast on the grapevine. It's time to activate my secret weapon."

"You have a thecret weapon?" Pippa's eyes widened behind her sparkly pink glasses.

Aunt True put her finger to her lips. "I certainly do. And her name is Ella Bellow."

CHAPTER 21

Score one for the town's biggest gossip.

Ella Bellow totally came through. By nine o'clock the next morning, there were two dozen people waiting for us on the bookshop doorstep.

Not only that, there was a news truck too. And not just any news truck, but the one from Channel 5 in Boston.

"Are you the owner of Lovejoy's Books?" someone called out, shouldering his way through the crowd. I recognized the questioner's face—well, his smile at least. Half the people on the planet knew that smile. A video of it flying across a room on its own and landing on a plate of cream puffs had been leaked onto the Internet a few years ago, and made him, his dentures, and his morning news show, *Hello, Boston!* famous.

Carson Dawson was smaller than he looked on TV—way shorter than me—and a lot wrinklier underneath his fake tan. In one leather-gloved hand he clutched a cup of coffee from

Lou's. In the other he held a microphone, which he thrust into Aunt True's face. *Peacock*, I thought instantly. Showy and loud.

"Co-owner," my aunt replied, unlocking the door.

"Is it true that your brother is a wounded warrior, Ms. Lovejoy? And that the two of you are struggling to turn around an ailing family business?"

Aunt True shot a sour look at Ella Bellow, who seemed to be fascinated by one of the buttons on her black coat all of a sudden. Our postmistress had been oversharing again. "Yes, it's true," my aunt admitted.

"I'd love to interview you!" gushed Mr. Dawson. "We're in town to film the famous waterfall, and when we saw the crowd, we came over to find out what all the commotion was about. This would make a wonderful companion piece. You know, 'small town pitches in to help wounded veteran.' Our viewers love local color."

Hatcher looked over at me and rolled his eyes.

"I'll agree to do an interview on one condition," Aunt True replied. Raising her voice to make sure everyone gathered on the sidewalk could hear her, she continued, "What we're doing this weekend is a surprise for my brother and his wife. They won't be home until Monday, and I don't want the story getting out beforehand." She leveled a stern gaze at Carson Dawson.

He nodded, chuckling. "Got it. Mum's the word."

Aunt True asked Hatcher and me to hold the door open for everyone, then taped a piece of paper to the window. I inspected it as the waiting crowd streamed past. My aunt had posted a wish list—furniture, mostly, and other items for the reading nooks she was hoping to set up.

Lou was first in line, carrying a stack of boxes filled with donuts. He winked at me as he passed. "Gotta keep everyone's strength up."

Mrs. Winthrop was right behind him with a big coffee urn. Lucas was next. Annie Freeman, who'd come with her brother Franklin and their parents, was talking his ear off.

"Hey, Truly," said Cha Cha as she trailed in behind the Freemans.

"Hey." I waggled my fingers at Baxter, who was with her. He smiled shyly.

"My parents can't come until after lunch," Cha Cha told me. "They've got Cotillion practice sessions all morning."

I was not looking forward to mine, but I didn't tell her that. "No problem" was all I said.

The Nguyens filed in, along with the Mahoneys from the antiques store next door, Bud Jefferson from Earl's Coins and Stamps across the street, and Reverend Quinn, the minister at Gramps and Lola's church. Mr. Henry the librarian smiled at me as he passed, and so did Ms. Ivey and Mr. Bigelow. Mr. Burnside, our principal, had brought his whole family, and there were a bunch of other people I didn't recognize.

ABSOLUTELY TRULY

"So happy to help Walt and Lola's family," said Mrs. Farnsworth, who ran the General Store with her husband.

Augustus Wilde swooped in after her, his silver hair brushed back from his forehead like the crest of a wave, and his trademark black cape fluttering in the chilly breeze. Hatcher looked over at me and grinned.

"We're saved! Captain Romance is here!" he whispered, and I smothered a laugh.

Augustus was Pumpkin Falls's resident celebrity. He wrote romance novels under the alias "Augusta Savage." His books fill up an entire shelf in the romance section, or as Hatcher calls it, the shirtless-men-kissing-beautiful-women section. Augustus drops by at least once a week. He sneaks over to the shelf that holds his books and turns them face out when he thinks no one is looking.

"Guerrilla marketing," he'd confided to me when I'd caught him at it. "We authors have to do what we can."

Danny and Hatcher's wrestling buddies swarmed in last, decked out in their team sweatshirts. Scooter Sanchez grinned at me as he sauntered past. I skewered him with a look that could have stopped an elephant.

"I didn't say anything!" he protested.

He didn't have to. I knew exactly what he was thinking.

Belinda Winchester was the final one through the door. I caught the faint strains of "My Girl" from her ever-present earbuds as she craned to see over my shoulder.

"Where's Miss Marple?" she demanded.

I pointed to the office, where Aunt True had corralled her for the day. Belinda marched over and clipped a leash to the dog's collar. "Too much excitement in here for this old girl," she announced, heading right out again. "I'm taking her for a walk."

Carson Dawson and his crew trotted around behind Aunt True as she gave them a tour of the bookshop. She unlocked the rare book cabinet and showed off the first edition of *Charlotte's Web*, which it turned out was Mr. Henry's favorite book.

"Mine, too!" exclaimed my aunt. "It's the perfect novel, isn't it?"

"Sublime," he replied as she passed it to him.

"I'm rather fond of it myself," the TV host admitted.

Mr. Henry held the book reverently. "I'd give anything for an autographed copy!" he said, and Carson Dawson got some footage of him talking with Aunt True about E. B. White, and the author's farm in Maine, where he'd raised actual pigs and observed actual spiders, and how he'd called the book his "hymn to the barn."

"Fun fact," said Mr. Henry. "Did you know that E. B. White did the narration for the audiobook? And that it took him seventeen takes to get through the passage about Charlotte's death without crying?"

"I can never get through it without crying, either," said Aunt True, and Mr. Henry nodded sympathetically.

ABSOLUTELY TRULY

I couldn't help noticing that Scooter had managed to wedge himself in front of the camera. I also couldn't help noticing Calhoun when he showed up a few minutes later, after the *Charlotte's Web* lovefest was over. This was mostly because my aunt made such a big deal out of it.

"Truly!" she called from across the store, with one of those big "your secret is safe with me" smiles. "Your friend is here!"

My face flamed. Scooter gave me an odd look. Calhoun didn't even glance my way, just went over and joined the wrestlers, who had formed a human chain and were ferrying boxes to the basement.

"Keep the books in the exact same order you find them, please," Aunt True instructed them, then crossed the store to organize the group in charge of rearranging the bookshelves.

Lucas and Franklin and Amy Nguyen were put to work dusting, and Cha Cha and Jasmine and I were assigned two jobs: keeping the little kids out of everyone's hair, and washing the glass globes on all the light fixtures.

"You can set up headquarters in my apartment," said Aunt True. "Don't let Memphis out, okay? There are board games in the trunk in the living room, and you'll find rubber gloves and dish soap and whatever other cleaning products you need under the kitchen sink."

"I have a practice session at the Starlite at eleven thirty," I told her.

"That's fine. Just see if someone can cover for you with the little ones while you're gone."

"I can do that no problem, Ms. Lovejoy," Jasmine told her.

While Jasmine rounded up the younger kids, Cha Cha and I went to join Mr. Jefferson and Mr. Freeman, who had brought a ladder up from the basement. The two men started dismantling the light fixtures, handing the white glass globes down to Cha Cha and me.

"Wow," said Cha Cha, as we carried the first two up to Aunt True's apartment. She looked around in amazement. "Your aunt's been everywhere."

"I know, right?"

"Can I show Annie Aunt True's scrapbooks?" begged Lauren, who had plunked herself down on the floor by the coffee table.

"I guess so," I told her. "Be careful with them, though."

In the kitchen, Jasmine was setting up a game of Candy Land for Pippa and Baxter. While Cha Cha returned downstairs for more glass globes, I rummaged under the sink for the rubber gloves and dish soap, and a few minutes later was up to my elbows in scummy water.

"This is disgusting," I said, holding up a sponge that had quickly turned black with grime. "You think dissecting a frog was bad, Jazz, you'd faint if you saw all the dead bugs floating around in here."

ABSOLUTELY TRULY

I rinsed the globe and handed it to her. She dried it carefully and set it on the countertop.

"One down, eleven more to go," she said.

It took us a while to clean them all. When we were done. Cha Cha and I began carrying the now-sparkling results back downstairs. I paused in the bookshop doorway and looked around. The last time I'd seen so many people working together on a project was when all my Texas uncles showed up to build a deck for our new house in Austin. The one we sold. The one I'd still move back to in a heartbeat.

"Gotta go," said Cha Cha, grabbing her jacket off the bench by the door. "I'm due over at the Starlite."

"Oh, yeah," I replied. "Calhoun's first practice session, right?"

She nodded. "Wish me luck."

"Truly! Could you bring your sisters down here for a minute?" called my aunt, who was standing by the sales counter with Carson Dawson. "Channel 5 wants a family shot to go with the interview."

I nodded and trotted back upstairs.

"Hey, Truly, have you seen your aunt's prom picture?" said Annie, holding up one of the scrapbooks. "Check out her B-O-U-F-F-A-N-T!"

She and Lauren dissolved into giggles.

"Very funny," I said, glancing at it. Then I looked a little closer. What caught my eye wasn't so much the picture of my aunt in her prom dress and huge hair—almost as huge as the hair on the guy she was with, whose picture I was pretty sure I'd seen somewhere before—but rather the program on the opposite page. It was for a West Hartfield High School drama production of *Much Ado About Nothing*, starring none other than Calhoun's parents.

As I hustled my sisters back downstairs to the waiting camera crew, my brain shifted into sudoku mode, puzzling over this new piece of information.

"Smile, everyone!" said Carson Dawson, baring his own toothsome grin as he bounded out in front of the camera.

"*Helloooooooooo, Boston!*" he announced, launching into his show's trademark opening cry. Work in the bookshop ceased as our friends and neighbors crowded around to watch. "Greetings from beautiful Pumpkin Falls, New Hampshire! I'm here today at Lovejoy Books, where an entire town is banding together to give a wounded warrior a helping hand."

Hatcher pinched me, and I pinched him back. Could this possibly be more embarrassing?

Mr. Dawson quickly zeroed in on Pippa. "What's your name, sweetheart?" he asked, crouching down and holding out the microphone.

"Pippa Lovejoy," my little sister replied, twisting one of her strawberry blond ringlets around a forefinger.

"And is this your family?"

She nodded, her sparkly pink glasses flashing in the bright spotlights.

"You have a big family!" the TV host exclaimed.

Pippa nodded again. "Theven."

"What?"

"There are theven of uth," Pippa repeated, holding up seven fingers.

"Ohhhhhh," chuckled Carson Dawson. "Theven of you!" He winked at the camera. "Isn't she just the cutest, folks?"

"Get me out of here," muttered Danny under his breath.

Carson Dawson straightened up and turned to face the rest of us.

"Whoa, tall timber!" he said when he spotted me. Chuckling, he made a show of craning his neck to look up into my face. Which was in the process of turning bright red. "What's your name, young lady?"

"*Drooly Gigantic*," said Scooter in a stage whisper from somewhere in the crowd.

My face went from red to five-alarm fire. I gritted my teeth and promised myself that I would flatten Scooter Sanchez the minute I had the chance.

"My name is Truly," I managed to tell the TV host.

"You grow *truly* tall timber up here in the Granite State, don't you?" Carson Dawson quipped, looking over at my aunt. Sizing her up, he added, "but then, I can see that your niece here is a chip off the old block."

I winced.

"Uh-oh," muttered Hatcher. "Incoming!"

Aunt True gave Carson Dawson a withering look. Stepping forward, she put her arm around my shoulder. "Ayuh," she replied in a broad, fake New Hampshire accent, "but then we Granite Staters always have preferred tall timber to *splinters*." She looked down from her considerable height at the TV host and sniffed.

His smile faltered. He turned to the cameraman and whispered, "Remind me to edit this bit later."

Smiling his big fake smile again, Mr. Dawson blathered on about our family, and the bookstore, and Dad's injury, and what we were doing this weekend to surprise him. "It's a veritable 'Bookshop Blitz,' folks! I'm told we won't recognize the place when they're done with it tomorrow."

The lights were hot, so was my face, and my cheeks hurt from smiling. Would this ever be over?

"Good one, Aunt True," whispered Danny, as the camera finally stopped rolling and the news crew began packing up. "Way to put that twerp in his place."

"I have no idea what you're talking about," Aunt True replied, the picture of innocence.

Carson Dawson promised to return the following afternoon for some "after" footage of the remodeled bookshop. On his way out, he and his news crew posed for the photographer from the *Pumpkin Falls Patriot-Bugle*, who'd been prowling around snapping pictures for the past hour.

"Never apologize for being 'tall timber,'" Aunt True told me, slipping her arm around my waist. "You and I were born to stand out in a crowd, Truly, and there's nothing wrong with that."

I gave her a rueful smile. That was the difference between an owl and a parrot. I didn't want to stand out in a crowd—I much preferred stealth mode. But I thanked her anyway.

"This is great!" the photographer said happily to my aunt as the Channel 5 crew left. "Definitely A-section material. I'm going to push for front-page placement in this week's issue."

The minute she said that, something clicked. I knew where the next clue was!

But first, I had an appointment at the Starlite Dance Studio.

CHAPTER 22

At least my practice session was Scooter-free.

We'd been told to come solo to our first private appointment at the Starlite, so that Cha Cha's parents could assess our abilities. Which were pretty much zero in my case.

It was a little weird dancing with Cha Cha's father. He wasn't that much taller than Cha Cha, so I towered over him, for one thing. He was really nice, though, and didn't make me feel at all awkward about it. Plus, even when I made mistakes he didn't act like I had two left feet.

"Slow, slow, quick quick," he said, moving me around the dance floor as easily as Pippa and Baxter had moved their game pieces around the Candy Land board. "That's it, you're getting the hang of it!"

I surveyed the spacious studio over his shoulder. It had hardwood floors and cushioned benches lining the mirrored walls. Potted trees twined with twinkle lights stood in all four corners of the room, and chandeliers blazed overhead. Maybe ballroom dancing wasn't so bad after all.

"Oops, sorry," I said as I stepped on Mr. Abramowitz's foot again.

"Not to worry," he replied quickly, smiling up at me. "That's why I get hazardous-duty pay." The smile vanished as he realized what he'd just said. Hazardous-duty pay is extra money soldiers receive for really dangerous jobs. Like flying a helicopter in a war zone. Flustered, Mr. Abramowitz stopped dancing. "I am so sorry, Truly. That was a thoughtless remark, considering all that your father has been through."

I shook my head. "It's okay, really."

"I hope your family knows how proud we all are of his service," Cha Cha's father continued. "And I think it's very brave of him, moving all the way across the country to take over the store from your grandparents. It can't be easy, having to suddenly shift gears like that."

"Um, yeah, I guess," I said.

I was quiet as we started to dance again. I'd never really thought about it that way. Was Mr. Abramowitz right? Had my dad done a brave thing, moving to Pumpkin Falls?

Cha Cha's father hummed along to the music, and I felt myself starting to relax. There was a flow to dancing that was not unlike swimming. Maybe I really was getting the hang of it.

Or maybe not.

"Oops," I said again, and Mr. Abramowitz winced.

"I think that's enough for today." He gave my arm a consoling pat. "Perhaps you and your partner could schedule a practice slot together before our next session at school? We'll be reviewing fox-trot this week, then moving on to the waltz."

Fat chance, I thought. I wasn't planning on spending any more time with Scooter than I absolutely truly had to. But, remembering my Pumpkin Falls manners, I thanked Mr. Abramowitz politely, then went to get my jacket.

Hearing music from the other, slightly smaller dance studio off the lobby, I peered through the window. Cha Cha and Calhoun were practicing the fox-trot. This must be where Pippa and Lauren took their lessons, I thought, noting the ballet barres in front of the mirrors.

Calhoun looked up just then and spotted me. He stopped dancing and scowled.

Cha Cha scurried over and popped her head out. "Hang on a sec, okay? We're almost done."

"Sure," I replied, and wandered over to the bulletin board to read the notices: upcoming classes (*learn to tango!*), local events (*bean supper at the church!*), and items for sale, including a tractor, a rooster, and a snowplow. Life sure was exciting in Pumpkin Falls.

A few minutes later, the music stopped and my classmates emerged. Calhoun brushed past me without a word.

"Pumpkin Falls manners!" I called after him, and Cha Cha grinned at me. "Not going so well, I take it?"

ABSOLUTELY TRULY

"He's not entirely hopeless," she replied.

As we crossed the street a few minutes later, I spotted the man in the green jacket who I'd seen before hanging around outside Lovejoy's Books. He reminded me of a stork, with his long, skinny legs and the way he was craning to peer through the window again. He wasn't wearing his hood this time, and I watched as he ran a hand through his bushy dark hair. I nudged Cha Cha. "Do you know that guy?"

She shook her head. "Nope. Why?"

I shrugged. "No reason." It was probably nothing—just somebody looking at a book. That's why we put them in the window, after all.

"Where's Calhoun going?" said Cha Cha, gazing down the block.

I turned to see our classmate heading into the offices of the *Pumpkin Falls Patriot-Bugle*. Suddenly, every nerve in my body went on full alert.

"Get Jasmine and Lucas and meet me there!" I told Cha Cha as I took off down the street. "I think Calhoun's trying to double-cross us."

CHAPTER 23

"What is this, kiddie day?" said the *Patriot-Bugle*'s receptionist, looking up from her magazine and snapping her gum.

"Um, we'd like to look at old issues of the paper," I said.

"Funny, young Clark Kent just said the same thing." She pointed a scarlet-tipped nail toward the door at the end of the hall. "Archives are downstairs to the left. Know how to use a microfiche machine?"

Cha Cha and Lucas and I hesitated.

"I do," said Jasmine.

"Good. Be sure and turn it off when you leave." She went back to her magazine.

"Since when do you know how to use a microfiche machine?" asked Cha Cha as the four of us headed down the hall.

"Since my parents are lawyers, duh," Jasmine replied. "They're always looking stuff up. Why are we here, anyway?"

ABSOLUTELY TRULY

"The next clue," I told her. "I overheard the photographer talk about putting our story in the paper. She said it was 'A-section material,' so it hit me that B-4 might be a section of the newspaper too."

Cha Cha snapped her fingers. "Truly Lovejoy, private eye, strikes again!"

"Yeah, only not soon enough. Calhoun's trying to beat us to it."

"Why?" asked Jasmine.

"I'm not sure."

The lights were on downstairs, and Calhoun was deeply engrossed in the microfiche screen across the room.

"What are you doing?" boomed Cha Cha.

He jumped, then glanced back over his shoulder at us. "None of your business."

"It is our business," I replied as we went over to join him. "It looks to me like a rat trying to steal the cheese."

His face flushed. "I would have told you if I found anything."

"Yeah, right," said Jasmine. "For a price."

I looked over his shoulder. "So what is B-4, anyway?"

"Classified ads."

Of course! The classifieds were the perfect place to leave a message for someone. "How far have you gotten?"

"I've checked through January, February, and March of the year the stamp was issued. Nothing so far."

The four of us crowded around him as he continued to scroll through the back issues. There was lots of news that year, some of it involving people we knew: My dad's wrestling team won the state tournament. The covered bridge was scheduled to be repainted. Ella Bellow and her husband visited the Grand Canyon and gave a slideshow afterward at the library. The destination for the senior class trip was announced: Montreal! Reverend Quinn of First Parish Church lectured at Lovejoy College on the Paul Revere bell; Aunt True was interviewed about the gap year she was planning to take in Patagonia; Belinda Winchester went home to Maine to visit her sister. Also, Calhoun's father was accepted to Dartmouth, and Bud Jefferson was headed to UNH.

We finally found what we were looking for, on Wednesday the third in the first week of June.

"There it is!" said Lucas, pointing to a boxed item. *For B* was at the top, and below it was another quote:

> *When you depart from me, sorrow abides and*
> *happiness takes his leave.*

Calhoun nodded. "Shakespeare," he said, sounding pleased.

I looked at him. Something was up.

ABSOLUTELY TRULY

Beneath the quote was another capital *B*, of course, just like before, but no numbers this time, only words. Exactly two of them: *HIGH NOON*.

The five of us stared at the screen. Seconds ticked by.

"I've got nothing," I said. "You guys?"

My friends shook their heads. So did Calhoun.

"You'd tell us if you did, right?" I asked him, and he nodded.

"'When you depart from me'—it kind of sounds like the writer is talking about somebody taking a trip," mused Cha Cha.

"There were a lot of people going places that year," said Jasmine. "Ella Bellow. Belinda Winchester. The entire senior class."

"I suppose Belinda could be one of our Bs," I said doubtfully. It was still hard to imagine anyone writing a love letter to the former lunch lady, though.

My friends and I pondered this idea, then we all burst out laughing.

"Yeah, that's what I thought," I said. My stomach rumbled. "We'd better get back. My aunt is counting on us, plus Lou's is catering lunch."

Jasmine went directly upstairs to Aunt True's apartment, where she'd left Lauren and Annie temporarily in charge. The rest of us filed back into the bookshop.

During the hour that we'd been gone, the space had been transformed. The carpet had vanished; all the books had been boxed up and taken to the basement; and dropcloths had been spread over the floor to protect the newly exposed hardwood, which would be washed and waxed tomorrow once the volunteer paint crew was finished. They were already hard at work, spreading the yellow paint that Aunt True and Pippa had picked out on the walls.

"Wow," I said.

"No kidding," echoed Cha Cha.

"Check out the office," said Hatcher, who was behind the sales counter handing out sandwiches and sodas.

I poked my head in to see Aunt True's entire wish list—armchairs, lamps, rugs, tables, and a bunch of other furniture—piled in the middle of the room. Belinda Winchester had brought Miss Marple back, and the dog was curled up on one of the donated chairs.

"People just keep dropping stuff off," my brother told me, shaking his head.

"Wow," I said again. Maybe there really was something to small-town living. "Where is Aunt True, anyway?"

My brother jerked his chin toward the back of the store. "In the children's section."

As I rounded the sales counter to go find her, something caught my eye. I froze in my tracks.

"Aunt True!" I shrieked.

ABSOLUTELY TRULY

She came running. So did everyone else within earshot, including Miss Marple, who started barking furiously.

I pointed to the rare books cabinet. It was unlocked, and the glass door was standing wide open. The autographed first edition of *Charlotte's Web* was gone!

CHAPTER 24

By the time Carson Dawson and his camera crew returned on Sunday afternoon, the bookstore shone. Its freshly painted walls glowed a sunny yellow, the washed and waxed hardwood floors gleamed, the windows and light fixtures sparkled, and the books were all neatly arranged on the newly repositioned shelves.

On the walls above them, just like Hatcher had suggested, Aunt True had hung colorful book posters, maps, and even some of Lola's artwork. Aunt True's vision of comfortable reading nooks scattered around the store was a reality now too. The donated rugs and armchairs and tables and lamps had been set up in several corners, and there was even a makeshift window seat in the children's room created from a blanket chest flanked by a pair of bookcases. Lauren had installed herself there among a pile of plump throw pillows, deep into a copy of *The Wolves of Willoughby Chase*.

ABSOLUTELY TRULY

There was only one thing missing: *Charlotte's Web*. The book had disappeared, and our excitement about what Carson Dawson was calling "the Bookshop Blitz" had evaporated along with it.

"This looks like a whole new store!" gushed the TV host. Pausing to face the camera, he added, "Folks, you couldn't ask for a cozier bookshop in all of New England!"

"Books bring people together, and people bring communities together," said Aunt True with a stoic smile.

"Great quote," said Carson Dawson. "I like that." He quickly replaced his big grin with a concerned expression, though, when Aunt True went on to tell him about the missing copy of *Charlotte's Web*.

"Looks like there's trouble," he intoned to the camera, "right here in River City—I mean Pumpkin Falls. Anyone having information about this crime should contact the local authorities."

The police—actually, Pumpkin Falls only had one policeman—interviewed Aunt True and dusted the cabinet for fingerprints, but with so many people coming and going all day, there were too many of them and they were too jumbled and smeared to be of any help.

"What about video footage from the security cameras?" asked Carson Dawson.

Aunt True snorted. "I don't think there is such a thing in Pumpkin Falls. We certainly don't have one."

The TV host's eyebrows shot up. "Well, then perhaps the dog saw something?" He winked at the camera, which promptly panned over to Miss Marple. But if she knew who took *Charlotte's Web*, she wasn't telling.

"Not much of a watchdog, I take it," chuckled the TV host.

"It's not Miss Marple's fault," said Lauren, rushing over to put her arms around the dog's neck.

"I never said it was," said Carson Dawson hastily. He turned to face the camera again. "That's it for this weekend's update, folks! From frozen waterfalls to a literary makeover, Pumpkin Falls is a happening place. And don't forget to check out next month's Winter Festival! It's the celebration's one hundredth anniversary, and I hear there's lots of fun in store. Until next time, this is Carson Dawson signing off for *Hello, Boston!*"

"Good-bye and good riddance," said Aunt True after he and his camera crew left. "What a phony."

She was even madder at him later that evening, though, when we turned on the TV at dinner and discovered that while Mr. Dawson had technically kept his promise—he hadn't leaked any footage of our remodeling project—somehow word had gotten out to the local news affiliate about the missing copy of *Charlotte's Web*.

The result was that Dad knew all about it by the time he got home.

"I never should have left you in charge!" he hollered at

ABSOLUTELY TRULY

Aunt True, thirty seconds after he came through the front door.

I understood why he was upset, of course—he was counting on the money from the sale of the book to help pay off the bank loan. Everybody was. But blaming it on Aunt True wasn't fair.

And if any of us had thought that a new high-tech bionic arm would magically transform Silent Man into the father we knew and missed, we were wrong. Way wrong.

"Can we see it?" begged Danny as we all crowded around, dying of curiosity.

"Later," Dad said shortly. "Right now I need to talk to your grandparents. They're in for an unpleasant surprise."

And before he even took off his jacket, he steered Aunt True to the living room, where he set up a videoconference under the watchful eyes of Nathaniel Daniel and his wife Prudence.

Dad was the one who ended up being surprised, though.

"We don't have an autographed first edition of *Charlotte's Web*," Lola said after he'd finished talking.

"Of course you do, Mom," Aunt True told her. "I saw it with my own eyes. Truly did too, right?"

I nodded.

My grandmother shrugged. "Well, I certainly don't remember it."

"Me neither," said Gramps. "And trust me, we'd remember something like that."

As for the rare books cabinet, it turned out that there was a key stashed on a hook behind it. A key everybody in town knew about it. It was there just in case any customers wanted to take a closer look at something in the cabinet and nobody was around to show it to them. Like the "mystery swap," the rest of Lovejoy's Books operated on the honor system too.

My father shook his head in disgust. "Great," he said. "That means anybody could have taken it."

He got up and stalked out of the room. Mom hurried after him. The rest of us crowded around the computer, eager to talk to our grandparents. They gave us a quick tour of their house—more of a concrete hut, really—in Namibia, told us a bit about the classes they were teaching and the library they were helping to build at the local school, then asked for all the news from Pumpkin Falls.

"Ella Bellow ith a bithybody," Pippa informed them, which made everybody laugh.

"You're a smart cookie, to figure that out so fast," said Gramps.

"Truly told me," Pippa replied, and my family laughed again.

"Has the January thaw finally arrived?" asked Lola.

"Nope," said Danny. "Everything's still frozen solid."

"A TV news crew came up from Boston over the weekend to film the falls," Hatcher told them. "They filmed us at the bookstore too."

"Really?" Lola looked surprised to hear this. "Why?"

Keeping her voice low and checking over her shoulder to make sure our parents were out of earshot, Aunt True filled Gramps and Lola in on the bookshop makeover.

"Well done!" said Lola, when she finished. "Our instincts were right to hand over the reins. We knew you and your brother would do wonders with the business."

Gramps looked out at me from the computer screen and smiled. "So, have you added anything to your life list, Truly?"

"Not much," I told him. "It's been too cold and snowy. There've been lots of cardinals and jays and chickadees around the feeders, of course, and I spotted a woodpecker the other day."

"Downy or pileated?" asked Gramps.

"Downy."

"My favorite!"

I shrugged. "Yeah, but they're nothing special."

"Every bird is special, Truly," Gramps said. "Backyard magic, remember?" He smiled at me again. "Be patient and keep your eyes peeled, and Pumpkin Falls might surprise you."

It already had. But I couldn't tell him that, of course.

CHAPTER 25

The third clue was much harder than the first two.

It took us nearly two weeks to figure out. And, surprisingly, a lot can happen in Pumpkin Falls in two weeks.

Like Math Boot Camp.

After I got an 83 percent on the next algebra test (or "17 percent more to 100 percent," as Lieutenant Colonel Jericho T. Lovejoy was quick to point out), Ms. Ivey sat up and took notice.

"Do you think your father would be interested in tutoring other students?" she asked me.

I shrugged. "Um, maybe?"

"He could charge a fee, of course. I think I'll stop by the bookshop this afternoon and ask him."

She walked me there after school and explained her idea to Aunt True.

"Of course he'll do it," said my aunt, who was dressed all

in black and wearing a Sherlock Holmes–style hat she called a "deerstalker." She was setting up chairs for the Mystery Mavens book club meeting.

Lovejoy's Books had four different book clubs gathering regularly now, thanks to the ad that Aunt True placed in the *Pumpkin Falls Patriot-Bugle*, and the blurb in our new bookshop newsletter. In addition to the Mystery Mavens, there were the Heart Throbs, who read romance novels (Aunt True wears flowery skirts and dresses for that one and serves high tea), the Highbrows, who like what Aunt True calls "literary fiction," and the Reel Readers, who read books that have been turned into movies and spend most of their meetings arguing about which version is better.

"We offer a wide range of services for our community here at Lovejoy's Books, including Math Boot Camp," Aunt True told Ms. Ivey, roping off the corner where the Mystery Mavens would meet with yellow "crime scene" tape.

I stared at her, openmouthed. Since when?

"Wonderful!" said Ms. Ivey. "I'll definitely be sending some students your way."

Afterward, when Aunt True told my father what she'd signed him up for, he protested, of course.

"It's extra money," she reminded him. "You're the one who keeps talking about the need for additional income streams."

My father continued to grumble for a while, but he

eventually agreed to do it. And that's how come I'm now sharing my tutor with Lucas (which really means Lucas and his mother, since, naturally, Mrs. Winthrop feels it's important to sit in on the sessions), Scooter Sanchez, and Annie Freeman, who may be the Grafton County Junior Spelling Champion but whose multiplication and division skills are sorely lacking.

Dad, of course, runs it like a military operation. The one time Mrs. Winthrop couldn't come, Scooter took advantage of her absence and started teasing Lucas. Dad caught him at it and told him to drop and give him twenty.

"Twenty what?" asked Scooter, mystified.

"Twenty what, *sir*," my father corrected him sternly. "And that would be push-ups, young man."

Scooter hasn't picked on Lucas since. At least not at Math Boot Camp.

The other thing that happened is that I went to the movies with Calhoun.

Well, not exactly. Cha Cha and Jasmine and Lucas were there too.

The way it happened was that I saw a flyer on the bulletin board at the General Store. I swear, every store in Pumpkin Falls has a bulletin board. Anyway, this particular flyer was squeezed in between a three-by-five card advertising free kittens (courtesy of Belinda Winchester, naturally) and another ad for a snow-shoveling service. The flyer caught my eye because it was bright yellow. CLASSIC WESTERN FILM SERIES was printed in large letters across the top, along with a picture of a cowboy on a horse. The first movie listed in the lineup? *High Noon.*

We had to investigate. The film was showing at Lovejoy College, and Calhoun made us bribe him again (dessert at Lou's afterward) in exchange for getting us tickets.

They'd scheduled it on a Friday at noon—I guess whoever organized the film festival thought this was funny—and on Wednesday at dinner I asked my mother if I could go.

"Friday's a no-school day because of parent-teacher conferences," I reminded her.

"It's also the day of Hatcher's first wrestling tournament," she replied. "We're all going, remember?" Her eyes slid over to Dad, who was focused on eating his pork chop. The fingers of his new bionic hand were gripping the fork while he sawed away with the knife in his left hand. So far, the new prosthesis seemed to be working well.

"Please, Mom?" I begged.

"Well, I suppose I could ask True if she'd be willing to stay with you. We won't be back until late."

"Mo-om! I don't need a babysitter!"

My father glanced up from his pork chop. "Truly," he warned. Talking back is one of Lieutenant Jericho T. Lovejoy's pet peeves.

"True isn't a babysitter; she's your aunt," my mother told me.

"Wait, you're going to miss my tournament?" said Hatcher.

"Sorry," I told him, not sorry at all. Wrestling tournaments are about as exciting as watching paint dry. You sit in the bleachers in a gym somewhere with a zillion other families, watching a zillion other wrestlers from a zillion other schools. It takes forever. The only time it's even remotely interesting is during the few minutes when somebody you know is out on the floor for their match. Maybe people feel the same way about swim meets, but I'm not stuck in the bleachers for those, I'm in the water.

"There'll be other tournaments," my mother told Hatcher. She turned to me and smiled. "I'm glad you're making friends, Little O. I really like the Abramowitzes' daughter."

"You mean the kazoo?" said Hatcher with a sly smile. That's what he calls Cha Cha behind her back. He thinks her deep voice is hilarious.

"Shut up, Hatcher," I said.

"Don't say 'shut up,'" my mother chided as my father looked up at me again and frowned. It was another of his pet peeves, of course.

"Yes, ma'am," I replied meekly, kicking my brother under the table instead.

On Friday, when I stopped by Lucas's house to pick him up, Mrs. Winthrop met me at the door. She was grinning from ear to ear, as excited as if Lucas and I were going on a date or something. Which we absolutely truly weren't. I was worried for a minute there that she was going to take a picture of the two of us.

"You'll drop him off at Lou's afterward, right?" she asked about fifty times, fluttering around nervously as she made sure Lucas had money, hat, mittens, an extra scarf, and anything else she could think of. Poor Lucas looked like he wished the floor would open up and swallow him.

I reassured her that I'd return him in one piece, and finally managed to pry him away. It was snowing again outside, and Lucas was quiet as we scuffed our way down Hill Street to the rendezvous point at Calhoun's house.

"Sorry about that," he said finally.

"Hey, you have to put up with my father," I told him.

He glanced over at me. "Your father's really nice."

I snorted. "Used to be. He's pretty cranky these days."

"Yeah, but I was kind of glad the day he got cranky with Scooter." Lucas smiled at me, and I smiled back.

A few minutes later we arrived at the ornate iron gate in front of the college president's house.

"Fancy schmancy," I said.

A freshly shoveled brick path led to the front door, which was flanked by twin urns containing small fir trees. They stood at attention like a pair of evergreen sentries. I resisted the urge to salute, and lifted the heavy brass knocker instead.

"Hello, Lucas," said the tall, sandy-haired man who

answered a moment later. "How nice to see you again. And you must be the Lovejoy girl that my son has been talking about." He smiled, and I gave him a tentative smile back. Calhoun had been talking about me?

"Make yourselves at home," said Dr. Calhoun, ushering us into the living room. "R. J. will be right down."

Lucas and I sat on the sofa. I surveyed the room. It was twice as big as my grandparents' living room, and decorated with all sorts of medieval-looking stuff. There was an actual suit of armor in the far corner, tapestries hanging on the walls, and a portrait of Shakespeare over the mantel. On either side of the fireplace were floor-to-ceiling built-in bookcases filled with books by and about Shakespeare.

"No wonder Calhoun knows so much," whispered Lucas.

The coffee table in front of us was piled with more books and magazines, most of them about Shakespeare too, and in the middle was a replica of a roofless building shaped like a circle.

"That's the Globe Theatre," said Dr. Calhoun, noticing my interest. He took a seat across from us, his dark eyes alight with enthusiasm. "The open-air theater in London where Shakespeare's plays were performed. The one that's there now is a reconstruction, of course."

"Cool," I said politely.

He smiled. "I like to think so. This room is my tribute to the Bard. His works are my great passion in life. Do you like Shakespeare?"

ABSOLUTELY TRULY

Before I could answer, the doorbell rang and he went to answer it, reappearing a moment later with Cha Cha and Jasmine. We all made polite conversation—mostly about Shakespeare—until Calhoun finally appeared.

"Have a wonderful time," said his father as we got up to leave. "I spoke with the film department and they've reserved a whole row of seats for you. I think you'll enjoy the movie; it's one of my favorites. Grace Kelly is at her most incandescent!"

I wasn't sure what that meant, but from the expression on Dr. Calhoun's face, I figured it must be something good.

My friends and I were by far the youngest people at the movie. Most of the audience were college students, but there were a few older people too, including Belinda Winchester. She was sitting in the back row, plugged into her music as usual and eating yogurt out of a cup. Spooning it into her pocket, actually. Or at least that's what it looked like at first, until I saw a furry little head pop out. She was feeding yogurt to a kitten.

Belinda waved her spoon at me. I waved feebly back.

"Friend of yours?" whispered Calhoun, giving me a sidelong glance.

"Uh, customer from the bookstore," I whispered back.

Black-and-white movies aren't my favorite, although I've seen a lot of them over the years, thanks to all the night-owl visits with my mother. She's a big fan. This one grabbed me right away, though. It started out with Gary Cooper, who played a marshal in the Wild West, getting married to a Quaker lady—that was Grace Kelly. "Incandescent" must mean really pretty, because she was gorgeous. Anyway, after the wedding, Gary Cooper turns in his badge so he can retire and go be a shopkeeper, but then he finds out this outlaw is coming to town on the noon train. The outlaw wants revenge on the marshal for putting him in jail. Being a Quaker and all, the marshal's new wife is against violence, so the newlyweds start to leave town. But then the marshal's conscience bothers him, because he feels like it's his duty to defend the place, so they turn back. This doesn't go over too well with his bride.

Things quickly go from bad to worse. The townspeople are too afraid to help, and as the countdown continues to the arrival of the train—clocks are constantly ticking onscreen, and people keep looking at their pocket watches—the marshal frantically tries to round up some deputies. Meanwhile, his wife is still mad at him for going back on his promise to quit being a marshal, and she tells him she's leaving on the same train. Time is running out for everyone and everything.

Halfway through the movie, I was pretty sure I knew where the next clue was.

"What are we waiting for?" said Calhoun after I whispered my theory to him and the others. He started to stand up. I grabbed his sleeve and pulled him back into his seat.

"Hang on, I want to see how it ends!" I protested.

ABSOLUTELY TRULY

"Shhhh!" Belinda Winchester hushed us sternly from the back row. "Pipe down!"

We did.

After the movie was over, we left in a hurry. "It's got to be the clock in the steeple," I told my classmates. "There was so much stuff about time and everything—and all those images of clocks! What else could it be?"

Cha Cha gave me an admiring glance. "Truly brilliant."

Calhoun snorted. "Maybe, if she's right. That's a big 'if,' though."

"So, we owe you dessert at Lou's, right?" Jasmine said to him as we made our way across the quad.

Calhoun looked a little embarrassed. "Actually, my father wanted me to invite you all back to our house for dessert. He made cupcakes."

I tried to imagine Lieutenant Colonel Jericho T. Lovejoy making cupcakes for my friends. Nope. No way. Not even before Black Monday.

"If the clue is somewhere in the steeple clock, how are we going to get up there to look for it?" I said a few minutes later, pulling a stool up to the island in Calhoun's kitchen. I selected a vanilla cupcake piled high with chocolate frosting.

"It's a church, duh," said Jasmine. "It's open to the public."

"I know *that*," I replied, stung. My grandparents were members of Pumpkin Falls First Parish Church, and we always went with them when we visited. "What I meant was how are we going to get into the *steeple?*"

"Don't look at me," said Cha Cha, whose family was Jewish. "We go to the synagogue in West Hartfield."

"Maybe we can ask for a tour?" Jasmine suggested.

"Reverend Quinn is really nice," said Lucas. "I'll bet he'd take us up there."

"It's settled, then," I told my friends. "We'll meet at the church on Sunday."

Lucas shook his head. "Reverend Quinn won't be there. He had dinner at Lou's last night and I heard him tell my mother that he was going away this weekend to some conference."

"Well then, that gives us a week to make plans," I said. "We can schedule another meeting of the, uh, Pumpkin Falls Private Eyes." My cheeks grew pink as I said this, knowing it would prompt a smirk from Calhoun. Which it did.

"Hey, bro!" A dark-haired girl poked her head into the kitchen. She was dressed in a cheerleader's uniform, and I recognized her from Danny's last wrestling meet.

"Hey, Jules," Calhoun replied.

"Make sure you and your friends clean up when you're done," she told him. "You know how Dad is about the kitchen being messy." She turned to walk away, and I noticed her name emblazoned on the back of her uniform: Juliet Calhoun.

Not Jules—*Juliet*. I didn't know much about Shakespeare,

but even I knew the title of his most famous play. I glanced across the kitchen island at Calhoun, who was absorbed in chocolate frosting.

No way.

No one would do that to their kid! Not unless they were nuts about Shakespeare.

Calhoun's father was nuts about Shakespeare.

I'd just figured out Calhoun's first name.

CHAPTER 26

I heard it before I saw it—a soft fluttering in the pine tree branches overhead. I held my breath and waited, arm extended, palm up, standing absolutely still.

Was I finally going to witness some backyard magic?

It was just barely light out. The rest of my family was still asleep, including my father, which was highly unusual. Lieutenant Colonel Jericho T. Lovejoy doesn't do sleeping in. But for once, he'd taken a day off from the bookshop and gone along to Hatcher's wrestling tournament yesterday. It was way upstate in Lancaster, and what with the snow and everything, my family hadn't gotten home until nearly midnight.

After the movie, I had spent the remainder of the afternoon at the bookstore with Aunt True. She'd unofficially hired me to be her Story Hour helper, and we worked on organizing craft supplies and making treats—little bullfrogs made out of kiwis, with grapes for eyes, since she was planning on reading *Frog and Toad Are Friends* at this morning's event.

"Right now it's just for glory, but we should be able to pay you soon," Aunt True told me. "Business has picked up a bit, thanks to the *Hello, Boston!* feature."

Even though *Charlotte's Web* was still missing and we only had a few weeks to go until Dad's deadline, Aunt True was thinking positively. I liked that about her.

Ella Bellow had come in as we were setting out cushions on the children's room floor.

"Brought your mail," she said, which I learned was code for *I've got some hot gossip*.

"Thanks, Ella," Aunt True replied. "Just set it on the counter."

"Did you hear about the Mahoneys next door?" the postmistress said, unwinding her black scarf. "They got picked to be on that TV show about antiques. *Attic Treasures*, or some such."

My aunt and I exchanged a glance. Ella was so predictable.

"By the way, I saw Bud Jefferson at the Savings and Loan yesterday morning," she continued, not even waiting for a reply. "He seemed worried. He headed straight for the loan department."

"Is that right?" murmured Aunt True, not paying the slightest bit of attention.

Ella's eyes glinted behind her black-rimmed glasses. "How's business for you folks?"

Aunt True's face flushed. She really hates having to fend off Ella's nosy questions. "Fine," she said shortly, and changed the subject. "By the way, any word on when we can expect that January thaw?"

"Nope. Longest I've ever had to wait for it, with February just around the corner." The postmistress shivered, rubbing her arms. "This cold is seeping into my bones."

Aunt True sprang into action. "I have just the book for that!" she said, suddenly all smiles. She handed Ella a copy of *Retirement in the Sunshine State.* "It just came in, and it's selling like hotcakes."

This was an overstatement. We'd sold exactly two copies.

Ella's mouth pruned up as she leafed through it. "Florida does sound tempting this time of year."

"It's always good to keep one's options open," Aunt True agreed, nodding sagely. She looked over at me and winked.

I smothered a smile. Word around town had it that our postmistress was thinking about retiring—maybe Aunt True was hoping to help spur it on.

Ella bought the book, which I took as a hopeful sign.

Later, after we closed up shop, Aunt True had come over to the house to stay with me.

She'd made us blueberry pancakes for dinner, with maple syrup from Annie and Franklin's family farm, and then she'd taught me how to play cribbage. While we played, we talked. We talked about swim team tryouts, which were on Monday, and which Dad still hadn't made up his mind about, except to tell me to quit bugging him, and we talked about the movie. It turned out that *High Noon* was one of Aunt True's all-time favorites.

"If you liked Grace Kelly, you should watch *To Catch a Thief*," she'd said. "Trade Gary Cooper for Cary Grant, the Wild West for the French Riviera, add in Alfred Hitchcock's trademark suspense, and—well, I won't spoil it for you."

I'd promised her I'd watch it.

My aunt told me about growing up in Pumpkin Falls, and stuff that she and my father had done when they were my age. It was a great place to be a kid, she'd said, but just like Dad she couldn't wait to go experience more of the world.

"I left the day after high school graduation, and I've only been back for brief visits in the years since," she'd told me. "This is the longest stretch of time I've spent here since I was a teenager, in fact."

"Are you planning to leave again?" I'd asked, surprised at how anxious that thought made me feel.

She'd hesitated. "Not any time soon. I'm actually having fun running the bookstore. I'd forgotten how much time I spent there when I was your age. It used to be my job to tidy up every night before closing. Plus," she added, "I know it's helping your father."

She and my mother kept saying that, so I figured they must be right, even though I hadn't seen much sign of it.

"Cha Cha's father said that Dad was really brave for moving here. Do you think that's true?"

Aunt True considered this. "There are all different sizes of brave, Truly. There's warrior brave, of course, and there's everyday brave, and everything in between. I happen to think Mr. Abramowitz is right. Your father is one of the bravest people I know. And not just because of what happened in Afghanistan. It's not easy to completely change course in life the way he has—especially when it wasn't his choice. I'm very proud of him."

I thought this over for a moment. "What about the bookstore—do you think it's going to make it?" Again, I was surprised at how anxious the thought of it failing made me feel. I'd spent a lot of time at the shop this past month, and most of it had actually been fun.

Aunt True hesitated again. "Well, I won't lie to you, we were really counting on selling *Charlotte's Web*. But Lovejoys can do anything, right?" She smiled. "We'll pull through somehow."

And if we didn't? I had wondered later, upstairs in bed. There was only one way to make sure we did, and that was to get *Charlotte's Web* back. It was time to catch a thief. The Pumpkin Falls Private Eyes already had one mystery to solve, though, so I decided to tackle this one on my own.

Which was why I'd gotten up early this morning. I had some work to do.

ABSOLUTELY TRULY

My grandfather's hat slipped forward, slightly obscuring my view. I was tempted to reach up and adjust it, but I knew I'd ruin everything if I did. So I continued to stand in the middle of the backyard and wait, the only movement the rise and fall of my chest and the steady puffs of my frosty breaths.

And then it happened. Backyard magic. There was another flutter of wings followed by the very lightest touch as a chickadee landed on the palm of my hand. It cocked its head and regarded me for a couple of seconds with a bright black eye—probably wondering who the stranger was wearing Gramps's hat—then it plucked a sunflower seed from my mitten and flew off.

A huge smile spread over my face. I wanted to laugh out loud, but I resisted the urge, hardly daring to breathe now for fear of scaring away the winged visitors that began darting toward me in a steady stream.

I glanced over at the house and spotted a face in one of the upstairs windows. It was my father. His eyes met mine and he smiled. A flutter of a smile, like bird wings. Then, swift as flight, it was gone and so was he.

I fed the birds until my toes were numb. Then I went back inside to have my own breakfast, get ready for Story Hour, and figure out how I was going to catch that thief.

CHAPTER 27

"His name is *Romeo?*" Mackenzie gaped at me from my laptop screen, incredulous. The two of us were talking while I got ready to go to the bookstore. "Are you sure?"

I nodded. "Pretty sure." What I wasn't so sure of was whether I was going to say anything to Calhoun. It was obvious that he didn't want anyone to know. I wouldn't either, if my name was Romeo. That was even worse than Truly.

"I guess it's kind of romantic, if you think about it. Tell me more about him," Mackenzie coaxed. "What does he look like?"

I sat down on the edge of the bed to pull on my socks, and frowned. "Why?"

"Is he cute?"

"I don't know! He's—Calhoun."

"What color is his hair?" she asked, as I started to brush my own.

ABSOLUTELY TRULY

"Kind of blondish-brownish, I guess."

My cousin heaved a sigh. "You're impossible!"

I grinned at her. Not only could Mackenzie describe the exact shade of Mr. Perfect Cameron McAllister's hair, she could probably tell you the exact number of hairs on his head. The difference was, she had a crush and I didn't. Absolutely truly not.

She tried one last stab at it. "Is he short? Tall?"

"Tallish," I told her.

"Ish? What's ish? Is he as tall as you?"

I grinned again. "Nobody's as tall as me, Mackenzie."

Walking downtown a little while later, my thoughts turned from Romeo Calhoun to the missing copy of *Charlotte's Web*. The more I thought about it, the more I realized how many people might have had a motive for taking the book.

For starters, there was Mr. Henry, the children's librarian. He'd flat-out said he would give anything for an autographed copy. Carson Dawson seemed pretty interested in it too. So was Aunt True, but she didn't count, of course. The Mahoneys could have taken it, I supposed, to show off on the TV show Ella told us about yesterday. And then there was the tidbit she'd shared about seeing Bud Jefferson at the bank looking worried. Was she right about him talking to a loan officer? Maybe he was in trouble and needed money. It would have been an easy thing to slip a book into his jacket pocket. Which reminded me, what about the man in the green jacket who was always hanging around outside the bookshop like he was casing the joint?

I sighed. Catching the thief wasn't going to be easy. There'd been so many people in the store during the Bookshop Blitz!

There was a big crowd at the bookstore this morning too, waiting for Story Hour to start. Aunt True had been talking it up on the bookstore's website and she'd even convinced the *Patriot-Bugle* to run a feature story about it. Attendance had doubled since the makeover.

After my dad had cooled off about the missing *Charlotte's Web* that day, we'd all taken him down to the store to show off our handiwork.

He didn't say much at first, just walked around inspecting everything. "You all did this?" he'd said, finally, and we nodded.

"Me too!" Pippa did a pirouette. She loved doing pirouettes on the bookstore's newly polished wooden floors.

My father had turned abruptly to Aunt True. "I owe you an apology," he said stiffly. The stiff part was because apologies aren't easy for Lieutenant Colonel Jericho T. Lovejoy.

"For what?"

"For what I said earlier. You were *exactly* the right person to leave in charge."

My father had been especially thrilled when he learned that she'd managed to do everything on a shoestring, and we all had basked in the glow of his approval. Especially Aunt

ABSOLUTELY TRULY

True. Unfortunately, it didn't last long, and the two of them soon returned to their bickering.

Which was what they were doing this morning.

"J. T., can you take Memphis upstairs?" Aunt True asked, thrusting her cat at him. "He's hissing at the toddlers again."

Memphis did not like toddlers. Or Story Hour.

"Blasted cat," grumbled my father, as Memphis hissed at him, too. Memphis didn't like the bionic arm either. "Can't Truly do it?"

"She's got her hands full," Aunt True told him, pointing to the tray loaded with little kiwi-grape bullfrogs that I was carrying to the children's room.

"Like I even have two hands to be full," my father muttered. Aunt True shot him a look. He heaved a sigh, somehow managing to corral Memphis, and the two of them disappeared upstairs.

Story Hour was a big hit, but what happened afterward was even better. Some fairy dust from this morning's backyard magic must have settled on me, because my father finally agreed to let me try out for swim team.

I brought the subject up as I was putting away the craft supplies in the office storage closet. "Please, Dad?" I begged. "Tryouts are Monday. You saw that last test—my grade has come way up!"

"Yes, it's come up, but there's still room for improvement," he insisted.

Aunt True came in just then. Hearing this exchange, she put her hands on her hips and glowered at my father. "Jericho Lovejoy, wake up and smell the coffee!" she said. "Look at how hard your daughter is working! She's done exactly as you've requested: She's been here every day for tutoring after school, right on time and without complaining. And she's gone above and beyond to help us here in the store—including working on weekends. Don't you think you could cut her a little slack?"

"I'll thank you not to tell me how to raise my own child," my father replied.

"Haven't you heard?" countered Aunt True. "It takes a village to raise a child—which is an actual fact, by the way, because I've been in many villages in many countries—"

"I don't need a travelogue, True."

My aunt grabbed him by his good arm and towed him out into the store. I followed at a safe distance—I didn't want to get caught in the brother-sister cross fire.

"Have you seen our front window this week?" said Aunt True. "It's all Truly's doing." She gestured at the sign I'd made that read WELCOME TO WINTER... BIRDING. I'd found a little fake evergreen Christmas tree downstairs in the storage room and placed it on the display table, which I'd covered with a white cloth, and hung some of Gramps's carved wooden birds from the tree's branches. Then I'd scattered birdseed underneath it, and propped a pair of binoculars alongside a stack of field guides from the shop's birding section, a couple

ABSOLUTELY TRULY

of life-list journals, and a copy of *Owl Moon*, of course."

"It's brilliant!" Aunt True continued. "She's a born bookseller. I've sold out of the journals, and I've had five orders for *Owl Moon* this week alone. Five!"

The muscles in my father's jaw worked. Lieutenant Colonel Jericho T. Lovejoy doesn't like being told what to do. Especially not by his big sister. Aunt True must have been a star debater in high school, though, because in the end she managed to broker a deal.

"How about you let her try out for swim team, but she continues with the tutoring until you're satisfied with her grade?" she said.

Please oh please oh please oh please, I thought as my father pondered her suggestion.

"I suppose that could work," he said finally, and I started jumping up and down and squealing.

A nearly six-foot-tall person with size-ten-and-a-half shoes makes a whole lot of noise when she's jumping up and down. Especially on wooden floors. And that's not even counting the squealing.

"Enough!" said my father. "There's a condition, Truly."

"Anything," I promised.

"No backsliding. If your math grade slips, you're off the team."

I nodded. I could live with that. I could live with anything, as long as it meant getting back in the water.

CHAPTER 28

Water is my natural element.

At least that's what my father always says. He says that I was swimming practically before I learned to walk. Mom says I did a cannonball in the baptismal font, which I know is a Texas tall tale, but I'm never quite sure about the one she tells about bathtime. She says I used to get so excited splashing around in the tub that she had to put floaties on my arms.

What I know for sure is that I've always loved the feeling of being in the water. Plus, it doesn't matter where you live or how often you move, there's always a pool and the water is always the same. Water doesn't care how tall you are either.

Right now, I couldn't wait to dive back in.

"Swimmers on the block!" shouted the coach, and my toes curled automatically over the edge of the starting block. The 50 Freestyle was the first of several hurdles here at tryouts that would determine whether I'd become a member of the Pumpkin

ABSOLUTELY TRULY

Falls Youth Swim Team. I just hoped I wasn't too out of shape from not having been in the water for several weeks.

"Take your mark!"

I moved into the track start position, placing one foot behind me and grabbing the block on either side of my forward leg, focused like a hawk on its prey as I waited. At the sound of the buzzer, I arced forward, launching myself into the air. For a brief moment I heard the shouts and cheers of the onlookers from the bleachers, and then the water closed over my head and the world fell away.

A current of pure joy coursed through my body. Swimming is probably as close as I'll ever get to flying.

As for being out of shape, I needn't have worried. It was like I'd never been away. I quickly fell into the familiar rhythm as my arms and legs sliced through the water, and I hit my pace after just a few strokes. A quick flip-turn at the end of the lane, push off and glide, and I was in the home stretch. I cranked up the tempo, pouring it on until I practically flew the last few yards. I slapped the edge of the pool and glanced up at the clock.

Not my best time, but not bad, either. Especially if you considered the fact that I hadn't been in the water since we moved to New Hampshire. Plus, I was the first one at the wall by a long shot.

The coach looked at me in surprise over the top of his clipboard. "I wasn't expecting that."

I smiled. No one ever is.

The thing is, I don't necessarily look like a jock. Most people figure girls my age who are as tall as I am and have feet as big as mine (helpful brother that he is, Hatcher calls them "flippers") are uncoordinated, like maybe we've sprouted too fast or something. Although I'm not always supergraceful—especially not on the dance floor—I'm not a total klutz, either. But put me in the water and it's like my body has found its reason for existence.

"You've got mermaid DNA," Dad used to tell me.

I glanced over at the bleachers and waved to him. He gave me a brief two-finger salute in return. Aunt True was next to him with Pippa and Lauren. She'd sprung them from after-school daycare so they could come watch. Well, Pippa was watching. Lauren had her nose in a book, as usual.

Cha Cha and Jasmine had come to cheer Lucas and me on, and my mother was going to try and make it for the last bit too. She had a late-afternoon history class with Professor Rusty. Danny and Hatcher were both at wrestling practice.

"Go, Truly!" my aunt shouted.

I grinned at her and hauled myself out of the pool. Grabbing my towel from the nearby bench, I looked over to where the next batch of hopefuls was lining up. Lucas Winthrop was among them. Lucas in a swimsuit was not a sight for sore eyes. Skinny as a whistle and pale as milk, he was easily the sorriest excuse for a seventh grader I'd ever seen. He had determination, though. When the coach blew his whistle, Lucas was the first one in the water, and if he churned his way across the pool with more grit than grace, he still ended up with a respectable time.

"Way to go, Winthrop!" I called, and he looked over, startled, then smiled shyly.

Behind me, some of the moms were talking in the bleachers.

"Swimming is the perfect sport for Lucas," I heard Mrs. Winthrop say. "My son was delicate when he was younger, you know, and contact sports are far too dangerous. Plus, he comes home from the pool so wonderfully clean."

Glancing over my shoulder, I saw the other mothers exchange amused looks. Mrs. Winthrop rattled on, oblivious.

Maybe Lucas and I had more in common than I thought. The pool was probably the one place he could go to get away from his mother. It's always been my refuge too. Being underwater is the ultimate form of stealth mode.

A little while later I was on deck again for the 100 Individual Medley. My mother waved to me from the stands. I was glad she'd made it in time, because the medley has always been my favorite race—twenty-five yards each of butterfly, backstroke, breaststroke, and freestyle.

"Let's see what you can do," said Coach Maynard.

At the sound of the bell I dove in, launching myself a few inches below the surface of the water into a streamline propelled by a mighty dolphin kick. Every muscle in my body zinged as I surged forward. The butterfly is my favorite stroke. I love that split second when I lunge out of the water and am almost airborne. It's like flying.

Thinking about flying made me think of my father. Would he be able to pilot a helicopter or plane again someday? Not commercially—he'd explained to us why that was out—but just for fun? I knew how much he hated being grounded. It was probably the same for him as not swimming was for me. I couldn't imagine not ever being able to swim again.

I would feel like a bird without wings.

I finished the medley not too far off my own personal best time. When I got out of the pool, Coach Maynard shook my hand.

"Welcome to the team, Truly," he said. "I don't need to see any more. Stick around for the rest of the tryouts if you want, but I'll expect you here starting tomorrow afternoon. We practice every day from four until six."

I nodded happily. Glancing up in the stands again, I gave my family and friends an exuberant thumbs-up. Then I headed to the dressing room to shower and change.

"Congratulations, honey," my mother said a little while later when I emerged. She gave me a big hug. "Not that I had any doubt."

"Thanks, Mom."

My father gave me an awkward squeeze. "I expected no

less from a Lovejoy," he said. This was high praise coming from Silent Man, and I practically floated to the parking lot.

Outside, snow was falling thick and fast.

"Can you believe this?" Aunt True marveled. "It's like something out of a Russian novel! I swear I don't ever remember a winter like this when we were growing up, do you, J. T?"

My father shook his head.

Mom turned her face up to the sky and closed her eyes. "Do you remember the part in *Anna Karenina*—"

"You mean when—" Aunt True began.

"Yes! Wasn't that incredibly—"

"Totally!"

"Tolstoy is the best!"

Aunt True and Mom are soul mates when it comes to books. They speak in this weird literary shorthand that none of the rest of us can understand at all.

"Would you guys mind if I walk home?" I asked, spotting Cha Cha and Jasmine emerge from the swim center. The Pumpkin Falls Private Eyes needed to talk.

"Not at all," said my mother, sliding into the driver's seat of our minivan. My sisters climbed in the back. "Are you coming, J. T., or are you heading back to the bookshop?"

"I should head back to the shop," he told her. "The accountant is dropping by in a bit to go over the end-of-the-month financials."

"I'll keep you company," said Aunt True, linking her arm

through his good one. "And just because you're my favorite brother, I'll even make you dinner."

My mother laughed. "Now, there's an offer you can't refuse. I'll see y'all later, then." She waved at us and drove off.

I said good-bye to my father and my aunt, then headed over to find Cha Cha and Jasmine, who had disappeared around the corner of the swim center. I followed and quickly came upon Calhoun stuffing snow down the neck of Lucas Winthrop's jacket again, while Cha Cha and Jasmine tried to stop him.

I ran over to help. "Knock it off, Romeo!" I hollered.

Calhoun froze.

I did too. I hadn't meant to drop the R-bomb that way. Once again, I'd put my big foot in my mouth.

Cha Cha and Jasmine and Lucas gaped at us.

"Romeo?" said Cha Cha. "Who's Romeo?"

I pointed wordlessly at Calhoun.

"Your name is *Romeo*?"

Calhoun's face flamed.

"I always wondered what the *R* in 'R. J.' stood for," said Jasmine. "I figured the *J* was for 'James,' like your dad, but I never would have guessed 'Romeo' for the *R*."

Calhoun abruptly let go of Lucas's jacket. "I'm outta here," he muttered.

Thinking quickly, I realized that I could use this to my advantage. "No, actually, you're not," I told him. "I've had to put up with 'Truly Gigantic' and 'Truly Drooly' for weeks now. You can deal with Romeo. Which," I added, "we won't tell a soul about, on one condition."

He regarded me warily.

"Quit picking on Lucas. And while you're at it, see if you can get Scooter to stop picking on him too. And on me."

Calhoun lifted a shoulder, then gave a reluctant nod.

"Good. Your secret is safe with us."

"Promise?" he asked, darting a glance at me.

"Cross my heart and hope to . . ." My voice trailed off. "Whatever. Our lips are sealed."

"Sealed," said Cha Cha solemnly, holding up three fingers in the traditional Boy Scout salute. Then her dimple appeared and she grinned broadly. "Scout's honor . . . *Romeo!*"

I grinned back. "Guess what?" I told my friends. "I think I have a plan for getting us into the steeple."

CHAPTER 29

With two weeks to go until Winter Festival, there was a change in the air in Pumpkin Falls.

It wasn't the January thaw. That still hadn't arrived, even though the calendar now said February. It was more a sense of anticipation, a crackle of excitement you could feel around town, at school, and in the shops as people talked about "the big weekend."

Aunt True says Winter Festival is Pumpkin Falls's answer to homecoming. She says people who grew up here or used to live here often come back for it, although if you ask me, which nobody ever does, I could think of better ways to spend a weekend than stuck in freezing-cold Pumpkin Falls, New Hampshire.

My math grade crept up a few notches, which pleased my father and made me feel a little more secure about my spot on the swim team. At practice, I did planks and push-ups and sit-ups and swam endless laps in preparation for our first race. The Pumpkin Falls Youth Swim Team always kicked off its season with a face-off against Thornton during Winter Festival.

Everywhere I've ever lived, there's always an archrival, and for Pumpkin Falls, Thornton is it. And everywhere I've ever lived, it's always the coach's job to get his or her team whipped into a frenzy over this rival. Coach Maynard droned on every day at practice about how we need to do our best and believe in ourselves and get out there and show Thornton what we're made of, blah blah blah. I'd heard it all before.

Casting a shadow over all of this, at least for me, was the bookshop's make-or-break deadline. I wished I could be more like Aunt True, who sailed ahead thinking positively and planning for the future, but the spike in sales after Carson Dawson's TV feature on Pumpkin Falls had leveled off, and with no *Charlotte's Web* in sight, I didn't see how we were going to make it. I saw all the long hours my father still spent behind closed doors with the accountant, and how he worried constantly over things called "profit margin" and "overhead" and "cash flow."

The other shadow was Cotillion. I was so not looking forward to the exhibition dance, even though Scooter and I were doing marginally better in class. This was mostly because Scooter had stopped goofing off. He'd caught wind of Calhoun's extra practice sessions—which he thought Calhoun was paying for—and that had lit a fire under his competitive streak.

"Oh good, the kittens are here," said Jasmine as she and Cha Cha and I took off our jackets and piled them on the bench by the bookshop door.

Ever since the remodel, Lovejoy's Books had become Belinda Winchester's home away from home. She and at least one kitten showed up pretty much every afternoon now, right around the time that Aunt True took her mini pumpkin whoopie pies out of the oven. When Saturday rolled around, though, the treats—and Belinda—arrived earlier, for Story Hour.

Cha Cha and Jasmine had volunteered to help Aunt True and me on this particular Saturday. Plus, my friends were eager to check out the new shipment of jewelry. They really liked all the new stuff that Aunt True had started to stock as part of her scheme to add more income streams.

The three of us helped ourselves to some of the whoopie pies that were waiting on the sales counter. My father emerged from the office to grab one too. He still complains about the expense, but I've noticed he's first in line when Aunt True brings them down from her apartment.

"She never leaves," he grumbled, casting a baleful eye on Belinda Winchester, who had settled into an armchair over by the front window with her latest paperback from the mystery swap. "And she never buys anything either."

"So? It's her happy place," my aunt replied from her perch on a stepladder behind the counter. She fiddled with the clothesline she was anchoring to the ceiling. "Pass me a thumbtack, would you please, Truly?"

Cha Cha and Jasmine and I poked around in the pile of literary T-shirts (EAT SLEEP READ! LITGEEK! I ♥ MR. DARCY!) that were heaped by the cash register, waiting to be strung up. The T-shirts were one of the new sidelines Aunt True had decided we should stock.

"You're turning us into the General Store," my father said, picking one up and grimacing at its slogan (SO MANY BOOKS, SO LITTLE TIME!).

"If it brings in customers, why not?" Aunt True replied cheerfully.

Mom and I think the sidelines have really livened things up. Cha Cha and Jasmine agree. They drop in often after school now to check out the new stuff on display, from cool little notepads and pens and tote bags to stationery, mugs, jewelry, and locally made soaps and candles. We've started stocking maple syrup and maple candy from the Freemans' farm too.

"Have you girls seen Truly's new Valentine's Day window?" Aunt True asked.

"It's not mine, exactly," I said. My aunt and I had worked on it together last night after dinner.

"You did the lion's share of the work," Aunt True replied.

I followed Cha Cha and Jasmine as they went over to the front of the store to check it out.

"Sweet!" said Cha Cha.

Across the top of the window was a banner with WE ♥ HAPPY ENDINGS on it, and I'd taped red construction-paper hearts and Cupids on the glass. The display table was covered in a floor-length red tablecloth and piled high with things that my aunt and I had gathered from the far-flung corners of the store: Valentine's Day cards; a red leather-bound copy of Shakespeare's sonnets; heart-shaped chocolates and soaps; a pink mug with white hearts on it, pink notebooks, pink sticky notes, pink pens—everything we could think of that celebrated love and romance. There were piles of books too: *Pride and Prejudice*, *Cinderella*, *Jane Eyre*, and a whole bunch more.

"I love happy endings too," sighed Jasmine. "They're so romantic."

Cha Cha and I looked at each other and grinned.

"Here are the new necklaces I was telling you about," I told my friends. "The ones made of Scrabble tiles. See? There's a letter on one side, and a design on the other."

"Cute!" said Cha Cha.

"I have a ballerina on mine," said Pippa, emerging from her favorite hideout under the table. "And a *P* for 'Pippa.' Aunt True gave it to me."

Jasmine and Cha Cha fussed over her necklace, of course,

and Pippa let them each take a turn wearing it. Then she disappeared back under the table again.

"Ooh, look at this one!" Jasmine held up a tile with a picture of a bear on it reading a book.

Aunt True was wearing one just like it in honor of Story Hour.

"So, all systems go for tomorrow?" I asked my friends, and they nodded.

"I'm sleeping over at Jazz's tonight," Cha Cha told me. "And my parents said I could go to church with her tomorrow."

"Perfect. We'll all be there—Calhoun's coming too."

Jasmine looked over at Cha Cha. "How are his private lessons going?"

"He's making progress, but he's not exactly Romeo on the dance floor," Cha Cha replied, and the three of us giggled. It was going to be hard to keep the lid on Calhoun's real name.

The bell over the door jangled, and Mrs. Abramowitz came in with Baxter. I pointed to where Pippa was hiding and he dove under the table to join her. Mrs. Abramowitz took off her coat. She looked like she'd just breezed in from a dance competition. She often looks that way. She has thick, curly dark hair like Cha Cha's, but Mrs. Abramowitz's is always swept into an elegant updo, and unlike my mother, who dresses mostly in jeans these days now that she's a college student again, or Aunt True, who dresses like, well, a parrot, sequins are a staple in Cha Cha's mother's wardrobe. Even her snow boots have high heels.

"I don't know about you girls, but I am ready for spring," she said, unwinding her scarf. "Where is that January thaw when you need it?" She glanced around the store. "Is your mother here, Truly?"

I shook my head. "She's coming in later. We're driving down to Manchester this afternoon."

"Let me guess—dress shopping?" Cha Cha's mother smiled at me. "Your mother told me you've grown another inch since your move to Pumpkin Falls."

There really are no secrets in small towns.

"That's the best part of Cotillion, I think," Cha Cha's mother continued. "It's such fun to have an excuse to get all dressed up."

Um, not really, I thought. I don't do dresses. They're way up there on the list of things I'm not good at.

Maybe Mrs. Abramowitz saw the worried look on my face, because she slipped an arm around Cha Cha, and smiled at Jasmine and me. "You girls are all going to shine, no matter what you wear."

Over at the sales counter, Aunt True pinned the last of the T-shirts to the clothesline, then climbed down from the stepladder and picked up the old-fashioned handbell she'd bought next door at Mahoney's Antiques.

"Story Hour!" she called, ringing it loudly.

Pippa and Baxter popped out from under the table and dashed to the children's room. Mrs. Abramowitz and my friends and I followed. So did Belinda Winchester, who was quickly surrounded by an admiring crowd of young kitten-lovers.

"She's like Mary Poppins or Mrs. Piggle-Wiggle or something," Aunt True said, watching her.

Dad looked mystified. "Who?"

Aunt True sighed. "Never mind." My father is so not a bookworm.

Initially, my father had been worried that Belinda might scare kids away, and more important, their parents—who were the paying customers, after all, as he pointed out—but she hadn't. In fact, she's kind of turned into another store mascot.

Of course, it helps that she almost always has a furry creature or two with her. Dad was not thrilled about allowing more pets into the shop, but the kittens have proved to be a huge hit.

"They're free advertising!" Aunt True had argued, and it's true. Some people—especially those with little kids—drop by the store now just to see the kittens, and most of them end up buying something.

"Girls, why don't you go ahead and pass these around," said my aunt, handing us each a plate of mini whoopie pies.

We dutifully distributed the snacks, which disappeared in nothing flat. The silver-dollar-size treats are almost as popular with the Story Hour crowd as the kittens are.

"Are these the same ones you brought in last week?" Aunt True asked Belinda, peering into the basket beside the chair where she was sitting.

"Maybe," Ms. Winchester replied slyly.

Aunt True frowned. "These are orange, though. I thought last week's were gray."

Belinda Winchester drew a large cotton handkerchief from her pocket and blew her nose loudly.

"How many do you have, exactly?"

"Handkerchiefs?"

"Kittens."

A slow smile spread across Mrs. Winchester's face. "Hundreds of cats, thousands of cats—"

"Millions and billions and trillions of cats!" Aunt True finished, laughing. "Perfect choice for today's Story Hour." She winked at me. "Change of plans," she said, then went over to the picture-book section and plucked a slim volume from one of the shelves. Holding it up, she asked, "Who knows the name of this book?"

A flock of little hands flew into the air.

"Baxter?" said Aunt True.

"*Millions of Cats,*" he replied, and she nodded.

"That's right. It's *Millions of Cats,* by Wanda Gág." Aunt

ABSOLUTELY TRULY

True sat down, and the little kids crowded around her as she started to read.

The bell over the front door rang again. I glanced over to see Ella Bellow come in. My heart sank as I realized that my father had vanished. Again. He had an uncanny way of doing that whenever Ella showed up.

It was up to me to man the sales counter. "Back in a sec," I whispered to my friends, and crossed the store to greet her. "Can I help you?"

"*May* I help you," she corrected.

Whatever, I thought, but aloud I replied meekly, "May I help you?" adding, "ma'am" for good measure and plastering a smile on my face. Paying customers are paying customers.

There was a burst of laughter from the children's room, and the postmistress and I looked over to see what the commotion was about. Aunt True and Cha Cha and Jasmine had the kids on their feet now, and they were all singing "Three Black Cats" to the tune of "Three Blind Mice" as they marched around Belinda's chair.

Ella Bellow sniffed. "So unsanitary."

I wasn't sure if she was talking about Story Hour, or Belinda Winchester, or the kittens, or what.

"I'm sure it's a violation of our town's health code to have so many animals on the premises," she said, casting a sour look at Miss Marple, who was sleeping peacefully in her dog bed on the floor below the sales counter.

I didn't reply, grateful that Memphis was upstairs in Aunt True's apartment. Ella Bellow was another item on the list of things my aunt's cat didn't like.

"You left a message that my special order is in." Ella picked up one of the flyers stacked by the cash register and scrutinized it while I retrieved her book from behind the sales counter. I looked at its title: *Second Acts: Starting a New Career in Your Golden Years.* So maybe the rumors really were true! Maybe Ella really *was* thinking about retiring.

"Grand Reopening Celebration, huh?" the postmistress said, peering down her knife blade of a nose at me.

"Yes, ma'am."

She waved the flyer. "You're holding it during Winter Festival?"

I nodded. That was Aunt True's idea, of course. She wanted to do something splashy to spotlight the bookshop's makeover.

"The paper says they're expecting a record crowd, since it's the centennial," Aunt True had told my father, who as usual was skeptical of her plan. Mostly because he didn't want to spend any money. "The bed and breakfast and all the motels up along Route Four are booked solid. What better time to show off our store?"

Ella Bellow frowned as she peered over her black-framed glasses at the schedule of events. In addition to next weekend's Valentine's Day Story Hour, featuring special guest star Mr.

ABSOLUTELY TRULY

Henry from the local library, there was a love poetry open mic night, prize drawings and giveaways all weekend, special gift bags with all purchases, a cooking demonstration by Franklin and Annie's mother with maple syrup from the Freeman farm, and a reading and book signing by Augusta Savage, aka Augustus Wilde, a.k.a. Captain Romance.

Ella Bellow arched an ink-black eyebrow at me. "Don't you think you might have bitten off more than you can chew? Do you really think that visitors will want to bother with all this?"

I stared at her. This was the real reason that she'd come in! The old crow was in fishing mode, not shopping mode, snooping around for gossip about our family's business as usual. Well, I wasn't about to give her the satisfaction of leaving with any.

"Of course they will!" I gushed in reply. "Business has been fantastic ever since *Hello, Boston!* Thank you so much, by the way, for telling Carson Dawson about us. That was brilliant."

Ella seemed taken aback. "I see. Well, I—that's good news, then," she said, and after paying for her book she beat a hasty retreat to the door.

It was almost as if she was hoping for bad news, I thought. But why? What possible difference could our bookstore's struggles make to a soon-to-be-retired postmistress?

CHAPTER 30

"Hey, Little O," said my mother.

"Hey, Mama Owl," I replied.

We smiled at each other.

"Can't sleep?" I shook my head and she set her book aside and patted the sofa. "Come sit by me."

I curled up next to her and she rearranged the quilt to cover us both. The remnants of a fire crackled softly in the fireplace. I stared at the glowing embers while my mother sipped her tea.

I'd missed this. We hadn't been Little Owl and Mama Owl for ages, not since before Black Monday. I was probably getting too old for it, but still, it was really nice.

"Seems like old times, doesn't it?" my mother murmured, resting her chin on my head. "So, are you happy with your dress?"

I nodded. The two of us had actually had a lot of fun

shopping earlier. And the dress we'd finally settled on was okay, as far as dresses go.

"And are you happy with your new friends? Cha Cha and Jasmine sure seem like great girls," my mother continued. "And that Winthrop boy has taken a shine to you too."

"Yeah," I replied. "They're all really nice. I still miss Mackenzie, though."

"We were going to keep this as a surprise, but your dad and I have been talking. We know this move hasn't been easy for you, and we really appreciate the way you've pitched in to help here at home and at the bookstore. So we're getting you something special for your birthday." My mother smiled at me. "Mackenzie!"

I sat bolt upright. The quilt dropped from my shoulders. "Really?"

She nodded. "Really. I've already checked with Aunt Louise and Uncle Teddy, and they said she can come for spring break. Aunt True donated some frequent-flier miles, and the ticket is booked."

I started to squeal, but my mother quickly put her finger to her lips, so I threw my arms around her instead. "Thank you so much, Mom!" I whispered, doing a quick calculation in my head. Spring break—and my birthday—was in the middle of March. That was only a little over a month away!

"Bedtime for bonzos," my mother announced a few minutes later. She gave the embers a good stir with the poker and secured the fireplace screen. "Come on, I'll walk you upstairs."

The following morning I woke at the crack of dawn. Between the rendezvous with my friends at church in a few hours and the thought of my cousin's upcoming visit, I was too excited to sleep. I glanced at my alarm clock. Still too early in Texas to call Mackenzie. I could text her, though.

Throwing back the covers, I slid my feet into my fuzzy slippers and grabbed my bathrobe from off the bedpost.

Thump. Thump. Thump. Miss Marple was awake too, her tail smacking softly against the bedspread as she wagged it.

"Hey, girl," I murmured, giving her a pat. Over the past month I'd had to resign myself to the fact that I was Miss Marple's favorite Lovejoy, at least while Gramps and Lola were away. I'd given up trying to foist her off on Lauren, and totally caved on letting her into my room. Miss Marple even slept in here most nights. She'd start out on the floor, but somehow she always ended up at the foot of my bed by morning.

The house was silent, except for the telltale clank and rattle from the radiators as they roused themselves to their daily business of keeping us warm. I dashed off a quick text to Mackenzie, telling her to call me the minute she woke up, then crossed to the window. It was still dark outside, except for a patch of light on the snow below me. My bedroom was directly over the kitchen, so someone was up. Most likely my father. Lieutenant Colonel Jericho T. Lovejoy is an early bird, up at zero dark thirty every morning for his daily run.

Sure enough, I found him in the kitchen, drinking coffee and reading the paper. The radio on top of the fridge was on low, a melodious male voice letting listeners know that the record-breaking cold that had gripped the valley for weeks now might finally be coming to an end.

"According to the National Weather Service, we can expect a warming trend by the end of the week," the announcer said. "Nothing like the January thaw finally showing up in February!"

"Too bad it's not showing up today," I said, glancing at the thermometer outside and shivering.

"What?" said my father, looking up from his paper. "Oh, right."

"Morning, by the way," I said.

"Morning," he replied.

"Hey!" I blinked in surprise when I spotted the big box of donuts on the counter, along with a pitcher of juice. That's what we always used to have on Sunday mornings, whenever Dad was home on leave. Yet another family tradition that got shelved after Black Monday.

"Hey, what?" Dad asked.

"Um, nothing." I gave him a sidelong glance. Silent Man seemed to have made a donut run. I helped myself to a chocolate-covered old-fashioned with sprinkles, poured myself a glass of juice, and sat down at the table across from him.

He was wearing the Terminator. The new prosthesis had made a lot of things easier for him to do, and I watched as he gripped the newspaper in its high-tech fingers and turned the page.

My father has three prosthetic arms to choose from now: the Terminator, Captain Hook, and the one he's dubbed Ken, which is his least favorite, even though it's the one that looks the most human. Ken is made of this plastic stuff that's matched to Dad's skin color. He named it after Barbie's companion, because all it does is hang around looking pretty.

"It's useless," I heard him tell Mom in disgust. "It doesn't move; I can't pick anything up or do anything with it—what's the point?"

My father had shocked us all at dinner one night recently when he'd made a joke about the "arms race" in his closet. It was a tiny joke, but still, it was a joke. It made me think that maybe Mom and Aunt True are right, maybe Pumpkin Falls has been good for him.

"Dad, what do you know about Ella Bellow?" I asked, taking a bite of my donut.

He peered at me over the top of the paper. "Why do you want to know?"

I shrugged. "Just curious. She's really nosy."

"That she is." He was quiet for so long I figured I'd been

dismissed. Then he said, "I've known Ella all my life. She's a good woman, and she's good at her job, but she's never been good at staying out of other people's business. And it seems to have gotten worse since her husband died a couple of years ago. I hear she's retiring soon—maybe she'll move to Florida and leave Pumpkin Falls in peace."

With that he returned to his paper. Now I was dismissed. And still left with more questions than answers.

CHAPTER 31

"You're not planning on wearing that to church, are you?" My mother frowned at Danny, who'd pulled his wrestling sweatshirt on over his freshly washed and pressed button-down shirt and tie.

"Fine," he said and stomped back upstairs to take it off.

This happens to at least one of us every time we go to church. Well, except for Pippa, who adores dressing up. This morning she was wearing her favorite pink velvet dress, and she'd added her pink tutu plus a tiara for good measure.

We don't always make it to church during wrestling and swim season, but on the Sundays that we do, I'm required to wear girl clothes. This morning I had on a turtleneck sweater and a skirt, beneath which I'd added wool tights and my sheepskin-lined boots. No point freezing to death up in the steeple.

Dad came downstairs last. He'd traded the Terminator for Ken, I noticed. Church was almost the only place he ever wore it.

ABSOLUTELY TRULY

It was too cold to walk, plus we were late, so we all piled into the minivan and headed down the hill toward town. The Paul Revere bell was pealing its Sunday welcome as we pulled into the parking lot. I glanced up and watched it swinging in the steeple. If everything went according to plan, I'd be up there soon too.

Entire books have been written about the Pumpkin Falls First Parish Church steeple, thanks to the Paul Revere bell. The bell is the main reason the church is featured on so many postcards at the General Store, but the other reason is because the steeple is ridiculously picturesque. It looks like a square-tiered wedding cake. The bottom "layer" is the actual bell tower, which has arched openings on all four sides. Above that is the clock tower, which sports a giant round black disk of a clock face with gilt numbers and hands. Both of these layers are decorated within an inch of their lives with ornamental railings and little pillars and curlicues and stuff. Perched on top of the whole thing is the spire, which looks like an upside-down ice-cream cone, and on top of *that* is the weather vane.

Lots of churches have weather vanes. I've seen some decorated with roosters and others with angels, stars, fish, and doves. What does the Pumpkin Falls First Parish Church have on its weather vane? A pumpkin, of course.

The early church leaders clearly had a sense of humor.

I wondered if Nathaniel Daniel was one of the ones

responsible for the choice. From his portrait, he didn't look like all that much fun, but you never know about people, I guess.

Glancing up, I could see a trio of pigeons perched on top of the brass pumpkin weather vane, their feathers fluffed up against the cold. I hoped that was a good omen.

"See you afterward, kids," my mother said, handing Pippa over to me as we went inside. "Behave yourselves."

My brothers and sisters and I trooped downstairs to the Sunday School, where I was relieved to see that all of my friends had made it.

"Um, I sorta kinda had to tell my brother," Jasmine whispered as I slid into the seat next to her.

"You *what*?!" Aghast, I looked across the table at Scooter, who bared his braces at me in a wide grin.

Jasmine raised her hand and asked the teacher if we had time to visit the ladies' room before class started, then grabbed my arm and towed me down the hall.

"He knew something was up," she told me, when we were safely out of earshot. "He saw the five of us heading to the movie a couple of weeks ago, and then he overheard Cha Cha and me talking last night in my room. He wouldn't stop bugging me about it."

"So? You didn't have to tell him anything!" I was furious.

"He said he'd bring my underwear to school and run it up the flagpole if I didn't," Jasmine said miserably.

I sighed. "Brothers," I said in disgust. I'd probably have caved too.

This was not good. Not good at all. No way did I want Scooter Sanchez tagging along. He would totally wreck everything!

I didn't have time to deal with him right now, though. Right now, I had to put our plan into action.

Sunday School couldn't be over soon enough. When class finally finished, I bolted for the fellowship hall. My friends—and Scooter—were right behind me. I spotted Reverend Quinn chatting with Aunt True, and trotted over to join them.

"You've met my niece, haven't you?" my aunt said to the minister.

"Certainly," Reverend Quinn replied warmly. "How is Pumpkin Falls treating you these days, young Truly?"

"Fine," I replied. "Except for one thing."

"And what is that?"

"I've never seen the Paul Revere bell." I tried to look super disappointed.

"We need to remedy that, don't we?" said the minister, and Cha Cha gave me a discreet thumbs-up. Then he added, "Tours of the steeple are given every weekend throughout the warmer months."

"I have to wait until spring?" I didn't have to fake my disappointment now.

"Isn't there a way we could see it before that?" said Cha Cha. "I've never been up to the steeple either."

Jasmine and Lucas and Calhoun all nodded in agreement.

"You kids can't be serious!" said Reverend Quinn. "I know for a fact that every student at Daniel Webster School is given a tour."

"Yeah, but that was way back in kindergarten!" Lucas trotted out his most pathetic expression.

Scooter, who was clearly enjoying this exchange, flashed his braces at me again. I tried to ignore him.

"Looks like you have a captive audience," said Aunt True.

"Really? You all want to see the bell? In this weather?" Reverend Quinn frowned. "It's terribly cold up there—there's no insulation in the steeple, and the bell tower itself is completely open to the elements."

"We'll put our jackets on," I told him. "Please?"

He sighed. "I'll get my coat." He turned to my aunt. "Would you like to come along, True?"

I held my breath. Having my aunt along was a complication I hadn't counted on.

"Tempting," she said. "I haven't been up there since high school. But I think I'll wait for warmer weather."

We grabbed our jackets and followed Reverend Quinn upstairs. Lucas was careful to avoid his mother, which was smart of him. She'd hyperventilate if she heard he was planning on going up into the steeple.

ABSOLUTELY TRULY

Our destination was a small vestibule just beyond the church's cloakroom. Two ropes hung from the ceiling; one was floor-length, the other dangled just above our heads. Reverend Quinn grabbed the one above our heads and tugged on it, pulling down a set of fold-up stairs.

"What's the other rope for?" Scooter asked.

"Ringing the bell," the minister told him. "Don't touch it." He pulled his wool hat down over his ears and started to climb. "Follow me, and mind your step."

I made the mistake of being first in line after him.

"I see London, I see France," whispered Scooter as I headed up the ladder. "I see Truly's gigantic under—"

"*Scooter!*" I whisper-hollered down at him. At least he couldn't really see my underpants. Which are absolutely truly not gigantic. I'd never been so grateful in my life for my wool tights.

A moment later I emerged in the middle of an atticlike room.

"Step to the wall, please," said Reverend Quinn. "It's going to be a little crowded up here."

I did as he asked, and something crunched beneath my feet. Looking down, I spotted frozen mouse droppings.

"Eew," I said, just as Scooter's head emerged through the opening in the floor.

"What did I do now?" he protested, scrambling to his feet. He looked around. "Cool!"

"Very," quipped Reverend Quinn, the word emerging in a puff of frost. He hadn't been kidding; it was freezing up here. "Let's make this snappy," he said as the rest of my friends joined us. "Built in 1803, the Pumpkin Falls Parish Church steeple is one of the finest examples of Georgian architecture in all of New England."

I could tell that this was a speech he'd given to a zillion tourists over the years.

"Steeples served several purposes for early settlers," he continued. "First and foremost, they generally housed a bell inside. Bells can ring a warning, mark the passing of hours, celebrate, and call the congregation to worship. By pointing heavenward, the steeple also serves as a reminder of loftier things." The minister paused a moment and raised his eyes toward the ceiling for effect. Jasmine stifled a giggle.

Reverend Quinn cleared his throat sheepishly, then checked his watch. "Five minutes is all I can really spare today, kids," he said. "Let's go on up, shall we?"

We followed him up the next ladder and through a trapdoor in the ceiling, emerging this time into the bright sunshine. The view from the bell tower was amazing. To the north, I could see the covered bridge. To the east, the village green spread like a carpet—a white one at the moment—toward the college campus; to the south I could just make out the rooftops of the houses up the hill along Maple Street, including Gramps and Lola's, and to the west were the lower slopes of Lovejoy Mountain, bristling with spruces and pines.

"And there it is in all its glory—our famous Paul Revere bell," said Reverend Quinn, directing our attention overhead.

He pointed out the inscription engraved around the top of it, which read REVERE & SON BOSTON 1804, then swung into his canned speech once again. "Cast in Revere's foundry in Boston's North End, this bronze bell has graced our church for more than two hundred years. It weighs over half a ton—one thousand and twelve pounds, to be exact, including the clapper, which weighs thirty-six pounds. Note the headstock—that's the wooden beam or crosspiece, as it's called, from which the bell hangs. And wrapped around that wooden wheel is its pull-rope."

Scooter inspected it closely. "Is that the same rope we saw downstairs?"

Reverend Quinn nodded. "The very same. Pulleys guide it down through the steeple. The rope turns the wheel, which swings the headstock and sets the bell in motion. Most people don't know that it's the bell that swings, hitting the clapper, rather than the other way around."

"How often do you ring it?" I asked, curious.

"At one o'clock every afternoon, before the church service on Sunday, for weddings, and at noon on New Year's Day and the Fourth of July."

"Why not every hour?" asked Jasmine.

"Our bell is in semiretirement," the minister said drily.

"Would you want to work all day if you were over two hundred years old?"

"I'll bet it's loud up here when the bell rings," said Scooter, reaching up to touch it.

"Extremely. You wouldn't want to be in close quarters without earplugs." Reverend Quinn glanced at his watch again. "Okay, kids, feel free to snap some pictures if you'd like—do NOT lean over the railings, young man"—he was talking to Scooter, of course—"and then we'll head back down."

"The envelope is up in the next level, with the clock, right?" whispered Cha Cha as we moved away.

I nodded and took a picture of her and Jasmine with my cell phone. "Almost time," I told them, then zipped the phone back into my jacket pocket.

Reverend Quinn started down the ladder. "Make it snappy, kids. I'll wait for you below."

This was the chance we'd been waiting for.

"Time to distract him," I whispered to my classmates. "I'm going after the clue."

"How come *you* get to go?" asked Scooter.

"Because that's the plan," I told him. "I know what we're looking for." I started toward the wooden slats that were nailed to the wall and served as a crude ladder.

Scooter shouldered past me. "It's an envelope, duh," he said. "Jasmine told me. How hard can that be to find?"

ABSOLUTELY TRULY

"Get down from there!" I ordered as he stepped up onto the first slat.

"Dude, do what she says," said Calhoun.

I looked over at him, surprised. Then I remembered the pact we'd made. Romeo was holding up his end of the bargain.

"Hurry up now, kids," Reverend Quinn called to us, and Calhoun jerked his thumb at Scooter, who reluctantly hopped down.

"All I need is five minutes," I told my friends and started up for the clock tower as they disappeared through the trapdoor in the floor.

CHAPTER 32

The platform of the clock tower was just like the one below, covered with frozen mouse droppings—and also pigeon poo. Piles and piles of pigeon poo. I knew this because I'd just stepped into one of them.

Grimacing, I scraped my boot on a clean spot on the floor and looked around. It was darker here than in the bell tower below; there were no arched openings in the walls to let in light. Enough leaked in from the open trapdoor in the floor that I could see fairly well, though.

I could hear fairly well too, and what I heard was a shriek. It sounded like Jasmine. The distraction we'd planned was under way.

I examined the back of the clock—nothing. No hidden compartments, nothing taped to it, just a bunch of gears whirring and clicking away. The rafters above were empty too. I checked the walls, the floor, every inch of the clock tower. No envelope.

I stood there, puzzled. It had to be here! I was certain of it. The second hand ticked loudly in the background as I searched again. I felt like Gary Cooper in *High Noon*. Time was running out. Reverend Quinn was bound to notice my absence soon.

I searched again, but the envelope wasn't here. And I had been so certain that it would be!

The scavenger hunt was over.

Discouraged, I went back over to the ladder. As I placed my foot onto the top slat, I caught a glimpse of something flapping on top of the thick piece of wood below—the one from which the bell hung. What had Reverend Quinn called it? The headstock?

I climbed down closer for a better look. Sure enough, something was stuck to the headstock's flat surface, and a corner of whatever it was had come loose and was flapping in the chilly breeze. It looked like a length of duct tape. Peering closer, I could see that it had been painted over with white to match the rest of the wood. It was nearly invisible, except for the telltale flash of silvery gray beneath the paint on the loose piece.

I stretched out an arm to see if I could reach it. No such luck. I climbed all the way down to the bell platform below and stretched up, but I couldn't reach it from there, either. There was only one option. I'd have to climb back up, scooch my way out onto the rafter directly above the headstock, then see if I could lean down and reach it from there.

It wasn't easy. The rafter was frosted as thickly as one of Dr. Calhoun's cupcakes with everything that was icky in the steeple. Dirt, mouse droppings, and probably two hundred years' worth of pigeon poo.

Pulling off my wool hat, I smacked it against the wood, sending up a cloud of dust and scattering frozen mouse droppings in every direction. Still gross, but better. I hiked my skirt up and straddled the rafter. As I inched forward, I heard something rip. I'd snagged my tights. So much for wearing my Sunday best—I was going to have some explaining to do when I got home.

Using my hat as a makeshift pigeon-poo snowplow, I continued inching my way out until I was directly above the flapping edge of duct tape. Then I leaned forward until I was lying flat on my stomach. Holding tight to the rafter with one arm, I cautiously extended the other. My fingertips grazed the upcurled edge of tape. I strained to grab it, but it was still too far away.

Frustrated, I sat up again. The only way I was going to be able to do this was if I swung my knees over the rafter and lowered myself down backward, the way I used to do on the jungle gym when I was Pippa's age.

There was no other choice. And if I wasn't quick, Reverend Quinn would be back up here looking for me. Before I could talk myself out of it, over I went. And suddenly I was really, really glad Scooter wasn't up here. He'd be singing "I

ABSOLUTELY TRULY

see London" at the top of his lungs, because my skirt had flipped completely over my head. I swatted it away from my face, tucking the front part into the waistband of my tights. A gust of frigid wind found the open gap between my turtleneck sweater and my back as I did so, and I choked back a screech.

I dangled there upside down like a frozen bat, face-to-face with Paul Revere's bell. I was close enough to touch the inscription with my nose if I'd wanted to. Which I absolutely truly did not.

I also didn't want to be spotted. People were starting to leave the church, and I was in full view of anyone who might happen to look up at the steeple from the street. I needed to hurry.

I pulled myself halfway up and grabbed hold of the headstock with one hand, then reached for the loose corner of duct tape with the other. Grasping it, I tugged. And tugged again, harder. *R-i-i-i-i-i-p!* The duct tape parted ways with the paint and the wood, and sure enough, there was something stuck to the underside. An envelope! Clutching it tightly, I hauled myself back up on top of the rafter.

I lay there for a second or two, panting. Suddenly, the big wooden wheel below me began to move. I scrambled for safety as the bell began to sway back and forth. And a moment later, all I could think about was covering my ears.

CHAPTER 33

I was partially deaf until Tuesday, thanks to Scooter Sanchez.

Ringing the bell was not part of our plan. Jasmine was the one who was supposed to create a diversion by pretending to fall off the ladder and sprain her ankle. In the end, though, everything worked out okay. In all the fuss over the unauthorized ringing, as Reverend Quinn hauled Scooter off by his ear, I was able to come down from the steeple without being spotted.

"What happened to you?" asked Cha Cha, staring at me wide-eyed as I climbed down the ladder into the vestibule behind the coat room.

"WHAT?" I hollered. I could see her lips moving, but no sound was coming from them. Or if it was, it was drowned out by the ringing in my ears.

Cha Cha's dimple emerged and she started to giggle.

"WHAT'S SO FUNNY?"

ABSOLUTELY TRULY

She pointed to my hair, my dust-streaked face, my pigeon-poo-smeared clothes, and my torn tights. By now, Jasmine and Lucas and Calhoun were laughing too.

"Did you get the envelope?" Calhoun made an envelope shape in the air with his fingers.

I pulled it out of my jacket pocket. Everybody crowded around, eager to see what was inside. I opened it. There were the usual *B*s at the beginning and end of the letter, along with another single line of text:

> *I do love nothing in the world so well as you—*
> *is not that strange?*

We all looked at Calhoun, who nodded. "*Much Ado*," he confirmed.

All it said underneath the quote was *our meeting spot*.

"That's not fair!" cried Cha Cha. The ringing in my ears had started to subside, but her voice was still like the faint buzz from a far-off mosquito. "How are we supposed to know where they liked to meet?"

"Total dead end," said Jasmine in dismay.

It certainly seemed like it. I didn't see how we'd ever be able to solve this clue.

"Maybe not," said Calhoun. "My father might be able to help."

Cha Cha swatted at my jacket with the edge of her scarf.

"We have to get Truly cleaned up first," she told him.

She texted her mother and a couple of minutes later it was all settled. We were invited over to the Abramowitzes' for lunch. Somehow, with my friends forming a human shield around me, I managed to make it out of the church unseen.

"Hey, wait up!" called Scooter, who had been released from Reverend Quinn's custody, unfortunately. He caught up as we were halfway across the village green. "Whoa—you are one big Drooly Gigantic Mess," he said when he caught sight of me.

I shoved him into a snowbank.

Cha Cha's mother was much kinder.

"Good heavens, what happened to you, Truly?" she asked as we came through the front door.

"I fell into a snowbank," I replied, shooting Scooter a look.

When I saw myself in the bathroom mirror, I was surprised Mrs. Abramowitz hadn't called an ambulance. I looked like Belinda Winchester on one of her worst days. Soap and water helped, and I managed to get my hair looking more normal, but the tights were a lost cause. I stuffed them into the trash, then opened the door a crack and handed my skirt and turtleneck to Cha Cha. I could only hope that the washing machine wouldn't ruin them. I'd tried dabbing them with a wet washcloth, but that mostly just smeared the pigeon poo around.

"Put these on for now," said Cha Cha, handing me back a pair of her sweatpants and a shirt that belonged to her father.

"You've got to be kidding me," I replied, holding the sweatpants up. They barely reached my knees. I put them on, though—what else was I supposed to do?

Cha Cha started to giggle again as I slouched into her room.

"Shut up," I said, grateful that the boys were downstairs. I knew how ridiculous I looked. Then I started to laugh too. Jasmine joined us, and pretty soon the three of us were howling so hard that we scared Fred and Ginger, the Abramowitzes' cats, who ran under Cha Cha's bed to hide. Our hilarity drew Cha Cha's mother upstairs to check on us.

"Everything okay in here?" she asked. "Lunch is ready."

As I looked around the kitchen table a few minutes later, it occurred to me that six weeks ago I could never have imagined being here. Not just in Pumpkin Falls, but here with these new friends, trying to solve a twenty-year-old mystery. It felt really strange.

And even stranger when we arrived at Calhoun's house to talk to his father.

"Interesting," said Dr. Calhoun, after he scanned the sheet of paper on which Calhoun had written the Shakespeare quotes. "They're definitely all from *Much Ado About Nothing*, just as you said."

"Do they remind you of anything?" Calhoun asked.

His father shook his head. "Should they?"

Calhoun lifted a shoulder. "I dunno. I thought maybe they would. You know, maybe something from a long time ago?" He looked at his father with a hopeful expression.

Suddenly, the pieces fell into place—*snick!*—like a sudoku puzzle. Calhoun thought his *parents* were the B and B in our mystery letters! It made perfect sense, since they'd played Beatrice and Benedick together back in high school. I'd seen it on the theater program in Aunt True's apartment.

Maybe he'd been hoping the mystery letters would get them back together again somehow. I held my breath as Dr. Calhoun frowned at the piece of paper.

But again, he shook his head. "Sorry, son. Doesn't ring a bell."

Bad choice of words, I thought, scowling at Scooter. He shot me one of his trademark *Who me? What did I do?* looks back.

"I was just trying to help," he whispered. "You know, with the diversion?"

Yeah, right, I thought.

"So is this for a school project or something?" Calhoun's father asked us.

"Or something," Cha Cha told him. "We're just interested, that's all."

"Glad to hear it. Nothing better than being interested in the Bard. It's a lifetime pursuit." Dr. Calhoun checked his watch. "Well, I'd better go. The pipes have frozen in one of the dorms, and I want to check in with the maintenance staff and see how the repairs are coming along. Juliet is upstairs if you need anything. You kids have fun now." He left, closing the door behind him.

"Sorry, Calhoun," I said. "You were hoping it was them—your parents, I mean—weren't you?"

Calhoun looked down at the floor. "Yeah, I guess. My mother loves Shakespeare almost as much as my father does. She was the one who named my sister and me."

"Named you what?" asked Scooter. "R. J.?"

"Never mind," said Cha Cha and Jasmine and Lucas and me, all at the same time.

And we started to laugh.

CHAPTER 34

On the morning that the Pumpkin Falls Centennial Winter Festival began, I awoke to the sound of dripping.

"Listen, Miss Marple!" I cried, throwing back the covers and leaping out of bed. "Do you hear that?"

The hardwood floor was freezing, and I hopped quickly over to the window, dancing from one foot to the other as I peered outside. Sure enough, the icicles on the eaves were starting to melt.

The January thaw had finally arrived!

"Better late than never," said the weatherman on the kitchen radio a few minutes later. He sounded jubilant. "Looks like the warming trend will linger into early next week, so all you maple farmers out there can take a deep breath and relax—your sap run is safe."

Lauren had beaten me downstairs to breakfast, and hearing this she ran to the closet under the front stairs to call Annie.

ABSOLUTELY TRULY

Not that the Freemans wouldn't have figured it out for themselves by now. All they had to do was open their front door.

Which is exactly what I did a few minutes later. I stood on the doorstep a moment, inhaling deeply. For once, my nostrils didn't freeze together the way they had ever since I'd arrived in Pumpkin Falls. The air was practically balmy.

Miss Marple dashed past me and scampered down the path, as frisky as a puppy. I was feeling pretty frisky myself, even though I knew it wouldn't last. Dad had explained to us one night at the dinner table recently that New England's famous January thaw is only a sneak preview of warmer months ahead.

"Old Man Winter is a tease," he'd said. "Every January he relents just a bit, and takes pity on us by opening the window a crack and giving us a peek at spring, then he slams it shut again and hammers us with more cold."

"J. T., you have the soul of a poet," Mom had told him, kissing the top of his head. My father had snorted, but he'd looked pleased.

As I stood there, soaking up the sunshine, I didn't care if it was just a sneak preview. I'd take weather like this any day.

Energized, I took a shower and dressed in record time, then walked to school as usual with my brother and sisters. Pumpkin Falls looked anything but usual, however.

Flags were flying everywhere, and there was bunting on the steeple and a big PUMPKIN FALLS CENTENNIAL WINTER

FESTIVAL! banner had been hung across the front of the Town Hall. The streets around the village green were lined with cars, as spectators and the news media crowded around to watch the sculptors at work.

The Pumpkin Falls Winter Festival is famous for its snow-sculpture competition, and people come from all over to enter it and to watch the sculptors at work. Gramps and Lola send us pictures of it every year. Last year there was a fairy-tale theme, which meant the village green was covered with dragons and knights and castles and lots of familiar characters—Snow White and all the dwarves, Jack and the beanstalk, Rapunzel, Cinderella, the three little pigs, that sort of thing. Cinderella won—probably because of the huge pumpkin carriage.

Pippa tugged on my hand. "Look! There'th Nathaniel-Daniel-lookth-like-a-thpaniel!"

I glanced over at the sculptures on the green, and sure enough, there was a larger-than-life snow sculpture of our famous ancestor, big nose and all.

Because it's the centennial, this year's theme celebrates the history of Pumpkin Falls, so in addition to Nathaniel Daniel Lovejoy there was a giant 100! in the center of the green, a big maple leaf, and a nearly life-size replica of the covered bridge complete with frozen waterfall. Plus, there was a huge Paul Revere bell and the façade of the General Store. A long line of people stretched in front of it, waiting to have their pictures taken on the front porch in the giant rocking chair carved out of snow.

"Can I thit in it too?" Pippa begged. "Pleathe?"

"We'll come back later, Pipster, when it's not so crowded," Hatcher promised.

School was mercifully brief. Nobody could concentrate anyway—everyone was too keyed up over the three days of activities ahead, which kicked off right after lunch with the Winter Festival Spelling Bee, for which Annie Freeman had been practicing for weeks. In addition, there were a bunch of sporting events—ski races, figure skating, and speed skating on the rink at the college, and other games and meets, including basketball, hockey, wrestling, and of course our swim team's grudge match against Thornton. Coach Maynard had been firing us up for that all week.

Tomorrow morning was the famous Polar Bear Swim at Lake Lovejoy, which is about the dumbest idea in the history of the world if you ask me, which nobody ever does. Who'd be stupid enough to jump into a frozen lake? A bunch of people, apparently, because the *Patriot-Bugle* was reporting a bumper crop of entrants.

All of the stores in town were offering special sales and promotions for the weekend too. Donuts at Lou's would be three for a nickel, the same price they were one hundred years ago, haircuts at the Kwik Klips were going for "two bits," which my father told us used to mean a quarter, and the

General Store employees were giving out free bags of penny candy with every purchase. The *Patriot-Bugle* had published a special commemorative edition, complete with "Then and Now" photographs of Pumpkin Falls, along with interviews with the town's oldest citizens.

The highlight of the weekend—at least for everybody but me—was the big dance tomorrow night at Town Hall. Of course, since the festival weekend happens to coincide with Valentine's Day this year, they're making an even bigger deal of it than usual. Mrs. Abramowitz is chair of the entertainment and decorating committee, and my mother, who's been helping her out since she's still working as the Starlite's receptionist, says Cha Cha's mom has been in a dither for weeks.

"I've never been involved in so many decisions involving hearts in my entire life," my mother told us at dinner last night. "Paper hearts! Sparkly hearts! Hearts that light up and hearts that spin and hearts that blow bubbles! Did you know that you can even order heart-shaped ice cubes?"

I did not, and I didn't care. I was so not looking forward to Cotillion. I hated the thought of being on display for the whole world to watch and laugh at. I'd probably trip over my own big feet, right in front of everybody.

I pushed the thought away. No point stewing about tomorrow when I had enough to stew about today—mainly our meet against Thornton.

The bleachers at the swim center were packed by the

ABSOLUTELY TRULY

time I came out of the locker room. I spotted my friends and family—they were all there, even Dad. Only Aunt True was missing. She'd volunteered to stay behind at the bookstore so that my father could come and watch me. She'd sent a text earlier that made me laugh, though. There was just one word in it: VICTORY!

Aunt True is a total Lovejoy when it comes to sports.

I was swimming a trio of races—the 200 Medley Relay, the 50 Freestyle, and last but by far from least, the 100 Individual Medley. Not for a while, though. First up were the younger kids and the newbies, including Lucas.

"That's my boy," I heard Mrs. Winthrop announce proudly to no one in particular, as Lucas stepped up onto the block.

Aunt True says it's positively painful to look at Lucas in a bathing suit, and she's got a point. I've shared the pool with some skinny swimmers before, but Lucas Winthrop takes the cake. From his knobby knees to his protruding ribs and collarbone, he's practically a walking anatomy lesson.

Mrs. Winthrop stood up, her video camera clutched nervously in her hands. She's still convinced her son is going to drown somehow. When you think about it, it's amazing he's even allowed out of the house.

Whenever I see Mrs. Winthrop, I remind myself to be grateful that I still have a dad, and not just one overprotective parent. Lucas doesn't seem to miss his father too much—at least, he never talks about it—but then again, he was just a baby when his father died, so he's never known any different.

Lucas didn't drown, of course. In fact, not only did he swim his best time ever, he won his first race ever. The Pumpkin Falls half of the bleachers exploded as he churned his way down the home stretch and slapped the wall. Mrs. Winthrop almost dropped her video camera, she was cheering so hard. I was yelling my head off and so was the rest of the team. Lucas looked at the clock in disbelief, then looked over at us with this huge grin on his face. I wanted to jump in the water and hug his little hummingbird self.

As I got ready for my first race, I hoped that Lucas's win was a good omen. And it seemed like it was, because I won the 50 Freestyle handily and our relay team, which had been performing unevenly, posted a faster time than in any of our practices, even though technically we lost to Thornton. I didn't care as much about those races, though—it was the 100 Individual Medley I was most worried about. That one's always been my race.

"Good luck," said one of the Thornton swimmers as we stepped onto the blocks.

I hate it when my opponents are cheerful. It makes them impossible to dislike.

"You too," I told her, trying to mean it.

The bell rang and I arced forward, my dive perfectly aimed to hit the water in the best possible position. *Half a dozen strong dolphin kicks, break the surface, arms spread like wings*, I told myself. I flew down my lane, did a quick double-touch on the gutter, then pushed into backstroke, every breath, every movement exactly as I'd imagined it.

The thing about swimming is, it's all mental. Yes, of course it matters that you've been working hard in practice, but that's all second nature when it comes down to the actual race. The trick is to picture yourself swimming every lap, picture your time, how many breaths you'll take, how far each stroke will take you, all of it. And most of all, you've got to picture yourself winning.

Which I had been doing for days.

I didn't hear the crowd; I didn't hear anything but my own breathing and my own fierce wanting to win. I moved effortlessly from butterfly to backstroke to breaststroke. As I approached the flip turn that would take me into the final freestyle stretch, I was neck-and-neck with the swimmer in the lane next to me. I tucked under, certain that my height would give me the advantage in the home stretch.

Or not.

As my legs flew over my head and I corkscrewed into the turn, my left heel slammed against the tiles.

Hard.

Jolted by the pain, I faltered. Only for a split second, but that was long enough to throw me off my rhythm. I scrambled to recover, pouring it on as I powered toward the finish, but it was too late.

I lost by three-tenths of a second.

I looked up at the clock in disbelief. The extra inch I'd grown since moving here had knocked me off balance and cost me the race! I'd been betrayed by my stupid Amazon feet!

Out of the corner of my eye, I could see Hatcher up in the bleachers tapping his fingers under his chin in our chin-up shorthand. I shook my head at him and closed my eyes. Why oh why did I have to be so freakishly tall? I dragged myself out of the pool, not even stopping to congratulate the winner. I didn't care if it was rude; I just wanted the shelter of the locker room.

"Tough luck, sweetheart," my mother said a while later, when I finally emerged. She gave me a hug.

"Way to hang in there," added my father, which is Lovejoy-speak for *Loser*.

Which was exactly how I felt for the rest of the day.

CHAPTER 35

"This is embarrassing," said Hatcher.

"Tell me about it," I replied.

The two of us were at the bookstore the next morning, helping Dad and Aunt True. I was still trying to blot out yesterday's disastrous swim meet. My family was being supernice to me, which only made me feel worse, of course. I'd tried to be happy for Danny and Hatcher, who were total rock stars at their wrestling meets last night (people around town are starting to refer to them as "The Lovejoy Brothers," like they're a circus act or something), and I tried to be happy for my mother, too. She could hardly contain herself when Dad wandered down to the mats and started talking to the coaches. It was the first real sign of interest he's shown in wrestling since Black Monday.

None of it made any difference to me, though. All I could think about was that stupid mistake I'd made in the final turn at the pool. And now here I was, about to be humiliated again. For some unknown reason, Aunt True had gotten it into her head that we should dress up in honor of Valentine's Day for the bookshop's Grand Reopening events. She'd even persuaded Dad to agree to spring for a pair of costumes.

She waited until this morning, when we were trapped at the store under Dad's watchful eye, to surprise us with them. Danny took one look and quickly played the homework card—*So sorry, big physics test first thing Monday morning, gotta go study, yada yada.*

Dad wouldn't let Hatcher and me off the hook, though. "Your aunt talked me into wasting money on these foolish things—someone is going to wear them!"

And those someones were us, of course.

"Thanks for throwing us under the bus," Hatcher muttered as our older brother made his escape.

Danny grinned and gave us a thumbs-up as he headed out the door. "Lookin' good!"

We didn't, of course—we looked ridiculous. Hatcher was dressed as Cupid, complete with a Roman toga, gold-painted plastic bow and arrow, and gold wings. My outfit was even more horrible. I was stuck with a hooded red unitard, whose matching headband had sparkly red hearts bobbing on a pair of wobbly antennae, and a poufy heart-shaped pillow that strapped over my body like a sandwich board. It was shiny and red, just like my face.

ABSOLUTELY TRULY

"At least we didn't have to dress up for the walk over here," said Hatcher grimly, tugging at his toga. "It could have been worse, right?"

The two of us had dropped Lauren and Pippa at Belinda Winchester's before heading to the bookstore. Belinda had offered to watch them until Story Hour, since the rest of us had a lot of work to do—setting up chairs for this afternoon's reading, baking piles of mini whoopie pies, and filling the goodie bags we would be giving out with purchases.

Belinda had met us at her back door wearing shorts, sandals with wool socks, a T-shirt, and a straw hat. "Groovin' to the Beach Boys," she said by way of a greeting, pulling out an earbud. She'd gestured at the blue sky and grinned. "Can you believe the weather this weekend? Made to order."

Pippa had given her a swift hug and run past her into the kitchen. Belinda Winchester's house looks pretty much the way you'd think it would, except that it's spotless. Cluttered as all get-out, but absolutely spotless.

"I was expecting *Tales from the Crypt* and instead I found Mrs. Clean," my mother had told my father the first time she stopped by.

"Hi, Fern," Lauren had said, bending down and scooping up the big tabby cat who'd been curled up by the woodstove. Belinda didn't actually have as many cats as people thought—there were just two permanent residents: Fern and Avery. But there were a whole lot of visitors. Word was out in Grafton

County that she'd take good care of strays, so baskets and boxes and even bags were dropped off on her doorstep, filled with felines in need of new homes. And somehow, Belinda always found them one. She had deputies in all the nearby towns scouting for potential kitten adopters, and she even had her own blog where she featured new arrivals.

I'd handed Mrs. Winchester a loaf of my mother's homemade banana bread. "My mom said to tell you thanks, and that she'll see you later this morning."

Belinda had nodded, her earbud already back in, head bobbing to the strains of "Kokomo."

"Here, Truly," said my aunt, thrusting a book at me and pulling my attention back to the task at hand. "Add this to 'Miss Marple's Picks,' would you? It will make Augustus happy when he comes in this afternoon for his reading."

"Miss Marple's Picks" was another one of Aunt True's bright ideas.

"Every bookstore on the planet has a 'Staff Picks' display," she'd said one afternoon as I was finishing up a tutoring session. "I think we should do something different."

"Who's going to care what the dog reads?" grumbled my father, after she explained her plan. Then he slapped his palm against his forehead in mock self-reproach. "Wait, what am I saying—dogs don't read!"

Aunt True laughed. "Everybody will care, J. T.—you'll see."

And she was right. It's been a huge hit with our customers.

ABSOLUTELY TRULY

"What's Miss Marple reading this week?" they'd ask, making a beeline for the shelf by the front door. Miss Marple has her own page now on the bookstore website (ghostwritten by Aunt True), which gets more hits than all the other pages combined. Just last week, the *Pumpkin Falls Patriot-Bugle* featured Miss Marple in their "Around Town" column, along with a fake interview and a picture of her sitting proudly by her namesake shelf. The story was picked up by the news wires, and we got a flurry of media interest from as far away as Australia. People everywhere love dogs, I guess.

Mom says Aunt True is a marketing genius.

Catching a glimpse of my poufy heart-shaped reflection in the front window, though, I wasn't so sure. I sighed and placed *Summer's Siren Song* by Augusta Savage face out on Miss Marple's shelf. Looking at it more closely, I was tempted to turn it over. Someone should give the women on the covers of romance books turtlenecks to wear. It's embarrassing.

I went back to the counter to continue stuffing gift bags.

"I keep thinking it just got misplaced and someone will find it," Aunt True was saying to a customer. "I still can't believe that someone would actually take it."

She was talking about *Charlotte's Web*, of course.

I'd come up empty-handed in my efforts to catch the thief. The mystery of the missing book was still unsolved.

Two hours later, I'd replenished our supply of gift bags filled with bookmarks, discount coupons, a copy of our newsletter, and chocolate kisses, and I'd helped Aunt True bake several dozen more mini pumpkin whoopie pies. Hatcher, meanwhile, had set up all the chairs for this afternoon's reading, waited on customers, sorted all the special orders, and was just finishing up getting things organized for Story Hour.

"Mr. Henry!" said Aunt True as the bell over the door jangled. "Right on time. I see you're dressed for the occasion."

The children's librarian, who was wearing his trademark red-and-white striped sweater, laughed. "I'm always dressed for the occasion," he replied. "You're looking very Valentine-y yourself."

Aunt True wasn't in a costume, exactly, but she'd decked herself out in red from head to toe—red skirt, red sweater, red tights, and red cowboy boots.

"I'm not sure," my aunt replied, plucking at the strands of silver paper hearts she'd strung around her neck. "I think I kind of look like Mrs. Claus."

"You couldn't look like Mrs. Claus if you tried," said the librarian gallantly.

My mouth fell open. Was Mr. Henry *flirting* with Aunt True?

Mr. Henry looked over at me. His eyebrows shot up as he eyed my costume. "And you're, uh, very fancy."

I made a face.

"The kids will love it," he told me with a wink. "Trust me."

He was right. Hatcher and I might have felt humiliated, but we were the stars of Story Hour. The kids laughed themselves silly as we circled the children's room with our trays of mini whoopie pies and heart-shaped shortbread cookies. Hatcher totally got into it, smiling his sunflower smile as he pretended to shoot his bow and arrow. I just stuck to handing out treats.

Afterward, the kids all ran over and lined up to have their pictures taken with us, and with Miss Marple, who was also dressed for the occasion, thanks to Pippa and Lauren. My sisters had tied a big red bow to her collar and painted her toenails bright pink. With sparkles, of course.

"Whoa," said a voice behind me. I turned around to see Scooter standing there. Calhoun was with him.

I didn't even give Scooter a chance to open his mouth. Looking him straight in the eye, I said, "If you call me 'Truly Gigantic' or 'Truly Drooly' or anything else ever again, I swear I will deck you!"

Scooter looked at the tray in my hand and laughed. "With what, a whoopie pie?"

"Leave her alone, Scooter," said Calhoun, giving the revolving greeting card rack a twirl.

Scooter over at him. He frowned. "What's up with you, dude? You're no fun at all lately."

They didn't stick around for long after that, thank goodness. They'd just come for the free treats anyway. Believe it or not, though, that wasn't the low point of the afternoon. The low point was after lunch, when the *Patriot-Bugle* showed up to cover Augustus Wilde's book signing.

"Ooh, look how cute you are!" said the photographer when she spotted me in my ridiculous costume. "Come on over—we need a shot of you standing next to Augustus."

Reluctantly, I did as she asked.

"This is definitely front-page material," the photographer assured us.

Augustus, of course, was thrilled. I, on the other hand, was not.

Just what I need to make my day complete, I thought sourly. Immortalized forever with Captain Romance.

Hatcher, the booger head, was nowhere to be seen during all this, of course.

I stomped off to look for him, fuming.

"What are you doing back here?" my father asked when I poked my head in the office. "Aren't you supposed to be helping man the cash register?"

"Hatcher can help," I said shortly. "Where is he, anyway?"

My father shrugged. "Haven't seen him. Go on back out there now, Truly. You know we're counting on you."

"Yes, sir," I said sullenly. *How come you get to hide back here?* I wanted to ask him, but I gritted my teeth and did as he asked.

ABSOLUTELY TRULY

The book signing dragged on forever. I stood politely with Aunt True and listened while stupid Augustus in his stupid cape (a red one this time, in honor of Valentine's Day) read from his stupid book. I stacked copies of stupid *Summer's Siren Song* on the table and herded his stupid starstruck fans into line for the signing. I passed out stupid sticky notes so they could write their names down in case Augustus was too stupid to spell them correctly, and even submitted to posing for stupid pictures afterward.

By the time everyone left and it was finally time to close up, I really, really wasn't in the mood to go to the stupid dance.

"Shouldn't you be getting ready?" Mom asked me back at home a while later. I was dawdling at the dinner table, picking at my macaroni and cheese. Hatcher and Danny and my sisters had already gone upstairs to change.

I lifted a shoulder.

"Come on, honey," she coaxed. "It's Winter Festival!"

What it was was a disaster. It had been a terrible, horrible weekend so far, and it was far from over.

"You've got such a pretty dress, and you've been practicing so hard for Cotillion," my mother continued. "Time to strut your stuff."

I dragged my stuff upstairs to the shower. I didn't feel like strutting anything, ever again.

CHAPTER 36

My spirits lifted slightly when I put on my new dress. Like I said, girl clothes are way up on the list of things I'm not good at, but this dress wasn't so bad. It was close-fitting black satin on top, with spaghetti straps and what Mom called a "sweetheart" neckline, and white poufy material on the bottom. Not poufy like the horrible pillow-shaped heart costume, but poufy like one of those flowy ballerina skirts. For contrast there was a wide red velvet belt, plus the skirt part was sprinkled with red polka dots. It sounds weird, but it wasn't. It was actually okay. And just the right length too.

I slipped into my size-ten-and-a-half black heels—low ones, like Mrs. Abramowitz recommended, so I wouldn't completely tower over my partner—ran a brush through my hair one last time, and grabbed my white gloves. Pausing to look in the mirror, I told myself that I was ready for anything. Even Scooter Sanchez.

ABSOLUTELY TRULY

"Oh, honey," said Mom as I came downstairs. "You look beautiful! Doesn't she look beautiful, J. T.?"

She nudged my father, who was trying to stuff his Ken hand into the arm of his jacket. He glanced up at me briefly. "Sure."

"Jericho Tobias Lovejoy, look at your eldest daughter!" Mom said sternly.

My father knows an order when he hears one. His eyes widened as he turned to look at me. *Really* look at me.

"How old is she, Dinah?" he asked.

"Twelve, but only for another month," Mom told him. "She's not our little girl anymore."

He shook his head. "I can see that. Our Truly-in-the-Middle is truly growing up." He smiled at me. "Your mother is right—you look beautiful, honey."

"Thanks." A warm feeling flooded through me. I felt bashful all of a sudden, and dropped my gaze toward my toes. My great big Truly Gigantic toes, which had cost me the 100 Individual Medley. The warm feeling evaporated.

"If it's okay with you," my father said to my mother, "I'm going to leave Ken home tonight. The useless thing is more bother than it's worth."

"So will you go with the Terminator, or with Captain Hook?" Mom asked him.

"Not sure yet. The Terminator was acting up a bit this afternoon—I'll go take a look at it." My father started back upstairs.

I had a sudden wild urge to giggle. Did other amputee families talk like this?

Silent Man had seemed a little more relaxed recently, and was even joking around a bit. Maybe my mother and Aunt True were right—maybe there had been a change in my father over the past weeks, a slow and gradual shift, quiet as the swing of a pendulum or the rise of a thermometer. He wasn't back to normal yet by any means, but maybe he was inching in that direction.

"Did you make vomit bars, Mom?" Hatcher asked anxiously as we pulled out of the driveway a few minutes later.

She pointed to a plastic container by Dad's feet on the floor of the van. "Right there," she said. "As requested."

This time I did giggle. Anybody listening to my family's conversations tonight would definitely think we were nuts.

Vomit bars were what my brothers call Mom's special seven-layer cookies. And it's true, with all the nuts and coconut and other stuff in them, from a distance they do kind of look like somebody barfed. They're our favorite dessert, though. Once, when we were little, our Texas cousins came to visit—all seventeen of them—and Hatcher and Danny were so afraid they wouldn't leave any for us, they decided to try and gross them out. That's when they came up with the name "vomit bars." It worked, kind of. At least until the older cousins saw us eating them and realized they'd been tricked.

A few minutes later we pulled up in front of Town Hall.

ABSOLUTELY TRULY

"Here, Truly," said my mother, passing me the container and giving Hatcher a stern look. "See that these get to the refreshment table safely, okay?"

"Sure, Mom," I replied, taking it from her.

Hatcher grinned.

"Mind the slush!" Mom called, just as Danny stepped out of the car and directly into a puddle.

"Oh, man!" he groaned, and we all laughed.

My sisters were beyond excited—unlike me, they couldn't wait to show off their dance moves for the crowd, plus they had their own party to look forward to in the Town Hall basement afterward. I'd overheard Mrs. Abramowitz tell my mother that a magician had been hired to entertain them.

My brothers, on the other hand, well, they might not have been dreading the whole thing the way I was, but I knew they'd much rather be at home watching hockey on TV. I was pretty sure Dad felt the same way, but he had his Lieutenant Colonel Jericho T. Lovejoy game face on as he escorted us inside.

The hall was jammed. In one corner, a band was tuning up. In another, Annie Freeman's mother was organizing the refreshment table. I delivered the vomit bars, then went to drop my jacket off at the coat check.

People were streaming through the doors, greeting their neighbors and former neighbors and others who were in town for the weekend celebration. Everyone looked happy. Everyone but me, that is.

Time to put your game face on too, I told myself, and went off to find my friends. I spotted Lucas first, looking painfully clean and neat. His hair was slicked back with gel, and he was wearing a tuxedo. This seemed like overkill, and was probably his mother's doing, since the Cotillion guidelines only said that boys should wear a dark suit. Lucas looked like a licorice stick.

"Hey," I said.

"Hey," he said back.

"Nice tux."

He blushed. "My mother bought it for me."

Ha! I thought. *I knew it.*

Jasmine jumped out from behind a pillar, beaming. "Notice anything different?"

I looked her over. She was wearing a fire-engine-red dress that set off her shiny dark hair. "Your dress is really pretty," I told her. "I like the sparkles."

"No, you dork, my braces! I got them off!" She beamed at me again, and I gave her a high five. So did Lucas. "Scooter still has to keep his on for a few more weeks, though."

That was the best news I'd had all day, and I perked right up.

Cha Cha waved from across the room. "You guys look great!" she called in her deep voice, coming over to join us.

"You too," I replied, admiring her black velvet strapless mini. "You look at least fifteen."

ABSOLUTELY TRULY

A moment later the lights dimmed and the band struck a chord. Cha Cha's mother tugged her husband into the middle of the dance floor.

"Good evening, everyone," Mr. Abramowitz said into his microphone. His greeting echoed through the crowded room. "And welcome to the one hundredth annual Pumpkin Falls Winter Festival!"

A deafening cheer went up from the crowd.

"As has long been our town's tradition," he continued, "we ask our young people to help kick things off in style."

That brought another cheer.

"And so, without further ado, I present to you the Daniel Webster School square dancers!" He motioned to the orchestra, who struck up "Turkey in the Straw" as the younger kids all marched out in pairs for their square dance.

"Oh, how adorable!" squealed Jasmine, pointing to Pippa and Baxter.

The two of them were holding hands, and they both wore grave expressions. Pippa took her responsibility as the opening act for the big dance very seriously, and she and Baxter had been practicing their steps faithfully.

Cameras flashed and proud parents beamed from the sidelines as Mr. Abramowitz began to call the dance: "The lady goes right, the gent goes left, circle left so lightly . . ."

Pippa and Baxter didn't miss a beat.

"They are so cute together!" whispered Cha Cha.

"I know, right?" I whispered back.

Annie Freeman twirled past, her multiple braids bouncing almost as quickly as her feet. She was busy talking, of course—probably spelling out the moves to her partner. My sister Lauren was right behind her with Amy Nguyen's younger brother. She shot me a look as she danced by, one that clearly said, *I'm so over this dumb kid stuff and ready to tackle ballroom.* Lauren still had stars in her eyes about Cotillion.

They finished a few minutes later amid thunderous applause. And then it was our turn.

"Places, everyone!" whispered Ms. Ivey, frantically trying to line us all up. The sixth, seventh, and eighth graders had all been practicing separately during gym class at school, and this was the first time we'd all be together. I waved to Hatcher, who was standing with his partner on the other side of the dance floor. He smiled his sunflower smile at me. Nothing rattled Hatcher.

When we were all in place, Ms. Ivey gave Mr. Abramowitz a thumbs-up. She looked really pretty tonight in her long white satin sheath and red heels. It occurred to me that I didn't know if there was a Mr. Ivey. If not, maybe Cupid would visit Pumpkin Falls and find her one.

"I still think this is stupid," said Scooter as he took my hand, placing his other on my shoulder.

"Yeah," I agreed. "Totally lame."

"And now, folks, it's time for this evening's Cotillion ballroom showcase!" announced Mr. Abramowitz.

ABSOLUTELY TRULY

I could feel Scooter's palms sweating right through his cotton gloves. He was as nervous as I was. This was not a good sign.

My parents both waved, and I saw something glint at the end of my father's sleeve—apparently he'd decided to go with Captain Hook tonight. And then the music started and Scooter and I were off and running. Dancing, rather. *Slow, slow, quick, quick.* I concentrated hard on making my feet go where they were supposed to, and Scooter must have too, because somehow we made it through the fox-trot without a misstep.

As the music segued into the waltz—*one, two, three, one, two, three*—I relaxed a little. Mr. Abramowitz had really helped me with this one during our practice sessions. I hummed along to the music and looked over Scooter's shoulder at my classmates.

Cha Cha and Lucas were zipping around the dance floor like old pros. Franklin Freeman was a little robotic, but he and Amy Nguyen were managing to keep the beat too.

The real surprise was Jasmine and Calhoun. Cha Cha had definitely put some polish on him during their secret practice sessions, because not only was Calhoun totally moving in time to the music, he actually looked like he was enjoying himself. He caught me watching him and smiled.

"Oops," I whispered to Scooter as I stumbled. "Sorry."

"Totally my fault," Scooter whispered back. And then he smiled too.

I almost lost my balance again. Smiles from both Scooter and Calhoun? What was going on?

"Very nicely done!" said Mr. Abramowitz as we all twirled to a finish. "Splendid job!"

The band gave a flourish as Mrs. Abramowitz stepped forward. She and Cha Cha's father conferred briefly, then she passed her husband some envelopes. He jotted down something on each of them.

"This year also marks the beginning of a new Pumpkin Falls tradition, one we hope will last for the next hundred years," Mr. Abramowitz told the crowd. "Prizes for our young dancers, who have worked so hard this winter!" A patter of polite applause rippled through the hall.

"The square dancers each received a ribbon and a gift certificate to Lovejoy's Books"—that had been Aunt True's idea—"but for the members of our Cotillion, we have cash prizes. The first category is best dressed."

This ignited a buzz in the room, and even though fashion isn't my thing, my heart beat a little faster too. I couldn't help it; I'm a Lovejoy and I'm competitive. Plus, this was by far the nicest dress I'd ever owned. Was it nice enough for a prize?

"This was a tough one, folks," said Cha Cha's mother, "but the prize goes to—Lucas Winthrop!"

Lucas turned as red as Jasmine's dress. Mrs. Winthrop leaped to her feet and started filming as he scuttled out to claim his prize.

"Oh, man," muttered Scooter. "That's totally unfair! His mother bought that tux for him."

ABSOLUTELY TRULY

"Shut up and clap, Scooter," I told him.

"Next we have best dance partners," Mr. Abramowitz continued. "There's a prize for each grade level."

I didn't know the sixth-grade winners, but they sure looked happy when they got their envelopes. Then it was time for the seventh grade. No way did Scooter and I even stand a chance for this one.

"Another tough category," said Cha Cha's father, "and in all fairness, Mrs. Abramowitz and I decided we would eliminate our daughter and her partner, because, as most of you know, our wonderful Charlotte, better known as Cha Cha, practically grew up in a dance studio."

The onlookers laughed.

"And so the prize goes to Jasmine Sanchez and Romeo Calhoun!"

Calhoun looked like he couldn't decide how to react—mortified that his real name had been so publicly revealed, or happy that his hard work had paid off.

"Romeo?" said Scooter in disbelief. "*Romeo?* Are you kidding me? That's what the *R* in 'R. J.' stands for?"

"Yup," I replied, then shouted "Way to go, Calhoun!"

Calhoun glanced over at me and smiled again.

After giving out the eighth grade prize—someone from Hatcher's wrestling team and his partner—it was time for the final category: most improved.

"This was also a tough decision," said Mr. Abramowitz.

"Knowing where these students started six weeks ago, and how far they've come, we feel they each deserve recognition. So how about another round of applause for all of this year's Cotillion members?" The crowd responded with enthusiasm, and then Cha Cha's father continued, "That being said, we would like to recognize one set of dance partners who got off to a *truly* rocky start"—my heart did a hopeful little skip at this—"but who have come through with flying colors: Truly Lovejoy and Scooter Sanchez."

Hatcher pulled his white gloves off and stuck his forefingers in his mouth, whistling shrilly. Scooter grabbed my hand and towed me across the dance floor. Mr. Abramowitz passed us each an envelope and shook our hands. Mrs. Abramowitz gave me a hug. "Well done, Truly," she whispered.

Dazed, I followed Scooter back to where my friends were waiting. How was this possible? Dancing was at the top of the list of things I wasn't good at.

"Hey, you know, about 'Truly Gigantic' and all," Scooter said uneasily.

That snapped me out of my daze. "Don't start," I warned him.

He shook his head. "No, I'm not—I mean, well, I'm sorry."

I stared at him. Two apologies in one evening? What on earth had gotten into Scooter?

"Truce?" he said.

"Uh, okay, I guess," I replied.

ABSOLUTELY TRULY

The music started up again, and the audience crowded onto the dance floor. My parents were among them, my father gamely resting Captain Hook on top of my mother's shoulder. My father said something and my mother threw back her head and laughed, the light glinting in her strawberry-blond curls. She looked really pretty tonight.

I saw Aunt True dancing with Mr. Henry, and Danny with Calhoun's older sister, Juliet. Meanwhile, the boys from my class made a beeline for the refreshment table, leaving us girls standing by the wall.

"Figures," said Cha Cha.

"Cowards," added Jasmine in disgust.

We watched the dancers, and a few minutes later Hatcher wandered over to join us.

"So, does that make up for yesterday?" he asked me, pointing to the envelope in my hand.

I considered his question. Cotillion was hardly a 100 Individual Medley. "Maybe a little," I admitted.

He smiled at me, then turned to Cha Cha. "May I have this dance?"

My mouth dropped open. My brother wanted to dance with the girl he called "the kazoo"?

"Sure," said Cha Cha, and he led her onto the dance floor.

Franklin reappeared, cramming the rest of a vomit bar into his mouth. Mumbling something, he held his hand out to Jasmine. She smiled a braces-free smile at him, and they joined my brother and Cha Cha. One by one my classmates were whisked away until I was left standing there all by myself.

I reminded myself that I didn't like to dance. That I wasn't any good at it. Okay, maybe not as bad as I used to be—I was holding a prize for most improved, after all—but still.

That didn't make me feel any better.

It wasn't so much that I *wanted* to dance, it was just that *not* dancing was worse. Way worse. Not dancing meant I was a wallflower. Not dancing meant I'd probably end up an old cat lady, like Belinda Winchester.

Who happened to dance by just then with Augustus Wilde. She'd traded the shorts I'd seen her wearing earlier for jeans and a red plaid flannel shirt. A plastic bag was looped over one of her wrists. I watched, incredulous, as Captain Romance gallantly dipped and twirled the former lunch lady, his red cape and silver hair streaming behind him.

Are you kidding me? I thought.

"Truly?"

I turned around. It was Calhoun. "Hey," I said.

"Would you like to dance?"

My mouth dropped open for the second time that evening. "Uh, sure," I managed to squeak out.

"You snooze, you lose," said Calhoun, his dark eyes gleaming in triumph. This time he wasn't talking to me, though. He was talking to Scooter, who was standing behind us with two cups of punch and a shocked look on his face.

ABSOLUTELY TRULY

Across the room, Aunt True beamed and gave me two enthusiastic thumbs up.

No, I wanted to tell her, *it's not what you think!*

Or was it?

The music shifted to a waltz, and Calhoun swung me smoothly into the *one, two, three* rhythm. I focused intently on not stepping on his toes. I really didn't want to step on his toes, for some reason.

We passed my brother and Cha Cha, and then almost bumped into Ella Bellow, who was dancing with Lou from the diner.

"It shouldn't be much longer before I can move in," she told him loudly, so that he could hear her above the music. "It's the perfect spot for my new shop."

Wait, what was Ella Bellow talking about? I steered Calhoun a little closer.

"I feel badly, of course," she continued. "You never like to see someone's business struggle. But it's certainly worked in my favor."

I came to an abrupt stop. Ella was talking about Lovejoy's Books!

I pulled away from Calhoun and marched over to her. "You're the one who took it!"

Ella Bellow looked at me in surprise. Then she stopped dancing too. "What on earth are you talking about?"

"*Charlotte's Web*! I overheard you just now, and you

practically admitted it!" I told her, my voice rising. The couples around us spun to a stop. "You had us special order that book about starting a new career in your retirement, and you've been prowling around the bookshop for weeks now, snooping. You're just waiting for us to fail so you can take over our space!"

"I most certainly am not!"

"You took it!" I shouted at her. "You need to give it back!"

Ella looked shocked. "How dare you accuse me of such a thing!" she sputtered.

My parents and Aunt True were making their way toward us through the crowd now.

"What's going on?" asked Belinda Winchester, dancing by with Augustus Wilde.

Ella pointed to me. "She just accused me of stealing from the bookshop! As if I'd ever do such a thing!"

The music had stopped by now, and everyone in the room was staring at me.

"Stealing what?" said Belinda.

"*Charlotte's Web*!" I replied.

Belinda looked puzzled. "How could anyone steal *Charlotte's Web*?" she said. "It's bolted to the wall."

It took me a minute to realize she was talking about the bronze sculpture in the library.

"I'm talking about the *book*," I told her. "The autographed first edition that was in the cabinet in our shop."

"Oh," said Belinda. "No one stole that. I have it right here." She reached into the plastic bag she was carrying and pulled it out.

A gasp went up from the crowd. My father stepped forward.

"Where did you get that?" he demanded.

"From Andy," she replied mildly. "He gave it to me for my ninth birthday."

"Wait a minute, you're the 'Bee' in the inscription?" said Aunt True.

Belinda Winchester nodded.

"Who's Andy?" asked my father, his head whipping back and forth as he tried to keep up with the conversation.

"E. B. White," said my sister Lauren. "It was in my book report, remember?"

"See? I told you I didn't steal anything," Ella Bellow said triumphantly. She turned to me. "And just in case you're wondering, Miss Think-You-Know-It-All, I have absolutely no designs on Lovejoy's Books. Bud Jefferson is going to rent out half his space for my new shop."

Once again, I'd gone and put my big foot in my mouth. I was Truly-in-the-Middle-of-a-Mess.

"Truly, I think you owe someone an apology," my father told me sternly.

My shoulders slumped. "Yes, sir," I said. I turned to face

the postmistress. I'd been so sure she was the thief! "I'm really sorry."

Her mouth pruned up. "As well you should be."

"Show's over, folks!" my father announced. He took me by the arm and hustled me over to a corner of the room, near where Annie Freeman was being interviewed by a *Patriot-Bugle* reporter about winning yesterday's spelling bee.

"And then this boy from West Hartfield messed up on a trick question," Annie told him. "The *P* is silent in P-T-A-R-M-I-G-A-N. Which is a bird."

One that happened to be on my life list. I'd been lucky enough to spot it when we lived in Colorado.

It took us a while to get everything straightened out. Once Belinda explained that she'd grown up in Maine, and that her family lived on the farm next door to E. B. White, it all made sense—the lunch-lady entry in the yearbook that talked about lobsters, the news report about her trip back to the seacoast to visit her sister, the cats named after Fern and Avery Arable in *Charlotte's Web*. Only two things still puzzled me.

"How did you manage to lose the book in the first place?" I asked her.

Belinda shrugged. "Things go missing," she said. "And things get found." She rummaged in her plastic bag again, emerging this time with a kitten and a half-eaten vomit bar. She took a bite—of the vomit bar, not the kitten.

The other thing I didn't understand was how Belinda

could possibly not have known that we all thought the book was stolen. It had been all over the news.

Except she didn't own a television, and she never read the newspaper. Plus, she had her earbuds in most of the time, listening to her music. Somehow, she'd managed to miss the whole thing.

The mystery was solved, at least, but not in a way that was going to help the bookstore. No way could my father and Aunt True use the book to pay off the bank loan now.

"Erastus Peckinpaugh, do you want to ask me something or not?" Aunt True said suddenly. Startled, I looked over to see the man in the green jacket—only tonight he was wearing an ordinary suit—hovering behind her.

"Punkinpie?" said Pippa. "That'th a funny name."

My mother turned around too. "Professor Rusty! How nice to see you here."

The man in the green jacket—the stork—was Professor Rusty? And Professor Rusty was Erastus Peckinpaugh? I felt something in my brain stir and come to life. Where had I seen that name before?

"Out with it already!" Aunt True put her hands on her hips as she turned to face him, tapping the toe of one of her red cowboy boots. "I'm tired of you creeping around like some silly high school boy. Do you think I haven't noticed you lurking outside the bookstore these past few weeks?"

And then Annie spoke up again behind us. "Finally, I got

the winning word," she told the reporter. "'Thespian.' T-H-E-S-P-I-A-N. It means actor."

Snick! The last puzzle pieces fit together as neatly as a sudoku puzzle. I leaned over to my friends.

"I know where the final clue is," I whispered.

CHAPTER 37

We ran straight to the bookshop.

"There's something I need to check on," I told my friends as we clattered up the stairs to Aunt True's apartment. The key was still under the mat where she always left it, and I unlocked the door and led everyone inside. "Don't let Memphis out."

"Thespian" had been Annie Freeman's winning word, and Aunt True and Erastus Peckinpaugh had both been in the Thespian Club back in high school! I'd seen it in my aunt's yearbook.

The scrapbooks were still piled on the coffee table, where Lauren and Annie had left them. I started leafing through them, and it didn't take me long to find what I was looking for. "Ha!" I said triumphantly, showing my friends the program for *Much Ado About Nothing*.

"Hey, that's the show my parents starred in," said Calhoun, spotting their names. "My mom has a copy of that program too."

"Yes, but check out their understudies," I said, pointing to the cast list, which confirmed my suspicions.

My friends' mouths fell open when they saw the names: True Lovejoy and Erastus Peckinpaugh.

"My aunt and Professor Peckinpaugh—Professor Rusty, the guy in the green jacket—were Beatrice and Benedick too. Unofficially, of course."

I pointed to the prom picture on the opposite page. "Now check this out—"

"Whoa, that's some hair," said Scooter.

"Whose, her aunt's or her date's?" asked Calhoun.

"Both of them," said Lucas, and everybody laughed.

"Erastus Peckinpaugh is my aunt's old boyfriend," I said, pulling out my cell phone. "Don't you get it?" I scrolled through the pictures on it, hoping I hadn't deleted the one I'd taken on our field trip to the covered bridge. Nope, there it was. I enlarged the bit that showed the graffiti on the rafter. "See there, inside that lopsided heart? Where it says 'E and T Forever'? That's got to be Erastus and True! That's the exact place she chose for her yearbook picture, and I think it's their meeting spot."

My friends stared at the program and the picture, digesting all this information. Then Scooter looked up and grinned.

"What are we waiting for?"

Two minutes later, we were running down the road that led out of town, the only light to guide us the full moon above

ABSOLUTELY TRULY

and the faint beams below from the flashlight apps on our cell phones.

We heard the river before we saw it. It was flowing freely again, thanks to the thaw, and as we approached we heard a loud *CRACK*, followed by a tremendous splash, as a great chunk of ice crashed from the falls into the water.

"Cool," said Scooter, aiming his light in the river's direction. "It's like the *Titanic* or something."

We jogged through the mouth of the covered bridge, our footsteps echoing in the dark as the sound bounced off its wooden floor and walls.

Jasmine giggled nervously. "Spooky," she said.

I shone my light up at the rafters, trying to remember where I'd been standing when I'd seen the graffiti. "It was somewhere in the middle, I think," I told my friends. "Can you guys all shine your lights up here too?"

They did, and it didn't take long to spot what I was looking for. "There it is! See? That heart with 'E and T Forever' inside? This has to be their meeting place."

"The envelope's probably taped to the top of the rafter, just like it was in the steeple," said Lucas.

"I'll take a look." Scooter climbed up onto the railing.

"Watch out!" cried Jasmine, grabbing her twin's lower legs to steady him. The X-shaped crosspieces along the wall of the bridge left too many wide gaps for comfort.

Scooter batted her away. "Relax, Jazz, I've got it."

Grasping a crosspiece with one hand, he stretched his other up toward the rafter. I glanced down at the moon's reflection in the river and shuddered. It would not be fun to take a nosedive into that dark, frigid water.

"I can't quite reach," Scooter said finally. "I'm not tall enough."

"I'm the tallest," I said as he hopped down. "Let me try."

"No, Truly, don't," begged Cha Cha. "Please."

"I'll be careful," I assured her. "Don't you want to know if it's up there?"

I hoisted myself onto the railing. The soles of my new heels were slick, and I edged my way cautiously along until I was standing directly under the graffiti. A sharp gust of wind made my coat and dress billow around my legs. I shivered. The tights I was wearing offered little protection, except perhaps for keeping Scooter from singing any more ditties about my underpants.

Holding tight to a crosspiece, I stretched up on tiptoe and reached for the rafter, just the way Scooter had done.

"There's something here!" I said after a moment of fumbling around.

"Is it an envelope?" Jasmine's voice was shrill with excitement.

"I think so—hang on a sec." I took off my mitten with my teeth and picked at the edge of whatever it was with my fingernails. "Got it!" I mumbled triumphantly a moment later, my mouth full of wool. "It's an envelope!"

ABSOLUTELY TRULY

I waved my duct-tape prize in the air in triumph, then handed it down to Jasmine. The others crowded around as she held it under the beam of Cha Cha's flashlight app.

I was climbing down to join them when my left shoe slipped.

"Whoa!" I cried. My arms windmilled as I tried to regain my balance. For a heart-stopping split second I teetered on the railing. And then my big feet betrayed me once again. Or, rather, my big shoes did. Both of them slipped out from under me completely and I landed on the railing with a spine-jolting bounce, then toppled through a gap between the crosspieces.

And then—well, then I did the Polar Bear Swim.

The last thing I heard before the river closed over my head was Cha Cha and Jasmine screaming. The next thing I heard was me screaming. Or what would have been me screaming, if I'd had breath enough to scream. The frigid water had knocked every scrap of it out of me.

I'd never felt *anything* that cold.

I thrashed in the icy current, gasping and choking. I couldn't think, I couldn't see, and worst of all, my jacket was dragging me down. Somehow I managed to wrestle myself out of it. The river swept it away under the bridge, and then it started to sweep me away. I panicked. Flailing blindly in the water, I smacked my hand against one of the pillars that held up the bridge and grabbed at it frantically, trying to get a grip on one of the stones in its base.

I clung there for a few seconds, trying to catch my breath. Somewhere far above my friends were shouting, but I barely heard them. I was too focused on not being swept away again. My shoes were long gone by now, and I jammed my ice-numbed toes and fingers into the crevices between the rocks, scrabbling clumsily as I pulled myself onto the base of the pillar.

Slowly, painfully, I began to inch my way up, collapsing in tears when I finally reached the top of the pillar's rough, narrow ledge. Only a minute or so had passed, but it felt like an eternity. My head ached. My teeth were chattering like a woodpecker on a tin roof. I was even colder now than I had been in the water, if that were possible, thanks to the bitter wind.

"Truly!"

Someone was calling my name.

"Here!" I croaked. "I'm here!" I looked up and saw Calhoun leaning over the wall of the bridge.

"Scooter and the girls ran for help!" he hollered down.

"We called nine-one-one, too," added Lucas, who was beside him.

I gave a feeble nod.

Calhoun stretched out his hand. "See if you can reach up and grab hold!"

I eyed the distance between us and shook my head. I didn't want to risk slipping again. The ledge was so narrow!

"Come on, Truly!" he urged.

With Lucas holding on to Calhoun's belt for all he was

worth, Calhoun stretched even farther down toward me.

"Bravery comes in all sizes," Aunt True had once said. I took a deep, raggedy breath. Did it come in mine?

I absolutely truly hoped so.

Shaking, I rose to my knees.

"You're almost there," Calhoun called down in encouragement as I forced myself to my feet and reached an arm up overhead. "A little to the left."

His left? My left? My knees were knocking and I was afraid my legs were going to collapse under me. I waved my hand back and forth. My fingertips grazed something. Or someone.

"That's it!" Calhoun shouted. "I nearly had you!"

It was my height that saved me. That and my Truly Gigantic, size-ten-and-a-half Amazon feet. Summoning every ounce of strength that I had left in me, I stretched myself up on tiptoes as high as I could and reached for Calhoun one more time.

"Gotcha!" he cried.

I promised myself right then and there that I would never, ever complain about being tall again.

It was agonizing. I was afraid to move even a fraction of an inch, for fear I'd plunge back into the river, dragging my friends with me. My toes, my legs, my fingers—my entire body was cramped with cold. I ventured a glance downward, which was a bad idea.

This is definitely at the very top of the list of things I'm not good at, I thought, closing my eyes to block out the terrifying sight of the dark water flowing swiftly past.

My arm felt like it was being pulled from its socket. *What am I good at, then?* I listed the things that came to mind: Swimming. Bird-watching. Sudoku. Window displays at the bookstore. And pre-algebra, thanks to my father's tutoring.

My father.

Lovejoys can do anything, he'd tell me if he were here.

Even this?

I wasn't so sure.

And then, finally, I heard a siren in the distance, followed by the sound of voices shouting my name. Footsteps pounded on the wooden floorboards of the bridge overhead. There were more shouts directly above, and then a voice I recognized. I opened my eyes and looked up to see that it was my father. A great sob of relief burst from me.

"Hang on, Truly!" He anchored himself to an eyebolt with his hook and reached down to me with his good hand.

"Don't let go, Dad!" I begged him as his fingers closed around my wrist. "Please don't let me go!"

"Never," he told me. "Cross my heart and hope to fly."

CHAPTER 38

"I'm really, really glad you went with Captain Hook tonight, Dad," I said later, when we were safely back at the Town Hall. The music had stopped and people were milling around everywhere. They'd burst into spontaneous applause when the rescue vehicles finally pulled up out front.

"Me too, honey," he replied, putting his good arm around me and kissing the top of my head.

The rescue was a bit of a blur. My father held on to me until the fire department arrived and pulled me to safety. I was shoeless, of course, and practically blue with cold, and I'd gotten pretty bruised and scraped up too. But at least I was alive. The firefighters bundled me into blankets and made me take off what was left of my wet, tattered dress so I wouldn't get hypothermia, and then they took me directly to my mother.

She started to cry when she saw me. "You're safe!" she kept repeating, hugging me tightly as if to assure herself that I wasn't going to go flinging myself from another bridge at any moment. "My brave girl!"

I shook my head, which was buried in her shoulder. "It was Dad," I told her. "Dad's the one who's brave. He didn't let go, and neither did Calhoun and Lucas."

I smiled at my two friends, whose faces were pink from all the praise they'd been showered with. Lucas's mother had him in a death grip, though. The poor kid would probably never be allowed out of the house again.

My mother kissed the top of my head. "What were you thinking, sweetheart, going down to the bridge like that?"

"We were looking for something," I told her.

"This," said Cha Cha, pulling the duct-tape-covered envelope out of her jacket pocket.

Erastus Peckinpaugh, who had been hovering at the edge of the crowd that surrounded me, looking more stork-like than usual, suddenly froze.

My mother's forehead puckered. "That trash was worth risking your life for?"

"It's not trash; it's for Aunt True," I told her. "From Professor Rusty—I mean Professor Peckinpaugh."

At this, Pippa, who had barnacled herself to my leg the second I climbed out of the fire truck, finally let go. "Punkinpie! Punkinpie! Punkinpie!" she chanted, twirling, and the people gathered around us started to laugh.

ABSOLUTELY TRULY

Cha Cha took out the envelope and passed it to my aunt.

"You really should read the other letters first," I told Aunt True. "But they're back at home."

We explained about finding the envelopes, and the quotes that were on the letters. Calhoun recited a few, and when he stumbled, his dad stepped in to help him. Aunt True listened silently as we told her how we'd followed the clues, casting a glance up at Professor Peckinpaugh now and then.

"Astounding," she said when we were done. "You did this all on your own?"

My friends and I nodded.

"Please read the last letter to us," begged Jasmine. "We have to know how the story ends."

"Why not?" said Aunt True. Opening the envelope, she drew out the faded piece of paper inside. "'For B,'" she began. "'When I said I would die a bachelor, I did not think I should live till I were married.'"

"Is that it?" asked Cha Cha. "Just another Shakespeare quote?"

"No, there's more. It also says, 'True, will you . . .'" My aunt's voice trailed off. She looked up at Professor Peckinpaugh, her eyes wide with surprise.

"True, will you what?" I reached for the letter, but Aunt True clutched it to her chest. Wait a minute, had Erastus

Peckinpaugh just asked my aunt to marry him?

Aunt True shot to her feet. "Why didn't you say something, Rusty?" she demanded, advancing on the bushy-haired professor. "After I left town you never wrote, you never called—I never heard from you again!"

"I thought you'd followed the clues and found the letters, and you weren't interested," he protested, taking a step back.

"How could I *possibly* have followed the clues?" Aunt True sputtered. "You hid them in a book that didn't belong to you, and that I never found! What were you *thinking*, Rusty?"

Erastus Peckinpaugh looked miserable. "I was trying to be clever," he told her. "I knew that *Charlotte's Web* was your favorite book, and when I saw it lying there on the floor that day at the bookshop it seemed like a good idea. You were always the one who tidied up at night; I figured you'd find it right away."

Aunt True shook her head. "You should have just mailed the letter to me. At least I'd have gotten it that way."

Professor Rusty sighed. "I was planning to. I'd even picked out a stamp to remind you of all those Civil War reenactments I dragged you to."

Cha Cha and I exchanged a glance. Another piece of the puzzle solved.

"The point is, I didn't even *see* the stamp!" Aunt True snapped.

He glanced at her ruefully then hung his head. "I just

assumed you would, just as I assumed you'd put two and two together."

"What, and get *five?*" Aunt True threw up her hands.

Dr. Calhoun winked at my friends and me. "'There is a kind of merry war betwixt Signior Benedick and her,'" he quoted in a whisper. "'They never meet but there's a skirmish of wit between them.'"

Aunt True and Professor Peckinpaugh were still bickering as we gathered our things to leave. On the way out, we passed Ella Bellow, who was collecting her coat from the big rack near the door.

"Hold on a minute, what's this doing in there?" she demanded as a fuzzy white head poked out from one of the pockets. "This doesn't belong to me!" Ella's voice rose in alarm. She spun around, sweeping the crowd with her eyes. Her gaze narrowed when she spotted Belinda Winchester. "Did you put this creature in my pocket, Belinda?"

"Don't look at me; it isn't one of mine," Belinda replied. Turning away from Ella, she gave Lauren and me a mischievous smile. "And that's not a lie," she murmured. "Technically speaking, it isn't one of mine. I didn't give birth to it."

My sister and I giggled.

In the end, Ella Bellow went home with a kitten, and the rest of us went home with both mysteries solved at last.

EPILOGUE

The January thaw lingered for three more days after my dramatic rescue, or what everyone in town was calling "a truly big splash."

That was the headline that had appeared on the front page of the *Pumpkin Falls Patriot-Bugle* the morning after my rescue. I was mortified at first, but the publicity really gave our bookstore a boost. The news wires picked up the story of the brave wounded-warrior-turned-bookseller who'd saved his daughter, and while Dad isn't thrilled being in the spotlight—he's been giving interviews to the media right and left ever since—he's definitely happy about the effect that the rescue had on our store's bottom line.

The Winter Festival Committee gave me an honorary blue ribbon for the Polar Bear Swim, which I pinned to the bulletin board above my desk, and Principal Burnside held a special assembly at school. He commended Calhoun and

ABSOLUTELY TRULY

Lucas for their part in the rescue, and me for what he called my "valor and panache" (I think that's another way of saying "bravery"), even though, as he pointed out sternly, we had absolutely no business being at the covered bridge in the first place without adult supervision.

Lots of people have been stopping by the bookstore to meet Dad and check up on me, both locals and tourists passing through. And just like Aunt True predicted, they sample our mini pumpkin whoopie pies and end up buying books.

So everything worked out for the best in the end.

The warm west wind that blew into town along with all the publicity carried with it the promise of spring. It melted the snow sculptures and released the frozen river from the grip of the ice, and ensured what Annie Freeman says will be a S-T-U-P-E-N-D-O-U-S maple syrup harvest this year.

I've been spending lots of time in the backyard since that night at the covered bridge, making friends with more of my grandfather's chickadees. I also added a cedar waxwing and an evening grosbeak and a ruffed grouse to my life list.

There would be more birds to add, come spring. Spring meant the return of meadowlarks and barn swallows, orioles and towhees, tanagers and buntings. And out on Lake Lovejoy, there would be osprey to watch diving for fish.

It might not be so bad to be stuck here in Pumpkin Falls, I decided, come spring.

Plus, my birthday was just around the corner, and that

meant Mackenzie's visit. I was looking forward to introducing her to my new friends.

"You know, I could have saved myself a whole lot of trouble if I'd just given that envelope to Aunt True in the first place," I mused to Cha Cha and Jasmine, stepping carefully around a puddle of slush as the three of us made our way downtown after school one afternoon.

"Yeah, but if you had, we might not all be friends," Cha Cha replied.

"And there'd be no Pumpkin Falls Private Eyes," added Jasmine.

They had a point. I was going to miss our adventures, but a town this small couldn't have any more mysteries to solve, could it?

"And don't forget the bookstore," added Jasmine. "You were the one who saved it."

That was a bit of an exaggeration. Yes, I'd inadvertently found *Charlotte's Web,* and yes, our business had gotten a boost from all the news about "a truly big splash." It still wasn't enough to turn the tide, though. What really turned the tide was Belinda Winchester.

She may look homeless, but it turns out Belinda invested her lunch-lady earnings shrewdly over the years, and she's rich. Her earnings support her kitten rescue, and she also fessed up to being the anonymous donor who gave the

ABSOLUTELY TRULY

Charlotte's Web sculpture to the local library years ago.

When Belinda realized what losing that autographed first edition meant for our family—and when she learned about the deadline hanging over our heads—she offered to become a silent partner in the business. Or maybe not-so-silent, since she's working part-time at the bookshop now. She knows everything there is to know about mysteries, so Dad and Aunt True have put her in charge of that section. She's as happy as a clam.

Aunt True also took her shopping for some new clothes, which is kind of like the blind leading the blind if you ask me, which nobody ever does. At least Belinda doesn't look like such a bag lady anymore. Well, except for the kittens. She almost always brings one or two along with her to work.

Dad says he still thinks Belinda Winchester is odd, but Aunt True reminded him that while books bring people together, it's people who bring communities together.

"A community is like a family," she told him, "and every family has a few odd ducks. The important thing to remember is that they're still family."

Belinda Winchester is definitely an odd duck, and so is Ella Bellow. We all kind of wish Ella had moved to Florida, but she's opening a knitting shop across the street from us next month instead. The sign is already up over her half of Earl's Coins and Stamps. She's calling it "A Stitch in Time," but Dad calls it the "Stitch and Snitch," since he says it's destined to be our town's new gossip central.

Ella also decided to keep her new kitten. She named it Purl, or as Annie Freeman tells everyone, "P-U-R-L, like the knitting stitch."

On the night before winter swooped in again, I heard something outside as I was getting ready for bed.

Tu-whoo! Tu-whoo!

I crossed to the window, threw it open, and leaned out to listen more closely. There it was again—*Tu-whoo! Tu-whoo!*

I held my breath. Could it be? I looked up at the full moon—an owl moon!—that hung in the sky. Its light reflected on the sodden snow below and shone through my window, puddling at my feet in a silvery glow.

I looked over at the picture book displayed on my shelf and thought of the father who takes his child owling.

Which in my case has never happened.

What if I rewrite the story? I thought. *What if in my story, the girl asks her father to go owling instead?*

"Dad!" I called, grabbing Gramps's barn coat and wool hat and stuffing my feet into my sneakers.

He didn't answer, so as I clattered downstairs, I reached for my cell phone and called him. A moment later, I heard the sound of his ringtone from the kitchen.

It was the theme song from *The Magnificent Seven*!

ABSOLUTELY TRULY

And right then and there I knew for sure that our family was going to be okay.

And that's exactly how it all happened, absolutely truly, cross my heart and hope to fly.

AUNT TRUE'S MINI PUMPKIN WHOOPIE PIES

Cookies

½ cup butter, softened

1 ¼ cups sugar

2 large eggs, at room temperature, lightly beaten

1 cup pumpkin

1 tsp. vanilla extract

2 T. molasses

2 cups all-purpose flour

1 tsp. baking powder

1 tsp. baking soda

1 tsp. ground cinnamon

½ tsp. ground ginger

½ tsp. ground cloves

¼ tsp. ground cardamom

¼ tsp. salt (only if using unsalted butter, otherwise omit)

Filling

4 ounces cream cheese, at room temperature

6 T. butter, softened

½ tsp. vanilla extract

1 ½ cups powdered sugar

Preheat oven to 350° F.

FOR COOKIES: Cream butter and sugar in a large bowl. Add eggs and beat well. Add pumpkin, vanilla extract, and molasses; beat until smooth. In a separate bowl, whisk flour, baking powder, baking soda, and spices. Add to pumpkin mixture and stir well. Using a teaspoon-size cookie scoop (or a heaping teaspoon), drop onto greased or parchment-lined cookie sheets.

Bake for about 12 minutes, until the cookie springs back to the touch, or a toothpick inserted into center comes out clean.

Cool on baking sheet for 5 minutes, then transfer to wire rack to cool completely.

FOR FILLING: Beat cream cheese, butter, and vanilla until fluffy. Gradually mix in powdered sugar and beat until light and fluffy. Generously frost the flat side of one cookie with filling, then top it with the flat side of another one to make a "sandwich." Repeat with remaining cookies and filling.

MISS MARPLE'S PICKS

The Borrowers by Mary Norton
Charlotte's Web by E. B. White
Cinderella by the Brothers Grimm
Frog and Toad Are Friends by Arnold Lobel
Jane Eyre by Charlotte Brontë
Little House on the Prairie by Laura Ingalls Wilder
A Little Princess by Frances Hodgson Burnett
The Long Winter by Laura Ingalls Wilder
Mary Poppins by P. L. Travers
Millions of Cats by Wanda Gag
Mrs. Piggle-Wiggle by Betty MacDonald
Owl Moon by Jane Yolen, illustrated by John Schoenherr
Pride and Prejudice by Jane Austen
The Wolves of Willoughby Chase by Joan Aiken

ACKNOWLEDGMENTS

Heartfelt thanks to Ellen Ingwerson and Clara Germani, whose expert knowledge of competitive swimming helped keep me out of deep water; and to MG (R) Lee Baxter for guidance on all things military. Any errors that managed to slip through the net are entirely my own. And a great big shout-out to my friend Victoria Irwin and to René Kirkpatrick and the entire staff at Eagle Harbor Book Co. on Bainbridge Island, Washington, for letting me play in their sandbox one long winter weekend. The world is absolutely truly a better place with bookstores like this one in it!

ALSO BY HEATHER VOGEL FREDERICK

Absolutely Truly

The Mother-Daughter Book Club
Much Ado About Anne
Dear Pen Pal
Pies & Prejudice
Home for the Holidays
Wish You Were Eyre
Mother-Daughter Book Camp

Once Upon a Toad

The Voyage of Patience Goodspeed
The Education of Patience Goodspeed

Spy Mice: The Black Paw
Spy Mice: For Your Paws Only
Spy Mice: Goldwhiskers

Hide and Squeak
A Little Women Christmas

Yours Truly

A Pumpkin Falls Mystery

HEATHER VOGEL FREDERICK

Simon & Schuster Books for Young Readers
NEW YORK • LONDON • TORONTO • SYDNEY • NEW DELHI

SIMON & SCHUSTER BOOKS FOR YOUNG READERS
An imprint of Simon & Schuster Children's Publishing Division
1230 Avenue of the Americas, New York, New York 10020
This book is a work of fiction. Any references to historical events, real people, or real places are used fictitiously. Other names, characters, places, and events are products of the author's imagination, and any resemblance to actual events or places or persons, living or dead, is entirely coincidental.
Text copyright © 2017 by Heather Vogel Frederick
Jacket illustration copyright © 2017 by Charles Santoso
All rights reserved, including the right of reproduction in whole or in part in any form.
SIMON & SCHUSTER BOOKS FOR YOUNG READERS is a trademark of Simon & Schuster, Inc.
For information about special discounts for bulk purchases, please contact Simon & Schuster Special Sales at 1-866-506-1949 or business@simonandschuster.com.
The Simon & Schuster Speakers Bureau can bring authors to your live event. For more information or to book an event, contact the Simon & Schuster Speakers Bureau at 1-866-248-3049 or visit our website at www.simonspeakers.com.
Jacket design by Krista Vossen
Interior design by Hilary Zarycky
The text for this book was set in Fournier.
Manufactured in the United States of America
0821 SKY
First Edition
2 4 6 8 10 9 7 5 3
Library of Congress Cataloging-in-Publication Data
Names: Frederick, Heather Vogel, author.
Title: Yours Truly / Heather Vogel Frederick.
Description: First edition. | New York : Simon & Schuster Books for Young Readers, [2017]
| Series: A Pumpkin Falls mystery | Audience: Ages 8–12. | Summary: When someone tries to sabotage the maple trees on her friend Franklin's family farm, Truly Lovejoy rallies the Pumpkin Falls Private Eyes to investigate. | Sequel to: Absolutely Truly
Identifiers: LCCN 2016031402| ISBN 9781442471863 (hardback) | ISBN 9781442471887 (ebook)
Subjects: | CYAC: Mystery and detective stories. | Families—Fiction. | Farm life—New Hampshire—Fiction. | New Hampshire—Fiction. | BISAC: JUVENILE FICTION / Mysteries & Detective Stories. | JUVENILE FICTION / Humorous Stories. | JUVENILE FICTION / Family / General (see also headings under Social Issues).
Classification: LCC PZ7.F87217 Yo 2017 | DDC [Fic]—dc23
LC record available at https://lccn.loc.gov/2016031402

For my maple buddy, Jonatha

Yours Truly

PROLOGUE

It takes roughly forty gallons of sap to make a gallon of maple syrup.

How do I know this? Welcome to life in the sticks.

I never expected to become an expert on maple syrup, that's for sure. Then again, I never expected to become a middle school private eye, either, or to spend Spring Break hunting for Bigfoot and wind up tangled in cobwebs in a long-forgotten tunnel. A whole lot of unexpected things have happened to me ever since my family left Texas and moved to Pumpkin Falls, New Hampshire.

This isn't a story about maple syrup, though. Not really. It's the story of how I stumbled onto a secret in my grandparents' house and unraveled a mystery dating back to the Civil War. And it all started the week I finally spotted an owl and celebrated the worst birthday of my life.

PROLOGUE

It takes roughly forty gallons of sap to make a gallon of maple syrup.

How did I know this? We learn to do it in these oaks.

I never expected to become an expert on maple syrup, that's for sure. Then again, I never expected to become a middle-aged private eye, either, or to spend Spring skunk hunting in Rigby's, and kind up tangled in cobwebs and longeron brambles. A whole lot of unexpected things have happened to me ever since my fateful fall Trek and the visit to Pumpkin Falls, New Hampshire.

That this isn't a story about maple syrup, not really. That's the story of how it all began until it came a secret in my grandparents' house and uncovered a buyer evading back to the Civil War, and it all started the week I finally spotted an owl and explained the secret behind my life.

CHAPTER 1

"Knock it off, Lauren!" I stuffed my pillow over my head, trying to block out the noise on the other side of my bedroom door.

Sunday was just about my only day to sleep in, thanks to swim team. I was usually up and in the pool by zero dark thirty. Which was fine—no complaints. The pool had always been my happy place. But ever since my younger sister discovered a box of our aunt's old Nancy Drew books up in the attic and started reading *The Hidden Staircase*, she'd been wandering around the house at odd hours tapping hopefully on the walls.

It was driving us all crazy.

"Lauren!" I hollered again, and this time the racket finally stopped.

Burrowing down under the covers, I squeezed my eyes shut and willed myself to go back to sleep. It seemed like I was tired all the time these days. My mother said it was a symptom of impending teenage-hood. Maybe she was right, because my older brothers would sleep all day if she and my father let them. And I was turning thirteen soon.

Soon?

My eyes flew open. I sat bolt upright, flinging my pillow aside. How could I have forgotten? My birthday was *today*, not *soon*!

I swung my legs over the edge of the bed, toes scrabbling for the slippers that waited on the hardwood floor. Reaching for my bathrobe, I slipped it on and sniffed the air expectantly. Lovejoy family birthdays always started with one of Dad's special breakfasts: scrambled eggs, bacon, and homemade sourdough waffles with real maple syrup. I'd been looking forward to it all week.

I shuffled across the room and out into the hall. There was no sign of Lauren, except for the fact that Miss Marple was sitting by my door, wearing a University of Texas T-shirt. Miss Marple is my grandparents' golden retriever. We were taking care of her while my grandparents were in Africa.

"Hey, girl," I said, and leaned down to give her a pat. She looked up at me and whined. Lauren loved dressing her up, but Miss Marple was not a fan.

I extricated her from the T-shirt, and she wagged her tail gratefully and followed me across the hall into my bathroom.

I still wasn't used to having one of my very own. It was pretty sweet, especially after having to share one with my brothers and sisters for so many years. Two older brothers—Hatcher and Danny—and two younger sisters—Lauren and Pippa, to be exact, putting me smack-dab in the middle. My dad was retired military, and for as long as I could remember we'd lived in base housing—Alabama, Colorado, Germany, Texas. Now, though, we were living in my grandparents' house, the one my dad grew up in. How we ended up here was kind of complicated, but the short version was, my father lost an arm in the war in Afghanistan, and because of that he lost his chance to be a commercial airline pilot, and partly because of that and partly because they wanted to, Gramps and Lola joined the Peace Corps and moved to Namibia so my dad could have a job running the family bookstore with his sister, and we traded our home in Austin for living here in their house. Complicated, right?

As Miss Marple settled happily onto the rug by the radiator, I got in the shower, humming the "Happy Birthday" song to myself and wondering if my parents had gotten me any presents. My cousin and best friend, Mackenzie, was my main gift—she was flying in from Texas tonight to spend Spring Break with me—but I'd spotted my mother sneaking a big bag inside the house yesterday, and I was pretty sure there was something for me inside.

Hopefully, it was the new feeder I'd been eyeing in one of my grandfather's birding catalogs. I'd placed the catalog strategically on the kitchen table a couple of weeks ago, open to the page in question. There was no way my parents could have missed it.

I was planning to put it outside one of the windows in my room. I figured it would be almost like having pet birds.

A person couldn't have enough bird feeders. Especially when that person was as crazy about birds as I was.

The house was still quiet when Miss Marple and I emerged from the bathroom.

"They're probably in the kitchen already, waiting to surprise me," I whispered to the dog as I got dressed and then tiptoed downstairs. Correction: I tiptoed; Miss Marple galumphed. She wasn't exactly the daintiest of dogs.

The only surprise waiting for me, though, was an empty kitchen. There was no sign of my family, no sign of any presents, and, tragically, no sign of waffles.

Disappointed, I glanced out the window. The driveway was empty too. Was there a wrestling tournament today that my parents and sisters had taken my brothers to? I'd almost forgotten my own birthday; maybe I'd forgotten about one of Hatcher's and Danny's wrestling matches as well.

Just then I heard the door to the garage open, and a moment later my father walked in.

Finally, I thought happily. *Waffles.*

"Why are you dressed like that?" He eyed me, frowning.

"Um . . . ," I replied, looking down at my clothes. I'd made an effort for once—I was always getting scolded for not dressing up enough for church—and picked out what I thought was a pretty nice outfit.

"Go get changed, Truly!" My father sounded impatient. "We haven't got all day."

I looked at him, bewildered. "Aren't we going to church?"

"Not this morning. We're needed at Freeman Farm."

My mother came into the kitchen behind him. "They have a syrup emergency," she said, like that explained everything. "We just dropped your brothers and Lauren off to help, and Pippa is waiting in the car. You were in the shower when we left—didn't you get our note?"

I turned around and looked to where she was pointing. Sure enough, right there in plain sight leaning against the salt and pepper shakers was a tented piece of paper with *TRULY* written on it.

"Don't worry, honey, we haven't forgotten you," my mother promised. "We'll have your special birthday breakfast tomorrow, after Mackenzie gets here."

Tears sprang to my eyes. We weren't going to celebrate my birthday until *tomorrow?*

Seeing the expression on my face, my mother bit her lip. "It's the right thing to do, Truly. The Freemans are swamped, what with the Maple Madness rush."

Maple Madness! I was sick of hearing about stupid Maple Madness. Our whole town had gone maple syrup crazy. The minute the weather conditions cooperated, all the farms and small backyard operations around town had begun scrambling to harvest the sap from the trees and turn it into liquid gold. And now, with April just around the corner, all anyone could talk about was Maple Madness.

Every autumn New Hampshire flung its doors open wide for the leaf peepers—tourists obsessed with fall foliage—and every spring they did the same for the maple maniacs. All over the state there were special events and tours and other celebrations during "sugaring off" season, including Pumpkin Falls' own week-long Maple Madness.

And this year my birthday had the misfortune of falling right in the middle of the kickoff weekend.

"But Mom, it's my *birthday*," I said, trying not to whine. *An extra-special one*, I wanted to add. The one I'd been waiting for forever, because today I was finally a teenager, which was practically a grown-up.

"Truly." My father's voice had the warning note in it that meant business.

I sighed. "Yes, sir."

My mother stretched up on her tiptoes and gave me a quick kiss on the cheek. At six feet tall, I towered over her. In fact, I pretty much towered over everybody in my family, except for my aunt.

"Thanks, sweetheart," my mother said. "And don't worry—we'll make it up to you tomorrow."

Fat lot of good that does me today, I thought bitterly, and went upstairs to change my clothes.

CHAPTER 2

By the time we arrived at Freeman Farm, the line of cars waiting for the parking lot to open stretched halfway down Lovejoy Mountain.

I still got a kick out of the fact that everybody around here called it a mountain. It was more of a molehill, really—and the ski run was a joke, compared to the ones we used to live near in Colorado.

"Good thing we took the back way," said my father, scowling at the traffic. "It's practically at a standstill over by Maynard's Maple Barn."

The farm next door to the Freemans was what's called a "hobby farm." It belonged to my swim coach. Like many people across New England, Coach Maynard and his wife had a small-time maple operation that they cranked up this time of year for fun and a little extra income. For the Freemans, though, maple syrup was their main business.

My father tooted the horn to announce our arrival, and Mr. Freeman trotted over to move one of the sawhorses blocking the entrance to the lot.

"I can't thank you enough for coming," he called, directing us into a parking spot. We all piled out of the minivan. A crowd of volunteers in orange aprons milled around nearby, including my brothers and two of my classmates from seventh-grade homeroom, Scooter Sanchez and Romeo Calhoun, who just went by "Calhoun" because he hated the name Romeo. I couldn't blame him. Truly was bad enough—I was named for one of my ancestors—but Romeo? He and Scooter and I waved at one another.

"Happy to help, Frank," said my mother with one of her sunny smiles. "Where do y'all want us?"

"Grace is hoping you'll join her in the Snack Shack." Mr. Freeman pointed toward a small shed at the far end of the puddle-strewn parking lot. "She's been up since before dawn making donuts, and by the look of things she's going to be busier than a one-eyed cat in a fish market today."

My mother laughed. "That busy, huh?" She took Pippa by the hand. "Come on, sweetheart, you can be my helper."

Mr. Freeman turned to my father. "J. T., how do you feel about taking over the parking detail? I need to prep the sugarhouse for the first tour."

"I'm on it," said my father.

Mr. Freeman frowned at the line of waiting cars. "I'm not

sure how we're going to squeeze everybody in. I can't ever remember having a kickoff weekend this busy before."

"Good problem to have," my father told him, and he brightened.

"You've got a point." Mr. Freeman started to go, then paused. "You'll probably need to open the satellite lot in the field across the street soon. Franklin and I cleared the last of the snow away this morning, so it's good to go. He and Annie know the ropes if you have any questions."

Annie Freeman detached herself from the gaggle of volunteers and came over to us as her father headed for the sugarhouse, a small wooden cabin beyond the barn and the Snack Shack.

"These are for you," Annie told my father and me, handing us each one of the bright orange aprons. On the front was the outline of a giant maple leaf with the words FREEMAN FARM printed inside. "My mother designed them—aren't they cute? They're for sale in the barn shop. Only you'll probably get to keep yours for free, as a thank-you for volunteering. But act surprised when my mother tells you, okay? Volunteers have to wear them at all times," she continued, without pausing to take a breath. "My father says it's safer that way, and safety is our top P-R-I-O-R-I-T-Y during Maple Madness."

Annie Freeman was in the same fourth-grade class as my sister Lauren. She never stopped talking—or spelling. Annie was the reigning queen of the Grafton County Junior Spelling

Championship, as she was quick to tell anyone who stood still long enough to listen.

Lauren emerged from the barn just then, clutching a stack of orange flyers. Annie motioned her over and took a bunch. She thrust them into my hands. "One per car," she told me.

"Got it," I replied, glancing down at the piece of paper on top of my pile.

WELCOME TO MAPLE MADNESS!
Tour the sugarhouse!
Grab a treat at the Snack Shack!
Stop by our barn store for more maple goodness and our special MAPLE MADNESS SALE!

"Madness" is definitely the right word, I thought, wincing. Could this whole thing possibly be any more lame?

My father checked his watch. "Okay, troops, it's oh-nine hundred hours," he announced crisply. "Time to get this show started!"

Annie's brother Franklin grabbed Scooter Sanchez and Calhoun and my brothers, and they all began moving the sawhorses that blocked the entrance to the parking lot. A moment later cars started streaming in.

"Scooter and Calhoun, I'm stationing you two here with Franklin," my father told my classmates. "Danny and Hatcher, you boys get the satellite parking lot across the street ready. By the looks of it, we're going to need it for overflow soon."

He doled out a few more assignments, then turned to me. "Truly, you're my floater. Look for anyone who needs extra help, cover for anyone who needs a break, take coffee to Mr. Freeman and any of the volunteers who look like they could use something hot to drink, that sort of thing."

I held up the orange flyers, and he nodded.

"That too. Hand them out to the incoming—I mean the customers."

In thirty seconds flat, Lieutenant Colonel Jericho T. Lovejoy had slipped back into his element, barking orders at everyone in sight. As I headed off to do as he'd asked, I glanced back over my shoulder at him. With his leather flight jacket and glove covering his titanium arm and hand, my father looked like anybody else's dad.

He wasn't, though. He was still adjusting to his "new normal," as he and my mother called it. A new normal that for him meant no more military and no more flying helicopters and airplanes. Grounded by his injury, he'd traded that life for a new life in this teeny town where he'd grown up. I could tell he still missed the old life, though, even though he was doing a really good job running the family bookstore with his sister.

"Where's your aunt?" asked Annie, who apparently had a gift for mind reading as well as spelling.

"Holding down the fort at the bookshop," I told her. "It's kind of a busy weekend, in case you haven't heard."

Annie grinned. "Too bad Jasmine and Cha Cha aren't here. They love Maple Madness."

Jasmine was Scooter Sanchez's twin. She and Cha Cha Abramowitz were my closest friends in Pumpkin Falls. The two of them were in Florida for Spring Break, visiting Cha Cha's grandparents. I'd been invited to go along, but I couldn't because of Mackenzie.

Who would be here in just a few more hours! There was one bright spot in this dud of a birthday, at least.

"We'll take that half of the parking lot; you take this half," said Annie. She ran off to join my sister Lauren, her bouquet of dark braids bobbing.

I made my way slowly toward the Snack Shack, passing out orange flyers as I went.

"Need any help?" I asked when I reached my destination.

"Thanks, Truly, but I think we're okay for now." Annie's mother nodded toward Pippa, who was perched on a box behind the window counter, flirting with one of the customers as only a kindergartner can flirt. "This one's quite the lucky charm."

I had to smile at that. With her gap-toothed grin, pink sparkly glasses, and halo of strawberry blond curls, my baby sister had the world wrapped around her little finger.

"I don't think I've ever seen this many people turn out for Maple Madness kickoff weekend before," Mrs. Freeman continued as she boxed up a dozen donuts for a waiting customer.

YOURS TRULY

"I think people are just grateful for a reason to celebrate spring, after the winter we've had," my mother told her, adding hastily, "Not that they aren't eager to sample your maple products too."

Pumpkin Falls and the rest of New England had just emerged from the coldest winter on record. It made the national news and everything. The snow in our town was epic—even the famous waterfall froze, which it hadn't done for a hundred years. Spring was finally on its way now, though, and the ground, so recently blanketed in white, was a patchwork of brown as the remnants of the last snowstorm faded away.

Of course, the beginning of spring also meant the beginning of what locals call "mud season." We didn't have that back in Texas, and it was just another in the long string of strikes against Pumpkin Falls, if you asked me, which nobody ever did.

"Now that I think of it, we could use more paper plates and napkins," Mrs. Freeman said. "Would you mind, Truly? They're in the kitchen, on the bottom shelf in the pantry."

"No problem," I told her, starting back across the parking lot. The sun felt good on my face, and my grumpy mood began to melt right along with the last of the snow. From all the weather reports I'd been hearing, conditions couldn't be more perfect for a successful sap run—the weeks when the maple trees released their sugary liquid. "Cold nights plus warm days make for a busy season in the sugar bush," one of the radio announcers had said just this morning on the drive over.

I can't believe I even pay attention to news like that, I thought in a rush of embarrassment. I'd have to watch my step once Mackenzie arrived. She'd never let me hear the end of it if I started spouting random facts about maple syrup.

"Isn't this a beautiful farm?" my mother asked me a few minutes later when I returned with the plates and napkins.

I shrugged. "I guess."

"You guess! Truly Lovejoy!" She took me by the shoulders and spun me around. "Just look at that view, darlin'!" Shading her eyes, she gazed out across the road at the long sweep of meadows that sloped down toward the Pumpkin River. She turned to Mrs. Freeman. "How long has it been here?"

Mrs. Freeman laughed. "The view or our farm? I suspect the view has been here longer."

My mother laughed too.

"The farm was built shortly after the Civil War, by one of my husband's ancestors," Annie's mother told us.

Annie's family were the first African Americans to settle in Pumpkin Falls. I knew this because we'd learned about them in school a few weeks ago, during Black History Month. Our social studies class had even taken a field trip to the old Oak Street Cemetery. Oak Street paralleled Maple Street, where my grandparents' house was—the house we were living in now. At the far end of our backyard there was an overgrown cut-through to the cemetery. Hatcher and I had discovered it one summer when we were visiting Gramps and Lola.

On our field trip my classmates and I had wandered around looking at the graves of long-departed Freemans and learning a bit about their history. For instance, Franklin's grandfather had marched with Martin Luther King during the Civil Rights movement back in the 1960s, which was pretty cool. I took a bunch of pictures of the tombstones. I still had some of them on my cell phone, including Fanny Freeman's (because who doesn't love the name Fanny?), an earlier Franklin Freeman (I took that one because of the awesome owl carved into the headstone), and, of course, the tomb of Frank Freeman, the original ancestor who had built Freeman Farm. That particular grave was one of the most famous in the Oak Street Cemetery.

"The whole namesake thing is as bad for Franklin's family as it is for mine," I'd remarked to Calhoun as the two of us had stood there looking at it.

He'd flashed me one of his rare smiles. "No kidding. Way too many Franklins, Franks, and *F*'s in general. But the epitaph is pretty sweet."

Two hearts forever entwined, one forever yearning to be free. I looked at it again, then slanted my friend a glance. Calhoun was a bit of a puzzle. He had this übercool exterior, but underneath he was smart as a whip and knew a ton about Shakespeare, of all things, thanks to his Shakespearean scholar father, and he could be funny and really nice when he wanted to. Which had been a lot more than usual lately. He'd even asked me to dance at the Valentine's Day party. I was beginning to think that maybe he liked me.

We'd both taken photos of the sculpture on top of the lid to the tomb and agreed that a mother cradling her infant was kind of a weird thing to have on a guy's grave. But then, there were a lot of weird things on the tombstones in the old Oak Street Cemetery, including a stone pumpkin on the one belonging to my ancestor Nathaniel Daniel Lovejoy. *Way to represent the Lovejoys, Nathaniel,* I'd thought, staring at it.

"You folks certainly ordered up some fine weather for the Maple Madness kickoff," commented one of the customers standing in line at the Snack Shack.

My mother nodded. "Couldn't be prettier."

A pretty day for a birthday, I almost blurted out, but didn't. Even I had to admit that helping the Freemans was the right thing to do. Still, being a Good Samaritan didn't completely erase the sting of missing my birthday breakfast.

I swear, moms must have radar that tells them when their kids are unhappy, because just then mine handed me a maple donut and a cup of hot chocolate. "I know it's not sourdough waffles," she whispered, "but maybe it will tide you over until tomorrow."

"Thanks, Mom," I said, and we smiled at each other.

YOURS TRULY

"That'll be two dollarth," my little sister announced smartly, holding out her hand. Her front teeth are finally starting to grow in, but she still has a bit of a lisp.

My mother arched an eyebrow. "You drive a hard bargain, young lady," she said, reaching into her pocket for some coins. "But I'm happy to pay for the birthday girl."

As she plunked a pile of quarters into Pippa's palm, I bit into the donut. It was so good I groaned out loud. "Oh man, these are *fantastic*, Mrs. Freeman."

Annie's mother handed me another one. "Why, thank you, Truly! It's an old family recipe." She winked. "This one's on the house, since it's your birthday."

Scooter Sanchez, who was walking by just then, turned and looked at me in surprise. It seemed like he was about to say something, but before he could, my father bellowed at him to double-time it back to his station. He sketched a wave and ran off.

Scooter was a lot nicer to me now than when we first moved here. He was still kind of a pain, though. It was really, really hard for him to resist teasing people, for one thing. On my first day at Daniel Webster School, we got off on the wrong foot when he called me "Truly Gigantic." Things got worse for a while, especially after he discovered that my brother Hatcher's nickname for me was "Drooly." It's one thing for your brother to call you something like that, and another when a complete stranger does it.

"Truly?" Mrs. Freeman handed me a cardboard box containing two cups of coffee and a paper plate piled with donuts. "Would you please take these to Ella and Belinda? They're manning the barn store for us this morning, and I'm guessing they could use a break about now."

Picking my way around the puddles, I headed toward the barn. I was more than a bit curious to see how our former postmistress and the local cat rescue lady were getting along. Things had been a little tense for a while between Ella Bellow and Belinda Winchester after last month's Valentine's Day dance, where Belinda had slipped a kitten into Ella's coat pocket. Of course she never admitted to it, but who else had a ready supply of kittens and handed them out like popcorn at a movie? Maybe Belinda had sensed that Ella was lonely and needed a friend—Ella was widowed a few years ago—or maybe Belinda was just being Belinda. Whatever prompted it, Ella had not been happy about the kitten surprise, at least not at first. She and Belinda had since patched things up, mostly. It helped that Ella had quickly fallen head over heels in love with little Purl—the name she picked for the kitten, to go with the new knitting shop she'd opened as a retirement project.

"Having fun yet?" Hatcher loped up behind me and slung an arm around my shoulders.

"You've got to try a maple donut," I told him. "They're amazing."

My brother reached for the cardboard box I was carrying,

but I whisked it out of his reach. "Go get your own. These are for Ella and Belinda."

"C'mon, Drooly," he coaxed, following me into the barn.

"Quit it, Hatcher!" I scowled at him. The Scooter Sanchez fiasco was still a bit of a sore spot between us.

"Sorry." He grinned, obviously not sorry at all. "Can't you let me have just one? Ella and Belinda will never notice."

"Aren't you supposed to be in the satellite lot?" I replied, keeping a firm grip on the donuts.

My brother shrugged. "I'm just taking a break."

"Better not let Dad catch you slacking."

"He won't. Cross my heart and hope to fly."

I gave him a rueful smile. That particular family saying had been off-limits for months after Black Monday—our name for the day Dad had been injured. I'd gotten into huge trouble earlier this winter for accidentally using it. The catchphrase was something my father and his best friend Tom Larson made up a long time ago when they were in flight school. But when Dad returned from Afghanistan and Mr. Larson didn't, the words stirred up too many bad memories for my father. Recently, though, the ban had been relaxed, and I'd even caught Dad using it himself a few times. Another sign that he was on the mend, according to Aunt True.

"Whoa," said Hatcher, looking around the store. "This is over the top."

The Freemans had pulled out all the stops for Maple

Madness. I had no idea there were so many maple products in existence. In addition to the usual jugs of every size filled with maple syrup, the shelves were crammed with a bunch of other stuff: maple sugar, maple candy, maple coffee and tea, maple-scented candles—even maple-scented soap. *Who in their right mind wants to smell like breakfast?* I wondered.

But that wasn't all. There was also maple hot sauce, maple fudge, maple cookies, maple cotton candy, and maple pepper, along with maple leaf key chains, maple recipe books, stacks of Mrs. Freeman's orange aprons, matching T-shirts, bumper stickers, and, I noted with chagrin, tote bags with MAPLE SYRUP—APPEARING SOON ON A BREAKFAST PLATE NEAR YOU! emblazoned on the side.

Not on one near me, I thought with a stab of self-pity, thinking wistfully of the sourdough waffles that had gone AWOL—military-speak for "absent without leave."

"Kids!" cried Belinda, waving at us from the far side of the store. Belinda Winchester looked a little less like a bag lady than she had when I first met her—Aunt True's recent wardrobe makeover had helped, sort of—but Belinda was still a few tacos short of a fiesta platter, if you asked me, which nobody ever did. Belinda had been on kind of a purple streak lately, but today she'd traded that in for head-to-toe orange. Not just any shade of orange, either, but fluorescent hunter-in-the-woods orange. I was guessing this color scheme was inspired by the apron that Mrs. Freeman had designed, which

Belinda was wearing over orange overalls, orange turtleneck, orange socks, and orange plastic clogs. With the bright green beret she'd plopped on her snowy owl white hair, Belinda looked like a carrot—an observation I whispered to Hatcher. He laughed.

"How's it going out there?" Belinda asked, trotting over and reaching for a donut. Hatcher gave me a mournful look, which I ignored.

"Busy," my brother and I replied at the same time.

Belinda nodded, sending the wires to her ever-present earbuds swinging back and forth. "Busy in here, too. Oh, happy birthday, by the way. Your aunt told me."

"Thanks."

"You having a party?" she asked hopefully as I handed her a cup of coffee. Belinda loved parties. Correction: Belinda loved the *food* that accompanied parties. "I have a great playlist I could bring."

She bit into the donut, her earbuds leaking the tinny strains of "Surfer Girl." Out of the corner of my eye I could see Hatcher grinning broadly. He got a huge kick out of Belinda. I did too, as a matter of fact. The thing was, you couldn't help but like her. As odd as she was, she had a lot of spunk for an older lady, along with a mischievous streak a mile wide.

Still, a senior citizen DJ-ing my birthday party wasn't exactly my idea of a fun time. Not that there was anything wrong with her oldies mixes. Belinda always played them during her bookstore shifts, and I liked the Beatles and the Beach Boys as much as anybody.

I shook my head. "Nope. No party. My cousin's coming tonight, though. She's going to spend Spring Break with me."

"Your aunt said something about that." Belinda took another bite of donut, then reached into the pocket of her orange apron and pulled out a kitten. "Would you like a present?"

I had to admire her persistence. "My mother would kill me, Belinda. And so would Lauren—she's been begging for one for months now."

"You could keep him at the bookstore."

Belinda worked part-time for us now—or maybe we worked for her, I wasn't exactly sure which. When the bookshop was teetering on the verge of bankruptcy earlier this winter, she'd saved our bacon by becoming a silent partner. She might look like a slightly crazy cat lady, but it turned out she was a shrewd investor, too, and those deep pockets of hers contained far more than just kittens. Anyway, Aunt True put her in charge of the mystery section, since that was Belinda's favorite genre and she knew pretty much everything there was to know about it.

I shook my head. "A resident kitten wouldn't go over well with Memphis."

"He'd get used to it."

Fat chance. My aunt's cat didn't like anyone except my

aunt. As for other animals, well, he'd made it his job in life to make Miss Marple as miserable as possible.

"Are you sure you don't want him? He's awful cute," Belinda coaxed, holding out the little bundle of gray fuzz. "So are his six sisters, if you'd rather have a girl. They're in a box behind the counter."

"Oh, look, honey, a KITTEN!" shrieked a woman wearing an orange I WENT MAD FOR MAPLE MADNESS sweatshirt. She dragged her husband over to where we were standing.

Belinda pulled out her earbuds and smiled. "They're free with a purchase," she told the customer. "Better act fast, though—we're almost out."

My mouth fell open. Belinda winked at me. She was never above stretching the truth when it came to finding homes for her furry charges.

"Going, going, gone!" added Ella Bellow, materializing just then.

I handed the former Pumpkin Falls postmistress a cup of coffee and a donut, and she gave me a chilly smile. Tall and rake thin, Ella had thawed a bit since I'd falsely accused her of stealing a rare book from our store, but despite my public apology we were hardly pals.

"I'd better get back," said Hatcher, who'd been watching for an opening and finally managed to swipe the last of the donuts.

"Yeah, me too," I said. "Bye, Belinda. See you later, Ella."

"You certainly will," Ella replied, her mouth pruning up in a smug I-know-something-you-don't smile.

"What was that all about?" my brother whispered as we headed out of the barn.

"No idea," I whispered back.

As we emerged into the sunshine, Hatcher trotted off toward the parking lot. I rounded the corner of the barn and nearly flattened Scooter Sanchez.

"Watch where you're going!" he said, startled.

"Like I did it on purpose!"

We stood there awkwardly for a moment, glaring at each other, and then all of a sudden Scooter lunged at me. Before I realized what was happening, his face loomed close to mine and he kissed me.

On the *lips*.

I stepped back, too astonished to speak.

Scooter's face flamed. "Happy birthday," he mumbled, and loped off.

That's when I spotted Calhoun. I could tell by the look on his face that he'd seen everything. Before I could say a word, he spun on his heel and stalked off.

It's not what you think! I wanted to shout in protest. *I didn't have anything to do with it!*

But he was already gone.

I slumped against the side of the barn. I never used to give boys a second thought. They were just there, like my older brothers. Now, though, they were kind of on my radar screen. Not the way they were on my cousin Mackenzie's radar screen—she was totally boy crazy. At the moment, she was head over heels in love with Cameron McAllister. They were both on the same swim team in Austin. Behind Mackenzie's back, I call him Mr. Perfect.

The thing was, though, it had recently begun to dawn on me that not only was there a chance Calhoun liked me, but that maybe, just maybe, I liked him back.

Except now, thanks to the kiss he'd just witnessed, he probably thought I liked Scooter.

Running behind the barn, I grabbed a handful of snow and scrubbed my lips. Why did my first kiss have to be from Scooter Sanchez, of all people? And why did Calhoun have to be there to witness it?

My birthday couldn't possibly get any worse.

CHAPTER 3

Actually it could, as it turned out.

That bag I saw my mother sneaking into the house? There was a gift for me inside, just as I'd suspected, but it wasn't what I'd been hoping for.

At breakfast the next morning after swim practice—waffles! finally!—I found a pile of presents waiting for me on my chair. On top was a big blue gift bag covered in sparkles.

"What's this?" I asked.

"Must be something for the birthday girl," said my father, setting a loaded plate in front of me and planting a kiss on top of my head.

"But it ithnt her birthday anymore," said Pippa.

"A technicality," my father told her.

Pippa's forehead furrowed.

"He means you're right, but she gets presents anyway," said Hatcher.

I opened the envelope taped to the bag. Inside was a birthday card containing a slip of paper. I pulled it out and read it aloud: *"This gift certificate enrolls the bearer in 'Spring Break Socks!' at A Stitch in Time."*

Hatcher's eyes met mine across the table. So this was what Ella had been all mysterious about at Freeman Farm yesterday.

"We're going to take knitting lessons!" my mother said, her Texas twang growing twangier as her excitement bubbled over. "The class starts tonight. I thought it would be something fun we could do together. You know, a little mother-daughter bonding time."

My eyes slid over to where my cousin Mackenzie was sitting. We'd barely had time to say hello since she'd arrived late last night. She smirked at me. Mackenzie had turned thirteen just last week, and when I called to wish her a happy birthday, she told me that her mother had enrolled the two of them in a yoga class as part of her present. The whole mother-daughter bonding thing must kick in automatically when you become a teenager, like zits or something.

"You and I haven't had much time to spend together since the move," my mother continued.

She was right about that. I'd been busy with swim team and school and helping out at the bookshop, and between her full-time college classes, part-time job as receptionist at the Starlite Dance Studio, plus the fact that there are five of us Lovejoy kids, my mother had been spread a little thinner than usual lately.

I reached into the gift bag and pulled out two skeins of pool blue yarn and a pair of knitting needles.

"I thought it would be a nice way to support Ella's new business venture too, Little O," my mother added, her voice trailing off as she sensed my lack enthusiasm.

Little O was what she used to call me when I was, well, little. Which I hadn't been for a long time. It's short for "Little Owl," because I was a night owl back then and never wanted to go to bed. My mother even knitted matching sweaters for us with owls on the front and our initials on the back: L. O. for me, and M. O.—Mama Owl—for her.

Across the table, Hatcher was frowning at me.

"Uh, yeah, mom, I'm sure it will be fun," I chirped as brightly as I could. But knitting was her thing, not mine. On a scale of one to ten, my interest in learning how to rub two sticks together and make socks was about minus a zillion.

"The class meets in the evenings," my mother continued. "I figured that would give you and Mackenzie plenty of time together during the day. And Ella says we'll each have a finished pair of socks by the end of the week."

"Awesome!" said Mackenzie, and I shot her a look.

My mother turned to her. "Why don't you join us, sweetheart? My treat."

My cousin's fork paused halfway to her mouth. "Uh, that's okay, Aunt Dinah. I'm happy just to hang out here with Lauren and Pippa."

YOURS TRULY

"Yay!" cried Pippa, bouncing in her seat.

"Nonsense," my mother said. "I'll call Ella right away. I'm sure there's room for you in the class. It will be fun!"

Now I was the one with a smirk on my face.

"I wish I could take knitting lessons," said Lauren enviously, looking up from her book. Breakfast was the only time my bookworm sister was allowed to read at the table. Another Nancy Drew, I noticed: *The Secret of the Old Clock*.

"You're taking dance right now, sweetie," my mother told her. "We can do a knitting class together another time."

"Open my prethent next!" Pippa demanded, plucking a package wrapped in bright pink paper from the pile and handing it to me.

"Wow, thanks!" I told her when I opened it. She'd given me a photo of herself in a homemade frame made of Popsicle sticks covered in purple glitter.

"Belinda helped me," Pippa explained. "You can put it on your drether, and that way you won't ever forget me."

Hatcher kicked me under the table. I studiously avoided looking at him.

"No chance of that, Pipster," I said solemnly.

Lauren gave me a bookmark with an owl on it—she must have overheard me admiring it at the bookshop—and my brothers had pooled their resources on a gift certificate to the sporting goods store in West Hartfield.

"For those new swim goggles you've been wanting," said Danny.

I beamed at my family. "Thanks, everybody!"

"Wait, there's one more," said Mackenzie, and passed me a small box she'd been hiding on her lap.

"Owl earrings!" I cried happily. I don't wear much jewelry—it's too much of a pain taking it on and off all the time, what with swim practice and everything—but these were really pretty. The flat, round disks were made of sterling silver, and each one had a great horned owl etched onto it, tufted ears and all.

"Nice," said my mother as I put them on and showed them off. "Your cousin knows you well."

"Maybe they'll bring you luck in finally spotting one," Mackenzie added.

"I hope so." Adding an owl to my life list—the list all birders keep of the different species they spot—was something I'd been trying to do practically forever.

My father placed another platter of sourdough waffles on the table, and my brothers and I dove for them. I managed to snag two.

"Truly!" scolded my mother. "Leave some for the rest of us."

"How come you aren't yelling at Hatcher and Danny? They've had, like, four each already!"

Across the table from me, Hatcher held up five fingers and grinned.

My mother sighed. "I swear, it's like feeding a pack of

wolves." She spiked a fork into one of my waffles and whisked it onto Mackenzie's plate.

"Hey!" I protested.

"You have a guest," she said.

"It's just Mackenzie!"

"Truly, you know better than to sass your mother," my father chided.

"Sorry," I mumbled, not feeling sorry at all. This was my birthday breakfast, and I'd been a good sport—well, sort of—about postponing it. What was wrong with making the most of it now that it was finally here?

"What was that?" my father replied, cupping his hand behind his ear.

"Sorry, *sir*," I corrected myself. Lieutenant Colonel Jericho T. Lovejoy was a stickler for protocol.

I slathered my waffle with butter, then drenched it with syrup.

Hatcher pretended to look shocked. "Have a little waffle with your syrup, why don't you?"

My mother took the pitcher away from me and passed it to Mackenzie. "This is real maple syrup from Freeman Farm."

"The place where you guys helped out at yesterday?" my cousin asked, perking up. She glanced over at me. "The one where—"

"*Yeah*," I said, giving her the stink eye. I could feel my face growing pink.

On the way home from helping the Freemans out yesterday, I'd texted Mackenzie about Scooter's ambush. She was at the airport in Chicago waiting for her connecting flight to Boston, and had called me back immediately demanding the gruesome details.

"Can't talk now. I'm in the car. I'll tell you more when you get here," I'd whispered, and hung up.

"Tell who what?" asked Hatcher, who had ears like a bat.

"Nothing."

I hadn't had a chance to tell Mackenzie more last night, though, because her flight ended up being delayed. She didn't arrive until nearly midnight, and thanks to daily doubles—the Spring Break camp I'd signed up for that had me at swim practice both morning and afternoon—I hadn't been allowed to go pick her up at Logan Airport.

"Are you kidding me?" I'd blurted when my father told me the news.

"I am not," he'd replied. "You made a commitment, and Lovejoys always honor their commitments. Coach Maynard is expecting you at the pool at oh-six hundred, and we won't get back until the wee hours."

Most of the time I didn't think swim practice was stupid. Swimming was one of my favorite things in the entire world, and usually there was no place I'd rather be than in the pool. But when it's your birthday, and your cousin who's your best friend and whom you haven't seen since Christmas is coming to visit, trust me, you'd think it was stupid too. My father's decision was a supreme act of parental unfairness, and I told him so. Then I asked—begged—him to make an exception for once.

"Sorry, Truly," said Mr. Military. "No means no."

"But Dad, it's my *birthday*."

"You girls will have all week to visit," he'd said stubbornly.

I'd tried to stay awake anyway until Mackenzie arrived, but between running around all day at Freeman Farm and the whole drama of my close encounter with Scooter Sanchez, my eyes slammed shut the minute my head hit the pillow.

When I woke up, it was morning, and Mackenzie was snoring lightly a few feet away. My grandparents' house was huge, and there were actually two extra bedrooms for guests, but we'd wanted to be together so I'd set up the air mattress for her in my room instead.

I'd pulled on my swimsuit and sweats, then tapped her on the shoulder. "Hey."

One of Mackenzie's eyelids had fluttered open. "Huh?"

"I'm going to swim practice."

"S'nice," she'd murmured, then rolled over and went back to sleep.

And now here we were at the breakfast table, and she was about to spill the beans about my first kiss. But she took the hint, thank goodness.

"—the one where you spent your birthday?" she finished smoothly.

"Truly was a good sport," my father said, patting my shoulder.

"She sure was," said Mackenzie, grinning broadly. I gave her the stink eye again.

"Happy day-after-your-actual-birthday, fellow namesake," said my aunt, breezing in through the back door just then. She leaned down to kiss my cheek. The two of us are both named after the first Truly Lovejoy, and one of the best things about moving to Pumpkin Falls had been getting to know Aunt True better. She'd always been the family free spirit, a world traveler who rarely stayed anywhere very long, but ever since Black Monday she'd given up her "wandering ways," as Gramps and Lola put it, and moved here to Pumpkin Falls to help run the bookshop with my father. She was totally in his court.

"Nothing's more important than family," she'd said simply, when I asked her about it once.

Leaning down again, my aunt took my empty plate away and replaced it with two brightly wrapped packages.

Across the table, Pippa started bouncing in her seat again. "Open them! Open them!"

I did. Inside the bigger of the two was the bird feeder I'd wanted. I looked up at my aunt, mystified. "How did you—"

"A little bird told me," she quipped, and everyone groaned. "Sorry, I couldn't resist. It was your mother."

"Did you think we didn't notice all the hints?" said my mother, and suddenly I felt ashamed of the way I'd reacted to her present.

"Thanks, Aunt True—and thank you for the knitting lessons too, Mom," I said, jumping up to hug them both.

The second package was from Gramps and Lola. It was a book, of course. When your grandparents own a bookstore, you pretty much know what to expect every time Christmas and birthdays roll around.

"*Owls of North America*," Mackenzie read the title aloud over my shoulder in her Texas twang. "Sounds like a real page-turner."

I grinned. "Shut up."

Mackenzie loved to tease me about being a birder, but I didn't really mind. She said it was an obsession, and she was probably right. I couldn't help it, though—birds fascinated me, especially owls. The fact that I hadn't yet spotted one wasn't for lack of trying. The last time there was a full moon, I'd dragged my father out into the woods to look for owls. We'd had fun, but unfortunately that's all we'd had, and I returned home without anything to add to my life list.

My father checked his watch. "Boys, you'd better hit the road if you don't want to be late to wrestling practice." As Hatcher and Danny got up from the table, he turned to me. "Truly, you and Mackenzie may be excused as well."

"Why don't you show Mackenzie around the house, and

then take her downtown," my mother suggested. She crossed the kitchen and kissed my father. "Thanks for breakfast, handsome. I'll be at my desk if anyone needs me."

My mother's "desk" these days was the dining room table. She'd pretty much taken it over since going back to college.

"Be sure and come see me at the bookstore," Aunt True told my cousin and me.

"We will," I assured her.

My father looked over at my little sisters. "And you two young ladies have KP this morning," he said, which was military shorthand for "Kitchen Patrol."

"But it's Truly's turn to do the dishes!" Lauren protested.

"The birthday girl doesn't do dishes," I reminded her.

Pippa frowned. "No fair! Yethterday wath your birthday, not today!"

Leaving them to argue their case to Dad, I escaped to the front hall. Mackenzie was right behind me. She grabbed my arm the second we were out of earshot. "Now, tell me about the kiss!"

CHAPTER 4

"Please," I groaned. "I just ate."

"That bad, huh?" Her blue eyes sparkled with anticipation. "I want all the gory details! Scooter's the one you had to dance with at that cotillion thing, right?"

Of course she had to bring that up. "That cotillion thing" was the mandatory dance class at Daniel Webster School that I'd been forced to enroll in right after we moved to Pumpkin Falls. It was part of this stupid town tradition that had its grand finale at the annual Winter Festival, when the whole school participated in an exhibition dance. I'd gotten stuck with Scooter for my partner. In the end, it wasn't all that horrible, especially after the two of us won the "most improved" award, which came with a cash prize of $25 each. And of course there'd been that dance with Calhoun. . . . Still, dancing would never top the list of things that I was good at, or that I liked to do. Especially not with Scooter Sanchez.

"So c'mon, Truly, what happened?" Mackenzie begged.

I made a face, then gave her a play-by-play account of Scooter's surprise ambush behind the Freeman's barn. I left out the part where Calhoun saw us, though. If Mackenzie suspected that I maybe, even a teeny tiny bit, might like Calhoun, she'd pounce on it like an owl on a field mouse. I'd never hear the end of it.

"So that's it?" she said when I finished. "Scooter just walked away?"

"Uh-huh."

"He didn't try and talk to you later, or call you?"

I shook my head.

"Weird! Well, we have all week to get to the bottom of it."

"Or not," I said. Analyzing Scooter Sanchez's romantic intentions was not my idea of a fun way to spend Spring Break. "How about we drop the whole subject instead, and I give you a tour?"

She sighed. "Fine."

We started in the living room.

"Mom told me to be sure and take lots of pictures," my cousin told me, pulling out her cell phone and snapping one of the baby grand. "Nice piano. Are you taking lessons again?"

"Maybe this summer. I haven't had time yet, between swim team and everything else that's happened."

"Everything else" meaning uprooting from Texas and moving across the country, starting over at a new school, stupid cotillion, stupid math tutoring, helping out at the bookstore, solving two mysteries, and falling into a frozen river. It had been a busy winter.

"Are those the ancestors you told me about?" asked Mackenzie, pointing to the oil portraits that flanked the piano.

"Yep. That one's Nathaniel Daniel Lovejoy, and the other is his wife, Prudence."

"Nathaniel's the one who founded Lovejoy College, right?" said Mackenzie, taking another picture. "The one with the big stone pumpkin on his grave?"

I nodded. I'd sent her a picture of it that day of the field trip to the cemetery. Mackenzie loved all the oddball stuff here in Pumpkin Falls.

"Yeah, and he named a mountain and a lake after himself while he was at it," I added. "It's kind of embarrassing."

"At least he used his last name," my cousin pointed out. "It could have been worse." She struck a pose and summoned her fake radio announcer voice. "And now, a word from Nathaniel Daniel Lovejoy, founder of Nathaniel Daniel College."

We both burst out laughing. My ancestor's parents must have been total morons to pick a pair of rhyming names like that. Didn't it occur to them how much the poor kid would get teased at school? Even Pippa called him "Nathaniel Daniel looks like a spaniel."

Mackenzie stared up at the painting. "You weren't kidding when you said he has a big nose."

The "Lovejoy proboscis," as Gramps had dubbed it, was a topic of great concern at the moment for my brother Hatcher. Gramps inherited Nathaniel Daniel's nose, and so did Dad, and now Hatcher was convinced that he was starting to follow in their footsteps. At least once a week he asked me if I thought his nose had gotten bigger. I said yes, of course, just to torture him, but to be honest I didn't think it looked any different.

"This is such a cool house," Mackenzie said, gazing around.

I nodded. Coming here for our annual visits used to be the high point of the year for me. When you grow up in a military family, you move a lot, and this was the one place I could count on never to change.

My cousin gave an envious sigh as we started upstairs. "You're so lucky you get to live here."

"Except for the fact that it's in Pumpkin Falls, not Austin."

"What's so bad about Pumpkin Falls?"

I shrugged. "It's not that it's bad, it's just—not Austin."

I still really missed Texas.

I skipped the squeaky stair, but I'd forgotten to warn Mackenzie about it, and it let out a screech as she stepped on it. "That's the original Truly," I told her, pointing to the portrait hanging above it.

"J. T.!" my mother called from the dining room before I could continue.

My dad emerged from the kitchen, frowning. "What?"

"Could you maybe find time this week to fix that stair, darlin'?" my mother asked, poking her head out into the hall. "I hate to keep nagging you, but it's driving me crazy. I'm trying to work in here, and every time anyone goes upstairs or down, all I hear is *squeak squeak squeak.*"

My mother was working on a research project for her American History for Educators class at Lovejoy College. Professor Rusty was the instructor. Professor Rusty's real name was Erastus Peckinpaugh, and he was my Aunt True's boyfriend. At least we suspected he was her boyfriend. Nobody was really quite sure. Ever since the Valentine's Day dance, when my friends and I delivered his long-lost love letters to Aunt True, Professor Rusty had been spending a lot of time hanging around the bookstore with a hopeful expression on his face, and my aunt had been acting a little odd.

My father flapped his good hand. "Put it on the honey-do list, and I'll get to it soon, I promise," he told her. "I'm late for a meeting at the bookstore."

"It's been on the list for weeks," my mother grumbled as he disappeared back into the kitchen.

"What's a 'honeydew' list?" asked Mackenzie.

"Oh, you know, 'Honey do this, honey do that.'" My mother smiled. "I'm guessing Teddy has one too."

Teddy was my uncle Teddy, Mackenzie's father. He was one of my mother's six Texas brothers.

Mackenzie smiled back. "Yeah, I'm pretty sure he does too."

My mother went back to her research, and I turned to the portrait again. "So, as I was saying, that's the original Truly Lovejoy."

"The one you and your Aunt True are named after?"

I nodded.

"She's pretty."

"You think?"

"She kind of looks like you."

I knew she meant it as a compliment, but I didn't see the resemblance at all. The original Truly and I were both tall, a fact I know because it said so on her German passport, a faded document that was hanging in a frame in the upstairs hall. Aside from her name, though—which clearly said "Trudy" and not "Truly," so the idiot at U.S. customs had no excuse for messing it up and forever changing her legal name—I couldn't decipher the German script. Aunt True could. She'd lived all over the world and spoke half a dozen languages, and she translated the passport once for me. The original Trudy/Truly came from a town called Lutterhausen in Germany, shortly before the Civil War. She had just turned eighteen when she arrived in the United States. Aunt True and I both beat her by two inches, heightwise, but she was still nearly six feet, which was really tall for a woman back in those days. The passport described her as "*schlank*," which my aunt told me means "slender," and her hair and eyes were listed as *"braun"*—"brown," like both of ours. There was no mention of freckles, though, and I hadn't detected any on her portrait. I, on the other hand, had a generous helping of them.

Mackenzie took a selfie of the two of us standing in front of the portrait.

"Perfect!" she said, showing it to me. "We look adorable."

Adorable? More like an ostrich and a finch, I thought. If my cousin were a bird, she'd be something small and cute, for sure. Definitely a finch, or better, a painted bunting, like the one I'd spotted last year in Texas and that had birders in New York City all atwitter a while back when one was seen in Brooklyn. Colorful as a box of crayons, the painted bunting was one of the most eye-catching species in North America. It fit Mackenzie to a tee.

"Cameron will love this," my cousin said, tapping on her cell phone as she sent off the picture. "He still can't believe your name is actually Truly."

Her phone vibrated almost immediately in response. She read the incoming text and smiled. "Cameron says hey."

I rolled my eyes. "Hey back."

We climbed up a few more steps.

"Who's that?" Mackenzie asked, pointing to another portrait. My grandparents' entire stairwell was lined with long-gone Lovejoys.

"Matthew Lovejoy," I told her. "He was Truly's husband.

She met him just a few weeks after she arrived in New York. He was staying at the hotel where she got a job as a maid, and it was love at first sight. At least Gramps told me once that's how the story goes."

My cousin sighed. "That's so romantic! I can see why she fell for Matthew. He's really cute." She took another picture. "Is that a uniform he's wearing?"

I nodded. "He was a soldier in the Union army." Our family's military tradition went way back, lots farther than just my dad. Matthew fought in the Civil War, and there were Lovejoys who fought in the Revolutionary War too.

Mackenzie wrinkled her nose. "The Union army was the Northern one, right?"

I grinned. History had never been my cousin's thing. "Yeah."

We continued upstairs, pausing at each of the remaining Lovejoys so Mackenzie could take their pictures. "What's that jingle you told me that you made up, to help remember their names?"

"Obadiah, Abigail, Jeremiah, Ruth," I singsonged, pointing to each one in turn. "Matthew, Truly, Charity, and Booth. But it only works going downstairs."

We decided that Mackenzie should finish unpacking before I gave her the rest of the tour. I'd cleared out a couple of drawers and made space in my closet for her stuff, but there still wasn't enough room.

YOURS TRULY

"You're only here for a week!" I exclaimed, emptying another drawer. I jammed the clothes it contained under my bed. "Did you have to bring everything you own with you?"

"Just because you always dress like you're on your way to a wrestling match doesn't mean I have to," she said loftily.

I glanced down at the ratty sweats I'd thrown on after swim practice this morning. She had a point.

The corner of her mouth quirked up in a smile. "Your room looks good, at least."

Up until now Mackenzie had seen my bedroom only on her computer screen, when the two of us videoconferenced. It was Aunt True's bedroom when she was growing up, and it had always been called the "Blue Room," since it was decorated in blue and white. I had a blue bedroom at our old house back in Austin, too—our old new house, really, because we'd only lived there for a few months before we moved here to Pumpkin Falls. Mackenzie had helped me pick out the perfect shade of aqua for its walls: Mermaid. I still dreamed about that color sometimes, and I'd been thinking of asking Gramps and Lola if they'd let me repaint my room here, too. *If* we stayed, that was, which it looked like we were going to, now that the bookstore was on more solid footing.

After Mackenzie finished unpacking, I showed her the rest of the second floor.

"Six bedrooms and three bathrooms?" she said, incredulous. "This place is huge!"

"And that's just the second floor," I pointed out. "There are more in the attic."

"Really? Wow."

"People had big families back when they built the house. At least that's what Gramps told me."

Mackenzie gave me a sidelong glance. "Even bigger than the Magnificent Seven?"

That was what my father called our family. It was the title of his favorite old movie, and the theme song was the ringtone on his cell phone. I nodded. "Even bigger than the Magnificent Seven."

Mackenzie was an only child, and I knew sometimes she envied the fact that I had so many brothers and sisters. That was because she didn't actually have to live with them.

We made a quick detour to Lauren's room so my cousin could say hi to all of my younger sister's pets.

"I'd forgotten how many you have!" Mackenzie said as she made the rounds.

"Nibbles is my hamster—" Lauren began.

"And Thumper ith the bunny, and Methuthelah ith the turtle," Pippa finished.

"I want a kitten too, but Mom and Dad keep saying no," Lauren said.

"No kittens for me, either," Mackenzie sympathized. "Hooper wouldn't like it."

Hooper was my cousin's beagle. He was old as the hills

and always rolling in gross things, but she loved him anyway.

Pippa tugged on her sleeve. "Want to play Barbieth with me?"

"Um, we've got plans, Pipster," I said. "Maybe later."

We finally managed to extricate ourselves, and I led Mackenzie to the door at the end of the hallway that led to the third-floor stairs. "If you thought Lauren's room was kind of stinky, brace yourself. This is where Hatcher and Danny live."

Mackenzie followed me up the steep, narrow staircase that led to my brothers' lair. "Whew!" she exclaimed, waving her hand in front of her face when we reached the top.

"Told you so. Total man cave. That's why I mostly don't come up here. What is it about teenage boys, anyway? Their rooms always smell like a cross between sweaty gym socks and wet dog."

My cousin giggled.

"So Aunt True told me that back in the old days, the maids and hired help lived up here," I continued. "Check out their bedrooms."

I showed her a row of closet-size rooms that branched off the big, central, open area my brothers had commandeered for their headquarters.

"Are you kidding me?" Mackenzie's eyes widened. "Where are the closets?"

Nowadays, my grandparents used the tiny rooms for storage, but back when there were servants living in the house, there would have been just enough room for a twin bed and a small chair or night table. At least there were windows.

"People in those days didn't have many clothes, and servants had even fewer," I explained. "Gramps said they just hung everything on hooks." I pointed to a trio lining one of the walls next to the door.

I watched as my cousin absorbed this information.

"Not exactly Mackenzie-friendly, right?" I said with a grin.

She stuck out her tongue at me. "Hey, I can't help it if I've gotta have my closet space." Looking around, she added, "Where are the bathrooms?"

I held up a single finger, and she gave me another incredulous look. "Are you kidding me? *One?* For all those servants?"

"There probably wasn't even indoor plumbing back in the early days," I told her. "Gramps said that when he was a kid, there was still an old outhouse behind the barn."

"Eew."

"No kidding."

"So is there an attic too, or is this it?" Mackenzie asked.

"This is it, mostly. There's a little more storage space through there." I waved a hand at a door at the far end of Hatcher and Danny's lair.

"Can I see?"

"Sure."

Someone had left the light on inside. Lauren, most likely. She'd been spending a lot of time up here lately, rooting around through all the old stuff. There was a lot of it—Lovejoys hated throwing anything out. The attic was where Lauren had found all of Aunt True's childhood books, including the set of Nancy Drew mysteries, and a bunch of other relics belonging to earlier generations of ancestors. She kept showing up at the dinner table dressed in the strangest outfits. White leather gloves that nearly reached to her armpits, moth-eaten shawls, hats with veils, that sort of thing. Mom thought it was funny, but my brothers and I thought it was weird, and told Lauren so.

Mackenzie surveyed the scattered jumble of boxes and trunks and moldering magazines and random pieces of broken furniture that littered the cramped space. A dressmaker's dummy sporting a sun hat leaned against an old armchair with the stuffing hanging out of it; a battered table covered with dust held an old birdcage, one of those ancient record players you had to wind up to play, and some fishing tackle; off in the shadows toward the eaves were a bicycle and an ancient wicker baby carriage and more boxes than I could count.

"Look at all this cool old stuff!" Mackenzie took another picture.

I snorted. "You and Lauren should start a club."

"How old is this house, anyway?"

"1769. It was built the same year that Nathaniel Daniel founded the college."

"This is seriously amazing," she said. "I can't wait to tell Cameron all about it."

Cameron will love this, Cameron will love that, I thought. I could tell I was going to get really sick of hearing about Mr. Perfect by the end of the week.

It was getting close to lunchtime, so I decided to save the rest of the house, including the barn turned garage and my grandmother's art studio above it, for later. "We'd better get going, if you want to see some of Pumpkin Falls before afternoon swim practice."

We stopped by my room to pick up our gear. Since Mackenzie was on a swim team back in Austin, I'd been given special permission from Coach Maynard to bring her along to practice this week at Spring Break camp.

"We can leave our stuff at the bookshop and pick it up right before practice," I said. "That way we don't have to come all the way home for it. Oh, and I have one more thing to show you," I added as we fished our jackets out of the front hall closet.

"What?"

I led my cousin to the tiny phone booth under the stairs and opened the door. "This."

My grandparents were just about the only people on the planet who still had a landline, and the dank closet with the faded, peeling wallpaper was where they kept their ancient rotary phone. My dad claimed it was the same one that was there when he was a kid.

"Gramps and Lola are true Yankees," he liked to tell us. "Thrifty to the core. You know your grandfather's favorite saying, right? 'Use it up, wear it out, make it do, or do without.'"

The phone booth was one place in the house that I could certainly do without. "I hate it when I have to take a call in here," I told Mackenzie.

She poked her head in and wrinkled her nose at the musty smell. "Yeah, but it's still kind of cool. That phone is totally retro—check out that vintage dial!"

I closed the door. "Um, yeah. My point exactly."

Glancing over at another door just beyond the phone closet, Mackenzie asked, "Where does that go?"

Now that I thought about it, there were two places in the house that I could do without.

"The basement," I replied. "Trust me, you don't want to go down there."

"Sure I do! I want to see everything!"

I sighed. "Don't say I didn't warn you."

I watched from the safety of the hallway as she tiptoed down and took a quick peek around. Quick, because the basement was always freezing cold, for one thing—the house still had its original dirt floor and stone foundation—and quick, because, well, my brothers didn't call it the spider farm for nothing.

I wasn't afraid of a whole lot of things, but spiders

combined with my grandparents' dark, creepy basement? I shuddered.

"Okay, you were right," Mackenzie said, clattering upstairs again a moment later.

I closed the door firmly behind her. "We definitely don't need to go down there again."

CHAPTER 5

"This whole place is like a movie set," Mackenzie said happily a few minutes later, as we headed down Hill Street into town. "Fade in to Pumpkin Falls," she intoned, slipping into her fake radio announcer voice again, "a small, charming New England college town—"

"Emphasis on *small*," I added.

"—complete with historic houses," she continued, ignoring me, "a church with a steeple that I want a tour of, by the way, so don't forget, a village green, a world-famous waterfall—"

I snorted. "World famous? Right."

"—and crowning it all, a spectacular covered bridge."

Snapping pictures right and left, my cousin continued her breathless narration all the way to the bookstore, where she made me stand under the LOVEJOY'S BOOKS sign so she could take yet another picture for Mr. Perfect.

"It's Miss Marple!" she cried when we finally went inside.

My grandparents' golden retriever, who'd been napping on her dog bed by the sales counter, heaved herself up and trotted over, tail wagging.

"Take a picture of us," Mackenzie ordered, passing me her cell phone.

"Greetings and salutations, girls!" said Aunt True, emerging from the back office. "You're just in time for a snack."

"Pumpkin whoopie pies?" asked Mackenzie hopefully.

My heart sank. I'd sung the praises of our bookshop's signature treat to my cousin, but, to be perfectly honest, I was kind of tired of pumpkin whoopie pies. They'd certainly proven a success—my mother says Aunt True is a marketing genius, and one of her bright ideas was to create a treat designed to lure customers into the store. The strategy had worked, as people often stopped by for a whoopie pie and rarely left without buying something. But I'd eaten so many in the past month that I didn't think I could choke down another one.

"Sorry, Mackenzie, but I decided to switch it up in honor of Maple Madness," my aunt told her. "May I present . . . Bookshop Blondies!" She pulled a tray out from beneath the sales counter and whipped off the tea towel that was covering it.

"Mmm," said Mackenzie, reaching for what looked like a brownie, only lighter in color. I took one too.

"Oh man, these are *delicious*," said my cousin, grabbing a second one before she'd even finished her first.

"That would be the secret ingredient," Aunt True told her, looking pleased.

I paused midbite. One of my aunt's last secret ingredients had been yak milk.

"Maple sugar," she continued, and I relaxed. "I'm going to enter them into the Maple Madness Bake-Off."

The annual Bake-Off was another Pumpkin Falls tradition. From what I heard, the competition could get pretty heated, which was kind of ridiculous, especially since there weren't any prizes. Just a blue ribbon and stupid Maple Madness Bake-Off winner bragging rights. But that was Pumpkin Falls for you.

There was a commotion in the back corner of the store just then, and my aunt looked over and sighed. "If you have time, girls, maybe you could help Belinda," she said. "We're just about ready to send another shipment to Namibia."

A couple of weeks ago my aunt had come up with another marketing idea. One of my grandparents' Peace Corps projects was building a library for the school in the Namibian village where they're staying, and Aunt True decided that it would be fun to help fill its shelves—drumming up a little extra business for our store while we were at it.

The Buy a Book, Send a Book campaign invited every customer who bought a book to buy a second one to donate to the new school library in Africa. If they did, they got a 50 percent off coupon for their next purchase. My aunt downloaded photos of our grandparents with the village kids, and used the pictures to design a really cool flyer and poster for the window. She advertised the program on our website and in our newsletter, and she got the *Pumpkin Falls Patriot-Bugle* to write an article about it too. Everyone in town knew Gramps and Lola, and their faces, along with all those smiling village kids, had been like catnip to our customers. So far, we'd shipped off three big boxes of books for the new library.

"Add this to Miss Marple's Picks while you're at it, would you, Truly?" my aunt said, passing me a book. "Face out, please."

Miss Marple's Picks was another of my aunt's promotional ideas, a twist on the typical "staff picks" shelf that most bookstores offer. Not only had it increased sales, but it had also turned my grandparents' dog into a minor celebrity. Miss Marple had been profiled by newspapers all over the world, and she even had her own column in our bookshop newsletter (ghostwritten by Aunt True, of course).

Helping myself to another Bookshop Blondie, I made a quick detour to Miss Marple's Picks, where I shelved the book my aunt had given me. Then, trailing Mackenzie in my wake, I headed back to the children's section to help box up more books for Namibia.

"No, Harold, you may not go to Africa!" I heard Belinda

scolding as we approached. Her voice was oddly muffled, thanks to the fact that she was leaning so far down into an open cardboard box that only her bottom was visible. The bottom in question appeared to be covered with another pair of overalls—white ones this time.

"Um, anything we can do to help?" I asked.

Belinda straightened. Swiveling around, she removed one of her earbuds and thrust a kitten at my startled cousin. "Here," she ordered. "Hold Harold."

Mackenzie blinked in surprise, but did as she was told.

"Wait a minute!" Belinda peered more closely at her. "You're not Lauren!"

"Um, no," my cousin replied meekly. "I'm Mackenzie."

Belinda's eyes narrowed. "Mackenzie-from-Texas?"

My cousin nodded.

"Well, all right then." Fishing in the pocket of her overalls, Belinda pulled out a lint-covered breath mint and popped it in her mouth. Sucking on it loudly, she smiled. "Welcome to Pumpkin Falls."

"Uh, thanks?" said Mackenzie.

I smothered a grin, watching as my cousin got her first dose of Belinda Winchester. I'd told her lots of stories about our retired lunch lady turned bookseller, but it was nothing like having the full experience for herself.

Belinda had shucked off yesterday's orange and reverted to her purple phase. My cousin's eyes drifted from Belinda's white painter's overalls to the purple-and-white-striped turtleneck underneath, then on down to the purple-and-white-striped socks and purple sneakers. For once, Belinda wasn't wearing a hat, and she'd combed her dandelion fluff of white hair into a semblance of neatness. Reaching into another pocket, she pulled out a long purple feather, which she twirled between her fingers, a thoughtful expression on her face.

To celebrate Belinda becoming a silent partner in the bookshop and taking over the mystery section—and to help her be a little more presentable to the public, I suspected—Aunt True had taken her on a clothes shopping spree a few weeks ago. This was a prime example of the blind leading the blind and a big mistake, if you asked me, which nobody ever did. Between the two of them, there was more "local color," as they called it in New England, here in our bookshop now than just about anywhere else in town.

"I have a gentleman caller," Belinda announced abruptly, with another twirl of her feather.

"Um, that's nice?" I replied, not quite sure what a gentleman caller was. It couldn't be what it sounded like. Belinda was way too old to have a boyfriend.

The bell over the bookshop door jingled, and Belinda quickly thrust the feather behind her ear. She removed it just as quickly as my father came in.

He looked around as if he were expecting someone to salute. That rarely happened in Pumpkin Falls—never, actually—but my father hadn't completely transitioned out of military mode yet, even though he'd been a civilian for nine months.

"True?" he called, frowning.

My aunt emerged from behind the sales counter. "You rang?"

"Memphis is on the loose again," my father reported. "Lou said that Mr. Henry said that Ed Sanchez saw him just now sitting in one of the rocking chairs down on the General Store porch."

I was guessing that wasn't a sentence my father ever imagined coming out of his mouth back before Black Monday. Pumpkin Falls was the kind of place that did that to you, though.

Aunt True sighed. "Spring fever. Happens every year, no matter where we're living. I'll take care of it."

As she headed out to round up her cat, my father waved to Mackenzie and Belinda and me, then disappeared into the back office.

A few minutes later, as we were finishing up the shipment for Namibia, the bell over the bookshop door jangled again. Belinda's purple feather instantly swooped back behind her ear as someone bounded across the bookstore toward us.

"My angel!" cried the someone.

Beside me, Mackenzie gasped. "Is that—"

"Yep," I whispered. "Captain Romance, in the flesh."

Captain Romance was what Hatcher and I called Augustus Wilde. He was our town's resident celebrity, a romance writer whose books were published under his pen name, Augusta Savage. There were a whole bunch of his titles over in what my brother had dubbed the "shirtless men kissing beautiful women" section. Augustus liked to come in every few days and check on sales. He also liked to rearrange the shelves so that his books were facing out, and I'd caught him trying to sneak them in with Miss Marple's Picks too.

Augustus was kind of a pest.

"Purple becomes you, my sweet, like heather on the bonnie highland moors," he cooed to Belinda, who made a noise I'd never heard her make before. It sounded alarmingly like a giggle.

Wait a minute, I thought. Was Augustus Belinda Winchester's *gentleman caller*? No way! I turned toward my cousin and surreptitiously mimed sticking my finger down my throat. Mackenzie pressed her lips together, trying hard not to laugh.

"As I wrote in my latest *New York Times* best seller, *Sweet Savage Siren*, 'Spring is here, the sap is rising, and so is love,'" Augustus continued.

This time my cousin couldn't contain herself, and neither could I.

"Mock me if you must," said Augustus, clearly wounded by our laughter. He flipped back his mane of silver hair and struck a dramatic pose. Which was easy to do when you were wearing a purple cape. Eyeing it, it suddenly dawned on me why Belinda had been decking herself in purple lately. "But as the great poet Tennyson says, 'In the Spring a young man's fancy lightly turns to thoughts of love.'"

I stared at Augustus. Seriously? A young man's fancy? He had to be eighty if he was a day, and Belinda, well, Belinda had been ancient when my dad was a kid.

The bell over the door jingled once again. This time it was Aunt True, with Memphis tucked firmly under one arm. She crossed the bookstore to join us.

"Greeting and salutations!" she said to Augustus, then turned to me. "Truly, would you mind putting Memphis upstairs? I think there's less of a risk of him escaping again if I just keep him in my apartment for now."

I took the cat eagerly, glad for any excuse to be spared more senior citizen lovebird talk. Before I could head off, though, the bell over the door jangled yet again.

"Uh-oh," I muttered under my breath to Mackenzie, when I saw who it was. "Incoming."

"What is the meaning of this?" demanded Ella Bellow.

"Greetings and salutations to you, too!" Aunt True replied mildly. "What is the meaning of what?"

Ella shook a finger toward the front of the store. "That window, is what!"

Aunt True and I exchanged a glance. What could Ella

possibly find objectionable about our front window? The two of us had stayed up late Friday night to finish it in time for Maple Madness kickoff weekend, and we'd devoted an entire corner to welcoming Ella's new knitting shop to the neighborhood.

"You have *Maple Country Mufflers* on display!" Ella sputtered. "It's one of the exact same books I'm selling at A Stitch in Time—you're competing with me!"

"Have a Bookshop Blondie, Ella," my aunt said soothingly, scooping the tray off the sales counter and holding it out. "We'll take the book out of the window. It's nothing to get worked up about—I had no idea you were planning to stock it too. Competing with you is the farthest thing from our mind."

Somewhat mollified, Ella selected a treat. Her dark eyes gleamed as she spotted my cousin. "You must be Mackenzie."

My cousin nodded warily.

"I heard you were coming to town—"

"Told you this place was small," I whispered to Mackenzie.

"—and I want to know all about you."

Memphis squirmed in my arms as Ella began pumping Mackenzie for information. She might have retired as the Pumpkin Falls postmistress, but Ella Bellow was still in the full-time gossip business.

"I see Rusty has been spending a lot of time here at the bookshop lately," Ella said to my aunt when she was done extracting Mackenzie's age, height, grade in school, hobbies, favorite color (green), and parents' names and occupations.

Aunt True nodded. "Indeed."

My aunt likes to torment Ella by giving one-word answers to her "fishing expeditions," as she calls Ella's nosy interrogations.

"I suppose it's only natural, seeing as how he's still a bachelor and seeing as how you're still single. You two used to date back in high school, right?"

"Yes," said my aunt.

"The two of you aren't getting any younger, you know."

"No," agreed my aunt.

Ella's mouth pruned up, but Aunt True just smiled sweetly. I smothered a grin. My aunt was rapidly elevating her evasion technique to an indoor sport.

Ella tried a different tack. "Speaking of couples, you two aren't the only ones in town keeping company. I've noticed that Amelia Winthrop has been spending a great deal of time at the coin and stamp shop."

Really? I thought in surprise. I knew Lucas liked spending time with Bud Jefferson, but his mother did too?

"Interesting," was my aunt's only comment.

Nothing escaped Ella's eagle eye, it seemed. I was just glad she hadn't seen Scooter kissing me behind the Freemans' barn, or I'd be the one undergoing the third degree right now.

Before Ella could ask any more questions, the bell over

the bookshop door jangled once again, and Franklin Freeman came in hefting a large box.

"Need some help?" asked Aunt True.

As I started to follow her to the front of the store, Memphis twisted out of my arms and made a dash for freedom. In a furry flash of spring fever, he squeezed through the door just before it swung shut.

"Blast that cat!" My aunt put her hands on her hips and scowled.

"Mackenzie and I will round him up again, Aunt True," I told her.

My father emerged from the office. "What's going on out here?" he asked, then saw Franklin. "Oh good, more maple supplies. Those little jugs of syrup sold like hotcakes this weekend, and we're running low." Lovejoy's Books did a brisk business in "sidelines," the official term for all the stuff besides books that our store sells, and the merchandise from Freeman Farm was among our most popular. "Nice turnout at your place yesterday!" my father added, clapping my classmate on the back with his good hand. "Your parents must be pleased."

Franklin nodded. He didn't look pleased, though. He looked miserable.

"Is something the matter, son?" my father asked, peering at him.

"Someone's been stealing our sap!" Franklin blurted.

We all stared at him.

"You mean from the barn store?" I asked.

He shook his head. "Not syrup, *sap*! They're taking it right from our trees!"

Ella's dark eyes gleamed again. At last, a piece of gossip she could sink her teeth into!

"Bad blood—or should I say bad *sap*—right here in Pumpkin Falls," she said with a delighted shiver. "Imagine that!"

CHAPTER 6

Lucas Winthrop was in love with my cousin Mackenzie.

He might as well have fallen in love with my left shoe.

Mackenzie was oblivious, of course. She was too wrapped up in Mr. Perfect Cameron McAllister to notice someone else. Especially someone else like Lucas Winthrop.

Everything seemed normal at first when we got to the pool for afternoon practice. Mackenzie and I changed into our suits and went out onto the pool deck, where we started the warm-up stretches that Coach Maynard had posted on the whiteboard.

"Who's the kid who looks like a stalk of celery?" Mackenzie whispered as Lucas emerged from the men's locker room.

"Lucas Winthrop," I whispered back. "I told you about him, remember?"

I still sometimes felt the need to avert my eyes when I saw Lucas in a swimsuit. He was so skinny, it was painful.

"Oh yeah—helicopter mother."

Lucas went about seven shades of red when I introduced them.

"Uh . . . hi," he stuttered, then just stood there looking at Mackenzie, dazed.

"Okay, everyone in the water!" said Coach Maynard, clapping his hands. He flipped the whiteboard over to reveal the afternoon workout. I groaned. He obviously wasn't planning to go easy on us over Spring Break.

Everyone got into the pool except Lucas, who continued to stand rooted to the spot. He looked like he was going to throw up.

"What's the matter with you, Winthrop?" Coach frowned at him. "You'd better not barf on my pool deck!"

"I'm fine," Lucas squeaked, his voice shooting up an octave as he jolted out of his trance and scuttled into the water.

It was clear he was anything but, though. He kept lifting his goggles and peeking at Mackenzie, for one thing. He did it once right in the middle of one of his laps, and swallowed so much water that he almost choked. Coach Maynard had to fish him out with the pool's lifesaving hook.

When it finally dawned on me what was wrong with him, I almost laughed out loud.

Lucas was a nice guy and everything, but crushing on my cousin? There wasn't a girl on the face of the planet—well, in Pumpkin Falls, at least—who would describe Lucas as Mr. Perfect. Mr. Scrawny and Undersized was more like it. He didn't stand a chance.

Despite Lucas's erratic behavior, swim practice went well, and Coach Maynard singled Mackenzie out several times for praise. He told her he'd be proud to have her on our swim team if she lived in Pumpkin Falls, which I could tell pleased her.

"I think we can do something this week to put some polish on that flip turn of yours," he added with a wink. "We'll send you back to Texas all charged up and ready to go."

Later, in the locker room, Mackenzie brought up the subject of Lucas. "I know he's your friend and all, but what's with the way he stares at people?"

I smiled. At "people"? *You're the only one he was staring at*, I wanted to tell her, but we had a whole week together, and she'd eventually figure things out for herself. Meanwhile, there was no point depriving myself of the fun of watching the *Lucas in Love* show.

So all I said was, "He's actually really nice," and then changed the subject. "You want to stop by the General Store on the way home? We could get ice cream."

Lucas was lying in wait for us outside the rec center.

"Why, thank you," drawled Mackenzie, her voice all full of Texas honey as he sprinted over and held the door for us. "Aren't you the gentleman!"

I don't think Lucas's feet actually touched the pavement the entire length of Main Street.

YOURS TRULY

When we reached Lou's Diner, the door flew open and Mrs. Winthrop popped out, like a bird from a cuckoo clock. She'd obviously been watching for her son. Lucas's mother kept him on a really tight leash and tended to panic if he was the least bit late for anything.

"There you are, sweetie!" she said. "I was beginning to get worried. You're usually so prompt."

Lucas looked like he wished the sidewalk would open up and swallow him. As Mackenzie and I said good-bye, his face flushed scarlet. His mother looked at him anxiously. "You're not coming down with a fever, are you?" She held the back of her hand to his forehead.

Spring fever, maybe, I thought, suppressing a smile. Could Augustus Wilde be right with all his poetic talk about springtime and rising sap? Was love bubbling up around Pumpkin Falls the way the sap was rising in the maple trees? The thought of maple trees made me think of Freeman Farm, and my smile faded. Between the sap theft and Scooter's ambush, I had plenty of reasons not to want to be reminded of that right now.

"We'd better get some chicken soup into you," Mrs. Winthrop added, hustling her son inside. "Bye, girls!"

Mackenzie and I continued on past the Starlite Dance Studio and Mahoney's Antiques and the Suds 'n Duds, then paused to look at the window display at the *Pumpkin Falls Patriot-Bugle*.

"This maple thing is a big deal around here, isn't it?" said Mackenzie.

"Everything's a big deal around here," I replied, eyeing today's headline: MAPLE MADNESS KICKOFF WEEKEND DRAWS RECORD CROWDS! From the newspaper's breathless coverage, you'd think alien life had been discovered on Mars.

We crossed the street to the General Store. Inside, I spotted Scooter and Calhoun at the ice cream counter. My stomach lurched. So much for not being reminded about Freeman Farm. I really wasn't ready to face either of my classmates again just yet.

Running into them was unavoidable, though, in a town the size of this one. *Might as well get it over with*, I thought glumly.

"Hey, guys," I muttered, and they turned around.

"Hey, Truly!" said Scooter, all smiles.

Calhoun didn't say a word. He didn't smile, either.

"This is my cousin Mackenzie," I told them, suddenly conscious of the fact that my damp hair was still plastered to my head. Mackenzie's hair was perfect, of course. She'd taken the time to blow-dry her strawberry blond Gifford curls—the very same kind that Pippa was born with—and they looked as perky as she did.

"Hello, boys!" My cousin's voice was dripping with Texas honey again, and she smiled the same Gifford sunflower smile at them that I see every day on my mother and Hatcher.

A funny expression settled over Scooter's face, somewhere between dazed and thunderstruck. It was a look I'd seen before. Quite recently, in fact. Lucas had been wearing it back at the pool. *Another one bites the dust*, I thought in amazement.

I didn't know whether to be annoyed, disgusted, or relieved. Annoyed, because even though I absolutely truly didn't care a speck for Scooter, it still hurt my pride a little to be passed over so quickly. Disgusted, because, well, Mackenzie and Scooter Sanchez? Eew. And relieved, because at least I wouldn't have to worry about Scooter trying to kiss me again. In the space of a split second, he'd transferred his affections to my cousin.

Mackenzie turned to Calhoun. "What did you say your name was?"

"Calhoun," he replied. "That's not my first name, though. My first name is Romeo."

My mouth dropped open. This was the first time I'd ever heard Calhoun voluntarily offer up this bit of information. He hated his real name.

Mackenzie laughed her breezy little laugh. "Romeo! I like it."

He smiled.

"Hey, did you guys talk to Franklin yet?" I asked, more by way of inserting myself into the conversation than anything else. It was becoming increasingly clear that with Mackenzie in town, I might as well be invisible. Which was kind of ironic, since for a long time after we first moved here I'd actually wished that I *were* invisible—"stealth mode," I called it. I didn't like sticking out, and stealth mode had always been my fallback position after one of our moves, which were numerous, since we were an active-duty military family until recently.

But I didn't like being ignored, either.

And if I were honest with myself, I'd have to admit I particularly didn't like being ignored by Mr. Romeo Calhoun.

At my question, my classmates managed to drag their eyes away from Mackenzie.

"No," said Scooter. "Why?"

I explained about the sap theft and how worked up Franklin had been about it.

"Sounds like a job for the Pumpkin Falls Private Eyes," said Calhoun, flicking me a glance.

My mouth dropped open again. Calhoun hated that name almost as much as he hated Romeo. He was the one who'd teased me the most about how dorky it was when I made it up last month after my friends and I got involved solving a couple of mysteries.

"Or not," he added coolly, looking away.

"I didn't know we were still a thing," I said. "The, uh, private eyes, I mean," I added quickly, when he glanced over at me again.

He shrugged.

"Great idea!" said Scooter, looking at my cousin to see what she thought. "It's pretty exciting, solving mysteries."

I could barely watch this. He was practically flexing his muscles for her.

"Cha Cha and Jasmine aren't here," I objected. "There is no Pumpkin Falls Private Eyes without the two of them."

"I could help," Mackenzie offered.

Scooter lit up at this suggestion. "Yeah!"

Everyone seemed to be looking to me to decide, even Calhoun. I stood there awkwardly, conscious of his gaze.

He's probably just eager to spend time with my cousin, I thought. *Same as Scooter.*

On the other hand, did it really matter, considering what hung in the balance? A major loss of sap—and the syrup it was turned into—could spell disaster for Franklin's family. Their farm really depended on all those maple sales. If there was something we could do to help, didn't we owe it to our friends to try?

"Well, okay, I guess," I said finally.

The four of us agreed to meet at my house the next morning after swim practice. From there we'd head to Freeman Farm to examine the scene of the crime.

"We'll tell Lucas on our way home," said Scooter as we took our ice cream cones outside and headed to the rocking chairs lining the General Store's porch.

The sun dipped behind the trees and the wind began to pick

up. Mackenzie shivered. "Y'all are nuts, eating ice cream in this weather," she said, but I noticed she didn't stop licking her cone.

"Maple *wal*nuts," I quipped, and my friends all groaned obligingly.

A few minutes later Scooter and Calhoun took off for Lou's, and Mackenzie and I started up the hill for home.

"You're really lucky, you know, getting to live here," she said.

I grunted. "You told me that already. I'd still trade it for Austin in a hot second, though."

"Seriously? Why?"

It was hard to explain. I didn't hate Pumpkin Falls the way I did when we first moved here—it was growing on me, in fact—but it didn't feel like home yet, either. And life in Austin seemed so simple in comparison, especially right now. There were no mixed-up feelings about Romeo Calhoun in Austin.

We turned off Hill Street onto Maple, and Mackenzie suddenly stopped in her tracks. "Whoa!" she said, pointing at a tree branch overhead. "Is that what I think it is?"

I looked up. Peering through the dusk, I stared at the large bird perched on the limb above us. It stared back, unblinking. "Uh, yeah," I replied, stunned.

It was an owl.

Mackenzie whipped out her cell phone and began furiously snapping pictures. "Cameron won't believe this! What kind of owl is it?"

"A barred owl," I whispered. I'd seen only about a zillion pictures of them, including one in the new book that Gramps and Lola had given me for my birthday. "Scientific name *Strix varia*; native to North America; also known as the hoot owl. It's the only owl in the eastern United States whose eyes are brown, not orange or yellow."

Brown eyes just like mine, I thought, transfixed.

"Well, aren't you just a fountain of information," drawled my cousin, still snapping away.

The owl didn't seem in any hurry to leave. It posed obligingly as Mackenzie continued to take pictures, and then, after a minute or two, finally spread its wings. Flapping once, it swooped away over our heads.

My heart squeezed tight with happiness as I watched its silent flight. I'd never seen anything more beautiful in my entire life.

Mackenzie clutched my arm. "How cool was that?" she squealed as we watched the owl glide into a thicket of trees across the road and disappear.

"Unbelievably cool!" I squealed back. Even as I said the words, though, I could feel a sour aftertaste of disappointment curdling my joy.

Joy, because finally—*finally*—after so many years of trying, I'd seen an owl in the wild!

Disappointment, because Mackenzie was the one who'd spotted it, not me.

It shouldn't have mattered, but somehow it did. I followed my cousin home, feeling deflated.

This was almost worse than yesterday's kiss.

And being overlooked by a boy I might actually like.

I was pretty sure I wanted to go back to being twelve again.

CHAPTER 7

"Directly into the shower, boys," my mother said, pointing to the back stairs as Hatcher and Danny barged into the kitchen.

"Something smells good!" said Danny, sniffing the air appreciatively.

"It sure isn't you!" I retorted, backing away. There was nothing worse than post–wrestling practice brothers.

"I want your dirty clothes in the wash too," my mother continued. "All of them. I was upstairs earlier today and found things lurking under your beds that could have walked to the laundry room all by themselves."

My brothers laughed.

"I'm serious," said my mother, putting her hands on her hips. But she was smiling, too. She shook the wooden spoon she was holding for emphasis. "No roast chicken unless you—and your clothes—are spotless."

Hearing this threat, my brothers quickly trotted off.

"Whew!" Mackenzie held her nose as they wafted past.

"And you keep saying you wish you had brothers," I reminded her.

"Truly, would you mind popping next door and feeding Bilbo?" My mother turned back to the stove. She was stirring something. Mashed potatoes, from the looks of it. Dinner couldn't come soon enough for me, despite our recent ice cream break.

"Who's Bilbo?" asked my cousin.

"A ferret," I told her. "Our neighbors are in Bermuda for Spring Break and we're taking care of him."

"That's a funny name for a ferret," Mackenzie said.

"They named him after Bilbo Baggins in *The Hobbit*," I explained. "Because he likes to explore."

Technically, my sister Lauren was the one who was supposed to be ferret-sitting. She was the big animal lover in the family. Me? If it had feathers and wings, I was all over it. Fur or scales? Not so much—although I had to admit I'd taken a shine to Miss Marple. Probably because she'd taken a shine to me. I seemed to be her favorite Lovejoy, at least while Gramps and Lola were away.

"Where's Lauren?" I asked my mother. "She's the one in charge of Bilbo."

"She and Pippa are still at Belinda's."

Belinda's Spring Break camp kicked off this afternoon. My sisters both whined so much about the fact that I got to have

Mackenzie come visit that Belinda offered to do something just for them. Nobody was exactly sure what—arts and crafts projects like Pippa's glitter and Popsicle stick frame, maybe, or a little baking, maybe. A whole lot of kittens, that was for sure.

I turned to Mackenzie. "Want to come with me?"

She shook her head. "Mind if I skip it? I'm a little jet-lagged, and I should probably call my parents. I promised I'd check in today."

"No problem."

She headed upstairs, and I grabbed my barn jacket from its hook by the kitchen door and went back outside.

The house next door looked a lot like my grandparents' house, except that the shutters and front door were painted black instead of green. I was guessing it was built around the same time that Nathaniel Daniel built ours.

The Mitchells had been Gramps and Lola's neighbors for as long as I could remember. They both worked at Lovejoy College. They didn't have any kids of their own, but thanks to their jobs—they were both professors—there were always lots of students hanging out at their house.

Not this week, though.

I made a short detour to fill our bird feeders and top off the water in the birdbath. Gramps left me with a list of instructions for caring for his "feathered friends," as he called them, and I'd been really good about keeping up with everything.

Thinking about his list of instructions reminded me that I needed to add "barred owl" to my life list tonight. Mine was still pretty measly compared to my grandfather's, but then he'd been keeping his a lot longer than I had.

I collected the mail from the Mitchells' mailbox, then fished the spare key out from under the welcome mat by the back door. Not the most original place to keep a key, but the fact was, hardly anybody locked their doors here in Pumpkin Falls. Gramps and Lola went to Mexico for a vacation one winter a few years ago and accidentally left their house unlocked the entire month they were away! They were also the ones who kept the bookstore cash inside a hollowed-out trigonometry textbook—I guess they figured nobody in their right mind would think of stealing that. Dad about had a fit when he found out. One of the first things he did when he took over the store was open a proper bank account.

Inside, I plopped the mail into the basket on the kitchen counter, then crossed the room to the enormous cage where Bilbo spent most of his time. Mr. Mitchell was crazy about ferrets—"the smartest pet imaginable!" he liked to boast—and Bilbo was completely spoiled. He had all sorts of toys and plastic tubes to run around in, plus a little ferret-size hammock for sleeping.

I tapped tentatively on his cage. "Hey, buddy."

Bilbo was already pacing back and forth. He knew what was coming next.

YOURS TRULY

"That's right, it's playtime," I said, gingerly unlatching the cage door.

I let out a screech and jumped back as the ferret darted past me. I watched as he ran in circles around the room, then began gleefully romping on the furniture in a way that would get us Lovejoy kids hollered at big-time if we did the same thing at home. Leaving the ferret to his fun, I changed his litter and fixed him a snack.

"Mmm, your favorite," I said, reaching into the container of ferret treats and holding one out to him.

Bilbo dashed across the room and snatched it from me, then made a beeline for the basement door.

Someone had left it open.

"Wait, no!" I cried. *My stupid sister! How could she have forgotten?* Lauren was the one getting paid for this, not me. I chased after the ferret, but he was too quick for me. He slipped through the door lickety-split. I heard his little feet pattering down the stairs, and then—silence.

I stood at the top, staring down into the darkness. Flipping on the light didn't help. The Mitchells' basement was just as creepy as Gramps and Lola's. Plus, the house was deserted, which made it extra creepy.

"Bilbo?" I called, embarrassed at how shaky my voice sounded. I descended the stairs reluctantly, every hair on the back of my neck standing at attention. Pausing at the bottom, I called the ferret's name again.

A moment later, something raced across my feet, and I nearly leaped out of my skin.

"Bilbo! Get over here!" I shouted.

There was no point trying to chase him. There were too many places in the basement to hide. I'd have to outwit him instead.

Running back upstairs, I grabbed the container of treats and stepped behind the open basement door. "Bilbo!" I called again, rattling the container enticingly.

Silence.

I gave it another shake, and this time there was a tentative scrabbling at the base of the stairs.

"Bilbo! Cookies!"

The ferret knew that word. In a flash, he came bounding up the stairs, and the second he was through the door I slammed it shut behind him. "Gotcha!"

Bilbo skidded to a stop and eyed me reproachfully.

"Sorry for spoiling your fun," I told him. "But I don't have all night."

Inching backward across the room toward his cage, I placed ferret treats on the floor like bread crumbs on a trail. "Come on, buddy," I coaxed. "This way."

He gave the first one a suspicious sniff, but the treats proved irresistible, and in a few moments he was back in captivity.

"You be a good boy now," I told him, latching the cage

firmly. "Lauren will be over to play with you tomorrow."

My pest of a sister owed me big-time for this one. Grabbing my coat, I locked the door, then slipped the key back in its hiding place and went home.

"There you are," said my mother as I came through the back door. "Right in time to set the table."

"But I just—"

"No buts, young lady. Your birthday is officially over."

"Yes, ma'am," I said meekly.

"I'll help," offered Mackenzie, reappearing in the kitchen just then.

"How are your folks?" my mother asked.

"Surviving without me."

"We're eating in the dining room tonight, girls," my mother continued. "I've cleared my books and things away. We'll need places for ten."

"Ten?" I frowned. "Who else is coming?"

"Your aunt and Professor Rusty."

I made a face at Mackenzie. "Prepare to be bored out of your gourd."

"Truly!" my mother frowned.

"Sorry, ma'am," I said.

It was true, though. Professor Rusty—a.k.a. Erastus Peckinpaugh a.k.a. Professor Punkinpie, as Pippa called him—was a full-fledged nerd. He was really nice and everything, and sometimes he could be funny, so I could see why my aunt liked him, but he was totally fixated on history. I mean *totally*. Especially the Civil War. He felt the same way about the Civil War as I did about birds, and swimming, and sudoku.

Last time he came to dinner, we were treated to a lecture on the Fighting Fifth, New Hampshire's most famous Civil War regiment. Professor Rusty belonged to a group of Civil War reenactors—excuse me, "living historians" was the proper term, according to him—who were named for soldiers in the Fighting Fifth. He was all excited that we'd moved here, because Matthew Lovejoy, the original Truly's husband, belonged to that regiment, and he was trying to talk one of my brothers into joining the group and portraying him. Danny wasn't interested, but Hatcher, surprisingly, was seriously considering it. When I gave him a hard time about it, he just looked at me and said "life list."

In other words, people who live in glass houses shouldn't throw stones.

I guess he had a point. Everybody has their obsessions.

My cell phone buzzed as we were finishing up setting the table. "It's Jasmine and Cha Cha," I told Mackenzie. "Check it out."

"No fair!" she cried, peering over my shoulder to see the selfie they'd sent of the two of them lounging on a beach. "Where are they again?"

"Key West."

"Sweet."

YOURS TRULY

I texted back, telling them briefly about the sap theft at Freeman Farm and the resurrection of the Pumpkin Falls Private Eyes. CHECKING OUT SCENE OF CRIME TOMORROW, I added. WILL LET YOU KNOW IF WE FIND ANYTHING.

SAY HI TO FRANKLIN FOR ME! Jasmine texted back.

Franklin Freeman was Jasmine's Mr. Perfect. Except he didn't know it yet.

"Anything else we can do to help, Aunt Dinah?" Mackenzie asked as we returned to the kitchen.

"That's sweet of you to offer," my mother replied, "but I think I have the rest of it under control."

Hatcher and Danny and Lauren and I had been doing a lot of the cooking these past few months since our move to Pumpkin Falls. My father was the one who came up with that plan, as a way to help Mom now that she was going back to college full-time. She'd told us we were all off the hook for Spring Break, though.

"Y'all have been juggling a lot, and I appreciate it," she'd said. "You've earned a real vacation."

There was a knock on the front door just then.

"Truly, would you get that?" asked my mother, pulling the roast chicken out of the oven.

I watched Mackenzie's face as I introduced her to Professor Rusty. I could hardly wait to ask what she thought of him. They're kind of an odd couple, my hippie-dippie aunt and her absentminded professor.

Professor Rusty would almost be handsome, if it weren't for that wild hair of his, which was dark and bushy and way too long, in an Albert Einsteiny kind of way. He'd been perpetually underfoot ever since the Valentine's Day dance, when the Pumpkin Falls Private Eyes revealed him to be the author of some love letters that had never made their way to my aunt. In a classic case of missed connections, the two of them had gone their separate ways after high school, Aunt True to travel the world, and Professor Rusty to college and graduate school.

If Erastus Peckinpaugh was clearly interested in rekindling the romance, it was harder to tell with Aunt True. For as long as I'd known her, my aunt had proudly classified herself as a nomad and a rolling stone. Was she ready to settle down? I honestly had no idea. Aunt True was being completely close-lipped about it, and not just with Ella Bellow.

Dinner was the usual Magnificent Seven mayhem. My brothers held court, recounting their day at wrestling camp; Pippa spilled her milk twice; and Lauren, who was wearing another of her attic finds—a glossy black hat with a fishnet veil—got reprimanded for reading at the table, although Aunt True argued for leniency. "She has such excellent taste in literature, Jericho!" she protested, when my dad took the book away. "*The Westing Game* was one of my favorites when I was in fourth grade."

I didn't even bother trying to get a word in edgewise.

"How's your research going, Dinah?" Professor Rusty asked my mother. "Have you settled on a topic yet?"

YOURS TRULY

"I can't decide between the Hatfields and the McCoys or the Underground Railroad," she told him.

"I know about the Underground Railroad!" Pippa piped up excitedly from the far end of the table. "Mr. Henry read about Harriet Tubman at library thtory hour!"

Professor Rusty nodded. "Indeed, Pippa. She was a very important conductor along those invisible rails, leading dozens of slaves to freedom." He turned back to my mother. "They're both excellent subjects, Dinah. Hmmm. Which would I choose? The famous feud that has entered both the annals of American folklore and our national lexicon, or one of the most exciting chapters in nineteenth-century history, featuring a network of brave souls and safe houses, secret tunnels and passwords, disguises and subterfuge? An organization that involved whites and blacks alike, men and women who risked everything to help some hundred thousand slaves to freedom? Slaves who faced danger at every turn as they risked recapture, punishment—even death?" He pretended to rub his chin, considering.

My mother laughed. "I think it's pretty clear which one you'd choose."

"You know my weakness for the Civil War era," he admitted. "It really is a fascinating subject, however. And did you know that the Underground Railroad may have a Pumpkin Falls connection? It's been the basis for much speculation over the years, although nothing has ever been proven."

"Is that so?" said my mother.

Professor Rusty ran a hand through his hair, warming to his theme. "Have you read about Henry 'Box' Brown, the slave from Virginia who mailed himself to freedom in a box?"

We looked at him blankly.

"Just one of many fascinating stories," he continued, turning to me. "Truly, you'll appreciate this one—there was a Canadian man by the name of Alexander Milton Ross, known as 'Birdman' to the workers on the Underground Railroad, because he traveled through the Southern states helping slaves escape while pretending to be an enthusiastic ornithologist."

"An orni-what?" asked Pippa, frowning.

"A bird watcher," I told her.

Across the table, my cousin gave me a frantic get-me-out-of-here-before-I-die-of-boredom look. Not that I wanted to sit through another of Professor Rusty's lectures, either, but history was so not Mackenzie's thing.

"May we be excused?" I asked politely. "Mackenzie and I set the table, so it's Hatcher's and Danny's turn to do the dishes."

"Don't go too far, girls," said my mother. "We'll be leaving for our knitting class in about half an hour."

Like I could forget.

"We'll be ready," I promised, forcing myself to smile sweetly, and I followed my cousin upstairs to my room.

CHAPTER 8

"Cute place," said Mackenzie, peering out the window of our minivan as we pulled up in front of A Stitch in Time.

Ella Bellow's new shop was carved from half of the building that housed Earl's Coins and Stamps. Bud Jefferson's business hadn't been doing too well—I guess people didn't collect that stuff the way they used to—and the two of them had struck a deal for Ella to take over part of his space. I examined the window display as I got out of the car. I was hardly an expert on store windows, but I'd been helping Aunt True with the one at our bookstore for a few months now, and I could tell that Ella had done a good job with hers. It was cheery and colorful, and she'd even managed a very un-Ella-like touch of whimsy: a near-life-size plush sheep in the center of the display, surrounded by baskets spilling over with skeins of bright wool. Decked out in a knitted hat and scarf, the sheep was wearing a sweater sporting a maple leaf design. A sign around its neck announced: MAPLE MADNESS IS BAAAAAAA-CK!

I couldn't help noticing the book propped up by the sheep's front hooves—*Maple Country Mufflers*, the one Ella'd had her gym shorts all in a twist about when she'd spotted it in our bookshop window.

"Ooo, that sheep is *adorable*!" Mackenzie squealed. "I have to get a picture. Go stand in front of it. You too, Aunt Dinah. Now smile!"

My mother slipped her arm around my waist and put her head on my shoulder. I rested my chin on top of her head. It still felt weird being taller than her, but I was getting used to it.

"Hey, Little O," she whispered as Mackenzie snapped the picture.

"Hey, Mama O."

"Happy birthday!"

"Thanks." I felt myself start to relax. Knitting might be my mother's thing, not mine, but that was no reason not to have fun.

"Come in, come in!" said a voice behind us. We turned around to see Ella holding the door open, beaming. Ella didn't usually beam, especially at me. I gave her a cautious smile in return and followed my mother inside.

A circle of chairs had been set up. Most of them were occupied. The other students in the Spring Break Socks class besides my mother and Mackenzie and me were Lucas Winthrop's mother; Alice Maynard, who was married to my swim coach; Belinda Winchester; Mr. Henry, the Pumpkin Falls children's librarian; and Annie Freeman and her mother.

Belinda jerked her chin at me and patted the seat next to her. I plunked myself into it. My mother and Mackenzie sat down on the other side of me.

"I'm so happy you all are joining me for the inaugural class in A Stitch in Time's knitting instruction series," Ella began rather primly. "As you can see, there's a snack table set up, and I hope you'll all help yourselves to tea and currant scones, my signature treat."

I elbowed my mother sharply. Ella had a nerve, making us take a book out of our window, when she was stealing Aunt True's idea for a signature treat!

My mother frowned and shook her head at me. "It's not a big deal."

I wasn't so sure Aunt True would feel the same way.

"Let's get started, shall we?" Ella continued. "We'll begin by winding our skeins of yarn into balls. It's so much easier to work with that way, I find."

Before she could show us how, there was a tap on the door in the new wall that divided her shop from Earl's Coins and Stamps.

"Got everything you need, Ella?" asked Bud Jefferson, poking his head in. "How's the temperature in here?"

"Such a thoughtful landlord!" Ella said. "It's just fine, thank you, Bud. There's an extra seat if you'd like to join us."

Across the circle from me, I noticed Mrs. Winthrop's cheeks turn as pink as the yarn she was holding. I remembered what Ella had said at the bookshop earlier, about Lucas Winthrop's mother and Bud Jefferson spending a lot of time together recently. Sap really did seem to be rising all over Pumpkin Falls these days.

"Uh, knitting isn't really my thing," he replied.

I could see why. Bud Jefferson looked like a bear, and he had hands like hams. It was hard to imagine them clutching a pair of knitting needles.

"Did you know that knitting used to be considered men's work?" Mr. Henry told him. "In fact, in some cultures women weren't even allowed to knit."

Mr. Jefferson's bushy eyebrows shot up. "Really?"

Mr. Henry nodded. "During the Renaissance, only men were allowed to join knitting guilds. The word 'knit' itself is derived from the Old English *cnyttan*, meaning 'knot'—probably because it grew out of the knots with which fishermen crafted their nets. They've been knitters for centuries, as have sailors and shepherds. The craft has a fascinating history. It started in ancient times, with the Romans and Egyptians."

It has been my experience that librarians know a lot of stuff.

"Huh," said Mr. Jefferson, digesting this information. "Interesting."

"Oh, come and join us, Bud!" said Ella. "You can at least

be sociable if you don't actually want to try your hand at knitting. I made some of those currant scones you like."

That clinched it. Closing the door behind him, Mr. Jefferson tiptoed in and looked around for a seat.

"Amelia could use your help." Ella's dark eyes gleamed as she gestured toward the empty chair next to Lucas's mother. "It takes two to wind wool, you know."

Beside me, my mother gave a quiet snort. I had a feeling that Ella was talking about more than just knitting. I wondered what Lucas thought about his mother and Mr. Jefferson. Did it freak him out that they might be "winding wool," as Ella put it?

"Here, Bud, hold your hands out straight," Ella directed. "Like a robot. Now, Amelia, untwist the skein. See how it forms a loop?" She placed the loop of wool over Bud Jefferson's hands and passed the loose end to Mrs. Winthrop. "Off you go—start winding."

I watched for a few moments as she wound and a ball began to form, then took my yarn out of my bag.

"We'll wind yours first," Belinda Winchester told me. I nodded, untwisted the skein, slipped it into place over her waiting hands, and started winding.

"Blue socks, they never get dirty . . ." Belinda sang softly to herself.

"What?"

She shook her head. "Nothing. Just an old camp song."

At least my mother had chosen my favorite color for the yarn she bought me, I thought as I wound. *Blue as water, blue as sky.* Thinking of water made me think of my Mermaid-hued bedroom back in Texas, and I made a mental note to ask Gramps and Lola about painting my room here in Pumpkin Falls. Maybe as an extra birthday present?

The work went quickly, and before I knew it I had a fat ball of yarn, ready to be turned into socks.

"My turn," said Belinda. She'd brought along purple wool, and I wondered if maybe she was planning to knit socks for her gentleman caller.

Purl the kitten skittered past just then. Belinda paused her winding and reached for the purple feather tucked behind her ear. She dangled it in the air, and Purl stopped in her tracks, then leaped up and batted at it with her paws. Belinda was too quick for her and whisked it out of her reach.

"Stop teasing Purl, Belinda," said Ella severely.

"Not teasing. Playing," Belinda replied, dangling the feather again.

"Her name's spelled P-U-R-L," Annie announced, just in case anybody was wondering. "It's a knitting stitch."

I smiled at Mackenzie. I'd told her all about the reigning junior spelling bee champion of Grafton County, but, like Belinda, Annie had to be experienced firsthand.

My mother leaned toward me. "Now that I know Annie's here, I'm feeling a little guilty," she whispered. "Should I call home and have your father bring Lauren down to join us?"

Lauren again! "But this was supposed to be *our* thing!" I protested. "You know, Little O and Mama O?"

I didn't want Lauren tagging along. I never got a chance to have my mother all to myself, and as it was, I was already sharing her with Mackenzie, sort of.

"I suppose you're right." My mother didn't look convinced, though, and she kept shooting guilty glances over at Annie.

Once we all had our yarn tamed into balls, Ella showed us how to cast on. "You'll want to look carefully at the patterns I've given each of you, and find the exact number of stitches you'll need," she said. "I've tailored them to your shoe sizes."

Great, I thought, with a rueful glance at my size-ten-and-a-half feet. I'd be casting on all night.

Sure enough, I had to cast on nearly twice as many stitches as Mackenzie. My cousin had feet like an elf.

Those of us who had never knit before—me, Mackenzie, Annie, Mrs. Winthrop, and Mr. Jefferson, who had succumbed to the spirit of the evening and was as busy casting on as the rest of us—were shown the two basic stitches, and instructed to practice several rows of each of them.

"When you alternate rows of these two stitches, which we'll be doing shortly," Ella explained, "you'll have what's called 'stockinette stitch.'"

"S-T-O-C-K-I-N-E-T-T-E," Annie couldn't resist whispering.

"Nice and smooth," Ella continued. "And when you alternate those stitches, or pairs of those stitches, within a single row, you create ribbing, which we'll all do at the top of each of our socks."

The more experienced knitters were already off and running. I watched in admiration as my mother's needles flashed. She could seriously go pro. The socks she'd chosen to knit were for my father, in a complicated pattern called "argyle." Mr. Henry was making red-and-white-striped ones, of course. Nearly his entire wardrobe was red and white, and Hatcher said he looks like an African American *Where's Waldo?* Mrs. Freeman was starting on an orange leaf design, and I wondered if maybe she were planning to sell the socks in the barn store at Freeman Farm.

After a few minutes I paused to inspect my progress. I'd made a hash of casting on, and somehow I must have managed to knit some of the stitches together, because now I had three fewer stitches than when I started. Seeing my dismay, Ella came over and helped me rip out the mistaken rows, and I started again.

I glanced over at Mackenzie. Her head was bent over her needles, and she was frowning in concentration. She was way ahead of me.

"No fair—you've done this before!" I said.

She shook her head. "Never."

I sighed. Just one more thing to add to the long list of

YOURS TRULY

things I wasn't good at. At this rate, I'd be lucky to have one big toe finished by the end of the week.

After a while we paused for tea and scones, which were surprisingly good. Who knew Ella Bellow could bake? Then it was time for more knitting. The evening flew by. Class was just about over when there was a knock at the door.

"Come in!" called Ella.

I looked up to see Coach Maynard in the doorway. Spotting Mackenzie and me, he smiled and sketched a wave. "I'm a few minutes early, honey," he said to his wife. His smile faded as he noticed Mrs. Freeman in the circle of knitters.

"Good evening, Wyatt," said Annie's mother pleasantly.

"You've got some nerve!" Coach Maynard thundered.

Mrs. Freeman looked up in surprise. "Pardon me?"

"Someone cut one of our sap lines, and I have a pretty good notion who it was," my swim coach retorted. "I saw that son of yours out sniffing around my property earlier today, Grace."

Uh-oh, I thought. This didn't sound good.

"Franklin? He would never—"

"I heard all about what happened at your farm last night," Coach Maynard barreled on. "You think we did it, and now you're trying to get even!"

"That's a ridiculous notion!"

"R-I-D-I-C-U-L-O-U-S!" Annie sputtered furiously.

Ella Bellow's head swiveled back and forth, like a

spectator at a tennis match. Her dark eyes gleamed again, and I knew she was filing this information away to be used the minute we all went home. By morning the entire town would know what was going on.

Was Pumpkin Falls facing its very own feud, Hatfield and McCoy style?

CHAPTER 9

"That was more exciting than I expected a sock class to be," said Mackenzie as we were driving home.

"'Exciting' is Pumpkin Falls' middle name!" my mother joked. Then her expression grew serious. "Theft isn't anything to laugh about, though, and I sure hate to see our friends disagreeing. I hope it all gets sorted out quickly."

It will if the Pumpkin Falls Private Eyes have anything to say about it, I thought. Because my mother was right—it wasn't fun to see the Freemans and the Maynards feuding. What if people in town started choosing sides? Things could get seriously out of hand.

"So what do you girls have planned for tomorrow?" my mother asked, glancing in the rearview mirror at us.

"Nothing much," I told her, which wasn't entirely true. Especially if you counted making a field trip to the scene of a crime.

"We might hang out with Scooter and Lucas and Calhoun."

"I thought I'd take Pippa and Lauren out to lunch and a movie over in West Hartfield, if you two want to join us," she offered. "The girls have been begging to see that new cartoon about the robot and the hippopotamus."

Mackenzie and I exchanged a quick smile. My mother clearly thought we were still six.

"Um, no thanks, Aunt Dinah," Mackenzie replied.

"Yeah, that's okay, Mom," I added. "We'll find stuff of our own to do." *Like see if we can catch a sap thief*, I thought.

"Suit yourselves."

Lauren was waiting up for us at home. "Can I see your socks?"

"Later," I told her.

"They're hardly socks at this point, sweetie," my mother explained.

"Hey, guess who was there?" said Mackenzie before I could shush her. "Your friend Annie and her mother."

Lauren shot my mother a wounded look. "Mo-om! If Annie gets to go, how come I can't?"

"Because it's my birthday present, not yours!" I snapped.

"Truly!" My mother gave me a reproachful look.

"Sorry," I mumbled, not feeling sorry at all. It was true, wasn't it? Leaving her to sort things out with my sister, I headed upstairs.

Mackenzie and I changed into our pajamas and brushed our teeth. Grabbing my new bird book, I flopped onto my bed on my stomach and opened it, eager to see if it contained any new information about barred owls.

"So what do you think of Calhoun?" Mackenzie asked casually, picking up her hairbrush.

I froze. "Um, he's okay, I guess."

"He's kind of cute, don't you think?"

The barred owl is most often found in mature forests, I read, keeping my eyes glued to the page. Whatever had prompted this, I was not about to take the bait.

"Of course Cameron's hair is blonder, and he has blue eyes, not brown like Calhoun's, but still, Calhoun is definitely cute," my cousin continued. "And I can't believe his name is Romeo!" She sighed. "That's so romantic."

Clenching my teeth, I read on: *The barred owl's typical call sounds like "Who cooks for you! Who cooks for you-all!"*

"Hey, did you notice the socks Belinda Winchester is knitting?"

This time I looked up. "Huh?"

"Belinda's socks—they're purple. Guess we know who those are for, right?"

Mackenzie clearly had romance on the brain. I shook my head and returned to my book.

Owls can find their prey without even seeing it, thanks to hypersensitive hearing. At certain frequencies, an owl's hearing is ten times more sensitive than that of humans.

Right then I would have been happy not to hear anything at all. Especially not my boy-crazy cousin.

Mackenzie sighed, finally taking the hint. "Fine. I'll read too." Kneeling in front of my bookcase, she ran a finger over the titles that lined its shelves. "Sudoku, birds, sudoku, birds. B-O-R-I-N-G, as Annie Freeman would say."

"S-O-R-R-Y!" I quipped in reply. "Didn't you bring anything from home?"

"Come to think of it, I'm pretty sure my mother stuck something in my suitcase at the last minute in case I wanted to read on the plane. I totally forgot."

She went over to my closet and opened the door. A moment later I heard her rummaging through her luggage, and then "Yes! Thank you, Mom!" This was immediately followed by a loud thud, and then "Whoa!"

"Whoa what?" I asked, looking up again.

"Whoa, as in you'd better come over here and take a look at this!"

There was an urgent note in Mackenzie's voice. I put my book down and crossed the room. My cousin was squatting by her suitcase, holding a fat hardcover book. Looking up at me, she asked, "Do you have a flashlight?"

"Um, maybe with our camping gear out in the garage or something. Why?"

"I need a light."

"Hang on a sec." My cell phone was charging on my desk. Grabbing it, I switched on the torch app and went back to the closet.

"Don't point it at me, you dork, point it at the floor!" my cousin protested, shielding her eyes.

"Sorry." Redirecting the beam, I saw that the corner of one of the wide wooden floorboards was sticking up at an odd angle. "That's weird."

"I know, right?" Mackenzie said. "When I dropped my book, it just popped up like that."

I knelt down beside her and poked at the floorboard's raised edge, trying to work my fingers under it. No luck. Then I pounded on the other end, trying to see if that would jostle it loose, but it still didn't budge.

"Do you have something we can pry it up with?" my cousin asked.

Returning to my desk, I grabbed my letter opener. "Be careful with it, okay? It was a Christmas present."

She spotted the carved owl on the handle and smirked. "You are such a bird nerd!"

I don't mind it when Mackenzie teases me. Most of the time, anyway.

Inserting the point of the letter opener beneath the floorboard's raised corner, she carefully slid the slim blade in all the way to its hilt, then levered down on it gently. The floorboard inched up.

"Do it again," I told her, setting my cell phone down. I poked my fingers underneath the lifted edge as she continued to push. The top of the floorboard was worn smooth from centuries of use, but the underside was rough. I hoped there wasn't anything lurking beneath it. Like spiders, for instance.

This was no time to be squeamish. I redoubled my efforts, and my pulse quickened as I felt the board start to loosen. I told myself not to be silly. I told myself that this wasn't one of Lauren's Nancy Drew books. There weren't any such things as secret compartments.

Mackenzie pressed down again, and I gave one last mighty tug at the floorboard, tumbling back as it suddenly shifted and came loose in my hand. I scrambled up onto my knees and leaned over to peer into the open space that had been concealed underneath. Mackenzie did too, and our heads banged together with an audible crack.

"Ouch!" we both said, sitting back on our heels.

"You go first," Mackenzie told me, rubbing her forehead.

Wincing, I reached for my cell phone again and shined it into the shadowy crevice. There was something tucked into the far corner. A small bundle of some sort, wrapped in a piece of faded fabric and bound with a knotted leather cord.

"What is it?" Mackenzie could hardly contain her excitement.

"I don't know."

Reaching in cautiously, I lifted it out and felt its edges. "A box of some kind, I think?" I shook it, but whatever it was didn't make a sound.

We carried our discovery over to my bed, where there was more light. Mackenzie sat down beside me, bouncing a little on the edge of my mattress. "Open it!" she urged, sounding like Pippa.

"I'm trying!" I replied, working at the age-stiffened knot.

"It's silk, I think," my cousin said, reaching out and brushing the faded fabric with a finger. "Looks like it was a pretty shade of light blue once. Who do you think it belonged to?"

I shrugged. "It's probably Aunt True's. This used to be her room."

The leather knot finally came loose. Unwinding the cord from around the bundle, I peeled back the fabric.

"It's a book," I said, disappointed. When you find a secret compartment in your room, at least a tiny part of you can't help expecting gold and jewels and buried treasure of some sort.

Smallish but thick, the book was bound in dark blue leather worn around the spine and edges. The word "DIARY" was stamped on the cover in faded gold, along with the initials *T. L.* in the bottom right-hand corner.

"See?" I told my cousin, pointing to the letters. "True Lovejoy. It's my aunt's."

"We probably shouldn't open it, then," said Mackenzie. "I mean, since it's her diary and everything."

"Yeah. It could be really personal, or embarrassing."

We sat in silence, staring at it.

"Maybe just a peek?" Mackenzie said finally. She gave me a hopeful glance.

I chewed my lip, considering. "A peek," I agreed, and opened the cover.

CHAPTER 10

"Whoa," whispered Mackenzie. "It's not your Aunt True's."

We stared down at the date on the diary's first page: January 1, 1861. The flesh on my arms prickled. The book I was holding in my hands had been hidden away for over a hundred and fifty years!

I traced the words on the inside front cover: *Property of Truly Lovejoy.*

"This was *hers!*" I told my cousin, my voice rising in excitement. "The original Truly's—the one I was named after!"

"You mean the one in the portrait?" Mackenzie's blue eyes widened. "Are you sure?"

"I can prove it," I told her. "Come on."

She followed me out into the hallway, where I flipped on the light and pointed to the framed document hanging on the wall nearby. "See? That's her passport. Check out the signature at the bottom. It's exactly the same as in her diary."

My cousin compared the two. "But her last name isn't Lovejoy," she said, squinting at the faded writing on the passport. "It's—"

"Becker. I know. She got the passport in Germany, before she came here and met Matthew. And see? Her real name was Trudy, remember I told you that? And about the immigrations officials who misunderstood and wrote it down wrong in her official papers, so she got stuck with Truly?"

Mackenzie smiled at me. "And so did you."

My name has always kind of bugged me, but as I stood there holding the diary in my hands, something changed. *Blue*, I thought, looking down at the faded leather cover and the scrap of fabric it had been wrapped in. Goose bumps again. The original Truly had liked blue too. She was a real living, breathing person, not just a face in an old portrait. For the first time, I felt a flicker of kinship with my ancestor.

"So she arrived here in America in . . . let's see"—Mackenzie struggled to make out the faded writing on the framed passport—"September 1860. And by New Year's Day in 1861, just three months later, she was already married to Matthew? Wow, that's what I call a whirlwind romance! It really must have been love at first sight, just like your grandfather told you."

YOURS TRULY

"What are you guys doing?"

We swiveled around. Our voices had drawn my sister Lauren from her room.

"Nothing," I said quickly. Too quickly. Lauren may just be a fourth grader, but she's not stupid.

"Doesn't sound like nothing."

"I was showing Mackenzie the original Truly's passport."

Lauren's gaze fell on my hand. The one holding the diary. She didn't miss a trick.

"And I, uh, thought she might be interested in seeing my life list too," I added quickly. The fib was the only thing I could think of on the spur of the moment. Fortunately, the notebook I kept my list of birds in was about the same shape as the diary, if not the exact same color.

And, fortunately, my sister fell for it.

"Oh," she said, immediately losing interest. Lauren loves animals, but she's not at all into birding. She turned to go.

"Maybe we can all do something tomorrow, like play a board game," said Mackenzie.

Lauren brightened. "That sounds like fun!" And skimming lightly down the hall, she gave my cousin a quick hug. "Night, Mackenzie."

"Night, Lauren."

My sister returned to her room. Her message couldn't have been clearer if she'd spoken it aloud: no hug for the mean big sister. I felt a pang of guilt, followed swiftly by annoyance. The thing was, I wasn't deliberately trying to be mean. I just didn't get to see Mackenzie very often, and I didn't want to have to share her. Was that so awful?

Back in my room, Mackenzie and I sat down on the bed beside each other again and opened the diary.

"Look at her handwriting!" my cousin marveled, carefully turning the pages. Yellowed and brittle, they were covered with elegant cursive. "Nobody writes like that now." She looked up at me. "How about we read it out loud?"

"Okay." I turned back to the first page. Some of the words were in German, but I did the best I could:

> *January 1, 1861*
> *Liebes Tagebuch—Dear Diary,*
> *Mother Lovejoy gave me this diary for Weihnachten—* [this word had been crossed out, and "Christmas" carefully entered in its place]—*in hopes I will use it to practice mein Englisch. I promised her I would write as often as I could. Today begins my new life as Mrs. Matthew Lovejoy. We were married heute Morgen*—[again, the words were crossed out and "this morning" added in their place]—*by Reverend Josiah Bartlett of the First Parish Church.*

YOURS TRULY

"Hey," I told Mackenzie, looking up. "That's the same church my grandparents belong to—the one with the steeple!"

"Cool! Don't forget you promised to take me up there too."

"I won't." I turned my attention back to the diary.

> *How I wish my own Mutti had been here for my wedding! I miss her so. Matthew says I am very brave, traveling so far from home, but this morning I don't feel brave at all. Only full of Heimweh.*

"What's '*Heimweh*'?" my cousin asked, frowning.

"We're going to need a German-English dictionary," I told her. "Maybe we can get one at the bookstore tomorrow, or the library."

> *But I do so love my husband! And I will learn to love Pumpkin Falls, and it will become home too. This Matthew promises me.*
>
> *Deine Truly*

Yet another cross-out through the final two words, which had been replaced with "*Yours, Truly*."

"Poor thing, she sounds really homesick," said Mackenzie.

"No wonder!" I tried to imagine myself in my ancestor's shoes. She was only a year older than my brother Danny, and she'd left her family and her country and had just gotten married to someone she'd known for only a few months.

Mackenzie sighed dreamily. "Isn't it romantic, though?"

I made a rude noise.

She elbowed me. "Keep reading!"

I looked down at the diary. "We should probably show it to my mom and dad," I said reluctantly. "Since it's a family heirloom and everything."

Mackenzie made a face. "You're probably right. Maybe we could wait until tomorrow, though?"

I was quiet for a moment. For one thing, the minute word got out about the diary, Lauren would be all over it. Something this old—and something she could read, to boot—would be like catnip to my bookworm sister. And if it were valuable, my parents might want to stick it in a museum or a safe deposit box. Mackenzie and I might not ever get another chance to look at it.

There was a knock on the door, and I reflexively stuffed the diary under my pillow.

"Girls?" My mother poked her head in. "I saw the light under your door. Morning's going to come early, and you have swim practice. I think you should call it a night."

Neither my cousin nor I said a word about the diary. We just nodded and climbed into our beds.

"Good night, then." My mother turned off the overhead

light and blew us each a kiss, and we each pretended to catch it. It's a Gifford bedtime ritual.

"Good night, Aunt Dinah," said Mackenzie.

"Good night, Mom," I echoed.

The door closed behind her. The diary stayed where it was.

"Just until tomorrow," I whispered to Mackenzie.

CHAPTER 11

The alarm on my cell phone jangled me awake. I stretched a leg out from under the covers and poked a toe at the nearby air mattress, nudging the lump that was Mackenzie.

"Go away," the lump mumbled.

"Up and at 'em!" I said in my best imitation of Lieutenant Colonel Jericho T. Lovejoy. I sprang briskly out of bed and flipped on the overhead light. "Daily doubles await!"

Mackenzie groaned. "I plead jet lag!"

"Don't you want to wow Mr. Perfect with your new flip turn?"

She cracked open an eyelid. "Who's Mr. Perfect?"

I grinned at her. "Pardon me. I mean Cameron McAllister."

At the sound of her true love's name, Mackenzie sat up and rubbed her eyes. "I was just dreaming about him."

I made a gagging noise, and she threw her pillow at me. I caught it and grinned. "Last one downstairs is a rotten egg!"

YOURS TRULY

Except for that long, scary stretch of months after Black Monday, when my father had a serious case of the doldrums, as he puts it now, I'd rarely known him not to be up before I am. For as long as I could remember, he'd been an early bird, and this particular morning was no exception.

"Morning, ladies," he said, glancing up from his coffee and newspaper as my cousin and I entered the kitchen.

"Morning, Uncle Jericho," Mackenzie replied, yawning.

My father gestured toward the fridge. "Power smoothies await."

"Thanks." I dropped a kiss on top of his head.

My father was big on making sure that the athletes in the family ate right, and that included a little something before early-morning practices. Even when we didn't feel like it, he insisted. Sometimes it was just a banana with a swipe of peanut butter; sometimes it was an energy bar; this morning it was a smoothie.

"How about I drop you off on my way to the bookshop?" my father offered. "It's been a busy few days what with all the tourists, and I want to get a jump on things."

The three of us were quiet on the short ride to town. Neither Mackenzie nor I brought up the subject of the diary, which was still in its hiding place under my pillow. I stared out the window, wondering if Pumpkin Falls had looked much different back when the original Truly had lived here. Probably not.

The last remnants of winter were rapidly melting away, and rivulets of muddy water swirled across the streets. It wouldn't be long now before the migratory warblers returned, along with the chipping sparrows and Baltimore orioles and evening grosbeaks. I made a mental note to work up a list of the spring birds that I should be watching for.

"Work hard, ladies," my father said as we pulled up in front of the pool.

"Always do," I replied as Mackenzie and I got out.

He gave us a thumbs-up and drove off.

I groaned when I saw the workout posted on the whiteboard. We'd be working hard, all right—Coach Maynard had seen to that.

"I hate speed intervals," Mackenzie grumbled as we started warming up.

"No kidding," I said. "Especially first thing in the morning."

Lucas sidled up to us, his face as red as if he'd just finished a set of sprints. He flashed my cousin a shy smile. "Hey."

"Hey, yourself," said Mackenzie.

I didn't bother replying. What was the point? Lucas wasn't talking to me anyway.

Along with the rest of our teammates—the ones who had remained in Pumpkin Falls for Spring Break, at least—the three of us grunted our way through the required sets of warm-up crunches and planks.

A few minutes later there was a short blast from Coach Maynard's whistle as he emerged from the office. He seemed like his normal self; there was no mention of last night's outburst at A Stitch in Time. I certainly wasn't going to bring it up.

"Let's see how you two do against each other," he said to Mackenzie and me, assigning us to adjoining lanes.

Given our differences in height, you wouldn't think it was fair to pit my cousin and me against each other, but once we're in the water it actually balances out. Mackenzie's so petite she's like a water flea, zipping across the surface of the pool. But my long legs and arms give me an advantage too, and in the end our times are generally really close.

"Good job, girls," he said, checking his stopwatch as we completed our first set. "Truly, you keep turning in these kinds of times, and you'll be going to state championships this year."

While I continued with the posted workout, Coach Maynard turned his attention to honing Mackenzie's flip turn. Lucas spent too much time watching them—well, watching Mackenzie—but at least he wasn't swallowing water like he did yesterday.

"Good workout, people!" Coach Maynard said at the end of our session. "Stay away from the junk food today, and I'll see you this afternoon!"

Lucas was waiting for my cousin and me again when we emerged from the locker room a little while later.

"We're still meeting up after breakfast, right?" he managed to squeak, clearly still awed by my cousin's magnificence.

Mackenzie dazzled him with a smile. "Can't wait!"

Bolstered by this sign of favor, Lucas practically skipped off down the street. What was it about my cousin that boys found so bewitching? I wondered, watching him go. Whatever it was, one thing was for sure—I could use a big dose of it.

Mackenzie and I jogged home, more because breakfast was waiting than because we actually had any energy left.

"I'm starving!" I announced as we burst into the kitchen.

"You're just in time for banana walnut oatmeal," my mother replied, ladling me up a steaming bowlful as I took a seat at the table.

"Hello, thtarving, I'm Pippa," said my little sister, collapsing in giggles at her own wit. She was at the age where stuff like that was still funny.

"Nice to meet you, Pippa, I'm hungry," said Mackenzie, stretching out her hand across the table. Pippa shook it, delighted that at least one of us was joining in on the fun.

Lauren looked up from her book—she'd moved on from *The Westing Game* to *The Sasquatch Escape*—and rolled her eyes. She was at the age where she was eager to distance herself from anything that seemed babyish. Which meant pretty much everything Pippa did.

"So what's on the schedule today over at Camp Belinda?" my mother asked.

"We're going to make muffins," Lauren replied, with a noticeable lack of enthusiasm.

"And we're going to learn how to play cheth," added Pippa.

"That sounds like fun," said my mother. "I didn't know Belinda played chess."

"All of the pieces on her chessboard are cats." Lauren gave her a sidelong glance, adding, "and the pawns are kittens."

"The answer is still no, Lauren," my mother said firmly. "We don't need a kitten."

My sister heaved the deep, dramatic sigh of the misunderstood. Mackenzie's eyes met mine across the table, glinting with amusement.

"We're just going to do boring stuff," I announced to no one in particular. "Hang around here for a while, look at my bird books, that sort of thing."

"Well, I'll be picking Lauren and Pippa up from Belinda's around eleven thirty," my mother told us. "If you change your minds, you're welcome to join us for lunch and the movie."

Pippa scrambled down from her seat and ran around the table. Twining her arms around my cousin's neck, she pleaded, "Come with uth, Mackenthie! Pleathe!"

Mackenzie gave her a hug. "I'd love to, Pipster, but Truly and I have some stuff we want to do. How about we play a board game with you tonight instead?"

Pippa perked up at this. "Candy Land?"

"It's a deal."

As soon as my sisters were safely off to Belinda's, and my mother was settled at her dining room table desk, Mackenzie and I went back upstairs to my room. I drew the diary out of its hiding place. "Should we keep reading?"

"Pleathe!" Mackenzie replied, mimicking Pippa.

I opened to where we'd left off.

January 7, 1861
Today I baked Matthew's favorite Apfelkuchen—
apple cake auf Englisch. Mother Lovejoy says I am
a fine cook.
Yours, Truly

January 23, 1861
Matthew's sister Charity made us a visit today. She
lives in Boston. She brought with her much newspapers.
Matthew reads to us what they say. So much sadness!
So much cruelty! Mother Lovejoy and I both wept.
Yours, Truly

"What's so sad and cruel?" asked Mackenzie.

I shook my head. "She doesn't say."

I skipped over a bunch of shorter entries that just detailed the housework she did and the things she baked. This one caught my eye, though:

YOURS TRULY

February 2, 1861
Mother Lovejoy and Matthew have a secret. I hear them whispering sometimes late at night. I don't know what the secret is, and I am afraid to ask.
Yours, Truly

February 5, 1861
I ask. Matthew says the less I know the better. He tells me it is safer this way. "There is nothing to worry about," he tells me. But that is all I do, it seems.
Yours, Truly

"More housework, more worrying, more baking," I murmured, running my finger across the next few pages of entries. "Hey, she made pumpkin muffins! Aunt True would love that! And something called '*Zwetschgenkuchen.*'" I sounded the word out, but had no idea if I was pronouncing it properly.

"I'm pretty sure '*kuchen*' means 'cake,'" said Mackenzie, looking over my shoulder. "Go back to where she talked about baking that apple cake."

I flipped back a few pages. From the looks of it, my cousin was right.

"But what the heck is a *Zwetschgen*?" I asked.

Mackenzie shrugged. "Dunno. I'll add it to the list of words we need to look up. Can you spell it for me?"

"Z-w-e-t-s-c-h-g-e-n," I said, feeling like Annie Freeman. Mackenzie wrote it down.

March 4, 1861
I have a secret too! Matthew is so happy. I told him I am sure it will be a fine boy.

"Wait, does that mean she's going to have a baby?" Mackenzie exclaimed, perking up.

I reread the entry and nodded. "I think so. It's probably their son Booth. He's the one in the portrait at the bottom of the stairs."

I continued reading:

I would like to name him for my father. Gerhard is not very nice for a girl, Matthew said, making me laugh. I assured him that it will not be a girl. The firstborns in my family are always boys. I must write to Mutti with the good news. She will be glad for me, but also sad. Pumpkin Falls is so far from Lutterhausen!
Yours, Truly

"Why do you think she left Germany?" Mackenzie asked.

I shrugged. "No idea. More work here, maybe? We'll have to ask Gramps."

YOURS TRULY

The next few entries all just had the same word: '*Schwangerschaftsübelkeit.*' Mackenzie added it to the growing list.

And then came an entry with another single word. One I could read and easily understand this time:

April 12, 1861
War.

A pleat appeared between my cousin's eyebrows. "Which war?"

I heaved a Lauren-size sigh. "Duh—the *Civil* War, of course! It's 1861! Pay attention!"

Mackenzie made a face at me.

April 18, 1861
The war is all that we here in Pumpkin Falls can talk about. President Lincoln has called for volunteers. I am so afraid for Matthew, and for our baby. What will become of us, if Matthew goes to be a soldier?
Yours, Truly

"Well, we know he did," said Mackenzie. "He's wearing a uniform in the portrait, right?"

I nodded, the flesh on my arms prickling again.

May 3, 1861
This morning I felt the baby kicking for the first time. "See?" I told Matthew. "He doesn't want you to go either." Matthew promises he will not leave before harvest.

August 30, 1861
Matthew left us this morning. He has gone with his friend Booth Harrington to Concord to join the Fifth New Hampshire Volunteer Infantry. Booth's younger brothers will help us with the harvest. Matthew looks splendid in his uniform, but oh, how I wish he did not have to go! Mother Lovejoy and I cannot stop weeping.
Yours, Truly

"Booth was Matthew's friend's name, huh?" I said. "I wonder if that's where they got their son's name."

"Guess we'll find out," Mackenzie replied.

September 9, 1861
Mother Lovejoy told me her secret. I have sworn to keep it.

My cousin and I exchanged a glance.

"All this talk about secrets is driving me nuts," Mackenzie drawled, and I nodded in agreement.

YOURS TRULY

September 12, 1861

The wind was from the south tonight. Mother Lovejoy let me light the lantern. My hands were shaking as I did. She says with Matthew away, we must be brave together.

Yours, Truly

"What's she talking about?" asked Mackenzie, puzzled. "What's so scary about lighting a lantern?"

I shrugged. "No idea."

September 13, 1861

Reverend Bartlett spoke with us after church. He says the package was delayed, but should arrive today. Tomorrow at the latest. I pray for its safe delivery.

Yours, Truly

I stared at the diary. What was the original Truly up to? Secrets? Packages? Lanterns? It all sounded so mysterious—and dangerous.

A knock at the front door interrupted my thoughts.

"Girls!" my mother called up from the dining room. "Your friends are here!"

Truly and her secrets would have to wait. I shoved the diary back into its hiding place, and Mackenzie and I went downstairs.

CHAPTER 12

Scooter and Calhoun were waiting on the doorstep. Lucas was squeezed between them, scrubbed within an inch of his life. His hair was slicked back, and he was wearing a shirt I'd never seen before. It looked new. I peered at it more closely. It *was* new—he'd forgotten to take the price tag off. You had to give the kid points for trying, at least.

My trio of friends nearly trampled me in their eagerness to get inside, and apparently closer to where Mackenzie was standing. I might as well have been invisible as far as they were concerned.

"Hey, Truly," said Calhoun, who at least had the grace to acknowledge my presence.

"Hey."

"Are you guys ready to go?" asked Scooter, who only had eyes for my cousin.

"Yeah," I told him, and turned to Mackenzie. "You'd

better borrow a pair of Lauren's boots. It's mud season."

Mackenzie's brow furrowed. "Seriously? That's an official thing?"

"A-yuh," drawled Scooter in an exaggerated New Hampshire accent.

Mackenzie burst out laughing, and Scooter looked pleased.

"You won't laugh when you see where we're going," warned Calhoun. "We're taking the shortcut through the woods, and it's a mess out there."

"Bye, Mom!" I called, stuffing my size-ten-and-a-half feet into a pair of rubber boots and grabbing my jacket. "We're going to show Mackenzie around Freeman Farm!"

My mother waggled her fingers at us, barely looking up from her research project. "Have fun!"

At the top of the hill the five of us left the road and struck out on a path across a field that led into the woods. The sun was fully up now, its light dappling down through the trees. I breathed in the pine-sharp scent of evergreen. Somewhere nearby, an eastern phoebe sang out its raspy, two-note call, and in the distance I heard the brief, lilting trill of a song sparrow. "Heralds of spring," Gramps called them.

I was glad I'd worn my boots. The ground grew increasingly squishy as we approached the flanks of Lovejoy Mountain, and pretty soon we were squelching and sliding with every step.

"See? Mud season!" crowed Scooter. He stamped his

feet, sending up a spray of brown glop as he showed off for Mackenzie.

"Quit it!" I hollered, but my cousin just giggled. I frowned at her. "Don't encourage him."

While it was a relief to have Scooter fixated on something besides me—I wasn't hankering for another lip-lock, that was for sure—I still couldn't help feeling a little overlooked once again.

Fifteen minutes later we emerged onto the road across from Maynard's Maple Barn. Judging by the number of cars in the parking lot, my swim coach was doing a brisk business with the breakfast crowd.

We jogged on down the road to Freeman Farm. The parking lot was not nearly as packed as it was at Coach Maynard's, but then the Freemans didn't serve pancakes and waffles. Annie spotted us from her perch in the Snack Shack and waved.

"Greetings and S-A-L-U-T-A-T-I-O-N-S!" she said, trotting out a championship word borrowed from my Aunt True. "Anybody want a maple donut?"

"My treat," said Lucas, shooting a glance over at Mackenzie as he pulled his wallet from his back pocket.

"They're on the house," said Annie. "My mom heard you were coming."

Crestfallen, Lucas put his wallet back.

"Thanks," I said, helping myself to a donut.

"Hey!"

We turned around to see Franklin trotting over to join

us. "Hi, Mackenzie," he said, flashing my cousin a big smile. Scooter and Lucas both glared at him.

"Hi," she mumbled back, her mouth full of maple donut.

I was beginning to get used to being ignored.

"Do you guys want a tour of the sugarhouse?" Franklin asked Mackenzie. "I'm scheduled to give one right now."

My cousin nodded. The rest of us assumed his invitation meant us, too, and we followed them toward the cabin at the far end of the parking lot. I studiously avoided looking at Scooter as we passed the barn, but I couldn't resist flicking Calhoun a sidelong glance. His face was stony. I sighed and looked away. I still really, really wanted to explain about the kiss.

Woodsmoke drifted from the round metal chimney pipe poking out of the sugarhouse roof, and my cousin sniffed the air happily. "It smells like camping!"

"Yeah," I agreed, suddenly missing Texas again. Some of my happiest memories were of the camping trips that our families had taken together, along with the rest of my Gifford aunts and uncles and cousins.

"Welcome to Freeman Farm, everyone!" said Franklin, offering the handful of tourists waiting by the door a wide smile. "Who wants to see how maple syrup is made?"

From the practiced way in which my classmate kicked into tour guide mode, I could tell he'd done this before. He herded us efficiently through the front door and into a small entry room. The walls were paneled in rough wood and lined with tools and antique-looking buckets and other implements. We gazed at them curiously as Franklin launched into a history of the maple syrup industry.

"Native Americans were the first to discover the maple tree's sweet gift," he began. "For thousands of years the Abenaki—that means 'people of the dawn'—who lived in this part of New England harvested sap and made it into syrup. They called this time of year 'maple moon.'"

He held up a bowl crudely shaped from bark. "This is a *mokuk*," he continued. "It's made of birch bark and sealed with pine resin, and it's what the Abenaki used to collect sap. Later, the early settlers used wooden buckets." He plucked one from a peg on the wall. "Those evolved into the tin buckets with lids that have become an icon for the industry, and that you often see on syrup jug labels and postcards. Today, buckets are made of galvanized steel or food-grade plastic, although many large operations, like ours, have replaced buckets with plastic tubing that feeds from the trees directly into holding tanks."

As Franklin passed examples of each of these items around, Scooter took the opportunity to smack Lucas playfully on the head with a length of plastic tubing.

"Quit it!" I warned, but once again Mackenzie just laughed.

"So how do you get the sap out of the trees?" someone in the crowd wanted to know.

YOURS TRULY

"I'm so glad you asked!" Franklin replied.

He's really good at this, I thought, impressed.

My classmate held up a small object that looked like a wooden tube or spigot. "This is called a 'spile,' which comes from the Dutch word meaning 'splinter' or 'peg.' This one is made of cedar, but the Abenaki and other tribes also fashioned them out of sumac stems. The spile was inserted into a gash in the trunk of the maple tree, and sap would flow through it into the waiting container, such as a hollowed out branch or a *mokuk*." He held up the birch bark bowl again.

"Do people still use spiles?" asked Mackenzie.

Franklin nodded. "Pretty much, except today they're made of metal, not wood." He pointed to a display board on the wall behind us featuring all different styles and sizes of spiles. "And of course we don't gash the trees with axes these days—we use drills to make the holes."

I fingered the small metal spigot as it came around. A faint memory stirred. The sights and smells in the sugarhouse were giving me a flash of déjà vu, and I was pretty sure that Gramps and Lola had brought me someplace like this when I was little. Maybe even right here to this farm.

"All we need—well, besides maple trees—is for the weather to cooperate," Franklin continued. "Cold nights plus warm days equal a good maple harvest."

"Why is that?" asked another tourist.

"It's simple, really," Franklin told him. "The alternating

temperatures cause pressure changes in the tree, which makes the sap flow. If it's too cold at night, the sap takes longer to warm up during the day. It's a good thing the winter we just had finally decided to call it quits, otherwise we might not have had a sap run at all this year!"

"He sounds like Mr. Bigelow," Calhoun whispered, and I nodded. Mr. Bigelow was our science teacher.

We exchanged a smile, and for a split second I thought maybe this would be the moment to explain about Scooter. Before I could, though, the smile vanished, and Calhoun looked away.

I felt my face flush. I could also feel my cousin watching me. I forced myself to smile at her. If I wasn't careful, she might figure out how I felt about Calhoun, and I didn't need that complication right now.

"So how does the sap get turned into syrup?" asked a gray-haired man in a bright red fleece jacket.

"Early settlers boiled sap in metal cauldrons on tripods they set up over open fires," Franklin explained. "These days, though, we're a little more sophisticated." Crossing the small room to a door on the far side, he paused for dramatic effect. "Which brings me to the next stop on the tour: the evaporation room!"

"He's like Willy Wonka giving a tour of the chocolate factory," said Calhoun, and Mackenzie and I both laughed.

"I'm in heaven," Mackenzie murmured as Franklin flung

open the door and we were suddenly enveloped in a warm, maple-scented cloud of steam. She closed her eyes and inhaled deeply. "Wake me up when Spring Break is over."

"Hello, everyone, I'm Frank Freeman," said Franklin's father, who was waiting for us next to a long piece of gleaming stainless steel equipment. "As you can see, ours is a completely modern processing facility. Our wood-burning evaporator here can process about twenty-five gallons of sap per hour."

We watched as he opened a furnacelike door at the far end of the apparatus and threw in more wood. The coals and half-burned logs inside glowed a brilliant fiery orange. I could feel the heat all the way across the room.

"This is called the firebox," said Mr. Freeman, warming his hands briefly in front of the blaze before shutting the door again. "A storage tank outside feeds the collected sap into this stainless steel evaporator pan." He pointed to the long, low horizontal pan set on top of the evaporator's surface. "As the sap boils, water is released through steam, and the sap becomes more and more concentrated. When it reaches the proper density—a sugar content of sixty-six percent or more—it's officially syrup."

Mr. Freeman looked around the room. "I'm happy to stick around after the tour and answer questions for anyone who wants more technical information, but for the rest of you, I'll conclude by explaining the final step, which is when we filter the syrup to remove any niter, or sugar sand—a sediment of naturally occurring minerals. From there the syrup is bottled and graded and labeled"—he held up a bottle bearing one of Freeman Farm's distinctive orange labels—"and sent next door to our store in the barn, which you fine folks will be visiting next, if memory serves." He winked at the crowd, who all laughed obligingly. "Any questions?"

A hand at the back shot up. "How much sap does a single maple tree typically produce?"

"Good question," said Mr. Freeman. "Usually between ten and twenty gallons, which translates to a quart or two of syrup."

"Wow, that's not much syrup for all that sap," someone else noted, and Franklin's father nodded.

"You are correct. Maple farming is a labor-intensive process, which is one of the reasons that syrup isn't necessarily cheap." He waggled his dark eyebrows. "But every drop is oh so worth it, right?"

The onlookers laughed again.

"Can you put more than one spile in a tree?" asked a woman in a blue cable-knit hat.

"Yes, but you need to be careful not to overtap," Mr. Freeman replied. "The bigger the tree, the more taps you can place. Depending on the circumference of the trunk, you can use one, two, or three spiles."

"So you must have to tap a lot of trees in order to produce a decent amount of syrup," the woman added, and Mr. Freeman nodded again.

"Our farm has one of the biggest and best sugar bushes for miles around," he said proudly. "There are thousands of trees on our property."

"Do the trees mind having their sap taken?" a little kid in the front piped up.

Franklin answered this one. "Not at all. It's kind of like donating blood, in fact. Just as your body replenishes itself, so the tree gets busy producing more sap to replace what's been taken. And, by the way, some maple trees on our property have been tapped for over a hundred and fifty years and are still producing!"

A chorus of oohs and aahs went up at this. I looked over at Mackenzie. I could tell she was enjoying herself. The Freemans put on a good show.

The tour over, Franklin led us out of the sugarhouse and into the barn store next door. It took Mackenzie forever to decide what to buy. I followed her around, keeping an eye on Calhoun as I did. The good thing was, he wasn't hovering around my cousin the way Scooter and Lucas were doing. The bad thing was, he wasn't hovering around me, either. He ignored us both as he leafed through a coffee table book about maple syrup production.

Mackenzie finally settled on maple syrup and maple candy

for her parents. "And Cameron will love this," she said, grabbing a container of maple hot sauce and putting it in her shopping basket.

"Who's Cameron?" asked Scooter, popping up behind us.

"Mr. Perf—" I started to say, but Mackenzie stepped on my foot.

"My, um, friend," she finished, at the same time that I said "Ouch." "We're on the swim team together back in Austin."

I gave her a look. Since when was Cameron McAllister just a "friend"? Apparently my cousin was enjoying all the male attention here in Pumpkin Falls.

"I should be getting back," said Lucas, glancing anxiously at his watch. His outings always came with a time limit. "My mother said she'd treat us all to lunch at Lou's, if you guys want to come with me."

"I never turn down a cheeseburger," said Calhoun, who had rejoined us.

"I thought you were going to show us the scene of the crime?" I murmured to Franklin, glancing around to make sure we weren't overheard.

He nodded. "It'll just take a couple of minutes. We can stop there on our way to Lou's. Let me just ask my mom if I can go first."

As we were leaving the barn store, a car pulled into the lot and a woman in jeans and a down vest got out. I'd seen her before at Lovejoy's Books—she was one of the reporters from the *Pumpkin Falls Patriot-Bugle*.

"There you are, Franklin!" said his mother. "Would you mind showing Janet what we found out in the sugar bush yesterday?"

Franklin flashed us an apologetic look. "Sure," he said. "Can I go to lunch at Lou's afterward, Mom? Mrs. Winthrop's treating."

"*May* I go to lunch," his mother replied automatically. I guess all parents have the grammar reflex. "Make it a short one. We need your help here."

"Okay." Motioning to the reporter to follow, he headed for the woods.

"Why is it called a sugar bush?" asked Mackenzie as we trotted after them. "I thought the sap came from trees, not bushes."

"It does," Franklin replied. "But for some reason a stand of maples—especially sugar maples, which is mostly what we have on our farm—is referred to as a 'sugar bush.' It's tradition, I guess."

"Your family puts a lot of work into managing this operation, doesn't it?" asked the reporter, rapidly scribbling in her notebook.

Franklin nodded. "Yep. The sugar bush has to be constantly monitored and maintained. We clear out underbrush and dead wood in the spring and summer, thin the saplings to make sure there are no more than fifty to sixty trees per acre—lots of stuff like that. Then there's equipment maintenance and repairs, cutting and stacking enough wood to keep the evaporator fire going during the sap run, making sure everything is spotless, ordering supplies, setting up the tubing and vacuum pumps—it kind of never ends. Plus, the barn store is a year-round operation, and we do all our own packing and shipping."

I looked at my classmate with new respect. I'd known he was kind of obsessed with maple syrup, but over the past few days I'd seen firsthand how hardworking he and his family were, and how much pride they all took in their business. It was impressive.

The sun was directly overhead now, and I unzipped my jacket. A light breeze stirred in the branches. I looked up, on the alert for birds. It would be totally cool to see another owl.

"What was it Franklin said the Abenakis called this time of year?" I asked my cousin.

"Maple moon, I think."

We walked along in silence. *Maple moon.* I liked the way that sounded. Maybe the maple moon would bring me luck in spotting an owl of my very own. Or maybe my new silver earrings would. I touched a finger to one of them and glanced over at Calhoun again, wondering if he'd noticed them.

A couple of minutes later Franklin stopped in front of a trio of trees. They looked exactly the same as all the others in the woods to me, but he obviously knew his family's property better than I did.

"This is where the sabotage took place," he told us.

I looked at the network of plastic tubing that linked these trees with all the others in the sugar bush. "How can you tell?"

"See that vertical line?" He pointed to a length of black tubing that connected the spile on the tree in front of us to the fatter horizontal blue tubing below it that led downhill. "When we were doing a routine inspection yesterday, we found that it had been severed. We replaced it, but my dad left the piece that had been cut so that we'd remember the spot."

Leaning over, he picked up a slender piece of black tubing that was lying on the ground. The reporter took out her camera, and Mackenzie and I both snapped a few photos as well.

The reporter made us all pose for a picture, and then my friends and I all milled around inspecting the evidence. Suddenly, there was a crashing noise in the underbrush behind us. We turned around to see someone striding toward us through the woods.

It was Coach Maynard, and he did not look happy. Not one bit.

"So this is the way you Freemans want to play it, is it?" he said, shaking something at Franklin. It was a piece of black plastic tubing, identical to the one we'd just photographed. "You want to ambush me *again*? Well, two can play at that game. Where's your father?"

CHAPTER 13

Word travels fast in a small town.

Ella Bellow helped it along, of course. How she found out about the showdown in the sugar bush was a mystery, but I suspected that Janet-the-reporter had something to do with it. Whoever or whatever fed the flame, by the end of the day Pumpkin Falls definitely had a full-blown feud on its hands, and people had started taking sides.

After our photo session at the scene of the crime with the *Pumpkin Falls Patriot-Bugle*, my friends and I had continued into town to Lou's, where we'd discussed what we'd seen over burgers and fries.

"If Coach Maynard's place was hit a second time, do you think it might happen again at your farm too?" I asked Franklin.

"I don't know," he replied, his expression troubled. He dipped a French fry into the puddle of ketchup on his plate. "I hope not."

YOURS TRULY

"It seems like kind of a stupid thing to steal," said Mackenzie. "They'd have to take a ton of sap to even make a single gallon of syrup, right?"

Franklin nodded. "Yup. Forty gallons or so. My dad thinks it might just be vandals. You know, teenagers blowing off steam."

"From Pumpkin Falls?" Scooter looked doubtful.

Franklin shook his head. "He's thinking West Hartfield, maybe. Remember last fall, when some guys from their football team spray-painted their stupid bobcat mascot on the side of one of the Farnsworths' cows?"

Scooter and Lucas and Calhoun started to laugh.

"I'll never forget the look on their faces when Mr. Farnsworth drove up to their next home game with his trailer and unloaded the cow right onto the field during halftime," crowed Scooter. "He said, 'This belongs to you, apparently,' and then let it loose."

"It was epic," Calhoun told Mackenzie, grinning. "That cow chased their football team and marching band into the gym."

"Seriously?" My cousin's voice shot up in disbelief. "People actually do stuff like that here? Pranks with cows?" She paused, gave my classmates a mischievous grin, then trotted out her fake radio announcer voice. "Pumpkin Falls: the town that time forgot."

"Yeah, it's a hopping place," Calhoun replied. Then his

expression grew serious. "I hope your dad's right, Franklin, and it's vandalism. Because if it's sabotage, that means someone deliberately wants someone else's business to fail."

Lucas looked down at his plate. "Wow, I hadn't thought about that."

We were all quiet for a moment, considering this possibility.

"I just wish there was a way to find out for sure who's responsible," said Franklin finally.

Scooter got a funny look on his face. At first, I thought maybe he'd accidentally bitten his tongue or something, but then I realized he'd just had an idea.

"I have to go check something out," he told us, sliding off his counter stool. "I'll text you guys later, okay?"

"That was weird," I said, watching as Scooter sprinted out of the restaurant.

"Uh-huh," Mackenzie agreed.

We finished our lunch, thanked Mrs. Winthrop for treating, and then went our separate ways, agreeing to be in touch again later after we heard back from Scooter.

"So what else do you feel like doing today?" I asked my cousin when we were back outside.

"Weren't we going to try and find a German-English dictionary?"

"Oh yeah, I totally forgot."

I steered her down the street toward Lovejoy's Books,

pausing by the antiques store so she could gawk at the moth-eaten moose head in the display window. It was sporting a pair of sunglasses today, along with a "Maple Madness!" sign around its neck. The Mahoneys had jazzed things up for the celebration.

My cousin pulled out her cell phone and snapped a picture. "Cameron is crazy about—"

"Taxidermy?"

"Shut up. Vintage sunglasses. Those are really cool."

"Vintage sunglasses. I'll be sure and make a note of that," I said drily, and she made a face at me, then laughed.

"Greetings and salutations!" said Aunt True, looking up from the shipment of books she was unpacking as we came through the bookshop door. "You girls are just in time for afternoon treats."

I'd been hoping that was the case.

"Don't touch the ones on the red tray," she added. "I need to drop those off at the General Store later for the Bake-Off."

"I'll bet you win," Mackenzie told her, grabbing two Bookshop Blondies from the other tray on the counter. She took a bite out of one of them. "These are fantastic!"

My aunt looked pleased. "Why, thank you, ma'am."

Miss Marple, who'd heard the word "treats," roused herself from her nap and trotted over. She sat obediently before anyone could say a word—"the preemptive sit," my father has dubbed it—and looked at us expectantly.

"Yes, Miss Marple, you can have a treat too," Mackenzie told her, taking a dog biscuit from the cookie jar on the counter. My grandparents always kept it there for four-legged visitors.

"Dog people are book people," Gramps liked to tell customers. When Lola pointed out that cat people were book people too, my grandfather would wink and add, "But cats don't bring their owners into bookshops on a leash."

"Any chance there's a German-English dictionary somewhere around here?" I asked.

Aunt True's eyebrows shot up. "I didn't know you were taking German."

"I'm not."

"Oh?" She gave me a quizzical look.

"Um, actually, it's for me," Mackenzie said. "It's for this, uh, project I have to do." Out of the corner of my eye, I saw her slip one hand behind her back and cross her fingers.

"Really? Interesting." My aunt disappeared into the travel section, returning a moment later with a thick paperback. "Will this do?"

Mackenzie and I nodded, and my cousin reached for her purse.

"Absolutely not," said Aunt True, waving it away. "What's the point of having a family business if you can't do something nice for your family now and then?" She handed the dictionary to my cousin and smiled. "Good luck with your project."

Mackenzie's face flushed. She was obviously feeling guilty about the fib. Not too obviously, I hoped. "Thanks."

"So I was showing Mackenzie the original Truly's passport," I said quickly, changing the subject. "You know, the one that's hanging on the wall outside my bedroom door? Anyway, we were wondering if you knew what Matthew Lovejoy did for a living. Besides being a soldier in the Civil War, I mean."

"Farming, I think," Aunt True replied absently, turning her attention back to the box of books she was unloading. "I'm pretty sure most of our ancestors were farmers. When they weren't founding colleges and naming lakes and mountains after themselves, that is."

Mackenzie and I exchanged a glance. Whatever it was that the original Truly was so worked up about in her diary sure didn't sound like farming.

"Oh good!" cried my aunt. "The new Inspector Mistlethwaite mystery is here!"

I smiled at her. "You thound like Pippa."

She smiled back and passed me a stack of books. "I thuppothe I do. Stick two copies on the new releases table by the front door, would you? And put one with Miss Marple's Picks. The other three can go in the mystery section."

I nodded and took them from her. "Um, did Matthew maybe have another business on the side?"

Aunt True peered at me over the top of her zebra-striped reading glasses. "What makes you ask?"

I shrugged. "No particular reason."

"Your grandfather would probably know. He's the family historian."

I glanced up at the clock on the wall and frowned. "What time is it in Namibia?"

Aunt True made a quick mental calculation. "Let's see, they're six hours ahead of us this time of year, so early evening, I think."

I turned to Mackenzie. "Dang! We won't have time to call them before swim practice, and by the time we get home, it will be too late." We'd have to wait and try first thing in the morning.

"Sounds urgent." My aunt gave me a thoughtful look, her curiosity definitely piqued.

"Uh, no, not really," I said hastily, and grabbing my cousin, I scurried off to distribute the new mystery books.

The rest of the afternoon was uneventful, aside from the fact that Coach Maynard was uncharacteristically quiet during afternoon swim practice. I just figured he was embarrassed about losing his temper in front of Mackenzie and Lucas and me earlier at Freeman Farm. I wanted to tell him it was okay, and that I'd seen far worse from Lieutenant Colonel Jericho T. Lovejoy, but I didn't want to embarrass him. Plus, he didn't look like he was in the mood to chat, so I just kept my head down and focused on the workout.

By dinnertime, there'd been no further word from

YOURS TRULY

Scooter, and we were no closer to solving the sabotage mystery. Since it was Hatcher's and Danny's turn to do the dishes, after second helpings of my mom's awesome mac and cheese, Mackenzie and I went up to my room and got out the German-English dictionary. We looked up *"Heimweh"* and *"Zwetschgen"* and *"Schwangerschaftsübelkeit"*—they meant "homesick" and "plum" and "morning sickness"—and then I sent off an e-mail to Gramps. It was the middle of the night now in Namibia, but he'd get it first thing in the morning.

"Want me to read some more?" I asked my cousin when I was done. She was lounging on her air mattress, texting Cameron.

"Sure."

As I pulled the blue-bound diary out from under my pillow, there was a scrabbling noise in my closet. I froze. Had my sister's hamster gotten out of his cage again? The scrabbling didn't sound Nibbles-size, though. It sounded bigger. Bilbo-size, maybe. If Lauren had snuck that ferret into our house, she was in big trouble. Setting the diary down, I got up and crossed the room to check. When I opened the closet door, however, it wasn't Bilbo I discovered, but my sister herself.

"You little sneak!" I said furiously. "You're spying on us!"

"I am not!" Lauren protested.

"You are too!" Grabbing her arm, I yanked her from the closet and pointed to my bedroom door. "Out! Now!"

"But I just—"

"I am sick and tired of your stupid Nancy Drew stuff! We all are. Just quit it, would you?"

Mackenzie shot me a warning glance. "How about we play that board game I promised you and Pippa, Lauren?"

My sister gave her a grateful look. "That sounds good."

"Don't let me catch you spying on us again!" I snapped, still seething. "Ever!"

My cousin frowned at me as the two of them left, but I didn't care. Lauren deserved it—she was really getting under my skin.

I stayed in my room and fumed until it was time to head downtown to our knitting class.

Which was when the real fireworks started.

CHAPTER 14

The first hint we had that something was wrong was that Coach Maynard's wife didn't show up for class.

"That's odd," said Ella, frowning at the clock on the wall. We'd all been at A Stitch in Time for nearly half an hour, which unfortunately wasn't long enough to miraculously transform my project. My so-called sock still looked like a droopy dishcloth. "I ran into Alice this morning at the post office, and she said she was looking forward to our gathering tonight."

"Her car was parked in front of the General Store when I left the library earlier," Mr. Henry reported. "I figured she was dropping off her entry for the Bake-Off."

The other thing that Pumpkin Falls was all abuzz about, besides the string of sap thefts, was the Maple Madness Bake-Off. The General Store traditionally hosted the presentation table, where people could ogle the entries before the judges made their decision. Mackenzie and I had offered to drop off

Aunt True's Bookshop Blondies on our way home earlier, so we could scout the competition.

"She's definitely going to win," Mackenzie had said, eyeing the assortment of muffins, bars, cookies, candy, cakes, and other assorted treats on display.

"I don't know," I'd replied, my mouth starting to water. "I've had Mrs. Freeman's Maple Fudge, and it's awesome. And Mr. Henry's Maple Walnut Cupcakes look pretty great too."

Everything had looked pretty great, actually. I had no idea how the judges were going to decide.

Now, back at A Stitch in Time, the phone on Ella's sales counter rang. She got up to answer it. And then Mrs. Freeman's cell phone rang, and so did my mother's, and so did just about everybody else's in the knitting class.

"She said what?" said Ella.

"They're doing what?" said my mother.

"You've got to be kidding me!" said Mrs. Freeman, and sprang to her feet.

Ella ran for the door, and my mother shoved her knitting into the bag of books about the Underground Railroad that Mr. Henry had brought for her and got up to follow her.

My cousin and I looked at each other, mystified.

"What's H-A-P-P-E-N-I-N-G?" asked Annie.

My mother looked over at my cousin and me. "Come on, girls. That was your father. Your aunt needs reinforcements over at the General Store. It sounds like a riot's about to break out."

By the time our entire sock class arrived, the General Store was in an uproar.

"Absolutely no way!" I heard Mrs. Farnsworth shouting, as I peered over the crowd to try and see the cause of the commotion. Sometimes it really helps to be six feet tall.

Mackenzie tugged on my sleeve. "What's going on?"

I glanced down at her, grateful for once that I wasn't petite. The only thing my poor cousin could see was Bud Jefferson's back. "Mrs. Farnsworth—she and her husband run the store, remember?"

"I thought they raised cows."

"They do that, too," I replied. "She's upset about something, but I'm not sure what yet."

"This is ridiculous!" Aunt True was shouting back. "We can't let this divide our town!"

I edged my way through the crowd. My mother and Mackenzie followed, using me as a battering ram. The General Store owner was squared off against my aunt. Behind them were two long tables covered with maple leaf–printed fabric. The plates piled high with Bake-Off entries were evenly divided between the two.

"We've never had two tables before—just one," Aunt True continued. "What kind of a message does this send to our community?"

"The message that some of us don't agree with what's going on," Mrs. Farnsworth said stubbornly.

"Surely we're bigger than this!" my aunt protested.

That's when I saw the signs. One table was marked TEAM FREEMAN, and the other TEAM MAYNARD. My swim coach's wife was standing behind the Team Maynard table with her arms folded across her chest.

"Uh-oh," I said.

"What?" asked Mackenzie, tugging my sleeve again. "Uh-oh," she said, when I pointed to the signs.

"Hatfields and McCoys," said my mother grimly.

Just then my father stepped forward. "I'd like to offer a solution," he said, his deep voice booming.

One thing about having a father who's ex-military, he knows how to command respect. The crowd quieted down as he turned to face them. "The Farnsworths have generously hosted the Maple Madness Bake-Off here at their store for many years—since I was a boy, in fact!"

"Last week, you mean?" someone called. That got a laugh.

"We all owe them our thanks," my father continued, smiling. He clapped his good hand against his prosthetic one and a ripple of applause and nods of agreement ran through the gathered throng as people followed suit. "Perhaps it's unfair to ask Ethel to go against what she feels is her right, since it's her store. And so, if it's amenable to everyone—Joyce, are you here to count the vote?" He looked around for the town clerk, who raised her hand from the back of the crowd. "If you all agree, I'd like to offer Lovejoy's Books as host for this year's Bake-Off."

You'd have thought he'd just suggested removing Paul Revere's bell from the steeple of the church. People looked that shocked. His offer completely took the wind out of Mrs. Farnsworth's sails. From the expression on her face it was clear that she didn't know what to say.

"What an excellent idea!" The crowd parted as Ella Bellow swept forward. "Jericho, I heartily agree."

Ella Bellow may be many things, including gossip central, but she's also one of our town's oldest residents, and people respect her.

"I think it's a good idea too," said Mrs. Freeman. "And, Alice, I want to assure you again that my family had absolutely nothing to do with what has been happening on both of our farms. Can't we rise to the occasion here, together, for the good of Pumpkin Falls?"

Mrs. Maynard didn't look convinced.

"This will just be a temporary change of venue, of course," my father hastened to explain. "I'm not trying to steal the spotlight or undermine town tradition in any way. I'm simply offering a solution during what seems to have become a stressful time for our town. Think of Lovejoy's Books as Switzerland—neutral territory. No choosing sides, no swirl of rumors or counter rumors, just delicious baked goods being judged on their own merits."

"Switzerland? Are you kidding me?" murmured Mackenzie, who was having trouble keeping her face straight.

"Don't say it," I warned, but it was too late.

"The town that time forgot," she whispered in her radio announcer voice, grinning at me. I pretended I didn't hear her.

The vote was taken, and everyone agreed. Well, almost everyone. Coach Maynard's wife took her Maple Coffeecake from the Team Maynard table and swept past us without a glance. A couple of her close friends followed suit. The rest of the crowd formed a procession down Main Street as the baked goods were gathered up and transferred to our bookstore. My aunt and I ran ahead to grab a long folding table from the basement.

"We'll set it up back in the Annex," Aunt True said as we wrestled the table into place. In short order it was covered with a tablecloth and the baked goods and their entry cards arranged—all mingled together, this time, with no TEAM MAYNARD and TEAM FREEMAN signs. Then everybody stood around awkwardly for a few minutes trying to pretend nothing had happened. And then they went home.

"Well done, J. T.," said Ella Bellow, patting my father's good arm as the last of the crowd left.

"That was brilliant, honey!" My mother beamed at him. "I was worried for a moment there that a few people might grab pitchforks."

Mrs. Freeman looked tired but relieved. "This really has been a stressful couple of days."

YOURS TRULY

"Let's just hope the truce holds until the judging," said my father.

My aunt looked up from where she was busy covering all the Bake-Off entries with plastic wrap. "It will hold for you, J. T.," she said, smiling at him. "You're a hero in this town."

My father gave her an uncharacteristically shy smile in return. He doesn't like to think of himself as a hero, just a soldier who did his duty for his country.

As I watched the two of them, I thought about what Aunt True had told me, back when I'd asked why she'd given up her travels to work at the bookshop. "Family is everything," she'd said. Maybe she was right.

"Small-town life can be tricky sometimes, but when it works, there's nothing like it," my mother observed.

"Pumpkin Falls," whispered Mackenzie in her radio announcer voice, quietly so nobody but me could hear her. This time I didn't pretend to ignore her. Instead, I slipped my arm through hers and whispered back, "The town that time forgot."

CHAPTER 15

"You keep telling me that this town is boring," said Mackenzie, looking up from the *Pumpkin Falls Patriot-Bugle*. She was seated at the kitchen table, eating a bowl of cereal. "It's not boring at all."

Of course it's not boring when you're the center of attention all the time, I thought, glancing over at the front page. My cousin had been glued to it ever since we came downstairs for breakfast.

SABOTAGE IN PUMPKIN FALLS? blazed the headline. SAP RUSTLERS STAGE BRAZEN HEIST!

Prominently featured beneath the headline was the picture taken yesterday of my friends and me at Freeman Farm. We were standing in front of one of the maple trees at the scene of the crime, and Mackenzie was front and center, her trademark Gifford sunflower smile on full display. I was barely visible, just a part of my head poking up behind Franklin, Scooter,

Lucas, and Calhoun. Franklin and Scooter and Lucas were supposed to be examining the evidence, but the camera had caught them gawking at Mackenzie. It was hard to tell which way Calhoun was looking. Not at me, though. That much I could tell.

Mackenzie was my cousin and my best friend. It wasn't as if she were doing something on purpose to make me feel like I was in stealth mode. She was just being, well, Mackenzie. But I didn't like feeling this way either. Left out. Overlooked. Ignored.

And what she'd said about Calhoun the other day—that he was cute—bothered me too. I couldn't figure out what she'd meant by it. Was it just a casual observation, or was she interested in him? And, more important, was he interested in her?

I pushed back abruptly from the table. My mother held up her coffee cup wordlessly. She was engrossed in a picture book she must have pulled out of Mr. Henry's library bag—*Moses* was its title, and it looked like it was about Harriet Tubman. Apparently, she'd finally settled on a topic for her term paper. I poured her a refill, then grabbed my jacket from its hook by the back door and went outside to feed the birds.

A light breeze danced through the row of evergreens that marked the edge of my grandparents' property. The branches swayed like swimmers' arms. Closing my eyes, I leaned back against the door for a moment and inhaled deeply. I held my breath for a count of three, then exhaled.

"I hear you," I said, opening my eyes again. Judging by the excited chatter of chickadees in the trees, they knew breakfast was coming. "Be patient."

I took my time filling the feeders and checking the water level in my grandfather's prized heated birdbath, pausing to listen to the twitter and jabber of the juncos, jays, and—wait, was that a song sparrow? I cocked my head. It was! Spring had definitely sprung.

My spirits rising, I headed back to the house. I'd find a way to talk to Calhoun about Scooter and Freeman Farm, and this thing with Mackenzie would sort itself out too. One thing I knew about my cousin for sure—she was loyal. She might tease me if I confided to her that I liked Calhoun, but if her interest in him was more than casual and she knew that I liked him, she'd back right off.

It was all so ridiculous, really—the surprise kiss, the way the boys were falling all over themselves to get Mackenzie's attention, the showdown last night at the General Store—even the whole notion of sabotage in pokey Pumpkin Falls. Sap rustlers? Seriously? The whole idea made me want to laugh.

The problem was, though, that people I knew and cared about were involved, which didn't make it funny at all. The Freemans depended on a good sap run each year to help earn income for their farm, and even though Maynard's Maple Barn was more of a hobby than a livelihood for my swim coach, he was my friend too. That scene at the General Store last night had been ugly. I really didn't want to have to choose sides.

The only solution to the whole mess was to get to the bottom of it quickly, before things got out of hand. Pulling my phone from my back pocket, I scrolled back through the pictures I'd taken at the scene of the crime. Nothing had changed since I'd puzzled over them last night. A bunch of trees in a forest; muddy footprints around the base of several trunks; a length of severed plastic tubing. Something had happened, that much was obvious. But exactly what was anybody's guess.

I scraped the mud off my boots by the back door and went inside. There was no sign of my mother or Lauren, but Mackenzie was still dawdling over the newspaper. And I could hear Pippa in the family room, singing along to *Chicken Parade*, her favorite morning cartoon show.

"I'm going to check my e-mail," I told Mackenzie. "Maybe Gramps has gotten back to us."

"I'll come with you." Dumping her empty cereal bowl in the sink, she followed me upstairs.

My grandfather had indeed e-mailed back. I read his response aloud: *Sorry I missed you last night. Can we connect at nine a.m. your time?*

I glanced at the clock. We had fifteen minutes.

Sure, I wrote back. *Talk to you soon!*

My cell phone vibrated just then. "It's Scooter," I said, frowning at his text message.

PFPE STAKEOUT TONIGHT!

"'PFPE' means Pumpkin Falls Private Eyes, right?" said my cousin, reading over my shoulder.

I nodded.

"But what does he mean by 'stakeout'?"

WHAT DO YOU MEAN, STAKEOUT? I texted back.

SURVEILLANCE, DUH. AT FREEMAN FARM.

Scooter was such a pain.

YOU MEAN US? I texted.

DOUBLE DUH.

I sighed, and rolled my eyes at my cousin. WHAT TIME? I texted back.

NINE THIRTY.

I groaned. Besides the fact that Scooter was infuriating, the last thing I wanted to do was spend Spring Break hiding in the woods, freezing my socks off while we tried to catch a sap rustler.

FORGET IT, I texted back.

My cell phone rang instantly. It was Scooter, of course. I put him on speaker.

"C'mon, Truly," he coaxed. "Calhoun's in, and even Lucas said he'd go with us."

Of course he did. Lucas was hardly going to miss out on an opportunity to spend an evening with the new love of his life.

"I borrowed some stuff from one of my dad's colleagues," Scooter continued.

"What kind of stuff?" I asked suspiciously.

"Video surveillance equipment."

"Seriously?" said Mackenzie. "Cool!"

I could practically hear Scooter's ego inflating. "Yeah, this guy's a private eye—a real one," he boasted. "My dad's law firm hires him sometimes. Anyway, this is sophisticated stuff. We just need to set it up, turn on the camera, and it will relay video to my phone."

"Wow!" Mackenzie sounded impressed. I was too, but I wasn't about to tell Scooter that.

"Why can't we set it up in the daytime, if it's all automatic?" I asked.

"I can't pick it up until later this afternoon. And after that, Calhoun's father is taking us to the Burger Barn over in West Hartfield."

"You just had burgers yesterday."

Scooter's grin was audible. "Calhoun's not the only one who never turns down a burger."

I wasn't sure I liked this idea at all. Sneaking out of the house at night was not only way up on the list of things that I wasn't any good at, but it was also guaranteed to get me a permanent spot in Lieutenant Colonel Jericho T. Lovejoy's doghouse if I were to get caught.

"Oh, come on, Truly!" said Mackenzie, her eyes alight with excitement. "All we're trying to do is help the Freemans—and Coach Maynard."

I hesitated. "I guess."

"Trust me on this one," my cousin said. "I'm older and wiser, after all."

I shot her a look. "By a *week*."

"Kidding! Sheesh."

"We'll meet by the entrance to the shortcut off Hill Street," Scooter told us. "I'll see you at nine thirty sharp. Bring flashlights." He hung up.

I shook my head. "I hope we're doing the right thing."

My cousin shrugged. "If not, at least I'll go home to Austin with an exciting story to tell."

"Yeah, about how I got grounded for life! You're not the one who'll have to face the music with my father if we get caught."

"We won't get caught."

I looked over at the clock again. "Gramps should be calling any minute."

Grabbing the diary from its hiding place under my pillow, I crossed to my desk and sat down in front of my laptop. I didn't have to wait long. A moment later I heard the alert tone that signaled an incoming call.

"Truly!" cried my grandfather as his face flashed onscreen.

"Gramps!" I cried back.

We beamed at each other.

"Your grandmother sends her love," he said. "She's sorry she couldn't be here to talk to you, but she started a

YOURS TRULY

crafts class in the village, and today's the first meeting."

I laughed. "Sounds like Pumpkin Falls," I told him, and explained about Ella's knitting class.

"I'll be sure and tell her that you're with her in needlework solidarity." Peering closer at the screen, Gramps added, "My goodness, is that Miss Mackenzie I spy?"

My cousin leaned over my shoulder and waved. "Hi, Mr. Lovejoy!"

He waved back. "Are you girls having a fun Spring Break?"

We both nodded.

"How's that life list of yours coming along, Truly?"

I told him about hearing the eastern phoebe and the song sparrow. "And guess what? I finally saw an owl!" I left out the fact that Mackenzie spotted it first.

"Huzzah and wahoo!" Gramps gave me two big thumbs-up. "Congratulations, sweetheart! I remember my first owl like it was yesterday. What kind?"

"Barred," I replied.

"Lovely. One of my favorites. Those beautiful dark eyes!"

"I know! I could have watched him forever."

We beamed at each other again. My grandfather and I speak the same language.

"So I e-mailed you because we found something," I told him finally.

"What kind of something?"

I held up the diary.

He looked puzzled. "A book?"

"Not exactly." I explained about the diary, and how and where Mackenzie and I had discovered it.

"How extraordinary!" he exclaimed when I was done. "To think that it was hidden there all these years. Have you read it?"

"Some of it. It's kind of confusing, though, which is why I wanted to talk to you. Can I read you a bit?"

"By all means." He leaned closer to the computer screen, tilting his head in concentration as I read him the passages in question.

"Wind is from the south, she says?"

I nodded.

"And she definitely mentioned a package?"

I nodded again.

"You need to show the diary to your parents right away!" The excitement in my grandfather's voice crackled over the computer screen. "It sounds to me like Truly and Matthew were involved with the Underground Railroad!"

CHAPTER 16

"Where's Mom?" I cried, bounding downstairs to the kitchen. Mackenzie was right behind me.

"She must have gone out while I was feeding Bilbo," said Lauren, coming through the back door.

I pulled my cell phone out of my pocket and shot off a text to my mother: WHERE R U?

HEADING TO CAMPUS, she texted back a moment later. STOPPED BY BOOKSTORE TO SEE DAD.

STAY THERE! HAVE TO SHOW YOU SOMETHING!

NOT GOING ANYWHERE—CUSTOMERS COMING OUT OF THE WOODWORK. COULD USE YOUR HELP.

"Come on, Mackenzie," I said. "We're going into town."

Hearing this, Pippa detached herself from the TV in the family room. "But Mom thaid you have to walk uth to Belinda'th!"

I frowned at her. "Can't you and Lauren go by yourselves?"

Lauren shot me a dirty look. "Of course."

"But Mom thaid you'd do it," Pippa whined, clinging to Mackenzie's hand.

"I'd like to see Belinda's anyway," my cousin said. "You've told me so much about it."

I sighed. "Fine." And tucking the diary into my jacket pocket, I hustled everyone out the door.

Belinda's house was at the very end of Maple Street. A sprawling Victorian with a wrap-around porch, it was nearly as big as my grandparents' house. Belinda was outside, bundled in her favorite old army coat and sweeping the front path in time to a melody we couldn't hear. Seeing us approach, she paused and leaned on her broom.

"Good morning, ladies!" she called, pulling out her earbuds. "You're right on time."

I glanced down at her feet. The fuzzy slippers she was wearing were improbably pink. Belinda didn't seem like someone who'd wear pink. Maybe this was a new look for her, now that she had a "gentleman caller."

Inside, we followed her down the hall to the kitchen, which smelled of something cinnamony baking in the oven. A trio of plates and mugs were set out on the counter, ready for a midmorning snack at Camp Belinda. Mackenzie drifted over to the wood stove. Half a dozen cardboard boxes were clustered around it in a semicircle. She peeked inside the closest one and squealed in delight.

"Kittens!"

"You were expecting maybe lizards?" I murmured, and she swatted my arm.

"You could take one home with you," said Belinda, who never gave up. "That little gray one, maybe? I have an extra airline carrier. It fits right under the seat."

Mackenzie gazing longingly at the contents of the nearest box.

"Feel free to pick one out—I mean up," Belinda added, tossing my sisters and me a wink.

I had to get my cousin out of here, fast, or she'd be a goner. I grabbed her by the arm and steered her toward the door. "Sorry, but we can't stay," I told Belinda. "Mom says the bookstore is getting slammed, and she needs our help."

"I could come along too," Lauren offered.

I glared at her. I was still pretty angry about yesterday's little spying episode. "No way. You need to stay here with Pippa."

"But—"

"I need your help too, missy," Belinda added hastily, noting Lauren's mutinous expression. "And so do the kittens. Now that the Bake-Off has moved to the bookstore, Ethel Farnsworth said we could use the General Store to set up a kitten display. Cash in on all the tourists, you know." She turned to me. "Tell True I'll just be down the street if she needs an extra pair of hands. No reason Lauren and Pippa can't handle Kitten Central on their own for a bit if need be."

The minute we were out of the house, I broke into a run. Mackenzie and I were breathless by the time we reached the bookshop. It was jammed, just like my mother had said.

"I haven't seen this many customers since our grand reopening during Winter Festival," I told my cousin, scanning the crowd for my mother. Spotting her back in the children's section, I made my way through the crowded aisles.

"Can I show you something?" I asked.

"Not now, honey," she said. "Your aunt needs you up front."

She shooed us off, and Mackenzie and I maneuvered our way back through the throng to the sales counter.

"Girls!" said my aunt, looking uncharacteristically frazzled. "Thanks for coming—it's all hands on deck today."

She passed a tray of Bookshop Blondies to Mackenzie. "You're on treat patrol—just walk around the store and pass these out, okay?" Turning to me, she said, "And if you could take over the cash register for these lovely customers, that will free me up for—well, for everything else." She glanced around, frowning.

The diary could wait. Taking off my jacket, I stuffed it under the counter and turned to the first person in line. "May I help you?"

For the next hour, I did nothing but ring up sales. Tour bus after tour bus pulled up in front of the store, disgorging customers. Apparently, half the senior centers in Boston were offering midweek "sugaring off" tours, and Maple Madness in Pumpkin Falls was a priority destination.

"Want to swap assignments?" asked my father, leaving his station at the front door and coming over to the sales counter. He added in a whisper that only I could hear, "I've had about enough of charm detail."

My father was in charge of ferrying the new purchases—and their delighted owners, most of whom were elderly ladies—back to the buses. He wasn't the most sociable person on the planet, but he'd sucked it up and put his Lieutenant Colonel Jericho T. Lovejoy game face on today.

"I'll take over for you, J. T." Aunt True emerged from the back office. "You can take the cash register. I need Truly to do some restocking." She handed me a hastily scribbled list. "Everything maple themed is selling like hotcakes, if you'll pardon the pun. Grab as many of these titles as you can find and put them on the table near the door."

"Got it."

"Oh, and give Grace Franklin a call, would you? We can't keep their merchandise on the shelves this week. See if they can bring over more of whatever surplus they've got in the barn store."

I hurried off to do her bidding. After I made the call to Freeman Farm, I gathered up cookbooks, coffee table books, travel guides, children's picture books—whatever we had with even a vaguely maple theme—and stacked them on the big table with the new releases where they could easily be seen, and hopefully purchased.

"Do you have a copy of *Maple Country Mufflers?*" asked a petite woman in a bright red sweatshirt. Emblazoned on it was a picture of a crown and the words KEEP CALM AND KNIT ON.

I shook my head. "We sold the last one just a few minutes ago. Sorry. You could check across the street at A Stitch in Time, though. They had a few copies when I was there last night. Be sure and tell Mrs. Bellow, the owner, that I sent you!"

Maybe that would win me a brownie point or two with Ella.

"Aren't you a helpful young lady!" the woman told me, reaching up and pinching my cheek. I stared after her in astonishment as she headed for the door.

Mackenzie, who'd come by with a nearly empty treat tray just in time to witness this scene, burst out laughing. "The last time anybody did that to me, I was, like, six."

"No kidding."

"Is that all that's left of the Bookshop Blondies?" said Aunt True in dismay. "Truly, could you see if maybe there are more in the freezer up in my apartment? I may need to bake another batch." She lowered her voice. "These tourists are like locusts. It's all I can do to keep them away from the Bake-Off table in the Annex. They keep lifting the plastic wrap and sneaking bites—I'm worried there won't be anything left for the judges!"

YOURS TRULY

I dashed upstairs, making sure that Memphis was locked securely inside when I left Aunt True's apartment. Today was not a good day for him to escape.

A few minutes later I returned with the frozen Bookshop Blondies to find half the customers lining up to pose for pictures with Miss Marple, and the other half clustered around Augustus Wilde.

"He came in looking for Belinda, and someone recognized him," Mackenzie muttered. "Or maybe he told someone who he was."

I grinned. "That sounds more like Augustus."

"Either way, you missed a lot of fangirling."

"Believe me, I've seen it before."

Augustus had a very devoted group of readers, especially older ladies, among whom his colorful capes and shoulder-length silver hair were cause for heart palpitations.

Aunt True flew into high gear arranging an impromptu book signing. I brought up another folding table and chair from the basement while she sat Augustus down with a pen and the half-thawed Bookshop Blondies. My mother herded the eager customers into a line, and Mackenzie and I scooped everything by Augusta Savage off the shelves in the romance section (and from Miss Marple's Picks, where a couple of Augustus's paperbacks had mysteriously appeared) and stacked them in front of our visiting celebrity. The books were snapped up nearly as fast as we set them down.

Forty-five minutes later, the tour buses finally rolled out of town.

"Whew!" said Aunt True, collapsing onto the old church pew that served as a bench by the door. "That was intense."

My mother turned to Mackenzie and smiled. "And here y'all thought Pumpkin Falls was a sleepy little town, didn't you, sweetheart?"

"Too bad it isn't like this every day," said my father. "We'd be gazillionaires."

The bell over the door jangled, and we looked over to see Erastus Peckinpaugh come in. He smiled at my aunt. "Ready for our lunch date?"

Aunt True's cheeks turned pink. "Ready," she replied primly.

"Wait," I told her. "Before you go, Mackenzie and I have something you all need to see."

CHAPTER 17

"Shhhhhh!"

"Shhhhhh yourself!" I hissed back.

Scooter was driving me nuts. He was in full show-off mode again tonight, swaggering around in an attempt to impress Mackenzie.

Who seems to be in the mood to be impressed, I thought sourly, casting a sidelong glance at my cousin. Her pent-up excitement had found an outlet in giggling over Scooter's antics.

Mackenzie had been wound up ever since the two of us had managed to sneak out of the house. Not an easy trick, given the fact that my father had radar that didn't quit. Fortunately, he'd been worn out after the Maple Madness rush at the bookstore and had fallen asleep in front of the TV. As for my mother, the house could have burned down and she wouldn't have noticed. When we left, she was still totally absorbed in another book about the Underground Railroad.

My cousin and I had reached the rendezvous at nine thirty sharp, just as we'd all planned. Scooter and Calhoun were waiting for us, but there'd been no sign of Lucas, who was just now straggling into sight.

"Sorry, guys," he panted. "I wasn't sure how I was going to get past my mom. I ended up climbing out my bedroom window."

"Whatever," said Scooter. "Let's go."

We followed him into the woods, using our cell phone torch apps to illuminate the muddy path.

All of a sudden, a voice boomed out of nowhere: "WHAT ARE YOU KIDS DOING?"

I jumped and let out a shriek. Mackenzie and Lucas did too. Scooter dropped his cell phone, along with a word that's at the very top of Lieutenant Colonel Jericho T. Lovejoy's Ultimate No-No List.

"Scooter!" I said, shocked, then turned around and shined my cell phone at—"Hatcher?"

My brother grinned at me.

"I thought you were Dad!" I said, smacking his arm. "You nearly gave us all heart attacks!"

"I spotted you and Mackenzie sneaking out. What's going on?"

My friends and I looked at one another. What choice did we have? We were going to have to let him in on our secret.

"Um, Operation Sugar Bush," I said reluctantly, knowing even as I said the words that I was in for it.

Which I was.

"Operation *Sugar Bush*?" Hatcher's voice shot up an octave. "What are you guys, the marines?"

Squirming, I opened my mouth to retort, but before I could say anything, he continued, "Oh, wait—this is one of your 'Pumpkin Falls Private Eyes' things, right?" He smirked, clearly enjoying my discomfort. He'd teased me endlessly about my "dorky little club," as he called it, back around Valentine's Day when he'd found out about it.

"If you must know," I said hotly, "we're going on a stakeout."

Scooter held up his camera bag. "We have surveillance equipment and everything."

Hatcher eyed the bag doubtfully. "Real surveillance equipment?"

Scooter nodded.

Calhoun did too. "I've seen it," he assured my brother. "It's legit."

That got my brother's attention. His cocky grin faded. "So what's the plan?"

I explained about how we wanted to help the Freemans—and Coach Maynard—by seeing if we could get to the bottom of the sap thefts. "Franklin's meeting us in the woods by their farm at twenty-two hundred hours," I told him. "He's going to help us set up the video camera near the scene of the crime."

"That's not a bad idea," said Hatcher. "It might actually work."

"You're not going to tell Dad, are you?"

"Not if you let me come along."

"I want to come too!"

I whirled around to see my sister Lauren emerge from behind a tree. I gaped at her. "What are *you* doing here!"

She shrugged. "I saw you and Mackenzie sneak out, and then Hatcher did too. I wanted to see where you all were going."

"You need to go home on the double!"

She scowled. "No."

"Lauren!"

"I'll tell Mom and Dad."

"You, you—*weasel*!" I sputtered. "If you do, I swear I'll—"

Mackenzie placed a hand on my arm. "It's okay, Truly. I'll keep an eye on her."

Hatcher and I exchanged a glance over Lauren's head. He lifted an eyebrow. I knew exactly what he was thinking. He was thinking that if our parents got wind of this—if Lieutenant Colonel Jericho T. Lovejoy got wind of this, to be exact—we'd be grounded until we were thirty. Lauren had us over a barrel, and she knew it.

"Fine," I snapped at my sister. "You can come along. But

YOURS TRULY

I don't want to hear a word out of you, understand? Not a single word."

She held up a finger to her lips and nodded.

Making a big show of turning my back on her, I looked at my friends. "Let's go."

My brother took over the lead as we continued up the trail. Dad said Hatcher was a natural leader, and it was true. I hadn't spent much time with him lately, and it was nice to have him along. My brother and I used to be inseparable, but ever since the move to Pumpkin Falls, things had been different, especially now that wrestling season and swim team were in full swing. Practically the only time I got to see Hatcher anymore was at the dinner table.

Fifteen minutes later he held up a closed fist. I stopped abruptly, and my friends all piled into me.

"What's the *matter* with you, Truly Drooly?" Scooter demanded.

"Don't call me that!" I shot back. "And what's the matter with *you*—don't you ever watch movies?" We Lovejoy kids had known the military hand signals since we were still being pushed around in strollers. I held up a closed fist. "It means 'stop,' duh."

Scooter reddened and opened his mouth to retort. Before he could, though, my brother shushed him.

"Zip it," he said. "We're about to pass Coach Maynard's place, and he's got a dog."

I'd forgotten about that. We all fell silent as we snuck past Maynard's Maple Barn. A few minutes later we reached the edge of the Freeman family's property.

Franklin must have been watching for us, because he stepped out of the shadows almost immediately. "Hey, guys," he whispered, motioning us over. "Thanks for coming. My dad and I found more evidence of tampering today. It looks like the sap rustler is still at large."

As quietly as we could, we followed him single file to the spot where we'd been photographed yesterday morning by the *Pumpkin Falls Patriot-Bugle*.

"This is where we'll set up, then," said Scooter, putting his camera bag down. He unzipped it and rummaged inside, pulling out a video camera, a funny-looking tripod, and several attachments.

"It's freezing out here!" Mackenzie complained, hopping from one foot to the other.

"Cold nights plus warm days equal a good sap run, remember?" Franklin told her, moving closer and rubbing her nearest arm briskly.

Leaving his camera bag, Scooter sprang into action too, and began rubbing Mackenzie's other arm.

"Thanks, y'all," said my cousin, as a beet-faced Lucas shifted from one foot to another, looking for an opening. Only Calhoun was oblivious; he was too busy examining the surveillance equipment.

YOURS TRULY

The corner of my brother's mouth quirked up as he watched my friends. He looked over at me, and I stifled a giggle. I might not be seeing a lot of Hatcher these days, but at least our sibling shorthand was still working loud and clear. One of the things I liked best about my brother was that the same things strike us funny. That and the fact that we rarely even had to say a word to know what the other was thinking. And right now, we were both thinking that my classmates were completely twitterpated.

"How does this thing work?" asked Calhoun, who was still fiddling with the camera equipment.

Scooter pried himself reluctantly away from Mackenzie and picked up the tripod.

"See these flexible legs? You can wrap them around just about anything," he told us, demonstrating on a nearby branch. Once the tripod was secure, he attached the camera and angled it so that it pointed directly at the maple tree in question. "I've already programmed in my cell phone number." He glanced over to check and see if Mackenzie was impressed, and she smiled at him in encouragement. "Let's give it a test." He pressed a button on the camera, and a second later his cell phone vibrated. "Check it out!" he crowed. We clustered around him, and he showed us the image that had just been sent.

"That's really awesome," said my brother.

"How long will it record for?" I asked.

"For as long as it senses activity," Scooter said.

"What if the battery wears out?" Mackenzie wanted to know.

"It won't. The camera only comes on when something's actually moving." Scooter pointed to a small attachment that perched on top of the camera. "See? That's a motion detector."

"So now what?" asked Lucas.

"Now we wait," Scooter replied.

"Here?"

"Weren't you paying attention, Winthrop? The camera will send the video feed directly to my cell phone, so we can all go home. I'll let you know the minute it alerts me to any activity."

Franklin dropped us off at the edge of the path leading back to town, and we said good night and squelched off into the forest. The walk home seemed longer. We were all tired and cold. Lauren had kept her promise and hadn't said a word, but her teeth were chattering audibly. I glanced back at her. The little moron had run out of the house with only a sweatshirt on. I felt a prickle of guilt. *I should probably give her my jacket*, I thought. She was my sister, after all.

Before I could do it, though, Calhoun beat me to it.

I looked at him in surprise. His eyes met mine, and he shrugged and looked away. *Cool on the outside, marshmallow on the inside*, I thought. That was part of the mysterious equation that was Romeo Calhoun.

"I am so not looking forward to swim practice tomorrow

morning," said Mackenzie, who was shivering despite all of the arm rubbing earlier.

"Me neither," said Lucas.

Mackenzie looked over at me, a hopeful expression on her face. "Maybe we could skip it?"

"You could get away with it, but not me," I told her. "Dad would never let me skip."

"What if you told him you were sick?"

Hatcher snorted. "He knows every trick in the book."

"We'll just have to power through," I said, and Mackenzie made a face. I could see my brother grinning at us in the darkness.

"Gotta think like a wrestler," he said. "No pain, no gain."

Mackenzie groaned.

A few minutes later we reached the corner of Maple and Hill Streets.

"Don't forget to text us if the camera picks anything up," I whispered to Scooter.

"I won't."

My classmates vanished into the darkness. Hatcher and Mackenzie and Lauren and I turned down Maple Street and headed for home.

"Uh-oh," I said as we drew closer. The lights in the kitchen were on, and I could clearly see my parents sitting at the table. Aunt True and Professor Rusty were with them. "Do you think they noticed we were gone?"

"I hope not," said Hatcher.

"There's no way we're going to be able to sneak past them!" Mackenzie had a panicked look on her face. "Uncle Jericho will probably put me on the first plane home."

"Don't worry, I've got your six," my brother assured me, using Dad's military-speak for "I've got your back." "You guys go wait in the bushes by the front door. Give me a minute or two, and I'll let you in."

"You're going to get caught!" I protested.

He flashed me one of his sunflower smiles. "I'll just tell them I went for a run."

Mackenzie and Lauren and I did as Hatcher told us to. Sure enough, a minute later the front door opened a crack and he motioned us inside.

"Piece of cake," he whispered.

There was a burst of laughter from the kitchen. The three of us darted past him and started upstairs. Lauren and I automatically remembered to avoid the creaky step, but it let out a screech as Mackenzie stepped on it. We all froze.

"Hatcher?" my mother called.

"Yes, Mom?"

"Hurry up and get to bed—you need your rest for wrestling tomorrow."

"Just heading up now!" Hatcher called back.

"And don't wake the girls."

Hatcher grinned at us. "Too late," he whispered, and we grinned back at him.

The four of us tiptoed the rest of the way up as quickly and as quietly as we could.

"Let me know if you hear anything from Scooter," Hatcher murmured, and I nodded as he disappeared down the hall toward the third-floor stairs.

I took Calhoun's coat from Lauren and made sure she went directly to her room. I didn't want her sneaking back downstairs and double-crossing us. Back in my room, Mackenzie and I changed into our pajamas. My cousin flopped down onto the air mattress with a contented sigh.

"I'm exhausted!" she said. "That was fun, though."

"Yeah," I replied, crawling under the covers. "I hope Scooter's scheme works."

"Do you think Professor Rusty brought the diary back?"

At the bookshop earlier today, he'd about jumped out of his skin when we showed everyone the diary and told them what Gramps had said. He'd begged us to let him take it over to the college so his colleagues in the history department could examine it. My parents agreed only after he promised to bring it right back.

"Want to go downstairs and check?" I asked.

"I'm too tired," my cousin said, her eyes already shut.

I threw off the covers. "I'll go. Back in a flash."

I yawned and rubbed my eyes as I entered the kitchen, feigning sleepiness. "I heard voices," I said in my best you-just-woke-me-up voice. "What's going on?"

"Sorry, honey. We didn't meant to wake you," my mother replied. She glanced over my shoulder. "Or you, Lauren."

I turned to see that Little Miss Tagalong had followed me downstairs. She gave me a smug look, then pretended to yawn too. I glared at her.

"Just too much excitement around here today!" said Aunt True, smiling at us both.

"Is that the diary?" Lauren's gaze was riveted to the small blue leather-bound book that lay open on the kitchen table in front of my aunt. "The one Truly told us about at dinner?"

"It is indeed!" said Professor Rusty. His wild halo of hair was wilder than usual, as if he'd been running his hands through it a lot in excitement today. Which he probably had.

"Professor Rusty and his colleagues think your ancestor's diary is credible evidence of an Underground Railroad operation here in Pumpkin Falls!" my mother told us. "Isn't that thrilling, girls?" Her eyes were shining. Her professor's love of history was clearly contagious.

"'Packages' is definitely Underground Railroad code for runaway slaves," Professor Rusty had told us back at the bookshop, after I'd read a couple of the passages Gramps had told me to share. "This is amazing!"

Aunt True had immediately put the CLOSED sign up on the door.

"I don't know about you all, but I have goose bumps," she'd announced. "I need to see where you found the diary right this minute."

"No need to close the shop, True," my father had told her. "I'll man the fort."

"You will not! This is a Big Moment in Lovejoy History, and you need to be there too, J. T."

My mother nodded and linked her arm through my father's good one. "True is right. We're all going home."

Outnumbered, my father had shrugged, placed a sticky note on the door that said *Back in an hour*—"just so we don't miss out on too many customers"—and followed us to the minivan, where we all piled in for the short drive back to Gramps and Lola's house.

"I just can't believe it," Aunt True kept saying as Mackenzie and I showed off the loose floorboard in my closet and the crevice beneath it where the diary had been hidden. "All those years when this was my bedroom—it was right here waiting!"

Now, standing in the kitchen, I was glad that Professor Rusty had kept his promise. I very much wanted to find out what happened to the original Truly. I reached out to pick the diary up.

Lauren beat me to it.

"I want a turn too," she said, snatching it away.

"Lauren! I was the one who found it!" I tried to tug it away from her, but she gripped it tighter.

"Girls!" said my mother, sounding shocked. "Be careful!"

"Put the diary down this minute." The warning note in my father's voice meant business.

"Historical artifacts require special handling," Professor Rusty added anxiously as I let go, and Lauren reluctantly set the small blue book back on the table. Professor Rusty slanted a disapproving glance at the two of us, then turned to my parents. "I highly recommend that the diary remain at the college for safekeeping. There are professionals on staff who will know how best to preserve the fragile pages. Plus, our curator has offered to have it transcribed. That way, scholars and researchers can read it too. This is a find of major historical significance, and deserves a wide audience."

Aunt True must have seen the crestfallen expression on my face, because she said, "It's an important historical artifact, Rusty, true, but it's also a family heirloom, and one with a direct connection to me, and to my niece and namesake. We'd like a chance to read it first. All of us."

"True, you don't under—"

"Erastus Peckinpaugh," said my aunt, pulling herself up to her full height. Which is the same as me—six feet tall—and impressive, at least when she does it. "You can wait another day or two."

"Yes, ma'am," Professor Rusty replied meekly.

I smothered a smile. Lieutenant Colonel Jericho T. Lovejoy himself had nothing on my aunt when she was in full boss mode.

Aunt True looked over at me again. "If you want access to the diary, Truly, there's a condition."

"Fine. What?"

"Lauren gets to read it with you."

I groaned. "Aunt True! No! She'll ruin everything."

"Truly!" said my mother, shocked. She gave me that look she always gives me when I disappoint her.

I hurtled on, oblivious. "It's true, Mom! Ever since Mackenzie got here, all Lauren's done is get in the way. She never leaves us alone! She's a total pest."

"I am not!" my sister protested. "You're the mean one—you don't want to let me do anything with you! Mackenzie is my cousin too!"

"Maybe she doesn't want you around either—did you ever think of that?" The words came flying out of my mouth before I could stop them.

Lauren's brown eyes filled with tears. "I *hate* you!" she shouted. "Cross my heart and hope to fly! And I'm going to tell—"

"That's enough!" said my father severely.

We Lovejoys know an order when we hear one. The room fell silent. I clenched my jaw so hard my teeth hurt. If Lauren spilled the beans about what the Pumpkin Falls Private Eyes had done tonight, I'd—I'd—I didn't know what I would do.

"So," I said after a long moment, "can I take the diary back upstairs with me?"

"*May* I take it," said my mother automatically, "and not a chance. Not after that outburst."

"But—"

"No buts," said my father firmly. "It remains to be seen whether you get to read any more of it at all. We should probably just give it to Rusty and be done with it." He pointed toward the hall. "To bed. Both of you. Now."

Lauren heaved one of her dramatic sighs, shot me a murderous look, and stomped out of the room. I was tempted to do the same, but figured if I wanted a chance at the diary again I'd better watch my step.

"Yes, sir," I said meekly, and went back upstairs.

CHAPTER 18

I awoke to the sound of rain.

Rolling over, I gazed at the droplets spattering the nearest window and saw that Mackenzie was awake too.

"You're up early," I told her.

"Yeah," she replied. "I think I'm finally getting over the jet lag." She sat up. "So what was going on downstairs last night? I was too tired to come see."

I filled her in on my argument with Lauren—leaving out the part I still regretted saying—and Aunt True's ultimatum about reading the diary with my sister. "If we even get to read it, that is," I finished glumly. "My dad was pretty steamed at Lauren and me. He may have given it back to Professor Rusty already."

But when we went downstairs a few minutes later, the diary was still on the kitchen table.

"Power bar?" my father said nonchalantly, as if nothing had happened.

"Thanks," I replied, taking one. I looked at the diary. I wondered if I should mention it or just wait for my father to bring it up.

He didn't, though. He just grabbed his keys and headed out to the car.

"Calhoun's jacket!" Mackenzie exclaimed as we started to follow. "Weren't we going to return it after swim practice? Hang on, I'll go back upstairs and get it."

When we got to the pool, we found Coach Maynard in a grumpy mood again. He didn't greet us in his usual cheerful manner, but just paced up and down silently on the pool deck, arms folded across his chest as we completed the warm-up.

"Coach stopped by Lou's this morning for coffee," Lucas whispered to Mackenzie and me between sets of crunches. "The Farnsworths were there, and I overheard them talking. I guess he found more sap lines cut. Mom said the Freemans did too."

"Did you hear anything from Scooter?" I asked.

He shook his head. "Nope. You?"

I shook my head too.

"Pipe down over there!" hollered Coach Maynard. "Save your breath for the workout."

It was a punishing one, almost as if our swim coach was taking out his frustration by making us practice extra hard.

I trudged my way through the sets of intervals and sprints. Up and back, up and back, I churned down my lane in one unending, uninspired slog. Most days swimming cleared my thoughts, but this morning they stayed a stubborn jumble: Truly and Matthew. Scooter's ambush. Calhoun. Mackenzie. The severed sap lines. My pest of a sister.

I'd never been so glad in my life for swim practice to be over.

"Do you guys want to hang out today?" Lucas asked hopefully, as Coach Maynard blew the "all clear" signal on his whistle and we got out of the pool. "My mom said she'd drive us to the bowling alley over in West Hartfield if everybody wants to go."

"Sorry, Lucas," I told him. "We've got plans."

I watched as he drooped off toward the men's locker room. I couldn't help feeling a little guilty. But for some reason I wasn't ready for him or for any of my other friends to know about the diary just yet. It was bad enough that Mackenzie and I had to share it with Lauren.

Hatcher texted me while I was changing: ANY NEWS FROM SCOOTER?

NOTHING YET, I texted him back.

"Almost ready," Mackenzie told me, as I pulled on a pair of jeans and a clean sweatshirt. "I've just gotta dry my hair."

She headed for the mirrors on the far side of the locker room. My hair was still wet. I just couldn't see the point of using a blow dryer. It wasn't like I had a hairstyle, after all—just hair. It would dry on its own soon enough. Tucking it up under my Longhorns baseball cap, I pulled on my clothes, then stuffed my wet swimsuit and towel in my pool bag. I reached for Calhoun's jacket, which had fallen on the floor. As I did, something fluttered out of one of the pockets. It was a piece of paper.

I bent down to pick it up, and froze.

The handwriting on it was Mackenzie's.

Call me! I have something to tell you! she'd written, along with her name and cell phone number.

I stared at the note, numb. *So much for loyalty.*

"Almost done!" sang my cousin, and I crumpled the note in my fist and shoved it into the pocket of my jeans.

Mackenzie was her usual chatty self as we left the pool. We stopped briefly at Calhoun's house to drop off the jacket, but he and his dad had gone out for breakfast, so we left it with his sister.

"I still can't believe that Calhoun has a sister named *Juliet*," Mackenzie said as we splashed our way home.

I just grunted.

"Who wants omelets and bacon?" my mother asked as we came through the back door.

"Me!" Mackenzie replied, peeling off her raincoat and hanging it up in the mudroom. "I'm starving. Thanks, Aunt Dinah!" She slid into a seat at the table.

I hung up my raincoat and sat down too—at the opposite end of the table. The diary had moved, I noticed. It was now directly in front of Lauren.

"Did you remember to feed Bilbo this morning?" my mother asked my sister.

"Yes, ma'am," Lauren replied virtuously. "And I cleaned out his cage, too."

"Good girl." My mother set plates down in front of Mackenzie and me. My cousin dove into her breakfast, but I didn't even pick up my fork. My appetite had evaporated.

"Truly, I'm expecting you to keep your word and let Lauren read the diary with you and Mackenzie," my mother said.

I nodded.

"I'm heading down to the bookstore for a bit this morning. Aunt True has a new marketing idea she wants to run by me."

I nodded again, and she gave me a sidelong glance. "You girls promise me you'll try and get along—and remember what Professor Rusty said about the diary. It's very old and very fragile."

"Yes, ma'am," Lauren repeated.

"I'm putting Truly in charge of it," my mother warned her, and my sister made a face.

"Fine," she mumbled.

My mother placed two more strips of bacon on my cousin's plate, then glanced over at mine. "Truly? Aren't you going to eat your breakfast?"

"I'm not hungry," I said shortly. How could I possibly be

hungry after what I'd discovered in the locker room?

She gave me another look, then turned to Pippa. "How about you, Pipster? Would you like Truly's extra bacon?"

My little sister nodded vigorously.

"And do you want to go to Belinda's, or would you rather stay here with the big girls?"

My heart sank. It was bad enough that I was stuck with Lauren—the last thing I wanted to do was babysit Pippa, too.

But Pippa shook her head. "It'th kitten delivery day," she informed us, smiling her gap-toothed smile. "Belinda thaid I could ride along in her truck and help."

I could tell by the expression on Lauren's face that she was feeling torn. Kittens—all animals—were way up on her list of favorite things, and I was guessing that riding around the Pumpkin River Valley delivering kittens sounded like sheer catnip to her. At the same time, though, I knew how much she wanted to read the diary, especially after she'd made such a big stink last night about feeling left out.

Staying put won out.

"Great. It's settled," said my mother. "I'll see y'all later, then."

As she and Pippa left for Camp Belinda, Lauren got up from the table. I frowned at her. "Where are you going?"

She paused. "Aren't we going to read upstairs in your room?"

I shook my head. "Family room," I said firmly. I might

have to share the diary with her, but I wasn't about to share my room, too.

"Hang on a second," said Mackenzie. "I'm going to go grab my knitting. Want me to bring yours down too?"

"Whatever."

She gave me a funny look. I ignored her.

"Don't touch the diary," I told Lauren as Mackenzie went upstairs. "I've got to feed the birds."

I put the diary on the coffee table in the family room, then grabbed my rain jacket and rubber boots again. It was still pouring outside, and the backyard was a dreary, muddy mess. Pulling my hood up, I picked my way across the soggy lawn to the nearest feeder. There was no excited chatter from the birds this morning. I knew they were out there, though, huddled in the shelter of the tree branches, feathers fluffed as they tried to stay dry. Eventually, hunger would cause them to venture out, and the food would be waiting for them.

Not the owls, though, even if there were any in the neighborhood. Owls and rain didn't mix at all.

There was a price to be paid for that gift of silent flight—owl feathers weren't waterproof. Grounded by soggy feathers, an owl couldn't hunt, and an especially loud, driving rain made it hard for them to hear their prey even if they could. They had to wait it out, and prolonged bad weather could mean hypothermia and starvation.

Talk about kryptonite!

Was Mackenzie my kryptonite? I wondered, swiping angrily at my eyes. Here I thought Lauren was my biggest problem—who knew that it was actually my cousin? I couldn't believe she was writing notes to Calhoun behind my back.

After I was finished filling the bird feeders, I went back inside. Lauren was sitting on the family room sofa next to Mackenzie, who was almost done with her first sock. It looked pretty good—much more like a real sock than the hot mess hanging from my knitting needles, that was for sure.

"So, are you going to read to us?" Mackenzie asked.

"Whatever." As I took a seat in the armchair across from them, my cell phone vibrated.

My cousin looked up sharply. "Is it Scooter?"

I pulled my phone out of my pocket, looked at the screen, and shook my head. "Cha Cha." I read the text message aloud: JASMINE AND I WILL BE BACK TOMORROW! TELL MACKENZIE WE CAN'T WAIT TO MEET HER!

Mackenzie smiled. "Tell them I can't wait to meet them, too."

I grunted, tapped out the message, then shoved the phone back into my pocket and picked up the diary.

"Why don't you tell Lauren what's happened so far," Mackenzie suggested, and I grudgingly explained how the original Truly had received the diary as a gift, then described some of the entries that she'd written.

"Can I see it?" Lauren asked.

"Sure," said Mackenzie.

I didn't move.

"Truly! Let her see it!"

I heaved a sigh and passed the diary to my sister. "Remember what mom said about being careful, okay?"

"Duh." She opened it, took one look at the handwriting, and frowned. "It's in cursive."

"What did you expect?" The words came out sharper than I'd intended, and Lauren flushed.

"Isn't it beautiful?" gushed Mackenzie, moving closer to my sister and putting her arm around her. She glared at me. "I wish I could write that neatly."

Lauren examined the pages. "It's hard to read," she said, disappointed.

"Yeah," I told her, taking the diary back. "That's why I'm in charge."

She shot me a look. I pretended not to notice and began to read aloud:

> *October 15, 1861*
>
> *My little angel arrived early yesterday morning. I have named him Booth, as Matthew wished. But Matthew honors my wish as well, and his middle name is Gerhard, after my dear departed father. Little Booth is the light of my life already, and Mother Lovejoy says he is just the tonic she needed*

for missing her son. We have written to Matthew, sharing the happy news.

Yours, Truly

October 20, 1861
Another package arrived last night. I was not able to help this time, being still abed. Mother Lovejoy hid it safely, and tonight it will be shipped to its destination in Maple Grove, Maine.

Yours, Truly

"Professor Rusty said that 'package' was a code word for 'runaway slave,' right?" said Mackenzie.

I nodded.

"I'll bet they had Maple Madness in Maple Grove," said Lauren, snickering at her own dumb joke.

My cousin laughed obligingly. I didn't, and Mackenzie shot me another look. "It is kind of a funny name, isn't it, Lauren? But why Maple Grove, I wonder?"

"What do you mean?" I asked.

"I mean I wonder why they sent the slaves there."

I shrugged.

"We should find out," Mackenzie continued. "Maybe the Lovejoys had a family connection there or something. We could ask Professor Rusty, or your mother—she's been studying this stuff, so she might know, right?"

"I thought you didn't like history," I said.

"But this really happened!"

"So did history, duh."

"You know what I mean!" she retorted, stung. "This was real people—people who are related to us. Well, to you."

I knew what she meant. And actually, I was just as curious as she was, especially about the original Truly. Eighteen years old, living in a foreign country—a country at war, at that—newly married, and now a new mother, plus she was involved in this supersecret, dangerous work. How could I possibly not want to know more?

"Mr. Henry at the library could help," suggested Lauren. "He knows everything. You could ask him tonight—he's in your knitting class, right?"

"Good idea, Lauren," said Mackenzie. "Let's start a list of questions for him." She scrabbled around in the drawer of the end table for a pen and some paper as I continued reading:

> *November 2, 1861*
>
> *I pray daily to our heavenly Vater to keep Booth's papa safe. We have not heard from Matthew in many weeks. I am glad I have our boy to keep my mind occupied. He is growing splendidly fat, like a little Ferkel.*
>
> *Yours, Truly*

Lauren snickered again. "Splendidly fat!" she repeated in delight.

Mackenzie reached for the German-English dictionary. "'*Vater*' is 'father,'" she reported.

"I could have told you that," I muttered.

"And '*Ferkel*' means 'piglet!'" she added a moment later with glee, and she and Lauren both shrieked with laughter. Suddenly, my cousin got a stricken look on her face. "Do you know if something happened to Matthew? In the war, I mean. I don't know if I could stand it if it did!"

I shook my head, wishing I knew more about my family's history. "We'll find out one way or another, I guess."

November 10, 1861

Reverend Bartlett came to see us today. He says Booth is a fine boy, and he looks forward to the christening. Then our talk grew serious. There are slave hunters in the Pumpkin River Valley, he says. We must be very careful. Our work grows increasingly dangerous. We are always to wait for the sign of the owl before receiving a package, and we are not to trust anyone. There are whispers of money changing hands in exchange for information—yes, even here in Pumpkin Falls. I am much troubled by this news.

Yours, Truly

YOURS TRULY

I paused for a moment, wondering about the sign of the owl that she'd mentioned. Was it a physical sign, like a drawing perhaps? Or was it a sound—a fugitive hooting from the nearby woods, the owl's call a request for help? I wondered too, if Truly knew anything about owls, or was interested in them the way I was. She was feeling more real to me with every page I read in her diary.

> *November 17, 1861*
> *We have had a letter from Matthew! He has been ill, but is now recovered and has rejoined his regiment. He sends his dearest love to little Booth and me and says he cannot wait until our family is together again. Until that time, he begs me to write often and tell him of our baby, and of home.*
> *Winter is coming. I fear for my dear husband, sleeping in a tent out in the cold. Mother Lovejoy and I busy ourselves knitting. At least we can be sure our Matthew has warm socks.*
> *Yours, Truly*

I stared at the page. *No way*, I thought. Truly was knitting socks too? This was almost eerie.

My cell phone buzzed again. I glanced at the screen. "It's Scooter."

Mackenzie looked up from her knitting. "Any news?"

I read his text aloud: "APB to PFPE!"

"What does 'APB' mean?" asked Lauren.

"All points bulletin," Mackenzie explained. "He's alerting the Pumpkin Falls Private Eyes."

WHAT'S UP? I texted back.

GOT SOMETHING TO SHOW YOU, Scooter replied.

CAN U COME OVER? I'M BABYSITTING LAUREN.

"What's he saying?" Mackenzie begged.

"Hang on, hang on," I replied irritably.

BE THERE IN A FLASH, Scooter texted.

BRING LUCAS AND CALHOUN, I texted back. LOLA'S STUDIO.

K.

I put my cell phone back in my pocket and closed the diary. "They're coming over," I told my cousin and my sister. "I told them to meet us in Lola's studio."

My sister's face lit up. "An official meeting of the Pumpkin Falls Private Eyes!"

"You're *not* one of us," I warned her. "You're only allowed to come today because I'm stuck babysitting you."

"You're not babysitting me!" she protested. "I don't need a babysitter!"

I gave a short laugh. "Right."

"What is *wrong* with you, Truly?" Mackenzie demanded. "You're in such a bad mood today!"

YOURS TRULY

I looked at her. What was wrong with *me?* I thought about the crumpled note that was still in my pocket. How about the fact that I had a double-crosser for a cousin?

I knew I was being unfair—Mackenzie didn't know that I'd found her note, and I'd never told her how I felt about Calhoun. I knew that the two of us needed to talk, but right now I was still too upset, plus I didn't want to say anything in front of Lauren. I had enough problems without her knowing about Calhoun too. Talking would have to wait.

"Nothing is wrong with me," I snapped back.

Mackenzie threw down her knitting. "Fine. Have it your way. Let's go up to the studio."

Earlier this winter my grandmother's art studio in the barn ended up being the unofficial hangout for the Pumpkin Falls Private Eyes. I really hadn't expected we'd be using it again—Pumpkin Falls was such a small town, after all, that I couldn't imagine there would be any more mysteries for us to solve. But life was full of surprises.

We went out to the barn-turned-garage and up the stairs to the studio. I slipped the key from its hiding place behind one of Lola's paintings on the landing and unlocked the door.

"It's cold in here," said Mackenzie, shivering.

"It used to be a barn—what did you expect?" I switched on

the space heater. "It warms up pretty quickly, though."

Lauren prowled around the room, inspecting our grandmother's art supplies and books and knickknacks.

"Don't touch anything," I warned.

"Truly!" Mackenzie glared at me.

"What?"

"Quit it!"

"Quit what?"

"Quit being so mean to Lauren."

"I'm not being mean. She's a *pest*."

"You're hopeless." My cousin retreated to the sofa.

A few minutes later I heard footsteps pounding up the stairs. The studio door flew open, and Scooter and Calhoun and Lucas crowded in.

"She's not part of the, uh, PFPE now, is she?" Scooter asked, looking over at my sister Lauren.

"No," I said at the same time that Lauren said, "Yes."

Mackenzie put her arm around my sister's shoulders and shot me a look. "We'll talk about it later. What do y'all have to show us?"

"We're not sure," said Scooter. "We've watched it a few times, and we need you guys to take a look."

We all crowded around his cell phone. Somehow Calhoun ended up beside me, and I was suddenly very conscious of my cousin's note for him in my pocket.

"See the time stamp?" Scooter paused the surveillance video almost as soon as he started playing it, and pointed to a corner of the small screen. "It's just after midnight. That's when something tripped the motion detector and the camera started filming."

He clicked the PLAY button again and the video continued. Nothing was visible at first, just a lot of darkness and the vague outline of tree branches. Then two pinpricks of light swam into focus in the underbrush.

"What's that?" asked Lauren.

"Eyes," Scooter told her.

"Whose eyes?" asked Mackenzie, peering closer.

"Wait and see," said Scooter.

The pinpricks drew closer, glowing green in the reflected light of the camera. Suddenly, they vanished.

"Wait for it," said Scooter.

The picture wobbled. A second later it wobbled again, then began rocking wildly from side to side.

"What's happening?" I asked.

"Something's shaking the camera," said Calhoun.

The final few seconds of the video were a confusing blur of tree branches and dark sky and what looked like fingers and a lot of hair—or was it fur? Mackenzie gave a little shriek and Lauren and I both jumped, startled, as a set of very sharp teeth loomed large, and the hairy something snarled ferociously before the screen went blank.

"Did that . . . that *thing* just try and eat the camera?" I asked. "What the heck was it?"

Scooter shook his head. "Beats me. Calhoun and Lucas and I have watched it about a zillion times, trying to figure it out. Those teeth are huge."

"I think it's a wolf," said Lucas.

"Are there wolves in Pumpkin Falls?" Mackenzie looked genuinely freaked out.

Scooter grinned. "Don't listen to Lucas. He doesn't know what he's talking about."

"Could it be a bear?" I asked. I vaguely remembered Gramps telling Hatcher and Danny and me something about bears once.

"It's possible," said Calhoun. "There are black bears in New Hampshire."

"I think it's Sasquatch," Lauren announced, and five heads swiveled in her direction as we all turned and stared at her. "You know, Bigfoot?"

"There is no such thing as Bigfoot," I scoffed. "You read too much."

She scowled at me. "Nobody knows for sure. It might be for real—people have taken pictures and stuff."

"Those are fake."

She shrugged. "What if they're not?"

YOURS TRULY

My friends and I looked at one another. I thought of those fingers and sharp teeth we'd just seen on the video, and my skin prickled.

But there was no such thing as Bigfoot, right?

CHAPTER 19

"So what do we do now?" Lucas asked.

"Reset the camera and try again, I guess," said Scooter reluctantly. I could tell that Lauren's theory had gotten to him, too. "What else can we do?"

"No way am I going back out there, not if this place is crawling with bears and Bigfoot." Mackenzie crossed her arms over her chest. "Y'all are nuts to even think about it."

"I'll go," offered Calhoun.

If he thought he was going to impress my cousin by volunteering, he was wrong. She just looked at him like he'd lost his mind.

"It's not like it's dark out or anything," Calhoun told her. "It's broad daylight."

My cell phone rang just then. "It's Aunt True. I've gotta take this."

"Truly?" my aunt said when I answered. "We have a

situation here, and I could use your help. Your dad's at physical therapy, and I tried your mother but she didn't answer."

"I think she's over at Belinda's," I told her. "She probably can't hear her phone over all that meowing."

Aunt True didn't laugh at my joke, which was a lame one, admittedly, but still. She usually laughed at my jokes. "Could you come down here and help cover the cash register for a bit?"

"Sure. Is everything okay?"

"Uh, yeah. Mostly. Sort of. We're getting set up for tonight's Maple Madness Bake-Off finals, and we seem to have hit a, uh, road block."

That didn't sound good.

"I'll be right there." I hung up and turned to my cousin. "Something's going on at the bookshop," I told her. "I need to go."

"I'll go with you."

"Me too," Scooter said quickly.

"Dude, you need to come with me," Calhoun protested. "You're the one who knows how the camera works, after all."

Scooter didn't look too enthusiastic about that idea. *Wait a minute*, I thought, watching him. Was Scooter *scared*? Not that I blamed him—I wasn't eager to go back to Freeman Farm, either, after seeing that video—but this was a very un-Scooter-like reaction. Especially in front of Mackenzie.

"The sooner we get this thing fixed, the sooner we can

figure out who the thief is," Calhoun reasoned. "Lucas, we'll need your help too."

Lucas looked about as thrilled as Scooter did to hear this.

Scooter sighed. "Fine." His gaze drifted over to to my cousin. "We'll meet you guys at the bookstore afterward, okay?"

The three of them left, and Lauren and Mackenzie and I closed up the studio, then got our jackets and headed downtown.

Lovejoy's Books was in an uproar.

"What the heck is going on?" my cousin asked.

"I have absolutely no idea," I replied.

A tourist bus was parked outside, and its occupants were milling around inside the bookshop, craning their necks to try and see the cause of the commotion in the Annex. My cousin and my sister and I made our way back to where Aunt True was standing helplessly by the Bake-Off table.

"My Maple Snickerdoodles will *not* be sitting next to her Maple Banana Bread," we could hear someone insisting. It was Augustus Wilde, looking mad enough to spit, squared off against Mrs. Mahoney from the antiques store next door. Our celebrity author swept by in a blur of purple, grabbing his plate of cookies from one end of the table and marching it down to the other.

In a flash, plates of goodies started whizzing back and forth along the long table as the Bake-Off contestants separated back into the two camps. My father hadn't solved the problem at all—Pumpkin Falls was still feuding, and with or without signs on the table, the dividing line was Team Freeman and Team Maynard.

Bud Jefferson shouldered his way through the crowd just then holding a platter labeled BUD'S BODACIOUS MAPLE WALNUT MUFFINS. Spotting Lucas's mother at the far end of the table, where all the Freeman family supporters had gathered their baked goods, he stopped in his tracks. Mrs. Winthrop was hovering protectively over a plate of Maple Caramel Popcorn. She watched Mr. Jefferson hesitate, then slowly head for the opposite end of the table to join Team Maynard. Her face fell. *Uh-oh*, I thought, glancing from one of them to the other. *So much for winding wool together.* Was their budding romance doomed?

There was a crash as a plate fell to the floor. Aunt True leapt forward. "People, please!" she cried. Catching sight of me, she mouthed a single word: "Help!"

"This is unreal," said Mackenzie. I could tell she was preparing to launch into her radio announcer voice and offer a commentary on small-town living.

"Don't," I snapped. "Not now."

One good thing about being six feet tall—people tend to get out of your way. I elbowed my way through the crowd like Moses parting the Red Sea, and a moment later I was at my aunt's side.

"We need to get this under control, and fast," she whispered frantically, making a dive for a platter of Maple Oat Scones teetering on the edge of the table. "Rusty's in class, and I still haven't been able to get ahold of your mother. See if you can reach Mr. Henry, maybe. Or Reverend Quinn. Somebody—anybody!"

I nodded. As she returned to her refereeing, I grabbed Lauren by the shoulders. "Go. Library. Now. Get Mr. Henry and bring him back here on the double."

I turned to Mackenzie. "Keep trying my mother. Tell her it's an emergency. I'll . . ."

My voice trailed off as the bell over the door jangled and Ella Bellow swept in. *Oh no!* I thought. Ella was the last thing we needed at a time like this.

"Have you no decency?" she cried as I elbowed my way back through the crowd toward her. "I can hear the ruckus from across the street—you're driving my customers away!"

And right into our bookshop, I thought. That was the real reason for Ella's outrage. The last thing we needed right now was her interference.

"Sorry, Mrs. Bellow." I tried to sound contrite. "We're dealing with the Hatfields and the McCoys again."

"I don't care if the lost heir to the Romanov throne is making a personal appearance!" she barreled on. "You people need to take control of the situation." Her mouth pruned up indignantly.

"Unless we can calm everybody down, none of us will have any customers today," I pointed out.

That got her attention. Ella's eyes narrowed as she considered her options. Stepping gingerly onto a nearby armchair—my aunt had comfy reading nooks set up all around the bookshop—she braced herself against a bookshelf and cupped her hands around her mouth. "Attention, everyone!" she announced. "This is neutral territory, remember? If this doesn't stop, we're going to have to cancel the Maple Madness Bake-Off finals tonight!"

The angry buzz died down as the crowd looked over at her.

"Well, if it isn't our own Ella Bellow, bellowing orders," said Augustus snidely. "Who put you in charge?"

I wanted to smack him over the head with his plate of Maple Snickerdoodles. If Belinda were here right now, she'd make mincemeat out of her "gentleman caller," who wasn't being much of a gentleman, if you asked me, which nobody ever did.

As Ella climbed down from her perch and marched over to deal with Augustus, the bell over the door jangled again, and Calhoun, Scooter, and Lucas rushed in.

"We did it!" panted Scooter. "The video camera is up and running again!"

Mackenzie glanced around to see if anyone was listening. They weren't—the tourists were still completely transfixed by the squabble in the Annex. "Any sign of Bigfoot?" she whispered to my classmates.

"You should have seen the huge footprints out there!" said Lucas, his eyes wide.

"They could have been Mr. Freeman's," Calhoun noted cautiously.

"But it was probably Bigfoot," boasted Scooter.

Mackenzie shivered. "I think y'all are incredibly brave."

Scooter preened, and Lucas puffed out his skinny chest too. "Yeah, it was probably Bigfoot," he echoed.

I looked at my classmates. Could this really be true? Was Bigfoot on the loose here in Pumpkin Falls?

Behind us, the bell over the door jangled again, and this time Mr. Henry came in. Lauren was right behind him. Spotting the boys, she made a beeline for us. Mr. Henry headed directly to the back of the store, meanwhile, where Ella was wrangling with Augustus Wilde and my beleaguered aunt was trying to convince the owner of the Suds 'n Duds, who was Coach Maynard's brother-in-law, to put his pan of Maple Gingerbread beside Mrs. Freeman's Maple Fudge.

"Did you find signs of Bigfoot?" my sister asked breathlessly.

Scooter gave her a solemn nod. "It's almost a hundred percent certain."

I glanced over at Calhoun, who was fiddling with the

zipper of his jacket. I wanted to hear what he had to say, but before I could ask, Mackenzie put her hand on his arm and whispered something in his ear. He smiled down at her, and she laughed her perky little laugh.

I turned away. As usual, I might as well be invisible.

CHAPTER 20

I stared in the mirror, turning my head from one side to the other. I frowned. I was almost positive that I looked the same as I always had—same brown eyes, same freckles, same stick-straight Lovejoy brown hair. I didn't have the Lovejoy proboscis, as far as I could tell, and I had a nice enough smile. So why was it that I seemed to be in complete stealth mode these days, at least as far as boys were concerned?

Since when had I started worrying about boys, anyway? Since Calhoun, of course.

I told myself to quit stewing about it. I told myself I didn't really care, and that it was silly to wish that things were different. Wishing wouldn't shrink my size-ten-and-a-half feet. Wishing wouldn't make me petite, or blond, or perky. Wishing wouldn't turn me into Mackenzie. I was stuck just being me, Truly.

Down the hall, I could hear laughter coming from Lauren's room. My cousin and my sisters were playing with

Nibbles, Lauren's hamster. A series of crashes told me that his little plastic hamster ball was currently rocketing around her room. Closing my bathroom door behind me, I crossed the hall to my bedroom and flopped facedown on my bed.

I hated feeling so out of sorts, and I hated feeling jealous of Mackenzie. I could tell she was puzzled and hurt by the way I was acting. I wanted things to go back to the way they'd always been between us, but I didn't see how they could.

I buried my head under my pillow. This whole thing was just a big tangled mess. An even worse mess than the stupid pathetic socks I was trying—and failing miserably—to knit.

There was a soft knock at my door. I lifted the edge of my pillow and peeked out to see my mother standing in the doorway.

"Is everything okay?" She came over and sat down on the edge of my bed beside me.

To my horror, I burst into tears. "I don't know, Mom!" I sobbed. "One minute I'm fine, and the next I'm—"

"Thirteen?" My mother laughed softly. "Oh, honey, I remember only too well being your age!" She leaned down and put her cheek next to mine. "It's not easy being a teenager," she murmured. "Give yourself some time to adjust. There are physical changes, of course—"

"Yeah, Mom, I know all about that," I said hastily. The one thing I did not need right now was a lecture on *Your Changing Body and You!*

"—and emotional changes too. It's all part of growing up." She hesitated, then added, "Are things okay between you and Mackenzie? Y'all seem a little . . . I don't know, tense."

I lifted a shoulder, too ashamed and embarrassed to admit what I'd been thinking. "Yeah, we're good." I was quiet for a moment, then added in a low voice, "Mom, do you think I'm pretty?"

She laughed. "Pretty? Sweetheart, I think you're beautiful, inside and out!"

I scowled. "You're just saying that because you're my mother."

"I am not!" She ruffled my hair. "Cross my heart and hope to fly. Why, just the other day at the bookshop your aunt True was saying how pretty you are! Ella was there, and she agreed too."

Ella Bellow thinks I'm pretty? Great. Not exactly the target audience I was shooting for.

My mother stood up. "Pull yourself together and come keep me company in the kitchen. Professor Rusty's bringing his research assistant to dinner tonight, and I'm making Tex-Mex."

"Chicken enchiladas?" I sat up. Chicken enchiladas were one of my mother's specialties. My mouth watered just hearing the words.

She nodded, passing me a tissue. "Now, dry your eyes and blow your nose."

I did as she told me. Downstairs, I set the dining room table for eleven, then settled in at the kitchen counter to help prepare the enchilada toppings.

"You've been reading about the Underground Railroad for your term paper, right?" I asked.

My mother nodded. "Uh-huh."

"So have you ever heard of a place called Maple Grove, Maine?"

"Not that I can remember. Why?"

I told her what we'd read in Truly's diary, about the "packages" being shipped to Maple Grove.

"Interesting. You should ask Professor Rusty tonight at dinner. He's an expert." She gave me a sidelong glance. "This diary is getting under your skin, isn't it?"

I nodded. "Yeah, I guess. It's just that reading it makes it all feel so real, you know?"

The door behind us burst open. My mother didn't even wait for my brothers to greet us. She just pointed her spatula toward the ceiling. "Upstairs! Shower! Now!"

Hatcher and Danny grinned and loped off.

"Whew, those boys get stinky." My mother wrinkled her nose and waved her spatula in front of her face as if to clear the air, and I laughed.

A few minutes later the back door opened again. It was my father this time. He crossed the kitchen and gave my mother a kiss. "Mmmm," he said, wrapping his arms around her waist from behind and resting his chin on top of her head. "Could that be chicken enchiladas I smell?"

"Might could," she replied.

"What's the occasion?"

"Dinner guests." She explained about Professor Rusty and his research assistant.

"So is it okay if I keep the Terminator on, or should I accessorize with Ken?" My father raised his prosthetic arm. We called it "the Terminator" because it was made of black titanium and polymer, and it was super high-tech. He controlled it with electrical impulses from his brain, and it had a wrist that swiveled like a real one and metal fingers that could grasp even the smallest things. Ken was made of flesh-colored silicone and looked more like a real arm, but Dad said it was useless. He named it Ken after Barbie's boyfriend, because even though it was good-looking, all it did was hang around.

My mother tapped his prosthesis lightly with her spatula. "I think the Terminator is just fine. Very macho and handsome."

Dad laughed and kissed her again. "Glad to know it has the Dinah Lovejoy Seal of Approval."

I'm relieved my father can joke about these kinds of things now. For a long time after Black Monday, we were really worried about him. But he was adjusting to the loss of his arm, just like he was adjusting to life in Pumpkin Falls.

Hatcher materialized, his hair still wet from the shower. He'd changed into jeans and a clean T-shirt.

"You smell almost as good as my chicken enchiladas," my mother said, sniffing him appreciatively.

My brother grinned. "Operative word being 'almost.' *Nothing* smells as good as your chicken enchiladas."

"A charmer, just like your father," she replied, mirroring his sunflower smile back at him.

The doorbell rang.

"Would you kids get that?" she said to my brother and me. "It must be True and Rusty."

It was. Hatcher took everyone's coats as they came inside, and Professor Rusty introduced the girl he'd brought with him.

"This is Felicia Grunewald, my research assistant."

"Nice to meet you," I murmured, trying not to stare at her hair. It was braided into twin coils that perched on her ears like a pair of blond cinnamon buns.

"Looks like someone raided Captain Romance's closet," Hatcher whispered as the cinnamon buns and their owner followed my aunt down the hall to the kitchen. My brother held up Felicia's navy blue cape, and I stifled a giggle. He was right—it looked exactly like something Augustus Wilde would wear.

"And what's up with that hair?" I asked.

"Princess Leia just called—she wants her earmuffs back,"

my brother quipped, and this time I laughed out loud. I love Hatcher.

A few minutes later my mother called everyone to dinner. We took our seats, and my father went around the dining room table, introducing each of us. Then he turned to Professor Rusty. "I'll let you do the honors with your guest."

"Felicia Grunewald is my research assistant, and a history major at the college," Professor Rusty told us. "Her field is medieval studies, but she's also quite knowledgeable about the Civil War. She's working for me over Spring Break." He looked over at Aunt True. "True, you might remember her parents, Bridget and Hans Grunewald? They own the Edelweiss Inn."

"The place near Mount Washington that looks like a Bavarian chalet?" cried my aunt, delighted. "We used to go there for birthday dinners when we were kids! Remember, J. T.?"

Felicia inclined her head, like royalty accepting a peasant's compliment. "I'm gratified to know that our alpine retreat inspires such fond memories."

Across the table, Hatcher flicked me a glance. I flared my nostrils at him, and he smirked. I knew exactly what he was thinking: *Who is this girl, and why is she sitting at our table?*

"So," said Professor Rusty, looking over at me, "have you finished reading the diary? I'd love for Felicia to take a look at it after dinner."

"Almost," I told him.

"I hear congratulations are in order, by the way," he continued. "The Pumpkin Falls Private Eyes are working on another case!"

My fork, which had been in the process of conveying my first bite of chicken enchilada to my mouth, froze in midair. The table fell quiet as everyone looked at me.

"The Pumpkin Falls Private Eyes?" Felicia snorted. "Who made up that cretinous name?"

I had no idea what "cretinous" meant, but I could guess. I felt the blood rush to my face, staining it the same shade as the enchilada sauce dripping from my fork.

How on earth had Professor Rusty found out?

"Trying to snare the sap thief, are you?" asked Aunt True. "Not a moment too soon, in my opinion. I don't want a repeat of today's scene at the bookstore, that's for sure."

Across the table, my sister Lauren seemed way too fascinated with her place mat. *Busted*, I thought, my glance frosting into a glare. Lauren was the only one who could possibly have leaked the news. This was her revenge for our argument over the diary, and all the other stuff that had happened between us these past few days.

I needed a distraction to change the subject.

"Hey, Professor Rusty," I began, "I was wondering—"

"Hay is for horses," my mother corrected me, and I sighed. Living with an aspiring English teacher was like living with the grammar police.

"Sorry. Professor Rusty, I was wondering if you've ever heard of a place called Maple Grove, Maine?" Glancing at my mother, I added "sir" for extra credit.

He furrowed his brow, considering. "Can't say that I have. Why?"

"We were reading about it in the original Truly's diary earlier—she talks about 'packages' being shipped there, so I guess that's where some of the slaves she was hiding were sent."

"Is that so? Fascinating! I'll look into it right away. Remind me tomorrow, would you, Felicia?"

Her mouth full of chicken enchilada, Felicia nodded, sending her Princess Leia muffins bobbing.

"Also, how come Truly sounds so scared all the time?" I continued. "Everything's all so hush-hush."

"It was incredibly dangerous work she was involved in," Professor Rusty replied. "That they were all involved in, really. For the slaves themselves, it took an extraordinary act of courage—not to mention a huge leap of faith—to run. Remember, they had no maps, few if any supplies, and in most cases no knowledge of the landscape outside their plantation. Running meant being ripped away from everything that was familiar, and leaving everything behind, including family and friends. There was danger at every turn: hunger, exhaustion, possible injury or illness, and relentless pursuit by their owners. A runaway never knew if those offering to help were friend or foe. What he or she did know was that if they were caught, the consequences would be dire. Many lost their lives. But none of that mattered one speck, compared to their burning desire for freedom."

I could see why my mother liked Professor Rusty's classes. He had a way of bringing things to life, even if he was a bit long-winded.

Down at the end of the table, my sister Pippa shuddered. "I wouldn't want to be a thlave," she announced as she set her glass of milk down, nearly spilling it.

Aunt True's hand flashed out just in time.

"Nice save!" My father smiled at his sister, then reached over and patted Pippa's hand. "No one wants to be a slave, honey."

"I understand why it was dangerous for the runaways," I said, "but I guess I don't understand why it was dangerous for the people—the conductors, right?—who worked on the Underground Railroad helping them."

"Ah," said Professor Rusty. "That would be on account of the Fugitive Slave Act."

I dimly remembered reading something about that at school.

"The Fugitive Slave Act was enacted by Congress on September 18, 1850," Felicia suddenly spouted, making me jump in my chair. "It made it the federal government's job to capture and return runaways."

Professor Rusty nodded. "That's exactly right, Felicia.

The law meant U.S. marshals could force local authorities in the Northern states—including New Hampshire—to help them round up suspected fugitives. In fact, all citizens were obliged to aid in the recapture of runaways, or face imprisonment and fines."

"But that's so unfair!" I cried.

"The abolitionists thought so too," my mother added, passing me a plate piled with the avocado I'd sliced earlier. "They called it the 'Bloodhound Law,' because of the dogs that were used to track down runaways. I read that some of the fugitive slaves would rub themselves with things like onion and pine pitch, hoping the hounds wouldn't pick up their scent." She shook her head sadly. "Can you imagine it? Here in this country?"

Professor Rusty reached over and speared a slice of avocado. "The law also made helping fugitive slaves a more serious federal crime. The marshals had the legal right to search anyone's home for runaways at any time, and arrest anyone caught harboring or aiding them."

"What happened if they got caught?" asked Mackenzie, her blue eyes round with concern. I knew she was thinking of the original Truly. I sure was.

"There were stiff penalties," Professor Rusty told her, taking a bite of his dinner. "Oh my goodness, Dinah, these enchiladas are amazing!"

"Thank you," said my mother.

YOURS TRULY

"While the consequences weren't as dire, of course, as those facing the slaves if they were caught," he continued, "still, your ancestors could have been sent to prison for six months and had to pay a big fine. It was a very brave thing your Truly did."

No wonder she'd been so scared! I thought. Prison? What would have happened to little Booth?

"How big a fine?" asked my brother Danny from the far end of the table.

"A thousand dollars," Felicia told him. "Which doesn't sound like that much, but it translates to almost thirty thousand dollars today."

Danny gave a low whistle. "That's a lot of money!"

"No kidding," said my father. "A fine like that could have meant financial ruin."

I wondered if he was thinking of the bank loan that nearly put our bookshop out of business this past winter, before Belinda Winchester stepped in to help.

I turned to Professor Rusty. "So do you think that's why Truly hid her diary? Just in case the house was searched?"

He nodded. "Most likely. Others did. There was a famous African American abolitionist by the name of William Still, who lived in Philadelphia and was a conductor on the Underground Railroad there. He kept meticulous records of the hundreds of runaways that he helped, hoping it would help reunite them with their families later. He hid his journal every night in a crypt in a nearby cemetery."

"A crypt?" Lauren looked puzzled.

"A grave," he told her.

My sister shivered. "Eew! I guess he figured no one would look for it there."

Professor Rusty nodded again. "Exactly."

I digested this information, wondering if I'd have had the kind of courage that my namesake did. One thing still bothered me, though.

"How would anyone have even found out that Truly was involved with the Underground Railroad?" I asked. "New Hampshire is a Northern state. Wasn't everybody in favor of freeing the slaves?"

Professor Rusty shook his head. "New Hampshire abolished slavery in 1783, but some people still felt strongly that the Southern states had a right to determine their own laws. Whole towns were split over the issue of abolition. It pitted neighbor against neighbor in some instances, and even split families. Pumpkin Falls experienced some of that."

"Plus, slave catchers and bounty hunters offered rewards for those who turned in fugitives and those aiding them," my mother added. "Greed has always been a part of human nature, unfortunately, and some people succumbed to the temptation."

"Weasels," muttered Hatcher.

I thought of the diary entry I'd read earlier: *There are whispers of money changing hands in exchange for information*, Truly had written. Weasels indeed.

"The Fugitive Slave Act brought everything to a head," said Professor Rusty, warming to his theme. I'd wanted a distraction, and I was getting my money's worth. No one was thinking about the Pumpkin Falls Private Eyes now. "Harriet Jacobs, a fugitive slave living in New York at the time, called the law 'the beginning of a reign of terror.' The Northern states were no longer a safe haven. Slaves who had fled the South and who had been living freely in cities like Boston and Philadelphia were forced to leave the new lives they'd forged for themselves and flee even farther north to Canada."

"So they were safe from the slave catchers there?" Hatcher asked.

"Yes."

"Canada was part of the British Empire at that time, which abolished slavery in 1834," Felicia spouted again. The girl sure knew her dates. "Some forty thousand blacks took refuge there after the Fugitive Slave Act was passed, and before the Civil War and the passage of the Thirteenth Amendment."

"What amendment was that?" Mackenzie whispered to me.

"The amendment to the Constitution abolishing slavery, duh," I whispered back, and she reddened. "Don't you pay attention in social studies?"

"The Underground Railroad's code word for Canada pretty much says it all," Professor Rusty told us. "They called it 'heaven.' Former slaves weren't entirely free from racism in Canada, but they had the right to vote, and they could become citizens and own property—things that were denied them in the United States."

"It was a bad time here," my mother said. "I can hardly bear to read about it! Not only were runaway slaves captured and returned to the South, but many free blacks were also taken, and forced into slavery."

"But that's awful!" I cried. "Couldn't they do something about it?"

Professor Rusty shook his head. "Slaves had no legal rights. They were completely defenseless."

No wonder my ancestors had been so on fire to help! I thought, feeling a sudden rush of pride in their actions. I was beginning to wish that I could travel back in time and give them a hand. I glanced down the table at my brother Danny. Truly had been only a year older than he was when she started keeping her diary. She had a new baby to care for, a husband off fighting a war, and a farm to run. Getting caught could have meant prison and financial ruin. And yet she'd risked it all to help others to freedom.

Professor Rusty served himself another enchilada. "If there was any good thing that came from the passage of that inhumane bill," he said, "it was the fact that it steeled this country's resolve to put an end to slavery. The Fugitive Slave Act reenergized the Underground Railroad and got Northern folks thinking more about and caring more about the issue of slavery. Many who'd been on the fence about abolition joined the movement."

"It was the beginning of end, in other words?" asked Aunt True.

He smiled at her. "You might say that."

Felicia dabbed her mouth with her napkin and turned to me. "So from your perusal of the primary source document, have you been able to ascertain where the fugitives may have been concealed?"

Hatcher kicked me under the table. I didn't dare look at him; I wouldn't be able to contain my laughter. I knew exactly what he was thinking, because I was thinking the same thing: Was this girl for real? Who talked like that?

"Um," I said, uncertain how to reply. I didn't want to be called "cretinous" again, whatever that was.

"What I think Felicia is trying to say," said Professor Rusty, "is that thanks to the diary we now know that your family was definitely involved in harboring runaway slaves. But the question remains, where did they hide them?"

CHAPTER 21

We didn't have time to look just then. Not with the finals for the Maple Madness Bake-Off about to start down at the bookshop.

My thoughts swirled as I piled into the minivan with my parents and brothers and sisters. Between everything that Professor Rusty had just told us, worries about Bigfoot, the town feud, and Mackenzie's apparent interest in Calhoun, it had been a confusing day.

And it was about to get more confusing.

"I insist that Reverend Quinn be disqualified as head judge," announced Ella Bellow, who was lying in wait for us on the bookstore's doorstep.

"Really, Ella?" said Aunt True calmly, taking her keys from her pocket and unlocking the front door. "It's his turn this year, remember?"

"I don't care," Ella continued, following her inside. Hatcher raised an eyebrow at me as the rest of us went in too.

The bookshop looked great. My aunt had gone to a lot of trouble this afternoon decorating for the contest, after she and Ella and Mr. Henry finally managed to quell the rebellion. There were big fake orange and red maple leaves hanging from the ceiling, and signs pointing to the Annex that read THIS WAY TO THE FAMOUS PUMPKIN FALLS MAPLE MADNESS BAKE-OFF! The long table that held the baked goods showed no sign of the earlier skirmishes. Plates and platters were lined up in an orderly fashion, with no regard to Team Freeman or Team Maynard.

"Reverend Quinn is one of the only people in town without an entry in the contest," my aunt said mildly. "If anyone's going to be an impartial head judge, it's him."

"Ha!" said Ella. "Explain to me, then, why he was spotted talking to Grace Freeman this morning on the village green."

My aunt gave her a look. "She goes to his *church*, Ella. So do the Maynards."

Ella Bellow sniffed. "That's beside the point. He shouldn't be seen consorting with the finalists on the very day of the judging!"

"You think she was maybe trying to bribe him with some fudge?" My aunt laughed. "Come on!"

From the look on her face, our former postmistress clearly

felt this was a possibility. Hatcher elbowed me. He was getting a kick out of this. I could only imagine what Mackenzie thought, but the two of us weren't exactly on speaking terms at the moment.

"Ella, how about you dial it back just a whisker?" asked my father, stepping forward. "I've had your Maple Bread Pudding, and it's wonderful. A strong contestant, I'd say."

My aunt, who had bent down to open a large box containing what looked like the new espresso machine, looked up sharply. "Maple *Bread* Pudding? This wouldn't have anything to do with the fact that everyone knows Reverend Quinn is on a gluten-free diet, would it?"

"The idea!" Ella sputtered, but her face reddened.

Hatcher elbowed me again. "Busted," he whispered, grinning from ear to ear.

"You have two choices, Ella," my aunt informed her, straightening up and putting her hands on her hips. "You and your pudding can stay in the contest, but I don't want to hear any more on this subject."

"And if I refuse?" Ella bridled.

Aunt True pointed to the door. "There's the door. Don't let it hit you on the way out."

An awkward silence descended on the bookshop. I'd never seen my aunt like this. The feud must have really gotten to her.

"Well, I never!" Ella suddenly seemed aware that we were

all looking at her. She scowled at us. "You Lovejoys think you're—"

It was Pippa who saved the day.

"I like your bread pudding too, Mithith Bellow," she said, stepping forward and taking Ella by the hand. "Belinda gave Lauren and me thome of your tetht batch yethterday. I think it dethervth a blue ribbon."

"You do, do you?" Ella replied, some of the wind going out of her sails.

Pippa nodded vigorously.

"Maybe we should ask Pippa to judge," my father joked. "Would that satisfy you, Ella?"

"Pleathe, Daddy?" begged Pippa, jumping up and down. "I want to hand out ribbonth!"

In the end, that's exactly what happened. My parents and my aunt decided that Pippa's presence might help defuse the tension, so she stepped in as last-minute assistant to Reverend Quinn. My little sister's irresistible charm once again worked its magic—at least for the hour that the finals lasted—and Pumpkin Falls managed to pull itself together and be civil while Reverend Quinn and the other two judges considered the entries.

Which was more than could be said for Mackenzie and me. Or at least for me. When Calhoun and his family came into the bookshop—Calhoun's sister Juliet had entered her

Maple Macaroons—my cousin started over toward him.

"Can't you just leave him alone for once?" I growled, grabbing her arm.

Mackenzie turned and looked at me, shocked. "What are you talking about?"

"I'm talking about how you already have a boyfriend!" I said hotly. "Stop being so boy crazy!"

She pulled her arm out of my grasp. "And you stop being just plain crazy!" she shot back.

Ella Bellow's Maple Bread Pudding didn't win, but neither did Mrs. Freeman's Maple Fudge or Coach Maynard's Maple Cream Pie. It was Mr. Henry who won, coming from behind with his Maple Walnut Cupcakes and scooping up the blue ribbon.

"Let's go home and see if we can salvage what's left of the evening, shall we?" my father said to us when it was all over and the last picture of the winner and his entry had been taken and the bookshop was empty again.

Fat chance, I thought, my eyes sliding over to Mackenzie. She'd been ignoring me ever since our blowup earlier.

"And how exactly do you plan to do that, J. T.?" asked my aunt.

"For starters, with some of your Bookshop Blondies, which are a winner in my book," my father said gallantly.

"Mine too," echoed Professor Rusty. "How about I swing

by the General Store and pick up some vanilla ice cream to go with them?"

"You said 'for starters,' J. T.," my mother said. "What else do you have in mind?"

My father looked around at all of us. He smiled. "Anyone interested in searching for the Underground Railroad's hiding spot?"

CHAPTER 22

"Team Lovejoy will scour the main part of the house, top to bottom, while Team, uh, History Department tackles the family room and the garage," ordered my father. We were back at Gramps and Lola's house, where he'd slipped effortlessly into command mode. "Hatcher and Danny, you two start in the basement."

My brothers exchanged a glance. "Can we maybe be in charge of the attic instead?" ventured Hatcher. He feels the same way I do about spiders.

"Show some team spirit, boys," said my father, pointing to the cellar door. "Downstairs, on the double."

Resigned to their fate, my brothers slouched off. The rest of us fanned out to search every nook and cranny we could think of, including closets, pantries, fireplaces—even bookshelves.

"Remember when we were stationed in Germany and

went to Amsterdam to see the Anne Frank house?" my mother said as the two of us began to explore the living room. While I rooted around in the window seats—nothing but blankets and board games there—she ran her fingertips around the edges of the built-in bookcases that flanked the fireplace.

I nodded. Hatcher had read *The Diary of Anne Frank* as a school assignment that year, and he'd been the one who'd begged to go.

"Yeah," I said, recalling the hinged bookcase that had concealed the Frank family's hiding spot from the Nazis. "Do you think there's something like that in our house?"

My mother shrugged. "You never know."

In the end, though, we came up empty-handed. So did everyone else.

"Perhaps they just stashed the fugitives in one of the attic rooms until the coast was clear," said Professor Rusty, running a hand through his hair. Aunt True, who was seated next to him on the front stairs, reached over and patted it back into place. Or tried to. Professor Rusty's hair was pretty U-N-R-U-L-Y, as Annie Freeman would say.

"I thought for sure the fireplace in the family room held the key," he continued morosely. "That was likely a summer kitchen back in the day, and I've read about a number of those big old fireplaces concealing secret chambers and passageways and trapdoors leading to tunnels."

I could tell he was disappointed. So was I, actually. It

would have been really cool to find the hiding place.

Lauren was the only one who refused to give up. While Mackenzie and I were showing Felicia the original Truly's diary, my younger sister wandered around, knocking on walls and stairwells. She was still at it when bedtime rolled around.

"Good heavens, Lauren, let's give it a rest, shall we?" said my mother. "Go get ready for bed."

My sister's gaze slid over to me. "We were supposed to finish reading the diary tonight."

"I'm not reading anything with a double-crosser like you," I told her. "Not after what you did."

"I didn't do anything!"

"You told Professor Rusty about the Pumpkin Falls Private Eyes!"

Lauren's eyes widened in feigned innocence. "I did not!"

"You are such a bad liar!"

"So what if I did, anyway? Who cares about your stupid club!"

My mother put her hands on her hips, exasperated. "Girls! Just stop, would you? Between you two and the Bake-Off feud, I've had enough squabbling to last a lifetime. Lauren, get to bed. You can finish reading the diary in the morning. And, Truly, I don't want to hear another word about any of this, do you understand?"

"Yes, ma'am," I muttered.

Maybe she was feeling sorry for me because of my tears

earlier in the evening, or maybe she was just tired and forgot, but my mother didn't ask for the diary back. And I didn't bring it up.

"I'm too tired to read any more tonight," Mackenzie told me when we were back in my room. She'd been uncharacteristically quiet all evening, and I felt a pang of guilt. The two of us hadn't talked since I'd lashed out at her earlier at the bookstore.

"Mind if I read ahead?"

"Nope." She got into bed and rolled over, turning her back on me.

I gazed at her ruefully for a moment, then opened the diary to where we'd left off:

February 9, 1862

F arrived just before midnight. We have been waiting for weeks for this special delivery. Reverend Bartlett sent a note with one of the Harrington boys after breakfast, letting us know the shipment was finally on its way, and the reason for its delay. Mother Lovejoy and I were busy all day preparing.

Yours, Truly

February 11, 1862

Our single package is now two! F is terribly ill, however, with a rattling cough and fever. This was the reason for the delay. I am on duty as nurse, and doing

the best I can, but with my own wee Booth to care for, and the threat of house search hanging over our heads, it is not easy.
Yours, Truly

Wait a minute, I thought, going back and rereading the entry. What did she mean by *our single package is now two?* I frowned, wondering if I'd missed something.

The next entry was very brief:

February 15, 1862
I have grown fond of this package. F and I have much in common, and much to talk about.

And then a few days later, this:

February 20, 1862
We heard the bloodhounds in the woods on Lovejoy Mountain tonight. Strangers are going door to door in town, with promises of fat payments for information, and neighbor looks at neighbor with suspicion. The owner is determined to get this package back, Reverend Bartlett tells us. No one is to be trusted. I must find a way to ensure safe passage—but F is too weak to be moved.
Yours, Truly

YOURS TRULY

February 23, 1862
No word from Matthew in weeks. And worse, Mother Lovejoy has fallen ill too.
Yours, Truly

This did not sound good. I read on:

February 28, 1862
I have been awake for three days and am nearly at my wits' end. Last night there was a knock at the door. Men I did not recognize were on the doorstep. Mother Lovejoy was taken by the fever, I told them. We are a house of death, I told them. They didn't believe me, even when I showed them her coffin in the parlor, where it rests awaiting burial tomorrow. One man wanted to pry it open and see if I was telling the truth, but after I pleaded with him he relented. I am pale and hollow-eyed from lack of sleep, and they finally took pity on me and left, Gott sei dank.

I looked this one up in the German-English dictionary. "*Gott sei Dank*" meant "thank God."

But they will be back. This I know. So tonight, whether the packages are ready or not, and no matter how dear F has become to me, I must send them on to a safer place.

Yours, Truly

Mother Lovejoy *died*? I scanned the entry again, trying to understand. What safer place was Truly talking about? Maple Grove? Canada? How would the packages—the runaways—get there? Who was F? Could Truly manage it, right under the noses of the dogs and bounty hunters?

There were so many unanswered questions.

My eyelids were heavy by the time I finally closed the diary and switched off the light. Sleep didn't come easily, though. I lay there for what felt like forever, thinking about what I'd just read. I couldn't stop thinking about what I'd read. And when I did finally manage to drift off, my restless dreams were filled with baying bloodhounds and men with torches chasing desperate men and women on the run.

CHAPTER 23

"Knock it OFF, Lauren!"

I stuffed my head under my pillow, trying to block out the noise. Spurred on by last night's fruitless basement-to-rafters search, my sister had redoubled her efforts to find the Underground Railroad's secret hiding spot.

Sleep was impossible. I gave an exasperated sigh and threw my pillow over at Mackenzie. No response. Pushing myself up on my forearms, I glanced over at the air mattress. It was empty; my cousin was already up.

I found her downstairs, eating a banana with peanut butter and talking to my father. She was pleasant to me, but distant. Neither of us mentioned my outburst at the bookshop last night.

I yawned all the way to swim practice—never a good sign. This was the final morning of daily doubles. After today, regular once-a-day practice was going to be a breeze. I leaned my head back and closed my eyes, savoring the prospect of sleeping in.

At the pool, Coach Maynard barely said a word to anyone. He just wrote down our workout on the whiteboard and motioned us into the pool.

"More sap lines were cut last night, after the Bake-Off," Lucas reported in a whisper. "At the Freemans, too. I overheard people talking at Lou's."

Maybe Felicia Grunewald, Professor Rusty's know-it-all research assistant, was right, I thought as I carved my way up and down my lane. Maybe the Pumpkin Falls Private Eyes wasn't only a cretinous name, but also a totally cretinous idea.

I'd looked up "cretinous." It meant "extremely stupid," which we probably were. How on earth were a bunch of seventh graders supposed to solve a crime like this? Could even hope to end the feud?

Swimming usually helped clear my mind and cheer me up, but I was still feeling discouraged by the time practice finished. My cell phone buzzed as Mackenzie and I were in the locker room changing.

"It's a text from Cha Cha," I said. "She and Jasmine want to come over after breakfast."

"Whatever."

"Cha Cha says we can take you to see the steeple."

"Fine." Mackenzie's voice was still cool; she wasn't giving an inch.

The steeple on the First Parish Church is one of our town's claims to fame, thanks to its bell, which was made by Paul Revere. I got to see it up close and way too personal earlier this winter. Mackenzie knew all about that fiasco, of course, and she'd been pestering me all week for a tour of the steeple. Now it didn't seem like she cared.

"I can't believe you're only here for two more days!" my mother lamented to Mackenzie a little while later, when the two of us sat down to breakfast—French toast, my favorite. "This week has just flown by, darlin'."

"Yep." My cousin picked up her fork and started to eat, while I just stared at my plate.

My mother regarded the two of us thoughtfully. "Y'all better make the most of it," she continued lightly. "You won't get to see one another again until summer vacation."

I glanced over at Mackenzie, struck by another pang of guilt. The day after tomorrow she'd be on the plane back to Texas. I needed to patch things up somehow—if that was even possible at this point.

"How did the kitten deliveries go yesterday?" my mother asked, setting a plate in front of Pippa.

"We gave away thix," my little sister told her proudly.

"Six? That is impressive," my mother replied, leaning

down to kiss the top of her head. She turned to Lauren. "Did you feed Bilbo this morning?"

My sister looked up from her book—*The House of Dies Drear*, one of the ones from the stack that Mr. Henry had given to my mother—and nodded.

"I remember that book!" I told her, figuring I'd better start extending olive branches if I really wanted to patch things up with my cousin. "It totally creeped me out. All those secret tunnels and that weird guy who lived in that cave—"

"Annie wants me to spend the night," Lauren interrupted, ignoring me. Mackenzie didn't even look up from her French toast. So much for olive branches.

My mother frowned. "This is an awfully busy week for the Freemans. The last thing they probably need is a house guest."

"I told them I'd help on the farm," Lauren assured her.

"Why don't I call Annie's mother and see if Annie can have a sleepover here instead?"

My sister's face lit up. "Thanks, Mom!"

After breakfast, Mackenzie and I walked Lauren and Pippa down the street to Belinda's, where we found the former lunch lady grooving to the Beach Boys again as she vacuumed. Her house might be stuffed with cats, but it was spotless. Belinda loved to clean.

"Morning!" she shouted after we banged on the door

about a hundred times. Pulling out an earbud, she flipped a switch on the vacuum cleaner, and it whined to a stop. I could hear the faint strains of "Help Me, Rhonda" coming from her dangling earbud.

"Any more kittens need delivering?" asked Lauren hopefully.

Belinda shook her head. "Sorry, sweetheart, that train has left the station. There'll be more soon enough, though, never fear." She looked over at Mackenzie. "I'm still counting on you to take one home with you."

My cousin laughed. "I'll ask my mother, but I'm pretty sure the answer is 'no.'"

Cha Cha and Jasmine were already at my house by the time Mackenzie and I got back.

"I wish you could have come with us, Truly," said Cha Cha. "We had a blast!"

"We had a very good reason for keeping her here in Pumpkin Falls," my mother told her, and placing her hands on my cousin's shoulders, she nudged her toward my friends. "Cha Cha, Jasmine, I'd like you to meet Mackenzie Gifford, my niece and Truly's cousin."

My friends smiled at Mackenzie, and she smiled back.

Bunting meets raven, I thought, glancing from my cousin to Jasmine, whose glossy dark hair was a constant source of envy. I would kill for hair like that.

"Hey, we got you something," Cha Cha said, handing us each a gift bag. My friend Cha Cha isn't like any bird I've ever seen—she's more of a feline. Her hair is dark, too, but short, and as fluffy as one of Belinda's kittens. I opened my present to find a T-shirt with a picture of a chicken roosting on top of the logo I CHICKENED OUT IN KEY WEST!

"There are these wild chickens all over the place that roam around on the streets," Jasmine told us. "It's kind of hilarious."

"I love it!" I said.

"Me too," said Mackenzie. "I'm going to put mine right on."

She chattered away to my friends as the four of us went upstairs to my room, sounding so much like her usual self that my heart gave a hopeful lift. Maybe things would be okay between us after all.

But the tendril of hope quickly shriveled.

Mackenzie paused at the top of the stairs and turned to me as Cha Cha and Jasmine went on ahead down the hall to my room. "Don't wear your T-shirt today," she whispered. "I'm not into being twins."

Hurt, I mumbled, "Okay." The message couldn't have been clearer: I was not forgiven.

"Hey, I brought something for you guys too," Mackenzie said to Cha Cha and Jasmine, all smiles again as she went into my bedroom and crossed to the closet. I knew what she was getting; she'd brought one for me, too, and she'd given one each to Lauren and Pippa as well.

"Super cute!" said Jasmine, when my cousin handed her a small ceramic cowboy boot with a big Texas Lone Star on it.

"Thanks, Mackenzie!" echoed Cha Cha. She plunked down cross-legged on my rug. "Now, tell us everything."

CHAPTER 24

I left out the part about Scooter's surprise birthday kiss, of course. No need to publicize that disaster, plus Jasmine was Scooter's twin and would be seriously creeped out at the thought of her brother crushing on one of her friends. Not that he was crushing on me anymore. Mackenzie's arrival had taken care of that.

I also didn't bring up the fact that my cousin had bewitched every middle school male in Pumpkin Falls. Cha Cha and Jasmine would find that out for themselves soon enough.

I filled them in on the sap heist, and Jasmine's eyes widened when I told them about the stakeout. "You seriously think it could be Bigfoot?"

I shrugged.

"The guys think so," said Mackenzie, and Cha Cha shivered.

After that, my cousin showed them the loose floorboard

in the closet where we'd found the original Truly's diary. My friends listened openmouthed as I read aloud a few entries.

"That is the coolest thing *ever!*" said Jasmine. "I can't believe you have a secret compartment in your room!"

"I know, right?"

Cha Cha reached for the diary. I passed it to her, and she ran her hands over the smooth, worn leather. "This is amazing," she said. "When you read the stuff she wrote, it's like she's right here in the room with us. The person you were named after and everything!"

"I wish I could talk to her," I said. "There's so much I want to know." Before I could continue, though, my mother called to us from the front hall.

"Girls! That was Reverend Quinn on the phone—he says he's got time to give Mackenzie a tour of the steeple, if you head over to the church right now!"

Leaving the diary safely tucked under my pillow, the four of us went back downstairs.

"Lunch is on me, ladies," said my mother, handing me some money. "And take your swim things with you," she reminded Mackenzie and me. "You'll save yourselves a trip that way."

Mackenzie and I grabbed our swim bags—last practice!—and we all headed for town. The rain had cleared up, and everything smelled of freshly washed earth. Jasmine and Cha Cha rattled on about their vacation as we walked, but while Mackenzie hung on their every word, I listened with only one ear. Beaches, boys, bikinis—been there, heard all about that.

I scanned the trees for owls. Was it a barred owl call that the Underground Railroad used, I wondered? Or another one? A great horned owl, perhaps—now, that was a distinctive call. *Hoo-h'Hoo-hoo-hoo.* They sounded just like what you'd expect an owl to sound like.

Reverend Quinn was waiting for us at the church.

"Hello, girls," he said with a welcoming smile. "You must be Truly's cousin Mackenzie."

Mackenzie nodded.

"I'm sure you've heard all about our steeple from Truly."

I blushed. The last time I'd been up in the steeple, disaster had struck. Disaster in the name of Scooter Sanchez, who had accidentally on purpose rung the bell while I was in the belfry. I'd been deaf for days.

But Reverend Quinn didn't know about that. I'd managed to make a clean getaway while he was bawling out Scooter.

"This is so awesome!" Mackenzie said happily as we climbed the ladder leading to the steeple. "I can't believe I'm actually getting to go up here! With a bell made by Paul Revere and everything! Wait until I tell—"

"Mr. Perfect?" I said, the words popping out before I could stop myself.

Mackenzie's happy smile faded. Once again I'd put my size-ten-and-a-half foot into my mouth. Felicia was right—I really was cretinous.

YOURS TRULY

I hung back while Cha Cha and Jasmine explained the history of the steeple to my cousin and showed her the view. I was feeling worse by the minute. What was *wrong* with me? Could I never do anything right?

When Reverend Quinn offered to take a group picture of us after the tour, Mackenzie made a point of making sure she stood as far away from me as possible.

"What's up with you two?" Cha Cha murmured, watching her.

"Nothing," I lied.

"Doesn't seem like nothing."

I sighed. "It's just—you know, kind of hard to explain."

"She seems really nice," said Cha Cha.

I nodded. "She is." I blinked rapidly, fighting back tears. I really wanted things to be okay again between my cousin and me.

At Lou's, Mackenzie took a seat at the opposite end of the counter from me. I ended up with Jasmine on one side and Ella Bellow, of all people, on the other.

"How are those socks coming?" Ella asked just as I bit into my grilled cheese.

"Mmmph mmmph," I replied.

"That bad, huh?" Her dark eyes glinted with amusement. She seemed to have gotten over her snit at the bookshop last night. "We'll have to see if we can do something to remedy that."

After lunch Cha Cha took us across the street to the Starlite and showed Mackenzie around. One of the dance studios was empty, and she made my cousin laugh as she grabbed Jasmine and mimicked how Scooter and I looked together at first at Cotillion.

"It's amazing you have any toes left at all, Truly," Jasmine joked. "My brother really flattened them."

"The two of them got better, though," said Cha Cha. "Competition will do that."

"And you should have seen how Cha Cha transformed Calhoun!" Jasmine crowed. "She's a genius—he looked like someone on one of those dance competition shows by the time she was done with him."

I looked away, remembering how Calhoun had asked me to dance. Now, if he had the chance, he'd probably ask Mackenzie. I wasn't so cretinous that I didn't know that.

Glancing down at my watch, I frowned. "Gotta go," I told my friends, shouldering my swim bag. "Last swim practice of Spring Break awaits."

As I turned to leave, my cell phone buzzed. It was Scooter.

"What's up?" asked Jasmine.

I frowned at his text message. "Um, I'm not sure. It's from your brother. He says 'Big foot brigade reporting in.'"

Mackenzie gasped. "Did he get *footage?*" She and Cha Cha and Jasmine all crowded around.

WHAT ARE YOU TALKING ABOUT? I texted back.

GOTTA SEE IT TO BELIEVE IT, Scooter replied.

My cousin squealed. "He got Bigfoot on camera!"

My fingers flew over my cell phone keyboard. WHERE R U GUYS?

MY HOUSE, Scooter texted back. YOU?

DANCE STUDIO. MEET US AT THE BOOKSTORE?

I looked over at my cousin and my friends. "Wow, you guys! This could be huge. If we got Bigfoot on film, we're going to be famous!"

"You should tell Lauren too," said Mackenzie. "It was her theory, after all."

I made a face. Just what I needed. Little Miss Tagalong, tagging along again. *Olive branch*, I thought. "Fine," I replied, and sent my sister a quick text too.

The four of us left the dance studio and ran back across the street.

"What do you think of the name 'Cup and Chaucer'?" Aunt True asked as we came through the front door.

"Cup and what?" I looked around for the boys. They weren't here yet.

"Chaucer."

"Um, as a name for what?"

"For the mini café I'm thinking of adding over there," my aunt replied, waving a hand at the space to the left of the cash register. "We could serve tea and coffee to go with our signature treats. As another income stream."

Aunt True is always thinking up new ways for our bookstore to make money.

"There's room at the end of the counter for an espresso machine," she continued, "and I think we could squeeze in two or three little tables and chairs."

"Cool, Ms. Lovejoy," said Jasmine. "I'd totally hang out here if you do that."

"You already totally hang out here," Cha Cha reminded her with a grin.

"Cup and Chaucer." My mother nodded slowly. "That's cute, True."

"Who's Chaucer?" my father asked, emerging from the back office.

My mother and my aunt gave him a look.

He grinned. "Kidding! I'm not a complete philistine." And striking a pose, he began to recite aloud in what sounded like a foreign language:

> *Whan that Aprille with his shoures soote*
> *The droghte of Marche hath perced to the roote,*
> *And bathed every veyne in swich licour,*
> *Of which vertu engendred is the flour . . .*

We all stared at him, speechless.

"Um, what was that?" Mackenzie asked.

"Unless I'm mistaken, that was your uncle Jericho spouting

Middle English." There was a note of awe in my mother's voice.

"Middle English?" I asked. "Isn't that something out of *The Hobbit*?"

"That's Middle-*earth*," scoffed Lauren, the bell over the door jangling as she came in to join us. "Duh. Everybody knows that."

I glared at her.

"Middle English was the dialect spoken and written in the British Isles in medieval times," Aunt True explained hastily, spotting the look on my face. "I have to say, J. T., I'm impressed."

"Contrary to popular opinion, I didn't just wrestle at the University of Texas—I actually received an education," my father told her smugly. "My freshman English professor happened to be a Chaucer nut, and one of the requirements for passing his course was memorizing the opening stanzas of *Canterbury Tales*."

"Will wonders never cease," said Aunt True, shaking her head.

"Apparently not," my mother agreed.

The bell jangled again, and we all turned to see Mr. Sanchez stride into the bookshop. He had Scooter firmly in his grip. Calhoun and Lucas slunk in behind them.

"Was your daughter in on this too?" Mr. Sanchez demanded, his face like thunder.

My father frowned. "In on what?"

"This!" Mr. Sanchez shook the video camera at him.

Uh-oh, I slid a glance at Scooter.

He gave Mackenzie and me a hangdog look. "I kind of borrowed it without asking," he muttered.

My father pinned me with one of his signature Lieutenant Colonel Jericho T. Lovejoy glares. "Truly? Were you involved in taking this camera without permission?"

I squirmed, hoping that someone would jump in and help me out. But I was on my own. Nobody wanted to face the wrath of Lieutenant Colonel Jericho T. Lovejoy when he was in full commanding officer mode.

Lying wasn't an option. Not to my father. It was time to face the music. "Yeah," I admitted. "I mean, yes, sir."

Before either my father or Mr. Sanchez could say anything more, Scooter held up his phone.

"Here's the thing, though," he told us. "It worked."

CHAPTER 25

"What worked?" demanded Mr. Sanchez.

"The surveillance feed," Scooter explained. "We set up a stakeout at Freeman Farm to try and catch the sap rustler."

My father and Mr. Sanchez exchanged a glance.

"And you're telling us you caught the thief on film?" said my father.

Scooter nodded.

"This still doesn't excuse what you did," Mr. Sanchez told him sternly. "My colleague is hopping mad. He left his equipment at my office earlier this week, planning to pick it up first thing this morning for an assignment. He was worried that it had been stolen."

Scooter hung his head. "I know. I'm sorry. It's just that Franklin is my friend, and with all the stuff going on between his family and the Maynards, I thought—"

"The problem is that you didn't think!" Mr. Sanchez retorted.

"Let's see what you've got, son," said my father.

We crowded around and watched over Scooter's shoulder as he tapped on his cell phone screen to pull up the video feed.

At first there was nothing to see but a lot of dark. Then, some sort of movement must have triggered the motion detector, because all of a sudden the camera's flash kicked on, illuminating the sugar bush. A cluster of maple trees was clearly visible straight ahead, along with the network of plastic tubing strung between them. A moment later, a dark shape skulked into view.

Mackenzie and Lauren both gasped. I clutched my cousin's arm involuntarily. *Here it comes*, I thought. Bigfoot! Life as we knew it would never be the same. There would be magazine covers and movie offers. We should probably think about scheduling a press conference.

"Keep watching," said Scooter, slanting us a glance. Behind him, Calhoun and Lucas had the oddest expressions on their faces. As if they were trying not to—

"Are you kidding me?" I blurted, dropping Mackenzie's arm.

Behind me, Aunt True started to giggle.

"Oh my goodness," exclaimed my mother. "That's the funniest thing I've ever seen!"

The video camera had caught the sap rustler red-handed, all right. Or red-pawed, in this case. Out of the undergrowth waddled not Bigfoot—not even close—but rather a fat mama raccoon, followed by a trio of roly-poly babies. The mother raccoon climbed up one of the trees and ventured gingerly out onto a branch. Reaching down with her paws, she grabbed a section of the tubing that was attached to the spile and severed it neatly with her sharp teeth. On the ground below, one of her babies grabbed the dangling end and began sucking vigorously on it.

"Man, I can't believe we thought it was Big—" I stopped short as I realized that everyone had turned to look at me. Scooter and Calhoun were drawing their fingers across their throats, desperately trying to get me to shut up. So were Cha Cha and Jasmine.

"Big what, honey?" my mother asked.

"Uh, nothing," I mumbled, embarrassed. "Some big, uh, kids. You know, from West Hartfield."

So much for a press conference, I thought glumly.

We continued to watch as the mother raccoon repeated the crime for each of her babies. By the end, we were all howling.

"I love the way she keeps looking around!" my mother said, wiping her eyes. "As if she knows she's doing something wrong and might get caught!"

"You are so busted, Mama!" crowed Aunt True.

"So much for 'sabotage in Pumpkin Falls,'" said my father, shaking his head.

"You have to take this down to the *Pumpkin Falls Patriot-Bugle* right away," my mother told Scooter. "They can post the video on their website and get the word out. This will put a stop to any feuding. I'm going to call Grace Freeman and tell her the good news."

"And I'll call Coach Maynard," my father said. He turned to me. "You're not off the hook, young lady. I'll speak with you later."

My heart sank. I'd be lucky if I got to set foot outside the house before the Fourth of July.

"I'll let Ella Bellow know, and the rest of the town will hear within the hour," said Aunt True as my parents disappeared into the back office. "Thank goodness this is settled. Pumpkin Falls is too small a community for a full-blown feud."

Mr. Sanchez blew out his breath. He looked at Scooter for a long moment, considering. "Well, I guess your heart was in the right place," he said finally. "I'll go see if I can patch things up with my colleague."

"Thanks, Dad," Scooter replied. "I really am sorry."

"I'm still planning to take it out of your hide, though," his father warned. "I seem to recall that the garage could use cleaning."

Scooter's face fell when he heard this.

"Next time you get a bright idea that involves someone else's property, run it by me first, would you, buddy?" His father took the video camera and left.

As the adults scattered on their various missions, my friends and I were left standing alone in the middle of the bookshop.

YOURS TRULY

"So I guess we can chalk up another win for the Pumpkin Falls Private Eyes, right?" said Scooter.

"Some win," said Calhoun. "Talk about the biggest anticlimax ever. Even I can write tomorrow's headline: *Masked bandits unmasked!*"

Mackenzie giggled, and Calhoun grinned at her. I looked away.

"So, what's next?" Scooter asked. "You guys want to hang out or something?"

"Can't," said Cha Cha. "It's Shabbat." The Abramowitzes are Jewish, and Friday nights are special for their family.

I shook my head. "We can't, either. It's the last day of swim practice."

"After that, maybe?" Scooter gave Mackenzie a hopeful look.

"We're kind of in the middle of a project," I told him before my cousin could say anything.

He frowned. "What sort of project?"

"Knitting, mostly. We have our last sock class tonight."

Hearing this, Lauren looked over at me sharply. Before she could spill the beans about the diary, I added quickly, "Plus, we were going to head over to the library."

That quickly extinguished any spark of interest on Scooter's part. The library was not at the top of his list of Fun Things to Do in Pumpkin Falls.

"Okay." His eyes slid over to my cousin again. "Maybe we can all hang out tomorrow?"

"Sounds good to me," said Mackenzie.

"See you guys then!" Scooter said, beaming. Calhoun and Lucas both waved—at Mackenzie—and followed him out the door. Cha Cha and Jasmine went with them.

"Can you believe that video? It was so funny!" Lauren said to Mackenzie.

"I know!" Mackenzie replied. "I can't wait to send a link to Cameron!"

"So now you remember Cameron," I muttered.

She turned to me. "What?"

"Nothing. Forget it."

"No! I will not forget it! I'm sick of your snide remarks, and I'm sick of your attitude. You've been a total pain this week, Truly!"

"I've been a pain? You're the one who's boy crazy!"

Mackenzie's mouth dropped open. Lauren's head whipped back and forth as she watched us. Ignoring them both, I grabbed my swim bag and stomped off to the rec center.

"Pool party!" Coach Maynard announced as I came out onto the deck a little while later. Mackenzie was still in the locker room. Neither of us had said a word to each other while we were changing.

There was a smile on my swim coach's face and a spring in his step that definitely hadn't been there this morning. Word must have gotten out about the surveillance video. Ella

YOURS TRULY

Bellow's doing, most likely. Ella worked fast. "We have cause for celebration."

I knew that Coach Maynard was talking about a lot more than just the effort we'd put into daily doubles this week. He was clearly just as relieved as we all were that the mystery was solved and the feud was over.

My teammates and I jumped in the pool and played water polo for a while, then just horsed around, happy we didn't have to swim laps. There was cake and ice cream on the deck when we'd finished swimming, and Coach Maynard praised Mackenzie for her hard work and told her that she was bound to be a success, if she kept it up. He even gave her this goofy certificate he'd printed up, crowning her with the title "Flip Turn Ninja."

As we headed up the front walk to my grandparents' house a while later, I heard loud hammering coming from inside.

"What's going on?" I asked, opening the door and tossing my jacket and swim bag onto the bench in the front hall. I poked my head into the dining room. My mother was seated at the table as usual, working on her research paper.

"Your father's finally tackling the honey-do list," she said absently. "He's working on replacing the garbage disposal in the kitchen, and after that he promised he'd fix the squeaky step on the front stairs. Pizza should be here soon."

Fridays are always pizza nights for our family.

"So where is everybody?"

"Hatcher and Danny just got back from wrestling. They're showering, I think. And Lauren and Pippa are upstairs somewhere," my mother said, flapping her hand vaguely toward the ceiling. "Annie's with them." She finally looked up. "How was your last practice?"

"Good," I replied, and Mackenzie nodded.

"What are you two going to do now?"

"I want to finish my socks," my cousin told her, without so much as a glance in my direction. She was almost done with them and would be heading home with a completed pair, just as Ella had promised. I, on the other hand, was far from done. Probably because I'd had to unravel mine twice and start over.

"I'm going upstairs to read," I said. I didn't care if I was forging ahead without everybody else—I had to know what happened to Truly and the fugitives.

Mackenzie followed me just long enough to grab her knitting, then disappeared back downstairs. I flopped onto my bed and opened the diary.

> *March 2, 1862*
> *Disaster! The packages were mailed tonight, but something went terribly wrong. I had to leave Booth alone in his cradle and run for Reverend Bartlett. He told me to go home and keep the door closed and not let anyone in, no matter what.*
> *Yours, Truly*

YOURS TRULY

March 3, 1862
Much activity on Maple Street today, and on into the night. I stay hidden behind the curtains with my son and pray.
Yours, Truly

March 4, 1862
A letter from Matthew! But it brought sad news: Booth Harrington, his friend for whom our son is named, was killed by a sniper on reconnaissance at Manassas. I must go to his family as soon as it is safe and comfort them. We all have to drink from the cup of sorrow in life, but this is a hard, hard loss.
My letter telling Matthew of his mother's death must not yet have been received, for he did not mention it. I can only imagine how difficult this news will be.
No word yet on whether the delivery arrived safely. I am on pins and needles, as Mother Lovejoy used to say.
Is there more darkness ahead, or will we finally see some light?
Yours, Truly

March 5, 1862
Light! Reverend Bartlett reported that the packages were miraculously unharmed, though shaken from the

ordeal. They have gone on their way undetected. Next stop, Maple Grove. And then, God willing, heaven.
Yours, Truly

Heaven. That meant Canada, right?
Only three more entries. My eyes fairly flew over the pages:

May 15, 1862
I have had a letter from F! Both packages arrived safely. F promises to return someday. A love token was enclosed—a beautiful bracelet of intricately braided hair, black and brown so close in hue I almost cannot tell them apart. There are two bracelets, I am told. F has kept one. Our hearts are forever entwined by our ordeal. I will write back and promise again that the secret will be kept for always.
Yours, Truly

Wait a minute, I thought. Special friendship bracelets? Had Truly fallen in love with someone else? Was it the fugitive slave she'd harbored? The mysterious F? Was that the secret she had vowed to keep? What about Matthew?

October 7, 1862
These past months have been an agony. No further

word from F, and now this! Matthew has been captured by the enemy. I am closing up the house, which echoes with sadness and loss. Booth and I must travel to Washington, where I will try and arrange for his father's release. We will be back, God willing, and together again as a family. I pray for my beloved husband, and for F, and for an end to all pain and suffering. I pray for peace.

Yours, Truly

October 10, 1862
We leave Pumpkin Falls today, Booth and I, but our hearts are here in this home, always.

Yours, Truly

And then, nothing. That was it. The rest of the pages were empty. I flipped through to the end twice to be sure.

I lay there on my bed, trying to make sense of what I'd read. A few minutes later, my cell phone buzzed.

Probably Mom letting me know the pizza's arrived, I thought. But a split second later the buzz turned into a familiar tune: "The Magnificent Seven."

A moment after that, I heard cell phones ringing all over the house.

I sat up. It wasn't pizza—it was Dad's special signal, the one he'd programmed into all of our phones in case of an emergency. The one that meant RED ALERT! DEFON 1! ALL HANDS ON DECK!

In a flash, Lovejoys came out of the woodwork. I dashed out of my room as Hatcher and Danny thundered down from the attic. Pippa and Lauren popped out from wherever they'd been playing, trailing a puzzled Annie Freeman. Downstairs, my mother emerged from the dining room. Mackenzie was right behind her, clutching her knitting.

"What's going on?" my cousin asked, bewildered, as we all converged on the front staircase.

My father was standing just below the portrait of the original Truly. In his left hand he was holding a hammer, and in his right, firmly clamped in the titanium grip of the Terminator, was one of the wooden stair treads.

He smiled at us. "I found the Underground Railroad's hiding place."

CHAPTER 26

I couldn't see a thing.

Opening my eyes as wide as possible, I stared into the darkness.

Nothing.

Not even a glimmer of light.

It was pitch-black inside, and airless. It smelled of moldy newspapers and dust and time that had slowed to a crawl and then stopped altogether. It smelled of something else, too, something that I really, really hoped was the decaying rag rug beneath me and not spiders.

I tried to shift position, and smacked into the wall. It was unbelievably cramped, especially for someone my size. I couldn't stand, I couldn't stretch out, I could only sit or lie down curled up on my side. I couldn't even begin to imagine how anyone had spent more than a few minutes in here.

I was tempted to use the torch app on my cell phone, but I

resisted the urge. Instead, I held my breath, trying to envision what it would have felt like to be hidden away, terrified that you'd be discovered and returned to a life you'd risked everything to leave.

A minute later, a crack of light appeared above my head. My father peered in. "Had enough?"

I nodded, and he lifted the stair tread away, then reached down and gave me his good hand as I clambered out.

"My turn! My turn!" shrieked Pippa.

"Only Truly and Mackenzie get to go in tonight," my mother told her.

"No fair!" Lauren protested. "How come?"

"Because they were the ones who found the diary, and without it we wouldn't have known what this space was, even if we'd ever managed to find it," my mother told her calmly.

"Someone would have discovered it eventually," Lauren muttered. She was resentful about the fact that she hadn't been the one to find the hiding spot. *So much for all that tapping, Nancy Drew*, I thought spitefully.

"Chin up, Lauren," said Aunt True. "Good things come to those who wait."

My mother had called my aunt the minute Dad showed us his discovery, and she and Professor Rusty were here practically before my mother hung up the phone. Professor Rusty looked like he'd just won the lottery. He'd taken a zillion pictures already, and he kept shaking his head and saying things like "Amazing!" and "Incredible!" and "Extraordinary!"

Watching him, I suddenly realized something: This was his owl. This was the thing Professor Rusty had been waiting his whole life to see.

He'd been super anxious about us touching anything. "It's vital to preserve the integrity of a historical find of this magnitude," he'd said, shining a flashlight into the secret room and leaning in. "Look at the dates on these newspapers lining the walls!" he'd cried, his voice muffled. "1848! 1853! 1860! What a treasure trove! They prove this is the real deal."

"Why are the walls lined with newspaper?" Mackenzie had asked.

"For warmth," he'd explained, standing up again.

Hatcher and I snickered. Professor Rusty really looked like Albert Einstein now, what with all the dust in his hair. Aunt True reached over and swatted at it, sending up a small cloud.

Professor Rusty coughed. "It would have been drafty in there in the wintertime, and the newspaper would have helped with that. It also probably helped absorb sound, making it safer. Same thing with that rug on the floor." He grinned at us. "Isn't it just marvelous, to think that this secret has been here all these years, completely undisturbed? It's like finding Tutankhamen's tomb!"

"You do have a tendency to exaggerate, dear," said Aunt True drily.

I swiveled around and stared at her. This was the first time I'd heard her call him a pet name. Did this mean he was really her boyfriend?

We'd all taken turns peering inside, and then I'd managed to persuade Professor Rusty to let me climb in.

"I'll be careful," I said. "I promise not to touch anything."

He'd finally agreed, although reluctantly. "Once the team from the museum has examined and photographed everything, it won't be such a big deal," he'd explained. "You can spend all the time in the world in there if you want to."

"Just for a minute," I'd begged. "Seriously, I won't touch anything."

And I didn't, but I sure looked, at least until my father replaced the stair tread, plunging me into darkness.

Did you leave me a clue, Truly? I wondered. But no artifacts had been left behind, from what I could see. No initials were written on the walls or on the floor. If I'd been hoping for a message, there wasn't one. Or else it had been cleared away long ago.

"I can't believe nobody noticed this spot before," my father said after I climbed out and Mackenzie climbed in. "It's as plain as the nose on your face once you know it's there."

"Not really," said my mother. Opening the telephone closet, she turned on the light and pointed to where the sloping ceiling angled to the floor. "Whoever built it did a very clever job. This space doesn't extend all the way to the foot of the stairs—they built a false wall to conceal the hiding place."

Professor Rusty and my father got a tape measure to see if she was right.

"Extraordinary," said Professor Rusty when it turned out that she was.

"I wonder who built it?" said my father, helping Mackenzie climb out. She was clutching her camera and looking smug, which I was pretty sure meant she'd been taking pictures and texting Cameron. Or maybe Calhoun? I scowled.

"Matthew, perhaps," said Aunt True. "If he was the first one in his family to get involved with the Underground Railroad. Or maybe his father or grandfather."

"We might be able to figure that out, based on the dates of the earliest newspapers, once we've made a thorough examination," Professor Rusty told her.

"I'm still mystified why no one else in the family seemed to know about this," said my father.

"Gramps might be able to answer that," I pointed out. "We should call him."

"Not in the middle of the night, we shouldn't," said Aunt True, glancing at her watch. "We'll try him in the morning."

The doorbell rang. It was the pizza delivery guy. We must have looked like complete nuts, what with three of us covered in dust and all of us buzzing with excitement. Pippa was hopping up and down the stairs nonstop, squealing. Danny had come straight from the shower and was still wrapped in his bath towel. Lauren had temporarily abandoned her bad mood and was playing ring-around-the-rosy in the living room with Annie, who was spelling words at the top of her lungs. The pizza delivery guy arrived just as she'd gotten to A-B-O-L-I-T-I-O-N! I noticed that he left as quickly as he could.

We ate on paper plates, right there in the front hall. None of us wanted to peel ourselves away from our discovery.

"I don't suppose you girls feel much like going to knitting class tonight, what with all this excitement," my mother said as we finished up.

"No way, mom," I said. "Sorry."

Mackenzie shook her head too.

"I know how you feel because I feel the same way," my mother told us. "I'll call Ella and let her know we're not coming."

In the end, everybody skipped sock class, as it turned out. The minute Ella heard why we weren't coming, she invited herself—and our fellow students—over to view the secret room for themselves.

"I brought currant scones!" she announced breathlessly, barreling through our front door. Right behind her were Mrs. Winthrop, Bud Jefferson, Belinda, Augustus Wilde—who wasn't in our sock class, but seeing a flash of purple at his ankles, I figured Belinda had probably brought him along to model the socks she'd made—Mrs. Maynard, Annie's mother, and Mr. Henry.

"I ordered pizza," said Mr. Jefferson.

YOURS TRULY

"Uh, how kind," my mother replied.

My brothers looked pleased to hear this. But then, they were bottomless pits.

The rest of the Pumpkin Falls Private Eyes arrived just as the pizza truck pulled into the driveway again.

"How did they find out?" I wondered when I spotted my friends.

"I texted them." Mackenzie avoided my gaze—which probably meant she'd texted Calhoun.

"I won't even begin to try and explain," my mother said to the bewildered pizza guy, taking the stack of boxes from him and handing him a huge tip. Turning to my brothers and sisters and me, she added in a low voice, "FHB," which is Lovejoy family shorthand for "family hold back."

Like I wanted any more pizza. My brothers, on the other hand, waited until she wasn't looking and helped themselves to two more slices each.

We all crowded into the living room, and the sofas and chairs and window seats and even the big stone hearth in front of the fireplace quickly filled up. I started to take a seat on the floor next to Cha Cha, but my mother placed her hand on my arm.

"Truly, why don't you tell everyone about what you found, and maybe read us a little from the diary," she suggested. "That will provide a little background to tonight's discovery."

"Okay." I went upstairs to get it. When I came back

down, I couldn't help noticing that Calhoun had taken a seat by my cousin. I tried not to look at them as I explained how Mackenzie and I had found the loose floorboard and the package that had been hidden underneath it.

"A secret compartment? How come you didn't tell us?" Scooter looked hurt.

"We, uh, wanted to keep it a surprise," I replied lamely. "But you can see it now, if you want to."

Of course everyone wanted to. I led them all upstairs. My room wasn't at its tidiest, but at least I'd made my bed.

I studiously avoided looking at Calhoun, but out of the corner of my eye I saw him gazing around curiously. At one point he leaned over to Mackenzie, then pointed at the framed woodcut of the snowy owl that hung on the wall above my bed. It was one of my prized possessions. She said something to him, and he laughed.

My stomach lurched. *She probably called me a bird nerd*, I thought bitterly.

Back downstairs, everyone took turns looking at the hiding place while I skimmed through the diary, picking out some of the better entries to read aloud.

There were audible oohs and aahs of excitement as I read about the bloodhounds on Lovejoy Mountain, and sighs when my audience learned of Mother Lovejoy's death.

"It's all so mysterious!" cried Mrs. Winthrop when I

got to the part about the original Truly's unnamed visitor. "Packages! A disastrous ordeal! Something that went terribly wrong!"

"And a bracelet made of hair, did you say?" Mrs. Freeman asked sharply.

I nodded.

"Interesting."

"It all ends so abruptly," sighed Aunt True. "What a cliffhanger! Any insights for us, Rusty?"

He cleared his throat. "About the ending, and what happened afterward? Alas, no. We'll have to wait for the call to Namibia." He turned to me. "I did find an answer to your question about Maple Grove, however. It turns out there was quite an astonishing discovery made there several years ago at a small Quaker church. The town is just two miles from the Canadian border, and it had long been rumored to be one of the final stops on the Underground Railroad. A married couple who founded the church were conductors. But there was little hard evidence to go on."

Coach Maynard's wife leaned forward in her chair. "Why is that?"

"Lack of documentation has proven difficult for historians," Professor Rusty explained. "So much of what we know has been passed down through oral history—through stories," he added, seeing Pippa's puckered forehead. "It makes sense, really, when you think about it—the people who helped were otherwise law-abiding citizens, and they didn't want to be discovered breaking the law. So their activities weren't openly discussed, and in most cases never recorded. A diary like the original Truly Lovejoy's is a rare thing indeed."

"So what was this astonishing discovery you started to tell us about?" asked Bud Jefferson.

"Ah yes. Twenty years ago or so, some renovations were being made to the church in Maple Grove, and a layer of wood was stripped away from the raised platform in the main meeting area. Beneath it was a trapdoor leading to what was clearly a hiding place. And so it would seem that the rails from Pumpkin Falls indeed led to Maple Grove, Maine, and from there on to Canada."

"To heaven," I whispered.

Professor Rusty smiled at me. "Exactly."

"Well," said my mother, "I know this has been an incredibly exciting evening—"

"E-X-C-I-T-I-N-G!" shouted Annie, who was still wound up like a top.

"Shhh, honey," said Mrs. Freeman. "Settle down or I'm taking you home."

"—but I think it's time we called it a day," my mother finished.

As coats and jackets—and one purple cape—were rounded up and distributed, everyone took a last look at the

YOURS TRULY

hiding place. Everyone except Mackenzie and Calhoun, that was. They were deep in conversation. Another hot spike of jealousy surged through me as I watched the two of them. There was no way around it—despite tonight's discovery, my Spring Break was not destined to end on a good note.

CHAPTER 27

For once, I wasn't woken up by the sound of tapping.

Good, I thought, rolling over and stretching. Now that the hiding place had been found, Lauren must have abandoned her annoying hobby. We could finally have some peace and quiet around here again. And with daily doubles over with, I could finally sleep in. I burrowed into my pillow again, preparing to do just that.

Before I could, though, there was a knock on my door.

"Lauren!" I groaned in protest. But it wasn't my sister—it was my mother.

"Girls?" she said. "We're getting ready to call Namibia!"

Mackenzie and I dressed in frosty silence. We hadn't spoken since last night. Downstairs, we found my parents and Hatcher and Danny already up, seated at the kitchen table with Pippa. There was no sign of Lauren.

Maybe Nancy Drew finally wore herself out, I thought.

"We're just waiting for Rusty and True," my father told us. "I sent your grandparents an e-mail last night telling them when to expect our call."

When my aunt and Professor Rusty arrived a few minutes later, it turned out they'd brought Professor Rusty's research assistant along with them again.

"Oh, hello, Felicia," said my mother. "Coffee?"

"Tea, please," she replied primly. "Earl Grey, preferably."

Hatcher kicked me under the table. I flared my nostrils at him.

My father sat by his laptop, keeping one eye on the kitchen clock as everyone got settled. "Oh-eight hundred," he said finally, and dialed my grandparents' number. A few moments later, Gramps and Lola's faces popped up onscreen.

"That's quite a crowd you have there, J. T.!" said my grandfather.

"The more the merrier."

"Your e-mail was awfully mysterious," said Lola. "Apparently you have something to show us?"

"Wait until you see," my father said, picking up his laptop and carrying it out of the kitchen. We all trooped after him. In the front hall, he passed the laptop to Hatcher, who held it with the camera pointing toward the staircase as my father lifted the squeaky tread.

My brother Danny shined a flashlight inside, and my father motioned to Hatcher to angle the camera toward the concealed room.

"What on earth?" I heard Lola exclaim.

"It's a hiding spot, Mom!" Aunt True's voice rose in excitement. "It's where our ancestors put the runaway slaves."

"Well, I'll be darned," said Gramps. "First a secret compartment and a long-lost diary, and now this. That's what we get for skipping town—we miss out on all the fun!"

My father showed my grandparents the telephone closet and explained about the false wall, and then we all went back into the kitchen and settled in for a chat.

"This is just remarkable," said Gramps, who sounded nearly as thrilled as Professor Rusty. "To think that I never suspected it was there!"

"So you really didn't have any inkling?" Aunt True asked.

My grandfather shook his head. "Not a one. No one ever breathed a word. I'm sure my father and mother would have told me, if they had known."

"Your father was Booth's son, right?" said Professor Rusty.

Gramps shook his head again. "Grandson. He was my great-grandfather. I knew him when I was a boy. Booth lived with us for the last few years of his life, and he used to tell me stories about his boyhood in Germany after the Civil War. But he never mentioned a secret room, or the Underground Railroad."

"What about his mother?" Aunt True asked. "Did he ever speak of her?"

Gramps's face clouded. "Such a tragic tale."

Beside me, I felt Mackenzie stiffen. Suddenly, I wasn't so sure I wanted to know the ending to this story.

"We know some of the details from the diary," my father said. "Ruth—the one Truly calls 'Mother Lovejoy'—died in the winter of 1862, apparently."

"That's right," said my grandfather. He glanced over at me. "Truly, why don't you go get the old family Bible? It's on the bottom shelf in the bookcase next to the piano."

I scurried off, returning a few moments later with a big, leather-bound book.

"If you open it to the front flyleaf, you'll see a record of births and deaths," Gramps said, and everyone crowded around, peering over my shoulder as I did as he instructed. "Do you see Ruth's name there?"

I ran my finger down the page and nodded. "Yes. It's the same date as in the diary. In fact, I think the original Truly made this entry in the Bible. It looks like her handwriting."

"That would make sense," said Lola. "Truly was the only Lovejoy in the house when Ruth died. Aside from Booth, that is, but he was a just a baby."

"What else do you see?" asked Gramps.

My finger moved to the line below, and stopped. My eyes suddenly welled up with tears.

How is it possible that I can feel such sadness about someone who lived—and died—over a hundred and fifty years ago?

I thought. The diary had made them all so real!

"When Truly got word that Matthew had been captured, she took the baby and went to Washington to try and secure his release," said Gramps. "The house stood empty for a while, Booth told me. His aunt—Matthew's sister Charity—would come up from Boston and look in on it from time to time, and she and her family often used it as a summer retreat."

I nodded. Truly had said as much in one of her final diary entries.

"Sadly, Truly's mission was not successful, and Matthew passed away in Andersonville that summer."

Professor Rusty went pale.

"Andersonville!" he breathed. "The worst of the Confederate prisons!"

My grandfather nodded somberly. "Truly was devastated. She returned to Germany to be with her mother."

"Did she ever get married again?" Mackenzie wanted to know.

"No," Gramps told her. "She died fairly young, too—of a broken heart, my great-grandfather told me. After her death, he finally came back to Pumpkin Falls to claim his inheritance—our home on Maple Street."

We were all quiet for a bit.

"He would have been too young to remember the runaways," said Aunt True slowly. I could tell that she was feeling sad too. We all were.

YOURS TRULY

We all have to drink from the cup of sorrow, the original Truly had written. I glanced over at my father's arm. Our family had, that was for sure.

"Wouldn't his mother have told him about her involvement with the Underground Railroad?" asked my father. "It's not as if it were something to be ashamed of."

"No, but it was part of a tragic chapter in her life," Gramps replied. "She may simply have wished it to remain closed."

"What about the mysterious F, and the secret that Truly promised to keep?" I asked.

"What secret?" asked Lola.

"In the diary," I said. "Hang on, I'll read it to you." I retrieved the diary, then riffled carefully through the pages until I found the entry I was looking for.

"Here it is," I said. "May 15, 1862." I read aloud the passage about the bracelets.

"How odd," said Gramps. "A love token. *Our hearts are forever entwined* . . . It almost makes it sound as if Truly had fallen—"

"Wait, a bracelet made of hair?" Lola interrupted. She grabbed my grandfather's arm. "Oh my, Walt."

"Oh my what, Mom?" asked Aunt True.

Onscreen, my grandparents exchanged a glance.

"Truly," Lola said slowly, "I want you to go upstairs to the attic. I'm pretty sure it's in the second small bedroom on the left—"

"—one of the servant's bedrooms?" I asked, and she nodded.

"Somewhere in there amongst our things, you'll find a box marked 'Family Keepsakes,'" she told me. "There are a lot of boxes, and I don't remember exactly where I put it, but you'll find it. Bring it downstairs, would you?"

"I'll go with you," said Hatcher.

It took us a while, but we found the box. Back downstairs, my brother held it up to the laptop camera. "Is this it?"

Lola nodded. "That's the one. Open it up, would you?"

My mother helped me, and we carefully removed the contents—old photographs, mostly, and mementos from when my father and Aunt True were little. There was a crib-size quilt and some baby shoes and a Cub Scout sash filled with sewn-on badges, and some toys and a silver rattle.

"You're looking for a small, square, black velvet box," said my grandmother.

"Got it," I said, spotting it buried beneath Aunt True's debate team trophy. I plucked it out and handed it to my mother. "You open it."

"Are you sure?"

I nodded. My heart was racing, and I could hardly breathe. I was pretty sure I knew what it contained.

My mother lifted the lid. "Oh my," she said, echoing my grandmother. "Would you look at this, J. T.?"

"This has certainly been a week full of surprises," said my father, peering into the box.

There was a bracelet inside. Black hair and brown braided together, just as the original Truly had said, *so close in hue I almost cannot tell them apart.* I almost couldn't either.

"Look at that braidwork!" Aunt True reached out a finger and gently stroked the bracelet. "It's exquisite."

"Sentimental hairwork was a common handicraft in the Victorian era," Felicia Grunewald suddenly spouted, setting her teacup down with a rattle. "Bouquets, wreaths, artwork, and jewelry made of human hair were viewed as a way of showing affection—you were literally wearing part of a loved one—and honoring them, or of memorializing the dead."

We stared at her, stunned into silence. How was anyone supposed to respond to that?

"Eew," said Mackenzie finally.

"Your father's mother gave the bracelet to me when we married," Lola told Dad and Aunt True. "All she knew was that it had belonged to Booth's mother."

"But what does it mean, *our hearts are forever entwined by our ordeal?*" I asked.

"That, it would seem, is destined to remain a mystery," Gramps replied. He glanced at his watch. "I hate to have to leave you all, but we have an appointment with the builders over at the new library."

We said our good-byes and promised to call with any new developments.

Annie Freeman, rubbing her eyes and yawning, wandered

in as Mackenzie and I were starting to clear the table. She spotted the bracelet and frowned. She opened her mouth to say something, but before she could, my mother asked, "Where's Lauren? You girls must be starving."

"She probably has her nose in a book," said Hatcher.

Annie's brow furrowed. "She's not down here with you?"

My mother shook her head. "Nope."

"Maybe she went over to the Mitchells' to feed Bilbo," said Danny. "Isn't she ferret-sitting this week?"

Something about the expression on Annie's face caught my mother's attention, and she set the cereal box she was holding down on the counter. "What is it, Annie?"

Annie looked at her, wide-eyed. "Last night," she said, "after everybody went to bed. We stayed up for a while, and Lauren was reading—"

"See? I told you," said Hatcher.

"—and all of a sudden she got really excited. She said something about figuring out what happened to the packages. She wanted me to come with her, but . . ." Annie's voice trailed off.

"Go on," urged my mother. "But what?"

Annie's voice dropped to a whisper. "But she said it might be a little S-C-A-R-Y."

My mother's face went ashen. "And she didn't come back?"

Annie shook her head.

My mother grabbed her cell phone and punched in Lauren's number. We all stood there, waiting, as it rang and rang and rang. "Nothing," she said, pressing her lips together and giving my dad an anxious look. "It went to voicemail. Either she doesn't have her phone with her, or the battery ran out."

My father turned to Hatcher and Danny. "Upstairs on the double, boys," he ordered them crisply. "Check the bedrooms, the bathrooms, and the closets. Make a sweep of the attic while you're at it too—she's been spending a lot of time up there." He grabbed his jacket. "I'll go next door and check the Mitchells'," he told my mother. "I'm sure it's nothing. She's probably feeding Bilbo, like Danny said."

He returned to the kitchen at the same time my brothers did. They all shook their heads.

"No sign of her upstairs," said Hatcher.

"And she's not next door," my father reported grimly.

As my mother sank into one of the chairs at the kitchen table, my father turned to my brothers. "She's not in the attic? Are you sure?"

"I checked all over," Danny assured him.

"Check again," my father ordered, and my brothers immediately vanished.

My mother turned to Annie. "When did you see her last?"

Annie's face crumpled, and my mother put her arms around her. "It's okay, sweetheart, it's okay."

"I fell asleep!" Annie wailed. "I tried to stay awake,

waiting for her, but I fell asleep! She told me not to tell anyone. She said—"

Annie paused, gulping back tears.

"She said what?" my mother asked gently.

Annie wiped her nose on her pajama sleeve and flicked a glance at me. "She said she was going to show those stupid Pumpkin Falls Private Eyes," she finished miserably.

Across the table, Mackenzie's eyes met mine.

My sister was missing.

And it was all my fault.

CHAPTER 28

Owl eyes, I thought. *I need owl eyes and ears.*

Owls could find their prey without even seeing it, my new birthday book had informed me. Their round faces were shaped like a satellite dish, specifically designed to detect sound. The ring of stiff feathers surrounding their face channeled sound toward the ears, which were hidden at the side of the face. At certain frequencies, an owl's hearing was ten times more sensitive than that of humans.

If I were an owl, I might be able to hear my sister, or somehow sense where she had gone.

I hated the idea of Lauren out there somewhere, alone all night and probably scared out of her wits. She was a pest and she drove me nuts sometimes—okay, a lot of the time—but she was my *sister*.

What on earth had possessed her to run off?

My mother called Belinda Winchester to see if Lauren had

gone to visit the kittens. My father called Mr. Henry to see if she was at the library. They tried the General Store and the Starlite Dance Studio and Lou's. Nothing. Professor Rusty and Felicia went back to the college to scour the campus; Aunt True headed down to the bookstore and checked there and her apartment. But Lauren was nowhere to be found.

"She can't have gone far," my mother kept saying. "It's just not like her to wander off!"

In all the confusion, no one had remembered to feed Bilbo.

"Truly, would you mind?" my mother asked.

"No problem." It was the least I could do. I grabbed my barn jacket and slipped out the back door.

The Mitchells' house was quiet. The clock above the mantel in the living room ticked loudly. *Lau-ren. Lau-ren. Lau-ren*, it seemed to say.

"You haven't seen her, have you, buddy?" I asked Bilbo, passing him a ferret treat.

But if he had, he wasn't telling.

Back in our kitchen, I heard Aunt True on her cell phone enlisting Ella Bellow to activate the town grapevine. Professor Rusty was in the telephone closet talking to campus security. My father had called the police—well, our town's lone policeman—and my mother was talking with the *Pumpkin Falls Patriot-Bugle*.

"The boys are checking the barn and the backyard," my father told me after he hung up. "Your mother and I will probably need to go out, so I want you and Mackenzie to stay here at the house just in case anyone comes to the door or calls on the landline."

"Yes, sir," I replied.

My cousin, who was on her cell phone with her parents, nodded too.

Belinda was enlisted to babysit, and she and Augustus Wilde—still sporting his purple socks—came over to get Pippa and take her back to Belinda's house.

"The kittens will keep her calm," Belinda whispered to my mother.

Professor Rusty slipped his arms around my aunt. "We'll find her," he assured her.

Definitely boyfriend, I thought, watching them.

In the space of an hour, the entire town had mobilized to search for Lauren.

Mr. Henry closed the library. Ella closed A Stitch in Time, and Bud Jefferson closed the coin and stamp shop. The Freemans shut down their maple syrup operation, and Maynard's Maple Barn, and the General Store, Mahoney's Antiques, and Suds 'n Duds all closed as well. Only Lou's Diner stayed open, so it could serve as downtown headquarters for the search.

I texted the Pumpkin Falls Private Eyes to tell them what had happened, and they immediately offered to join in the hunt. Scooter Sanchez texted back to tell me that his father had offered us his colleague's video surveillance equipment, if we needed it.

All across Pumpkin Falls, friends and neighbors and complete strangers fanned out to look for my sister. But as the hours dragged on, there was still no sign of her.

"Lou's is handing out sandwiches to the volunteers," Hatcher reported as he and Danny swung by at noon with a plate for my cousin and me. "Mrs. Winthrop sends her love."

"Mackenzie! Lunch!" I called up the front stairs. She'd been staying out of sight up there somewhere all morning.

"Not hungry!" the answer floated back down.

I was, though. Grabbing a chicken salad sandwich, I paced back and forth in the kitchen. *Think, Truly, think!* I told myself. *Think like an owl hunting her prey.* Single-minded. Focused. Alert. Where could Lauren be?

Annie had said something about her reading a book last night. Which one, I wondered? Could it offer a clue? Leaving my half-eaten sandwich on the counter, I ran upstairs to check.

I found Mackenzie in Lauren's room, making the rounds of the cages.

"Her pets were hungry," she whispered, swiping at her eyes. "Nobody remembered to feed them."

All of a sudden I couldn't take it anymore.

"Mackenzie, I'm so sorry for how I've been acting," I blurted. "It was stupid! I don't have an excuse and I'm really, really sorry."

"Don't—" she began, but I plunged on before she could continue.

"I had no right to be snarky about Cameron McAllister or call you boy crazy. I'm an idiot and a total jerk and cretinous, just like Felicia Grunewald said! If you like Calhoun, that's fine. You can have him."

She looked at me, confused. "Calhoun?"

I lifted a shoulder.

"*Romeo* Calhoun?"

"Uh, yeah," I mumbled, frowning.

"What are you talking about? 'You can have him'? Why would I want Calhoun?"

"Um," I replied, "you said you thought he was cute."

My cousin pulled herself up to her full five feet one inch and placed her hands on her hips. "Is *that* what this snit was all about, Truly Lovejoy?"

Now I was the one who was confused. "Isn't it?"

"You're absolutely right—you *are* cretinous!" Mackenzie snapped. "I don't like Calhoun!"

"You don't?" I stared at her, astounded.

"Well, I like him, but I don't *like* him. You know what I mean. Besides, you're the only one he talks about."

I blinked. "I am?"

"He thought you liked Scooter."

My heart sank. Of course. The kiss behind the Freemans' barn.

"But I set him straight," said Mackenzie.

I gaped at her. "You did? When?"

"Last night. I knew you liked him, and I wanted to help."

So that's what she'd been doing when I saw them talking! "How did you know?"

She made a rude noise. "I've known you forever, you moron. I can read you like one of Lauren's books."

We regarded each other for a long moment.

"You're welcome," my cousin said finally.

I started to laugh, and a second later, she did too.

"I hated being mad at you!" I told her.

"I hated you being mad at me!" she replied. "You're my best friend in the whole world!"

"And you're mine!" I crossed the room and gave her a Bigfoot-size hug, lifting her off her feet and into the air. Then I set her down again and smiled. "Now, let's go figure out what happened to my sister."

CHAPTER 29

Lauren's room looked like a mini library. She went through books the way I went through sudoku puzzles. There were books piled on her dresser, books piled on her desk, books piled on her chair and on her bedside table and on her pets' cages and on the floor.

I didn't even know where to start.

So I called Annie Freeman.

Her mother answered the phone. "Any word yet about Lauren?"

"Not yet," I said. "May I please speak to Annie?"

Mrs. Freeman hesitated. "She's awfully upset."

"I just want to ask if she remembers what Lauren was reading last night. It might be important, Mrs. Freeman."

"Okay."

There was a pause, and then Annie got on the line. I repeated my question.

"Um," she said. "I think it was something about a house, maybe?"

I relayed this information to Mackenzie, who took a quick look around the room and then shook her head.

"Okay, Annie. If you remember anything else, call me."

Something about a house, I thought as I hung up. That rang a faint bell, but I couldn't put my finger on it. I tried Aunt True next, but that proved to be another dead end.

"Sorry, Truly—I honestly have no idea," she said. "Your sister devours books the way Rusty devours my Bookshop Blondies. How about Mr. Henry? Could you try calling him? Lauren's always at the library. He might be able to help."

"Good idea!"

Mr. Henry answered on the first ring. "Truly Lovejoy!" he replied eagerly when I told him who was calling. "Any news about Lauren?"

"Nothing yet," I replied. "Hey, I was wondering, do you remember if she checked something out recently about a house?"

"A house? Hmmm." He was quiet for a moment, thinking.

"It might have had something to do with the Underground Railroad," I added.

"Lauren didn't check anything out about the Underground Railroad, but there may have been something in that stack I brought to sock class for your mother. Tell you what, let me check the computer. I should have a list here."

It was quiet for a minute. I could hear him typing.

"Let me see . . . yes, here we are." He read off the names one by one.

"Nope," I said to each of the titles. "Nope. Not that one either."

He listed several more, then said, "Wait, was it *The House of Dies Drear*?"

I gave a little yelp. "I think that's it! That's the one I saw her reading the other night at dinner!"

"It has a black cover, as I recall."

"Thanks, Mr. Henry."

Mackenzie and I took the room apart. We finally found the book in the unlikeliest spot—stuffed down at the foot of Lauren's unmade bed.

Her bookmark was still in it. I opened to where she'd left off reading and scanned the page. *Snick!* The pieces slid into place as neatly as one of my sudoku puzzles.

I looked up. "I think I know where Lauren is," I told my cousin. "Sort of."

CHAPTER 30

I ran down the hall toward the stairs. Mackenzie was right on my heels.

"Obadiah, Abigail, Jeremiah, Ruth," I chanted as we flew down the stairs. My cousin joined in, and we singsonged the rest in unison: "Matthew, Truly, Charity, and Booth!"

I pulled up the stair tread that marked the entrance to the hidden room and shined my cell phone light into it. As I'd suspected, it wasn't exactly as we'd left it yesterday.

"Remember Professor Rusty told us not to touch anything until the history department had a chance to look everything over?" I said, and Mackenzie nodded. "Check it out."

She peered inside.

The tattered rag rug had been shoved over to one of the far corners of the cramped space.

"No one thought to look in here when Lauren went missing," I said, sitting down on the step above the gaping hole and reaching out a hand toward my cousin. "Steady me, would you?"

She did, and I climbed inside. A cloud of dust flew up. "I could use a little more light," I told her, coughing.

"Hang on, I'll grab the big flashlight. Danny left it on the hall bench."

She returned momentarily and aimed a strong beam downward.

"Much better." Kneeling down, I peered closely at the floor.

"What are you looking for?" Mackenzie asked.

"A trapdoor," I said, and explained about *The House of Dies Drear*, and how it involved this family who moved to a creepy old house riddled with secret passages and tunnels that runaway slaves had once used to hide in and escape.

"Wow, that must have been catnip to Lauren," said my cousin, and I nodded.

"Ha! Gotcha!" I crowed, slipping my fingers into a small groove in the wood floor. The trapdoor squawked as I lifted it, its hinges stiff from a century and a half of disuse.

"Wow," breathed Mackenzie. "No way! I can't believe we missed that yesterday."

"Professor Rusty would hardly let us touch anything, remember?"

My cousin squeezed into the hiding space beside me. We peered down into the darkness. "Where does that ladder go?"

"I guess we're going to find out," I told her, and taking the flashlight, I swung my legs over the edge.

The air grew colder as I climbed down. I waited at the foot of the ladder for Mackenzie, playing the flashlight beam around what appeared to be another small room.

"They must have walled this section of the basement off," I told my cousin, my voice echoing against the stone. Straight ahead, a tunnel curved past the fieldstone foundation. It was narrow and dark and brick lined, and the walls and ceiling were thick with cobwebs.

I froze.

Cobwebs meant spiders.

I couldn't believe that Lauren had had the courage to come down here by herself.

She'd come this way for sure, though. I could plainly see her footprints in the dust.

I had to go after her, even though every fiber of my body was screaming *Stop! Stay back!*

"Shouldn't we call your parents?" Mackenzie whispered, clutching the back of my sweatshirt as I stepped slowly forward.

"As soon as I find my sister," I told her, then called, "Lauren?"

There was no answer.

I called again, louder this time. My voice bounced off the brick walls, echoing weirdly back to me. I took a few more steps forward.

Mackenzie peered into the darkness. "Do you think this leads to the barn?"

"No idea."

We inched our way forward through the cobwebs and dust, following my sister's footprints.

"Which direction do you think we're going?" my cousin asked, coughing as she accidentally kicked up a cloud of dust.

I made a face, swatting at the strands of cobweb that clung to my hair. "Toward the Mitchells' house, maybe?" I guessed. It was disorienting down here in the dark.

"Didn't your mother say something about houses connecting in some communities? Maybe the people who used to live at the Mitchells' were involved with the Underground Railroad too."

"That would totally make sense!" I quickened my pace, buoyed by the thought of my sister so close at hand.

A few minutes later, I stopped. "Does the tunnel feel like it's getting narrower?"

Mackenzie grunted. "Maybe."

We pushed on. Now I definitely could feel the tunnel growing narrower. Panic welled up in me—Mackenzie was right, we should have told my parents.

And then we turned a corner, and I stopped short.

"Whoa!" said my cousin as she slammed into my back. "What is it?"

"The footprints," I replied. "They disappeared."

"Huh?"

I shined the flashlight on the floor. "They're gone. See?" My sister's trail ended at a pile of rubble.

Mackenzie stared at it, and then understanding dawned. "The tunnel caved in!"

We fairly flew back to the ladder. I called my parents the minute I clambered out of the hiding place. They arrived at the same time that Pumpkin Falls' lone police car pulled up. The rest of the town soon followed, and in the space of ten minutes our house looked like Grand Central Station.

My mother cleared off the dining room table, and my father got to work organizing the search and rescue teams. Before long, one crew was hard at work in the basement of the Mitchells' house, looking for a possible tunnel exit. Another crew was assigned to the tunnel beneath my grandparents' house, where they cautiously began trying to clear away the rubble.

Professor Rusty threw caution to the wind. "Nothing matters but rescuing Lauren," he said to the work crew as he followed them down the ladder in the hiding place that led to the basement. "Don't worry about damaging anything. Life always trumps history."

"What is taking them so long?" my mother asked a short while later, pacing up and down the front hall. "Shouldn't they have found her by now?"

"It's slow going," Professor Rusty reported when he emerged a few minutes later. "They're trying to avoid another cave-in."

By midafternoon neither the crew over at our neighbors' house nor the crew in our basement had found anything. I was heading to the kitchen to get myself some water when I saw my parents talking quietly in the dining room.

"Oh, J. T.!" I overheard my mother say. "What if she's—"

"We're not going to think that way, Dinah," my father told her firmly. "We can't. There's no reason to give up hope. Lauren is a Lovejoy, after all. And Lovejoys are made of strong stuff."

"She's a little girl, and she's down there somewhere in the dark," my mother whispered.

"I'm sure she took a flashlight with her."

"But how long can a pair of batteries last?" My mother leaned her forehead on the windowpane, watching the shadows lengthen in the yard. My father put his good hand on her shoulder and squeezed.

Tears pricked my eyelids. I backed away. I hated to think of my sister trapped in the dark too. But there wasn't anything I could do. It was up to the search and rescue crews now.

Friends stopped by, bringing food and offering comfort. Lucas Winthrop's mother and Mr. Jefferson arrived together with a fruit basket, and peeking out the window I was pretty sure I saw them holding hands as they came up the front path. Bud Jefferson's were back in his coat pockets when I opened the door to greet them, though.

The Abramowitzes brought a casserole, Scooter and Jasmine's parents brought a ham, and Mr. Henry came with what looked like a lifetime supply of his award-winning Maple Walnut Cupcakes.

I was in the dining room with my mother when Mrs. Freeman came in. "Dinah!" she said.

"Grace!" my mother replied, and the two of them embraced.

"I brought homemade bread," Mrs. Freeman told her. "I'll just leave it in the kitchen. And I have something I want to show you. I don't know why, but I think it may be important." She turned to me. "Something you said last night, Truly, made me think of it."

She drew a small box out of her jacket pocket. "It's a family heirloom."

She lifted the lid, and I stared at the contents, confused. Nestled on a piece of white velvet was a bracelet made of intricately braided hair.

A bracelet identical to the one that belonged to Lola.

There are two bracelets, Truly had written in her diary. The mysterious F had kept one, she had said.

"It was my husband's great-great-grandfather's," she said. "His mother gave it to him."

YOURS TRULY

His *mother*! I thought. *Snick!* The last puzzle piece clicked into place.

Our hearts are forever entwined.

And all of a sudden I knew where my sister was. For real this time.

CHAPTER 31

"This way!" I cried, squelching across the backyard. My family and half of Pumpkin Falls were right on my heels. My flashlight bounced wildly off the birdbath and the evergreens that lined my grandparents' property. In the distance, an owl hooted: *Who cooks for you! Who cooks for you-all!*

Barred owl, I thought automatically, wondering if it was the same one Mackenzie and I had seen that first night she was here.

Which seemed like a million years ago now.

The original Truly had listened for owls too, a hundred and fifty years ago. She had listened, and responded, and saved lives. Could I save one now?

Lauren! I thought desperately. *Hang on! We're coming!*

This must have been what happened back in the winter of 1862. A cave-in. That must have been the disaster that Truly mentioned in her diary. Her two "packages," trapped beneath the earth. And no one able to dig them out for days, thanks to the slave hunters lurking everywhere. There'd been a happy ending to that tale—the runaways were miraculously unharmed, Reverend Bartlett had told Truly. Would there be another miracle now?

"Are you sure you know where you're going?" said my father, smacking at the underbrush with the Terminator.

"Pretty sure," I told him as my flashlight picked out the overgrown path that led from Gramps and Lola's property to the old Oak Street Cemetery.

The hill behind my grandparents' house was steep. We bushwhacked our way up, panting from the effort, and finally emerged by a line of tombstones at the back of the graveyard.

I grabbed Mrs. Freeman's arm. "Where's your ancestor's grave?"

"Which one?" she asked.

"The first Frank Freeman's."

She pointed her flashlight to the left. "Over there."

I ran over toward where her beam was shining. There it was! The sculpture on the lid of the tomb was unmistakable. I pointed my flashlight at the headstone:

> FRANK FREEMAN
> *Two hearts forever entwined, one forever yearning to be free*

Frank Freeman was the original Truly's mysterious F! I was sure of it. *Our hearts are forever entwined by our ordeal*, F had written to her. It had to be Frank.

I looked over at Professor Rusty. "Remember William Still?"

He ran a hand through his hair as he pondered my question, then his eyes lit up. "Of course!"

I looked at the most-photographed grave in the cemetery, considering. I pushed on the epitaph. Nothing. I ran my fingers around the edge of the headstone. Nothing seemed out of place; nothing had any give.

It had to be the statue, then, the beautiful carving of the African American mother cradling her infant, which stood in the middle of the slab covering the crypt.

As my family and friends looked on in bewilderment, I nodded at Professor Rusty. He reached out and grabbed the statue by its base and gave a mighty heave. At first, nothing happened. He heaved again, and this time there was a loud scraping sound as the slab moved slightly.

"Some help, gentlemen?" Professor Rusty looked over at my father and my brothers. They leaped into action, crowding around.

All four of them heaved, and stone ground against stone with a mighty screech. With one final piercing squawk, the slab shifted, revealing the open crypt.

I flung myself onto the edge, hardly daring to look down inside.

YOURS TRULY

My sister was huddled in the darkness beneath us, her pale face streaked with dirt and tears.

"Truly!" my sister sobbed as I lifted her out. "I knew you'd find me!"

"Lauren!" my mother cried out. "Oh, Lauren!"

We wrapped our arms around her, both of us sobbing in relief too.

"Can I be one of the Pumpkin Falls Private Eyes?" Lauren asked, gulping back tears. "Please?"

I nodded, hugging her fiercely. "Cross my heart and hope to fly."

EPILOGUE

April 12th
 Dear Diary,
 My sister is safe. She was cold, hungry, tired, and very, very frightened by the time we found her, but she's safe and that's all that matters.
 Aunt True is right—nothing is more important than family. I know that now. Not world travel, not swimming, not owls, not sudoku or best friends or boys. Family is everything.
 After the dust finally settled from the excitement of the search and rescue and the hoopla that followed—we got our press conference after all, though there was no mention of Bigfoot—Aunt True gave me this diary, and a fountain pen to go with it.
 "We have to do something to celebrate," she told me. "And this seems appropriate."
 Professor Rusty took the original Truly's diary to the college, where the museum's curatorial staff (including cretinous Felicia

Grunewald) is busy studying and transcribing its faded pages. It turns out the diary is a big deal. Several collectors have asked to buy it, but Gramps and Lola told them it's not for sale. I'm glad.

Our house is a big deal too, thanks to the hiding place and the tunnel. Aunt True is working with her boyfriend (she calls Professor Rusty that openly now, so it's official) to get it listed on the National Register of Historic Places.

I'm kind of a big deal too. At least our local newspaper thinks so. I was on the front page of the Pumpkin Falls Patriot-Bugle, along with Lauren, of course, and Annie Freeman says I'm a H-E-R-O-I-N-E for rescuing my sister, and for solving her family's mystery too.

The Freemans are still wrestling with the fact that their ancestor Frank Freeman was actually a she, not a he—a runaway slave named Frankie who was the original Truly's dear friend, and the mysterious F in her diary.

Like many other runaway slaves, Frankie had concealed her identity and passed for a man. It was safer for women that way, Professor Rusty told us. Part of the "ordeal" that she and my ancestor and namesake shared was the birth of Frankie's son. That's what the whole *our single package is now two!* riddle in the diary meant.

"You mean my great-great-great-grandfather was actually my great-great-great-grandmother?" said Franklin, who was incredulous when he first heard the news. "Why would someone want to keep that a secret?"

YOURS TRULY

Professor Rusty explained that it probably started when his ancestor fled the South. "In the end, Frankie simply kept her disguise," he told us. "After reaching Canada, she probably stayed for a while, but her dearest wish was to return to Pumpkin Falls and her new friend Truly."

It wasn't easy for women to own property in those days, he told us—especially African American women. Frankie might have risked losing her farm if people knew she was a woman. So she'd kept her secret, but she left a clue: the statue on the crypt of a woman and infant. And sure enough, when Professor Rusty and his team of colleagues examined the statue closely, they found her name scratched in tiny letters on the bottom: FRANKIE.

As promised, Truly had kept her friend's secret faithfully, taking it with her back to Germany, and eventually to her grave. We'll never know for sure why she didn't tell Booth about Frankie, but the secret remained for us to discover.

Professor Rusty had DNA tests done on the hair in the twin bracelets, and they came back 100 percent positive as Freeman and Lovejoy, further proof of the activity of the Underground Railroad in our tiny town. Frankie's and Truly's lives were entwined back then, just as our neighbors' lives and ours are here in Pumpkin Falls still.

The whole sap rustler thing turned out to be kind of a big deal too. Scooter's surveillance video of the raccoon saboteurs went viral, and Aunt True made hay with it, designing a bookshop window that featured blown-up stills of the mama raccoon and her babies, along with cookbooks, picture books featuring raccoons, and more stuff on maple syrup. Lauren got in on the act too, adding Rascal, one of her all-time favorite stories.

My aunt really is a marketing whiz. Cup and Chaucer, her new micro cafe, is starting to take shape. The two little tables she set up are almost always occupied, even though she's only serving tea right now. The directions that came with the espresso machine were in Italian, and as soon as we get them translated, Aunt True is going to train Hatcher and me to be baristas.

Ella Bellow took pity on my poor pathetic socks, and I was invited to Stitch and Snitch—I mean A Stitch in Time—for a remedial class. "Free of charge," she told me. "I did advertise successful socks in a week, after all."

With her help, I finally finished them. They're kind of lumpy, and they itch, but they don't look all that bad, so I'm wearing them anyway. I worked too hard on them not to.

Mackenzie and I talk all the time, just like always. We videoconference a couple of times a week, and she loves to show me what Frankie, her new kitten, is up to.

Yes, Mackenzie took a kitten home. Belinda's persistence paid off. And yes, my cousin named her Frankie, after Franklin's ancestor. "That way I'll never forget our Spring Break together," she told me.

Like there's any chance either of us could.

My cousin is still crazy about Mr. Perfect Cameron McAllister, although I think she's keeping her options open with both Scooter

YOURS TRULY

and Lucas, because I've overheard them vying with each other about who gets more texts from her. She backed away from Franklin, though, after I told her that Jasmine liked him.

The two of us are cooking up a plan to get together this summer. Cha Cha and Jasmine might come along too. I can hardly wait.

I'm still adjusting to life as a teenager. I still cry unexpectedly sometimes, and I still find myself wishing I were a chickadee instead of an ostrich more often than not, but at least I don't wish I were twelve anymore.

Thirteen is just fine with me, thanks to a certain boy whose initials are Romeo Calhoun.

Mackenzie's little talk with him seems to have lit a bit of a fire under Calhoun, because he volunteered to go owling with me. I take this as a good sign. I'm hoping maybe there'll be another kiss, eventually, to erase the memory of that first disastrous one with Scooter behind the Freemans' barn.

I have to go now. There's a full moon in the sky outside—a maple moon!—and Calhoun is waiting. I'm wearing the owl earrings that Mackenzie gave me for my birthday, and I can hear a barred owl in the distance. Wish me luck!

Yours, Truly

AUNT TRUE'S BOOKSHOP BLONDIES

Please ask a grown-up for help.

6 T. butter, softened
1 cup maple sugar
1 egg
½ tsp. maple flavoring
½ tsp. vanilla extract
1 cup all-purpose flour
1 tsp. baking powder
½ tsp. salt
1 cup chopped walnuts (optional)
Sea salt for sprinkling

- Preheat oven to 350° F. Grease an 8" square pan.
- In a large bowl, cream the butter and maple sugar together; beat in egg, maple flavoring, and vanilla. Whisk flour with baking powder and salt and add to egg mixture, stirring to combine. Add nuts.
- Pour into greased pan and bake for about 25 minutes, until edges are lightly brown and just beginning to pull away from pan.
- Remove from oven and cool on a rack. Sprinkle the top of the blondies with sea salt, if desired.

MISS MARPLE'S PICKS

The Canterbury Tales by Geoffrey Chaucer
The Hidden Staircase by Carolyn Keene
The Hobbit by J. R. R. Tolkien
The House of Dies Drear by Virginia Hamilton
Moses by Carole Boston Weatherford and Kadir Nelson
Rascal by Sterling North
The Sasquatch Escape by Suzanne Selfors
The Secret of the Old Clock by Carolyn Keene
The Westing Game by Ellen Raskin

Really Truly

ALSO BY HEATHER VOGEL FREDERICK

Absolutely Truly
Yours Truly

The Mother-Daughter Book Club
Much Ado About Anne
Dear Pen Pal
Pies & Prejudice
Home for the Holidays
Wish You Were Eyre
Mother-Daughter Book Camp

Once Upon a Toad

The Voyage of Patience Goodspeed
The Education of Patience Goodspeed

Spy Mice: The Black Paw
Spy Mice: For Your Paws Only
Spy Mice: Goldwhiskers

Hide and Squeak
A Little Women Christmas

Really Truly

A Pumpkin Falls Mystery

HEATHER VOGEL FREDERICK

Simon & Schuster Books for Young Readers
NEW YORK • LONDON • TORONTO • SYDNEY • NEW DELHI

SIMON & SCHUSTER BOOKS FOR YOUNG READERS
An imprint of Simon & Schuster Children's Publishing Division
1230 Avenue of the Americas, New York, New York 10020
This book is a work of fiction. Any references to historical events, real people, or real places are used fictitiously. Other names, characters, places, and events are products of the author's imagination, and any resemblance to actual events or places or persons, living or dead, is entirely coincidental.
Text copyright © 2020 by Heather Vogel Frederick
Jacket illustration copyright © 2020 by Charles Santoso
All rights reserved, including the right of reproduction in whole or in part in any form.
SIMON & SCHUSTER BOOKS FOR YOUNG READERS
is a trademark of Simon & Schuster, Inc.
For information about special discounts for bulk purchases, please contact Simon & Schuster Special Sales at 1-866-506-1949 or business@simonandschuster.com.
The Simon & Schuster Speakers Bureau can bring authors to your live event. For more information or to book an event, contact the Simon & Schuster Speakers Bureau at 1-866-248-3049 or visit our website at www.simonspeakers.com.
Jacket design by Krista Vossen
Interior design by Hilary Zarycky
The text for this book was set in Fournier.
Manufactured in the United States of America
0420 BVG
First Edition
2 4 6 8 10 9 7 5 3 1
Library of Congress Cataloging-in-Publication Data
Names: Frederick, Heather Vogel, author.
Title: Really Truly / Heather Vogel Frederick.
Description: First edition. | New York : Simon & Schuster Books for Young Readers, [2020] | Series: A Pumpkin Falls mystery | Audience: Ages 10 to 14. | Audience: Grades 4-6. | Summary: "Truly Lovejoy is excited for the perfect summer in Pumpkin Falls, New Hampshire: swim practice outside, working at the bookstore, one-on-one time with her mom, and best of all, time with the dreamy R. J. Calhoun who may just like Truly back. But the idyllic falls apart when she's sent off to mermaid academy—sparkly tail and all. Luckily, a mystery is never too far behind the Pumpkin Falls Private Eyes, and this one may just encourage Truly to come out of her shell, in more ways than one"—Provided by publisher.
Identifiers: LCCN 2019041522 (print) | LCCN 2019041523 (eBook) | ISBN 9781534414372 (hardcover) | ISBN 9781534414396 (eBook)
Subjects: CYAC: Mystery and detective stories. | Camps—Fiction. | Swimming—Fiction. | Buried treasure—Fiction. | Community life—New Hampshire—Fiction. | New Hampshire—Fiction.
Classification: LCC PZ7.F87217 Re 2020 (print) | LCC PZ7.F87217 (eBook) | DDC [Fic]—dc23
LC record available at https://lccn.loc.gov/2019041522
LC eBook record available at https://lccn.loc.gov/2019041523

For Naomi

PROLOGUE

There's a mermaid tail hanging in my closet.

And it's all my cousin Mackenzie's fault.

Look, I love anything to do with water—especially swimming. I've been on a swim team since I was five years old, and my father likes to tease that H_2O is my native element. But mermaid lessons? That would never have occurred to me in a million years. Maybe a billion. Mackenzie, though, was all over the idea the minute she spotted the brochure at the library.

I should have known that a place with a name as lame as Sirena's Sea Siren Academy could only spell trouble. Which I've had my fair share of ever since we moved to Pumpkin Falls, New Hampshire, and I accidentally became a middle school private eye. This time, however, I found myself way over my head in the trouble department as I tangled with pirates onstage and off, suffered a very public wardrobe malfunction, and embarked on a near-disastrous spelunking expedition while hunting for long-lost treasure.

(I didn't know what "spelunking" meant either, until it was too late to turn back. It's a good word, well worth looking up.)

But before any of this happened, and before anything remotely resembling a mermaid tail showed up in my closet, I had one major hurdle to face: the annual Gifford Family Reunion.

CHAPTER 1

"Smile like you mean it!" My grandmother clapped her hands, trying to attract the attention of the seven adults who were lined up on the steps of the Pumpkin Falls Public Library, talking and laughing. She turned to the woman behind the tripod beside her. "Aren't they something?"

The tripod, and the camera attached to it, belonged to Janet Foster, ace reporter for the *Pumpkin Falls Patriot-Bugle*. If it were possible for a newspaper as teeny as the *Pumpkin Falls Patriot-Bugle* to actually *have* an ace reporter, that was.

"They certainly are," Janet replied, peering through her camera lens. Janet moonlighted as a professional pet photographer. I had no idea how she was with people pictures, but in a town the size of ours, you took what you could get. And my grandmother had done exactly that, hiring her to take our traditional family reunion photos.

Grandma Gifford beamed. "All my beautiful babies!"

My brother Hatcher let out a snort. Our grandmother slipped her arm around him and squeezed. "Just you wait! Someday you'll have kids of your own, and then you'll understand. Your babies are *always* your babies, no matter how old they are."

I gazed skeptically at the half dozen men and one petite woman who were being photographed. It was hard to imagine any of my big Texas uncles as babies. Or my mother, for that matter. She stood at the end of the lineup like the period at the end of a sentence. Or rather, an exclamation point. Dinah Gifford Lovejoy didn't have much to offer in the height department, but she wasn't lacking in spunk.

"So these are all your kids?" Janet asked, pulling a small notebook and pen from the back pocket of her jeans.

My heart sank as I watched her switch into reporter mode. Janet may have been hired to take our family reunion photos, but she clearly knew a story when she spotted one. Not that we were hard to miss: thirty-seven Giffords in matching T-shirts parading through Pumpkin Falls were a sight to behold, as my grandmother would say.

"You bet your sweet cowboy boots they're my kids!" Grandma G replied, her voice brimming with Texas sugar and sass. "A boy for every day of the week and a girl for Sunday."

I looked at my mother, wondering how she'd survived growing up with six brothers. Six! And I thought two was bad. Hatcher and Danny were a handful, but my mother had had

REALLY TRULY

to deal with Uncle Teddy, Uncle Lenny, Uncle Craig, Uncle Rooster (his real name was Richard, but no one ever called him that), Uncle Brent, and Uncle Scott.

Then again, she'd had our grandmother's example. Grandma G was petite like my mother, but she had a voice like a bullhorn and backbone to spare. There was no mistaking who was boss when my grandmother was around. She'd had to be strong to raise seven kids by herself after my grandpa died.

I'd never met my Texas grandfather, but I still felt like I knew him. He was practically a legend in our family—the penniless cowboy from West Texas who'd pulled himself up by his bootstraps, swept our grandmother off her feet, and built a ranch near Austin with his own two hands. Theodore Roosevelt Gifford. My uncle Teddy was named after him.

I didn't have a favorite uncle, not really. I loved them all. But if I *did* have a favorite, it would be my uncle Teddy. He was my cousin and best friend Mackenzie's father, and I knew him almost as well as I knew my own dad. The hardest part about leaving Texas and moving across the country to New Hampshire had been moving away from them. And I knew I wasn't the only one who felt that way. Uncle Teddy and my mother were at the tail end of the Gifford lineup, and the closest of the Gifford siblings in age, barely eleven months apart. The two of them were best friends when they were little, and they were still best friends now that they were grown up.

"How are you enjoying Pumpkin Falls so far?" Janet asked my grandmother, her pen hovering over her notebook.

"Mighty fine!" Grandma G enthused. "You've got yourself a real slice of American pie here."

I could tell by the way Janet was nodding and scribbling that she liked that quote. It was perfect headline material, and I braced myself for the fact that, thanks to my ridiculously quotable grandmother, my family was probably going to end up plastered all over the front page of the *Patriot-Bugle*.

If only we'd kept the reunion in Texas, where it belonged! The Giffords had gotten together every summer since before I could remember, but until now our reunions had always been at the ranch. That's where my mother and her brothers had all grown up, and everyone but us still lived within half a day's drive. This year, though, for the first time, we were breaking with tradition. This year, my mother had invited everyone to spend the Fourth of July with us here in Pumpkin Falls.

The town didn't know what had hit it. Giffords had started arriving yesterday morning, and they'd kept streaming in all day. My father had been put in charge of logistics for our reunions years ago, and he organized the weekends like a military operation. This was right up his alley, seeing as how he was a former lieutenant colonel in the United States Army. Everything ran like clockwork thanks to him, with rotating squads of Giffords in charge of transportation, food shopping, meal setup, cooking, cleanup, and more. This year, Mr. Mili-

REALLY TRULY

tary had rented a school bus, and he and my brother Danny had taken turns running shuttles to and from Logan Airport in Boston, and would now spend the holiday weekend ferrying all of us around Pumpkin Falls.

This morning, we'd all gone downtown and descended on Lou's Diner for donuts (Dad had called ahead of time to warn them that thirty-seven hungry customers were on their way, to make sure there would be enough). Afterward, we'd given everyone a tour of Lovejoy's Books, our family's bookstore, and then stopped by Mahoney's Antiques for a peek at the big silver pumpkin trophy that would be awarded later this weekend to the winning Fourth of July road race team. Finally, we'd headed to the Pumpkin Falls Library, whose front steps had been selected as the best place in town for our reunion photographs.

As I watched Grandma G looking over the shots that Janet had taken so far, Hatcher spotted the expression on my face and grinned.

"Cheer up, Drooly," he whispered, calling me by my least favorite nickname. My real name, Truly, was odd enough, but Drooly? Please. "It will all be over soon."

I shot him a look. Thirty-six more hours hardly qualified as "soon."

It's not that I didn't love our epic family reunions—I did. They were great, when they were in Texas where they belonged. We were invisible on the ranch, and safe from prying eyes. We could be as goofy and loud as we wanted, without the rest of the world looking on. Here? I glanced around. By my calculations, at this very moment fully half of Pumpkin Falls was gawking at us.

"That should do it for this group," said Janet, after she and my grandmother settled on the winning shot. "How about one with just the grandkids next, and then we'll go for—what is it you call it? The full Gifford?"

My uncles let out a collective Texas whoop. I scowled, not feeling nearly as enthusiastic. Our upstairs hallway was plastered with "the full Giffords"—group portraits that had started when my mom and her brothers were little, gradually swelling in size to include their spouses, and then us kids. Our parents and aunts and uncles had all looked ridiculously young when they were first married, hardly older than Danny and Hatcher, who dubbed the photos Hairstyles Through the Ages. Most of the men had long hair and mustaches back in the day, and a few had even sported mullets. ("Business in the front, party in the back," as Danny liked to say.) Not my dad, of course. Mr. Military's hair was even shorter back then.

The portraits had grown larger each year as more and more cousins and siblings came along. I used to love looking at baby me and toddler me, and all the rest of us as we grew over the years. Now, when he really wanted to needle me, Hatcher called the pictures "the full Truly," for the way they charted my astronomical growth. I'd been a normal-size kid for a long time, but at the beginning of sixth grade I'd started to shoot up like one of the giant sunflowers in Grandma G's garden. At six feet tall, I towered over all of my classmates and most of my immediate family, and I was happy not to be reminded of that fact.

"Hey!" said my cousin Mackenzie, slipping her arm through mine. "There's Cha Cha and Jasmine!"

Cha Cha Abramowitz and Jasmine Sanchez were my closest friends in Pumpkin Falls. They waved at us, grinning hugely. I could tell they were enjoying the Gifford reunion spectacle. Mackenzie and I waved back.

"Ooo, and there's Calhoun!" My cousin stretched up on her tiptoes to see over the crowd. Mackenzie was petite, like my mother and grandmother. Whenever I was with her, I felt like an ostrich standing next to a chickadee.

I could feel my face flush. I'd been studiously ignoring Romeo Calhoun ever since I'd spotted him at the edge of the crowd. I could only imagine what he thought of this sideshow. I slid a glance over to where he stood talking to his sister Juliet. Seriously, those were their names, Romeo and Juliet, thanks to their father, who was a huge fan of "the Bard," as he called Shakespeare.

Calhoun wasn't my boyfriend, but I liked to think that we were more than just friends. Or at least that we'd both like us to be. We weren't officially dating or anything—my father said I was much too young for that. "When you can drive, you can date, and not before," was his motto, and when Lieutenant Colonel Jericho T. Lovejoy laid down the law, us kids said "yes, sir" and fell in line. Calhoun and I hung out a lot, though. I'd taken him bird-watching a few times—my favorite hobby—and we went to the General Store for ice cream and stuff with our group of friends. But unlike Jasmine's brother Scooter, who had ambushed me on my birthday last Spring Break with a big smooch I wasn't looking for, Calhoun hadn't so much as tried to hold my hand. Mackenzie thought he just needed encouragement. I wasn't sure what to think. Despite the fact that I had two brothers, boys were still a mystery to me.

"Kids!" called my grandmother in her bullhorn voice, momentarily silencing the crowd. "Come and get your pictures made!"

As Mackenzie and I headed toward her, Aunt Angie appeared with the stroller containing our youngest cousins. Twins Bella and Blair were just six months old.

"Why don't you girls hold them for the picture?" our aunt suggested, passing a baby each to Mackenzie and me.

Mackenzie was a pro, thanks to all the babysitting she did back in Austin. Babies weren't my thing, though. In fact, they were way up on the list of things I wasn't good at. Blair must have sensed that, because the minute I took her, she started to cry.

"Jiggle her up and down, like this," said Mackenzie, bouncing Bella gently.

I tried to mimic her, but it only made my tiny cousin cry harder.

"I'm right here, peanut!" cooed Aunt Angie, waggling her fingers.

"Give her to me," said my younger sister Lauren, scooping Blair out of my arms. She made googly eyes and silly faces and bounced her expertly on her hip until Blair stopped crying and produced a toothless smile.

Aunt Angie gave my sister an admiring glance. "Don't you have the magic touch!"

Lauren turned pink with pleasure at the compliment. "Babies aren't that different from kittens."

"No, Lauren, you can't have a kitten," my mother said automatically. My sister had been angling for another pet ever since we'd arrived in Pumpkin Falls.

Lauren heaved the deep sigh of the misunderstood, then followed Mackenzie and me onto the steps to join the rest of our cousins.

"Two rows! Tallest in the back, shortest in the front!" ordered Grandma G.

"How about we try something different?" Janet suggested. "Let's put Truly in the middle, and then staircase down from there on either side."

I grimaced. I'd been hoping to hide in the back row. I knew Janet didn't mean anything by it, but Truly-in-the-Middle was my father's nickname for me, since I was the middle kid in our family. And ever since my growth spurt, it was like my family couldn't resist showing me off. My parents had put me smack-dab in the middle of our last Christmas card photo, where I towered over both of them, and over my brothers and sisters, all of us in our matching holiday sweaters my mother had knit for us. Talk about a sight to behold.

Aunt Louise, Mackenzie's mother, sorted us into place with help from Aunt True, who was a Lovejoy, not a Gifford. They went up and down the line, wiping noses and brushing stubborn cowlicks into place in an effort to make us presentable. This was Aunt True's very first Gifford reunion. If she was feeling a little overwhelmed, you'd never know it. My father's sister seemed to take everything in stride, including giving up a life of travel to move back to her old hometown and help run the family bookshop.

"I think that's as good as it gets," said Aunt Louise finally.

My aunts retreated to the sidelines as Grandma G gave Janet a thumbs-up. The camera whirred and clicked.

"Looking good!" said Janet. "How about one more, just in case? Smile, everyone!"

Just as the camera shutter clicked for the final time, my cousin Matt, who was ten and a show-off, made a face. This meant another retake, of course, and there were two more misfires after that, one because my little sister Pippa got distracted by a butterfly and another because Uncle Rooster's two youngest boys started swatting each other. Finally, Janet managed to take a picture that satisfied my grandmother. Which was a good thing, because my cheek muscles were starting to hurt from all the smiling.

"Time for the full Gifford!" Grandma G announced. She gave her lips a fresh swipe of her signature bright red lipstick as the rest of the Texas side of my family crowded forward.

"True, you get in the shot too," my mother said.

"Yes, True, come on up here and join us," said my grandmother. "And bring that long drink of water with you." She winked at Erastus Peckinpaugh, my aunt's gangly boyfriend, who taught history at Lovejoy College. Their romance—which my friends and I helped rekindle last winter—was finally out from under wraps. It was also a subject of keen interest to the residents of Pumpkin Falls, who were placing bets as to when Professor Rusty, as everybody called him, would propose.

"But we're not Giffords!" Aunt True protested.

"Neither am I," said my father, taking his place beside my mother. "But we're all still family."

"Honorary Giffords!" Aunt Louise decreed, and another big Texas whoop went up from my relatives.

Aunt True smiled and shrugged. Grabbing her boyfriend's hand, she squeezed in beside me. Suddenly I didn't feel like such a freak. Aunt True and I were the same height.

"Stand your ground, tall timber," she whispered, giving me an affectionate nudge with her shoulder.

Aunt True liked to refer to the two of us as "tall timber" and often joked that we were born to stand out in a crowd. Maybe someday I'd have her confidence. Right now, I was still getting used to my newly attained height. And my size-ten-and-a-half feet. I took a deep breath, straightened up, and smiled once again at the camera.

"And that's a wrap!" said Janet half a dozen clicks later.

My father stepped forward, thrust two fingers in his mouth, and gave a sharp whistle. "Head 'em up and move 'em out! The bus leaves in two minutes—there's just enough time before dinner for a swim over at Lake Lovejoy. Y'all know what's on the menu tonight: Teddy's famous ribs!"

This announcement brought another chorus of whoops. Uncle Teddy's barbecued ribs were always a highlight of our reunions. I could hardly wait. Pumpkin Falls didn't know the first thing about barbecue. New Englanders called it "having a cookout," and it mostly involved hamburgers and hot dogs, not brisket and ribs.

As I followed my family across the village green toward the waiting school bus, I waved to an elderly woman seated on a bench. She waved back. Thelma Farnsworth and her sister Ethel were married to a pair of brothers. Ethel and her husband Ike Farnsworth ran the General Store; Thelma and Elmer Farnsworth had a small dairy farm at the edge of town. Every summer, the Farnsworth sisters also helped out as cooks at Camp Lovejoy.

REALLY TRULY

"Are you part of a circus?" Thelma asked me, puzzled, as the stream of Giffords in matching T-shirts flowed past her bench.

"We might as well be," I muttered in response.

"Did you hear that, Elmer?" Thelma shouted to her husband, who was bent over a nearby trash bin, sorting through its contents. A bag full of empty soda cans was at his feet. Elmer loved collecting junk. "One man's trash is another man's treasure" was his motto.

"ELMER!" Thelma called again, louder this time. "THE CIRCUS IS IN TOWN!"

Elmer was hard of hearing but refused to wear a hearing aid. The reason I knew this pretty much summed up my life in Pumpkin Falls. There were no secrets in a town the size of ours. Everybody knew everything about everyone else—including the fact that Elmer Farnsworth had a stubborn streak which, combined with his pride, was keeping him from admitting that he didn't hear as well as he used to. This had been a topic of lively discussion recently on the General Store's front porch, where he and his buddies liked to hang out, and where I often overheard their conversations when I was eating ice cream with my friends.

Elmer snapped upright like he'd been poked with a pin. "I LOVE THE CIRCUS!" he bellowed.

I did a mental face-palm and ran for the bus.

I loved my family and I loved our reunions, but I didn't

love being such a public spectacle. Stealth mode was more my speed, my term for flying under the radar. I didn't love people staring at us or the prospect of being front-page news, and I especially didn't love our matching T-shirts—this year's were a blinding shade of neon green with a bright orange pumpkin on the front and THE GIFFORDS GO TO PUMPKIN FALLS! splatted on the back.

I hated to admit it, but as much as I'd been looking forward to our family reunion, I was looking forward to it being over, too. Because then my perfect summer could finally begin.

CHAPTER 2

I hummed to myself as I set out paper plates and napkins on the half dozen picnic tables that stretched end to end across our backyard. My dad had tacked a note to the bulletin board at the General Store last week, asking if anyone had any extra we could borrow, and just like that, trucks had started pulling into our driveway with picnic tables. Small towns had their drawbacks, but there were definitely advantages, too. I'd always thought that Texas was friendly, but Pumpkin Falls could give it a run for its money in the neighborly department any day of the week.

I plunked down another paper plate and thought about the perfect summer that would soon be mine. It shimmered in my mind like a lane in the pool first thing in the morning, before anyone else dove into the water. Smooth as glass, not a single ripple—perfection! Well, except for the fact that Mackenzie wouldn't be here. That definitely counted as a ripple. Still, I was looking forward to long lazy days, with plenty of time for bird-watching and bike rides and hanging out with my friends. Plus swim team. Summer swim team was the best. It was much more relaxed than during the school year, and practices were going to be outside, just like in Texas, since Coach Maynard had wangled special privileges for our team at Lovejoy College's outdoor pool.

Helping out at the bookstore was near the top of my list of things to look forward to as well, which was kind of a surprise. When we'd first arrived in New Hampshire, I'd thought the bookstore was stupid. Well, not exactly stupid—I'd loved visiting it when Gramps and Lola, my Lovejoy grandparents, had been in charge—but to me, the family business represented the whole reason we'd had to move away from our home in Austin, so I'd resented it at first.

That wasn't fair, of course. It wasn't the bookstore's fault that my father had lost his right arm in a bomb explosion in Afghanistan, and that he couldn't be a pilot anymore. But it had taken me a while to understand that.

Lovejoy's Books had been in a sorry mess when we'd first arrived, teetering on the brink of closure. But my dad and Aunt True—with help from all of us, and from Belinda Winchester, the town's resident cat lady, who had unexpectedly stepped forward to invest in the business—had done what had at first seemed impossible. These days, the bookshop's future was looking a lot less rocky.

REALLY TRULY

It still surprised me how much I loved spending time there. Unlike my sister Lauren, who loved books the way I loved water, I wasn't the world's biggest bookworm. But there was more to running a bookstore than just reading, as it turned out. I got to help Aunt True come up with creative displays for the windows, which I was surprisingly good at. I got to use the cash register and help set up for events, and I was Aunt True's assistant for Story Hour on Saturday mornings. And now that we'd added Cup and Chaucer, the mini café that was my aunt's latest marketing scheme, I also got to run the espresso machine and make hot beverages for our customers, which was fun.

And then there was the cherry on top of my summer sundae: Romeo Calhoun.

Calhoun loomed large in my plans for a perfect summer. Right after school had finished, he'd casually asked if maybe I'd like to go to the Lovejoy College Summer Film Festival with him. I'd tried to sound equally casual when I said yes, but inside I was jumping up and down. A whole week of movies! With Calhoun! I didn't care that his father was the one who'd suggested it, or who'd arranged free tickets for us, or that Calhoun had invited all the rest of our friends along too.

This year's film festival was featuring movies from the 1950s. Aunt True had pounced on the brochure when I showed it to her.

"Wait until you see *Rear Window*," she'd said with a

happy sigh, scanning the list of movie titles. "Grace Kelly is SO gorgeous! And so is Audrey Hepburn—you'll love her in *Sabrina*. And you'll love *Singin' in the Rain*, and *Born Yesterday*, and *Ben Hur*, and *Father of the Bride*!" She looked up at me and smiled. "What a fantastic series! I think I'll get tickets for Rusty and me too."

I wasn't sure what to say to that. Double-dating with my aunt and Professor Rusty did not exactly fit into my perfect summer plans.

"Truly!" My mother's voice snapped me out of my daydream.

"Yes?"

"Can you feed Bilbo?"

"Lauren's home for the weekend—that's her job!"

"I know, but she's busy. Rooster's organized a scavenger hunt for the younger kids."

"Can't Hatcher do it?" As usual, my brother had gone AWOL—military shorthand for "absent without leave."

"He's helping your father show Aunt Lily and Uncle Scott the Underground Railroad hiding spot," my mother replied.

Of course he was. My brother always managed to find something more interesting to do than chores. "Fine," I grumbled.

"Excuse me?"

"Fine, ma'am." My parents were sticklers for politeness. And in a military family, that meant plenty of sirs and ma'ams.

REALLY TRULY

This past Spring Break, the Pumpkin Falls Private Eyes—that was what my friends and I called ourselves—had solved another mystery in town. Two, actually. One involved maple syrup rustlers, or at least what we'd thought were rustlers, and the other involved the Underground Railroad. It turned out that one of my ancestors had been involved with helping runaway slaves. She'd hidden them right here in Gramps and Lola's house. We'd discovered the secret compartment under the front stairs that had concealed the runaways and the escape tunnel that led through the cellar and under the back lawn to the cemetery. After the tunnel caved in, my parents had decided it was too dangerous to preserve, despite its historical value. Professor Rusty had begged my father not to seal it.

"It would be an irreparable loss!" he'd protested, but my father hadn't budged. My aunt's boyfriend still hadn't quite forgiven him, although he was somewhat mollified by the fact that the secret compartment under the stairs was left intact.

I pulled my cell phone from my pocket and checked the time. I was going to have to hustle to make it over to the Mitchells' and back before dinner.

The Mitchells were our neighbors. They were away for a few weeks and had offered us the use of their house for the reunion. It had six bedrooms, just like Gramps and Lola's house, and half the adults were staying there. Most of my cousins were sleeping outside in tents. Only Mackenzie and I opted to stay indoors.

"Smart girls," Grandma G had said when she'd heard this. "I like my creature comforts too."

I double-timed it around the picnic tables, slapping down the rest of the paper plates and anchoring them with silverware, then setting out rolls of paper towels. Uncle Teddy's blackberry jalapeño ribs were famously messy. The aroma wafting over from the grill was making my mouth water. Uncle Teddy was the undisputed king of barbecue in our family. "Low and slow" was his motto when it came to smoking meat, and he knew exactly how much heat to put in his signature sauce: enough so your lips tingled a little, but not so much that it made your nose run. That didn't stop half my family from adding extra hot sauce. I smiled, thinking about the surprise that would be waiting for them at dinner.

One thing about our family reunions—the food was always fantastic. Everyone contributed their favorites, from Uncle Rooster's signature lasagna to Aunt Sally's famous banana French toast to Uncle Teddy's ribs and more. On the final night, we always "splashed out," as my mother called it, and chipped in to have dinner catered. And being Texans, and being Giffords, there was no such thing as too much barbecue, so we always had the catering for that meal done by the Salt Lick, a family favorite near Austin.

This time around, though, we were in Pumpkin Falls, not Texas, and my parents had opted to host a clambake for our final meal. Not that we were anywhere near the ocean—you

REALLY TRULY

pretty much couldn't get any more landlocked than the Pumpkin River Valley—but clambakes were a New England tradition, and my mother was determined to send everybody home having had what she called "a genuine taste of Yankee food." And this year that meant a house call from Lobster Bob, instead of the catering team from the Salt Lick. But the clambake wasn't until tomorrow night. Tonight, there was barbecue!

I sniffed the air again greedily, then loped off across the lawn toward the neighbors' house. Lauren was the animal-lover in our family, and she was usually the one who looked after the Mitchells' pet ferret. This summer, though, my younger sisters were both away at camp, so most of the time I was the one who ended up stuck with cleaning Bilbo's litter box and giving him his meals.

Another part of my perfect summer was the fact that, with Lauren and Pippa at Camp Lovejoy, and with my brothers shortly heading off to a weeklong wresting clinic at Boston University, I would have my parents' undivided attention.

As the middle kid, it was easy to be overlooked. But this summer, for a whole week, I wouldn't be Truly-in-the-Middle, I'd be Truly-the-Only-Child! My mother had already promised to fix my favorite foods and take me to West Hartfield shopping for a new swimsuit and treat us to pedicures. She'd even mentioned driving down to Boston for the day, just the two of us. I was looking forward to being pampered and spoiled a bit. It was going to be perfect.

"Hey, Bilbo!" I called, opening the Mitchells' back door. I heard scrabbling from across the kitchen. The ferret was waiting by the door of his cage, pacing back and forth and looking at me with his bright little eyes. I wasn't wild about any animals except birds, but even I had to admit Bilbo was pretty cute. We'd almost become friends.

After I'd fed him, given him a little playtime, and made sure he was settled for the night, I headed back outside. There was no fence between my grandparents' backyard and the Mitchells', so my father had commandeered the entire expanse of twin lawns for our reunion. The picnic tables were on our side, closest to the kitchen. The fire pit and lawn chairs were just beyond, also on our side. The tents and hammocks were spread out pretty evenly across both backyards, and the far side of the Mitchells' back lawn had been arranged with separate zones for badminton, croquet, and horseshoes.

"Organized mayhem" my dad called it. He was more cheerful this weekend than I'd seen him in months. There was nothing Lieutenant Colonel Jericho T. Lovejoy liked better than bossing people around, and the reunion had given him a real boost in that department.

Just then our back door banged open, and Hatcher finally appeared. "Need any help?"

I shot him a look. "Not anymore."

He shrugged and sauntered off. I glared at his back. I'd hardly seen Hatcher all weekend. He'd vanished into the herd

REALLY TRULY

of older male cousins, all of whom were sharing one of the huge tents that Hatcher and Danny had set up at the far end of our lawn. It shouldn't have been that big of a deal, Hatcher spending time with his favorite cousins. I was spending time with mine, after all. But I hadn't seen a whole lot of Hatcher since summer started—and for months before that, now that I thought about it. He'd been involved with the Pumpkin Falls Private Eyes, at least for a little while over Spring Break. But other than that, he always seemed busy with wrestling and his school friends. It wasn't like it used to be. Back in Texas, Hatcher and I had always been a team—the two of us against the world. Now things were changing. I'd seen them change before, after my brother Danny started high school. He'd gotten his driver's license and a girlfriend and a part-time job, and after that he was hardly around anymore. This fall, Hatcher would be starting high school too. Would the same thing happen to him?

Does anything ever stay the same? I wondered. My gaze wandered over toward my dad. That question was easily answered. Things could and did change in the blink of an eye.

I watched as he picked up a spatula with the Terminator and started showing off for some of my uncles. The Terminator was what we called my father's fancy prosthetic arm, the one made of black titanium. He'd gotten it this past winter, after our move to Pumpkin Falls, so none of my relatives had seen it in action before. Some of the littler cousins had been afraid of it at first, just like Pippa had been, but fascination eventually won out over fear.

"Having a bunch of brothers-in-law around is good for him," said Aunt True, coming up behind me.

I turned around. "Huh?"

She nodded toward the grill. "Your father. It's good for him. All that male-bonding stuff."

She was probably right—my aunt usually was. My father did seem like he was in his element this weekend. Besides the whole I-get-to-organize-everything-and-boss-everyone-around thing, he adored my uncles, and they adored him. The seven of them had always had fun together. My father had even agreed to an arm-wrestling competition, for old times' sake. The tale of how my uncles had made my dad arm-wrestle every single one of them before they'd allow him to date their little sister—now my mother—was part of Gifford family lore.

After his injury had forced him to become a lefty, though, my father wasn't as invincible as he used to be. Last night, Uncle Lenny had finally managed to beat him—something he'd been waiting years to do.

"Time for Rooster Rover!" hollered Uncle Rooster, popping through the back door like a jack-in-the-box. The scavenger hunt was over, apparently.

A herd of younger cousins spilled out of the house behind him, squealing with excitement. I smiled. I used to squeal like that too.

REALLY TRULY

Uncle Rooster had made up the game years ago. It was just like red rover, except instead of chanting "Red rover, red rover, let so-and-so come over," he'd changed it to "Red Rooster, red Rooster." And before a player could run toward the opposing team to try to break through the line of linked arms, he or she had to crow like a rooster. Of course the little kids thought this was hilarious, and everyone tried to outdo everyone else. By the end, it wasn't much of a competition, just a bunch of kids collapsed in a pile of giggles.

I watched my uncle as he led the group to the far side of the lawn. His nickname suited him perfectly. Uncle Rooster was, well, like a rooster. Big, colorful, and loud. A bit of a show-off, he definitely liked to strut. And right now, he was strutting his stuff at the head of a line of little kids who would come to dinner worn out, hungry, and happy.

I did a final sweep of the picnic tables to make sure everything was ready, then headed to where I'd stashed tonight's surprise.

"Three at every table," my mother whispered from the kitchen window, startling me so much that I almost dropped the box I'd fished out from under the back steps.

"Yes, ma'am," I whispered back.

Acting as casual as I could, I distributed the bottles on the tables. No one paid me the slightest bit of attention except Hatcher, who suddenly materialized again.

"They turned out awesome!" he gloated, picking up one of the bottles. "You're a genius, Drooly!"

"Thanks," I said, and smiled at him. It was hard to stay mad at someone who was paying you a compliment, even when he called you by your least favorite nickname.

I stood there for a moment, admiring my handiwork. I'd worked hard on the design, with a little help from Aunt True. The bottles were tall and thin, with bright red stoppers and a shiny silver label. On the label was a flexed arm that looked identical to the black titanium one my father was currently wearing. In its fist was a flag with a skull and crossbones on it, along with two words in fiery red: THE TERMINATOR.

"Ribs are ready!" Uncle Teddy called just then.

It was the announcement we'd all been waiting for. Giffords swarmed from every direction. Mackenzie and her mother and a long line of aunts and uncles appeared from the kitchen, carrying platters and bowls piled high with corn bread, coleslaw, and Grandma G's baked beans, which were almost as famous as Uncle Teddy's ribs. Everyone raced for the buffet table, where we piled food on our plates like we hadn't eaten in weeks.

"What have we here?" cried Uncle Rooster as he took a seat and spotted the Terminator bottle nearest him.

"A little something to spice up your sad, bland life, Rooster," my father teased.

"It's homemade hot sauce!" blurted my sister Lauren, unable to contain her excitement any longer. "Dad made it, and everybody gets to take a bottle home, like a party favor!"

REALLY TRULY

"Is that so?" My uncle reached for the bottle nearest his seat. "'The Terminator,'" he read aloud. "I like it already."

"Fair warning," my father told him. "It packs a punch. You might want to try just a drop or two to start with."

A collective "oooh" went up around the long tables as Uncle Rooster grinned at him, then picked up a rib and defiantly shook three drops onto it.

Beside me, Mackenzie shook her head. "What is it with our uncles and hot sauce?"

"Beats me."

Our family's naturally competitive nature meant that our barbecues always ended up with a bunch of us—my uncles, mostly—trying to outdo each other in the hot sauce department, like the little kids with their Red Rooster crows. I was as competitive as the next person, maybe even more so, but I wasn't stupid enough to go to the mat over something like hot sauce. My stomach needed its lining.

We all watched as Uncle Rooster took a bite. "Hmmm," he said, shaking his head. "Sorry, Jericho, I'm not feeling it."

"You will," my father replied calmly.

After the second bite, Uncle Rooster leaped up and bolted for the house.

"If you can't stand the heat, stay out of the kitchen!" my dad yelled after him, and everyone shouted with laughter.

"Rooster never could hold his hot sauce," said Grandma G.

"Rusty, you stay away from that stuff!" Aunt True called

down the table to where her boyfriend was seated with my uncles. "You'll get blisters!"

"It'll just warm him up for you, True!" Uncle Teddy called back, making loud kissing noises. "Isn't that right, Professor Hot Lips?"

Aunt True's boyfriend blushed furiously. He still wasn't used to being teased. My dad said it was because Professor Rusty was an only child. I was pretty sure he was enjoying the attention, though. There was a hint of a smile behind the blush.

The back door banged open, and Uncle Rooster reappeared. He'd gotten ahold of Grandma G's lipstick and painted his lips bright red. We gaped at him, and then everyone started to laugh again.

Uncle Rooster gave my father a crisp salute. "I admit defeat. Duly *terminated*, sir!"

One thing you could say for Uncle Rooster, he wasn't a sore loser.

"I don't think I can eat another bite," said Mackenzie after a while. Then she grinned and reached toward the almost empty platter of ribs. "Well, maybe just *one* more bite."

I grinned back, licking the barbecue sauce off my fingers with a sigh of contentment. I'd really missed Uncle Teddy's barbecue.

"Who wants ice cream?" Aunt Louise called from the back steps.

"You've got to be kidding!" protested Uncle Rooster, clutching his stomach.

"Spoken like a man who's just eaten his weight in ribs," teased Aunt Sally.

"Nonsense!" Aunt True retorted, pushing back from the table. "There's always room for ice cream."

"True speaks truth," quipped Aunt Meg as she and Uncle Lenny got up too. Mackenzie looked at me and shrugged, and the two of us followed them.

"Mint chip, please," I told Aunt Louise when it was my turn. "Just one scoop."

"Two for me," said Mackenzie. "Chocolate and strawberry."

"Now there's a true Gifford," said Grandma G approvingly.

I looked at Mackenzie. Five feet nothing and about the size of my little finger, my cousin could really put it away. She smirked at me. "C'mon! After all that swimming we did this afternoon? I earned it."

The two of us took our cones over to the hammock, where we swung back and forth in contented silence.

"I am so full!" Mackenzie groaned a little while later.

"I wonder why, Ms. I'll Have Two Scoops?"

"It was worth it!"

We swung some more. Light streamed through the open window over the sink in the kitchen. I listened to the clatter of pots and pans as Aunt Rose and Uncle Craig did the washing up, and to the soft strumming of Uncle Brent's guitar over by the firepit, where conversation among the grown-ups was punctuated frequently by loud bursts of laughter. The clink of horseshoes and shrieks and giggles from my sisters and younger cousins playing hide-and-seek drifted over from the Mitchells' yard. Closing my eyes, I could almost imagine that we were back on the ranch.

Listening to my family reminded me of listening to birds. The twittering of sparrows would be the younger cousins; the piercing cries of jays the older ones; and the laughter from the adults was like the raucous cawing of crows. What was it that they called a flock of crows? Gramps and Lola had sent me a book on owls for my birthday, and it had a whole list of terms dating back to the Middle Ages for groups of different bird species. *A parliament of owls*—that one I remembered, of course. Owls were my favorite birds. *An exaltation of larks*, which Aunt True said was pure poetry. Ditto for *a charm of finches*. I couldn't remember the term for a flock of sparrows, but I did remember the one for blue jays—*a scold of jays*. That was spot on. The term for a flock of crows had been an odd one, I recalled, casting about in my memory for it. Oh right—*a murder of crows*!

I wrinkled my nose. That was awful. Not the right term for my family at all.

Seagulls, maybe? *A squabble of seagulls*. Better. No, wait— geese! *A gaggle of Giffords*. Perfect!

REALLY TRULY

Swaying lazily in the hammock, I watched my cousins and aunts and uncles, my brothers and sisters and parents. What would those people in the Middle Ages have thought of my family? I wondered.

"What are you snickering at?" asked Mackenzie, giving me a sidelong glance.

"Nothing."

She sighed deeply. "I wish we had more time together! I can't believe we only have one more day left."

"I know."

She sat bolt upright, sending the hammock swaying wildly. "Hey, what if you flew back with me to Austin?"

"What?" I frowned. I loved Mackenzie and would miss her, but Texas was not part of my perfect summer plans.

"I'm sure Coach would be happy to have you back on the Nitros' summer swim team. And we could hang out with all our friends and go to the mall and camping and play with Frankie!" Frankie was Mackenzie's new kitten. She'd taken him home with her when she'd visited in March, courtesy of Belinda Winchester.

I hesitated. My perfect summer dangled in the air between us, glimmering like an ornament on a Christmas tree. "What if you stayed here instead?"

She shook her head. "Can't. My parents have a big family vacation planned to Yellowstone. You could come with us." She looked over at me. "Plus, I've already been to Pumpkin

Falls twice now since you moved here, and you haven't been back to Austin even once. C'mon, Truly—everything will be just like it was before!"

That isn't true, I thought, as she continued to chatter on about all the stuff we could do together. Nothing was going to be like it was before. Not my father, whose arm would still be missing, and not my family, who was still getting used to the unexpected left turn in our lives that had brought us here to Pumpkin Falls.

"So, what do you think?" prodded Mackenzie. "Are you in?"

"I have stuff planned," I told her. "I can't."

She took my hand and gave it a squeeze. "I wish you still lived down the street, Truly. I really miss you. I miss *us.*"

I knew exactly what she meant. We'd hit a rough patch over Spring Break, but she was still my best friend in the whole world. Life just wasn't the same without her around. Pumpkin Falls wasn't as awful a place as I'd thought it was when we first moved here, but still, Mackenzie wasn't here.

"I know," I replied, squeezing back. "I miss us too."

CHAPTER 3

"It's going to be a scorcher!" my father announced as I yawned my way into the kitchen the next morning. Mackenzie and I had stayed up way too late talking.

My mother stretched up on her tiptoes and planted a kiss on my cheek. "Happy Fourth of July!" She handed me an apron, and I blinked at it sleepily. "Squad Lovejoy is in charge of breakfast, remember?"

"Where's Hatcher?" I said automatically. My brother was AWOL again, as usual.

My father cupped his hand behind his ear. "What was that? I believe the correct answer is 'yes, ma'am.'"

I sighed. "Yes, sir. I mean, yes, ma'am."

"Looks like your aunt could use some help," my mother said as I draped the apron over my head. I turned around so that she could tie it for me, then shuffled over to the stove, where Aunt True passed me a large spoon.

"Blueberry donut muffins," she said as I joined her in scooping batter into the waiting muffin tins. "My new recipe. You'll have to tell me what you think—I'm considering making a mini version as our signature treat at the bookshop this summer."

My aunt was in charge of marketing for Lovejoy's Books, and she was big on signature treats. She said people came for the treats and stayed to shop, and so far, she'd been right.

A few minutes later, Uncle Teddy and Aunt Louise wandered in, sniffing the air appreciatively. The kitchen smelled of sausage and coffee and muffins.

"Morning, everyone!" said my uncle. "Tables are all set up and ready to go outside, J. T. Anything we can do to help in here?"

"Nope," my dad replied. "Breakfast is still a few minutes out. Grab a cup of coffee and take a load off."

"That's an invitation we won't refuse," said Aunt Louise. She took two of the mugs stacked by the giant carafe that my mother had borrowed from church and poured coffee for my uncle and herself.

Uncle Teddy waggled his eyebrows at me. "Great day for a road race!"

I made a face. Running was so not my thing, and Uncle Teddy knew it. I'd much rather be in the water, especially on a day that was expected to be a "scorcher."

"Do we have to go?" I asked my father. "Can't we just

spend the day at Lake Lovejoy instead?" My voice sounded whiny even to my ears, but I couldn't help it. The prospect of trotting all over Pumpkin Falls in the blazing sun was not appealing.

"Too late! We're Team Lovejoy's Books, remember? I signed us up weeks ago."

Four on the Fourth—a 4K road race on the Fourth of July—was a big tradition in my new hometown. Nobody loved a holiday like Pumpkin Falls did, and nobody had more holiday traditions. Some were normal enough—twinkle lights on Main Street at Christmas, for instance—others, like the annual Halloween Pumpkin Toss, which dated back to before the Revolutionary War, were not. Our Fourth of July race was the oldest of its kind in New England and drew huge crowds of runners. Just about everyone in town got involved one way or another. Most of the local businesses sponsored a team of runners, and whoever's team won got to display the trophy (the big silver pumpkin we'd taken our relatives to see at Mahoney's Antiques) until the following Fourth of July. The winner also got the money raised by the race's entry fees. Well, *they* didn't, but their project of choice did.

Each spring at the town meeting, two finalists were chosen from a list of proposed Pumpkin Falls beautification projects, and those became the projects that the Four on the Fourth teams competed to fund. I knew this because my brothers and sisters and I had been forced to attend the meeting.

"This is democracy in action, kids!" our mother had told us on our way to the town hall that night. She'd gone back to college after our move to Pumpkin Falls, intending to become an English teacher. The American History for Educators class she'd taken with Professor Rusty had her bubbling over with patriotic spirit. "There's nothing more American than a town meeting. Consider it part of your civic education."

I'd heard Gramps and Lola talk about town meetings before, but they hadn't sounded very interesting. And mostly they weren't, if you asked me, which nobody ever did. There were a bunch of boring reports on stuff like budgets and tax revenues, and discussions about things like sewage treatment (eew!), graffiti, and the pros and cons of licensing a food truck. One of the top agenda items at the meeting we attended was a proposal to install parking meters on Main Street, which sparked a surprisingly lively debate. Surprising because seriously, who got worked up about parking meters? Pumpkin Falls, that's who.

Ella Bellow, who used to be the postmistress until she retired last January, had been elected town moderator and ran the meetings. Ella loved being in charge of things even more than my dad did. She had more energy than should have been legal for somebody her age. Giving up her job as postmistress seemed to have given her a new lease on life, too. Instead of retiring to Florida, as everyone in town had thought was her plan, she'd stayed put, opened a knitting

REALLY TRULY

shop, and become involved in town politics. She was busier and bossier than ever.

"As always, only two worthy causes will be chosen from this year's proposed list of beautification projects," Ella had announced that night. "Of course, I can't pretend to be impartial about one of the projects," she added coyly, flinging the fringe of her sparkly blue knitted shawl over her shoulder. Ella used to dress mostly in black, but she'd been wearing brighter colors since opening A Stitch in Time. My father had dubbed her new shop "A Snitch in Time," thanks to Ella's favorite sport, which was gossip. "It's a scandal, the shape that the Pumpkin Falls Grange is in!"

I nudged Hatcher. "What's a grange?"

"You know, that old building on the edge of town where they put on plays and stuff."

"My father was a founding member of the Pumpkin Players," Ella continued, "and he'd be as shocked and saddened as I am if he saw what poor stewards we have been of that historic building. Back in its heyday it was one of the crown jewels of this town. I should know; I practically grew up within its hallowed halls!"

"During the Jurassic era?" whispered Hatcher, which made me giggle and earned us a stern glance from my father.

After Ella finished trying to convince everyone to vote for her pet project, Mr. Henry, the children's librarian at the Pumpkin Falls Library, leaped to his feet.

"The Pumpkin Falls Grange is a worthy cause, of course," he said. "The arts are vital to the health of a community, as are its open spaces"—he tipped his red baseball cap at Reverend Quinn, who was slated to speak next on a project with the überthrilling title "Revitalizing our Village Green"—"but what could be more important to the future of Pumpkin Falls than its children? And providing them with an attractive, modern space in our library, which is undeniably one of the gems of our community, is an investment in that future. Let's use this year's earnings to revitalize the children's room!"

Ella Bellow tried and failed spectacularly to keep a neutral face. I could tell she was itching to snatch the microphone back from Mr. Henry.

"May I remind you all," she snapped, finally doing just that, "that the Pumpkin Falls Grange is even older than the library—"

"Jurassic Ella," Hatcher whispered again, more quietly this time, so as not to attract my father's attention.

"—and therefore more historic."

"Your point is interesting," Mr. Henry conceded, deftly plucking the microphone away from her again. "However, age alone does not equate with value." The two of them continued in ping-pong fashion until Scooter Sanchez's father, who was assistant moderator, had to step in and ask them to wind things up so that other people could speak about their proposed projects.

REALLY TRULY

The meeting ran late. Pippa fell asleep on the floor. My sister Lauren read not just one but two books, and my mother finished knitting an entire sock. Unlike my brothers who at least had their cell phones to distract them, I'd left mine at home and was stuck having to listen to Reverend Quinn try to whip up some enthusiasm for repainting the benches and bandstand on the village green, and then some guy I didn't know drone on about replacing the rusted rivets in the covered bridge, which he claimed were an eyesore and possibly an actual hazard. Ethel Farnsworth got excited during that discussion and leaped to her feet, recommending that the town expand on the project and install hanging flower baskets on the bridge as well, but she was quickly shushed by Ella.

When the vote was finally taken, Ella and Mr. Henry emerged triumphant. The children's room at the library and the Pumpkin Falls Grange would vie for this year's Pumpkin Falls Beautification Project. The outcome of the Four on the Fourth race would determine the winner.

Not surprisingly, Team Lovejoy's Books chose to support Mr. Henry and Team Library. Ditto for Team Starlite Dance Studio and Team Kwik Klips, our town's hair salon. Ella pledged Team A Stitch in Time to the Grange restoration, of course, and her friends fell in line behind her: the Farnsworths and Team General Store, the Mahoneys and Team Mahoney's Antiques, and Reverend Quinn and Team Speedy Geezers, which was made up of some of the older gentlemen from the men's choir at First Parish Church.

The screen door leading out to the backyard slammed shut, startling me. I looked up to see Uncle Brent come in. "When's chow?" he asked. "The troops are getting restless."

My father handed him a platter of scrambled eggs. "Perfect timing. We're ready to go. How about you ladies?"

"Enough muffins to get started," said Aunt True, putting the last tray into the oven and setting the timer.

"Look alive, then, Truly-in-the-Middle, and hustle outside with what you've got."

I opened my mouth to complain again about my brothers not pulling their weight when Hatcher sauntered in. He grabbed a tray loaded with yogurt containers and fruit and gave me a sly grin. "Yeah, Drooly, what are you standing there for?"

"Hatcher," warned my mother.

"Sorry," he said to me, as I stalked past him out the back door.

"BREAKFAST!" my brother Danny hollered from the back steps, which apparently was his contribution to our family's assigned task. In a flash, just like every other meal all weekend, hungry Giffords descended from every direction.

Mackenzie was the last one to appear. "Sorry I didn't get up in time to help," she told her father, rubbing her eyes sleepily. "I forgot it was our turn to set up."

REALLY TRULY

Uncle Teddy gave her a hug. "No big deal, petunia. We thought we'd let you sleep in."

I watched them, wishing my father could be more chill like Uncle Teddy. "Sleeping in" wasn't part of Lieutenant Colonel Jericho T. Lovejoy's vocabulary.

Hatcher came up behind me and gave me a companionable hip bump.

"What do you want?" I snapped. I hated it when he insulted me and then tried to act like nothing was wrong.

He took a bite of the muffin he was holding. "These are great."

"Thanks," I muttered.

He gave me a blueberry-stained grin. I scowled at him, but it was hard to stay mad at Hatcher. His smile was infectious, even when it was smeared with breakfast. Honestly, it could be raining toads, and my brother would still walk around smiling. He'd inherited the happy gene, along with the Gifford sunflower smile, as Grandma G called it. It was identical to the smile my mother almost always wore, as did my sister Pippa and my cousin Mackenzie and a bunch of my other uncles and cousins. Me? I was a Lovejoy through and through, and only smiled when I meant it.

"I can't wait for the race!" Hatcher said.

I grunted. My brother loved to run. "I can."

"C'mon, it'll be fun. I think our team has a good chance of winning, too."

I shrugged. "Maybe."

My father may have lost an arm in Afghanistan, but both his legs worked just fine. He was fast, and he'd been training hard. He and Danny had been running together just about every morning since it finally stopped snowing last spring. Hatcher joined them often, although he wasn't as fanatical about it as they were. Lauren was pretty zippy for an almost fifth grader, plus there was Professor Rusty, who apparently had been on the track team in high school and college. Aunt True called him our "secret weapon." *Emphasis on 'secret,'* I thought, looking over at her boyfriend's pale skinny legs and knobby knees. None of us had ever seen him so much as walk fast. As for me—

"I just hope I can finish," I said glumly.

"Don't be such a wet blanket, Drooly!"

"Shut *up*, Hatcher!"

My mother passed us, carrying a pitcher of orange juice. "That's enough, you two!"

"Sorry, ma'am," we replied simultaneously.

I waited until she was out of earshot, then turned to my brother and peered closely at him, feigning concern. "I think your nose looks bigger this morning."

Hatcher's hand flew up to his face. He gave his nose an exploratory squeeze, and I suppressed a smile. He was terrified that he was going to inherit the famous "Lovejoy proboscis," as Gramps called it—the big nose visible on our ancestor Nathaniel Daniel Lovejoy in the portrait in the living room, and on Gramps and our father, too.

"Come on, Mackenzie." I crossed to where my cousin was standing and grabbed her arm. "Let's eat."

CHAPTER 4

Breakfast was over practically before it started, the food vacuumed up by my hungry relatives in nothing flat. Afterward, everyone scattered to put on their race day clothes so we could head downtown. No school bus for us this morning—we were hoofing it, as Grandma G called it.

"Pumpkin Falls will be jammed," my father had warned our relatives last night. "As the oldest road race in New England, Four on the Fourth is a big deal. Runners come from all over to check it off their bucket list."

My sisters and the younger cousins all ran ahead along Maple Street, excited in the way that only little kids who don't know what's waiting for them can be excited. I slouched along next to Grandma G, who was pushing the stroller containing Bella and Blair. The rest of my family streamed down Hill Street, all of us in our matching T-shirts—red, white, and blue today in honor of the holiday. *Hey, kids! Check it out!* I thought, cringing inwardly. *The circus is in town! Step right up and see a gaggle of Giffords!*

"What's up with you?" asked Mackenzie, giving me a sidelong glance.

"Nothing."

"So, are you going to try out for the play?"

I frowned. "What play?"

"Weren't you paying attention? It was all Cha Cha and Jasmine could talk about."

"Really? When?"

"Yesterday. Downtown. After we all got our pictures taken."

I shook my head. I'd probably been too busy keeping an eye on Calhoun, but I wasn't about to admit that.

"Well, anyway, it's called *The Pirates of Penzance*, and tryouts are tomorrow at the Grange."

"The pirates of what?"

"Penzance."

"That's a play?"

Mackenzie nodded.

"Technically, it's a musical," Hatcher interjected, wedging himself between us. "A really famous one, by these guys called Gilbert and Sullivan." He draped his arms—already sweaty, thanks to the rapidly rising temperature—over our shoulders.

"Eew!" I protested, pulling away. "It can't be that famous,

if I've never heard of it before." But the names Gilbert and Sullivan sounded vaguely familiar. Had my mother mentioned them at dinner a few nights ago? Or maybe Aunt True?

"The flyers are all over town," said Hatcher. "You can't miss them."

I shrugged. Somehow I'd managed to.

"Cha Cha says that Calhoun's father is directing," Mackenzie continued.

This was a surprise. "I thought Dr. Calhoun was only interested in Shakespeare."

"Apparently he makes an exception for Gilbert and Sullivan," my cousin told us. "At least that's what Calhoun said."

"Since when were you talking to Calhoun?"

"Since you were feeding Bilbo yesterday. He rode his bike over to say hi."

"And you didn't tell me?"

"Sorry. I forgot. Anyway, Cha Cha and Jasmine are both going to try out."

"I might too," said Hatcher.

I gaped at him. My brother had never in his life expressed the remotest interest in acting. I wondered if this sudden burst of enthusiasm for the theater had anything to do with the fact that Cha Cha was planning to try out. Hatcher seemed unusually interested in Cha Cha Abramowitz lately.

"You should try out too," he added.

"Fat chance." Singing was way up on the long list of things

REALLY TRULY

I wasn't good at. My mother, who rarely said anything critical about anybody, liked to joke that I couldn't carry a tune in a paper bag. Even Miss Marple, my grandparents' elderly golden retriever, who had inexplicably latched onto me as her favorite Lovejoy, whined and scratched to be let out of the bathroom whenever I sang in the shower.

And it wasn't just the singing—I'd never had any desire to be onstage, period. It was the whole stealth mode thing, which had kicked in big time after my überweird sixth-grade growth spurt. I hated drawing attention to myself. Piano recitals were an agony, and I dreaded oral reports at school. I tolerated swim meets only because I was mostly underwater. Being onstage, in the spotlight, in a *musical*? No way.

We reached the bottom of the hill and crossed the village green. My father was right about the streets being jammed. Dozens of runners were already assembled by the church, signing in at the long registration tables and putting on their numbered race bibs.

"Huddle up, Giffords!" my father shouted, using his official Lieutenant Colonel Jericho T. Lovejoy voice in order to be heard about the crowd. My extended family crowded together as closely as thirty-seven people could. Thirty-nine, counting Aunt True and Professor Rusty.

My father proceeded to explain how things would work. Technically, our relatives wouldn't be running for Team Lovejoy's Books, since the officially sponsored teams were limited to six runners each. "But we hope you'll run alongside us for moral support anyway," he told them. "Pace us, pass us, cheer us on, make fun of us"—Uncle Rooster gave an enthusiastic whoop at this—"just get us across that finish line!"

That was the only catch to winning the Four on the Fourth race: The whole team had to cross the finish line in order for the official time to count.

"Once you've got your race bibs, we'll gather on the green for warm-ups and stretching," my father added as he led us over to the registration tables. While we were waiting in line to sign in, two big buses with CAMP LOVEJOY lettered on the sides pulled up to the curb. A little girl in a pixie haircut leaned out of one of the windows and waved at my littlest sister in excitement. "PIPPA!" she shrieked.

"TARA!" Pippa shrieked back. She flew over to the bus. Lauren was hot on her heels.

I watched as a river of girls in navy blue shorts and white polo shirts with the official Camp Lovejoy logo flowed from the bus, engulfing my sisters. Should I have gone to camp this summer too? Gramps and Lola had offered to pay for it, and my sisters were obviously having fun. But I'd turned down their offer in favor of my perfect summer.

After Mackenzie and I signed in, we joined the rest of my family on the village green. I looked around as my father led us through a series of stretches. Pumpkin Falls had gone all out for the Fourth of July. In addition to the requisite flags flying from every shop and building in town, all of the flower containers hanging from the lampposts had been planted in patriotic colors, and there was red-white-and-blue bunting hanging from every conceivable spot, including the bandstand.

"The town that time forgot," Mackenzie intoned in her radio announcer voice, as the Pumpkin Falls Brass Band struck up a Fourth of July medley. I had to smile. She was right. Pumpkin Falls was kind of stuck in a time warp.

Most of the benches scattered around the village green were full of racegoers and their families and friends. I watched as people set up lawn chairs in the shade and lined up by Emily's Eats, the town's sole food truck (the one that had been green-lighted at the town meeting this past spring).

"Looking forward to the race?" asked Aunt True, who had come to cheer us on.

I made a rude noise, and she laughed. Aunt True and my mother weren't part of Team Lovejoy. "For one thing, we're walkers, not runners, and for another, every team needs a cheering section," my mother had said firmly when my father had invited them to join.

"The only thing I'm looking forward to is the fireworks," I said, which was the truth. I loved fireworks, even though the ones they had in Pumpkin Falls couldn't rival the ones in Austin. As the capital of Texas, Austin always pulled out all the stops.

"Cassidy!" Aunt True called out suddenly, waving to a

tall red-haired girl who was stretching nearby with a bunch of campers.

The red-haired girl waved back, then loped over to join us. She was older than me, and obviously a counselor. "Nice to see you again," she told my aunt.

"Truly, this is the girl I was telling you about," said Aunt True. "Cassidy Sloane and some of her fellow counselors are the ones who started the book club for their campers." I vaguely remembered her saying something about that.

"How are you enjoying *Understood Betsy*?" asked Aunt True.

"We love it so far," Cassidy replied. "And we *adored* your pumpkin whoopie pies!"

Pumpkin whoopie pies were one of Aunt True's signature treats. She'd been alternating between those and her Bookshop Blondies in the store for the past few months. I'd be sorry to see either of them retired for the season—but Hatcher was right, the blueberry donut muffins were pretty great too.

Aunt True laughed. "Stop by the bookstore anytime, and I'll make sure you head back to camp with goodies as well as books."

"I'll definitely take you up on that," Cassidy replied. Just then, one of the campers trotted over and grabbed her hand, tugging her back toward their group. "Gotta go! Good luck, Team Lovejoy!"

Hatcher poked me in the back as she left. "Hey, Professor

REALLY TRULY

Rusty's research assistant is here!" He pointed to Aunt True's boyfriend, who was standing in the shade talking to a girl in a Camp Lovejoy uniform. "I'd know those cinnamon buns anywhere."

I grinned. He was talking about her hair, which she wore coiled over her ears in Princess Leia–style poufs. "What's her name again?"

"Felicia something."

"Grunewald," Aunt True told us. "Felicia Grunewald." She gave us a sly smile. "Maybe I should add cinnamon buns to our signature treats at the bookshop."

Hatcher and I stared at her, then burst out laughing.

"What?" said Aunt True, the picture of innocence.

The loudspeaker crackled. "Runners, make your way to the starting line, please!"

"Team Lovejoy's Books!" barked my father. "Follow me!"

As Hatcher, Danny, Lauren, Professor Rusty, and I set off after him, I surreptitiously sized up the other teams.

Team Library was led by Mr. Henry, who had pulled his dreadlocks back into a ponytail for the occasion. Beneath his racing bib he wore a red-and-white-striped tank top over red shorts. No surprise there—Aunt True called red and white Mr. Henry's signature colors. Hatcher said he looked like Waldo in *Where's Waldo?*

"I'm so E-X-C-I-T-E-D!" squealed Annie Freeman, skipping along beside Mr. Henry. Annie was the reigning winner of the Grafton County Junior Spelling Championship and my sister Lauren's best friend. Annie herself wouldn't give us too much of a run for our money today, but there was also Annie's brother Franklin to consider, along with Calhoun and his sister, Juliet, and my friend Jasmine's brother Scooter.

Jasmine herself was running for Team Starlite, which was definitely stiff competition. Jasmine was a star basketball player, and Cha Cha and her parents were in great shape, thanks to all the dancing they did at their studio. Plus, they'd recruited two guys from the high school track team.

The Team Kwik Klips "krew members," as they called themselves, were looking pretty competitive too. They'd all sprayed red, white, and blue streaks into their hair, and were clearly fired up for the race.

Oh well, I thought, whether or not we won, at least we were all running together in support of Mr. Henry's library project. That was the main goal. Our real competitors were the teams running in support of Ella Bellow's Grange project.

Ella wasn't running in the race herself, but she'd twisted the arms of a bunch of her customers to join her team, including my swim coach's wife and Bud Jefferson. Mr. Jefferson was a huge bear of a man who I hoped was as slow as he was big. Technically, he was Ella's landlord, not her customer, although he'd taken up knitting after getting roped into a class on socks that my mother and I had signed up for over Spring Break.

Team Mahoney's Antiques looked stronger. Like my

REALLY TRULY

father and Danny, the Mahoneys were both dedicated runners, and their friends on the team looked equally fit. Team General Store, on the other hand, was a bit of a wild card. None of the Farnsworths were running—they were all older than Grandma G, for one thing, and hardly what you'd call athletic. Four of the people on their team I'd seen around town but had never met. The only two that I knew were Mr. Burnside, our school principal, and Mr. Bigelow, my science teacher. Like Professor Rusty, Mr. Burnside was tall and skinny—thanks to my weird habit of classifying people as birds, I'd always thought of him as a flamingo—and he had the look of a runner, with long legs and a lean build. But any potential edge he might give to the team was probably offset by Mr. Bigelow, who was short and kind of tubby and reminded me of a duck. On the other hand, I knew from experience that Mr. Bigelow had an enormous amount of enthusiasm—he was one of our school's most popular teachers—and sometimes that made up for lack of athletic ability.

The only team I was almost positive that we'd be able to beat were the Speedy Geezers. Reverend Quinn had been bragging about his team for weeks and making pronouncements about "dark horses" and "underdogs," though, so maybe he knew something the rest of us didn't.

I scanned the crowd of onlookers, searching for my mother. I spotted her and waved. She waved back, and so did Aunt True, Pippa, and Grandma G, who coaxed Bella and Blair into waving their chubby little fists from their stroller too.

"Go, Team Lovejoy!" shouted a deep voice. I caught a flash of purple and recognized Augustus Wilde, the romance author who was our town's celebrity. For once, Augustus wasn't wearing a cape. Instead, he sported a purple T-shirt emblazoned with the words GO TEAM LOVEJOY! Belinda Winchester was dressed in an identical T-shirt, and both of them were fanning themselves with matching purple baseball caps. I gave them a thumbs-up.

"Runners, take your marks!" cried the voice over the loudspeaker.

My mouth suddenly went dry. The dread that I'd been feeling earlier came flooding back in a rush. Why had I let myself be talked into running this stupid race?

Hatcher leaned over to me. "Remember, Drooly, all you have to do is finish."

"Don't call me Drooly."

He grinned. "That's the spirit!"

Finish, I thought. I could do that.

Couldn't I?

CHAPTER 5

As it turned out, I could, though just barely.

Even my little sister Lauren beat me to the finish line, which I knew I'd never hear the end of. How was it that I could swim as fast as lightning for what felt like hours on end and barely be short of breath, but an easy 4K loop completely knocked me out?

Mackenzie had doubled back at one point to run alongside me. "How's it going?"

I'd given her a curt nod. My cousin hadn't even broken a sweat, which was almost as irritating as the fact that she felt she needed to check on me.

She'd trotted alongside me as the two of us turned onto Main Street, the official halfway mark in the race.

"There are the girls!" called my mother, who was standing in front of Lovejoy's Books, and my family cheered for us. Aunt True was balancing a baby on one hip. Bella, maybe? I couldn't tell. The twins were dressed alike today, both wearing matching red, white, and blue onesies and floppy stars and stripes sun hats.

My friend Lucas Winthrop and his mother were there too. Lucas was smeared with industrial-strength white sunscreen, his face practically hidden beneath a floppy hat similar to the ones worn by the twins. Poor Lucas! His mother still thought he was six. He'd wanted to run, but she wouldn't let him.

"Heatstroke," she'd warned when he asked. "We can't risk that."

A huge smile spread across Lucas's face when he saw Mackenzie. He waved, trying to attract her attention. Ever since she'd come to visit last Spring Break, Lucas had been smitten with my cousin.

"Go, Bud!" Mrs. Winthrop shouted, and I looked over my shoulder to see Mr. Jefferson lumbering along behind Mackenzie and me. He was red in the face and sweating profusely, and if you asked me, which nobody ever did, he was the one that Mrs. Winthrop should have been worried about when it came to heatstroke, not Lucas.

After a disagreement last March during the big Maple Madness Bake-Off (Maple Madness, a celebration of all things maple, was another of our town's traditions), the blooming romance between Lucas's mother and Bud appeared to be back on track. The town's residents were keeping a close watch on all of the current couples, thanks to Ella Bellow's frequent

REALLY TRULY

bulletins from A Stitch in Time. Over at the General Store, I'd heard a number of bets placed as to who'd get engaged first: Mrs. Winthrop and Bud, Belinda Winchester and Augustus Wilde, or my aunt and Erastus Peckinpaugh.

Secretly, my money was on Aunt True. And secretly, I couldn't help thinking it would be fun to have a wedding in the family. I hadn't been to a family wedding since I was eight, when Uncle Brent married Aunt Angie.

"Go on ahead," I panted, flapping my hand at Mackenzie as we spilled out the other end of Main Street.

She nodded and broke away, and I didn't see her again until I managed to huff and puff my way up Hill Street and then circle back to the finish line, where what seemed like the entire gaggle of Giffords was waiting for me.

"Well done, Truly-in-the-Middle!" said my father, giving me a sweaty hug, and Hatcher dumped a bottle of water over my head.

After all of the runners were accounted for, the judges withdrew inside First Parish Church to tally the scores. Meanwhile, the crowd drifted over to the bandstand to wait for the results.

"We still have a chance," Hatcher told me as the brass band struck up another medley of tunes, John Philip Sousa this time.

"You've got to be kidding! I was one of the last ones across the finish line."

"Yeah, but Professor Rusty delivered the goods. Aunt True was right about him being our secret weapon. Our average time is way up there."

A podium had been set up on the bandstand, and behind it stood Augustus Wilde, who had been selected by the race organizers to hand out the prizes. I watched as he taped a poster of his latest novel to the front of it. Augustus didn't have a stealth mode. He was what Aunt True called a guerrilla marketer, someone willing to go to great lengths to promote their own work. Not surprisingly, after the judges emerged and passed him an envelope with the results, during his moment in the spotlight he also managed to wedge in a plug for his new book.

"As I wrote in my latest best seller, *Fortune's Forbidden Fruit*," he told the crowd with a sweeping gesture toward the poster on the front of the podium, "there are no winners in life, only finishers."

This didn't strike me as the most inspiring of quotes, but it brought a ripple of polite applause anyway. Pumpkin Falls supported its own.

Hatcher nudged me with his elbow. "Captain Romance strikes again."

I smiled. "Captain Romance" was our secret nickname for Augustus.

The awards presentation began with the low-hanging fruit—gift certificates for free ice cream cones at the General

REALLY TRULY

Store, which were given to everyone in the crowd wearing a race bib; a prize for the youngest racer to finish (Annie Freeman got that one, which she accepted with a squeal of "G-R-A-T-I-T-U-D-E!"); another for "most improved time from last year" (that went to Principal Burnside); and finally, an award for the last person to cross the finish line—which I was really truly grateful I didn't win.

Reverend Quinn took a bow as he stepped forward to accept the bright orange ribbon with LAST BUT NEVER LEAST emblazoned on it. "Blessed are the meek," he quipped, holding it up.

Overall fastest time was awarded to an elite runner from Connecticut who regularly qualified for the Boston Marathon.

"This race has been on my bucket list for years," he told the crowd. "I'm only sorry we out-of-towners don't qualify for your famous trophy. There's nothing I'd like better than to add that to my shelf. In fact, I may have to move to Pumpkin Falls so I can have a shot at it next year!"

He took his seat again to cheers of encouragement from the crowd.

"And now," said Augustus, striking a dramatic pose, "the award we have all been waiting for—the silver pumpkin!"

Ella Bellow was standing beside me, arms folded tightly across her chest. Much to her displeasure, Team A Stitch in Time had been disqualified. Bud Jefferson had dropped out halfway up Hill Street. On the other hand, one of the Team

Kwik Klips members had stumbled and hurt her ankle, and they had also ended up disqualified. That meant the odds were still even, as far as the Pumpkin Falls Beautification Project competition went. As for the winning team, Hatcher had said our time was solid. Was there a chance we might pull it off? I started envisioning a window display at the bookstore featuring the coveted trophy.

Augustus turned to the brass band behind him. "May I have a drumroll, please?" They obliged. He opened the envelope and peeked inside. "And the trophy goes to"—he paused again to wring every last drop of drama from the moment—"Team Starlite!"

Hatcher and I exchanged a rueful glance.

"Oh well," said Mackenzie. "At least Mr. Henry's project won, right?"

I nodded. The children's room at the library would get its renovation.

"There's always next year," Mr. Henry said to Ella, whose expression looked like she'd soaked it in pickle juice. She gave a curt nod and stalked off. Ella was not a good sport.

The gaggle of Giffords were, though. My relatives and I all whooped and cheered as Cha Cha, her parents, and the other members of Team Starlite climbed the steps of the bandstand to collect their prize. The big silver pumpkin was going to look great in the Starlite Dance Studio window, gleaming under the twinkle lights.

Augustus bent down and reached under the podium for the trophy. A moment later, he snapped upright again. He was frowning.

"Where did you put it?" he asked Belinda in a stage whisper.

"Under the podium," Belinda whispered back. "You saw me."

"Well, it's not here!"

Belinda clambered up the bandstand steps to look for herself. Ella joined her, as did Mr. Henry. The four of them scoured the podium, then the bandstand itself and the bushes that surrounded it.

But Captain Romance was right—the silver trophy was gone!

CHAPTER 6

One good thing came from the Great Pumpkin Trophy Heist, as the *Patriot-Bugle* quickly dubbed it: The Gifford Family Reunion got knocked off the front page.

At first, everybody thought that Belinda Winchester was confused, and that maybe she'd just forgotten to retrieve the trophy from the window of Mahoney's Antiques before the race. But she protested that she most certainly had retrieved it, and she even had a cell phone photo to prove it—one she'd taken on the bandstand earlier in the day that showed Augustus Wilde hoisting the trophy in mock victory.

Residents and tourists alike quickly spread out all over town looking for it, but in the end, everyone came up empty-handed. The silver pumpkin was definitely gone.

"Who would want to steal a dumb trophy?" I asked, as Mackenzie and Cha Cha and Jasmine and I retreated to the shade of one of the trees on the village green. The rest of my

REALLY TRULY

family was gathered nearby, and over by the bandstand, the town council was holding an emergency meeting with the police—well, policeman. Pumpkin Falls only had one: Officer Tanglewood.

"It's not dumb," Cha Cha scolded in her deep voice, the one that had earned her the nickname "the kazoo" from Hatcher. "It's tradition." She was obviously disappointed. I'd be disappointed too if my team had won, and the trophy we were entitled to show off all year had vanished.

"You have a point, though, Truly," said Jasmine. "I can't think of anyone around here who would do something like that."

We were quiet for a moment, considering.

"Ella?" I suggested, glancing over at the bandstand, where our former postmistress-turned-knitting-shop-owner was lecturing Officer Tanglewood. "She was pretty unhappy about losing."

Cha Cha didn't look convinced. "Ella wouldn't sink that low, would she?"

"It could be anybody!" said Mackenzie. "A local, a visitor—there were a ton of people at the race today who aren't from around here. Including all of us Giffords."

I looked at her, astonished. "None of us stole it!"

"I *know* that. I'm just saying!"

"I'll bet it was one of those marathoners." Jasmine's dark eyes narrowed as she watched the runner with the winning time laughing with his friends. "That guy, for instance. I'll bet he made that joke about moving here so he'd be eligible to win the trophy next year just to throw everyone off track."

"We shouldn't jump to conclusions," Cha Cha cautioned. "Don't forget what happened over Spring Break."

This past March, during Maple Madness, the sap lines at Freeman Farm and Maynard's Maple Barn had been cut. Everyone suspected sabotage, and things had gotten pretty heated for a while. It had been like the Hatfields and the McCoys around town, with accusations flying and neighbors taking sides against neighbors before my friends and I had finally caught the real culprit.

"Hey," said Scooter, sauntering over. Calhoun and Lucas were with him.

"Hey back," I replied.

"Did you guys have any luck?"

We shook our heads.

"Neither did we," said Calhoun.

The three boys sat down on the grass beside us.

"If the trophy were smaller, I'd say maybe a magpie took it," I told my friends.

"What's a magpie?" asked Scooter.

"A bird that likes shiny things."

The problem was, you'd need a bird the size of an ostrich to carry away a trophy like the silver pumpkin, and ostriches were in short supply in New England. We did have eagles,

REALLY TRULY

though. Gramps had taken me to see them out at Cherry Island on Lake Lovejoy.

"Sounds to me like a case for the Pumpkin Falls Private Eyes," said Scooter, glancing at Mackenzie. Like Lucas, he had a crush on her too.

"This is the last day of our family reunion," I told him. "We don't have time for that."

"Where's your civic spirit?" he protested. "We should at least pool our knowledge and do a little preliminary investigating together."

I didn't want to investigate. I wanted to go the lake, where Grandma G had a big picnic prepared, and where there were paddleboards and kayaks and swimming. It was my reward for running the stupid road race.

"Mackenzie's leaving tomorrow," I told him. "We want to spend the day together."

"You would be," Lucas pointed out, crossing his pale arms over his chest and trying to sound grown-up and important. "Plus, the trail's going to go cold if we don't hop on it."

"Lucas is right," Calhoun agreed. "We should move on this."

"Fine," I snapped, getting to my feet. It was unlikely we could solve this mystery before tomorrow, but it was also unlikely that my friends would shut up about it if we didn't at least try. There was one obstacle, though. "Our parents will say no," I warned. "They're sticklers about us all staying together during our family reunion."

Surprisingly, though, this time they weren't.

"Sure," said both my father and Uncle Teddy, when Mackenzie and I asked if we could hang out with our friends for the afternoon instead of joining everyone at the lake.

"Just be back home in time to freshen up for the clambake," my mother added.

My sister Lauren, who had officially become a member of the Pumpkin Falls Private Eyes over Spring Break, was torn between staying with us and going swimming with our younger cousins.

"This is a wild-goose chase," I told her. "Go to the lake. You have to go back to camp tonight after the fireworks, remember? It's the last chance you'll get to hang out with everyone."

"Promise you'll tell me if anything interesting happens?"

I nodded. "I promise."

Hatcher opted for the lake too. "Sorry, Droo—I mean Truly," he corrected himself. "I won't see our cousins for a whole year otherwise."

Uncle Teddy gave Mackenzie money to treat us all to lunch at the food truck, and then my family left. After we ate, we retreated to Lovejoy's Books, which was air-conditioned, for our meeting.

The bookshop was busy. We'd been planning to close for the Fourth of July, but with all the tourists in town, my father and Aunt True had changed their minds.

REALLY TRULY

"Gotta make hay while the sun shines," Aunt True had said.

Good call, I thought, eyeing the throng of customers. Belinda had volunteered to man the fort so that my father and aunt could spend the afternoon at the lake, and she'd corralled Augustus into helping. He was holding court over at Cup and Chaucer, dispensing beverages along with recommendations for books—most notably his own.

"I see you like Earl Grey tea," I overheard him tell an older lady who was hanging on his every word. Augustus had a lot of fangirls. "You may enjoy my own *Earl of Hearts.*"

I smothered a grin. I'd have to tell Hatcher about that one later.

"It's too crowded to meet here," said Calhoun, glancing around.

I agreed. "The library is open. How about we go there?"

The library was usually closed on Sundays, but Mr. Henry and the staff had decided to keep it open for race day, so that visitors could use the restrooms. No unsightly porta-potties for Pumpkin Falls, no sirree. We headed back down Main Street toward the village green. Our town's lone police car was parked outside the library. Inside, we found Officer Tanglewood at the front desk, chatting with Mr. Henry.

Officer Tanglewood smirked at us. "Well, if it isn't Nancy Drew and—what is it you call yourselves? The Pumpkin Falls Private Eyes?"

"As I recall, John," said Mr. Henry, giving us a discreet

wink, "these enterprising young people were the ones responsible for finding the sap rustler last March. And Truly here proved herself a real-life Nancy Drew indeed! You'll remember that she was the one who found her sister when she went missing."

That wiped the smirk off Officer Tanglewood's face.

"What can I do for you?" asked Mr. Henry, and I explained that we were looking for a quiet spot to meet.

"There's no one in the children's room at the moment," he told us. "It's all yours. I assume you're turning your attention to the missing trophy. Any strategies you can share?"

My friends all looked over at me. For some reason they'd decided I was in charge of the Pumpkin Falls Private Eyes. Which I wasn't.

"Well," I began, then stopped. We didn't really have a plan yet. Officer Tanglewood saw me hesitate. His lips started to curl again, and I felt my face flush with annoyance. "I thought we'd ask Janet at the *Patriot-Bugle* if we could look over the photographs she took of the race this morning," I said, plunging ahead with more confidence than I felt. "She may have taken one that shows where the trophy went, or who took it, if it's been stolen."

"Brilliant!" said Mr. Henry. "Now we're getting somewhere. Unless you've already taken care of that, John?"

Now it was Officer Tanglewood's turn to redden. "I was just about to."

REALLY TRULY

"Crowdsourcing!" blurted Lucas. We all turned and stared at him, and not just because his voice had cracked.

"Crowd what?" asked Jasmine.

"Sourcing," said Mr. Henry, who was a walking dictionary. Most librarians are. "Also brilliant. It means tapping the collective wisdom of the public—asking for their help, often through social media."

"Plenty of people besides Janet took pictures," Lucas continued. "I saw them. We can put the word out online to send us anything that looks suspicious."

Mr. Henry turned to Officer Tanglewood. "I'm sure you've thought of that, too."

"Of course," the policeman blustered, making it perfectly obvious that he hadn't.

"Well, it certainly can't hurt to have these intrepid young people here duplicate your efforts," Mr. Henry said smoothly. "The more the merrier when it comes to solving a mystery, right? Especially one involving such an important symbol of our town's heritage."

Officer Tanglewood looked like he was wishing we'd all just disappear, Mr. Henry included. My friends and I headed upstairs, only too happy to oblige.

"I love this place!" said Mackenzie happily.

I did too. I'd been coming to the children's room at the Pumpkin Falls Library since I was a little kid, and despite the fact that it was definitely in need of renovation—the paint was faded and peeling, for starters, and the chairs and sofas were nearly threadbare, and I suspected that the weird blotch on the ceiling meant there was a leak in the roof—it was one of the coziest places in town.

We headed automatically for the floor pillows under the big bronze sculpture in the corner that depicted a scene from *Charlotte's Web*. Everyone in the room except Calhoun, who had only moved here a couple of years ago, and Mackenzie, who had visited for the first time over Spring Break, had grown up sitting in the doorway of Zuckerman's barn for story hour, beneath the bronze cobweb that contained Charlotte. At least now, at our age, we didn't fight over who got to sit next to Wilbur and who got stuck next to Templeton.

"What do we have so far?" I asked, pen poised over my notepad to start making a list. We almost always began our meetings by making a list. I jotted down two headings: *What We Know* and *What We Don't Know*.

"We know the trophy is missing," said Lucas.

Scooter shot him a look. "Duh!"

"Scooter!" Mackenzie chided, which earned her a worshipful glance from Lucas.

"Sorry," mumbled Scooter. If anyone could make him behave, it was my cousin.

"Maybe add a column for 'Suspects,' and one for 'Action Items,'" suggested Calhoun. "I like Lucas's idea for crowdsourcing—and yours, Truly, for looking at Janet's photos."

REALLY TRULY

He smiled at me, and I smiled back, then wrote down his suggestions.

"We should find out what time Belinda picked up the trophy from Mahoney's," said Jasmine.

I wrote that down under *What We Don't Know*.

"And when it was last seen," added Cha Cha.

I wrote that down too. "How about suspects? Do we have any?"

In the end, we came up with the marathon runner, an older man whom Lucas claimed to have seen lurking outside Lou's Diner and, after some discussion, Ella Bellow. I stared at the list glumly. There was discouragingly little to go on. We brainstormed for a while, not making much progress. When I finally looked up at the clock, I realized with a start that Mackenzie and I had less than half an hour before Lobster Bob was due to arrive for the clambake.

"To be continued," I told my friends, leaping to my feet. "Our parents will have our heads on a platter if we aren't home in time to change for dinner."

As we were leaving, Mackenzie paused by a rack of brochures advertising all the tourist attractions in the area. Gramps and Lola had taken us to a lot of them over the years. We'd been to Story Land when we were little (kind of like a smaller, lamer version of Disneyland) and hunted for souvenirs at Clark's Trading Post. We'd climbed Mount Monadnock when we were older and gone swimming and boating at

Lake Winnipesaukee and ridden the Mount Washington Cog Railway to the highest spot in the northern Appalachians. Other places I hadn't been to and had no interest in visiting included the World's Second-Largest Chainsaw (the largest was in Michigan, apparently) and New Hampshire's Favorite Dairy Museum. I knew that some people called our state "Cow Hampshire," but who would want to visit a museum about cows? And did "favorite" mean that there was more than one?

"Hey, check this out!" Mackenzie plucked a brochure from the bottom row.

"Check what out?"

"This." She thrust it into my hands.

A woman wearing a bikini top and a fish tail floated on the brochure's aquamarine cover, smiling broadly and waving. I read the words in her thought bubble aloud: "'Do you dream of being a mermaid?'"

Can't say that I do, I thought, and handed it back.

"Sounds like fun, right?" said my cousin.

"For Lauren and Pippa, maybe," I replied.

For me? Not in a million years.

CHAPTER 7

By the time we got home, the school bus filled with my relatives had returned from the lake, and the house was awash in Giffords getting ready for the clambake. Mackenzie and I took quick showers and changed out of our sneakers and smelly race clothes into sandals and sundresses—Grandma G liked us all to dress up for our annual "farewell banquet," as she called it.

"Obadiah, Abigail, Jeremiah, Ruth," Mackenzie sing-songed as the two of us headed back downstairs from my bedroom. I'd made up the rhyme when I was younger, to help me remember the names of all my Lovejoy ancestors in the portraits that lined the staircase.

"Matthew, Truly, Charity, and Booth!" I finished, pausing momentarily to blow a kiss at my namesake. I'd gained a new respect for the original Truly Lovejoy this past Spring Break, when I learned how she'd risked everything to help runaway slaves on the Underground Railroad.

"Here come my two beautiful eldest granddaughters!" announced Grandma G as Mackenzie and I entered the kitchen. She was sitting at the table with Professor Rusty and Aunt True, who was holding one of the twins while Aunt Angie nursed the other. At least I assumed that was what Aunt Angie was doing. There was a blanket draped over her shoulder, and I figured that the slightly squirmy lump she was cradling underneath it must be either Blair or Bella. I watched Professor Rusty making silly faces at whichever baby Aunt True was holding, startled by an unexpected thought: *Do they want a baby of their own?*

I figured the two of them would get married someday, but it had never occurred to me that they might want to start a family. Would Aunt True still want to work at the bookshop if she had a baby? My stomach lurched as I realized what a huge hole it would leave in my life if she didn't.

My father poked his head in the back door. "Truly! Grab some newspapers from the recycling bin, would you? Brent could use a hand out here."

"Yes, sir."

"I'll help too, Uncle Jericho," said Mackenzie.

The two of us rummaged through the recycling bins in the mudroom and took a stack of old newspapers outside. Uncle Brent was the sole member of tonight's setup squad, since Aunt Angie was busy with the twins. We helped him spread the newspapers on the picnic tables, then set out paper plates

REALLY TRULY

with a plastic bib on top of each one. Clambakes were notoriously messy.

"Where's that hot sauce of your father's at?" my uncle asked me.

I wrinkled my nose. "Hot sauce? On lobster?"

Uncle Brent grinned. "First rule of Texas cuisine, darlin': Ain't nothing on the menu that hot sauce don't improve."

I laughed and retrieved the box from the kitchen. After Mackenzie and I set the little Terminator bottles out on the tables, there wasn't much else to do, since dinner was being catered. And from what I could tell, it was nearing completion. Over by the portable stoves that had been set up, Lobster Bob, a white-haired gentleman with big bushy white eyebrows and a mustache to match, was tending a pair of huge, steaming pots.

We Lovejoys were on cleanup duty tonight, which would be a snap. All we'd have to do was roll everything up in the newspapers, stuff it into garbage bags, and boom, we'd be done. Mackenzie and I would have plenty of time afterward to enjoy our last evening together.

A few moments later, Lobster Bob started banging a wooden spoon on a pot. "Who's ready for a CLAMBAKE?"

In the stampede that followed, Giffords scrambled for seats as the caterers paraded over to the tables bearing platters of freshly-boiled lobsters and buckets of steamed clams, piles of corn on the cob and homemade rolls, and giant bowls of coleslaw. I'd been skeptical about the whole clambake idea, especially after so many years of great barbecue from the Salt Lick. But my mother's instincts had been right. The clambake was a huge success, after a bit of a rocky start when some of the littlest cousins ran away screaming at their first sight of the fire-engine red lobsters. It didn't help that my cousin Matt egged them on by chasing after them with one in each hand. Lobster Bob was clearly used to this reaction, though. He'd set up a lobster-free zone for the younger kids at the far end of the tables, complete with a hot dog station.

"I see you waited until now to reveal your true colors, J. T.!" teased Uncle Rooster, as my father took a seat across from him. He pointed to my father's baseball cap. Unlike my Texas uncles, who were all sporting matching Longhorn caps—University of Texas is practically a religion in the Gifford family—my father had chosen to wear his favorite faded Red Sox cap.

"Hey! My team is playing the Yankees tonight, and it's my lucky hat." My father had been a Red Sox fan since he was a little kid. Most New Englanders are.

"No hats of any kind at mealtime, boys," Grandma G decreed from the head of the table, and despite the fact that they were grown men, not little boys, my father and uncles obeyed her instantly, removing their caps and setting them down beside their plates. Grandma G's word was law.

Since it was our farewell banquet, my grandmother made

us all hold hands while she said grace. Then it was time to dig in.

"Messy little suckers, aren't they?" said Uncle Rooster, showing Mackenzie how to extract a clam from its shell and remove the membrane from its tubelike neck. "Think of it as rolling down a turtleneck."

She grimaced but did as he instructed, dubiously eyeing the unappealing lump that dangled from her fork.

"I know," I told her. "They look kind of gross. But trust me—they're delicious."

"Dip it in hot water first to clean it and then in the melted butter," said Hatcher, pointing to the paper cups lined up in front of her plate. "Your taste buds will thank you."

Mackenzie hesitantly followed his directions. A big smile spread across her face as she ate her first steamer, as this style of cooked clam is called in New England.

"Told you so," said my brother smugly.

"Even better with hot sauce," said Uncle Brent, shaking a couple of drops of the Terminator into his butter.

Mackenzie shuddered. Like me, she's not a fan of hot sauce.

Lobster Bob inspected one of the Terminator bottles curiously. "May I?" he asked, and Uncle Brent handed him a clam. Lobster Bob dipped it into the spiced butter and took a bite. His bushy eyebrows nearly disappeared under the brim of his chef's hat. "Wow! That'll make your eyes water—but in the best possible way." He ate the rest of the clam enthusiastically.

"Where'd you get that stuff? Bring it with you from Texas?"

Uncle Brent jerked his thumb at my father. "Nope. J. T. made it."

"Seriously?" Lobster Bob looked over at my father. "Are you willing to part with a few bottles? You can name your price. If it catches on, we'll make it an exclusive line."

My parents exchanged a glance. Our family was always looking for ways to make extra money. "Income streams," my parents called them.

My father nodded. "Sure, why not?"

"It can't be exclusive, though," Aunt True said firmly. "We already carry the Terminator at Lovejoy's Books. It's one of our best sellers."

I happened to know that this was a teeny white lie. Maybe even a medium-size one. I'd overheard my parents and Aunt True *talking* about carrying the hot sauce at the bookstore as one of our sidelines—the official name for everything that bookstores sell that aren't books—but nothing had come of it yet, as far as I knew.

Lobster Bob nodded. "I understand. Still, I'm definitely interested."

Teaching Mackenzie how to liberate the lobster meat from its shell was harder than teaching her how to eat a steamed clam. We Lovejoys had all had lobster before, of course. Gramps and Lola had taken us over to the seacoast plenty of times when we visited. But most of the Gifford clan hadn't.

REALLY TRULY

Lobster wasn't exactly a Lone Star State specialty. It took a lot of work to get through that armorlike outer shell, and the nutcrackers and picks that Lobster Bob had brought along to help were practically airborne as my family members passed them back and forth.

"Check it out!" crowed my father. We looked over to see him pick up a lobster claw in his prosthetic hand's titanium fingers. He squeezed, and there was an audible *CRACK!*

"Sweeeet!" hollered my cousin Matt. "Do it again, Uncle Jericho!"

The younger cousins abandoned their hot dog feast at the far end of the table to scamper over and watch this new trick. "No one wins against . . . *the Terminator*!" my father cackled, and they all squealed obligingly as he cracked another claw.

Across the table, my mother gave Aunt True a misty smile. Aunt True smiled back. I knew exactly what they were both thinking. They were thinking what I was thinking, that my father had come a long way this past year since his injury. He'd gone from soldier to civilian, pilot to entrepreneur, and most importantly, from Silent Man—our name for the brooding stranger who had returned to us from Afghanistan—back to his own silly, fun-loving self, the father we'd always known and adored, who could joke around with his brothers-in-law, effortlessly entertain his nieces and nephews, and make light of his own hardship.

"That high-tech device of yours could come in mighty

handy in this line of work," deadpanned Lobster Bob. "If you ever need another job, Mr. Lovejoy, I'll hire you."

My father raised the lobster claw in a mock salute.

"Clambake coma!" declared Hatcher a little while later, slumping forward and pretending to do a face-plant on his paper plate.

"No kidding," I groaned. I hadn't been this full since—well, since dinner last night.

As the catering crew circled the long row of tables passing out warm washcloths so we could wipe off our hands and faces, I helped my brothers bundle up the lobster shells and clamshells and corncobs and other trash in the newspaper table coverings and carry them away to the garbage cans in the barn. Then I helped Uncle Brent pass out clean plastic silverware and napkins. The clambake came with dessert, too—homemade blueberry pie and vanilla ice cream, which Lobster Bob was busy serving up.

"What have we here?" asked Uncle Teddy, taking the piece of paper that Mackenzie handed to him along with his fresh napkin. He read it aloud: "'Sirena's Sea Siren Academy'?"

I looked over, surprised to see him holding the brochure from the library.

"I was wondering if maybe we could go," said Mackenzie. "Me and Truly."

I stared at her, aghast. She shrugged and smiled. "You said

REALLY TRULY

you wished we could spend more time together this summer."

"Yes, but—"

"And since you don't want to come to Texas, how about I stay and we do something fun together instead? We don't just have to hang around Pumpkin Falls."

Not wanting to go Texas didn't mean I wanted to go to some dumb mermaid camp. But before I could say so, my cousin turned back to her father. "Please?" she begged. "Could we? It's just for a week. I'd be home in plenty of time for our trip to Yellowstone."

Uncle Teddy passed the brochure across the table to Mackenzie's mother. "What do you think, Louise?"

"What do I think of what?" Aunt Louise paused her conversation with my mother and Aunt True and glanced at the brochure. She looked up at Mackenzie and smiled. "Aww, honey! Mermaid camp!" Panic rose inside me. "You'd have loved this when you were little."

The panic subsided a bit. Aunt Louise understood exactly—Sirena's Sea Siren Academy was for little kids. Not teenagers like Mackenzie and me.

"You have to be thirteen to attend," Mackenzie continued, pointing to the fine print at the bottom. "Truly and I are just the right age."

Was this conversation really happening? "But I don't want to go!" I protested, my panic level spiking again. No one seemed to be listening to me.

Mackenzie had always been the one fixated on mermaids, not me. When the two of us were little, she used to make me call her Ariel, like in the movie. She wore Ariel pajamas and slept under an Ariel bedspread and dressed up like Ariel for three Halloweens in a row, and probably would have done it for a fourth, except she couldn't stuff herself into her toddler-size costume anymore.

I'd always loved being in the water, but I'd never actually dreamed of *living* there. The closest I'd ever gotten to the whole "under the sea" thing was swim team. That and painting my bedroom back in Texas a gorgeous shade of aqua called Mermaid. Although now that I thought about it, Mackenzie had been the one who had picked the paint out for me.

Aunt Louise inspected the brochure more closely. "Cape Cod, huh?" She passed the brochure to my mother. "That's just a few hours south of here, right, Dinah?"

My mother nodded, slowly turning the pages.

"We'd be happy to pay for Truly to go along and keep Mackenzie company," said Uncle Teddy. That was his polite way of saying, *I know money is tight in your family—let me help out.* Uncle Teddy was really generous.

This was one time that I wished he weren't, though. I shook my head violently at my mother behind his back, drawing a finger across my throat and then pretending to stick it down inside for good measure. Didn't she understand that I had no interest in learning to be a mermaid? None! But my mother pretended not to see me.

"Well, it would certainly be a nice opportunity for her," she said, glancing over at my father. "And for us, too, don't you think, J.T.? Just imagine! All five of them away at once!"

I couldn't believe my ears! She was trying to get rid of me! What about all our plans for pedicures and shopping and day trips to Boston?

"What about me?" I asked indignantly. "Don't I have a say in this?"

"Really, Truly," said my father, frowning. "You could be more gracious. Your aunt and uncle are offering to do something very nice for you."

For you, you mean, I thought, but for once I didn't put my size-ten-and-a-half foot in my mouth and say so. I cast around frantically for another reason not to go. "But you need me at the bookstore!"

My father wasn't budging an inch. "Your aunt and I can handle things just fine without you. Right, True?"

My aunt nodded. There was no support there, either. They were all traitors!

"Who'll take care of Bilbo?" I said, playing my trump card. "You need me for that—Lauren has to go back to Camp Lovejoy tomorrow."

That would definitely get me off the hook. No way would my mother want to deal with changing ferret litter.

"I'm sure Belinda will watch him if I asked," she replied calmly.

I opened my mouth to retort and shut it again. There wasn't much I could say to that. My mother was right. Belinda Winchester was very much like my sister Lauren when it came to animals. At least in the kitten and cat department, which was pretty close to the ferret department.

"What on earth are you two going to do without any children underfoot?" asked Aunt Louise in mock horror.

My mother didn't even hesitate. "Sleep. Go to the Fabulous Fifties film series with Rusty and True. Not have to cook for anybody, or do laundry for anybody, or drive anybody anywhere."

My father reached over with his good hand and gave hers a squeeze, smiling. "Sounds like heaven."

And just like that, my perfect summer flew out the window.

CHAPTER 8

The rest of the Fourth of July passed in a shell-shocked blur. After the clambake, my father loaded us all into the school bus and drove back to Lake Lovejoy for the fireworks. I sat slumped in my seat in a daze as Mackenzie prattled on about Sirena's Sea Siren Academy. My perfect summer hadn't just been whisked out from under me—it had been turned inside out and flipped end to end. It was enough to make anybody's head spin.

Things only got worse when we reached the lake. The beach was packed with people in lawn chairs, happily anticipating the fireworks to come. My friends spotted our bus as it pulled in and came over to join us.

"Any news?" asked Lucas, screeching to a halt in front of Mackenzie. Scooter was right behind him.

My cousin smiled her Gifford sunflower smile. "About what?"

"The missing trophy."

Mackenzie looked over at me.

I shrugged. "Don't look at me—I don't know anything."

His main reason for conversation exhausted, Lucas dangled there, growing pinker by the minute until my cousin took pity on him.

"We do have a bit of news, though, don't we, Truly?" she said.

I shook my head grimly. "Nope. We do not. No news at all."

She turned to my friends. "Truly and I are going to mermaid camp!"

Lucas was rendered even more speechless, if that were possible. Scooter and Calhoun stared at us. So did Cha Cha and Jasmine, before they started squealing so loudly that they attracted a herd of my younger cousins, who came charging over to see what was going on.

"What the heck is mermaid camp?" asked Scooter.

Mackenzie took out her cell phone and showed our friends the video ad she'd found online for Sirena's Sea Siren Academy. It sent the boys into gales of laughter—and sent Cha Cha and Jasmine running off to ask their parents if they could go too. The result was that in nothing flat all four of us were signed up and would be heading together to Cape Cod.

"I can't wait!" exclaimed Jasmine happily. "C'mon, Truly, how could this not be fun?" she added, noticing the sour expression on my face.

REALLY TRULY

Let me count the ways, I thought bitterly. First of all, it turned out that it wasn't just a camp for teenagers; it was for adults, too, which meant we were going to be spending a week with a bunch of seriously deranged people obsessed with mermaids. Second, I was going to have to wear a stupid clamshell bra, or at least something that looked like one. Competitive swimmers didn't do bikinis. Okay, maybe some of them did, but not me. And then there was the tail!

Aunt Louise had called the number on the brochure right after dinner. "You girls are in luck—they still have a few open slots this week," she told us. "Sirena says we'll have to rush-order mermaid tails for you, though. I'll have them shipped directly to Cape Cod."

This was rapturous news to Mackenzie, who had begged my mother to knit her a mermaid tail back in second grade (who knew there were knitting patterns for mermaid tails?) and then happily worn it to shreds. She made a beeline to the computer and found the website.

"What do you think—Calypso, Waverly, Oceana, or Marina?" Aunt Louise asked me. "Those are the styles that Sirena told me were most suitable for teen mermaids."

I scowled. Like there even were such things!

"Blue or green?" asked Aunt Louise, when I finally settled on Marina.

"Blue," I muttered.

"Sequins?"

"No sequins."

Mackenzie went with Calypso in green—with sequins, of course.

My mother sucked in her breath when she saw the price. "Say thank you, Truly," she urged. "This is incredibly generous of your aunt and uncle."

Aunt Louise smiled. "How often do I get to spoil my daughter and my niece in one fell swoop?"

The only bright spot in the rest of the evening, was, quite literally, the fireworks show. Well, that and the fact that I got to spend a few minutes alone with Calhoun. While waiting for the festivities to start, I drifted down to the edge of the lake, leaving Mackenzie and Jasmine and Cha Cha to hyperventilate about mermaid camp. I was skipping rocks morosely when Calhoun wandered over to join me.

"Sorry you won't be around for the film festival," he said, bending down and picking up a rock. "I was looking forward to it."

Looking forward to the movies, or to going with me? I wondered, but couldn't quite work up the nerve to ask. Instead, I just nodded. "Yeah, me too."

He hurled his stone, and we stood watching as it skipped far out across the water.

"Good one."

"Thanks." There was a pause. "I guess your camp thing will be fun, though."

I snorted.

"You don't think so?"

"You saw the video! Would you want to spend a week at something called Sirena's Sea Siren Academy?"

The corners of his mouth quirked up. "I guess not, but mermaids aren't my thing."

"They're not mine, either!"

"Really?" He looked surprised. "I figured since you like to swim so much—"

"Just because I like to swim doesn't mean I want to be a mermaid!"

"You don't have to be so touchy about it!"

I blew out my breath. "Sorry. It's just that I'd planned for my summer to go one way, and now it's turned into something completely different and completely awful."

We picked up more rocks and skipped them.

"I'm thinking of trying out for the play tomorrow," Calhoun told me.

This was a surprise. But Calhoun was full of surprises. He could be cool and aloof on the exterior, but he was a bit of a marshmallow on the inside. That much I knew. I also knew that he was almost as knowledgeable about Shakespeare as his father. "I didn't know you liked to sing!"

He lifted a shoulder. "In the shower mostly. But yeah, I kind of like to sing." He skipped another stone. "So Mackenzie said you're not planning to try out."

I shook my head.

"Not even for the chorus? They just sing and dance in the background."

"Nope."

"You play the piano, right? They always need accompanists for rehearsals."

I shook my head again. "No way. I'm not good enough."

"Seriously, Truly, working on a show is fun! How about stage crew? They have a blast building stuff."

I gave him a sidelong glance. Calhoun was being unusually persistent. And he seemed to know an awful lot about theater. But then, he knew a lot about a lot of things. Romeo Calhoun was smarter than he let people know.

One thing I knew for sure—*The Pirates of Penzance* was not for me.

CHAPTER 9

Exactly twelve hours after the last of the fireworks flickered out over Lake Lovejoy, I was on a bus to Cape Cod.

My cousin and friends and I napped most of the way, worn out from the mad dash to get packed, say good-bye to our families, try out for *The Pirates of Penzance* (Cha Cha and Jasmine, who actually ended up singing for Calhoun's father right there at the lake), and stumble out of bed at zero dark thirty to catch the early bus to Boston. Hatcher and Danny traveled with us as far as South Station, where they saw to it that we made our connection before heading off to their wrestling clinic at Boston University.

"Have fun!" Hatcher called over his shoulder to us as he trotted off after Danny.

"You too!" I called back.

A couple of hours after that, we finally pulled into the bus station in Hyannis.

"Oh great," I mumbled.

Mackenzie yawned, rubbing her eyes. "What?"

I pointed wordlessly out the window. Our ride to Sirena's Sea Siren Academy was waiting for us. It wasn't hard to spot. For one thing, the minivan was aqua, the same color as the manicure on the woman standing next to it. For another, there was a huge mermaid painted on its side.

Mackenzie squealed, waking Cha Cha and Jasmine. "Check it out!"

Our friends did, and then they squealed too.

"Wheee!" I muttered, as we gathered our things and clambered off the bus. "We get to ride in the mermaid-mobile."

"Knock it off, Truly!" Mackenzie sounded exasperated.

I'd been doing my best to suck all the fun out of our upcoming "adventure," as my mother persisted in calling it, ever since my cousin had roped me into it. I figured it was the least I could do to thank her for derailing my perfect summer.

"Welcome to Cape Cod, ladies!" gushed the woman by the minivan. She trotted over to meet us, her shoulder-length red corkscrew curls bobbing like a buoy at anchor. "I'm Sirena."

Sirena didn't look like mermaid material. Not that I knew what mermaid material looked like, but for some reason I'd expected someone with a name like Sirena to be tall and willowy. Sirena was even shorter than my mother and round as an apple.

She helped us load our luggage, then slid in behind the

steering wheel. "We've got about a half-hour drive ahead of us. You girls just sit back, relax, and I'll have you there in time for lunch. Most of the other guests have already arrived."

Mackenzie bounced up and down on the seat beside me. "We're going to mermaid camp!"

"Mermaid *academy*, please, mermaid *academy*," Sirena corrected, wagging an aqua-tipped finger in the rearview mirror. "This is not *camp*! What we are undertaking this week is much too serious an endeavor to be trivialized by that term."

I snorted, and Mackenzie elbowed me in the ribs.

As we left bustling Hyannis, Sirena turned onto a quieter, tree-lined road. It wound along past tidy houses whose white picket fences spilled over with roses and hydrangeas. We passed through several little towns, some of them with village greens nearly identical to the one back home.

"Cape Cod looks like an overgrown version of Pumpkin Falls," said my cousin.

"Isn't it awesome?" Jasmine replied. "The Cape is one of my favorite places in the whole world! We come here on vacation every year—wait until you see the beaches!"

We drove along in silence for a while. My eyelids drooped. A few minutes later Jasmine shrieked, and they flew open again.

"What?" boomed Cha Cha, and the minivan swerved as Sirena glanced at her in alarm. Cha Cha's voice always surprised people the first time they heard it.

"It's the Brewster Store!" Jasmine exclaimed. "It's like our General Store back in Pumpkin Falls, only better. Their penny candy counter is amazing. And they have homemade ice cream, and fudge, and all sorts of cool stuff for sale!"

Sirena smiled. "The Brewster Store is always a big hit with our guests. It's just a short walk from the academy."

A few moments later she turned onto a narrow lane. Up ahead, I spotted Sirena's Sea Siren Academy. Like the minivan, it was hard to miss, thanks to the sign out front with a life-size mermaid painted on it.

I peered out the window as Sirena pulled into the driveway. The academy was a little more run-down than it appeared in the flyer. The white clapboards of the large house at the front of the property were peeling, and the lawn was ragged around the edges and rapidly turning brown in the summer heat. The window boxes were cheery, though, painted a soft blue and filled with bright red geraniums. And there were matching window boxes on the row of tiny cabins that stretched out behind the main building.

"Here we are," said Sirena, parking the minivan next to an identical one. She gestured toward the main house. "This is Mermaid Headquarters—Mermaid HQ for short—where you'll find the dining room, the communal living room, and everybody's favorite, the screened-in porch. We call it Mermaid Crossing."

Of course you do, I thought crossly. I was already sick of all the mermaid references. This was shaping up to be a long week.

"And that will be your second home while you're here!" Sirena pointed toward a large pool beyond the cabins. Its blue water gleamed invitingly. There were bleachers set up on the far side, partially shaded by the fringe of pine trees that I assumed marked the edge of the property.

I caught a quick flutter of yellow on a branch high up in one of the trees, and my spirits lifted a bit. A goldfinch! Maybe I'd end up adding a bird or two to my life list while I was here. That would be some consolation. That and the fact that I'd be in the water most of the day. I wondered if I'd have time to sneak down to the pool for a quick dip before lunch.

"One of the most important rules of Sea Siren Academy," Sirena warned, as if reading my thoughts, "is to never swim alone. Always make sure you have an experienced buddy to watch you when you're in the pool. Now, let's get you girls settled into your quarters. Delphine will be ringing the lunch gong shortly."

Lunch gong? Seriously? My gaze slid over to my cousin. Normally, something like this would strike Mackenzie as funny too, and we'd share a smirk, if not an outright laugh. But she was oblivious, her eyes shining in rapturous anticipation of all things mermaid.

We unloaded our luggage and followed Sirena down the path toward the cabins. Like the driveway, the path was made of what looked like white gravel, but on closer inspection turned out to be some sort of crushed seashells. They made a pleasant crunching sound underfoot. I figured it must be a Cape Cod thing, as I'd seen a lot of similar driveways on the ride over from Hyannis.

"We've put you down at the end, in Whelk," Sirena told us.

What the heck is a whelk? I wondered. Then I noticed the signs over the doors to the cabins. They were painted the same shade of blue as the window boxes, with each cabin's name carved into them and painted a contrasting gold: NAUTILUS, ABALONE, OYSTER, and SAND DOLLAR. There was a pattern here, I quickly realized. A whelk must be a shell.

"Your quarters, ladies," Sirena told us, opening our screen door with a flourish.

It was dark inside. As my eyes adjusted to the dim light, I could see that the space was small and cramped. Two bunkbeds, two dressers, two windows in front, two in back. One tiny bathroom, and one even tinier closet.

Good luck with that, I thought, eyeing our collective suitcases.

"Your tails arrived earlier this morning," Sirena told us, gesturing to a pile of packages at the foot of one of the lower bunks.

This brought fresh squeals from Mackenzie and my friends.

REALLY TRULY

"Please don't try them on yet," Sirena cautioned. "The unveiling and tailing ritual is part of our evening activity tonight."

Unveiling and tailing? My gaze slid over to Mackenzie again, but there wasn't even a flicker. She was taking this all completely seriously.

"Yes, ma'am," I said automatically, knowing an order when I heard one. *No calling it mermaid camp. Never swim alone. No trying on of tails.* Sirena had as many rules as Lieutenant Colonel Jericho T. Lovejoy.

After Sirena left, there was a scramble for the bunks. Jasmine and Cha Cha each claimed a top one; Mackenzie and I ended up on opposite sides of the room on bottom ones. I pressed my nose up against the screen on the window at the foot of my bunk and gazed longingly at the pool. Laughter floated over from Sand Dollar, the cabin next door.

"How many other people are here this week, do you think?" I asked.

"Maybe twenty?" Cha Cha ventured. "If the four other cabins are like ours."

They weren't, as we learned during introductions at lunch. Not quite, anyway. Two of them, Abalone and Oyster, contained just two beds each. Abalone was occupied by the two eldest "aspiring mermaids," as Sirena referred to all of us.

"This is Zadie Malone and her friend Lenore Sullivan," she announced, peering at her clipboard through aqua-framed reading glasses as we took our seats around the dining room table. "They worked together years ago in Los Angeles before marrying and moving to opposite ends of the country—Oregon for you, Lenore, and Vermont for you, Zadie, correct?"

The two ladies nodded.

"But you've remained best friends all these years—"

"—and every year we go on an adventure together, don't we, Lenore?" finished the one named Zadie.

There was that word "adventure" again. Had Zadie been talking to my mother?

Lenore nodded again. With their halos of white hair and wrinkled, smiling faces, the two of them reminded me a bit of Belinda Winchester. I felt a pang of homesickness. If I were back in Pumpkin Falls right now, I'd be hanging out at the bookshop with Aunt True and Belinda instead of a bunch of "aspiring mermaids."

"Last year we went on a raft trip through the Grand Canyon," boasted Zadie. "And the year before that we went bungee jumping in Australia."

"My, aren't you the thrill seekers," said Sirena admiringly.

"Next year we're planning to celebrate the big nine-oh by learning how to skydive."

Wait. *What?* I stared at them. "The big nine-oh"—did that mean what I thought it did? As in Zadie and Lenore were eighty-nine going on *ninety*? I was at mermaid camp with ladies older than Grandma G!

REALLY TRULY

I was still digesting this bit of information when Sirena introduced the mother-daughter duo who were staying in Oyster, the other cabin with just two beds. "Meet Helen and Hayden Drake, who have come all the way from Seattle!"

"We're here for some special mother-daughter time, aren't we, princess?" said the mother part of the duo, reaching over and patting her daughter's hand.

"Princess," who looked to be around my age, rolled her eyes. "Yes, Mom."

The other guests were a mix of adults and teens. Nautilus was occupied by four girls from St. Louis who'd been given the week together as a high school graduation gift. Sand Dollar, the cabin next to ours, housed four women who didn't know each other at all, but who were quickly bonding over the tuna fish salad that Delphine—Sirena's daughter and the academy's only other employee—had served up for lunch.

"Mermaids eat fish," Sirena announced, as if it were a fact. She poked her fork into a chunk of tuna and hoisted it aloft. "I hope you like seafood, because you'll be eating a lot of it this week."

The conversation ebbed and flowed around me as we ate. I glanced around the dining room. The table and chairs had seen better days, as had the faded seashell-themed wallpaper. The air conditioner in the corner wheezed and grumbled as it grudgingly eked out a coolish breeze. Instructing aspiring mermaids didn't seem to be a very lucrative business. If the property was a bit shabby inside and out, though, at least the food was good. I wasn't a huge fan of tuna fish salad, but this wasn't gloppy with mayonnaise, and it had an unexpectedly yummy twist: chopped apple. I was pretty sure the rolls were homemade, and the gingersnap cookies, which finished off our meal, most definitely were. Somebody knew how to cook—Delphine, maybe?

I watched Sirena's daughter as she circled the table, clearing away dishes. She was in her late twenties, I guessed, and as tall as Sirena was short. Nearly as tall as me. The differences between mother and daughter didn't end there. Delphine's fingernails were free of polish, and her hair was blond, short, and spiky, not curly and red. I caught a glimpse of a mermaid tattoo on her left ankle as she passed by.

"We'll take an hour's siesta back in our cabins," Sirena informed us when we finished our meal. "Mermaids need their beauty rest! After that, I have a special treat in store to provide us with a little inspiration before we plunge into the hard work of learning to be mermaids. I've booked us seats at *Beauty and the Buccaneer*, the daily matinee at the Jolly Roger!"

If she'd expected us to be overjoyed at this announcement, we disappointed her. The table fell silent as we all looked at each other, puzzled. *Jolly Roger?*

"You mean the pirate museum?" said Jasmine finally, and Sirena nodded. "Oh, I love that place! We go every summer!"

I perked up at this. Pirates beat the pants—or should it be

REALLY TRULY

tails?—off mermaids any day of the week. But my hopes were quickly dashed when Sirena went on to explain that the daily show featured not only pirates but also professional mermaids.

"There are professional mermaids?" I blurted, astounded at this news.

"Yes, indeed," Sirena replied. "I used to be one myself."

As we got up from the table to return to our cabins for rest hour, Sirena looked me up and down. "My, you are a tall one, aren't you?"

There was really no point in replying to that kind of comment.

"Delphine!" Sirena called, and her daughter poked her head in from the kitchen. "What do you think? We haven't had any guests in a while who were tall enough to pull off the sea serpent costume."

Delphine gazed at me, considering. She nodded slowly. "That would certainly spice things up a bit."

I could feel my face redden. I wanted to be a sea serpent even less than I wanted to be a mermaid. Folding my arms across my chest, I gave the two of them my best impression of a Lieutenant Colonel Jericho T. Lovejoy glare. If my mother could see me now, I knew exactly what she'd say: *Really, Truly, where are your manners?* I didn't care. No way was I going to spend a week at stupid mermaid camp learning how to be a stupid sea serpent.

Sirena and Delphine were too busy discussing the idea to

notice my expression, though. A moment later, Sirena clapped her hands. "Ladies! The vans will be leaving Mermaid HQ at two o'clock sharp! Don't be late."

I stalked out of the dining room after my cousin and friends, who were chattering happily about the Jolly Roger and tonight's unveiling and tailing. There was no talk of any of them being sea serpents, I noted bitterly. Obviously they were perfect mermaid material.

Me, on the other hand? Mermaid camp—pardon me, mermaid *academy*—hadn't even started yet, and I was already flunking out.

CHAPTER 10

"Wow!" Mackenzie whispered. "Those ladies can really swim!"

We were sitting front and center in the Jolly Roger's "showquarium," as the theater was called, watching *Beauty and the Buccaneer*. Any closer and we'd have been onstage ourselves.

Onstage underwater, that is.

All that stood between us and the quartet of mermaids currently performing their routine was a thick pane of glass. It was like sitting in front of a giant fish tank. Most of the showquarium, including the seats we occupied, was underground. All we could see was a carefully constructed "amazing undersea world," as the program trumpeted, complete with a fake castle, fake seaweed, fake seahorses that the mermaids rode in on, and a fake sparkly coral reef. A fake treasure chest in one corner spilled over with the kind of plastic jewelry that my sister Pippa loved to play dress up with. The only thing that was real, as far as I could tell, were the fish that darted here and there. Far above, sunlight filtered down through the water, illuminating the whole scene.

It was incredibly cheesy.

If only Hatcher were here to poke fun at it with me! This kind of thing was right up his alley. It was usually up Mackenzie's alley too, but when I glanced over at her, I could tell by her shining eyes that she was not in the mood for mockery. Ditto Cha Cha and Jasmine. I seemed to be the only one who noticed how silly it all was. Especially the pink seahorses. They looked like giant pool toys.

Mackenzie was right about one thing, though, I had to admit. The professional mermaids really could swim.

I watched the four women glide through the water, propelling themselves with an effortless flip of the flukes at the bottom of their surprisingly realistic tails. They swam in and out of the castle, waving at us from the windows (Mackenzie waved back, like she was five). They looked at themselves in hand mirrors and pretended to brush each other's hair. They performed what looked like underwater ballet moves, arcing forward and back in graceful somersaults. They swam over to the treasure chest, where they pulled out strands of fake beads and pearls and hung them around each other's necks. Occasionally, one of them would dart over to the back corner, grab one of the long black tubes hidden among the fake seaweed—

REALLY TRULY

oxygen tubes, I presumed—and take a quick breath. Otherwise, they just swam around with their eyes open, big smiles on their perfectly made-up faces (hello, waterproof mascara), as if water really were their natural element.

"Ooo, look! Here comes Beauty!"

Behind us, Hayden suddenly came to life. She'd been watching mostly in silence until this moment, when the quartet of mermaids pointed in excitement toward the castle as a fifth mermaid emerged. She wore a gold bikini top and a gold crown, and she was riding in a carriage shaped like a giant gold shell. It floated toward us, pulled by two of the pink seahorses, although I was pretty sure there was a motor involved somewhere.

"Check out her tail!" Mackenzie whispered, mesmerized, as the carriage stopped directly in front of us, and Beauty emerged. She swam out and hovered before the window, waving and smiling at us as she showed off her long golden tail, which was much fancier than the ones belonging to the other mermaids.

"A *shimmertail!*" breathed Hayden.

I was impressed in spite of myself. Glimmering scales in iridescent shades of peacock blue and green were scattered up and down the tail's golden surface, and the oversized flukes at the bottom looked like butterfly wings.

"Wow!" Mackenzie exclaimed, her eyes shining again. I was guessing "shimmertail" had just shot right to the top of her Christmas list.

All of a sudden the mermaids drew back in mock horror.

A sinister figure plunged into the water from above. Dressed in a black-and-white-striped T-shirt and what looked like the bottom half of a wetsuit, he descended toward the bottom of the showquarium on a big black anchor. In one hand he held a fluttering black flag with a white skull and crossbones on it.

"The buccaneer!" exclaimed one of the girls from St. Louis at the same time that Mackenzie said, "The pirate!"

"Boo! Hiss!" called Zadie, who was enjoying the show almost as much as my cousin.

The pirate gave an evil grin, revealing a gold tooth. He hopped off the anchor and swam toward the mermaids, who fluttered their hands in pretend panic.

"C'mon, Team Mermaid!" I shouted. "Whack him with your tails!"

Whether it was my encouragement or just the script, the mermaids finally sprang into action, forming a guard around Beauty. The pirate tried to reach over them and grab her crown, but they successfully fended him off. Finally, he gave up and turned his attention to the treasure chest.

"Not the treasure!" hooted Zadie, who was surprisingly feisty for someone who was nearly ninety, if you asked me, which nobody ever did.

As the pirate rifled through the contents of the chest, the mermaids set off after him in furious pursuit. I knew they were furious because of the way their tails lashed the water. In the end, he was no match for them, though. Everyone cheered

REALLY TRULY

when Beauty gave him a final thwack with her shimmertail, sending him somersaulting across the bottom of the showquarium. Her mermaid guards snatched away his pirate flag, put him in handcuffs, and sent the buccaneer back to the surface on one of the seahorses in defeat.

"That was amazing!" said Mackenzie as we emerged from the theater. "I can't believe how long they all could hold their breath."

"At least ninety seconds, and some of them for up to two and a half minutes," Sirena told her. "I used to be able to hold mine for two minutes, back when I was performing."

I tried to imagine her as a professional mermaid. Sirena was shaped more like one of the bobbers my brothers used when they were first learning how to fish, but when she was younger, she was probably built more like Cha Cha or Mackenzie, pint-size and cute.

"Were you a mermaid here at the Jolly Roger?" asked Hayden's mother.

Sirena shook her head. "No—Florida. But that was many years ago. Delphine worked here every summer during college, though." She clapped her hands. "Ladies! You have about forty-five minutes to enjoy the museum before we head back to Mermaid HQ."

As the rest of the group made a beeline for the gift shop, Cha Cha and Jasmine and Mackenzie and I entered the "Wreck of the *Windborne*" exhibit.

"Ooo, spooky," said my cousin, shivering in anticipation as we pushed past a curtain of fishing nets into a dark tunnel. We emerged onto a gangplank that led onto a replica of a ship. A costumed guide motioned us over.

"The tour is just getting started," he told us, adjusting his tricorne hat. A fake stuffed parrot was perched on his shoulder. "Welcome aboard the *Windborne*, mateys!"

Mateys? Seriously? I glanced at my oblivious cousin. Where was Hatcher when I needed him!

"The tale of the *Windborne* is a tragic one," our guide began. "While sailing home to England in 1765 with a hold full of South American gold and silver, she was attacked off Jamaica by Benjamin 'Black Tooth Ben' Buttonwood and his band of pirates. They trussed the *Windborne*'s captain up like a Thanksgiving turkey and set him ashore on a small island. His crew was given the choice of being marooned with him or joining the buccaneers. Most chose to go rogue."

"I want to be a pirate too!" announced a little boy about Pippa's age.

"Arrrrgggghhh!" growled our guide approvingly. "Bully for you, lad!"

Frustrated actor, I thought. Couldn't get a real job, ended up here. That's what my father always said about the employees these kinds of museums.

The guide continued with his tale. "The *Windborne* spent the next couple of years sailing under the black flag—that's what they call the skull and crossbones, that or the 'Jolly Roger'—preying on other ships. Then, in the spring of 1767, she set a course for Black Tooth Ben's home port in Maine. Legend has it he planned to meet his sweetheart there and spirit her off to a life of luxury in the West Indies. Alas, fate had other plans. The *Windborne* was nearing Nantucket when she ran afoul of a nor'easter. The monstrous storm blew them back toward Cape Cod, and they foundered on a sandbar just off Marconi Beach."

Jasmine gasped. "I've been swimming on that beach!"

The guide nodded solemnly. "As have I, lass, as have I." His voice dropped low. "As the ship's bell tolled the alarm, the *Windborne* broke apart. Nearly all hands were lost, including that of the cabin boy, who was just about your age." He pointed at the little boy who'd announced that he wanted to be a pirate. He didn't look so certain now. "Only two men made it to shore. Isaiah Osborne, the ship's carpenter, was quickly found, arrested, and hanged for piracy. The other managed to escape and was never seen or heard from again. Dandy Dan, his shipmates called him, but his real name has been lost in the mists of time."

"What happened to the treasure?" asked Cha Cha.

"They say that Dandy Dan spirited some of the booty away with him when he vanished, but no trace of it has ever been found. The *Windborne* lay in her silent grave at the bottom of the sea for three hundred years. Bits and pieces of her washed ashore from time to time, tantalizing beachcombers and treasure seekers alike. But her exact location eluded all who sought to find her."

The tour guide knew how to spin a tale. We were hanging on his every word.

"All, that is, except Skipper John Dee, Cape Cod's own intrepid underwater explorer. Ten years ago, after spending most of his life searching for the *Windborne*, he mounted one final expedition, and this time he found her! Thanks to his recovery efforts, we now have this museum and all of the priceless historical artifacts that it contains." He whipped off his hat and threw it into the air. "Huzzah for Skipper Dee!"

"Huzzah for Skipper Dee!" echoed the tour group.

I laughed out loud, which earned me a puzzled look from the tour guide. Just the other night Mackenzie had read *Eloise*, Pippa's favorite book, to a group of our younger cousins. Skipperdee was Eloise's pet turtle's name. I looked over at my cousin, expecting to see her grinning too, but she was too busy huzzahing to notice.

After the tour, we meandered on through the other exhibits, looking at the cannonballs and swords and other artifacts that had been recovered from the ocean floor.

"Hey! There's the ship's bell!" said Jasmine.

We followed her to the large tank in which it hung submerged. It reminded me of the Paul Revere bell in the steeple of our church back in Pumpkin Falls. This one was similar in style, only smaller. The name WINDBORNE was engraved around the middle. I stared at it, imagining the storm and the howling wind and the cries of all those doomed men, including the poor little cabin boy. And above it all, the ringing of the bell as the ship sank beneath the waves.

I jumped as someone touched my arm. It was Mackenzie.

"What's the matter?"

"Nothing."

"Come on," she said, "this room gives me the creeps. Let's go look at some pirate treasure."

CHAPTER 11

There was plenty of treasure to see. The *Windborne* sank loaded with plunder from nearly two dozen ships, and my cousin and friends and I lingered over the displays of gold and silver coins and jewelry from Africa and South America.

Another costumed guide was standing by one of the exhibit cases, letting people hold a real coin—a silver piece of eight. When it was my turn, I held out my hand as directed.

"Wow!" I exclaimed as she placed the coin in the center of my palm. My fingers closed over it reflexively. "I wasn't expecting it to be so heavy."

She smiled. "Nobody ever is."

I managed to find some decent souvenirs in the gift shop, including fake pieces of eight for Hatcher and Danny, a plush stuffed parrot toy for Pippa, a book called *The Pirate Queen* for Lauren, and for my mother and Aunt True, the museum's special blend of *Windborne* tea. I hesitated by a rack of T-shirts, wondering if my father would get a kick out of one that said CAPTAIN HOOK on it. I finally decided that he would. Lieutenant Colonel Jericho T. Lovejoy had a good sense of humor, and I was guessing he'd wear it proudly with his matching prosthetic arm with the hook on it, the one he'd received before upgrading to the Terminator.

"Ladies!" called Sirena, poking her head in the door of the shop. "Time to set sail for home. Dinner awaits! It's fish and chips night, our traditional welcome meal."

We arrived back at Mermaid HQ just in time to stash our loot in our cabins before the dinner gong sounded. *Sirena wasn't kidding when she said we'd be eating a lot of fish this week*, I thought, surveying my plate. It was a good thing that I liked seafood.

"Oh man, this is so good!" said Mackenzie, and Delphine smiled.

"You know your way around a kitchen, that's for sure," agreed Zadie.

"Indeed she does," said Sirena proudly. "I'd say she's a chip off the old block, except I can't even boil water! I'm hopeless at cooking."

"I had to learn in self-defense," joked Delphine.

After dinner, it was time for the "unveiling and tailing."

"Change into your swimsuits, gather your tails, and meet at Mermaid Crossing—the back porch—in fifteen minutes," Sirena told us, and we all scattered to our cabins.

Mackenzie skipped happily down the path toward Whelk. "I can't wait to try mine on!"

I could. Watching the professionals today at the showquarium had given me a little more respect for the whole mermaid thing, but I still wasn't looking forward to turning myself into one. And my mood did not improve when I got my first glimpse of Mermaid Crossing.

"Over the top much?" I muttered at the same time that Mackenzie exclaimed, "It's perfect!"

Twinkle lights in the shape of seashells were draped across the porch's broad screens, and there were fishing nets and glass floats strung up everywhere. Big cushy chairs and sofas covered in faded blue denim were arranged in a semicircle, and scattered atop them were throw pillows that sported jaunty sayings like LIFE IS BETTER AT THE BEACH! and SEAS THE DAY! and MERMAIDS AHOY!

I eyed the enormous full-length mirror that leaned against the back wall of the house. It was encrusted with a haphazard pattern of seashells glued to its frame and looked like something Pippa might have made in kindergarten. Above it was a colorful mural featuring a trio of mermaids seated on a rock, brushing their long hair while whales frolicked in the distance. MERMAID CROSSING was written above their heads in shiny silver paint.

We all found seats and looked over at Sirena, who had changed into a gauzy white dress that fluttered and swirled around her knees as the ceiling fan spun overhead in slow circles. Sparkly flip-flops, full makeup, and yards of costume jewelry completed the look.

"And now," she said dramatically, "it's time for the unveiling and tailing!"

At Sirena's signal, we all opened the packages containing our tails. At first glance, Marina, the style I'd chosen, didn't look all that bad. I held it up. The tubelike part at the top was made of shiny blue fabric printed with scales, and the flukes fluttered limply at the bottom. I gave it a tentative tug. The whole thing didn't look very long, but it was stretchy.

"You'll need to insert the monofin first," Delphine told me. Unlike her mother, she was dressed simply in denim shorts and a Brewster Store T-shirt.

I gave her a blank look.

Leaning over my shoulder, she rummaged in the box that the tail had arrived in and pulled out a stiff, black crescent-shaped thing. "It's like a single swim flipper," she explained. Picking up the fluttery fabric at the bottom of the tail, she inserted the monofin into a hidden opening along the edge, then pulled the stretchy fabric back in place to cover it.

"Voilà!" she said, smiling. "Flukes!"

When everyone was finished prepping their tails, we all held them up.

"We're quite the rainbow, aren't we?" said Zadie, whose tail was hot pink.

"It always ends up this way," said Sirena. "Mermaids are a colorful bunch."

"Isn't mine gorgeous!" Mackenzie crowed, scattering audible exclamation points like the glittering sequins on her green Calypso tail.

The last time I'd seen Mackenzie this happy was over Spring Break, when her parents had given her permission to bring a kitten home. But even the thrill of picking Frankie out of a litter seemed to pale in comparison to this.

No two tails were alike, except for Hayden's and her mom's. They had ordered matching ones covered in flat, pearly disks.

"I think those are a style called Atlantis," Jasmine whispered to us. "I saw them on the website. They're custom and *really* expensive."

This didn't surprise me. Mrs. Drake was clearly a nothing-but-the-best-for-my-princess kind of mom.

"Delphine, would you like to demonstrate how a mermaid puts on her tail?" Sirena asked her daughter.

Delphine nodded and stepped out of her shorts, revealing her bathing suit underneath. She picked up a shiny turquoise tail that was draped over the back of the sofa and rolled it down like a sock. Then she sat down and deftly placed her feet into the openings in the monofin. With one graceful movement, she stood up again, pulling the fabric upward while she shimmied. The tail unfurled smoothly over her long legs. She gave a final tug to the waistband, removed her T-shirt to reveal a matching turquoise bikini top underneath, then perched on the arm of the sofa, smiling at us as she swished her flukes back and forth.

"Couldn't have done it better myself," said Sirena, as we gave Delphine a round of applause. "Now it's your turn, ladies. Let the tailing begin!"

The porch grew quiet as we concentrated on copying Delphine. Sixteen pairs of legs were inserted into sixteen fabric mermaid flukes. Thirty seconds after I started to pull my tail up, though, I knew something was wrong. Marina was supposed to fit mermaids five foot eight and over, but no matter how hard I tugged and shimmied and yanked on it, the stupid thing wouldn't go past my knees.

"Oh, honey," said Zadie, looking over at me, "they sent you the wrong size!"

Cha Cha laughed her raspy laugh until her legs went weak and she collapsed on the floor. That set Jasmine and Mackenzie off, and pretty soon everyone was laughing. Everyone except me. I stood there wearing half a mermaid tail and feeling like a big idiot.

Sirena finally took pity on me. "Don't worry," she said, wiping her eyes, "if there's one thing we have here at Mermaid HQ, it's plenty of tails." She crossed the porch and flung open an old trunk that was serving as a makeshift coffee table. "See if you can find one that fits you."

As the rest of the group hopped around looking at themselves in the full-length mirror and snapping selfies, I tried on one tail after another. A couple of them almost worked, but nothing was quite right for my size-ten-and-a-half feet and extra-long legs.

"Any luck?" asked Sirena a few minutes later.

I shook my head.

"Delphine, surely there must be one of your old tails floating around here that would work for her."

"I'll go check," said Delphine.

"And while you're upstairs, bring down the sea serpent costume, would you?"

Delphine nodded, shimmied back out of her tail, and disappeared into the house. I steeled myself to put my foot down. I'd rather be sent home than have to be a sea serpent!

In the end, though, I didn't have to. Delphine returned a few minutes later bearing a rueful expression and a sad, droopy brown mess riddled with so many holes it almost looked like lace draped across her shoulders. At one end lolled a sea serpent head, grinning spitefully at me.

"Moths," Delphine reported to her mother. "They got into the old practice tail of mine, too."

"Oh no! What a shame!" Sirena frowned, drumming her aqua-tipped fingers on the arm of her chair.

"There's always my tail from the Jolly Roger," Delphine suggested. "It would fit her."

REALLY TRULY

REALLY TRULY

"That's against the rules," said her mother sharply.

I perked up at that. "Against the rules" sounded a whole lot better than "sea serpent."

"She's probably got the strength for it," Delphine continued, the two of them discussing me as if I weren't standing right there. "It said on her application that she's on a swim team."

Sirena thought it over. "Well, perhaps we could make an exception." She nodded at Delphine, who withdrew inside the house again, and returned a few moments later carrying what looked like a floppy rubber tube made of glimmering aquamarine.

"A *shimmertail*!" cried Hayden. "No fair! Only professional mermaids are supposed to wear shimmertails!"

Sirena silenced Hayden with a stern wag of her finger. "Mermaids are never envious. And this is a special case. Truly is too tall for any of the other tails that we have on hand."

"Truly *enormous*," Hayden muttered resentfully. She said it under her breath, but I heard her just fine. My face flushed.

"Now, Hayden," said her mother, half-heartedly scolding her.

Delphine handed over the shimmertail. I gasped and nearly dropped it.

"Thirty pounds of sculpted silicone," she told me. I was familiar with silicone. My father actually had three prosthetic arms to choose from, and silicone was what Ken, his name for the lifelike but useless option, was made of.

I hefted the tail. It was going to be interesting trying to swim in this thing. I might as well strap a cinder block to my feet. I sat down to put it on.

"Wait," said Delphine, "you'll need these first." She passed me a pair of black socks. "They're neoprene and will keep your feet from slipping out of the heel straps." She also handed me a spray bottle.

I squinted at it. "What's this?"

"Hair conditioner mixed with warm water. Spray your legs with it, and the tail will go on easier."

I wrinkled my nose but did as I was told. Putting first one foot in and then the other, I felt around for the heel straps that would secure my feet in place.

"Take your time," said Delphine. "Pull it up inch by inch."

The silicone tail didn't stretch as much as the fabric tails had. It took a lot of encouragement and instruction from Delphine, and I was red-faced and sweaty by the time I was done, but I finally managed to wiggle into the gleaming tube.

Mackenzie's eyes widened in admiration. "Wow! You look amazing, Truly."

"Truly amazing," quipped Zadie. "Right, Lenore?"

Lenore nodded.

Delphine turned to her mother. "See? I told you. Fits like a glove."

More like a corset, I thought. The waistband was so tight I could hardly breathe.

"Don't try and stand up," Delphine instructed. "That's pretty much impossible in a shimmertail."

"Okay," I said, scooting myself awkwardly over to the mirror. The shimmertail *was* pretty awesome, I had to admit, smoothing it over my hips. Realistic-looking 3-D scales were molded along the length of it, and glitter had been embedded into the silicone itself, giving the surface an iridescent sheen. The graceful arch of the fluke at the bottom was nearly twice as big as the ones on the fabric tails. I looked—well, I looked like a real mermaid.

If there were such things.

Over my shoulder, I caught a glimpse of Hayden's face. She was staring at my tail with unmistakable envy.

"There's a matching bikini top," said Delphine, handing me what looked like two aquamarine potholders sewn together.

I gulped. "I don't—"

"Come on, Truly!" Mackenzie begged.

I sighed. *In for a penny, in for a pound,* I thought. Awkwardly tugging my arms inside my Pumpkin Falls Swim Team T-shirt, I managed to pull the top of my one-piece racing suit down and squirm into Delphine's bikini top.

"It's perfect!" said Mackenzie, after I reluctantly removed the T-shirt to show off the results. "Right, Cha Cha? Right, Jazz?"

My friends nodded enthusiastically.

"I think we've found our queen," Sirena said to Delphine.

Wait. What? I thought in alarm. Who said anything about a queen?

I looked in the mirror again. There was nothing remotely regal about what was looking back at me. My worst nightmare had just come true—I was wearing a clamshell bra!

I grabbed my T-shirt and yanked it back over my head.

Sirena arched an eyebrow. "We've got our work cut out for us," she murmured.

Delphine patted her on the shoulder. "We've dealt with worse."

As everyone wriggled onto the sofas and chairs, Delphine went back inside, reappearing a few moments later with a tray.

"Mermaid snacks!" Sirena announced. "Time to celebrate your new tails!"

The snacks turned out to be a flavored sparkling water and shortbread cookies cut into fish shapes. We helped ourselves while Delphine passed around some handouts.

"You'll be choosing a mermaid name for the week," Sirena told us. "This list will provide you with some suggestions, but feel free to let your imagination take you where it will."

Mine was taking me right out the door and onto the bus for home, I thought as I glanced down at the name at the top of the list. Malibu? Seriously?

"If your mermaid name has an interesting meaning, please share it with us," Sirena continued. "Sirena, for instance, is

Greek for 'enchantress'—a siren was a mythical sea creature whose beauty and song lured sailors to their deaths."

That sounded like something to aspire to, I thought, suppressing a smile. I made a mental note to add this to the growing list of things I couldn't wait to tell Hatcher.

"And Delphine is French for 'dolphin,'" Sirena went on. "We encourage you to come up with a backstory for yourself as well. Spin us a tale! Who is your mermaid? Where did she grow up? What are her hopes and dreams?"

"My mermaid name is Shellina," blurted Hayden, like she couldn't hold it in any longer.

If I'd been drinking anything just then, it would have spurted out my nose for sure. Shellina? Even Mackenzie let out a sound that was close to a giggle.

"I was born in the undersea kingdom of Tritonia," Hayden continued, throwing us side-eye. "My father is the ruler there, and I have six younger sisters, and I will grow up and marry a prince."

Shellina's backstory sounded suspiciously like the plot to Pippa and Lauren's favorite mermaid movie, but nobody else said anything, so I didn't either.

"And someday, I shall be queen." Hayden looked pointedly over at me as she emphasized this last bit.

Queen Shellina? I sat up a little straighter in my shimmertail. Not if I had anything to say about it. I didn't ask to be queen, but I wasn't about to just hand the role over to a spoiled brat, either.

"Wonderful!" said Sirena. "You've obviously come prepared, Hayden. The rest of you have a little homework to do. But don't stay up late! Remember, mermaids need their beauty rest. 'Early to bed, early to rise, keeps mermaids fit and their fins looking nice!'"

I groaned inwardly. Where did she *get* this stuff?

"Off with your tails now, and then off to bed with you. Tomorrow is a big day. Class will convene at the pool before breakfast. We have less than a week before the revue to transform you into mermaids."

Review? I didn't like the sound of that. "You mean, like a test?"

"Not review, R-E-V-U-E," said Sirena, spelling the word out like Annie Freeman. "It's our performance for the general public. We do it at the end of every session here at the academy."

My face must have registered my shock.

"It's a very popular event here in Brewster," Sirena hastened to assure me.

"There wasn't anything in the brochure about a revue!" I protested. It was one thing to be forced to goof around privately in somebody's backyard, and a whole other kettle of fish to have to appear as a mermaid in public!

"Just think of it as a piano recital," said Mackenzie.

I shot her a look. She knew exactly how I felt about those. Plus, I'd never worn a bikini top to a piano recital in my life,

REALLY TRULY

let alone a tail. And only parents and relatives showed up for piano recitals, not the "general public."

So much for stealth mode. Unless I totally caved and let Hayden—make that Shellina—get her way, I was destined to be front and center in Sirena's Sea Siren Academy pool for all of Cape Cod to gawk at.

This was quickly shaping up to be the worst week of my life!

CHAPTER 12

I lay in my bunk, listening to the soft murmur of voices that floated in the window from the cabin next door. The ladies of Sand Dollar were busy getting better acquainted from the sound of it. All was quiet in Whelk, apart from Cha Cha's and Jasmine's steady breathing and an occasional snuffle-snore from Mackenzie across the room. I was the only one awake. I turned over again, trying to get comfortable. But sleep was impossible.

What was I doing here? How had I let myself get talked into coming to mermaid camp? I should be home, helping out at the bookstore and trying to find the missing trophy.

Unplugging my cell phone from its charger, I slipped out of bed and crept as quietly as I could across the bare wooden floor to the cabin door. Outside, I tiptoed behind Whelk, then sprinted across the back lawn toward the cover of the pine trees beyond the pool. I stood there for a moment in the shadows, hoping no one had seen me. But the windows in the main house and all the cabins remained dark, and the ladies of Sand Dollar were still busy whooping it up, clearly not interested in anything going on outside. Like a fellow aspiring mermaid making a desperate phone call.

Aunt True answered on the first ring.

"Truly? It's late—is everything all right?"

At the sound of her voice, I burst into tears.

"Oh, honey, what's wrong?"

"Everything!" I wailed. "I hate it here! I want to come home!" I knew I sounded like a homesick little kid, but I didn't care. The words came tumbling out in a rush. "My stupid mermaid tail didn't fit because they sent me the wrong size, and Sirena wanted me to be a sea serpent instead but it had moth holes and now I have to wear something called a shimmertail and be a queen in front of the *entire world!*"

There was silence on the other end of the phone as my aunt tried to digest this burst of information. "Um, I get the picture, I think?"

Just in case she didn't, I expanded on my list of complaints: Sirena and her dumb "mermaids eat fish" and "mermaids need their beauty rest" and other pronouncements; Mackenzie's complete lack of a sense of humor about all the things that struck me as funny; Hayden's designs on my throne, which I didn't really want anyway; the revue looming at the end of the week. "I even have to wear a stupid clamshell bra!" I finished indignantly.

I could hear Aunt True smiling. "You do realize, of course, that you're going to have great stories to tell about this experience for the rest of your life."

I grunted. "That doesn't help."

"I know, sweetheart." She sighed. "I wish I could fix this for you."

"You can! I really want to come home, Aunt True! I called you because I know Mom and Dad were looking forward to some time alone, but couldn't I stay with you?"

There was another long pause. "I tell you what," she said finally. "Before we go with the nuclear option, how about you sit tight for forty-eight hours? Things might get better. And if they don't, and you still want to come home, I'll drive down and get you, okay?"

I could live with that. "Okay."

"Good girl. Meanwhile, call me any time, or zap me a text. Tall timber sticks together. Now, go get some sleep. I hear that mermaids need their beauty rest."

I laughed grudgingly. After we hung up, I decided to text Calhoun and Scooter and Lucas. No point waiting until tomorrow.

ANY PROGRESS? I waited for a response. Nothing. They were probably all asleep. As I was slipping my phone back into my pocket, though, it buzzed.

It was Calhoun!

A LITTLE, he told me. LUCAS'S CROWDSOURCING—#MISSING

REALLY TRULY

TROPHY #PUMPKINFALLS #FOURONTHEFOURTH—IS STARTING TO PAY OFF. WE'RE REVIEWING THE PHOTOS AS THEY COME IN.

VIDEO CHAT TOMORROW?

SURE. HOW'S MERMAID CAMP?

DON'T ASK, I replied, adding an eye roll emoji.

LOL! NIGHT

NIGHT

There was one other person I thought about calling, but I knew from personal experience that athletes at sports camps went to bed early. I typed out another text instead: HELP! HAVE BEEN KIDNAPPED BY ALIENS DISGUISED AS MERMAIDS! I added an alien emoji, along with a mermaid one for good measure, and sent it to Hatcher. And then I went back to bed.

Morning came way too early. I trailed down to the pool behind my cousin and friends, yawning. I wasn't the only one who'd stayed up too late. The four women from Sand Dollar looked even less awake than me. They'd still been talking and laughing when I'd finally managed to fall asleep last night.

Sirena wagged a finger at them. "Next time, ladies, do as I tell you. Mermaids—"

"—need their beauty rest!" the four of them chorused in unison.

"That's exactly right." Sirena was bright-eyed and bushy-tailed, as Grandma G would say. Today she was wearing a bright floral swimsuit, matching floral flip-flops, sunglasses whose frames were studded with rhinestones, and a wide-brimmed hat. From what I'd seen, just about everything Sirena owned was decorated either with sequins, fake jewels, or glitter.

Delphine looked more like a normal person. Her racerback swimsuit was similar to the one I was wearing, and over it she'd pulled the same denim shorts she'd worn last night.

The high school girls from St. Louis were in high spirits, laughing and joking around with one another. Hayden still looked grumpy. Her mother, who was probably used to her moods, calmly sipped coffee out of a travel mug with MER-MAMA emblazoned on the side. Zadie and Lorena were going through a series of stretches on the pool deck. I watched them, impressed. They were pretty flexible for ladies pushing ninety.

Sirena clapped her hands. "Into the water with you!"

"What about our tails?" asked Hayden.

"We'll get to that later. First, morning mermaid exercises."

This sounded suspiciously like warm-ups at swim team practice, which it pretty much was. Sirena and Delphine led us through stretches along the wall first, and then made us swim laps while they watched.

"We want to get a sense of your overall comfort in the water, and of your general level of ability as swimmers," Sirena told us. Delphine stood beside her, taking notes.

REALLY TRULY

I felt myself relax the minute I slipped into the pool. Ever since I was a little girl, I'd loved the feeling of being in the water, whether it was a pool, a lake, the ocean, or even a bathtub. I loved that moment when the water closed over my head and the outside world fell away. As Sirena put us through our paces, the anxiety that had crowded in on me last night began to fade away. Was it really that big a deal if I had to swim in public? I'd done it a zillion times before, after all, at countless swim meets over the years.

Maybe Aunt True was right, and things would get better. And if not, all I had to do was stick it out for forty-eight hours. Forty-two, now.

I'd been happy to see that Sirena's pool was a regulation-size twenty-five-meter one. As I churned my way to the far end, I thought maybe I'd ask if I could swim some extra laps each day, to help keep me in shape for summer swim team. This mermaid stuff seemed like it was going to be a snap. I was easily the strongest swimmer here. Well, along with Mackenzie. When I reached the far edge of the pool, I paused, treading water as I awaited further instructions.

"Swim back to me underwater!" Sirena called. "Let's see how far you can go."

Like I said, easy.

I took a deep breath and pushed off, diving beneath the surface into the streamline I used for races, then dolphin-kicked my way back down the length of the pool. I inspected the bottom as I swam. The pool had been nice once, with tiny colored tiles that formed an intricate mural of King Neptune holding his trident aloft, surrounded by dolphins. Now, though, the picture had faded, and some of the tiles were missing.

Thirty seconds later, I reached the shallow end.

Sirena checked something off on her clipboard. "Excellent, Truly. Impressive breath control."

"Thanks." At least now they knew that I could swim.

So could Zadie and Lenore, as it turned out.

When Sirena asked if anyone knew any synchronized swimming moves, Zadie and Lenore looked at each other, smiled, and swam out to the middle of the pool. They extended their arms overhead like ballerinas, then slowly and gracefully arced backward through the water in perfect unison, one knee bent, one straight, toes pointed.

"Perfect knee-back dolphins!" gasped Delphine.

We all clapped as the two older ladies resurfaced.

"We appear to have a pair of ringers in our midst!" Sirena exclaimed, putting her hands on her hips. "Out with it, you two. Where on earth did you learn to do that?"

"From Esther Williams," Zadie replied smugly, swimming back over to join us. Lenore was right behind her.

Sirena's mouth fell open. "You're kidding, right?"

"Nope. We weren't much older than these girls here"— Zadie gestured toward Mackenzie and Cha Cha and Jasmine and me—"when a Hollywood talent scout discovered us in a

REALLY TRULY

water ballet class in Laguna Beach. That was the start of our film career."

"You mean to tell me that you two swam with Esther Williams in the *movies?*" If Sirena's jaw dropped any farther, it was going to hit the pool deck. I had no idea what she was talking about, but Delphine and Hayden's mom and the four ladies from Sand Dollar clearly did, as they all looked equally astounded.

Zadie and Lenore nodded again, clearly pleased by the attention.

"We thought about telling you ahead of time, but Lenore thought it might be more fun to surprise you," Zadie explained. "Isn't that right, Lenore?"

Lenore gave a modest smile.

"Oh. My. Goodness," said Sirena, for once at a loss for words. She stood there, shaking her head in disbelief. "Which of her movies were you in? I have them all!"

"Let's see, *Million Dollar Mermaid*, of course, *Neptune's Daughter*, and *Easy to Love*—a whole slew of them. They even brought us out of retirement to help choreograph the water ballet scene in *Funny Lady*."

Turning to the rest of us, Sirena announced, "I simply can't believe this. We are in the presence of underwater royalty, ladies. *Royalty!*" It must have been obvious that some of us were still clueless, because she went on to explain. "Esther Williams just about single-handedly popularized water ballet, which is what they used to call synchronized swimming. She was a huge movie star, and an amazing athlete—without her popularity and pioneering influence, synchronized swimming might never have become an Olympic sport! And for many of us who grew up watching her onscreen, she's part of the reason we became mermaids. You could say that, in a way, she was the spark that lit the fire beneath today's interest in all things mermaid."

Thanks a bunch, Esther, I thought.

"As a tribute to Zadie and Lenore, I'm switching up our post-siesta movie today," Sirena continued. "I'd planned to have us watch *Splash*, but we'll watch an Esther Williams movie instead!" She turned back to the two elderly ladies. "And did I hear you correctly? Do you have experience with choreography?"

Zadie nodded.

Sirena clasped her hands together beseechingly. "Would you be willing to help us out this week? Pretty please with mermaid glitter on top?"

"We were hoping you might ask," Zadie replied. "Isn't that right, Lenore?"

Lenore nodded again.

Sirena gave them a rapturous look. "Just think what a marketing hook we'll have! 'All-new mermaid revue, choreographed by Esther Williams's own protégées!' Every senior citizen on the Cape will be begging for a ticket!"

REALLY TRULY

I let the water close over my head and sank to the bottom of the pool. It was quiet down there, and sane.

Later, after breakfast—scrambled eggs, fresh fruit, and bagels with cream cheese and something called "lox," which turned out to be smoked salmon—we returned to the pool.

"Now that I feel confident in your swimming abilities, we're ready to try it with tails," Sirena told us. "It's time for your official mermaid training to begin, ladies!"

Excitement fizzed as everyone rushed to wiggle into their tails. Everyone except me. There was no rushing a shimmertail. Once again, I needed Delphine's help putting it on. I was the last one into the pool, slithering awkwardly across the deck to join Mackenzie and my friends, who were perched on the edge, swishing their flukes in the water.

"Group photo, ladies!" said Sirena, taking her cell phone out of a pocket in her swim cover-up. "Lean back on your elbows and lift those tails aloft—jaunty angle now, let's show them off! Smile and say—"

"Cheese?" I suggested.

"—seashells!"

Looking down the long row of multicolored tails sparkling in the morning sun, I had to admit we made a pretty sweet lineup.

"Wonderful!" Sirena gestured toward the water. "When you feel ready, hop on in. We'll stay down here at the shallow end to begin with. Please keep a grip on the edge for now. We're going to take this in baby steps."

I dangled my shimmertail in the pool, swishing its flukes and testing the resistance. I was used to swimming with my legs and feet close together—the dolphin kick was a staple on swim team, and the butterfly was my favorite stroke—but it was a completely different feeling having them encased in a heavy silicone tube.

Around me, my fellow aspiring mermaids began sliding in. Sirena watched the proceedings closely, standing poised with one of the long rescue hooks that Coach Maynard sometimes used to fish swim team members out when they accidentally swallowed a big mouthful of water and panicked. But Sirena was fairly small and some of the other guests—two of the Sand Dollar ladies in particular—were pretty large. If push came to shove, they might yank her right into the pool with them. I hoped I wouldn't have to try to put my junior lifeguarding skills to the test while wearing this heavy tail.

But nobody seemed to be panicking so far. Quite the opposite, in fact. All I could hear were shrieks of delight as the others tested out their tails for the first time. Mackenzie held on to the edge of the deck, flapping her flukes up and down behind her. She smiled up at me. "What are you waiting for?"

I shrugged. "Nothing." Scooting forward, I pushed myself in.

And sank instantly to the bottom of the pool.

CHAPTER 13

I thrashed around in a panic, struggling to heave the tail into a position that allowed me to stand. The water was only four feet deep, but it might as well have been forty. When the pool hook appeared beside me, I grabbed it and let myself be hauled up.

"I'm not so sure this is a good idea, Delphine," said Sirena when I emerged unharmed but flustered. "This may be beyond her abilities."

Beyond my abilities, my eye! I thought. I'd show her beyond my abilities.

Lovejoys are competitive. We can't help it; we just are.

Taking a deep breath, I let go of the hook, pushed off the wall, and launched myself into a streamline. Arms stretched out in front of me, I undulated back across the pool for several lengths, exactly the same way I'd done a few minutes earlier when Sirena tested my breath control. The tail was heavy, there was no doubt about that. I could feel the powerful resistance as I forced the flukes up and down, up and down through the water. But my legs were powerful too, their muscles honed from years of swim team practice.

Suddenly I felt a subtle shift as I found my groove. I was no longer fighting the shimmertail, and in a flash it went from enemy to ally, rocketing me forward with each dolphin kick. I shot to the surface and threw my arms overhead in the classic butterfly arm stroke, the shimmertail propelling me through the air faster and higher than I'd ever managed on my own before. I almost laughed out loud. So this was what flying felt like!

At the far end, I slapped my hands on the pool's edge, just the way I would during a race, rotated, then pushed off and swam back toward Sirena and the others.

Right before I reached them, I suddenly reversed into a backstroke position, whipped my tail up and out of the water, and smacked my flukes down as hard as I could.

My fellow aspiring mermaids squealed as a tsunami engulfed them.

"Really, Truly!" sputtered Sirena. "Was that necessary?"

Hayden glared at me. "Show-off."

Everyone else was laughing, though. Delphine grinned as she marked something down on her clipboard. "You have to admit that was quite an advanced move, Mom."

Sirena, who was mopping her face, grudgingly agreed. "I guess we don't need to worry about her abilities." She turned to the rest of the group. "That's quite enough tricks for one morning. I want to see laps now and plenty of them. Take it slow while you get used to swimming in a tail."

Sirena and Delphine put us through our paces for the next hour, alternating laps with stretches and basic ballet arm gestures. Nothing too strenuous, but I was definitely getting a workout, thanks to the heavy shimmertail.

"You've danced before, haven't you?" Delphine said, watching Cha Cha.

My friend smiled. "A bit."

"Her parents own a dance studio," Jasmine explained. "She doesn't just dance—she helps teach."

Sirena beamed. "We are just overflowing with talent this week! This is going be a standout revue. Definitely one of the academy's best, I can already tell." She looked at her watch. "Okay, ladies, let's take a break! We'll be back in the pool later this afternoon, and meanwhile, I'm going to give you a choice. You can stay in the water for another half hour with Zadie and Lenore, who are keen to share a few of their synchronized swimming moves, or you can enjoy a little free time before lunch."

The high school girls opted for free time. So did the Sand Dollar ladies. As Delphine headed for the kitchen, Sirena retreated to a seat by the cabana, as she referred to the shed where the pool supplies were stashed, and kept one eye on us and one on her cell phone. That left Mackenzie and

Cha Cha and Jasmine and me in the pool, along with Hayden and her mother.

If I'd ever thought synchronized swimming wasn't real swimming, I quickly learned otherwise. Zadie and Lenore started with a few basic moves. I already knew how to tread water, but they demonstrated how to do it invisibly, sculling our arms underwater with our elbows glued to our sides as we waved our flukes back and forth. It took a surprising amount of effort to stay afloat.

"Being a good synchronized swimmer takes the lung power of a long-distance runner, the leg strength of a water polo player, the grace and rhythm of a ballet dancer, and the muscle control of a gymnast," Zadie explained. "That's what Esther Williams always used to say."

Next, they had us try the ballet leg double position. Lying back in the water, we drew our knees in to our chests, then extended our legs straight up and waved our flukes in the air.

"See how I'm sculling underwater again to keep myself in place?" said Zadie.

We also tried the oyster, lying flat on our backs in the water and then closing up like clamshells—or oyster shells in this case—by bringing our legs and hands up and touching them together, then sinking down bottom first into the water.

"Good job!" said Zadie. "Now form a circle and try some of the moves in unison."

Swimming in a tail was a lot harder than the professional

REALLY TRULY

mermaids had made it look at the pirate museum. By the time Delphine rang the lunch gong, my legs were aching, and my arm and back muscles were sore from the constant sculling needed to counter the downward drag of the heavy shimmertail.

"This isn't mermaid academy; it's mermaid boot camp," I grumbled as we trooped back to our cabins to change.

At lunch, I nearly fell asleep in my clam chowder. My head was bobbing as Sirena outlined the rest of the day's packed schedule.

"And don't forget, we're all going to reveal our mermaid names tonight after dinner!" she told us. "Get busy on those backstories, ladies!"

Mackenzie and Cha Cha and Jasmine had to practically carry me back to Whelk for our siesta. I flopped onto my bunk as the three of them huddled together to work on their backstories. I was too tired to lift my head off the pillow, let alone lift a pen. They'd been swimming all morning in tails made of spandex and neoprene, not thirty pounds of silicone. I was out like a light in ten seconds flat.

I awoke with a start as Mackenzie shook my shoulder.

"Siesta is over, Truly!"

"Already?" I groaned. "We were supposed to have a Pumpkin Falls Private Eyes videoconference." I checked my phone. Sure enough, there was a whole string of text messages from the boys.

"We can do that later," my cousin said. "Hurry up! You'll miss the movie!"

I texted Calhoun to let him know the change of plans, then headed back to Mermaid HQ, where Sirena and Delphine had giant bowls of popcorn waiting for us in front of the big-screen TV.

"Which movie did you decide on?" Zadie asked Sirena.

"*Million Dollar Mermaid*, of course!"

Zadie laughed. "I figured you might choose that one." She patted the sofa next to her. "Come on, Lenore. This is going to be fun."

The movie was as cheesy as the rest of mermaid camp. Zadie was right, though—it was fun. It wasn't about a mermaid, but rather a real woman named Annette Kellerman who was a famous Australian swimmer a century ago. She had to wear leg braces as a kid, but overcame them by learning to swim. She went on to win all sorts of prizes before moving to America and becoming a star, performing in this giant aquarium theater in New York called the Hippodrome. I liked how feisty Annette was, sticking up for herself when she got in trouble with the law for wearing a one-piece bathing suit. That was considered scandalous back in 1907, when women were supposed to wear "bathing costumes" that looked like long dresses, or bloomers with stockings.

The best parts, though, were when Annette—Esther Williams—dove and swam. I could tell the minute I saw the muscles in her legs that she was a real athlete. Sirena had been right about that. Esther did her own stunts, and even without knowing much about synchronized swimming, I could appreciate the level of difficulty most of the dives and tricks took.

I had to admit that I liked the choreographed water ballet stuff, too, even if it was over the top Hollywood, with Esther almost always wearing full makeup and something sparkly.

"There we are!" yelled Zadie at one point, and Sirena immediately hit pause on the remote. Zadie sprang out of her seat and rushed to the TV screen, pointing to a circle of girls in gold swimsuits and matching caps who were emerging from the water on a platform. "That's us, right behind Esther!"

Sirena hit play again, and we watched as the swimmers all rose into the air, thanks to what Zadie explained was a hydraulic lift. Esther Williams was wearing a glittering gold bodysuit and matching crown for this scene, and Zadie and Lenore framed her like a pair of shiny gold bookends.

I glanced from the youthful onscreen images to the two wrinkled faces beaming at us from across the room. Would I look like that when I was their age, I wondered? On the other hand, if I could swim as well as they could when I was nearly ninety, who cared?

My favorite scenes were the ones filmed from above. As the swimmers' arms and legs moved in changing formations, they created a sort of human kaleidoscope, which was really cool to watch.

"Such precision! Such artistry!" cried Sirena, pausing the movie again a few minutes later when the camera zoomed in on Zadie and Lenore. The two of them were smiling big red-lipstick smiles and laughing as they were towed across the Hippodrome pool by an invisible underwater mechanism.

"That was our big close-up!" Zadie said. "And those smiles weren't fake—we were genuinely having fun. We thought we had the best job in the world!"

We all clapped after the grand finale, when the two of them were once again lifted out of the water on a platform with Esther Williams and a bunch of other swimmers, this time against a backdrop of fireworks that fizzed and flamed.

Zadie sighed with satisfaction. "Esther really knew how to make an entrance—and an exit."

"How come they don't make those kinds of movies anymore?" asked Cha Cha.

"Aqua-musicals, you mean?" said Zadie.

"There's an actual name for them?" Cha Cha's deep voice went up an octave.

"Oh yes. Aqua-ballet, aqua-musicals—they even named us in one of the films. We were billed as 'the Neptunettes' in *Neptune's Daughter*."

For some reason this struck Mackenzie as funny. She

started to laugh. "That could be your mermaid name, Truly—Neptunette!"

I gave her the stink eye. But she'd reminded me that I still needed to pick a name and a backstory. So far, I had nothing.

"Were you ever in the Olympics?" asked one of the girls from St. Louis.

Zadie shook her head. "No. By the time synchronized swimming became an Olympic sport in 1984, we were way too old. But they asked Esther to be an official commentator. She was wonderful! We watched together from my house that year, cheering her on."

Sirena stood up. "Ladies, you have about an hour of free time until our afternoon pool session. If anyone wants to make a trip to the Brewster Store, the van is available."

"Or you can walk," suggested Delphine. "It's less than half a mile from here."

My cousin and friends and I chose that option, and a few minutes later we were crunching down the shell-covered driveway toward the road.

"I'm going to live here when I grow up," Jasmine announced. "Cape Cod is so cool! I love being near the ocean."

Cha Cha shook her head. "Not me. New York City is where I want to be. It's the only place for a dancer. Well, that or San Francisco or London, maybe."

"I'm a Texan through and through," said Mackenzie firmly. "It's the Lone Star State for me. You too, right, Truly?"

I lifted a shoulder. I had no idea where I wanted to live when I grew up. I was still trying to get used to Pumpkin Falls.

Just as Jasmine had promised, there was a long counter at the Brewster Store where they served ice cream and fudge and penny candy. I looked around as we waited for our cones. The creaky wood floors and high ceilings and big windows reminded me a bit of our bookstore back home. The rest of it was similar to the Pumpkin Falls General Store, as Jasmine had said, except that instead of selling mostly practical everyday stuff like seed packets and tools, the Brewster Store was geared completely to tourists. The displays were crammed with postcards and souvenirs, sweatshirts and T-shirts and baseball caps with I LOVE CAPE COD on them, plus beach toys and knickknacks and that sort of thing.

"Hey, check it out!" Cha Cha pointed to a sign in the window:

BOOK SIGNING THURSDAY NIGHT!

AMANDA APPLETON, PHD, PRESENTS HER NEW BOOK—

SAGA OF A SHIP: THE LOST TREASURE OF THE WINDBORNE

REALLY TRULY

"Isn't the *Windborne* that wreck we learned about at the pirate museum?" she asked.

"Yeah," said Jasmine. "Let's tell Sirena. Maybe she can schedule a field trip."

Fine by me, I thought. Pirates were more interesting than mermaids any day of the week.

CHAPTER 14

By four o'clock, we were back in the pool.

"Lenore and I spent our siesta with Sirena, working up a routine for the revue," Zadie told us.

"We focused on simple moves that should be easy to learn and easy to perform," Sirena added, "but the girls"—it took me a moment to realize she was talking about Zadie and Lenore —"put them together in combinations that will add a little razzle-dazzle."

Razzle-dazzle? Did anyone actually use that term? Anyone except Sirena, that was? My eyes slid over to Mackenzie, but predictably, there was no answering smirk.

"And," Sirena continued, "we've got a killer finish that will really show off our mermaid queen."

I wasn't sure I liked the sound of that.

Hayden definitely didn't. I could tell by the look on her face.

"You'll probably recognize a few of the moves," said Zadie. "It's a bit of a nod to *Million Dollar Mermaid*—but without the fancy special effects."

"Unless you call sparklers special effects," said Delphine.

Sirena beamed at Zadie and Lenore. "I can't thank you two enough!" she gushed. "This is going to be our best revue ever! I'm going to call it *A Tribute to Esther Williams*. Delphine, you can help me make up flyers tonight, and we'll distribute them around town tomorrow."

Zadie had us all take seats on the edge of the pool opposite the bleachers while Sirena and Delphine headed for the cabana. They emerged a moment later with a boom box and a whiteboard on an easel. Zadie wrote DECK WORK on the whiteboard.

"We're going to break it down into individual positions and strokes," she told us. "Then we'll work on transitions—the movements that connect everything into a routine. But first we're going to start with some deck work."

"Think of deck work as a preshow routine," Sirena added. "You'll perform this part right where you're sitting now, before you get in the water."

Zadie nodded at Delphine, who fiddled with the boom box. A moment later, music wafted from its tinny speakers.

"As the lights go up and the music starts," said Zadie, "you'll all be sitting along the edge of the pool just like you are now, but with your backs to the bleachers and your knees drawn up to your chins. Would you try this, please, ladies?"

We pulled our tails out of the water and swiveled around obediently.

"Sirena? Delphine? Can you see the tails?"

Sirena and her daughter, who had taken seats in the bleachers, both shook their heads.

"Now, I'll be positioned here at the end of the row"—Zadie scampered down to where Jasmine was sitting—"and at my signal, Delphine is going to switch on the spotlight. She'll point it at each of you, one by one. When the light hits you, I want you to turn around, lean back on your elbows, kick your tail up into the air, and hold it for the count of five. Lenore? Would you please demonstrate?"

Lenore did.

"Make the most of it, ladies," said Sirena, as Lenore leaned back and kicked her tail up into the air. "This is your close-up, as they call it in Hollywood!"

"Absolutely!" Zadie agreed. "Flaunt those flukes, smile and wave at the audience, show off a little. After you count to five, you'll sit up and drop your tail in the water. Give it a good splash when you do." She pointed at Lenore, who obediently dropped and splashed. "After the tail drop, the spotlight will move on to the next mermaid. Everyone will get their moment to shine. All except you, Truly. Our mermaid queen will be safely hidden in the cabana until closer to the grand finale."

Hayden looked pleased for the first time all day.

REALLY TRULY

It was our turn next. Even though I'd be waiting in the wings—well, the cabana—during the opening number, Zadie had me practice with them anyway. She went down the row, tapping each of us on the shoulder to represent the spotlight. We spun around one by one to face the bleachers, leaned back and hoisted our tails into the air and waved them around for the count of five, then sat up and dropped our tails into the pool.

The next move involved diving into the water like a row of dominoes. Once again, Lenore demonstrated as Zadie walked us through it.

"After the final tail drops, the lights will come up, and on my cue, it's arms up, palms together"—Lenore put her arms over her head and pressed her palms together—"and you'll peel off one by one and dive into the water from where you're sitting, just like we did in *Million Dollar Mermaid*. And don't forget that big smile!"

Lenore dove neatly into the pool, smiling for all she was worth. Zadie had us run through the domino dive a few times, and then it was time to connect the moves together.

"What do you think, Sirena?" asked Zadie when we were done.

"I think we have ourselves a genuine school of mermaids!" Sirena replied, doing a little victory shimmy. Her red curls shimmied happily too.

"Excellent work, ladies!" said Zadie. "That's our deck work, done and dusted."

Sirena told us we'd learn the next part of the routine tomorrow, and suggested we swim laps while Delphine got dinner ready.

A few lengths of the pool later, Mackenzie surfaced beside me. "This is great, isn't it?"

I grunted.

"Mermaid camp—I mean mermaid *academy*—is even better than I thought it would be. I love it here, don't you?"

If anyone had told me a few days ago that I'd find myself in a pool on Cape Cod, wearing a mermaid tail and learning synchronized swimming moves from a pair of elderly ladies, I'd have told them they were crazy.

What was crazier was the fact that Mackenzie was right—it was better than I thought it would be. I was actually starting to enjoy myself. At this rate, I might not need Aunt True to come rescue me.

"It's okay, I guess."

Mackenzie laughed. "C'mon, Truly! Admit it—you're having fun."

I grinned at her. "Yeah," I admitted. "I'm having fun."

And then I flipped over onto my back and splashed her with my shimmertail.

CHAPTER 15

"Ladies!" Sirena clinked her knife against her glass to get our attention. Dinner had been another Delphine special—crab cakes, salad, and corn on the cob—and rumor had it that it would be followed by something called Mermaid Chip Cookies, which sounded intriguing. "Let's take a quick break and then gather at Mermaid Crossing for dessert, and the big reveal of your mermaid names!"

I stiffened. I'd completely forgotten to pick one!

"I'm eager to hear your backstories, too," Sirena continued. "See you in ten minutes!"

I hadn't made a backstory up either! I raced back to Whelk, glancing up at the sign over the door as I entered our cabin.

Hmm, I thought. Whelkina?

No. That was worse than Shellina. I'd have to come up with something better.

Mackenzie and Cha Cha and Jasmine were right on my

heels. The three of them huddled on Mackenzie's bunk, discussing something in low murmurs as I crossed to mine. I started hunting for the handout that Sirena had given us on our first day. I finally found it wadded up under my bed. Uncrumpling it, I scanned the list. No, no, and no. Each of the suggested names sounded worse than the one preceding it.

"It's time to go, Truly!" said my cousin a few minutes later, heading for the door as the gong sounded back at Mermaid HQ.

"I'll be there in a sec. Save me a seat." I scanned the handout again, starting to panic. None of the names were something I wanted to be stuck with all week. Harbor? Please. Echo? Jewel? Stormy? They sounded like something Belinda Winchester would name her kittens. There had to be *something* decent I could call myself! I looked frantically around the room for inspiration.

My gaze fell on the stack of presents I'd bought for my family at the pirate museum. The title on the spine of the book I'd picked out for Lauren caught my eye: *The Pirate Queen*. I grabbed it and flipped through the pages. The story looked interesting. It was about an Irish woman named Grania O'Malley, whose exploits on the high seas back in the 1500s rocked the Elizabethan world.

"Grania." I repeated the name aloud slowly. I could live with Grania.

Slamming the book shut, I ran out the door, spinning

my backstory as I sprinted toward Mermaid Crossing. I flung myself onto one of the sofas beside Mackenzie just as Hayden—make that *Shellina*—began to speak.

Hayden droned on for at least five minutes about her stupid fishy alter ego. We learned that Shellina's favorite color was the deep green of emeralds, and that her favorite hobby was collecting shells (of course), and that she had a pet hermit crab named Crabby. My smile grew broader with each passing minute. I couldn't wait to tell Hatcher about this!

Hayden probably would have gone on for a lot longer, but Sirena finally cut her short. "Thank you, Shellina, for the delightful word-picture you've painted for us," she said smoothly. "Now, how about you, Mrs. Drake?"

Hayden's mother kept it short and sweet. "My name is Coralina. I, too, live in Tritonia, where I serve the princess Shellina." This sounded pretty true to life. Princess Hayden clearly had her mother wrapped around her little finger.

It was Zadie's turn next.

"I'm Isla, which is Spanish for 'island,'" Zadie announced. She gestured to Lenore. "And this is Merissa, which means 'of the sea.'"

"Beautiful names," said Sirena, nodding in approval. "Two of my favorites."

Zadie had come up with a pretty good backstory about a pair of mermaids who were captured and forced to perform in an underwater circus—an "aqua-circus," as she called it.

One by one, everyone shared their chosen names and backstories. The four high school girls from St. Louis had picked Chantal, Morwenna, Genevieve, and Bijoux. Morwenna, who was a really good artist, had drawn a detailed map of the undersea realm where they lived, and we all oohed and aahed over that. The four ladies in Sand Dollar introduced themselves as Rilla, Avalon, Oceana, and Bahari, which we learned was Swahili for "ocean." Some of their stories were pretty good, too—especially Bahari's. She'd invented this whole African legend about an underwater world populated by slaves rescued from ships heading to the New World. They'd been freed by King Triton, who turned them into mermaids and mermen.

Then it was our cabin's turn.

"I'm Nixie," said Cha Cha. "That's German for 'little water sprite.'"

Sirena beamed. "Very appropriate for you, Cha Cha. Good choice."

"This is my twin sister Pixie," Cha Cha continued, pointing at Jasmine. "We live in a cave whose walls are lined with sparkling gems."

I wondered if that idea was inspired by the Starlite Dance Studio, whose walls may not have held sparkling gems, but certainly held twinkle lights.

"Nixie and I were orphaned in a storm when we were just mer-babies," Jasmine said, picking up the thread of the story.

REALLY TRULY

"Fortunately, we were adopted by a dolphin, who taught us how to dive and play and who caught fish for us to eat. And then one day, we happened to meet—"

"Me, Neptunette!" said Mackenzie, with a flash of jazz hands. "I'm their best friend."

So that's what the three of them had been working on back in our cabin! I tried not to feel left out as they giggled their way through their joint backstory.

Sirena arched an eyebrow at my cousin when they finished. "Really? You're going with Neptunette?"

Mackenzie nodded. "As a tribute to Zadie and Lenore, who are awesome."

Zadie jumped up off the sofa, ran over to where we were sitting, and kissed my cousin on both cheeks. "And we think you are awesome too, Miss Neptunette." She made a sweeping gesture that encompassed the entire room. "In fact, we think you are *all* awesome, don't we, Lenore—I mean Merissa?"

As usual, Lenore just nodded and smiled.

Finally, it was my turn. *Last but no way am I gonna be least*, I thought, my Lovejoy competitive spirit kicking in. "I'm Grania," I began in a low and mysterious voice.

"Interesting," said Sirena. "We've never had a Grania before, have we, Delphine?"

Delphine shook her head.

I plunged ahead, channeling Aunt True at our bookshop's story time, and Augustus Wilde at one of his dramatic readings, and Gramps, who'd told the best bedtime stories in the world when we Lovejoy kids were little.

"They called me the pirate queen, back when I had land legs," I continued. "I ruled the Emerald Isle, roving the high seas and plundering all ships that crossed my path. But I ran afoul of the law. They chased me from Dublin to Dover, until I did the only thing I could. I sailed to—" I paused. Sailed to where? My gaze fell on the MERMAID CROSSING sign, and I continued, "Mermaid Bay, a place of dark magic, where I called on all the gods of the watery deep to aid me in my time of peril." This was all completely made up, of course. The real Grania O'Malley had done no such thing. But my audience obviously didn't know that. They were hanging on my every word. Even Hayden. "A great wave sprang up, as if from nowhere, and swept me off my ship before I could be caught and punished for my dark deeds. I tumbled down, down, down, deep beneath the surface of the sea, where King Triton awaited me." I thought about the mosaic at the bottom of the pool. "He touched me with his trident, and suddenly I could breathe underwater! Dolphins came and transported me to a castle, and a bed made of soft seaweed, and when I awoke, I had this fish tail you see before you." I finished with a sweeping gesture like Zadie's, pointing at my legs.

The room burst into enthusiastic applause.

"Now *that's* a backstory!" said Delphine, which earned me a dose of stink eye from Hayden.

REALLY TRULY

The Mermaid Chip Cookies were just as good as they sounded, studded with pastel M&M's and sprinkled with sea salt. When it was time to head back to our cabins for bed, I grabbed a couple of extras when nobody was looking and stuffed them into my pocket.

"Should we try to get ahold of the guys?" I asked when we got back to Whelk.

Mackenzie frowned. "It's kind of late."

"Yeah, but we promised." I punched in Calhoun's number on the videoconferencing app. Scooter's face was the one that appeared on my cell phone screen, though.

"Where have you guys been?" he demanded, scowling. "We've been waiting for hours! Didn't you get our texts?"

"We've been kind of busy."

"Doing what?"

I pulled a cookie from my pocket. "Eating delicious Mermaid Chip Cookies, for one thing!" I took a long, slow, exaggerated bite, just to torture him.

"Being mermaids is hard work," Jasmine explained. "It's not like we're just sitting around on our, uh, tails. We have a lot of stuff we have to do. We're going to be starring in a show later this week."

Scooter's scowl softened into a sly smile. "Wish we could see that!"

Calhoun's face appeared beside Scooter's. "Hey!"

I smiled at him. "Hey back!"

"We may have some leads," he told us.

I paused midbite. "Seriously? That's great!"

"Lucas knew what he was doing with those hashtags. It seems like just about everybody who was at the race that day took pictures and posted them on social media. There's this one guy in particular—show them, Lucas."

Lucas's pale hand shot into view, holding his phone up for us.

"Um, who exactly are we looking for?" asked Cha Cha.

"See the old guy in the Grateful Dead T-shirt and aviator sunglasses?"

"By the bandstand?" Mackenzie squinted at the screen.

"Yeah. He's the guy I saw hanging out near the diner, too," said Lucas. "He shows up in a bunch of the pictures before the race, and then he disappears."

I chewed on that bit of information. "Does that automatically make him a suspect, though? Maybe he was just passing through."

"Just passing through near the *bandstand*? He's right there when Belinda and Augustus are fooling around with the trophy, and he's right there when they put it back in the paper bag under the podium. Then he vanishes. Definitely suspicious."

Lucas had a point.

"So what now?" Jasmine wanted to know.

"Now we see if anyone knows him," Calhoun told her. "We're going to start asking around."

REALLY TRULY

"Excellent work, guys," I said. "I wish we were there to help you."

"No you don't," said Scooter, scowling again. "You'd rather be right where you are, eating Mermaid Chip Cookies without us."

I smiled and took another bite. And then I hung up.

CHAPTER 16

At breakfast the next morning, a FedEx truck pulled into the driveway just as we were starting in on big steaming bowls of Delphine's deluxe oatmeal. Everyone watched with interest as the driver strode up the front path carrying a package. Sirena went to the door to meet him.

"It's for you, Truly," she told me a moment later, setting the package down on the sideboard beside a platter of homemade raspberry rhubarb muffins. I started to get up, but she held up her hand. "Breakfast first! Most important meal of the day for mermaids."

I sighed and sat back down. "Yes, ma'am."

"You need lots of fuel, ladies. We have a busy day ahead. Zadie and Lenore and I have scheduled extra pool time. We have a lot to learn before the revue this weekend."

When Sirena finally excused us from the table, I bolted for

REALLY TRULY

the sideboard and grabbed my package. I looked at the return address label. It was from Aunt True!

"See you all poolside in five minutes!" said Sirena. "Move your tails, mermaids!"

I dashed down the path to Whelk, where I flung myself on my bunk and tore the wrapping off the package. Inside, a big envelope with my name written on it in my aunt's bold handwriting was waiting. I pulled out a card featuring an oval picture of a tranquil forest scene—a stand of majestic redwood trees reflected in a pool of water. *Tall timber,* I thought instantly, and smiled. Aunt True knew how to make a point. A line of her crisp handwriting wound around the oval's edge: *To the Unsinkable Truly Lovejoy, my favorite eldest niece, who really truly knows how to make the best of everything.* Inside, she'd written, *Don't ever be afraid to stand out in a crowd. (Even if it's a crowd of mermaids!)*

Aunt True was the best!

I propped the card up on my bedside table and turned my attention to the rest of box's contents. My aunt had sent maple sugar candy, too! Before I could rummage any further, though, my cousin and friends burst in.

"Where's your bathing suit?" said Mackenzie. "Hurry up—we're due at the pool."

My care package would have to wait.

The rest of the day was a lot like the day before, except that we skipped siesta after lunch in order to squeeze in as much pool time as possible. We paused midafternoon for a snack (homemade energy bars, courtesy of Delphine) and another Esther Williams movie—*Easy to Love* this time, which had more over-the-top stunts, including Esther doing water-ski jumps and diving from a helicopter. Actually, her stunt double did that one.

"The helicopter scene is the only one she ever used a stuntwoman for," Zadie told us. "And wisely so. We found out later that she was pregnant at the time."

For dinner, Delphine whipped up an amazing soup she called "cioppino," which was full of big chunks of fish, along with scallops and shrimp and clams and mussels. She served it with crusty homemade bread.

"Mermaids have excellent manners," Sirena told us, "but dipping your bread in the cioppino is allowed."

As we were finishing, Sirena tapped her glass. "You worked very hard today, and Delphine and I are proud of all of you. As a reward for your efforts, we're rearranging our evening schedule slightly. Instead of Mer-mopoly and the other games we had planned, we're moving up one of the academy's most anticipated activities—Bling Night!"

A chorus of cheers filled the dining room. I looked over at Mackenzie and my friends. They were clearly as clueless as I was.

"Mermaids love bling," Sirena continued, trotting out

another of her fake mermaid facts. She reached into a drawer in the sideboard behind her and pulled out several long sparkly necklaces. She draped them over her head and added a trio of bracelets and half a dozen rings. The result was blinding. "How many of you brought yours with you?"

Every hand around the dining table flew up except ours.

"We didn't know we were supposed to," said Jasmine.

"It was right there in the brochure," scoffed Hayden.

Sirena gave her a warning glance. "Not to worry. You girls were last-minute additions, after all. You'll be making your own tonight! Let's meet at Mermaid Crossing in five minutes."

While our fellow aspiring mermaids scattered to retrieve their bling, Mackenzie and Cha Cha and Jasmine and I helped Delphine carry dessert out to the porch.

Mackenzie looked askance at the bowl full of what looked like green shaving cream that Delphine handed to her. "What *is* this?"

Delphine laughed. "Just whipped cream with a little food coloring in it."

Dessert was something she called "Fruit of the Sea," which was actually fresh strawberries topped with a cloud of the pale green whipped cream. It looked a little weird, but it tasted great. Mackenzie and I both had two helpings.

"Delphine always makes this for Bling Night," said Sirena happily, scooping a little more out of the bowl too. "Now, ladies, tonight is the night you've all been waiting for! You're going to make bling to your heart's content."

My heart was pretty content being bling free, I thought, watching as Delphine placed a large tray on the coffee table in front of us. It was piled high with seashells, fake gems, metallic tassels, glitter, and the like—all the kinds of stuff that I avoided like the plague in real life. Crafts were another item on the long list of things I wasn't good at. But then, mermaid camp wasn't real life, was it? I sighed and reached for a glue gun. The swimming part had turned out to be not so bad. Maybe this would be fun too.

I was just finishing up stringing my second strand of glitter-encrusted seashells when my cell phone vibrated. I pulled it from the pocket of my shorts. It was Hatcher!

"I'll be right back," I told the group, and headed for the powder room off the kitchen. Closing the door behind me, I put my phone to my ear. "Hey!"

"Hey yourself!" my brother replied. "I got your text—sorry I didn't have a chance to answer sooner. You know how wrestling camp goes."

"Yep." Exactly the same as swimming camp, and every other athletic camp on the planet. Eat. Sleep. Practice. Repeat.

We chatted for a few minutes. Aunt True was right about mermaid camp providing great stories. I got Hatcher laughing so hard he almost choked when I told him about Shellina and

REALLY TRULY

Skipper Dee and Sirena and her endless list of mermaid rules and sayings.

"Oops, gotta go," he said finally. "Coach is making us watch videos from practice today. See you back in Pumpkin Falls!"

"See you!"

We hung up, and I went back out to the porch to finish my bling.

Later, before she dismissed us for the evening, Sirena made an announcement.

"We have a special field trip planned for you tomorrow morning before breakfast!" she told us. "Instead of meeting by the pool, please meet in the parking lot at six thirty a.m. sharp. Wear your bathing suits and bring your towels and tails."

This didn't sound good. Especially the tails part. Was she planning to drag us out in public somewhere?

"And, ladies, don't stay up too late this time! I can promise you that this is a trip you won't want to miss. Remember, mermaids need their—"

"—beauty rest!" we all chorused.

Back in the cabin, Mackenzie and Cha Cha and Jasmine and I made another video call to the rest of the Pumpkin Falls Private Eyes. I sorted through the remainder of my care package while we chatted, pulling out a T-shirt with WELL-BEHAVED WOMEN SELDOM MAKE HISTORY on it, a new sudoku book, a stash of my favorite candy bars, a double strand of peacock blue and green glass beads that I recognized from our latest sideline shipment—more bling!—and the latest issue of *Bird Watcher's Digest* magazine.

"Pay attention," Scooter said irritably, watching as I flipped through it. "This is important."

"I'm listening," I replied, and pulled a pair of purple wool socks from the box. I frowned. What was Aunt True thinking? It was July! Then I saw the little note pinned to them. Belinda had knitted them for me.

At least she hadn't sent me a kitten, I thought. But she had included a picture of one, a really cute little gray kitten with a white tip on his tail, like he'd dipped it in paint. On the back she'd scribbled *I've named this little fellow Fog. He's the perfect mer-kitten, and he's up for adoption! Tell your mermaid friends!* Like Aunt True, Belinda had a flair for marketing. Unlike Aunt True, Belinda focused solely on her foster kittens.

"We've had some luck following up on the Grateful Dead guy," Scooter said, still glaring at me. "Lucas's mother remembers seeing him at Lou's that morning when he stopped in for coffee and a donut."

"And Mr. Henry is almost certain he spotted him heading for his car right before the award ceremony," Lucas added. "He remembers because he says the guy's car was awesome, a 1957 Chevy or something."

At the bottom of my care package was a trio of books. I lifted them out and examined the covers, frowning. Aunt True had gone full mermaid on me. There was a copy of *The Little Mermaid* (a sticky note on the cover assured me that this was the original fairy tale by Hans Christian Andersen, and that I'd like it much better than the movie) and something called *The Mermaid Handbook*. Lots of illustrations, gilt edges—I figured Mackenzie would love that one. The third book, at least, looked like something I might want to read.

"Check it out!" I said to my cabin-mates, holding up *Saga of a Ship: The Lost Treasure of the Windborne*. "This is that book we saw at the Brewster Store! The one whose author is doing a book signing tomorrow night."

"Truly!" My head snapped up. It was Calhoun. "Could you please put that down and pay attention?"

"Sorry," I replied meekly.

"We also have some new suspects, thanks to the crowd-sourcing."

"Really?" said Mackenzie. "That's great! Way to go, Lucas!"

Lucas gave her a shy smile.

"Take a look at this one," said Scooter, holding up the first picture for us to see. It was out of focus, but if I squinted I could just make out what was written on the suspect's baseball cap: DON'T MESS WITH TEXAS.

"Um," I began as Mackenzie blurted, "That's our Uncle Rooster!"

Lucas looked crestfallen.

"It's okay," she assured him. "It's still really good detective work."

Scooter showed us the other two pictures, both taken on the morning of the race. One was of a middle-aged woman wearing a Red Sox baseball cap. She was setting up a lawn chair on the village green and appeared to be all by herself. The other was of a pair of teenage boys about Danny's age who were lounging on the steps of the gazebo.

"Definitely suspicious," said Cha Cha.

"That's what we thought," said Calhoun. "We've asked around a little bit, but so far, nothing."

"Keep at it," I told them. "We're with you in spirit."

"Talk to you guys again tomorrow night?" asked Scooter, with a hopeful glance at my cousin.

I held up *Saga of a Ship*. "We might be at a book signing. How about you text us if you get any more new leads or learn anything about our suspects?"

After we hung up, Mackenzie reached over for the book I was still holding. "Can I take a look?"

I passed it to her. Cha Cha scooted closer. Jasmine climbed up onto her bunk and leaned over the edge, her long dark hair trailing down like seaweed.

"Looks kind of interesting," my cousin said, riffling through the pages.

"It's long, though," added Jasmine, yawning. "And

REALLY TRULY

there aren't many pictures." She reached out and fingered the strand of beads I'd looped around my neck. "Ooo, pretty!"

"Mermaids love bling," I deadpanned, and they all laughed.

"So are you really going to read a giant book about pirates?" asked Mackenzie.

I shrugged. "They're more interesting than mermaids. They were real, for one thing."

I shared my maple sugar candy with them, and the three of us talked for a while, and then it was time for bed.

"Night, Pixie. Night, Nixie!" Mackenzie called softly from across the room. "Night, Grania!"

"Night, Neptunette!" I called back, stifling a giggle.

There was an echoing giggle from Cha Cha's bunk, which got Jasmine going, and pretty soon we were all giggling.

"It's not that funny, you guys!" Mackenzie protested, but she was laughing too.

"Yes it is," I told her, which set us all off again.

Our giggle fit finally subsided, and the room grew quiet. Propping myself up with my pillow, I switched on the flashlight app on my cell phone and opened *Saga of a Ship*. I leafed through a few pages, then turned to the index and ran my finger idly down the entries. Something caught my eye under the listings for *C: Cherry Island, p. 87.*

I frowned. There was a Cherry Island on Lake Lovejoy.

The book couldn't be referring to that, though, could it? For one thing, Cherry Island was only our island's nickname. Its real name, the one that appeared on maps, was MacPherson's Island. Only locals called it Cherry Island. Curious, I turned to page eighty-seven and hunted until I found the reference: *Rumors persisted well into the 1800s about one of the survivors of the* Windborne. *It was said that he fled with his share of the treasure and buried it in a place called Cherry Island, where it has remained undiscovered to this day."*

I put the book down thoughtfully, then reached for my cell phone. CHERRY ISLAND'S REAL NAME IS MACPHERSON'S ISLAND, RIGHT?

A few seconds later my phone vibrated. PRETTY SURE, Hatcher texted back. WHY ARE YOU STILL UP? MERMAIDS NEED THEIR BEAUTY REST.

I smiled. I'M NOT A MERMAID, I'M GRANIA THE PIRATE.

WHAT?? DID YOU GET A PART??

HUH?

THE PLAY, DUH.

He thought I was talking about *The Pirates of Penzance.*

NO, I texted back. I DIDN'T TRY OUT, REMEMBER?

"Truly, turn that thing off, you're keeping us all awake," Mackenzie mumbled.

GOTTA GO, I texted. SURROUNDED BY CRABBY MERMAIDS. NIGHT!

NIGHT!

REALLY TRULY

I switched off my phone and lay there in my bunk in the dark, staring up at the bottom of Jasmine's mattress. *Saga of a Ship* had to be referring to a different Cherry Island. It couldn't possibly be our Cherry Island.

Pirates in Pumpkin Falls? Preposterous!

CHAPTER 17

I awoke at the crack of dawn the next morning and lay there with my eyes half-shut, listening to the low, soothing coo of a mourning dove. Above it floated the flutelike whistle of a Baltimore oriole, its song punctuated in turn by the insistent call of a cardinal. I smiled. The dawn chorus was in full swing. I heard a robin's refrain—*cheerily, cheer up, cheer up, cheerily, cheer up!*—and remembered how, when I was little and Gramps was trying to get me to wake up, he'd fooled me into thinking the bird was actually calling to me: *Truly, get up, get up, Truly, get up!*

Which I might as well do, I thought, throwing back the covers. There was time to squeeze in a little bird-watching before we left on Sirena's "mystery trip." I pulled on my bathing suit, then dressed in shorts and a T-shirt, grabbed my binoculars, and slipped out the cabin door. My flip-flops were where I'd left them on the front steps last night. As I slid my

REALLY TRULY

feet into them, I glanced toward the pool. An early-morning mist hovered over the water.

It looked irresistible.

Never swim alone, Sirena had said. It was one of her top ten Mermaid Commandments. I hesitated, torn. It wasn't like I needed a buddy—I was on swim team, for Pete's sake. Plus, I could be in and out before anyone else was even up. Nobody would ever know.

A moment later I was skimming over the grass. I couldn't help myself—the gleaming water drew me like a magnet.

When I reached the edge of the pool, though, I stopped short. Somebody had beaten me to it. Two somebodies, in fact.

"Truly!" said Zadie, beckoning to me. "I mean Grania—come on in and join us."

I gaped. "But—"

She gave me an impish grin. "Skinny-dipping is good for the soul. Isn't that right, Lenore?"

Lenore nodded. I quickly covered my eyes as she did a surface dive. "Um, no thanks."

"Suit yourself. Or not, as the case may be!" Zadie laughed and paddled away.

A bird walk it was, then, I thought, veering back toward the driveway. As I passed the hammock, though, I suddenly changed my mind. Switching directions, I detoured to Whelk and slipped inside, where I retrieved the book about the *Windborne* that Aunt True had sent. Then I headed to the hammock to read.

Twenty minutes later, I sat up so fast the hammock flipped over and I went sprawling onto the grass. Scrambling to my feet, I ran back to Whelk and burst through the door.

"Hey, guys, wake up!"

Jasmine groaned. Mackenzie buried her head under her pillow.

"Go away," growled Cha Cha.

"Seriously, you have to hear this!"

Mackenzie lifted a corner of the pillow and peered out at me. "Hear what?"

"It's from the book Aunt True sent!"

"Which one?"

"*Saga of a Ship*!"

"It's too early!" Jasmine protested, as Cha Cha let out another low growl.

"I mean it—this is big stuff! I think one of my ancestors was a pirate!"

"Oh for heaven's sake, you have pirates on the brain," said Mackenzie in disgust. She rolled over, pulling the pillow back over her head.

I pried it away, thrusting the book under her nose and stabbing my finger at the page. "Look, it's right here in black and white!"

She glared at me resentfully. "I'm *sleeping*, Truly."

"Right here, see? It's talking about one of the pirates who survived the shipwreck of the *Windborne*—the one who didn't get caught."

"Dandy Dan?" Jasmine mumbled.

"That's the one! It says that he was described by his shipmates as 'a man most generous of beak.'"

My cousin stared at me blankly.

"*Beak*. You know, nose?"

"What the heck are you talking about?"

"He had a *big nose!*"

"So?"

"So think about it—the Lovejoy *proboscis*?" Mackenzie looked at me like I'd completely lost my mind. "Nathaniel *Daniel*—"

"—looks like a spaniel," she concluded automatically.

"Exactly! My ancestor! You've seen his portrait—his nose is enormous! He's a man 'most generous of beak'!"

The lump in the bunk that was Cha Cha gave a raspy laugh. "Are you kidding me?"

Mackenzie sat up and threw her pillow at me. "You woke us up for *that*? Do you know how many people in this world have big noses, Truly?"

"A lot, that's how many!" said Jasmine. "It's just a coincidence."

"Yeah, but c'mon, guys, think about it—don't you think it's a little too many coincidences? It's not just the big nose, it's the name—Dandy *Dan*. Nathaniel *Daniel*. And there's more." As I explained about Cherry Island, my cousin and friends fell silent.

"It's still probably just a coincidence," Jasmine said finally.

"And even if it were true," said Cha Cha, "how would you ever find out for sure? It's been a secret all these years."

"So was the Underground Railroad hiding spot, and the original Truly's diary, and Professor Rusty's letters to Aunt True," I pointed out.

"Yeah, but we found all those by accident," Cha Cha continued. "The *Windborne* sank three hundred years ago, and people have been trying to solve the mystery of the pirate treasure ever since. And not just any people—really *smart* people. Historians and real-live treasure hunters, like the guy who founded the pirate museum."

Mackenzie nodded, pointing to the book. "The author has a PhD, remember?"

"We're smart too!" I protested. I couldn't believe they couldn't see what was right in front of their eyes.

Jasmine sat up. "Okay, so let's say it isn't a coincidence. Where do we even start?"

I waved the book at them. "We could start by talking to Amanda Appleton at her book signing tonight."

Mackenzie looked doubtful. "What if she doesn't want to talk to a bunch of kids?"

REALLY TRULY

"Authors always want to talk to potential readers," I told them. "Trust me. We've got to talk to this lady. She may know a bunch more than what she put in her book."

While my cousin and friends got dressed, I sat on my bunk and stared at the cover of *Saga of a Ship*. I thought about the portrait of Nathaniel Daniel Lovejoy on our living room wall back home in Pumpkin Falls. Could my distinguished ancestor really have sailed under the black flag?

If Nathaniel Daniel had actually been Dandy Dan, what made him decide to give up his life of crime and become a model citizen? One who founded a college and paid for the Paul Revere bell on our church? Facing the prospect of a public trial and hanging, I supposed it would have been a smart move, heading to a small town in the foothills of the White Mountains, far away from the sea. What better place to hide than in tiny landlocked Pumpkin Falls? No one would think of looking for a pirate there.

I thought of Nathaniel Daniel's wife, Prudence. She looked so prim and proper in her portrait, the very image of a perfect New England housewife—certainly not like someone who would marry a pirate or approve of him spending his ill-gotten gains. Had she known about her husband's wicked past? If he'd even had a wicked past, that was.

I had so many questions!

I wondered if any of my other relatives knew about Dandy

Dan, the pirate "most generous of beak." Was there a reason that Aunt True had sent me this particular book? Was she in on the secret? Was this some big skeleton in the Lovejoy closet that everyone had taken pains over the centuries to hide?

I needed to talk to Aunt True again.

CHAPTER 18

Talking to my aunt was going to have to wait, though.

"No shell phones today," Sirena announced as we gathered as directed at the minivans a short while later. She held out a basket. "It's time to unplug."

Mackenzie clutched her phone, horrified. "Is she kidding?" she whispered to me.

"I don't think so," I whispered back.

She wasn't. Sirena circulated among us, collecting "shell phones." Mackenzie wasn't the only one who was reluctant to part with her hers. Hayden looked equally appalled, as did the girls from St. Louis.

"You will thank me for this later, ladies, I promise," Sirena reassured us. "This is an exercise that all of our classes here at the academy find instructive and restorative. Just imagine—an entire day disconnected from the world, recharging body and soul!" She struck a dramatic pose, her mane of red corkscrew curls looking as if they'd just been plugged into an outlet and were recharging too. "And we're going to start our restorative morning by plunging into the silent world beneath the sea."

"You're taking us to the beach?" squealed Hayden.

"Indeed I am! Now that you are all comfortable swimming in your tails, it's time for me to release my mermaids into the wild. I shall take you to the ocean and set you all free!" She struck another pose, lifting her hands toward the sky. Delphine tapped her watch discreetly, and Sirena dropped her hands and motioned us toward the minivans. "Ladies, your chariots await! Time and tide wait for no man—and no mermaids."

As everyone loaded up their tails and towels, my cousin and friends and I told Sirena about the book signing.

"Hmmm. We have a pretty full slate for this evening. It's Sea Siren Night."

I gave her a blank look.

"It's an opportunity for the musically inclined to show off their vocal talent as we learn some sea shanties," Sirena explained.

Singing? I thought in dismay. *She's talking about singing?*

Noting my expression, she continued, "However, we do like to support community events, and a trip to the Brewster Store would give me a chance to talk to the owner about publicizing our revue. I'm sure she'd be thrilled to meet Zadie and Lenore—I happen to know she's a big Esther Williams fan."

Sirena took a quick vote. Half were in favor of Sea Siren

REALLY TRULY

Night, and the other half, including Mackenzie and Cha Cha and Jasmine and me, voted for the book signing.

"Very well then," said Sirena. "We'll do both. Delphine, you can manage Sea Siren Night without me, right?"

"Sure, Mom. No problem."

"We'll try and be back in time for dessert. I know you're planning something special."

I perked up at that, although I couldn't imagine how Delphine could top Mermaid Chip Cookies.

Sirena made a right turn out of the driveway, away from the Brewster Store. "This is Breakwater Road," she told us. "It leads to the breakwater, or jetty—sort of a wall of rocks that juts out into the water, creating a sheltered cove. You'll see when we get there."

Jasmine gazed out the window as we drove and gave a contented sigh. "The houses are all so pretty!"

Cape Cod was definitely Jasmine's happy place.

"Which house would you guys pick if you had to choose?" asked Mackenzie. This was one of our favorite games. The two of us had ben selecting our future fantasy homes since we were little.

Jasmine and Cha Cha joined in with gusto. Jasmine chose a huge colonial-style house that looked like Gramps and Lola's. Mackenzie did the same. Cha Cha and I went for cozier Cape Cod–style ones with rose-covered picket fences.

Sirena, who'd obviously been eavesdropping, pulled over

to the side of the road for a moment. "The house you like is called a 'half cape,' Truly," she said. "Only two windows on one side of the front door. A 'full cape,' on the other hand"—she pointed to Cha Cha's choice, directly across the street—"has four windows, two on either side of the front door."

Cha Cha's forehead puckered. "Why would somebody only build half a house?"

"Yeah, someone Truly's size wouldn't even fit in it," muttered Hayden. I pretended not to hear her.

"It was the starter house of its day," Sirena explained. "The story goes that sea captains would build a half cape so that their spinster daughters could live independently, and then, if they ever got married, their husbands would build the other half."

"What a dumb idea!" scoffed Mackenzie. "I'd much rather have a big house."

She wouldn't if she had to help clean it, I thought. Mackenzie's parents had a housekeeper who came once a week. Our family had—well, us. "Chores build character," my parents loved to remind us every Saturday morning, when they rousted us out of bed and organized a full-on blitz starring the Magnificent Seven, as my father called our family. I'd had enough dusting and vacuuming to last me the rest of my life. Half a house would suit me just fine. I'd take a quarter, even.

There weren't many people on the beach this early in the morning. I noticed a couple walking their dog, a scattering of

REALLY TRULY

joggers, some kayakers out on the water, and a lone fisherman standing far out on a line of boulders that must be the jetty, or breakwater, that Sirena had described. Down by the water's edge, a woman was talking on her cell phone while her daughter busied herself in the sand with a plastic bucket and shovel.

"Look, Mommy! Mermaids!" The little girl tugged on her mother's shorts, pointing to where we had spread out our towels and were busy wiggling into our tails. The woman turned, peered over her sunglasses at us, then began talking animatedly into her phone. She must have alerted the entire neighborhood, because inside of five minutes a line of cars started pulling into the parking lot.

Delphine was still helping me into my shimmertail when the news truck showed up and two people got out.

I looked at one of them and froze. *No way*. It couldn't be! But it was. I'd recognize that big phony anywhere. The last time I'd run into Carson Dawson, host of Channel Five's *Hello, Boston!*, had been right after we'd moved to Pumpkin Falls. He'd managed to embarrass me on television then. But I sure wasn't about to let him do it again now.

"Hurry up and get me into this thing!" I whispered frantically to Delphine, as we struggled to pull my tail into place.

She frowned. "What's the matter?"

"I can't let him see me!"

"Who?" She glanced back over her shoulder. "Oh wow! Mom's going to faint."

Sure enough, the minute she spotted Carson Dawson and his colleague, Sirena let out a yelp and made a beeline across the parking lot. Meanwhile, I scooted across the sand toward the water as fast as I could manage. My fellow mermaids were already sitting in the shallows, shrieking as each cold wave lapped over them. The Atlantic Ocean wasn't exactly the Caribbean. I inchwormed past them and flung myself into the water without a moment's hesitation. Freezing to death was a far better fate than facing Carson Dawson.

A few minutes later, Mackenzie finally got up the nerve to join me. "It's not like Texas!" she gasped, when she came up for air.

"Nope," I burbled. Stealth mode wasn't easy under these circumstances, but I was giving it my best shot. I hunched down in the water, only the top half of my face visible. With any luck, I'd be unrecognizable.

Zadie was next to take the plunge.

"Whoooo-eee!" she hollered, surfacing with a whoop. "Now that's what I call refreshing!"

One by one, the others joined us. Once past the initial hurdle, it didn't take all that long to get used to the chilly water, and pretty soon everyone was splashing each other and goofing around as we showed off our tails for the audience on the beach. I kept a low profile, staying at the back of the pack. *"Pack" isn't the right word*, I thought. Neither was "gaggle." What was it they called a bunch of fish? I giggled

REALLY TRULY

when I remembered the correct term—"school"—then started coughing as I accidentally swallowed some seawater. *School* of mermaids—mermaid *academy*—Hatcher and Aunt True would think this was funny too, and I added it to my list of things to tell them.

Swimming in the ocean in a shimmertail was way easier and way more fun than swimming in one in a pool. The salt water was more buoyant, for one thing, which helped offset the weight of the silicone. For another, I could really stretch out and take it for a proper test drive. Staying parallel to the jetty, I butterflied my way out toward the open water, pausing when I reached the end. Then I turned around and swam back.

Breakwater Beach was on the bay side of the Cape, so there wasn't any surf to speak of, but there were plenty of gentle waves. We all floated in the water for a while, bobbing like buoys and enjoying the soothing rhythm of the incoming tide.

"Yoo-hoo! Ladies!" Sirena called to us from across the parking lot. "Look who I found!"

Uh-oh, I thought, hunching lower in the water as she headed toward the beach with a determined look on her face. Carson Dawson and his cameraman were right behind her.

As the three of them approached the water's edge, the cameraman trotted ahead and turned to start filming Sirena and the television host.

"*Helloooooooo, Boston!*" hooted Carson Dawson,

launching into the famous opener for his TV show. "Real mermaids, folks! Right here on Cape Cod! And Channel Five is here to check it out!" He smiled his fake smile for the camera, then motioned to the cameraman, who slowly panned over to where we were all bobbing in the waves. "I'm here with Sirena of Sirena's Sea Siren Academy—say that three times fast"—he paused and chuckled at his own joke—"who assures me that we are in for a treat."

"Indeed you are, Carson," Sirena chimed in smoothly, leaning in close to the microphone he had in his hand. "A magical nautical treat."

"If the mermaid academy thing doesn't work out, she could always pursue a career on TV," I burbled to Mackenzie, who shushed me.

"Ladies? Are you ready to strut your stuff?" Sirena's question caught us off guard, and for a long moment nobody moved. Then Zadie leaped into action.

"Back layout, mermaids!" she ordered. "Tails in, heads out, arms interlocked."

A soldier's daughter knows an order when she hears one. I snapped into position. So did everyone else, and within seconds we had formed a circle on our backs in the water, flukes touching in the middle, arms extended to each side so that we were connected shoulder to shoulder. From above, we'd look like the spokes on a bicycle wheel.

"Ballet tails!" called Zadie, and we lifted our tails straight

REALLY TRULY

up into the air and flapped our flukes. Carson Dawson and the crowd of onlookers gasped in delight.

Zadie led us through a few other simple formations that she and Lenore and Sirena had taught us for the revue. We ended with surface dives, showing off our flukes again. I made sure to smack the water hard with mine and make the biggest splash that I could, in hopes of drenching Carson Dawson. Unfortunately, he was out of range.

"Mommy! I want to be a mermaid too!" piped the little girl who'd first spotted us.

"And you can do just that on Saturday night," Sirena told her, whisking the mic from the Channel Five host and smoothly serving up a pitch for our upcoming show. "Sirena's Sea Siren Academy is located right here on Breakwater Road. We'll be presenting our all-star mermaid revue this Saturday at seven p.m.—we're calling it *A Tribute to Esther Williams*."

"Esther Williams!" said Carson, reaching for the mic again. I could tell from the creases on his tanned forehead that he was worried his news segment was at risk of being hijacked. "Now there's a name I haven't heard in years."

Sirena's aqua-tipped fingers were closed firmly around the microphone. She tugged it toward her. "Yes, the *Million Dollar Mermaid* herself!" She bent down toward the little girl, who was looking up at her with shining eyes. I recognized that expression. It had been on my cousin's face all week. *Mermaid fever.* "Two of Esther's former protégées will be performing with us and offering pointers after the show for aspiring mermaids just like you! Come early to get a seat, and don't forget your swimsuit!"

Sirena straightened up again and beckoned to Zadie and Lenore, who swam closer to shore. I hung back, watching as they charmed the crowd with a few more of their synchronized swimming moves.

"Wow," said Carson Dawson, finally regaining control of the mic. "They're really something!" He looked over at the rest of us. "And these are all your students?"

"Yes, indeed. Sea sirens, all! Swim on over and say hello to Mr. Dawson, ladies!"

As the rest of the mermaids obeyed, I hung back, still keeping as much of me underwater as was humanly possible.

The TV host squinted in my direction. "What's wrong with that one?"

Sirena frowned. "Some mermaids can be shy."

"Is that a fact?"

"Oh yes," Sirena continued, nodding sagely. Her red corkscrew curls nodded too. "On the whole they prefer not to be seen by humans."

Suddenly the whole thing struck me funny—two adults, one with a fake tan and faker smile, the other with an aqua mani-pedi and a T-shirt that proclaimed MERMAIDS ARE MER-MAZING!— acting as if it were entirely natural to be discussing the emotions of mythical creatures. I started to laugh and immediately got salt water up my nose again. Turning my back to the shore, I struggled to suppress my coughing fit. The last thing I wanted to do was attract more attention to myself.

Fortunately, Carson Dawson was finished with us. "That's a wrap!" he announced. As he and Sirena retreated back toward the Channel Five news truck, deep in conversation, I rolled over onto my back and floated in the waves again. My cousin and friends swam over to join me.

"Mermaids can be shy," I said, smacking my tail on the water for emphasis.

Mackenzie grinned at me and smacked hers, too. "Mermaids need their beauty rest."

"Mermaids make waves," added Jasmine with an impressive whack.

"Mermaids eat lots of fish," Cha Cha chimed in, twirling around and splashing water in every direction.

"Mermaids talk on shell phones," I said, wondering when Sirena would return ours. Aunt True wasn't going to believe it when I told her about Carson Dawson.

The four of us kept a steady stream of stupid mermaid rules and puns flying back and forth for a while: "Mermaids are never shellfish." "Mermaids send messages by sea-mail." "Mermaids can be crabby." "Mermaids are fintastic." "Mermaid foes are anemones."

Later, as we tossed our tails and towels into the back of the minivans, Sirena reappeared.

"I can't believe our luck!" she said. "Mr. Dawson is here for the week, filming segments for a special about everyday life on Cape Cod. He's going to be spotlighting some local events, and he's going to stop by and film us! Ladies, the all-star revue is going to be featured on TV!"

Everyone cheered.

Everyone but me.

I felt like I'd been kicked right in the shimmertail.

I was going to be on *television*? It was bad enough to have to perform in front of a live audience. Being on television meant performing in front of practically the entire world!

My clamshell bra and I were on a crash course for complete and utter humiliation.

CHAPTER 19

HELP! I texted Aunt True later that day, when dinner was over and Sirena finally relented and gave us our "shell phones" back. GOT TIME TO TALK?

I'd barely pressed SEND before my phone rang in response.

"What's up?" my aunt asked.

"Carson Dawson, that's what!" I paced the back lawn, fuming as I filled her in on our morning at the beach. What I'd thought would simply be a funny story to share had exploded into a looming disaster.

"Don't worry," she said when I was done. "I've got your six."

That was military speak for "I've got your back." If anyone could fix this, it was Aunt True. I had no idea how, or if it were even possible, but I felt better just hearing this.

"So what else did you do today?"

I gave her the rundown. Aunt True was particularly interested in Zadie and Lenore.

"Wow, they're helping Sirena and her daughter choreograph your routine?"

"Uh-huh," I replied. "The stuff they have us doing is actually pretty sweet. Not that I want to perform in public," I hastened to add. "Especially not on TV. Oh, and we've been watching some of their old Esther Williams movies, too, like *Million Dollar Mermaid*."

"Is that the one where she wears a gold swimsuit and crown and dives off a really high platform?" Aunt True is a "cinephile," as she puts it—which is a fancy word for someone who is a big fan of movies.

"Yeah."

"I love that one!"

"I liked it too. And *Easy to Love*. They're kind of corny, but all the water ballet scenes were amazing, and Zadie gave us the behind-the-scenes scoop. Did you know that Esther Williams was pregnant when she did most of those water-skiing stunts?"

I could practically hear Aunt True's eyebrows shoot up. "That's amazing! Wait until I tell Rusty!"

"He likes Esther Williams?"

"Rusty is a man of surprising depths. So what's on the schedule for tonight?"

"A book signing."

"Really? At Sirena's?"

I explained about the Brewster Store, and *Saga of a Ship*.

REALLY TRULY

"That new book I sent you?"

"Yeah." I was just about to tell her my theory about Nathaniel Daniel and Cherry Island, when she interrupted.

"Oops, gotta go. Hair ball."

Memphis, my aunt's cat, was a feline conveyor belt for hair balls. Everyone in my family was used to Aunt True dropping everything when one appeared, which they did with alarming regularity.

"Okay. Bye!" I replied, but she'd already hung up.

I made a detour to Whelk to grab my copy of *Saga of a Ship*, then headed back to Mermaid HQ to meet up with the group that was heading to the Brewster Store. Zadie and Lenore had decided to join Mackenzie and Cha Cha and Jasmine and me, as had the ladies from Sand Dollar. Meanwhile, the four high school girls plus Hayden and her mother had opted for Sea Siren Night. Somehow Hayden had gotten it into her head that she might be able to sing on TV during the revue and get discovered by some big Hollywood talent agent. If you asked me, though, which nobody ever did, the only thing that was going to be discovered was the fact that she was a pain.

The staff at the Brewster Store looked happy to see us.

"Sirena!" cried the woman behind the fudge counter.

"Monica!" cried Sirena.

The two of them leaned in and made air-kissy noises.

"I see you've brought a crowd," said Monica. "We're

gathering upstairs, ladies. Treats are on their way."

"Fudge, I hope," murmured Cha Cha, eyeing the display behind the glass counter. "Mermaids love chocolate."

We took up the entire first two rows. A scattering of people were seated in the back, some with copies of the book in hand, others who were probably just there for the free treats. After working at Lovejoy's Books, I could scan an audience like a pro.

"How nice of you all to come!" The author made the rounds, shaking hands. I'd seen her type before. She was wearing what Hatcher called an I-am-an-artist outfit—the kind a person wears when they want to make a statement, like Augustus Wilde and his purple cape. In Amanda Appleton's case, her statement seemed to be, *I may have been a pirate in a previous life.* Oversize white shirt? Check. Wide black belt with a gold buckle? Check. Large gold hoop earrings? Check. All she needed was a red bandana and an eye patch to complete the outfit. "Are all of you together?" She peered at us from behind a pair of big, black-rimmed glasses, her blue eyes alert.

"We are indeed," Sirena answered.

"A family reunion?"

"You might say that." Zadie gave her an impish smile. "We're sort of a seafaring family."

"You've come to the right place, then!" enthused Dr. Appleton. "I have a salty tale to tell, so let's get started." She turned to face the audience. "The main question every author is asked is, 'Where do you get your ideas?' With *Saga of a Ship*, I didn't get the idea, *it* got *me*." She nodded at my cousin and friends and me. "When I was about your age, girls, I was walking on a nearby beach one day, and I spotted something in the sand. At first, I thought it was a piece of trash. For some reason it caught my attention. When I leaned down to take a closer look"—she paused dramatically, reaching inside the neckline of her shirt to draw out what looked like a slightly squashed fifty-cent piece on a silver chain—"I realized that I'd found something special."

"A piece of eight!" said Jasmine. "Just like at the pirate museum."

"That's exactly right," Dr. Appleton told her. "It's a Spanish coin called a 'cob,' worth eight reales—hence 'piece of eight.' Its shape is somewhat irregular, since they didn't have the equipment to make perfect coins back in the sixteenth and seventeenth centuries. They just sliced off pieces of a silver rod instead and stamped them by hand. This one was minted in Bolivia in the early 1700s."

She handed it to Monica, who passed it around so that we could all take a look.

"This one coin was all it took to shape the course of my life," Dr. Appleton continued. "I was hooked, and from then on pirates and pirate treasure have been my great passion. And since I live here on Cape Cod, it was only natural that I developed an interest in the wreck of the *Windborne*. Fortunately for me, I have friends and colleagues who share my interest, including one who built a whole museum devoted to it! Isn't that right, John?" She smiled at a man with a gray beard and a Jolly Roger T-shirt seated in the back row. *Skipper John Dee!* I thought as he smiled and waved back.

Dr. Appleton went on to explain her research process, and how, in order to try to track down the history of the ship, its crew members, and their tragic fate, she'd sifted through all sorts of stuff called "primary source material." I was pretty sure I'd heard that term before. Professor Rusty, maybe? No, wait—it was that research assistant of his with the weird hair: Felicia Grunewald, the one we'd seen at the road race. She'd used the term over Spring Break, when we were trying to figure out my ancestor's connection to the Underground Railroad. It meant original letters, diaries, newspaper reports, and stuff.

"Most of my research starts at the library," the author continued. "One of the most exciting primary sources I came across recently was a letter that had been accidentally filed with another document, and thus overlooked by previous scholars. It was written to Isaiah Osborne, the ship's carpenter who survived the wreck only to be caught and hanged as a pirate. We already knew from Isaiah's testimony at his trial that after he washed ashore, he'd entrusted his share of the treasure to a shipmate he called Dandy Dan. The two had split up and run in opposite directions, planning to meet up again later. This letter mentions Cherry Island"—I nudged Mackenzie when I heard this—"and names a date for the two to meet, but of course Isaiah never made it to the rendezvous."

Someone in the row behind us raised a hand. "Finding the pirate treasure would be a big deal, right?"

"Oh yes," Dr. Appleton replied. "A very big deal indeed."

"A real career maker," added Skipper John Dee. "Just like finding the *Windborne* was for me."

"Would you get to keep the treasure if you found it?" someone else wanted to know.

The author pursed her lips. "It would depend on where it was found. Many states have so-called 'finders keepers' laws, but they are interpreted differently. In this case, the statute of limitations would have long since run out for heirs to claim it, so I suspect that yes, I would get to keep it."

I blinked. So even if Dandy Dan were actually my relative, Amanda Appleton would get to keep his treasure? That hardly seemed fair.

"Whether or not you got to keep it, finding it would still be very good for book sales," Monica pointed out, and Dr. Appleton nodded.

No kidding, I thought. Forget guerrilla marketing—Skipper John Dee was right. Finding the lost pirate treasure would definitely be a career maker. Dr. Appleton wouldn't need Augustus Wilde–style tactics. All the publicity would send *Saga of a Ship* rocketing to the top of the best-seller lists.

She'd be on the cover of every magazine and newspaper, and interviewed on every news show on TV, including Carson Dawson's *Hello, Boston!*

Monica glanced toward the stairs. "It looks like the refreshments have arrived. Why don't we take a five-minute break, and then I'm sure our speaker will be glad to answer any other questions you might have."

Cha Cha's hand shot up. "My only question is, are you serving fudge?"

Monica laughed. "Of course!" she replied, setting off a stampede for the refreshments table.

"Oh man," I said a few minutes later, reaching for a second piece. "This is really good. You know, fudge would make a great signature treat at our bookshop. I'm going to talk to Aunt True about it."

"Mmmph mmm," replied Cha Cha, which I was pretty sure meant "great idea."

Mackenzie looked over at me. "Are you going to ask about Nathaniel-Daniel-looks-like-a-spaniel?"

"Um," I replied. "Maybe. I haven't decided yet." The discussion about the "finders keepers" laws had made me uneasy. I wasn't so sure now that I wanted to share my hunch.

Mackenzie and my friends went back to their seats. I headed for the drinks at the end of the table and poured myself a lemonade. It was obvious that Dr. Appleton was as obsessed with pirate treasure as I was with birds. Telling her that I might have a clue about Dandy Dan's identity and the treasure's whereabouts would be like somebody telling me they knew where I could go to see a great grey owl—the world's largest owl, and so notoriously hard to spot it was nicknamed "Phantom of the North." If I ever heard of the whereabouts of one, wild horses couldn't keep me away. I had a feeling it might be the same for Dr. Appleton if I told her about Dandy Dan. So the question was, did I really want a professional treasure hunter sniffing around our little town? What if I wanted to find out more about Dandy Dan first—and maybe hunt for his treasure myself? With the help of the Pumpkin Falls Private Eyes, of course.

In the end, I didn't have a choice.

"Excuse me, Dr. Appleton?"

I looked over to see Mackenzie's hand waving in the air. She was going to let the cat out of the bag! I scrambled back toward my seat, but it was too late.

"If you thought you might know who Dandy Dan was," she asked, "how would you go about figuring out for sure?"

Dr. Appleton went completely still. Behind her glasses, her blue eyes focused intently on Mackenzie.

"It's just that we think he might be my cousin's ancestor," Mackenzie continued. "The one who founded Pumpkin Falls."

I slid into my seat and clamped my hand down hard onto her knee.

"Ouch!" She looked over at me and frowned, yanking her leg away. "What's the matter with you?"

"Pumpkin Falls?" Amanda Appleton cocked her head, alert as a chickadee. No, not a chickadee, I thought, watching her. A hawk, maybe. Or a falcon. Definitely a predatory bird.

"No!" I whispered urgently, giving Mackenzie a look that Hatcher would have recognized instantly. It was the one that said, *Warning! Danger! Red Alert! DEFCON Three!*

Unfortunately, my cousin and I didn't share the Lovejoy sibling shorthand.

Mackenzie nodded. "It's a little town in New Hampshire."

I did my best impression of a ventriloquist and forced two words out of the side of my mouth: *"Shut. Up."*

"You might go the library and try to do some research yourself, I suppose," said Dr. Appleton, trying but failing to sound casual. She couldn't hide the rising excitement in her voice. "Or you might consult an expert like myself." She ventured a reassuring smile. "I'd be happy to offer some advice."

I'll bet you would, I thought grimly. Forget predatory bird—how about pirate, plain and simple?

CHAPTER 20

Mackenzie and I weren't speaking.

I was furious with her for spilling the beans about Nathaniel Daniel, and she was furious with me for being a "drama queen," as she put it.

"You're making a big deal out of nothing!" she'd protested as I grabbed her by the arm and hauled her outside after the book signing was over. I didn't even wait to get my copy of *Saga of a Ship* autographed. It was too risky—Mackenzie might give something else away.

"I am not!" I retorted. "A 'career maker,' that pirate museum guy called it! If we give Dr. Appleton any more information, she'll just use it to track down Dandy Dan and the treasure."

"Wasn't that the point?"

I glared at her. "Weren't you listening? *Finders keepers?*"

Mackenzie hadn't spilled the beans entirely, at least. Amanda

Appleton didn't know Dandy Dan's real name yet. And my cousin hadn't mentioned Cherry Island. But how long would it take for a trained researcher to find those things out?

Mackenzie stomped off to Whelk the minute we got back to Sirena's. Cha Cha and Jasmine stood in the driveway looking uncomfortable. I could tell they didn't know whether to stay with the group or console Mackenzie.

"You guys do what you want," I told them, flapping my hand. "No way am I missing out on one of Delphine's desserts."

I made the right choice.

"It's called Siren Song Cake," Delphine told us as she cut into a multi-tiered mocha refrigerator cake layered with whipped cream and something called mascarpone cheese. "Because it sings to you from the fridge, luring you in."

She passed me a slice, and I took a bite. "Oh man," I said for the second time that evening. "This is amazing."

"It's my mom's favorite," said Delphine. Sirena, whose mouth was full, waved her fork happily in agreement.

I ended up surrendering to the cake's siren song and asking for a second piece. The shimmertail had really added to my workouts this week, and I was hungry all the time. I was going to be in great shape by the time I returned to summer swim team.

Thinking about home and swim team got me thinking about our friends back in Pumpkin Falls. I drifted over to the corner of

REALLY TRULY

the porch where Cha Cha and Jasmine were standing—they'd both surrendered to the siren song of Delphine's dessert too. "Have either of you heard from the guys today?"

They both shook their heads.

I pulled out my cell phone and tapped out a text to Scooter and Lucas and Calhoun.

A few seconds later the three of them popped up onscreen.

"Are you eating *again*?" Scooter looked incredulous. "And it's always sweets!"

"Mermaids love dessert," I replied calmly, zooming in on the layer cake. I could almost hear him drooling.

"We had fudge earlier too," Cha Cha added helpfully.

Scooter groaned.

"Maybe my dad will make brownies for us if I ask," Calhoun told him. Calhoun's father was an enthusiastic baker.

Lucas peered over my shoulder. "Where's Mackenzie?"

"Back in our cabin," I said, without going into details. I didn't want to get into what had happened at the Brewster Store just yet. "So, anything new on your end?"

"Nothing," said Lucas.

"Nada," said Scooter.

"Zip," said Calhoun. "Well, not entirely zip. Officer Tanglewood's been giving us a hard time because we haven't found the trophy yet."

I wrinkled my nose. "Well, we'll be home soon. See if you can fend him off until then."

"What happens if nobody finds the trophy?" asked Jasmine.

I shrugged. "They'll just make another one, I guess. It's not that big a deal."

"But it won't be the *same*."

"Of course it will," I told her. "It's just a dumb silver pumpkin."

"It's not dumb!" she said hotly. "It's tradition!"

"Guys," said Calhoun, "it's not worth arguing about. And not to change the subject or anything, but my dad says the cast list will be posted tomorrow."

Cha Cha and Jasmine both squealed at this news.

"Ladies! Shell phones off!" said Sirena, who was seated on a nearby sofa deep in conversation with Zadie and Lenore. Well, with Zadie anyway. Lenore seemed to be mostly listening, as usual. "It's almost time for lights-out."

Jasmine grabbed Cha Cha's hand. "Let's go tell Mackenzie!"

I followed them outside, but I wasn't ready to return to Whelk just yet. I tried texting Hatcher to see if he was still awake, but he didn't respond. So I sat in the hammock for a while, brooding about Mackenzie spilling the beans to Dr. Appleton, the likelihood that I was going to make a complete fool of myself in the revue, and how complicated and tangled life seemed sometimes. And then I went to bed.

. . .

REALLY TRULY

Friday was a blur of rehearsals and preparations for Saturday night's show, punctuated by a flurry of excitement after lunch when Calhoun texted us a photo of the cast list.

"I can't believe I'm Mabel!" boomed Cha Cha, clutching her phone and hopping up and down in excitement.

Mabel was the female lead. Jasmine was excited too, even though she didn't have a major part. She'd been cast in the chorus as one of the "maidens"—the daughters of the Major-General.

"That means Hatcher is my father," she said, giggling.

My brother had gotten the part of the Major-General. I could only imagine the jokes that would be flying around our dinner table back at home, since a major general outranked a lieutenant colonel. My father was going to have something to say about that.

It was so typical of my brother to land the lead role! He'd never acted before, never sung in public before—well, besides church, which didn't count—he'd just tried out on a whim and knocked it out of the park. Sunflower smile, sunflower life. It was like he was sprinkled with stardust or something.

"Ooo, Cha Cha!" said Jasmine, looking at the rest of the list. "Calhoun got the part of Frederic, Mabel's true love."

Cha Cha turned pink and laughed it off. I laughed too, but I wasn't laughing on the inside. Neither of my friends knew about my crush. Mackenzie was the only one I'd confided in. I slanted her a glance, but she was still ignoring me.

Calhoun had talked Scooter into auditioning, and like his sister, he was in the chorus, and would be doubling up as a pirate and a policeman. Calhoun's sister, Juliet, had been cast as Ruth, Frederic's nanny, which we all thought was kind of funny. She'd hardly have to act at all—she bossed Calhoun around all the time anyway.

Lucas was the only one of my friends who, like me, hadn't tried out. I was pretty sure it was because his voice was changing and tended to go shooting off into the stratosphere unannounced.

"I wish I could stay and be in the play," said Mackenzie. "You guys are going to have so much fun!"

"Why don't you?" said Cha Cha. "I'm sure there'd be room for you in the chorus."

My cousin shook her head. "I can't—my parents have planned a vacation for us to Yellowstone National Park. We leave next week."

"How about you, Truly?" asked Jasmine. "Are you sure you don't want to get involved?"

I shook my head. "Not my thing."

The rest of the afternoon found us logging serious pool time. Zadie and Lenore put us through our paces, making us practice our routines over and over until we had them down cold. By dinnertime, we were all so tired that the only thing we had the energy for afterward was lolling on the sofas in the living room watching *Splash*.

REALLY TRULY

"Ladies, I think we should declare an early curfew tonight," Sirena said when the movie was over. "Tomorrow is a big day. You owe it to yourselves to be mer-mazing!"

Mer-mazing? Ha! Unless something "mer-aculous" happened, like I got sprinkled with some of Hatcher's leftover stardust, I was pretty sure I was still on a collision course for disaster.

CHAPTER 21

"This week has gone by so fast!"

I cracked open an eyelid. Mackenzie was sitting on the edge of her bunk across the room, swinging her legs back and forth. Was she finally talking to me?

No such luck.

"I know," Jasmine replied, padding out from the bathroom. She perched beside my cousin and put an arm around her. "I wish we could all stay here forever."

I pulled the pillow over my head. Not me. I was ready to go home. On the whole, mermaid camp—excuse me, mermaid academy—hadn't been as bad as I'd expected, but I was eager to salvage what was left of my perfect summer. Bird-watching? Couldn't wait. Swim team? Ditto. Working at the bookstore? Top of my list. And even if I'd missed the film festival, maybe I'd still get a chance to go to a movie or two with Calhoun. Plus, there was the missing trophy to find, and

REALLY TRULY

I was itching to try to solve the puzzle of my ancestor-who-might-be-a-pirate.

At breakfast, Zadie and Lenore and Sirena surprised us by announcing that our morning pool session was canceled.

"There's such a thing as over practicing, ladies," said Zadie. "Trust us, you're ready."

There was another surprise too.

"It's part of graduation day here at the academy," Sirena told us. "Along with the diploma that you will receive, of course, suitable for framing."

A mermaid diploma? Seriously? Who'd want to frame that?

One look at Hayden's face told me that she would. Mackenzie too.

Sirena's surprise turned out to be a professional photographer.

Oh great, I thought when she introduced him. More embarrassing photographs! I'd had my fill of them already this summer, thanks to the Gifford Family Reunion. But everybody else seemed thrilled at the prospect.

The cabana, which was providing the backdrop for our photos, was almost unrecognizable. Sirena and Delphine had stayed up late decorating it, and the little shed was glammed to the hilt, complete with fishnets, seashells, and buoys covered in glitter.

The photographer, a local friend of Sirena's who was used to ladies in full mermaid garb, put us each through a series of poses.

"Nobody better post these pictures on the Internet," I muttered when it was my turn.

Delphine passed me a tiara. "I'll make sure Mom doesn't use yours on our website," she promised. "Now suck it up and look royal."

After the individual photos came the big group photo, and then it was time for the smaller group photos. The girls from St. Louis went first, then Hayden and her mother, and then the Sand Dollar ladies, who had bonded over the past week and were already making plans for a mermaid reunion in Atlanta, where one of them had a pool.

After Zadie and Lenore posed together, it was our turn. As Mackenzie and Cha Cha and Jasmine and I wiggled into position beneath the fishnets, I couldn't help noticing that Mackenzie made sure to put Cha Cha and Jasmine between us.

"Let's get one with just the cousins, too," said Sirena, after our group shot.

Mackenzie gave me a look. And not one that said, *Boy, I can't wait to be in a photo with you.* Delphine must have seen it, because she came over and quietly offered some advice.

"Look, girls, I don't know what's going on, but I know best friends when I see them," she murmured, making a show of arranging our flukes. "Don't let anything spoil that."

There was a long pause, and then Mackenzie looked over and gave me a sheepish smile.

REALLY TRULY

"Sorry," she said. "I guess I shouldn't have spilled the beans at the Brewster Store."

"I'm sorry too. I shouldn't have snapped at you." I put my arm around her, and we both smiled for the camera.

Afterward, we changed back into our regular clothes, leaving our undersea finery in the cabana as Sirena had instructed.

"Graduation day will continue shortly with our farewell banquet," she told us. "We always have it at lunch instead of dinner. You'll be too nervous to eat anything tonight before the revue, and afterward there won't be time before you all head home."

As much as I was eager to sleep in my own bed again, and see Hatcher, who was also due home from wrestling camp tonight, I wasn't looking forward to the long bus ride back to New Hampshire. At least I'd be able to nap. I had a feeling I'd be tired after the revue.

We spent some time back in our cabins packing before the gong announced that lunch was ready. Place cards had been arranged around the dining room table with our mermaid names on them. I was seated next to Mackenzie/Neptunette, and Cha Cha and Jasmine—Nixie and Pixie—were across from us. Zadie (Isla) and Lenore (Merissa) were next to Cha Cha. We all took our seats and reached for our diplomas, which had been printed on parchment paper, rolled into a scroll, and placed on our plates. Each scroll was tied with a blue ribbon, from which dangled a silver shell charm.

"It's so cute!" gushed Mackenzie.

"One last bit of bling," said Sirena, smiling at her.

I unrolled my diploma and read the fancy script:

Sirena's Sea Siren Academy

By the powers of neptune invested in this institution,

I hereby proclaim that Truly Lovejoy

Has proved herself worthy of the name "Grania"

And is officially inducted into the sisterhood of mermaids.

Around the border was a colorful motif of mermaids and dolphins and shells, and Sirena had signed it at the bottom with a flourish.

"Isn't this just the bees' knees!" said Zadie. "Don't you think so, Lenore?"

Lenore nodded, adding her seashell charm to the bracelet that encircled her wrist and jangling it with satisfaction.

Delphine had pulled out all the stops for our farewell meal.

REALLY TRULY

"Can you believe it?" crowed Mackenzie when she spotted the platters that emerged from the kitchen. "Our second clambake in a week!"

As much as I loved lobster and steamed clams and corn on the cob, even they couldn't chase off the herd of leaden butterflies that were stirring in my stomach. I was pretty sure they'd work themselves into a full-blown stampede by the time the revue rolled around.

Dessert managed to distract me, at least temporarily.

"Let's hear it for Delphine!" cried Zadie, and we gave her a standing ovation as she circled the table with a tea cart, showing off the enormous mermaid cake she'd made for us. The mermaid's tail sported sparkly scales, and I figured her curly hair—made of red licorice laces—had to be inspired by Sirena. Fondant seashells coated in edible glitter lined the edge of the platter.

"I can't believe you made all those decorations from *frosting*!" said Cha Cha, and Delphine nodded modestly.

There was a longer-than-usual siesta after lunch, to give us time for naps and to make one last trip to the Brewster Store for souvenirs and to finish packing.

"I'm going to miss being a mermaid," Jasmine lamented as she folded a T-shirt and put it in her suitcase.

My cousin sighed. "Me too."

"At least we have our tails to bring home with us," said Cha Cha. "Maybe we can all get together for a swim next time you're in Pumpkin Falls, Mackenzie."

I wouldn't be going home with a tail—at least not one I could swim in. The shimmertail was only a loaner. I was tempted to throw away the stupid too-short reject I'd started out with, but then I remembered how much Aunt Louise had spent on it, and I stuffed it into my suitcase instead. Pippa would be thrilled to have the hand-me-down.

When the gong sounded again—"The last one!" Mackenzie said mournfully—we gathered back at Mermaid Crossing. There was a light meal of tuna fish sandwiches, chips, and fruit waiting for us, but Sirena was right, we were all too nervous to eat.

"Don't worry, this happens every session," she consoled us. "Delphine will pack everything up for you to take along on the ride home. You'll be starving after the revue."

I glanced up at the clock on the wall. Sixty minutes from now, I would be making a complete fool of myself in front of a bunch of strangers. The butterflies, which had been largely quiet since lunchtime, began to stir.

All too soon it was time to head down to the pool, where people were already starting to show up. Word had gotten out, thanks to Carson Dawson and *Hello, Boston!*

"Into the cabana, mermaids!" said Sirena. "Your tails and costumes are waiting. Delphine will be along shortly to help with makeup."

We crowded inside. Our tails were hanging on a row of hooks that lined the small shed, each one marked with a tag that had our mermaid name on it. Our swimsuit tops and bling were neatly piled on the benches below. I sat down under the hook labeled GRANIA and took a deep breath. There was no going back now.

"Oooo!" squealed Hayden a few minutes later, peeking out the window beside me. "Channel Five is here!"

The other mermaids wiggled over and crowded around us, and we all craned to see. Sure enough, Carson Dawson and his cameraman were just getting out of the news truck. The butterflies in my stomach were rocking and rolling now.

The Channel Five team weren't the only familiar faces to show up, though.

"Hey!" exclaimed Cha Cha, as the Abramowitz's SUV pulled in beside the news truck. "My family's here!"

We watched as her parents and little brother emerged.

"They brought my parents—and my brother!" said Jasmine.

My heart sank. I was going to have to perform in front of Scooter Sanchez?

That wasn't the worst of it, though. There was one more passenger in the SUV.

"I am not going out there in this thing in front of *Calhoun!*" I sputtered, clutching my clamshell bra to my chest and crouching down below the windowsill. The butterflies were legit stampeding now.

"You're the queen," said Hayden. "You have to, or you'll ruin the show, and the rest of us will look stupid."

You already look stupid, I was tempted to reply, but didn't. Not with Delphine standing right beside us. I just glared at her instead.

When it was my turn for what Delphine called the "glam chair," I sat quietly as she swiped bright red lipstick—a nod to Esther Williams—onto my lips. I didn't flinch as she brushed glitter onto my cheeks and eyelids, and onto the strands of fake seaweed she wove into my hair. But when she reached for the can of glitter spray to give me one final spritz, I pulled away. "I'll blind everybody when the lights go up!"

Delphine laughed. "Nonsense. Mermaids love glitter, and so do our audiences."

"Bling too, right?" I said with a reluctant smile, rattling the sparkly necklaces I was wearing. I was loaded with enough of them to send me straight to the bottom of the pool. We all were, I thought, looking around.

Some of the others had even decorated their bikini tops. Hayden and her mother had added plastic pearls to theirs to match their pearly tails, and the high school girls must have spent hours hot-gluing sequins and tiny shells onto theirs.

"Tiara time!" Delphine told me.

I sighed. "Are you sure I need to wear that thing?"

"Quit complaining, Queen Grania! You're going to look very regal."

I didn't feel regal at all. I felt like an idiot.

Hayden watched as Delphine pinned the glittering ornament to my hair. I'd caught her practicing my routine a couple of times this week when nobody was looking, and I was pretty sure she was hoping for a last-minute chance to switch places. *Not if I have anything to say about it,* I thought. Not even if it meant abandoning stealth mode. I didn't intend to give her the satisfaction.

"Truly!" Mackenzie grabbed my arm and pointed out the window.

"What?" I leaned over to take a look, then gave a little yelp of surprise.

My parents had come for the performance too! And not only my parents but also the rest of the Magnificent Seven—Hatcher and Danny and both of my sisters, who must have been sprung from camp for the occasion. As they took their seats, another car pulled into the parking area beside our family's minivan.

"It's Aunt True and Professor Rusty!" The butterflies retreated a bit. Aunt True had promised to help shield me from Carson Dawson. I couldn't imagine how, but she'd said she had my back, and my aunt always kept her promises.

Sirena stuck her head in the cabana. "Curtains up, ladies!"

Delphine flipped a switch by the door, and all the floodlights went out. Excited murmurs rippled through the audience.

"Positions, everyone!" Sirena said in a stage whisper.

All the mermaids except me scooted across the deck to

the edge of the pool. They sat there in the dark, backs to the bleachers and tails out of sight, just as we'd practiced. Delphine waited until everyone was in place, then nodded to her mother.

The loudspeaker crackled. "Ladies and gentlemen, families and friends!" Sirena's voice floated out into the warm summer night. "May I present to you Sirena's Sea Siren Academy All-Star Mermaid Revue!"

A single spotlight flared, illuminating Zadie at the far end of the lineup. As the music started, she swiveled around and leaned back, hoisting her tail into the air expertly. She smiled and waved, and the audience clapped enthusiastically. I watched, counting to myself: "One Mississippi, two Mississippi, three Mississippi . . ." On the stroke of five, down went Zadie's flukes into the pool with a splash, and her head snapped left as she looked over toward the next mermaid in line. The spotlight followed her gaze to one of the girls from St. Louis, who repeated the exact same moves. Each time the spotlight landed on a new mermaid, the audience clapped again.

"There's Cha Cha!" I heard Baxter, Cha Cha's little brother shriek. Cha Cha grinned and waggled her fingers at him.

After the entire row of mermaids was facing the audience, tails in the water, Sirena's voice came over the loudspeaker again: "And now, we bring you tonight's feature, straight from Hollywood—*A Tribute to Esther Williams*!"

REALLY TRULY

The bleachers erupted as the music swelled and the floodlights came up and one by one the mermaids peeled off the edge of the pool, diving into the water like dominoes. Carson Dawson's cameraman was filming everything. I glanced anxiously at Aunt True, who was busy whispering to Erastus Peckinpaugh. She hadn't forgotten me, had she?

Out in the middle of the pool, arms and legs began rising and lowering in unison, and flukes swished this way and that. The choreographed routine was proceeding like clockwork. The tails looked fantastic in the water, I had to admit, and so did the bikini tops, bling, and even the stupid glitter. It wasn't exactly *Million Dollar Mermaid*, but it wasn't half-bad, either.

Our revue didn't have an elaborate plot like the performance at the Jolly Roger showquarium, just a bunch of synchronized swimming moves leading up to my appearance in the shimmertail. The whole thing would actually have been kind of fun, if it weren't for the fact that there was a news camera out there just waiting to humiliate me on TV. And if the boy I liked hadn't been sitting smack-dab in the middle of the bleachers, where he was about to have an excellent view of me wearing mermaid underwear.

I glanced over at Aunt True again, hoping for a sign—something, anything!—that would let me know she had a plan to foil Carson Dawson. But she didn't even glance my way. This time she wasn't just whispering to Professor Rusty—she was kissing him. In public!

I was on my own.

Cut and run! urged the butterflies.

Mermaid up! ordered my conscience sternly. This was no time for stealth mode. It was time to step up and be tall timber, like Aunt True was always telling me. My fellow mermaids were depending on me. Besides, I wouldn't get very far in a thirty-pound tail anyway. Whether I liked it or not, Romeo Calhoun was about to get an eyeful.

Reaching under the bench for the skateboard that was stashed there waiting for me, I lowered myself onto it, hoisted my legs and shimmertail into place, and propelled myself into position by the door. As the music swelled, Mackenzie and Cha Cha and Jasmine and the rest of the mermaids formed a circle in the center of the pool and slowly sank beneath the surface of the water. Delphine cut the floodlights.

That was my cue! I rolled to the edge and slid into the water as quietly and unobtrusively as I could. Taking a deep breath, I did a silent surface dive and dolphin-kicked my way underwater to where the others were waiting.

When the lights came up again a few seconds later, I was hidden within a tight circle of bodies. And then it was goodbye, Truly Lovejoy, and hello, Grania the Mermaid Queen.

"Hey!" I heard Carson Dawson exclaim as the bodies fanned out like petals on a flower and I emerged, tiara sparkling in the spotlight. "I've seen that girl somewhere before!" The news host peered at me, his overly tan forehead wrinkling in concentration. He turned to his colleague. "Zoom in!"

Here it comes, I thought, bracing myself.

But nothing did.

Aunt True hopped down from her seat and disappeared behind the bleachers. She reappeared almost immediately, smiling a big Cheshire cat smile. I'd seen that smile before. It was the one that said, *I've been up to something*.

A few seconds later, Carson Dawson tapped his microphone and frowned. He said a few words to his tech, who inspected the camera, then shook his head and shrugged.

Aunt True must have unplugged their power cable!

As the two men trotted off to investigate, my fellow mermaids circled around me in formation while I used the powerful shimmertail to propel myself slowly straight up out of the water. Beneath the surface, my legs were pumping furiously back and forth. Above, I was cool as a cucumber, regally smiling and waving to the audience.

"Go, Truly!" Calhoun shouted, and he and my brothers and Scooter whistled and stamped their feet in the bleachers. A school—make that an *academy*—of mermaids rotated slowly around me, arms outstretched shoulder to shoulder.

Time for the razzle-dazzle, I thought. As the others fanned out even farther, allowing me more space, I slid down into the water again and leaned back in the ballet leg double position. Lifting my tail in the air, I sculled my arms the way Zadie and Lenore had taught me and waved my flukes back and forth for all I was worth. The audience gave an audible gasp as the shimmertail caught the light.

Out of the corner of my eye, I spotted Scooter filming me with his cell phone. I gritted my teeth and kept smiling. If he put that video online, I was personally going to stuff him into this shimmertail and send him to Davy Jones's locker!

The music shifted, and the circle of mermaids parted. I headed for the opening.

"Swim pretty, now!" Zadie whispered as I passed her, echoing Esther Williams's famous phrase. I could tell from the twinkle in her bright blue eyes that she was having fun. I was surprised to realize that I was too.

"I'll do my best," I whispered back, and began a slow circuit of the pool. The others peeled off and swam after me single file, like a mermaid parade.

We all smiled and waved as we glided by the cluster of little kids in swimsuits who were seated in the front row. They watched us, eyes shining in anticipation. They were obviously eager for the traditional swim-with-a-mermaid part of the show, which was scheduled to begin as soon as our revue was finished.

The music swelled, signaling the approach of the big finale. While I jackknifed into a surface dive, the other mermaids swam over to where Delphine was waiting by the edge of the pool. I brought my tail down on the surface of the water with a loud *SMACK!*, propelling myself into a streamline. Surfacing, I burst into the air and flung my arms forward into the butterfly stroke—my favorite. The rest of the mermaids were all back in the center of the pool by now, and I swam faster and faster around them until I was fairly flying through the air. The audience whooped and cheered.

For a moment, I forgot about being on display in a clamshell bra, and I forgot about the butterflies, and I forgot about everything but the feel of the water and the way the shimmertail rocketed me through it.

For a moment, I almost felt like a real mermaid.

And then disaster struck.

With one final *thwack* of my tail, I dove deep underwater and headed for the center of the tight circle that the others had formed again.

When I emerged this time, they crowded around, lifting me onto the shoulders of the two tallest girls from St. Louis. As they did, I felt a tug on my back and let out a horrified yelp as I started to rise into the air.

Someone had undone the clasp on my bikini top!

My clamshell bra was about to go AWOL, right in front of my family and friends! And possibly a TV audience too, if Carson Dawson managed to get his camera rolling again.

Instantly, I clamped my arms across my chest, trapping my top in place. This wasn't what I was supposed to be doing at this point in the finale. I was supposed to be collecting a fistful of sparklers from my fellow mermaids, who had retrieved them from Delphine just a few moments ago. It wasn't quite Esther Williams and her hydraulic-lift-and-fireworks finale, but it was the best imitation we'd been able to improvise.

"What's wrong with you?" Mackenzie whispered as I hunched over, terrified that I wouldn't be able to keep what was left of my dignity in place.

"Wardrobe malfunction!" I whispered back, and her eyes widened as she saw my bikini top closure flapping freely.

Zadie saw them too. "Just keep smiling," she told me, moving in to hide me from the Channel Five team, who had finally managed to plug the camera in again.

Over her shoulder, I caught a glimpse of Hayden. She was smiling the same Cheshire cat smile that Aunt True had worn a few minutes ago, the one that said, *I've been up to something*.

I gaped at her.

Shellina was the one who'd done this?

Anger surged through me, from the tip of my flukes to the top of my tiara. No way was she getting away with this, grand finale or no grand finale.

Without giving it another thought, I tipped backward into the water and smacked down as hard as I could with my shimmertail.

CHAPTER 22

I went home in disgrace.

My parents didn't even let me say hello—or good-bye—to Calhoun. I barely had time to grab my suitcase before they marched me off to our minivan.

I'd missed Hayden by inches with my tail. From the way she'd carried on, though, you'd have thought it was a direct hit. When my flukes smacked down on the water's surface, I'd unleashed a tidal wave that soaked not only her but also everyone else within a ten-foot radius. Plus it extinguished the sparklers, ruining the grand finale.

Hayden had hollered bloody murder, and I'd hollered right back. We'd gotten into a fight right there in the pool—or as much of a fight as two people in mermaid tails could get into, with one of them clutching her clamshell bra for dear life and the other coughing and spluttering and pretending she was almost drowned.

With some assistance from my father and the lifeguard's hook, Sirena had finally managed to haul the two of us out.

"Try and salvage what's left of the evening," I heard her hiss to Delphine and Zadie as she hustled us off to the cabana. After the ruckus, though, most of the little kids didn't want to get in the water with a mermaid anymore—they were probably afraid that they'd get smacked with a tail too. I felt bad about that. But I didn't feel bad about defending myself. Hayden had been needling me all week, and sabotaging my swimsuit top was the last straw.

Our parents—along with Aunt True and Professor Rusty—came barreling into the cabana behind us. Hayden denied everything, of course. Her mother started threatening to sue me, sue Sirena, sue all of Cape Cod. My mother told her to back off. Sirena was trying to get everyone to calm down. And then my dad started in on me, before I even had a chance to explain.

"You will apologize to this young lady, Truly, and you will apologize now," he ordered.

"J. T., for heaven's sake at least let her get dressed first," said Aunt True, draping me with a towel. My aunt was one of the only people I knew who could stand up to my father. To her, he was just her little brother, not Lieutenant Colonel Jericho T. Lovejoy.

"Stay out of this," my father warned.

"Why am I the one who has to apologize?" I protested,

determined to act like tall timber for once in my life and stand up to him too. "She's the one who tried to humiliate me in public!"

Hayden pretended to look shocked. "I did not! You're lying!"

The muscles in my father's jaw twitched. He was clenching his teeth. This was a warning sign I usually didn't ignore, but I was angry enough that I threw caution to the winds. "She undid my bikini top, Dad! I almost went the full mermaid out there!"

"Don't you dare speak back to me!"

My courage fled under his stern gaze. "No, sir," I mumbled in defeat. There was no point trying to be tall timber. My father always knew how to cut me down to size.

He inclined his head toward Hayden and tapped his foot, waiting for my apology. Hayden shot me a triumphant look.

You win, Shellina, I thought bitterly. Before I could open my mouth to get the words out, though, Professor Rusty held up his cell phone.

"Technically, Truly is right," he announced. "I was filming the revue, and it's all right here, clear as day. This girl *did* undo Truly's swimsuit top."

My father turned on him, his face beet red. "If I want your opinion, I'll ask for it, Erastus," he snapped. "This is a family matter."

"Rusty is family!" Aunt True retorted.

"He most certainly is not."

Aunt True drew herself up to her full height, towering over my father. "Well, he will be soon enough," she told him. "Rusty just asked me to marry him, and I said yes. We were going to tell you all tonight when we got home."

This unexpected announcement stunned everyone into silence.

So *that's* what the kiss in the bleachers had been about! My mother let out a screech of joy, then burst into tears. My father just stood there awkwardly for a moment before giving my aunt a hug and shaking Professor Rusty's hand.

With my side of the family happily distracted for the moment, Sirena swung around and wagged an aqua-tipped finger at Hayden and her mother.

"Given the evidence caught on video, your daughter has a great deal to learn about being a mermaid, Mrs. Drake," she said grimly. Hayden's mother started to protest, but Sirena bulldozed right over her. "Mermaids are polite. Mermaids are kind. Mermaids are honest. And mermaids never, ever bully other mermaids. In fact," she finished, "I am rescinding Hayden's diploma. She is not mermaid material."

It was Hayden's turn to let out a screech.

"Come along, princess," her mother said coldly. "We don't have to stand for this."

Sirena followed them out the door, her red corkscrew curls bobbing furiously. "And if you post one peep about this on social media, or give Sirena's Sea Siren Academy one negative review, I will sue you for slander! And don't think I won't—I have the video as evidence!"

The cabana door slammed shut behind them.

My father turned to me again. "This isn't over, Truly," he told me. "The fact remains that you acted abominably. You're a Lovejoy, and Lovejoys don't behave the way you did tonight."

"But—"

He held up his good hand, silencing me. "Not. One. More. Word. Your mother and I will be discussing your punishment."

Delphine poked her head in just then. "Um, okay if I come in? Truly needs my help getting out of the shimmertail."

My family withdrew to wait outside. Delphine closed the door again and turned to me, smiling broadly. "You were awesome tonight, and don't let anyone tell you otherwise! Hayden has been pushing everyone's buttons all week, including mine. If you hadn't given her a taste of her own medicine, I might have done so myself. What she did to you was unforgivable."

Her words of support were so unexpected, I felt myself tearing up. "But I ruined the whole evening for everyone!"

Delphine flapped her hand dismissively. "Nobody minds a little extra drama when they come to see a show," she continued, tugging at the waistline of the shimmertail and starting to roll it down. "Besides, it served that little blister right. We get a bad apple every once in a while, but I've never seen one who pulled a trick as rotten as that one. Hayden really got my mother's flukes in a flap."

I had to smile at that.

Delphine looked at me thoughtfully. "You're a really good mermaid, Truly. Best I've seen for an amateur. It's not easy to swim in one of these things."

"Um, thanks."

"I've kept this tail because I thought for a while that maybe I'd go pro, like my mother did. You know, move to Florida, join the famous mermaid revue there. But the thing is, I love it here on Cape Cod."

I nodded. "It's a pretty awesome place."

"And here's the other thing—I've discovered that I love cooking even more than I love being in the water. I've been thinking that maybe I'll start my own bakery or café."

"Wow! I'd definitely eat there if you did."

She smiled. "Thanks. It feels really right. I guess what I'm trying to say is, I'd like to give you this shimmertail as a gift."

I stared at her, open-mouthed. She had managed to extract me from it by now, and she rolled it up and stuffed it back into its enormous duffel bag. "Matching top, too," she said with a wink, tossing it in.

I stammered my thanks, although to be honest at that moment I would have been happy never to see a shimmertail—or a clamshell bra—again.

REALLY TRULY

Delphine wasn't the only one who was solidly in my court, as it turned out. Zadie and Lenore intercepted my parents and me on the way to the car. Zadie gave me a big hug good-bye and made me promise to keep in touch. Then it was Lenore's turn. To my astonishment, she spoke the first words I'd heard from her all week.

"Little brat got what she had coming to her," she murmured in my ear, wrapping me up in a bear hug. "There's nothing worse than a bully."

The only other bright spot was that Professor Rusty—I guess I'd be calling him Uncle Rusty pretty soon, which was a weird thought—wasn't the only one who had caught the finale on video. Carson Dawson had also managed to film "the tail end of things," as my aunt jokingly referred to it. With any luck, his video clip would become an Internet meme, and Hayden could relive that epic smack online for years to come.

I, on the other hand, was probably going to be grounded for life.

CHAPTER 23

The next twenty-four hours were painful.

Mackenzie rode home from Cape Cod with Aunt True and Professor Rusty—part of my punishment, I assumed, since it was our last night together before she went back to Texas.

"Really, Truly! I am so disappointed in you" was the only thing my mother said to me on the long drive north. That's what she always said when one of us messed up. Her disappointment was worse than any amount of my father's bluster, or his icy silence, which was what he dished out all the way back to Pumpkin Falls.

As for the rest of my family, Pippa and Lauren, who were returning to Camp Lovejoy first thing in the morning, quickly fell asleep. Danny had his earbuds in and mostly ignored me except for a few sympathetic glances. Hatcher was the only one who addressed the elephant in the room— well, minivan.

REALLY TRULY

"Too bad you're in the doghouse," he whispered. "That tail smack was epic!"

"Hatcher," said my father sternly, "I heard that."

"Sorry, sir."

When we finally pulled into our driveway several hours later, my father reached over the back of the driver's seat and held out his hand. "Cell phone," he said crisply, and I reluctantly handed it over. "Remainder of your punishment still to be determined."

Mackenzie flew home the next morning. I had been quarantined in my room overnight, while she was banished to the guest room, so we didn't get a chance to talk before she left. I wasn't allowed to go with her to Logan Airport, and I almost didn't even get to say good-bye. My father relented at the last minute, though, and let me come downstairs to see her off.

"Make it snappy," he said, grabbing her suitcase and carrying it out the front door.

We stood there for a moment under the watchful gaze of my ancestors' portraits. *They're probably judging me too*, I thought glumly. "Sorry I messed everything up."

Mackenzie hugged me. "You didn't! Hayden totally deserved it. Uncle Jericho is overreacting." She broke away and grinned at me. "Videoconference later tonight, when I get home?"

"If my dad doesn't take my laptop away."

Hatcher and Danny had volunteered to drive her to the

airport. I waved from the front steps as the three of them pulled out of the driveway.

"At least *you're* happy to see me," I said to Miss Marple, who'd been sticking to me like Velcro ever since I got home. She looked at me and wagged her tail. "Let's go back upstairs."

Even there I couldn't hide from trouble, though.

"Truly!" my mother called a few minutes later. "There's someone here to see you!"

I was flopped on my bed with my dog-eared copy of *Owls of the World*. Reading about birds, especially owls, was always soothing. "Tell them I'm not here!" I called back.

"Truly Lovejoy, come down here this minute!" I could tell by the tone of my father's voice that he meant business.

I closed my book reluctantly and stalked downstairs, halting in surprise when I saw Calhoun's father standing in the front hall. He smiled when he spotted me.

"Sorry to stop by so early in the morning," he said. "R. J. told me you were home."

"R. J." was what Calhoun's father called him, short for Romeo James.

"I hear there was a bit of excitement last night at mermaid camp!"

"Mermaid academy," I corrected automatically, the words flying out before I could stop them. My father smelled sass and frowned at me.

"'Academy,' of course." Calhoun's father nodded. "R. J.

showed me a photo of you in—the shimmertail, I believe it's called?"

I nodded, squirming inside. Calhoun had a picture of me in my mermaid outfit?

"It's quite an amazing feat of costumery, young lady. You look like a real mermaid."

I lifted a shoulder, not sure what to say to that. My father's eyebrows flew together as he frowned at me again.

"Thank you," I said, obeying the unspoken order. Like mermaids, Lovejoys were always supposed to be polite.

"I came by to talk to you about *The Pirates of Penzance*. You've probably heard that I'm directing it?"

"Yes, sir."

"Rehearsals start tomorrow afternoon, and R. J. told me that you might be interested in working on stage crew." Noting my surprise, he added, "I realize it's not glamorous, but it's much needed, and it can be a lot of fun."

"Um," I began, wondering why on earth Calhoun had told his father that I was interested in stage crew. Hadn't I made it clear that I wasn't?

"Your friend Lucas has agreed to join us," Dr. Calhoun continued, as if that was an incentive. "Plus," he added, "I'm hoping you might be willing to reprise your role as a mermaid for the opening scene, and perhaps the finale." He held up a hand as I started to protest. "R. J. told me that you're not interested in singing or dancing, and that's just fine. I had in mind a nonspeaking role—something along the lines of set decoration, if you will. You'd be the crowning glory to our briny 'improbable fiction,' as the Bard might term it."

"The Bard" was Shakespeare. Calhoun's father loved quoting him.

Set decoration? I didn't know whether to be flattered or insulted. Mostly I was just flabbergasted. I had no interest in being a "crowning glory," whatever that was, especially not onstage, and especially not while wearing the shimmertail—which was currently banished to the back of my closet, where it couldn't remind me of last night's disaster.

"Of course she'll do it," said my father, pinning me with his steely-eyed gaze. The message couldn't have been clearer: This was to be my punishment.

"Wonderful!" said Dr. Calhoun, rubbing his hands together happily. "Rehearsal starts tomorrow afternoon at four o'clock sharp at the Grange. I'll see you there!"

My father closed the door behind him as he left, then turned to me, looking pleased with himself. "A little community service never hurt anybody. After all, if I'm not mistaken, it was Gilbert and Sullivan who came up with the phrase 'let the punishment fit the crime.'"

"Yes, but that was *The Mikado*, J. T., not *The Pirates of Penzance*," Aunt True told him, emerging from the kitchen just then. She and my mother had been deep in conversation about wedding plans since breakfast. "And for the record, I

REALLY TRULY

think Truly has been punished enough." She crossed the hall and put her arm around my shoulders. "If she doesn't want to perform, she shouldn't have to."

I shot her a grateful look, but I could tell by the way my father's jaw was set that his mind was made up. Like it or not, I was going to be in *The Pirates of Penzance*.

CHAPTER 24

"Welcome, players! Come in, come in!" Dr. Calhoun flung open the door to the Grange.

My friends and I filed inside, along with all the other kids who'd gotten parts in the play or who were there, like me, to work behind the scenes. It was hotter indoors than out, thanks to another July scorcher of a day and the Grange's lack of air-conditioning. Overhead, an anemic ceiling fan was straining to stir up a breeze.

I looked around curiously. I hadn't been here since I was younger and Gramps and Lola had brought my brothers and sisters and me to see a production of *The Sound of Music*. "Shabby" was probably the kindest word I could think of to describe the Pumpkin Falls Grange. It was a wonder the place hadn't been condemned. In addition to the garden-variety old building issues—creaky floorboards, peeling paint, cobwebs on the light fixtures, moth-eaten curtains on the stage—there were more serious problems. Some of the glass panes in the dusty windows were cracked, there was a bird's nest in the rafters overhead, and I could actually see daylight through a hole in the roof.

"Ella Bellow is right—this place is a dump," said Cha Cha in a raspy stage whisper.

Calhoun's father pursed his lips. "It is somewhat lacking in charm," he admitted, "but as the Bard says, 'The play's the thing.' And once our stage crew weaves their magic, I guarantee you that by opening night these humble surroundings will be transformed and the audience will be transported." He made a sweeping gesture with his arm, as if seeing it in his mind's eye already. "And in this case, we're going to transport everyone to the 1950s!"

This stirred a ripple of interest.

"I was inspired by last week's film festival," Dr. Calhoun explained. "I had been thinking to myself, *What can we do to present Gilbert and Sullivan in a fresh new way?*—and there was my answer! Instead of nineteenth-century Cornwall, we'll give them midcentury modern, complete with malt shops, poodle skirts, and bobby socks."

I had no idea what he was talking about. And from the looks of it, neither did any of my friends.

Dr. Calhoun had us divide up into our respective groups—actors, costumes and makeup team, and stage crew. Mr. Henry, Lucas's mother, the Farnsworth sisters, and a few other people I didn't recognize were helping with costumes and makeup.

The stage crew consisted of me, Lucas, and three "old hands," as they called themselves: Bud Jefferson, Elmer Farnsworth (who may have been hard of hearing but who apparently was a whiz with a hammer), and Belinda Winchester.

"I've been working stage crew since 1963," Belinda told Lucas and me. "Same year that 'Surfin' USA' was on top of the charts." She popped an ear bud in and hummed along to the Beach Boys as Dr. Calhoun started taking roll call.

My eyes slid over to the wooden bench along the wall, where Augustus Wilde was seated with his laptop perched on his knees. Wherever Belinda went these days, Augustus went too, so it looked like we were getting him as a kind of bonus. Or mascot, more likely. I doubted he'd be much help when it came to actual work—at the moment he was ignoring us completely. He frowned at his laptop, typing furiously. Augustus was on a deadline for his new novel.

"Where's my Frederic?" Dr. Calhoun called, and Calhoun held up his hand. "Ah, there you are, R. J. How about Mabel?"

Cha Cha raised her hand too, and Dr. Calhoun checked her off on his clipboard.

"Major-General Stanley?"

Hatcher, who was seated next to Cha Cha, jumped up and saluted, which got a laugh.

"And Ruth, Frederic's nanny"?

Calhoun's sister Juliet waved from the back of the room. "Hi, Dad!"

REALLY TRULY

Her father smiled and waved back, then checked her name off too.

I noticed that Chanda Patel, my new piano teacher, was the accompanist. She was about Aunt True's age, with dark hair and eyes, and a shy smile. She taught in the music department at Lovejoy College, and we were supposed to start my lessons later this week. I looked at her with interest, wondering whether I'd like her as much as I had liked my teacher back in Austin. I hoped so. I'd really missed taking piano lessons. But there just hadn't been time up until now.

After roll call, Dr. Calhoun enlisted Juliet's help in handing out scripts.

"Friends, we have less than a month to put this show together," he told us as she moved through the hall with the stack of booklets. "It's going to be tricky, but I know we can pull it off."

Belinda Winchester offered to help distribute the rehearsal schedule and the sign-up sheet for costume fittings. When she got to me, she reached into the pocket of her overalls and handed me a kitten along with a clipboard.

I looked down at the ball of fluff in my hand and blinked. "What am I supposed to do with this?"

Belinda shook her head sadly. "Truly," she said, "it's a *kitten,* not a major appliance. It's not that complicated."

Augustus waited until she trundled off down the row of chairs, then took pity on me. "Here," he whispered, leaning over and holding his backpack open. "It's kitten proof—and kitten friendly."

I peeked inside. Sure enough, in the bottom of his backpack was a fleece vest covered in cat hair. Augustus had obviously been down this road before. I deposited the kitten gingerly inside and watched as it curled up on the fleece and started purring. The kitten had been down this road before too.

After all the handouts had been distributed, the three groups scattered to different corners of the Grange.

"Okay, huddle up, stage crew!" said Bud Jefferson. "In a nutshell, our work is pretty much everything the actors don't do. We're in charge of set design, getting props on- and offstage, lighting, that sort of thing. It's hard work, but we always have fun. Right, guys?"

Belinda gave a thumbs-up.

"RIGHT SIZE?" said Elmer, puzzled.

"I SAID 'RIGHT, GUYS'!" Bud repeated loudly, and Elmer gave a thumbs-up too.

Bud had mapped out a schedule of his own for us. I looked it over and winced. At this rate, we'd all practically be living at the Grange.

"When am I supposed to have time to do anything else this summer?" Lucas stared at the schedule gloomily. "The only reason I signed up for this is because my mother begged me to. She's hoping it will be a 'bonding experience' for me and Bud."

REALLY TRULY

I gave him a sympathetic glance. Lucas didn't like change any more than I did. And change was definitely in his future. Bud was probably going to marry his mother and become his stepdad. At least that's what practically everyone in town said. Pumpkin Falls was holding its collective breath waiting for Bud to propose.

"Okay, everyone! Good kick-off meeting," said Dr. Calhoun a few minutes later. "Actors, I want you all off book by the beginning of next week. The faster you memorize your lines, the faster things will start to come together. And speaking of coming together, tomorrow evening we will gather here to clean the Grange before we do a read-through. Bud Jefferson and the stage crew will be in charge. Please come dressed appropriately, and bring brooms, mops, cleaning rags, and any supplies you can spare from home. See you at seven o'clock!"

As we left, I turned to my friends and moaned, "How did I get myself roped into this?"

Calhoun gave me a sideways glance, a smile playing on his lips. "Technically, I got you into this. I didn't want you to miss out."

"Gee, thanks."

"Let's get ice cream," Jasmine suggested. "That will cheer you up."

"Um," I replied. My father had been quite clear about the fact that I was still grounded. Helping out with stage crew was part of my punishment, but I was to go directly home after every rehearsal. I explained my predicament to my friends.

"If we run into your father, we'll just tell him that we kidnapped you," said Scooter.

I snorted. Like that would fly with Lieutenant Colonel Jericho T. Lovejoy.

"I scream, you scream, we all scream for ice cream!" Jasmine teased in a singsong voice. "Mmmm—chocolate chip, your favorite!"

"Fine," I said, giving in. "But keep a sharp lookout for my father."

In the end, there was no sign of him, but I couldn't dodge Ella Bellow.

"Yoo-hoo!" she called, swooping down on me as we mounted the steps to the General Store. Her dark eyes gleamed. "A little bird told me that your aunt is engaged!"

The rocking chairs that lined the porch stopped in their tracks, and a row of gray heads all swiveled in my direction.

I sighed. "Yes, ma'am, that's right."

"Have they set a date for the wedding?"

"Not that I know of."

Ella tried to pry more information from me as the onlookers strained to hear. I didn't have any to give her, however, and wouldn't have shared it with her if I did. I finally managed to extricate myself and follow my friends inside.

Where I immediately froze.

REALLY TRULY

"What is *she* doing here?!" I whispered, grabbing Cha Cha and ducking behind the postcard rack.

Cha Cha looked around, mystified. "Who?"

"Shhhh! Keep it down! She'll hear you!"

We peered out from behind the postcards featuring all the wonders that were Pumpkin Falls—the church steeple with the Paul Revere bell, Lovejoy College, and of course the covered bridge.

Cha Cha's green eyes grew round as she saw who I was pointing to. "Amanda Appleton? What's she doing here?"

"My question exactly."

Jasmine, who had trotted off after the boys to the ice cream counter, came back looking for us. She frowned when she spotted us behind the postcards. "What's going on?"

"*She's* what's going on," I told her, pointing to Dr. Appleton, who was browsing the General Store's selection of local guidebooks.

"No way! What's she doing here?"

"That's what we want to know."

"Should I just go over and ask?"

I clutched Jasmine's arm. "No! I don't want her to see us."

The boys came around the corner with their ice cream cones just then. Hatcher was with them. He stared at me. "Who are you hiding from?"

Lucas looked around in alarm. "Is it your father?"

"He's here?" My whisper went up an octave. That was all I needed.

"Calm down, he's nowhere in sight," Hatcher told me. "But seriously, what's going on?"

"Emergency meeting of the Pumpkin Falls Private Eyes, that's what's going on!" As Dr. Appleton wandered away toward the housewares aisle, I leaped up and bounded past my brother and our friends, racing for the front door. "Follow me!"

I paused at the bottom of the porch steps, suddenly unsure where to go. Our usual meeting spot in Lola's studio wouldn't work. Not with me being grounded. The library was closed by now, and so was our family's bookshop. Aunt True often stayed late, though, and, fortunately, I had a key.

Unfortunately, my father did too, and there was a chance he might be there.

Was it worth the risk?

"Bookstore," I told the others, deciding that it was. "Give me a few minutes head start, then come to the back door and I'll let you in."

I arrived just as Aunt True was ringing up the last customer. She already had the CLOSED sign on the door, but I used my key to let myself in.

She looked up and smiled when she saw me. "Truly! Come and meet Artie Olsen. He and his wife run Camp Lovejoy."

I thought Bud Jefferson was a big guy, but Artie Olsen was

huge. I had to tip my head back to look him in the eye. He stuck out his hand, and mine all but disappeared as he gripped it.

"Howdy, Truly! I've heard a lot about you from your sisters."

I glanced at the counter, noting his purchases: *Men and Fire*—one of our most popular barbecue cookbooks—plus a bottle of my dad's Terminator hot sauce. Aunt True had been serious when she'd told Lobster Bob about adding it to the store's sidelines.

"I'm in charge of the weekly cookouts at camp," he explained. "You and your family have a standing invitation to join us, you hear?"

He left, and Aunt True locked the door behind him.

"Such a nice man," she said. "His wife's a sweetheart too." She sat down on the antique church pew that we used as a bench by the door and patted the seat beside her. "How was your first rehearsal?"

"Belinda tried to give me a kitten."

She smiled. "So not a total loss, then."

"How about you? Busy day?"

"Surprisingly so. Half of Pumpkin Falls came in, supposedly to shop for books but really to gawk at my engagement ring. Ella Bellow's grapevine is working overtime."

"She cornered me at the General Store just now, too, fishing for details." The minute the words were out, I clamped my hands over my mouth.

Aunt True grinned. "Busted! The lure of ice cream is hard to resist. Don't worry—your secret is safe with me."

"How the heck did Ella find out, anyway?"

"How does Ella find anything out? It's one of the mysteries of the universe."

"I still can't believe you're getting married!"

"I know, me neither." My aunt waggled her finger happily. The diamond in her new ring winked and sparkled as it caught the light.

"Want me to close up for you?"

"Would you mind? Rusty's taking me out to dinner, and I need to shower and change. I'd better check with your father first, though. I wouldn't want to get you in deeper trouble."

Apparently helping out at the bookstore didn't violate the terms of my grounding, because a minute later she gave me a thumbs-up as she emerged from the office. "But you're to go directly home afterward."

I nodded, crossing my fingers behind my back. The meeting would have to be quick.

Aunt True gave me a hug and left to go upstairs to her apartment. I counted to ten, then sprinted to the bookshop's back entrance, where Hatcher and my friends were waiting.

CHAPTER 25

The first order of business for our emergency meeting was bringing Hatcher and the other boys up to speed on Amanda Appleton.

"Wait. What? There were *pirates* in Pumpkin Falls?" Scooter's forehead puckered as he tried to grasp what I was telling them.

"Not pirates—pirate. Just one: my ancestor, Nathaniel Lovejoy. Maybe."

"Nathaniel-Daniel-looks-like-a-spaniel?" Lucas looked incredulous.

So did my brother. "You're kidding, right?"

I sighed. They weren't making this easy. "Look, guys, I know it's hard to believe, but trust me: It totally makes sense." I grabbed a copy of *Saga of a Ship* from the new releases table and showed them the passages that had caught my attention.

"It's a bit of a stretch," my brother said when I was done

explaining my theory about Dandy Dan's "generous beak" and Cherry Island.

"It's not that far-fetched if you think about it," Cha Cha insisted, and I shot her a grateful look.

Lucas was still skeptical. "How will we ever be able to find out for sure?"

"There's got to be some evidence somewhere," I told him. "A diary. Letters. Maybe a map. That's obviously what Dr. Appleton is in town to find. We just have to stay two steps ahead of her."

"Why?" asked Scooter, his forehead puckering again.

"Because if she finds the information first, it might lead her to the treasure, if there is one. Apparently there's this thing called a 'finders keepers' law, which means she'd have the legal right to it if she finds it."

"Even though Nathaniel Daniel is our ancestor?" Hatcher was indignant. "That's not fair!"

I nodded. "I know, right? Especially since I'm the one who figured out the connection. But that won't stop Dr. Appleton. She isn't the kind of person who gives up easily. There's too much at stake for her—including fabulous publicity for her book if she finds the treasure. We're going to have to be quicker and smarter than she is if we want to get to it first."

I could tell by the expressions on their faces that the boys were warming to the idea of a treasure hunt.

REALLY TRULY

"We should go explore Cherry Island," said Scooter. "There might be clues there."

I wrote that down.

"We should talk to Mr. Henry," added his sister. "He knows a lot about the town's history."

I wrote that down too.

"You and I should look around and see if there are any Lovejoy family papers at home, Truly," Hatcher suggested. "Like you said—letters, or a map or something. Maybe up in the attic or stashed someplace like the original Truly's diary was."

Last Spring Break, I'd found a diary belonging to my namesake, which had revealed some long-hidden family secrets. Could lightning like that strike twice?

Lucas raised his hand. "While we're here, can we talk about the missing trophy?"

In all the excitement over Amanda Appleton, I'd almost forgotten about the other mystery we were trying to solve.

"Sure," I told him, and he and Scooter and Calhoun showed us a couple more pictures they'd gathered and flagged as suspicious. After inspecting them carefully, we were able to identify one of the people in them.

"I'm pretty sure that's Reverend Quinn's cousin," said Jasmine, examining a picture of a skinny man in baggy shorts. "I remember him from the crowd along Main Street. He almost hollered himself hoarse cheering on the Speedy Geezers."

"We should still talk to Reverend Quinn about him, though," I said, and wrote down a reminder. "Just because we recognize somebody doesn't eliminate them as a suspect. Well, except for my uncle Rooster."

The other picture was a slightly out-of-focus shot of a woman at the finish line. She was wearing a red-and-white-striped sundress—Mr. Henry's signature colors—and her hair was styled in dreadlocks just like his.

"Do you think they're related?" asked Cha Cha.

"We can ask when we go see him at the library," I said, jotting that down too.

"So to recap, we have half a dozen potential suspects right now," said Calhoun, counting them off on his fingers. "The man in the Grateful Dead T-shirt, the lady in the Red Sox baseball cap, the two teenagers, and the man-who-may-be-related-to-Reverend-Quinn and the woman-who-may-be-related-to-Mr.-Henry."

"My money's still on the guy in the Grateful Dead T-shirt," I told my friends. "But let's keep showing the pictures around town and see if anyone has any more information. You guys will have to do it, though—my dad took my cell phone."

"What about trying to get more information about Dandy Dan?" asked Scooter, who was clearly more interested in pirate treasure than the lost trophy. "How are we going to do that? With you being grounded and all, I mean."

I pondered my dilemma. My grounding came with three

concessions: piano lessons, play rehearsals, and working at Lovejoy's Books. I'd tried to get my father to add swim team to the list of exceptions too, but he'd dug his heels in on that one.

"This is punishment, young lady, not summer camp," he'd snapped when I'd asked.

Maybe there was still a way, though. "I have a piano lesson tomorrow morning, and Ms. Patel's apartment is just around the corner from the library."

"Perfect!" said Jasmine. "We can meet there afterward and talk to Mr. Henry."

Out of the corner of my eye I could see Hatcher shaking his head. "You are going to be in so much trouble if Dad catches you!"

What was the worst that could happen? I'd be grounded for all of eighth grade, instead of just the foreseeable future?

"In for a penny, in for a pound, right?" I told my friends. "I'll see you guys there. Are you in too, Hatcher?"

My brother shook his head. "Can't. Lobster Bob hired me to work at a clambake tomorrow."

With our sisters away at camp and Danny still at work—now that he was home from the wrestling clinic, he'd gone back to his summer job washing dishes at a restaurant in West Hartfield—it was just Hatcher and me and our parents for dinner. Hatcher made the salad while I set the table, stepping carefully over Miss Marple's sleeping form. Mealtimes always found her under the kitchen table, pretending to nap but actually keeping a sharp eye on the proceedings. Miss Marple lived in hopes of food falling to the floor.

"Thank you for helping your aunt close up the shop," said my mother as we all took our seats a few minutes later.

A guilty flush crept over my face. I hoped nobody noticed.

"I went ahead and fed Bilbo, since you were both at rehearsal earlier." She passed a platter of chicken enchiladas to my brother. "How did it go?"

"Great!" he replied. "It's going to be really fun."

I focused on my plate as Hatcher offered a blow-by-blow of our first meeting at the Grange. When he was done, my mother turned to me. "And how about stage crew, honey?"

"Fine."

My father cupped his hand behind his ear and frowned.

"Fine, ma'am," I corrected myself. I told her we'd run into Ella Bellow after the rehearsal—I didn't say where—and that she already knew about Aunt True and Professor Rusty's engagement.

"Of course she does," said my father. "There's no keeping anything from that woman!"

"Now J. T.," said my mother, "Ella is—"

"—a busybody!"

"I was going to say inquisitive," my mother said mildly. She'd gotten into big trouble last winter when Pippa had overheard her call Ella a busybody and then repeated it in public.

My parents smiled at each other across the table. My father reached over and picked up my mother's hand and kissed it gallantly. The two of them had been all moony since their week alone. It was embarrassing.

"Inquisitive it is," he said.

"More like the Inquisition," Hatcher whispered to me, and I choked back a laugh, nearly expelling a bite of enchilada in the process.

"While you two are taking care of the dishes," said my father when we were finished with dinner, "your mother and I are going for a walk."

Hearing the word "walk," Miss Marple sprang to her feet.

"Okay if I head next door afterward?" asked Hatcher. "The Sox are playing the Minnesota Twins tonight and the Mitchells have cable."

My father nodded. "I'll come join you when we get back." He slipped Miss Marple's leash off the peg by the back door, clipped it to her collar, and turned to me. "But you, young lady, are still grounded."

"Yes, sir," I said meekly.

They left, and Hatcher and I cleared the table.

"Do you have time to look around before the game starts?" I asked him. "For Dandy Dan stuff, I mean."

"Sure."

We started in the living room. The two of us stood for

a moment in front of the portrait of our might-be-a-pirate ancestor. Did I detect a glint of mischief in Nathaniel Daniel's eye? He certainly looked the part of a dandy, what with the froths of lace at his collar and cuffs and his fancy gold signet ring with an eagle etched on it. The same ring appeared in Obadiah Lovejoy's portrait, and Jeremiah's, and on down the generations. Gramps wore it now, and someday it would be my father's.

"You sly dog," Hatcher scolded, wagging his finger at the portrait. "Thought you could keep it a secret, didn't you?"

"You don't think there could be something hidden on the back of the frame, do you?"

Hatcher shook his head. "Nah, too obvious."

We decided to check anyway. We carefully lifted the portrait off the wall and placed it facedown on the sofa. But Hatcher was right—there was nothing on the back to see.

"How about Prudence?" I asked.

Again, nothing.

"You'd think there'd be a clue *somewhere* as to Nathaniel Daniel's true identity," I said, disappointed.

My brother shrugged. "Maybe that *is* his true identity. Or maybe he was Dandy Dan, but he didn't want anyone to know and carried his secret to the grave. It's not like it was something he could brag about. It would have been a huge scandal! He probably liked being such a distinguished citizen and didn't want to rock the boat."

REALLY TRULY

Hatcher was right, of course. Still, after he left to go watch the Red Sox game, I poked around a bit more. I started by making a circuit of the room, examining the bookshelves and taking down anything that looked super old. I made a pile on the coffee table, then sat down on the sofa and picked the books up one by one and riffled through their pages. I had no idea what I was looking for, but I figured I'd know it if I saw it.

It suddenly occurred to me that this was the first time I'd ever been in the house alone. My skin prickled. Old houses tended to make a lot of weird noises, and Gramps and Lola's house was no exception. I found myself on high alert with every little creak and groan it produced. Was it my imagination, or did the shadows in the room's corners suddenly seem deeper? As I scuttled around turning on all the lights, I decided I was done snooping for the night. No way was I going up to the attic by myself!

The front hall stairs creaked again. Thoroughly creeped out by now, I jumped up from the sofa and went over to the piano. The pile of Fourth of July sheet music we'd had out for the family reunion was still on the rack.

Sitting down on the bench, I placed my hands on the keys and swung into "The Stars and Stripes Forever," one of my dad's favorite military marches. Nothing like a little John Philip Sousa for chasing away the ghosts of Lovejoys past.

CHAPTER 26

The next morning, on the way to my piano lesson, I stopped by the bookstore to say hi to Aunt True and Belinda. Well, that and to rustle myself up some free mini blueberry donut muffins. I was barely through the door when I spotted a poster propped on the table at the front of the shop. I stopped short and stared at it, horrified.

"What is THAT?!" I screeched.

Aunt True, who was standing by the cash register, looked up in alarm. I pointed wordlessly at the poster.

She frowned. "Um, it's an advertisement for a book signing?"

"I can't believe you invited *her* to do a book signing at our store!"

"Why wouldn't I?" Aunt True looked baffled.

Time to spill the beans, I decided, figuring my friends would understand.

REALLY TRULY

My aunt's eyebrows rose higher and higher as I explained about everything that had happened on Cape Cod. I showed her the passages I'd found in *Saga of a Ship* and told her my theory on Dandy Dan. I told her what had happened at the Brewster Store book signing and about the finders keepers law and how oddly Dr. Appleton had reacted to Mackenzie's question.

Aunt True was quiet when I finished. One of the things I loved best about my aunt was that she always took me seriously. She didn't waste time arguing with me that my theory was improbable or a "stretch," as Hatcher had called it. She read the passages in the book I showed her, then sighed.

"Here's the thing," she said. "I can't uninvite her. That would be rude and unprofessional. Plus, the best way to figure out what she's up to—if she's really up to something—may be to spend time with her and hope she lets something slip. The book signing will give us the perfect opportunity."

I hadn't thought of that. My aunt was not only a marketing whiz, she was also a genius.

"We can talk about strategy later," she added, crossing back to Cup and Chaucer and grabbing a handful of mini blueberry donut muffins. She passed them to me and shoved me out the door. "For now, though, you'd better get going or you'll be late."

I was still so rattled by this development—Amanda Appleton? at Lovejoy's Books?—that my piano lesson was pretty much a disaster. My fingers stumbled all over the keyboard, and everything I tried to play sounded horrible.

"Is everything all right, Truly?" Ms. Patel asked finally.

Her voice was soft and had a slight lilt to it. *Mourning dove,* I thought automatically.

"You seem nervous."

I folded my hands in my lap and nodded. That was as good an excuse as any. "I usually play a lot better."

"So I see." She flipped through the folder of sheet music and piano exercise books I'd brought along to show her. "These are fairly advanced pieces."

I sat there miserably, feeling like a musical failure.

She regarded me for a moment, then smiled. "I'll tell you what—how about we spend the rest of this lesson playing some simple duets—fun ones that are way too easy for us, just to loosen up and get acquainted a bit, musically. When I was your age, it was always a big deal to change piano teachers."

Things went a little better after that, and I was genuinely enjoying myself by the time we finished. I could tell I was going to like Ms. Patel.

ON MY WAY! I texted my friends as I left her apartment. I had my cell phone back, thanks to my mother.

"If you want Truly out at night working on stage crew, she might need it," she'd insisted to my father at breakfast this morning. He'd grumbled, but finally agreed.

REALLY TRULY

My friends were waiting for me on the front steps of the town library. Inside, we found Mr. Henry in his usual spot upstairs in the children's room. For once, though, he wasn't wearing his signature red and white. Or if he was, it was hidden under a pair of painter's coveralls.

"To what do I owe this pleasure?" he asked from where he was perched on a ladder, paintbrush in hand. The walls were empty of bookshelves and books and the Charlotte's Web statue was covered with drop cloths, as was the floor. The old carpet had been ripped up, and rolls of the new carpet were waiting in the hallway, covered in plastic.

Something else was different too. I frowned, trying to put my finger on it.

"How do you like the new skylight?" Mr. Henry asked. "It was installed over the weekend."

I glanced up. That was it! Light streamed in, brightening what was formerly a cozy but somewhat dim room.

"It's going to be brilliant, don't you agree?" He winked. "Literally as well as figuratively."

I smiled. "Mr. Henry, if someone wanted to find out about our town's history—and about some of its early residents—where would they start?"

He climbed down from the ladder and placed his paintbrush on one of its rungs, then wiped his hands with a rag. "Funny you should ask that question. A woman came in just yesterday wanting to know the same thing."

My friends and I looked at each other in dismay. Dr. Appleton had beaten us to it!

We followed Mr. Henry downstairs to the reference room, where he showed us a shelf of books about the history of Pumpkin Falls and a drawer full of old maps.

"If you really want to go way back, I believe the Lovejoy papers are in the archives over at the college," he told us. "They would most certainly contain information about the town's early history."

My ears perked up at that. "Papers? Like newspapers?"

"The term usually refers to a broad range of items," Mr. Henry explained. "For an author, it might mean manuscripts and research material and correspondence with an editor or publisher, that sort of thing. In this case, it may mean letters, diaries, account books, deeds, and more. And yes, newspaper clippings as well."

He looked over at Calhoun. "You'll have to get special permission to visit the archives. Perhaps your father can get you access, R. J." He turned to me. "Or you might try asking Professor Rusty. The fact that you're a Lovejoy should work in your favor."

This sounded promising. Dr. Appleton wasn't a Lovejoy, and she didn't have a father who was the college president or a soon-to-be uncle in the history department. Maybe we could still stay a few steps ahead of her.

"By the way, how's the case of the missing trophy going?" Mr. Henry looked at us expectantly.

"Um, slowly," I replied.

Scooter pulled out his cell phone and scrolled to the picture of the woman at the finish line in the red-and-white-striped sundress. "We were wondering if you knew this person."

Mr. Henry took one look and burst out laughing. "My sister Sarah? Yes, in fact I do know her."

My friends and I exchanged sheepish glances.

"The thing is," I continued, "we had to ask. Just because we recognize somebody or know them doesn't mean we can automatically eliminate them as a suspect."

Mr. Henry nodded soberly. "Just doing your due diligence," he said. "I understand." He placed his right hand over his heart—or where his heart would be under his painter's coveralls. "What is it your father always says, Truly? Cross my heart and hope to fly, my sister did not take the trophy."

I made a show of pulling my notepad out of my backpack and crossing her off our list.

"I suppose you heard about the special town meeting that Ella Bellow called while you girls were away," Mr. Henry told us. "Some folks are fired up to go ahead and have a new trophy made, but most of us voted to wait a bit longer. We're still hoping that the original will turn up." He winked at my friends and me. "Keep up the good work! Everyone in Pumpkin Falls is counting on you. Well, everyone except, perhaps, Officer Tanglewood. I for one hope you solve this before he does."

Mr. Henry went back upstairs. I looked at my friends. "Divide and conquer?"

Each of us took a stack of books from the shelf and started flipping through the pages, looking for information about Nathaniel Daniel, aka Dandy Dan, any mention of pirates, or anything else that might prove useful.

After half an hour, though, we came up empty-handed. Well, except for the fun facts that my ancestor won the town's very first Halloween pumpkin toss in 1769, the same year he founded the town, and that his wife Prudence was "possessed of a greene thumbe and civick spirit," as one newspaper of the era put it.

If we'd been hoping to discover a long-lost treasure map, that didn't happen either. The drawer that Mr. Henry had pointed out proved almost as much of a dead end, yielding only a topographical map of the Lake Lovejoy area that included MacPherson's Island, aka Cherry Island. Scooter took a picture of it with his cell phone for future reference.

"I have to get back to the bookstore," I told my friends, glancing up at the clock. "My father will notice if I'm gone much longer."

"We'll stop by the bookstore if we hear anything about the other suspects," Calhoun told me. "Otherwise, see you tonight at the Grange."

I nodded. I was stuffing my notebook into my backpack when I heard a sharp intake of breath from Jasmine. I looked

REALLY TRULY

up to see Amanda Appleton standing in the doorway of the reference room.

"Hello, kids." She cocked her head, a puzzled expression on her face. "Wait a minute—I recognize you girls! You were at the book signing on the Cape!"

Cha Cha and Jasmine and I nodded cautiously.

"Nice to see you again." Glancing at the open map drawer behind us, she pursed her lips. "What brings you all here?"

Her question caught me off guard. "Research," I blurted, and instantly could have bitten my tongue off. "For the play we're all in, I mean," I added quickly.

"Really? What play is that?"

"*The Pirates of Penzance.*"

She arched an eyebrow. "Pirates? How interesting." A smile flitted across her lips. "Well, happy hunting!" She walked briskly back across the lobby toward the bank of computers by the front desk.

"What was that all about?" Calhoun whispered.

"That was Amanda Appleton," I whispered back. "I shouldn't have told her anything."

"Do you think she suspects?" asked Cha Cha.

I lifted a shoulder. "I don't know. I hope not."

I was still wondering when I turned onto Main Street a couple of minutes later. Glancing across the street at the Starlite Dance Studio, I read the sign in the window: WINNER OF THIS YEAR'S PUMPKIN FALLS FOUR ON THE FOURTH ROAD

RACE! But the pedestal in the middle of the display was empty.

Between the missing trophy and Dr. Appleton, the Pumpkin Falls Private Eyes certainly had their hands full. If there was one thing I knew for sure, we weren't giving up just yet on either account.

CHAPTER 27

The afternoon passed agonizingly slowly. I was keyed up about Amanda Appleton and eager to talk to Hatcher. He was still with Lobster Bob, though. I channeled my nervous energy into vacuuming the entire store, helping Belinda unpack the latest shipment of books, and taking turns with Aunt True at the Cup and Chaucer counter.

Later, back home after my shift was over, I slam-dunked a quick dinner, then gathered the cleaning supplies that Dr. Calhoun had asked us to bring to the Grange. My mother was backing the minivan out of the barn when Lobster Bob's truck finally appeared and Hatcher hopped out.

"You're late," I told him, wrinkling my nose. "Plus, you smell like fish."

He grinned and tipped his new baseball cap at me. It was red, with a white lobster on the front. "You were expecting roses?"

"I was expecting maybe you'd take a shower before rehearsal!"

"Hey, all we're doing tonight is cleaning. I'm just going to get all sweaty and dirty anyway. Chill, Drooly."

The Grange was already abuzz with activity by the time our mother dropped us off. Elmer Farnsworth, Belinda, and Augustus, who must have finished the draft of his new book, because his laptop was nowhere in sight, were beating the curtains onstage with brooms. Bud Jefferson and Lucas trailed in their wake with a pair of vacuum cleaners, attacking the clouds of dust that had been stirred up. A group of actors was mopping the floor, and Mr. Henry and Lucas's mother and the rest of the costume and makeup team were tackling the windows with buckets of water and rags.

"Ah, the cavalry is here!" said Dr. Calhoun, swooping down on my brother and me. He handed us each a long-handled duster. "How does cobweb duty sound?"

We started with the chandeliers. As we swiped at the cobwebs, I filled Hatcher in on what had happened at the library, from our dead ends to Amanda Appleton's surprise appearance.

"So do you think she suspects anything?"

I shrugged. "That's what Cha Cha asked. I honestly don't know."

"Maybe I should get another perspective," he said a few

minutes later, and wandered off to talk to Cha Cha, leaving me on my own to start on the rafters. He'd been talking to Cha Cha a lot lately. I dragged a ladder into place and was halfway up when I heard a voice below.

"Hey!"

I looked down to see Calhoun standing there, smiling at me. I was suddenly acutely aware that I was covered in cobwebs. I smiled back. "Hey yourself."

"Want to take a break and help me?"

"Sure." I followed him out the back door to where a large, rectangular something was waiting, strapped to a dolly and covered with a drop cloth. It looked kind of like a refrigerator.

"You'll see" was all that Calhoun would say when I asked him what it was.

"Set it by the stage," his father called to us as we rolled it inside. "Gather round, people!"

Work around the Grange halted as everyone came over to stare at the drop cloth–covered object.

"What is it?" asked Jasmine.

"Our time machine to the 1950s!" Dr. Calhoun enthused. He reached for the drop cloth and pulled it away. "Behold, a genuine, bona fide midcentury jukebox!"

"Groovy!" said Belinda. "Does it work?"

He nodded. "Elmer was able to get it going for us."

Calhoun plugged it in, and the machine lit up like a

Christmas tree. Belinda punched a couple of the glowing buttons.

"*One, two, three o'clock, four o'clock, rock . . .*" The song began blasting from the built-in speakers.

"Five, six, seven o'clock, eight o'clock, rock," Belinda sang, her short white curls bobbing in time to the music. Augustus grabbed her around her ample waist, and the two of them started to dance.

"Nine, ten, eleven o'clock, twelve o'clock, rock," Bud Jefferson continued, as he and Mrs. Winslow followed suit.

"WE'RE GONNA ROCK AROUND THE CLOCK TONIGHT!" bellowed Elmer, twirling his broom around the stage.

The music was upbeat and irresistible, and bit by bit everyone joined in. My brother paired off with Cha Cha. Dr. Calhoun danced with his daughter, Juliet, and Jasmine danced with Scooter. Calhoun took my hand, and the two of us began bobbing up and down to the music too. He'd grown since the last time I'd danced with him during cotillion last winter. We were almost eye to eye.

Dr. Calhoun was grinning broadly when we finished in a breathless whirl. "I knew the 1950s was the right era! If we can bring this same kind of bounce and energy to Gilbert and Sullivan, we'll have the audience eating out of our hands."

We all took turns picking songs as we continued with our cleaning. We sang along to the ones we knew and tapped our toes to the ones we didn't. The rest of the evening flew by, and by the end of it the Grange looked as good as it was going to get without a complete renovation. The windows sparkled, the chandeliers and rafters were cobweb free, the floor was mopped clean, all the chairs were wiped free of dust, and the stage was neat and tidy.

"Good work, team!" said Dr. Calhoun. "You've earned a break. Juliet will hand out refreshments while I go over a few housekeeping items and give you a brief outline of my vision for the play."

"Chocolate with chocolate ganache frosting or carrot cake with spiced cream cheese frosting," whispered Juliet as she passed around a tray of cupcakes. "My father made them."

"The operetta usually opens aboard a ship or a beach along the coast of Cornwall," Dr. Calhoun continued. "But in this case, we'll open in a 1950s malt shop."

Lucas's hand flew up. "What's a malt shop?"

"Like a diner," Dr. Calhoun replied. "With lots of ice cream on the menu. A malted is kind of like a milkshake. Anyway, I thought we'd name it the Rockin' Mermaid to give it a nautical flair, as a nod to the traditional setting. As the prelude begins, a pair of pirates will wheel in the counter and stools, and atop the counter will be our own resident mermaid, Miss Truly Lovejoy, the Esther Williams of Pumpkin Falls!"

"Like a float in a parade," whispered Scooter.

More like a fish on a platter, I thought in dismay, feeling my face flame.

"This will bring in another nautical element and help set the scene a bit." Dr. Calhoun outlined his vision in broad strokes, from the pirates dressed in black leather jackets, white T-shirts, and a hairstyle called a ducktail, to the high school prom dance floor where the second act would take place. I tuned out after a while and focused on my chocolate cupcake with chocolate ganache frosting. It was delicious. Dr. Calhoun really knew how to bake.

When he got to the finale, though, I tuned back in again big-time.

"It's here that the pirates are revealed to actually be noblemen, and thus entitled to wed the daughters of the Major-General"—my brother hopped up and took a bow—"and then of course there's the big smooch between Frederick and Mabel at the end."

Dr. Calhoun added this last bit almost as an afterthought.

I sat in shocked silence. Scooter, being Scooter, gave a wolf whistle. Calhoun was expressionless in his seat beside me, staring straight ahead. Farther down the row, Cha Cha had gone beet red. This was clearly a surprise to both of them, too.

"I understand that this can be awkward for actors your age," Dr. Calhoun told his son and Cha Cha, "so fake it for now during rehearsals. We'll save the real thing for the performances."

REALLY TRULY

The real thing?

He couldn't mean it!

But he did.

This was really truly happening! My crush was going to kiss my closest friend in Pumpkin Falls onstage right in front of me, and there wasn't a thing I could do about it!

CHAPTER 28

"It's not fair!" I wailed, flinging myself into Aunt True's arms.

"What's not fair?" she asked, bewildered.

"Calhoun is going to kiss Cha Cha in front of everyone!"

"Oh, honey," she said, patting my back soothingly as I explained what had happened. "It sounds like you need a cup of tea." She drew me inside and shut the door behind us.

Hatcher and I and the others had all left the Grange shortly after Dr. Calhoun dropped the kiss bomb. On the drive home, I'd asked my mother if she could swing by Aunt True's apartment above the bookstore.

"I forgot to show her where I put the shipment of new teas she ordered for Cup and Chaucer," I fibbed. "I'll walk home afterward."

Now, as my aunt poured me a cup of her best Earl Grey, the floodgates opened.

"What if Calhoun *likes* kissing her?" I said, the tears starting up again. "I thought he liked me, but maybe he'll like her better."

"Well—" Aunt true started to reply, but I barreled on.

"And it's not just the kiss—it's everything! Being grounded. Mackenzie living so far away. The stupid mermaid stuff. Even Hatcher—all he wants to do these days is hang out with Cha Cha. My own brother likes her better too!" I was being irrational, but I didn't care. My voice rose and cracked. "Plus, you're getting married and you'll probably have a baby and not even want to work at the bookstore anymore!"

My aunt nearly spat out her tea. She looked over at me, astounded. "Whoa, how did we get from misplaced kiss to baby and quitting the bookstore?"

I shook my head, too miserable to answer.

"Look, things do change, Truly, I won't lie. Life is all about change. People grow up, people grow apart, they move on and move out of our orbit, or we move out of theirs. But not all change is bad, sweetie. There are happy surprises around every corner too. New people move into our orbit while others we thought were gone suddenly reappear. Look at Rusty and me! And new experiences, even the difficult ones, can bring unexpected blessings—just look at how far your father has come."

She handed me a tissue, and I wiped my nose.

"Have you talked to your mother about all this?"

I shook my head again. "She's too busy. Besides," I

added bitterly, "she didn't even want me around this summer, remember?"

"Truly!" My aunt gave me a reproachful look. "Your mother is never too busy for you, and you know it. And as for not wanting you around, don't you think maybe you're being just a little bit unfair? Try and think about things from someone else's perspective for a moment. It wasn't just your father's arm that was shattered in Afghanistan. Many of your parents' hopes and dreams and plans for the future were shattered too. And with your father struggling to recover, your mother had to completely reorient her life to help support him. Now, just like him, she's trying to build a future she didn't expect either."

"I know, but—"

Aunt True held up her hand. "There are no buts," she told me firmly. "This is one time in your life when you have to be completely unselfish. Your parents had the rare opportunity to spend a few short days together this summer all by themselves, and they took it. Can you really blame them?"

I stared at the floor. Memphis was sitting on the carpet, swishing his tail back and forth. Without warning, he coughed up a hairball, then glared at me like it was my fault. *Great*, I thought. Even the cat was judging me.

"It's not like your parents abandoned you by the side of the road!" my aunt continued, grabbing a paper towel and calmly cleaning up the mess. "You got to go to—"

"Mermaid camp?" I gave a short laugh.

"Come on, you know you had fun. I have the pictures to prove it! You were having a blast out there in the pool in that tail thing—at least before the wardrobe malfunction." She started to chuckle. I glared at her, but pretty soon we both were laughing.

"The look on that girl's face when your tail hit the water!" Aunt True gasped, struggling to catch her breath.

That set us off again. When we were finally able to compose ourselves, my aunt gave me another hug. "Better?"

I nodded.

"Good." She chucked me under the chin. "Now get back out there and be the tall timber that you and I both know you are. And as for the fake kiss, that's all it is—fake. Trust me, as a former member of the West Hartfield High School Thespian Club, I know! I've had my fair share of stage kisses, and they're nothing like the real thing."

Easy for her to say, I thought as I started for home. I hadn't had the real thing yet. And at this rate, it was entirely possible that I never would.

CHAPTER 29

Back home, I had just passed the portrait of my namesake on the stairs when my cell phone buzzed. It was Mackenzie.

GOT TIME TO VIDEO CHAT?

I texted back a thumbs-up and sprinted the rest of the way to my bedroom, shutting the door behind me. A moment later, her face appeared on my cell phone screen.

"Hey!" she said.

"Hey yourself! I thought you were on the way to Yellowstone with your parents?"

My cousin shook her head. "We don't leave until tomorrow morning. How's it going?"

I filled her in on everything that had happened since she left. Like me, she let out a screech when she heard about Amanda Appleton's upcoming appearance at Lovejoy Books, and another when I told her about our encounters at the

REALLY TRULY

General Store and the library. She also wanted to know if we'd found the silver pumpkin trophy yet.

"No, but we have five suspects. I still think it's the Grateful Dead guy, but the guys think maybe it was the teenagers." I explained about how our friends had been taking the crowd-sourced photos around town. "They were at Lou's this morning during Romeo hour, and one of the men was almost certain he'd seen the two teenagers before."

In Pumpkin Falls, "Romeo hour" had nothing to do with Calhoun and everything to do with what Reverend Quinn had dubbed the "Retired Old Men Eating Out" club. A couple of times a week, the Romeos arrived early at Lou's and lingered over coffee and breakfast.

When I told Mackenzie about the kiss at the end of *The Pirates of Penzance*, I had a hard time not bursting into tears again.

She was quiet for a moment. "Ouch," she said. "I get how tough that is. But you know, Truly, there's a simple solution to your problem."

I looked at her in surprise. "There is?"

"Sure. You kiss Calhoun first!"

My mouth dropped open. "But—"

"But what? Why not?" She gave me a sly smile. "That's what I did with Cameron, you know."

"Mr. Perfect?"

"Don't call him that."

"You never told me that's what happened!"

"You never asked! I could tell he was working up the courage, and I beat him to the punch, that's all. Maybe it's the same with Calhoun."

Was it possible she was right?

We chatted for a while longer, then I told her I hoped she'd have fun at Yellowstone and we said good night. As I was getting ready for bed, my cell phone buzzed again. This time it was Jasmine.

YOU GUYS WANT TO EXPLORE CHERRY ISLAND TOMORROW?

My cell phone buzzed like crazy as her question brought a series of enthusiastic texts from the other Pumpkin Falls Private Eyes.

DON'T KNOW IF I CAN SNEAK AWAY, I replied cautiously. I'LL TRY.

I gave it my best shot the following morning at the bookstore.

"Um, the books that Mom ordered for Lauren and Pippa just came in," I told my father a few minutes after I showed up for my shift. "Is it okay if I ride my bike out to camp and deliver them?" I quickly added, "Sir?"

"Nice try," he said calmly, not even looking up from his computer. "You're grounded, remember?"

Aunt True came to my rescue. "And you're being unreasonable, J. T.! It saves us time and money if she's willing to be our delivery girl—plus, Artie Olsen liked your Terminator hot sauce, and he put in an order for half a dozen bottles for the Parents' Weekend barbecue. Truly can take those with her."

Silence. Then: "Fine, but no dawdling. I expect you to come right back here."

Coming right back to the bookstore wouldn't leave me enough time to check out Cherry Island. I wondered what white lie I might be able to produce that would help with that. A flat tire on my bike, maybe?

But I didn't need to resort to a lie, white or otherwise.

"Nonsense! For Pete's sake, J. T., it's July!" said Aunt True sternly. My father looked up, opened his mouth to say something, then closed it again. Resistance was pointless when my aunt was in full big-sister mode. "The girl has been working her socks off for us this year—without pay, may I remind you—and it's a long ride out to the lake. She's earned a little R and R. You can ground her again afterward."

My father crossed his arms over his chest and frowned. "I'm clearly outflanked," he said, dismissing me with a flap of his hand.

Aunt True shooed me toward the door. "Take your towel and bathing suit with you and go for a swim if you get the opportunity," she whispered. "Just make sure you're back in time to help me set up for the book signing."

I wasn't looking forward to that.

"How are we going to get out to the island?" asked Jasmine when we all met up a little while later on the road to the lake.

"We'll figure it out when we get there," I said. "Swim if we have to. The island isn't that far from the public beach. Lauren says that kids from Camp Lovejoy swim to it all the time."

Luck was with us, though, in the form of Artie Olsen.

"You kids are going to do what?" he said, when he overheard us talking as I delivered his order of hot sauce. "Absolutely no way. Not a good idea to swim that far without supervision. We always send a canoe out with the campers when they do the Cherry Island swim. Why do you want to go, anyway?"

I thought quickly. "There's a bald eagle's nest out there," I replied, which was true. "My grandfather has taken me to see it a few times. I'm a birder." Which was also true.

Mr. Olsen smiled. "A birder! As am I." He eyed us thoughtfully. "How about if I lend you our war canoe?"

"War canoe?" Lucas's eyes widened in alarm. I could tell he was thinking that his mother wouldn't like the sound of that.

"Just another name for a big canoe, son. It can seat up to fifteen, but six can man it nicely."

"Wow—thanks, Mr. Olsen!" I said.

"No problem. It's the least I can do for a fellow birder—

and the daughter of the man who makes my new favorite hot sauce." He put a finger to his lips. "Don't tell a soul, though, or I'll have the whole town down here wanting to use our equipment." He made us promise to wear life preservers and, after glancing at the clock, said he'd go ask the kitchen staff to pack us a lunch. "Can't have you starving to death on camp property."

I asked at the front office about Lauren, who I learned was away on an overnight hike, so I left her new book in her cabin.

"Ooo, a mermaid book," said Cha Cha as I set it on my sister's bunk. "*The Tail of Emily Windsnap*—she'll love it."

My mother definitely had mermaids on the brain. She'd bought a copy of a picture book called *The Mermaid* for Pippa, who we found doing something with glitter in the arts and crafts studio.

"Truly!" she squealed, running over to give me a big hug. She turned to her cabin-mates and announced proudly, "She's my SISTER!"

"Is she a giant?" whispered one of them, and Scooter started to laugh.

"Don't," I warned him, but it was too late. He couldn't resist.

"Truly gigantic," he teased.

"Shut up, Scooter," said Calhoun, but he was smiling too.

Actually, to my surprise, so was I. *Maybe Aunt True was right*, I thought. Maybe people did grow and change—even me.

It was an easy paddle out to the island, thanks to Jasmine and Scooter, who knew their way around a canoe and told us exactly what to do. When we reached the shore, which was mostly rocky, Jasmine hopped out and guided the boat to a small sandy stretch that sloped up toward a tangle of bushes lining the shore. The canoe was heavy, and it took all six of us to pull it high enough out of the water that it wouldn't float away.

Calhoun shucked off his backpack and took a seat on a fallen log. "Eat first, then explore."

No one protested that idea. I sat down beside him. For one wild moment I wondered what he'd do if I grabbed him and kissed him. Not that I was actually planning to, of course.

He glanced over at me. "What are you laughing about?"

"Nothing."

I'd only had a couple of mini blueberry muffins since breakfast, and I was starving. Thelma Farnsworth and her sister Ethel, who worked in the camp kitchen during the summer, had packed substantial lunches for us, I was happy to see. Turkey sandwiches, potato chips, apples, peanut butter cookies, and bottles of water to wash it all down. I ate happily, enjoying the slight breeze that rustled the leaves in the trees above. I tipped my head back and closed my eyes, feeling the warmth of the sun on my face. A shadow fell over me, and I looked up.

"Check it out! It's an eagle!" I'd been hoping we'd see one.

REALLY TRULY

My friends all shaded their eyes and looked up too.

"Wow, it's huge!" said Scooter.

"Right? They're amazing."

We watched as the large bird circled overhead, then landed in a dark mass of branches high up in one of the trees.

"That's its nest," I explained. "Did you know that a bald eagle's nest can weigh up to a ton and measure up to eight feet across?"

"Ooo, 'Fun Facts with Truly'!" Cha Cha sounded like Mackenzie, who loved to tease me about what she called my obsession with birds. She quickly added, "But that's a really cool fun fact."

After lunch, it was time to explore. Scooter pulled out his cell phone and scrolled to the picture of the topographical map we'd found at the library.

"How about we start with the trail that circles the island," suggested Calhoun, squinting at it.

"What are we looking for?" asked Jasmine.

I shrugged. "I have a feeling we'll know it when we see it."

Our loop around the small island revealed exactly nothing, though.

"Guess we're going to have to bushwhack in toward the center," said Calhoun.

The island's tangled interior was not an inviting prospect. But Calhoun was right—there really wasn't an alternative.

"Let's head for that big tree with the eagle's nest in it," I suggested. "We want to look for something that might have been around when Nathaniel Daniel was here. A tree like that one, a big rock—some landmark that would have been easy for him to find again."

"Good thinking," said Cha Cha, but after another half hour we still had nothing, unless you counted the scratches on our arms and legs from pushing through the undergrowth.

"Too bad we don't have a treasure map." Jasmine leaned back against a tree trunk and pulled out her water bottle. The rest of us pulled ours out too. It was hot, even in the shade.

We were quiet for a while, listening to the lapping of the water on the shore nearby. It was disappointing to have come so far and not find anything that looked remotely like a pirate's hideout.

"If you were going to stash a treasure someplace," I mused aloud, "where would you put it?"

"Inside a hollow tree?" Cha Cha suggested.

I shook my head. "Lightning could strike, the tree could fall down in a storm—not safe enough."

"It's not like there's a bank vault out here," said Scooter.

"Not a vault, but someplace secure," I told him. "Dandy Dan had a lot of pirate gold to stash away, and he'd have wanted to keep it safe."

Calhoun dumped the rest of the contents of his water bottle over his head. "Let's take one more look, then call it a day. I want to go for a swim."

REALLY TRULY

We spread out this time, and for a while there was nothing but the sound of branches snapping underfoot and people slapping at mosquitoes. Then Scooter gave a yelp that brought the rest of us thrashing toward him through the underbrush.

"It's probably nothing," he said, pointing to what looked like a dark crevice beside a boulder. "It's so overgrown I almost missed it."

The six of us tugged on the vines and branches that covered the crevice, and a few minutes later were rewarded with what was clearly a genuine opening. My skin prickled in excitement. "This could be it, guys!"

"What if it's a bear's den?" asked Lucas.

My excitement fizzled. Jasmine took a step back in alarm. It did kind of look like it could be a bear's den.

Calhoun shook his head. "No scat."

"No what?" Scooter's forehead puckered.

"Scat," I told him. "Animal droppings—poop. Calhoun is right. I don't think anything or anyone lives here."

We turned on the flashlight apps on our cell phones and shined them inside. The opening led to a narrow passageway—too narrow for most of us—and blackness beyond.

I looked over at my friends. "Lucas, you and Cha Cha are the only ones small enough to fit."

Cha Cha scowled. "No way am I going in there!"

Lucas turned even paler than his usual shade of pale. "My mother would kill me."

"So don't tell her, duh!" scoffed Scooter.

"Shut up, Scooter," said his sister.

"Maybe we should come back tomorrow with better flashlights," said Cha Cha,

As we turned to go, Calhoun shrugged off his backpack again. "No time like the present," he said, and we paused to watch as he pulled out a length of rope, a bike helmet, a headlamp, and some duct tape. Noticing us staring at him, he straightened. "What? You can't go spelunking without the proper equipment."

Scooter's forehead pleated again. "Spe-what?"

"Spelunking—you know, cave exploring. I figured a cave might be one possibility that Dandy Dan would consider, and I thought I might as well come prepared in case we found one."

I stared at him, wondering if he would ever cease to amaze me.

"You can do this," Calhoun said, turning to Lucas and cinching the rope around his waist.

Swim team had been good for Lucas. He was still skinny, but he'd added muscle over the past months. He still looked anxious, though.

"You can't breathe a word about this to your mother!" I told him.

"Are you crazy?" He shook his head vigorously. "Not a chance."

REALLY TRULY

Calhoun settled the bike helmet on Lucas's head and strapped it firmly in place. Then he reached over and flipped on the headlamp he'd attached with duct tape. "Okay, buddy, in you go. Just take it slow and steady, inch by inch. There's no rush."

Squaring his narrow shoulders, Lucas nodded, then crouched down and squeezed into the opening. "Yuck," he said. "It's kind of damp in here." There was silence for a bit. We could hear him scrabbling around. "The tunnel gets bigger!" His voice echoed. He sounded nervous, but a little excited, too. And then there was silence again.

"Lucas?" Calhoun called.

There was no response.

"Lucas!" This time, Calhoun's question was answered by a squeak and more scrabbling as Lucas came backing swiftly out of the opening. He was covered with dirt and leaves and pine needles.

"Is it a bear?" asked Jasmine, her eyes wide.

Lucas shook his head. "Worse. There's a big hole in the ground, and I almost fell in!"

CHAPTER 30

It took some convincing, but we finally got Lucas to go back into the cave again.

"Take your cell phone this time," I told him. "See if you can get some pictures."

He reappeared a few minutes later, and we all gathered around. There wasn't much to see in his photos, mostly just the dim outline of rocks on the ground and roots sticking out overhead.

"There," said Lucas, pointing. "There's the hole."

It was difficult to make it out, but he was right. There was a hole in the ground.

I peered at a faint glimmer of light in the corner. "What's that?"

Lucas shrugged. "I'm not sure. I held my cell phone out over the edge, but I was afraid I might drop it, and I didn't want to lean over very far myself in case I fell in. I think maybe there's water down at the bottom, though. I could hear sloshing."

"I'm going in," I told my friends.

"You won't fit," warned Calhoun.

"Truly gigantic," Scooter added again helpfully.

I gave him a look. "I've got to try, at least. If you guys hold really tight to the rope, maybe I can lean down over the edge and get a better view. I'm a lot taller than Lucas." I looked over at Scooter. "Just don't."

He didn't. But he grinned.

"Okay, then," said Calhoun briskly. He transferred the bike helmet from Lucas's head to mine and fastened the rope securely around my waist. "One tug means yes, two means no. Three tugs from you means you're ready for us to pull you out."

Crouching down, I sucked in my breath—and the rest of me—and somehow managed to squeeze myself through the narrow gap beside the boulder. Lucas was right, the passage smelled like wet leaves and dirt. I winced as I scraped my head against the low roof.

"See anything?" called Cha Cha.

"Not yet."

"The hole sneaks up on you!" Lucas warned. "Be careful!"

Inching cautiously forward, I soon reached the edge of the hole. I knelt down on all fours, turning my head slowly as I shined the headlamp around its circumference. It was larger than I thought, probably at least as wide as I was tall. If I was expecting to see a big sign that said THIS WAY TO PIRATE TREASURE! though, I was disappointed.

There wasn't much to see anywhere else, either. Just dirt and roots and rocks. Nothing to indicate that this was anything but an ordinary cave.

"Doing okay in there?" I heard Calhoun's muffled voice in the distance and gave the rope one sharp tug in reply. Flattening myself onto my stomach, I crawled forward and peeked over the edge of the hole.

It was deep. Very deep. Lucas had been right about the sloshing sound—I could hear it too. I groped around for a rock and dropped it in. It seemed a long time before I heard a plunk as it hit the water below. I inched forward again until my entire head and shoulders were extended out over the edge, then aimed the headlamp directly downward. I peered into the darkness. Light from my headlamp reflected on the water, but I could also see light reflecting up *through* the water. It had to be coming from outside! There was another entrance to the cave!

I tugged on the rope three times and my friends started to haul me back.

"Ouch," I called in protest as my chest scraped against a sharp rock. I heard my T-shirt tear. "Slowly!" Flinging out an arm to steady myself, I grabbed on to what I thought was a root. It pulled away from the dirt, and I was still clutching it when I emerged into the sunlight.

REALLY TRULY

"There's another entrance," I panted, dropping the root and swiping at my dirt-encrusted clothes. "I could see daylight in the water down at the bottom of the hole. The underwater opening must be somewhere along the shore."

"Which direction?" Calhoun asked.

I looked around, disoriented. "I have no idea."

"What's that?" Cha Cha pointed at the ground.

"A root." I prodded it with my toe.

She bent down and picked it up. "I don't think so, Truly."

We all leaned in to examine it more closely.

"I looks kind of familiar," said Jasmine. "I think it's a piece of rope, like the kind we saw at the pirate museum on Cape Cod."

My friends and I stared at each other in awe.

"She's right!" I whispered. "I think we found Dandy Dan's cave!"

CHAPTER 31

We hid the opening to the cave as best we could, piling up branches and leaves until it was nearly invisible again. Covering our tracks back to the main path was almost impossible, though. We'd broken a lot of branches in our initial rush to get to Scooter. We could only hope that if anyone else came out to the island they wouldn't notice.

I really, really wanted to hunt for the underwater entrance, but it was getting late, and I was due back at the bookstore for Amanda Appleton's signing. "We can come back again tomorrow, maybe," I told my friends, tucking the length of tarred rope safely into my backpack.

Cha Cha looked Lucas and me up and down, smiling. "You guys had better wash off before we go back."

I glanced over at Lucas. If I looked anything like he did, she was right. He was streaked with dirt, there were wet leaves tangled in his hair, and as for his clothes—well, he was going to have a hard time explaining them to his mother.

I waded out into the water and dove in. Lucas followed, and so did the rest of our friends. We swam around for a few minutes, splashing each other and whooping with excitement over our discovery.

After we paddled back to the camp and returned the war canoe to Artie Olsen, we got on our bikes and headed for home. We were halfway to Pumpkin Falls when a red sports car with a kayak strapped to its roof passed us going in the opposite direction.

Cha Cha's head swiveled around. "Hey!" she called over her shoulder. "Wasn't that—"

"Yeah," I replied, steering my bike to the edge of the road. "Amanda Appleton."

My friends pulled over to join me, and we exchanged worried glances.

"She's headed toward the lake," said Lucas. "What if she goes out to the island?"

Calhoun shook his head. "She won't have time. The book signing starts in an hour."

Hopping back on my bike, I picked up my pace, arriving at the bookstore just as Aunt True and Belinda finished setting up the chairs. "Sorry I'm late!"

"No worries." Aunt True's eyebrows flew up when she looked at me. "You might want to freshen up before the customers start arriving, though. You can borrow something of mine."

I ran upstairs to her apartment. When I saw myself in her bathroom mirror, I almost burst out laughing. The swim in the lake had cleaned most of the dirt off, but my hair was sticking up every which way, and my T-shirt was torn in three places.

I washed my face and brushed my hair, then rummaged through my aunt's closet for something suitable to wear. Aunt True and I had totally opposite tastes in clothing. My aunt was a parrot, never happier than when she was parading around in bright colors and wild fabrics. I was—what was I, anyway? A partridge, maybe? I glanced in the mirror again. Yeah, a partridge. Mainly brown plumage, with just a few understated stripes in my feathers.

I settled on a pair of jeans, a T-shirt in a not-too-bright shade of teal, and a pair of sandals that weren't my usual style, but whose teal beads matched the color of the shirt I'd chosen. On a whim, I added a pair of dangly turquoise earrings. *Stripes in my feathers,* I thought, smiling to myself.

"Very nice!" said Aunt True approvingly when she saw me. "You should borrow my clothes more often."

"Guess what?" I started to tell her. "We—"

"You can tell me later," she said, twirling me around by the shoulders and giving me a little shove. "Right now, see if you can help Belinda at Cup and Chaucer. Things are hopping over there."

They certainly were. I barely had a moment to catch my breath for the next few minutes as we waited on the crush of

REALLY TRULY

customers eager to buy a beverage before the book talk started.

"I'll take a chai tea latte, please."

I looked up to see Dr. Appleton standing in front of me. She was dressed in the same outfit she'd worn for the book signing on Cape Cod—the one that screamed *I may have been a pirate in a previous life*. I blinked. "Uh, sure. Coming right up."

"Did you have a fruitful day yesterday?"

"Fruitful?" I tried not to sound panicked. *Why was she asking? Did she know about Cherry Island and the cave?*

"Successful. With your research. *The Pirates of Penzance*, was it?"

"Oh that!" I nodded, then busied myself with her drink order to cover my relief.

She smiled. "Wonderful. That's what I love about research—the thrill of the hunt."

I gave her a thin smile in return as I handed over her cup. *Definitely a pirate*, I thought, watching as she walked away. And not just in a previous life. In this one too.

"If everyone could take a seat, we'll get started," Aunt True announced.

"Go sit down with your friends," Belinda whispered to me. "I can handle things from here."

I made my way around the edge of the crowd to the back, where I took a seat between Lucas and Cha Cha. Farther down the row of seats, Calhoun leaned forward and waved. I waved back.

"We have a real treat for you today, folks," my aunt continued, holding up a copy of *Saga of a Ship: The Lost Treasure of the Windborne*. "Author Amanda Appleton will be sharing with us the story behind her new book. It's a stirring tale of piracy on the high seas, of skullduggery under the back flag, and of a mysterious missing treasure. Please join me in welcoming her to Lovejoy's Books!"

The crowd clapped enthusiastically as Dr. Appleton crossed to the podium. Before she could say anything, though, the bell over the door jangled, and Ella Bellow came in. Bud Jefferson and Lucas's mother were right behind her, holding hands. Beside me, Lucas's face flushed pink.

"Plenty of seats down front," Dr. Appleton told the latecomers. "You haven't missed a thing—we're just getting started."

As they made their way to the front row, Amelia Winthrop scanned the crowd for Lucas. She spotted him with us and blew him a kiss.

"Ooo, Lukey-pookey!" whispered Scooter. "Mommy loves you!"

"Could you please find another hobby, Scooter?" I whispered back, as Lucas's face went from pink to fire-engine red.

"I'm just teasing!"

"Nobody thinks it's funny but you."

I felt something brush past my ankles and looked down to see Memphis stalk by. My aunt's cat loathed book signings.

REALLY TRULY

Too many people. He crouched under my chair, glaring balefully out at the crowd. Miss Marple, on the other hand, was in her element, making her way up and down the rows of chairs collecting pats. My aunt shooed her onto her dog bed by the cash register as Dr. Appleton began to speak.

Her talk was almost identical to the one we'd heard on Cape Cod. She told the audience about herself and her background, explained her research and writing process, and then shared the story of how she got hooked on hunting for pirate treasure, showing off the silver coin on her necklace. This time, though, when she described the *Windborne*'s final tragic voyage, she zeroed in on Dandy Dan.

"I've recently learned that the *Windborne*'s sole survivor may have a Pumpkin Falls connection," she told the audience. "It's an exciting new development that I'm here in town to explore, in fact."

Ella Bellow's hand shot into the air.

"Yes?"

"If there is indeed a connection, can we expect an influx of visitors and treasure hunters once the news is out?"

Ella loved tourists. They were good for business, she said, which was true.

The author pursed her lips, considering. "It's entirely possible. Quite likely, in fact."

This caused a ripple of interest, particularly among the local business owners.

"How do you feel about that?" asked Bud Jefferson. "More treasure hunters means more competition, right?"

Dr. Appleton shrugged. "My motto has always been, 'May the best man—or woman, as the case may be—win.'"

Was it my imagination, or was she looking directly at me when she said that?

CHAPTER 32

The thing about Lovejoys? We were competitive.

Really competitive.

And unlike Four on the Fourth, this was one race I was determined not just to finish, but to win. Especially now that we'd had a taste of victory with the discovery of what was very likely Dandy Dan's cave. I didn't want Amanda Appleton unraveling my family secret before I did. This was my mystery to solve, not hers.

I said as much to my friends as we all crowded into the big booth at the back of Lou's Diner with my aunt after the book signing. My father didn't like my being there one bit, but he could hardly argue with the fact that I'd just worked another two-hour shift—for free—and that I needed to eat before rehearsal.

"I'll buy her dinner and then drop her off at the Grange," my aunt had told him. "No detours, I promise."

After we placed our order, we finally had a chance to show my aunt what we'd discovered on Cherry Island.

"This is astonishing!" she said, running a finger along the length of rope. "I mean, it's got to be, what, nearly three hundred years old?" She shook her head in amazement. "The tar must have helped preserve it from rotting. Rusty will be beside himself." Seeing the looks on our faces she added hastily, "But don't worry—I won't breathe a word to him until you give me the okay."

She made us promise we wouldn't go back to Cherry Island alone, though. "Caves are notoriously dangerous," she warned. "I don't want anyone getting hurt."

As for Dr. Appleton, Aunt True had come up with a brilliant plan for finding out what she was up to. She'd sicced Ella Bellow on her.

"It hit me the minute Ella walked in the bookshop," she told us. "If you have a secret weapon, you might as well use it, right?"

As everyone had lined up to get their books signed, Aunt True had pulled Ella aside and hinted that she thought something about the author was a little fishy. That instantly caught Ella's attention, and she'd spent the rest of the evening plying Dr. Appleton with questions. She'd managed to extract a fair amount of information, too.

Aunt True ticked the details off on her fingers. "She's staying at the Pumpkin Falls Bed and Breakfast; her plans are 'indefinite'—which means she probably won't be leaving anytime soon—and she's been fishing in the college archives."

My friends and I looked at each other in dismay. Once again, Dr. Appleton was one step ahead of us!

"Has she made the connection between Dandy Dan and Nathaniel Daniel?" I asked.

My aunt shrugged. "Maybe? She mentioned to Ella that she was looking into all the early settlers who arrived here in Pumpkin Falls soon after the wreck of the *Windborne*."

It wouldn't be long before she zeroed in on Nathaniel Daniel Lovejoy in that case, I thought glumly, if she hadn't already.

After dinner, Mrs. Abramowitz was waiting outside to drive us to the Grange. She'd volunteered to help with the choreography for the show.

"*The Pirates of Penzance* is one of my favorites!" she said as we piled into Cha Cha's SUV. "And the fifties setting is so fabulous—I'll have you all doing the bunny hop and the jitterbug in no time. You kids are going to have a blast!"

This did not sound like a blast to me. I stared down at my feet, which didn't always cooperate in the dancing department, grateful for once that they'd be safely encased in the shimmertail.

So far, stage crew had been less boring than I'd expected. Lucas was good company, despite his standoffishness with Bud Jefferson, who was clearly determined to make this the bonding experience that Mrs. Winthrop was hoping for. Plus, my knack for the window displays at the bookshop seemed to have carried over to stage design, as I'd come up with several good ideas that nobody had thought of, including the addition of an ice cream–themed mural on the back wall of the Rockin' Mermaid Malt Shop.

Tonight, while my brother and friends rotated between costume fittings, their first few scene run-throughs, and vocal and dance practice, the members of the stage crew were brainstorming details for props and set decorations. We figured that the second act, which would take place in a high school gymnasium during prom, was a no brainer.

"All we need is a disco ball, a bunch of streamers and banners, and boom we're done," Belinda said, and we all agreed.

The set for the first act, though, was more challenging. Recreating a 1950s malt shop was going to take a lot of work.

"I'm hanging up my hat after this production, and I want to go out on a high note," Belinda told us, hoisting her kitten-du-jour, a little orange tiger, into the air for emphasis. "This has to be a real showstopper."

"CORN POPPER?" said Elmer Farnsworth.

"SHOWSTOPPER!" Belinda repeated.

"I HAVE A CORN POPPER IN MY TRUCK!" he assured her, springing to his feet. "OTHER STUFF TOO."

Belinda heaved a sigh as Elmer darted off. "Come on, team. We might as well go take a look."

REALLY TRULY

She passed her kitten to Augustus, who reached for it automatically and put it in his backpack. We all followed them out back to where Elmer's truck was parked. It looked to be nearly as old as he was, and it was loaded to the gills. The junk pile in Elmer's barn was legendary around Pumpkin Falls, and he appeared to have brought half of it with him.

"All right, folks, dig in!" said Belinda. "We're looking for anything that might remotely work as a prop for a 1950s malt shop."

Before we knew it, we were wrestling a vintage red Coca-Cola machine, a couple of old diner booths, a set of heavy chrome stools, and assorted kitchenware into the Grange.

"These will make swell props, Elmer—thanks!" Belinda enthused. She looked over to where I was setting a toaster down on the floor of the stage. "Think you could handle an art project, Truly?"

I shrugged. "I could try, I guess."

A little while later, Hatcher wandered over and looked at the big piece of plywood propped up against the stage in front of me. "Not bad, Drooly," he said, watching over my shoulder as I sketched a mermaid onto it for the Rockin' Mermaid sign that Dr. Calhoun envisioned.

"Don't call me that," I said automatically. I frowned, concentrating on getting the sweep of her tail just right. "You didn't sound too bad just now either."

"Thanks. My solo is really hard, though. Do you think

you might have time to help me practice at home?"

I looked at him, surprised and pleased that he wanted to hang out with me. "Sure!"

Over on the other side of the Grange, Ms. Patel struck a chord on the piano, and Cha Cha started to sing. Hatcher and I both turned to watch. For someone so small, Cha Cha sure was loud. And if her speaking voice was low, her singing voice was just the opposite. She didn't sound like a kazoo at all. She could really hit the high notes, and most of them were even on pitch.

"Gather around, people!" Dr. Calhoun said when Cha Cha finished. "Parents' Weekend is coming up at Camp Lovejoy. Gwen and Artie Olsen, the directors, got wind of our production, and they've invited us to perform a sneak preview as entertainment for their big barbecue this weekend. I realize that's not much notice, but I told them yes. We'll do just a few songs—the first one featuring our pirates, of course. Then Mabel's 'Poor Wand'ring One,' which we just heard from Cha Cha and which is coming along nicely, and"—he looked over at my brother—"if you're feeling ready by the weekend, Hatcher, I thought we'd end with your solo. 'I Am the Very Model of a Modern Major-General' always brings down the house."

My brother gave a crisp salute. "Reporting for duty, sir!"

Dr. Calhoun scanned the cast and crew, his gaze settling on me. "While we won't be bothering with much in the way of sets or costumes," he continued, "I thought that since we'll

REALLY TRULY

be performing lakeside, it would be fun to wow everyone with our resident mermaid. I'd like you to open for us, Truly, since there's actual water for you to swim in. You'll be a big hit with the campers!"

My face turned the same shade as the vintage Coca-Cola machine. I was going to have to perform in public *again*? "Um, fine, I guess." At least I wouldn't have to worry about a wardrobe malfunction this time around.

"I'll leave the actual choreography up to you," Dr. Calhoun told me. "Just be sure to make a splash!"

That I could definitely do, especially in a shimmertail.

As I headed back to my art project, I passed Bud and Lucas.

"You'll love fishing!" I heard Bud assure my friend. "There's nothing better than being out on the water before dawn when the world is quiet."

Lucas looked like he could think of a lot of things that sounded better than that.

"You just name the time, and I'll take you," said Bud. "I don't even need advance warning. Canoe's always on my truck this time of year."

Later, while my brother and friends and I all waited for Mrs. Abramowitz, we told Hatcher about our trip to Cherry Island.

"That's awesome!" he said, inspecting the piece of rope I'd found. "I wish I could have been there with you. What's next?"

"The cave is off-limits for now," I told him. "Aunt True doesn't want us going back out there alone." I told him about Amanda Appleton and the information that Ella Bellow had extracted at the book signing. "Dr. Appleton has been fishing in the college archives, and she may have made the connection between Nathaniel Daniel and Dandy Dan. We need to find out what fish she's caught, if we want to get to the treasure first."

CHAPTER 33

The following morning, Lucas stopped by the bookstore after swim practice. "Ready to go?" he whispered, helping himself to a trio of blueberry donut muffins.

I glanced toward the office, where my father was frowning at his computer. "Um, not yet," I whispered back. "My dad hasn't left for physical therapy."

I continued tidying up Cup and Chaucer while Lucas killed time showing customers the crowdsourced photos of our suspects in the missing trophy case. It had been nearly two weeks now since the race, and it was hard not to get discouraged. We'd managed to narrow down our list of suspects a bit more—Reverend Quinn had vouched for his cousin in the baggy shorts—but we still hadn't had any luck figuring out who was behind the theft.

The bell over the door jangled, and Officer Tanglewood strolled in. "How about a cappuccino, Nancy Drew?" He snagged a handful of muffins while I prepared his beverage. Taking a bite of one he asked, "Mmmmph mmmmph?" which I was pretty sure translated to "Did you kids solve the case yet?"

I shook my head. "We're close, though," which wasn't necessarily true, but I wanted to wipe the smirk off his face, which it did.

My father left shortly after Officer Tanglewood did. I waited until Belinda arrived and Aunt True was busy with a sales rep, then slipped out.

"What happens if your father finds out?" Lucas asked as we jogged down Main Street toward Lovejoy College.

"He won't," I told him with more confidence than I felt. I was skating on thin ice these days, as Grandma G would say, and I knew it. My luck had held this far, though, and we really needed to get a look at the Lovejoy papers.

As we passed through the iron gates that marked the entrance to the college, I heard someone call my name. I turned to see Erastus Peckinpaugh coming toward us on one of the paths crisscrossing the campus.

Uh-oh, I thought in dismay. If Professor Rusty let it slip that he'd seen me here, my name would be mud.

"I thought you were grounded, Truly."

I nodded and crossed my fingers behind my back. "I'm just running a quick errand for the bookstore."

"Well, when you see your aunt, would you please tell her

not to forget we have an appointment with Reverend Quinn this afternoon at the church?"

Lucas looked surprised. "I thought my mom said the wedding wasn't until this fall."

My future uncle laughed. "We're not getting *married* today, Lucas. It's just some counseling that's required for engaged couples." He checked his watch. "Oops, duty calls—in this case my summer session class on American westward movement."

He loped off again. Lucas and I continued on to the college library, where we found our friends waiting for us on the broad granite steps.

"Where have you guys been?" rasped Cha Cha, rising to her feet. "We've been here forever!"

"Sorry," I told her. "We had to wait until my dad left."

Calhoun texted his father to let him know we were all here, then led us inside past the security guard. While we were waiting for Dr. Calhoun, I crossed the spacious lobby to the famous statue of my possibly pirate ancestor, who was also the college's founder.

"Time to give up your secrets, Nathaniel-Daniel-looks-like-a-spaniel," I whispered. Just like in his portrait at home, his nose was the most prominent feature on his face—and the shiniest, thanks to generations of college students who rubbed it for luck before exams. I reached out and rubbed it too. We could use all the luck we could get right about now.

"I think it's admirable that you want to learn more about our town's history," Dr. Calhoun told us a few minutes later as he steered us toward the stairs. "I'm impressed."

We followed him into the basement and down a long hallway to a door marked ARCHIVES. Inside, we had to surrender our backpacks and sign an official-looking form that basically said we promised not to steal or damage anything, or quote anything or take pictures of anything without permission.

Lucas glanced around the room. "It's kind of dark in here, isn't it?"

"Natural light isn't good for old documents and antiquarian books," Calhoun's father explained. "This area is climate-controlled. We have to keep it at just the right temperature and humidity levels to best preserve our college's treasures."

At the word "treasures," my friends and I exchanged glances. Calhoun's lips quirked up in a half smile. I knew exactly what he was thinking, because I was thinking the same thing—if his dad only knew what we were up to!

I recognized the archivist from the bookshop. She was a regular at our author events. She'd been at Amanda Appleton's, and she often hung out at Cup and Chaucer after work and on the weekends.

"You're the bookstore girl!" she blurted when he saw me.

"I see you're acquainted with our archivist, Peregrine Butler," said Calhoun's father.

REALLY TRULY

I looked at her with interest. Peregrine falcons were my second favorite bird, next to owls. I'd never met anyone named after one, though. The archivist didn't look much older than most of the college students on campus. Her short, spiky hair sported a broad green streak, and she also had a nose ring and a tattoo that spelled out *Dewey Decimal* circling her left wrist like a bracelet. I liked her immediately.

"I'll leave you in Dr. Butler's capable hands, then," Dr. Calhoun said. "I'll be upstairs in my office if you need me."

The archivist gave us a cheerful smile as he left. "Call me Peregrine, please. All this flurry of interest in Nathaniel Lovejoy! First Dr. Appleton, and now you kids. Of course, now that we know about a possible connection between Pumpkin Falls and the missing pirate treasure, it makes sense that people are looking into our town's early settlers. Is that what triggered your interest as well?"

"Partly," I replied. "That and the fact that he's my ancestor, and I've always wanted to know more about him."

Which was true, or at least true-ish.

"Well, let's see if we can satisfy your curiosity." Peregrine led us to a table at the back of the room, where she'd arranged an assortment of things for us to look at. Before we could touch any of them, though, we had to put on white cotton gloves.

"It's just like cotillion," said Scooter, waggling his fingers at me.

I groaned. "Don't remind me."

There was a lot of stuff to examine. The selection of Nathaniel Daniel's "papers" that had been set out for us included letters, account ledgers, deeds to his property, and his last will and testament.

"How are we supposed to read these?" Scooter complained, picking up one of the letters and squinting at the spidery script.

"I'm actually pretty good at deciphering old handwriting," said Calhoun, who apparently had no end of hidden talents. "My dad has a bunch of letters that my great-grandparents wrote to each other during World War Two. They're really interesting."

"Great," I told him. "You're in charge of the letters."

"I'll take the account ledgers," said Scooter quickly. "The numbers look easy to read."

His sister agreed to help him, while Cha Cha and Lucas zeroed in on the deeds. That left me with Nathaniel Daniel's last will and testament. I picked it up gingerly. It was old and fragile and looked like it would tear easily.

"That's been transcribed." Peregrine passed me two type-written pages. "You'll find this easier to decipher."

"No fair!" said Scooter.

"You chose the ledgers, you stick with the ledgers," I told him loftily. And settling into a chair, I started to read.

I, Nathaniel Daniel Lovejoy, being of sound mind, do hereby declare this document to be my last will and testament,

REALLY TRULY

the transcript began. Everything seemed pretty normal. He left his house—the one my family and I lived in now—and "all his worldly goods" to his wife, Prudence, except for a few bequests. There was money to help with the upkeep of the church, and some for the college, and even some to help with repairs on the covered bridge.

You wily fox! I thought. Nathaniel Daniel had covered his tracks well. Nobody in a million years would believe this public-spirited citizen was a pirate, which was likely just the way he'd wanted it.

There were also bequests of a few personal items. He left his gold pocket watch to his son, Obadiah, whose portrait I passed every day in the stairwell at home—and a harpsichord to his daughter, Abigail, whose portrait hung right beside her brother's. My eyes drifted down the page. A copper teakettle to a cousin, a horse to his friend and neighbor John Wainwright, blah blah blah, the list went on. I was just about to hand the pages back to the archivist when my gaze landed on the last item. It was tossed in almost like an afterthought, only it wasn't an afterthought.

It was the pot of gold at the end of the rainbow.

I sat up straight in my chair, every hair on the back of my neck at attention. *And finally, to my beloved wife, Prudence, I leave a parting gift—my signet ring engraved with an eagle in flight.*

That was the ring that Nathaniel Daniel was wearing in

his portrait at home! The one that had been passed down to my grandfather and would someday belong to my dad!

I continued reading. *May it serve to remind her of our courting days in the sunrise of our youth. Always remember, my love: Where the eagle flies, there lies the prize. Where the eaglet sleeps, harken to the deep.*

Where the eagle flies. Gramps had told me once that eagles had nested on Cherry Island for as long as anyone could remember. Had they nested there in Nathaniel Daniel's day too?

The clue fell into place as neatly as the final number in a sudoku puzzle.

To most readers, those words would seem just what they appeared to be—a sentimental gift from a loving husband to his wife. But they were likely much more than that. "The prize" had to be the pirate treasure, and Nathaniel Daniel was telling Prudence where she could find it! *Where the eaglet sleeps.* The eagle's nest in the tallest tree on the island was the key.

"May I take a picture of this?" I asked Peregrine, trying to keep the excitement out of my voice.

She glanced up from her desk. "Of the will? Sure."

I slipped my cell phone out of my pocket and snapped photos of the transcript. Then I kicked Cha Cha under the table and cut my eyes urgently toward the door.

She got the message.

"Hey, you guys," she said, setting a faded document back on the table. "I'm getting hungry. Can we break for lunch?"

The archivist looked surprised. "I told Dr. Calhoun I'd be happy to stay open as long as you need."

"Thank you, but we're starving," I said, handing her back the transcript. "This is really cool, though. Maybe we can come back again another day?"

I practically bolted out the door. I grabbed my backpack from the security guard and ran up the stairs two at a time. My friends were right behind me.

"What's your hurry?" asked Scooter.

"Look what I found!" I exclaimed, pulling out my cell phone and holding it up.

"'Where the eagle flies, there lies the prize,'" Calhoun read aloud, and I explained my theory about the nest.

"It can't possibly be the same tree," scoffed Scooter. "Nathaniel Daniel wrote that will back before the Revolutionary War!"

"There are plenty of trees around Pumpkin Falls that have been here for hundreds of years," I retorted. "My grandfather is always pointing them out. There's even one in our yard. Why not one on Cherry Island, too?"

"I guess it's possible," said Calhoun, but he sounded doubtful too.

"I just *know* this is it," I insisted. "This has to be the key to finding the treasure."

Jasmine frowned. "Do you think Dr. Appleton figured it out too? She's pretty smart."

"She may have figured out the connection to Cherry Island, and she may have figured out the part about the tree, but she still doesn't know about the cave."

"At least we hope she doesn't," said Lucas.

"So what do we do now?" asked Scooter.

"We 'harken to the deep.' We have to go back to the island. We have to find the underwater entrance and get to the treasure before Dr. Appleton does."

Cha Cha looked at me. "But we promised your aunt we wouldn't go alone!"

"We'll figure something out!" I called over my shoulder as I ran out the front door of the library—and smack-dab into my father.

CHAPTER 34

The thing about skating on thin ice is that you almost always fall in.

I should have known that my run of luck wouldn't last. My father was bound to find out about my escapades sooner or later, and now, thanks to a last-minute cancellation of his physical therapy session, he had. And he wasn't happy about it at all. In fact, I hadn't seen him this mad since I'd gotten an F-plus in math last winter.

Lieutenant Colonel Jericho T. Lovejoy did not like being lied to. Not one bit. He marched me home on the double.

"This is a breach of trust, young lady!" he stormed. "You knew the agreement—bookstore, piano lessons, stage crew." He ticked them off on the fingers of his good hand. "That's it! And now I find you've been sneaking around the whole time—"

"Not the whole time."

"Don't you talk back to me!"

"No, sir," I said meekly.

"I *knew* I was being too lenient! I never should have listened to your aunt."

When the dust finally settled, I was banned from the bookshop until further notice. The only reason I was still allowed to take piano lessons was because my parents had prepaid for the summer, and the only reason I was still allowed to be part of the stage crew was because my father considered it community service.

I was basically under house arrest.

"It's awful, Mackenzie!" I was sitting in my bedroom closet, video chatting with my cousin, who was at a lodge in Yellowstone. My father had taken away my cell phone again, but thanks to the fact that I'd kept my laptop hidden in my dresser drawer, he'd overlooked it. I kept my voice to a whisper since he was right downstairs. He'd set up a satellite office in the dining room now that I'd been deemed untrustworthy. "I can't even go out in the yard!"

"Hang in there," Mackenzie whispered back. "Your dad blows his top sometimes, but he'll calm down eventually. He always does."

I snorted. "Maybe by the time I'm twenty." My laptop dinged just then, and I glanced at the incoming request. "It's the PFPEs—gotta go."

"Say hi to everyone for me!"

REALLY TRULY

I promised I would, and we hung up. I clicked on the icon to answer the other call. "Hey!" I whispered.

My friends' faces appeared onscreen. "Sorry you're grounded again!" they chorused.

I gave them a wan smile. "I thought you'd be at Cherry Island by now."

Cha Cha shook her head. "Not without you."

"We're going to head over to the Pumpkin Falls Farmer's Market instead," Jasmine explained. "We figured that would be a good place to show the photos of our suspects from the Four on the Fourth."

"Somebody out there has got to recognize one of our suspects," said Lucas. "I can't believe we keep coming up empty-handed!"

Our suspects had dwindled to four people: the woman in the Red Sox baseball cap, the two teenage boys who locals thought might be from West Hartfield, and the older man in the Grateful Dead T-shirt and aviator sunglasses.

"Good luck," I told my friends. "Keep me updated." I told them to keep their eyes—and ears—out for any developments with Amanda Appleton, too, and then I hung up.

Bird-watching from my bedroom window killed some time, and I spent an hour practicing the piano. Miss Marple was at my heels as usual as I went back upstairs after that. She wasn't at the bookstore today because she'd been to the groomer this morning.

"At least I have you for company," I told her as the two of us settled onto my bed. Technically Miss Marple wasn't allowed up there, but I needed at least one friend by my side. I put my arm around her and buried my face in her fur. She smelled good, like coconuts. The bookstore's loss was my gain—Miss Marple was always fluffy and soft when she came back from the groomer.

I did a few sudoku puzzles and read another chapter in the book about eagles that I'd picked up at the library, but mostly I was bored. It was going to be a long summer if I had to spend it indoors.

By the following afternoon, I was still grounded and still bored.

The only bright spot was that between the rest of yesterday and most of today, I'd had plenty of time to help Hatcher practice his solo. We'd spent so much time at it, in fact, that our entire family knew the melody and words by heart. It was pretty catchy—more like a rap than a song. I'd overheard my mother singing it while she was washing the dishes last night, my father humming the tune at breakfast, and I'd even caught Danny, who between his summer job and hanging out with his girlfriend was hardly ever home except to sleep, whistling it to himself as he left on his late morning run.

Now I found myself whistling it, too, as I paced my bedroom. Miss Marple watched me anxiously, then clambered

REALLY TRULY

down from the bed and paced with me, whining. I had to find a way to be allowed out of the house! The chances of that happening, though, were slim to none. Not unless I could get my mother on my side, but that wouldn't be easy. My parents liked to present what they called a "united front" when it came to discipline.

I had one thing going for me, though. My mother felt my father was being too harsh. I knew this because I'd overheard them talking in the kitchen last night, after they finished the dishes. I'd gone downstairs to get a snack—I was still allowed to eat, as far as I knew—and paused on the stairs when I heard their voices.

"First no swim team and now no bookstore? Seriously, J. T.?"

"It's the principle of the thing!" my father replied stubbornly. My father was big on the principle of things.

"What's True going to do without her? She really depends on Truly, you know."

I could practically hear my father's jaw clenching. "That girl needs to learn a lesson. No means no."

Later, my mother had come upstairs to my room. "Hey," she said, poking her head in my door.

"Hey," I replied without enthusiasm.

She sat down on the end of my bed. "I've been so busy with summer school and work at the Starlite"—my mother had a part-time job at Cha Cha's parents' dance studio to help make ends meet—"that I feel like I haven't had time to spend with you, Little O."

Little O was her special nickname for me, short for Little Owl.

I lifted a shoulder.

"I'm sorry our plans got postponed by mermaid camp."

"Mermaid academy," I said automatically, and she laughed.

"You know what I mean. Anyway, I didn't want you to think I'd forgotten about you. I promise we'll squirrel away some mother-daughter time before you go back to school, okay?"

I nodded, and she leaned down and kissed the top of my head. "That's my girl."

She went back downstairs, leaving me to think about what she'd said. I recalled what my aunt had told me earlier, too, about my parents needing some time together. I felt a stab of guilt as I thought about how hard they were both working, my mother at her college classes and her part-time receptionist job at the Starlite, and my father at the bookstore. I knew money was tight these days, and it hadn't even occurred to me that I might be giving them more to worry about. I'd only been thinking about myself. Why was it so difficult to be unselfish and look at things from somebody else's perspective?

I took my binoculars out and watched idly as the postman made his rounds along Maple Street. Miss Marple, who had seri-

REALLY TRULY

ous postman radar, knew he was on his way even without binoculars. She woofed and ran downstairs to sit by the door as he came up the front path. Another woof announced that our mail had whooshed through the slot and landed on the entry hall rug.

"Truly!" my mother called a few moments later. "You've got mail!"

I never got mail, unless it was my birthday, which it wasn't. Puzzled, I went downstairs where I found a postcard and a letter waiting for me. The postcard was from Glacier National Park, where Zadie had somehow gotten wind of *The Pirates of Penzance*. "Break a leg—or a tail!" she'd written on the back, which I knew from the fountain of knowledge that was Calhoun was theater-speak for "good luck."

The letter was from Delphine.

> *Dear Grania,*
> *I did it! I signed a lease on a restaurant space and will be opening a café in Brewster this fall! I'm calling it Mermaid Crossing. My mother is trying to get Carson Dawson to feature me on* Hello, Boston! *Fingers and flukes crossed! I hope you're having a great summer, and that you come visit next time you're on the Cape. I'll make Mermaid Chip Cookies just for you.*
> *Love,*
> *Delphine*
> *PS How is the shimmertail doing?*

I tossed the letter onto my bed. *Hanging in the back of my closet,* I thought. I wasn't looking forward to wearing the tail—or the clamshell bra—again in public.

Later, at dinner, I stared glumly at the red-circled dates on our kitchen calendar. We had our next-to-last rehearsal tonight before the sneak preview of *The Pirates of Penzance* at Camp Lovejoy. After that, it was just ten days until opening night, when I'd have to watch Calhoun kiss Cha Cha Abramowitz.

Hatcher was working for Lobster Bob again, and Danny was at the movies with his girlfriend, so it was just my parents and me at the table. My father basically pretended I wasn't there. He read the newspaper while he ate, and my mother's few attempts at conversation fizzled.

"Are you going to drive her to rehearsal tonight, J. T., or should I?" she asked finally.

My father grunted.

"How about we both take her?" my mother suggested. "We'll drop her off, then swing by the General Store for ice cream. It seems to me you could use some cheering up."

My father grunted again, but it was an "okay, fine" kind of grunt. I slanted him a glance. Was it possible there was a thaw in the ice?

"We'll be back promptly at nine to pick you up," my father told me as they dropped me off at the Grange. "No dawdling."

"Yes, sir."

REALLY TRULY

Inside, I discovered that Elmer and Belinda had been busy. The set was nearly done! The two of them had stopped by for a couple of hours earlier in the day to finish painting the black-and-white-checkerboard pattern on the floor covering. It was almost dry.

"What do you think?" asked Belinda.

"I think it looks awesome!"

She looked pleased.

The ROCKIN' MERMAID sign was done too, so I turned my attention to putting the finishing touches on the mural. I still had a trio of larger-than-life sundaes to complete. As I painted, I hummed along with the cast, who were hard at work practicing the songs that they were scheduled to sing at tomorrow's sneak preview performance.

During the snack break—lemonade and Dr. Calhoun's homemade cowboy cookies—I had a few minutes to catch up with my friends. There'd been no new developments in the missing trophy case. The photos they'd been circulating around town had brought nothing but blank stares.

"And there's more bad news," said Cha Cha. "We saw Amanda Appleton heading out of town toward the lake again this morning with her kayak."

If Dr. Appleton found the treasure before we did, I'd never forgive myself! It was my own dumb fault that she had such a big head start on us, though. If it hadn't been for my pigheadedness in disobeying my father, I might have been free to rejoin the Pumpkin Falls Private Eyes by now.

I returned to my stage crew chores feeling discouraged.

An hour later, Belinda declared the paint on the floor dry enough to finish putting the set together. While Bud and Lucas nailed my ROCKIN' MERMAID sign over the fake door at the back of the stage, Belinda corralled Augustus into helping Elmer move the diner booths and jukebox and red Coca-Cola machine into place.

"Now this," said Belinda when we were done, "is what I call a showstopper!"

"Indeed," Augustus agreed, slipping an arm around her waist.

"All we need are some smaller props on the shelves and counters," she continued. "Plates, glasses, sundae dishes, that kind of thing. Maybe an old-fashioned milkshake mixer. Elmer!"

Elmer cupped his hand behind his ear.

"Do you have anything that could go on the shelves?"

"WHAT'S THAT ABOUT ELVES?"

"*SHELVES*, ELMER, *SHELVES!*" Belinda repeated. "WE NEED STUFF TO DISPLAY ON THE SHELVES!"

"YOU DON'T HAVE TO YELL! I'LL CHECK MY BARN WHEN I GET HOME."

"Gather round, people!" Calhoun's father called a few minutes later. "Our sneak preview performance is tomorrow. Since it's a Saturday, we'll be able to squeeze in a run-through

REALLY TRULY

first thing in the morning. Let's plan to meet back here at the Grange at nine a.m. sharp, okay?" He turned around and waved an arm grandly at the stage. "And how about a big round of applause for the stage crew for bringing our marvelous malt shop to life!"

The hall burst into cheers, and Belinda and Bud and Elmer and Lucas and I all took a bow.

Belinda crossed to the jukebox and punched a couple of buttons. "La Bamba" was one of my uncle Rooster's favorites, and as its familiar strains poured from the speakers, I joined in as everyone started jumping around to its infectious beat. It felt good to let off some steam.

"This looks amazing!" Surprised, I turned to see my mother gazing at the stage. My father was beside her. "You helped build this, Truly?"

I nodded. "I didn't do all that much. Just the 'Rockin' Mermaid' sign and that fake tile stuff behind the counter, and the mural."

"Well, I think it looks spectacular," said my mother. "Don't you agree, J. T.?"

My father gave a short nod. "Hard work always pays off."

Just five words, but they gave me hope. I knew it was pushing my luck, but I had to at least try. "Am I still grounded?"

My father snorted. "Of course you are!"

I looked over at my mother, who gave me a regretful look but didn't say anything. The united front was clearly still in full force.

I couldn't help myself. "Please, Dad! I'm really, really sorry I disobeyed you!"

"As you should be." He turned on his heel and stalked out.

I might as well just hand Dandy Dan's treasure over to Amanda Appleton, I thought bitterly as I followed him to the car. At this rate, the Pumpkin Falls Private Eyes would never be back in business.

CHAPTER 35

Dress rehearsal was a disaster in every possible way.

"People, people!" wailed Dr. Calhoun, clapping his hands over his ears. "Have you forgotten everything we've practiced? Listen to the piano and stay on pitch!" He shook his head wearily. "And you sounded so good last night!"

"It's okay," Belinda whispered, handing me a kitten for comfort. A tiny black one with a white splotch on its nose. "Dress rehearsals are traditionally terrible."

Lucas and I exchanged a worried glance. This terrible? Hatcher seemed to have forgotten all the words to his song, Cha Cha's high notes were in danger of shattering the glass on the chandeliers, and Calhoun and the other pirates were bumbling through their dance steps like—well, like Scooter and me at cotillion practice last winter.

We were going to be a laughingstock!

Bud Jefferson came up behind us and clapped a paw on

Lucas's shoulder. "Looking forward to our expedition tomorrow?" He'd finally worn Lucas down and, after promising Lucas's mother that he'd make him wear a life preserver, sunscreen with at least SPF 50, a hat, and wraparound sunglasses, they were scheduled to go fishing.

"Yeah, about that," Lucas replied, squirming away. "I don't think I'm going to be able to go after all."

Bud's smile wavered. "Oh, okay. Well, another time then?"

I stroked the kitten as I watched Bud droop over to join Elmer and Augustus.

"You know, Lucas," I said, thinking about my aunt's earlier advice, "not all change is bad."

He gave me a puzzled look.

"Bud's a really nice guy. Maybe you could give him a chance?"

"Maybe you could mind your own beeswax, *Drooly!*" Lucas snapped, my nickname shooting up an octave as his voice cracked.

I stared at him in shock as he stalked off. I'd never seen Lucas lose his temper before. When we broke for a midmorning snack a little later, he kept a wary distance as we gathered with our friends.

"We're down to just one suspect," Scooter said, helping himself to one of the donuts from Lou's that Mrs. Winthrop had brought for the cast and crew.

"Whoa!" said Cha Cha. "What happened?"

"It turns out that the woman in the Red Sox baseball cap is a client of my father's. I spotted her outside his office this morning, and, well, I guess I—"

"What my brother means to say is that he got hollered at for accusing her of stealing the trophy," said Jasmine.

"She took my question all wrong!" Scooter protested.

"And it gets worse," Jasmine continued smugly. "It turns out that the teenage boys are her kids. They were all at the race to cheer on their dad. My father hit the roof when he overheard Scooter questioning her."

At least I wasn't the only one whose father overreacted sometimes. "But this is good news, right?" I said. "This means the guy in the Grateful Dead T-shirt and aviator sunglasses has to be the thief!"

Scooter pulled out his cell phone, and we all stared at the picture of the older gentleman again. "How are we ever going to find him, though, since nobody knows who he is?"

"Who *who* is?" asked Augustus, who had wandered over to snag a donut. He peered over Scooter's shoulder and frowned. "Why do you have a picture of Frank on your phone?"

I looked up at him, startled. "Wait, you know him?"

"Sure. That's Frank Peabody, my agent. I've been his client for years. I invited him up to Pumpkin Falls to experience a real New England Fourth of July."

With all the people we'd shown the photo to, I couldn't

believe that we'd forgotten to show it to Augustus Wilde!

"So he didn't steal the pumpkin trophy?"

Augustus's eyebrows flew somewhere north of his hairline. "You kids didn't seriously think—*Frank*? Steal the silver pumpkin?"

"NAPKIN?" bellowed Elmer, who had spotted the donuts too.

"PUMPKIN!" Augustus bellowed back.

"I HAVE NAPKINS IN THE TRUCK!"

Augustus did a face-palm as Elmer trotted off.

My friends and I looked at each other in dismay. This was more than discouraging; this was disastrous for the Pumpkin Falls Private Eyes. Our final suspect had just gone down in flames. How were we ever going to face Officer Tanglewood now? We'd never hear the end of it.

One good thing came out of the rehearsal, though. We finally came up with a plan for getting back to Cherry Island. Or at least my friends did.

"You know," said Calhoun, taking a bite of donut, "since we're going to be at the lake later this afternoon anyway for our performance, it's the perfect opportunity to go back and look for the underwater cave."

"There'll be a ton of people around, though," Cha Cha pointed out. "How are we going to slip away?"

"Could we get our parents to drop us there early?" asked

REALLY TRULY

Jasmine. "Maybe tell them we want to spend the afternoon at the beach to relax before the show or something?"

"No way I can do that," I told them. "I'm still grounded. *Really truly* grounded this time."

"Okay, then, we wait until the barbecue to make our move," said Scooter. "People will be so busy eating and talking, they won't notice we're gone."

"What part of 'grounded' don't you understand?"

He looked at me and smiled. "C'mon, Truly! You found a way out of it before—you can find a way out of it again."

It was tempting.

Especially since a pirate treasure might hang in the balance.

But then I thought of my parents, and how hard they'd both been working this summer. They didn't need me adding to their worries. I was tall timber, I reminded myself. I could stand my ground and do the right thing for once.

"Nope," I told my friends. "You'll have to go without me this time."

CHAPTER 36

"'The play's the thing / Wherein I'll catch the conscience of the king,'" quoted Dr. Calhoun. We were in Camp Lovejoy's Lower Lodge, getting ready for our performance. It was stuffy inside, despite a whisper of breeze that drifted through the screened windows, and the large room smelled faintly of past fires in the giant stone fireplace. "That's the Bard, of course, from *Hamlet*. Not that our goal is to catch anyone's conscience! But if we can catch the *interest* of the audience, now that's a noble goal. With any luck, this sneak preview will whet their appetites and spur ticket sales."

We'd all been worried after this morning's dress rehearsal. Really worried. But Dr. Calhoun had tried to calm our fears. "Dress rehearsals are often less than perfect, to say the least," he'd said on the ride over in the camp bus that Artie Olsen had sent to pick us up. "Sure, you were a little rough this morning, but I've heard you practicing all week, and I have full confidence that you'll pull this off without a hitch."

Now he clapped his hands and beamed at us. "I have two surprises for you, people! First, we have been given special permission by Camp Lovejoy to use a very special stage for our performance—*Dreamboat*, the camp's floating cabin!"

There was a gasp of excitement at this announcement. Pippa and Lauren had told me about *Dreamboat*. One of the high points of camp was when each cabin got a turn to have a sleepover on it.

"And second," Dr. Calhoun continued, "Mrs. Winthrop stayed up late the last few nights, and she finished the costumes!"

A whoop went up as the cast crowded eagerly around Lucas's mother. She handed each actor his or her costume, and everyone scattered to the four corners of the room, which had been curtained off with bedsheets, to try them on.

Everyone except me. My costume was stuffed into the enormous duffel bag at my feet, and I wasn't planning on putting it on again until the very last minute.

"Check it out!" crowed Scooter, strutting across the lodge toward me a few minutes later. He was wearing jeans, a white T-shirt, and a fake black leather jacket with a skull-and-crossbones patch sewn on its breast pocket.

Calhoun was right behind him, dressed in an identical costume.

"Looking good, boys!" said Cha Cha, who resembled a

pint-size ball of fluff in her pink poodle skirt and matching pink cardigan.

"Thanks," said Calhoun, smiling at her. "You, too."

I'd been trying really hard not to think about their onstage kiss. At least the real thing was still over a week away. For this sneak preview performance, we were just doing a trio of numbers from the first act.

Hatcher emerged next in his Modern Major-General costume, which featured a ton of gold braid, rhinestone buttons, and big, flashy fake medals. Bling! Definitely nothing Lieutenant Colonel Jericho T. Lovejoy would ever be caught dead wearing, but it was going to look great onstage.

We all retreated to a quiet spot by one of the windows to go over the plan one more time. I glanced outside to see if I could spot my family and was dismayed to spot Amanda Appleton's familiar red sports car pulling into the parking lot. "What's she doing here?"

"My dad invited her," Calhoun replied sheepishly. "I totally forgot to tell you. He ran into her at the library again today after dress rehearsal and, well, I guess he thought that with her interest in pirates, she'd get a kick out of the show."

"Great." I heaved a sigh. "You guys will have to be extra careful when you head to the island, or she might try and follow you."

I scanned the crowd on the grassy lawn that led to the water-ski beach. My parents were here, of course—all of our parents were here. And so were Aunt True and Professor Rusty and both of my sisters. The wheelbarrow races were just finishing up, and there was a lot of shouting and cheering going on.

"After the show, when the barbecue starts, Hatcher will create a diversion," Scooter began. "On my signal, we'll peel off one by one and head for the kayaks."

"Wait, you're just going to take Camp Lovejoy's kayaks?" I said. "Without permission? This is your plan?"

"You've got a better one?"

I flapped my hand. "I'm sitting this one out, remember?"

"Like I was saying," Scooter continued, clearly enjoying the role of team leader for a change, "we head for the kayaks. Once we paddle out to the island, we'll find the eagle's nest tree, and Lucas will do the rest."

I looked over at Lucas, who had been avoiding me all day and still wouldn't look me in the eye. "Are you sure he's up to it?"

Calhoun shrugged. "He's the best swimmer we've got besides you."

Was it my imagination, or was Lucas looking paler than usual? I was guessing he didn't like this idea any more than I did, but he wasn't going to admit it. I chewed my lip. This whole thing had disaster written all over it. But what could I do to help? Nothing, that's what.

"Truly! I've been looking for you!" I turned to see Dr.

Calhoun crossing the room toward us. "Now that we're going to be using *Dreamboat* as our stage instead of the H dock, perhaps we should rethink your opening number."

We'd planned to have me embedded with the crowd of actors making their way toward the H dock—our original stage—before the performance. While they acted as a sort of human shield, I'd pull on the shimmertail and slip into the water unnoticed.

"*Dreamboat* is anchored in the cove on the other side of camp," Calhoun's father explained. "We're going to have Artie tow it around the point and surprise the audience after your opening number."

I saw the dilemma. With the cast aboard *Dreamboat*, how was I going to get into the water without the audience seeing me? Six-foot-tall mermaids were pretty hard to miss.

Suddenly I had a brainstorm. "Hey, Mr. Jefferson!" I called to Bud. He was standing over by Mrs. Winthrop as she helped make a few last-minute alterations to the Pirate King's costume. Hearing me call, he came right over.

"What's up, Truly?"

"Do you have your canoe with you?"

He nodded. "I always have my canoe with me."

That's what I'd been counting on.

"Would you be willing to be my camouflage? To help get me into place for the opening number, I mean. We could drive over to the public beach, and while you paddle I could hitch a ride back to camp along the far side of your canoe, where the audience won't see me."

"Brilliant!" said Dr. Calhoun. "What do you say, Bud?"

"Sure, no problem."

Five minutes later, Bud and I took off for his car as the pirates and maidens headed down to the cove where *Dreamboat* was waiting.

"I just have to put this thing on," I told Bud, patting my duffel bag as we pulled into a parking spot at the beach.

"No rush," he said. "It'll take me a few minutes to get the canoe into the water."

As I wiggled and squirmed my way into the shimmertail, the sensation was both familiar and strange. Sirena's Sea Siren Academy felt like a million years ago.

"Say, that thing looks real!" said Bud when I was done.

"Yeah, it's pretty cool." I scooted forward on the sand into the water, then propelled myself over to the far side of the canoe. Holding on to the gunwale while Bud paddled, I let myself be towed along the shoreline toward Camp Lovejoy. It was only a short distance from the public beach, and soon Bud was cutting over toward the center of the H dock. He drew up beside the leg closest to the water-ski beach. The waiting audience paid us no attention—to them, he was just another boat in the water.

"How's this?"

"Perfect," I said. "Thanks!"

As he paddled away, I held my breath and slipped below the surface of the water, emerging a moment later under the dock, where I clung to one of its supports and waited for my cue. I had a good view of the beach from here. People were spreading out towels and setting up folding chairs for the performance, including my parents, who were talking to Cha Cha's family. Bud had paddled his canoe to shore and joined Mrs. Winthrop; Ella Bellow was sitting with Belinda and Augustus. I spotted Amanda Appleton talking to Aunt True, who had a pleasantly bland expression on her face. I also spotted the tall red-haired girl from the road race—Cassidy something?—and Felicia Grunewald, Professor Rusty's assistant. They were both surrounded by their campers.

As the loudspeakers crackled and the first notes of the overture floated out over the water, Dr. Calhoun gave me a thumbs-up.

"Showtime," I whispered, determined to make Esther Williams—and Zadie and Lenore—proud.

Taking a deep breath, I dove down and dolphin-kicked my way underwater out to what I guessed was about the center of the area in front of the beach. Swishing the shimmertail back and forth mightily, I breached the surface like a rocket, then arced forward and dove down again, smacking my flukes against the water hard. Dr. Calhoun had asked me to "make a splash," and that was exactly what I planned to do.

The rest of my opening routine was made up of moves

...nging and sketched in the plot for the audience. It was lame but funny. Today was Frederic's—Calhoun's—twenty-first birthday, and he'd finally completed his years of servitude to the Pirate King. Now he'd decided to become an upstanding citizen. This wasn't going to be a smooth road, of course.

The maidens were up next, and after their opening chorus, Cha Cha—as Mabel—took center stage and belted out "Poor Wand'ring One" to Frederic, who had fallen in love at first sight.

Another synopsis from Dr. Calhoun followed. He explained that the girls were all the high-born daughters of the Major-General, and thus not marriage material for lowly pirates. Then it was Hatcher's turn. I held my breath as he began:

I am the very model of a modern Major-General,
I've information vegetable, animal, and mineral . . .

The lyrics to his rap-style song were complicated and silly. "Patter" was the term for it, Dr. Calhoun had explained to us, and it was one of the hallmarks of Gilbert and Sullivan. I sang along under my breath as the tempo increased. Had we practiced enough? Would Hatcher mess up? Faster and faster the music and lyrics went as the song neared its end, until Hatcher was flying along so fast I was sure he'd stumble.

But he didn't!

pieced together from the revue at Sirena's.
dolphin dives, I flipped over onto my back
water with my arms, held my legs up in the
waving my flukes back and forth.

"THAT'S MY SISTER!" I heard Pi
smiled wide and blew her a kiss.

Swim pretty, I reminded myself, and I di
and waving just like I'd been taught at merm
audience ate it up. As the overture neared
crossed the water in front of the beach in a
strokes, ending with one final dive and pow
flukes. As the onlookers clapped and cheere
the H dock and pulled myself up onto it, per
to watch the rest of the performance.

Hearing the low thrum of the water-ski
to watch as it came into view around the edg

"*Dreamboat!*" someone called, and the
and shouted "aaargh!" at the sight of the flag
and crossbones that fluttered from a pole o
the floating cabin was in position directly in f
Artie hopped aboard, dropped an anchor, t
into the ski boat and putt-putted away.

The music swelled, the front door and wi
boat flew open, and pirates came flooding
roared as they launched into the rousing ope

Dr. Calhoun stepped forward when the

ride back to camp along the far side of your canoe, where the audience won't see me."

"Brilliant!" said Dr. Calhoun. "What do you say, Bud?"

"Sure, no problem."

Five minutes later, Bud and I took off for his car as the pirates and maidens headed down to the cove where *Dreamboat* was waiting.

"I just have to put this thing on," I told Bud, patting my duffel bag as we pulled into a parking spot at the beach.

"No rush," he said. "It'll take me a few minutes to get the canoe into the water."

As I wiggled and squirmed my way into the shimmertail, the sensation was both familiar and strange. Sirena's Sea Siren Academy felt like a million years ago.

"Say, that thing looks real!" said Bud when I was done.

"Yeah, it's pretty cool." I scooted forward on the sand into the water, then propelled myself over to the far side of the canoe. Holding on to the gunwale while Bud paddled, I let myself be towed along the shoreline toward Camp Lovejoy. It was only a short distance from the public beach, and soon Bud was cutting over toward the center of the H dock. He drew up beside the leg closest to the water-ski beach. The waiting audience paid us no attention—to them, he was just another boat in the water.

"How's this?"

"Perfect," I said. "Thanks!"

As he paddled away, I held my breath and slipped below the surface of the water, emerging a moment later under the dock, where I clung to one of its supports and waited for my cue. I had a good view of the beach from here. People were spreading out towels and setting up folding chairs for the performance, including my parents, who were talking to Cha Cha's family. Bud had paddled his canoe to shore and joined Mrs. Winthrop; Ella Bellow was sitting with Belinda and Augustus. I spotted Amanda Appleton talking to Aunt True, who had a pleasantly bland expression on her face. I also spotted the tall red-haired girl from the road race—Cassidy something?—and Felicia Grunewald, Professor Rusty's assistant. They were both surrounded by their campers.

As the loudspeakers crackled and the first notes of the overture floated out over the water, Dr. Calhoun gave me a thumbs-up.

"Showtime," I whispered, determined to make Esther Williams—and Zadie and Lenore—proud.

Taking a deep breath, I dove down and dolphin-kicked my way underwater out to what I guessed was about the center of the area in front of the beach. Swishing the shimmertail back and forth mightily, I breached the surface like a rocket, then arced forward and dove down again, smacking my flukes against the water hard. Dr. Calhoun had asked me to "make a splash," and that was exactly what I planned to do.

The rest of my opening routine was made up of moves

singing and sketched in the plot for the audience. It was lame but funny. Today was Frederic's—Calhoun's—twenty-first birthday, and he'd finally completed his years of servitude to the Pirate King. Now he'd decided to become an upstanding citizen. This wasn't going to be a smooth road, of course.

The maidens were up next, and after their opening chorus, Cha Cha—as Mabel—took center stage and belted out "Poor Wand'ring One" to Frederic, who had fallen in love at first sight.

Another synopsis from Dr. Calhoun followed. He explained that the girls were all the high-born daughters of the Major-General, and thus not marriage material for lowly pirates. Then it was Hatcher's turn. I held my breath as he began:

I am the very model of a modern Major-General,
I've information vegetable, animal, and mineral...

The lyrics to his rap-style song were complicated and silly. "Patter" was the term for it, Dr. Calhoun had explained to us, and it was one of the hallmarks of Gilbert and Sullivan. I sang along under my breath as the tempo increased. Had we practiced enough? Would Hatcher mess up? Faster and faster the music and lyrics went as the song neared its end, until Hatcher was flying along so fast I was sure he'd stumble.

But he didn't!

pieced together from the revue at Sirena's. After a few more dolphin dives, I flipped over onto my back and, sculling the water with my arms, held my legs up in the ballet leg position, waving my flukes back and forth.

"THAT'S MY SISTER!" I heard Pippa shriek, and I smiled wide and blew her a kiss.

Swim pretty, I reminded myself, and I did my best, smiling and waving just like I'd been taught at mermaid academy. The audience ate it up. As the overture neared its finish, I crisscrossed the water in front of the beach in a series of butterfly strokes, ending with one final dive and powerful splash of my flukes. As the onlookers clapped and cheered, I swam over to the H dock and pulled myself up onto it, perching on the edge to watch the rest of the performance.

Hearing the low thrum of the water-ski boat, we all craned to watch as it came into view around the edge of the point.

"*Dreamboat!*" someone called, and the audience hooted and shouted "aaargh!" at the sight of the flag bearing the skull and crossbones that fluttered from a pole on the roof. When the floating cabin was in position directly in front of the beach, Artie hopped aboard, dropped an anchor, then hopped back into the ski boat and putt-putted away.

The music swelled, the front door and windows of *Dreamboat* flew open, and pirates came flooding out. The crowd roared as they launched into the rousing opening number.

Dr. Calhoun stepped forward when the pirates were done

REALLY TRULY

When he finished, the audience leaped to its feet.

"Bravo!" shouted Aunt True, and my brother took a bow, smiling his Gifford sunflower smile and looking enormously pleased with himself. I saw him shoot a glance at Cha Cha, who smiled back at him.

"There you have it, folks," said Dr. Calhoun, "a sneak preview of our upcoming performance at the Pumpkin Falls Grange, where we hope you'll join us for an evening of musical fun and fantasy! Tickets are available now at the General Store!"

While Artie returned with the water-ski boat to tow *Dreamboat* back to the cove, my little sister and a gaggle of her cabin-mates came rushing over to ooh and aah at the shimmertail. My parents trailed along behind them.

"Is it real?" asked one of the little girls shyly, reaching out a finger to touch it. I was pretty sure her name was Meri.

I shook my head. "No, but wouldn't it be cool if it were?"

Pippa gave me a hug, and so did my mother.

"Your daughter is doing a splendid job!" Dr. Calhoun told my parents. "Both as a mermaid and on our stage crew. She's proved herself an invaluable member of our team this summer and you should be proud of her."

My father leveled a gaze at me. "Should we now."

My mother elbowed him. "J. T.! For heaven's sake lighten up!"

He sighed, then leaned down and gave me an awkward

one-armed hug. "Sentence completed with honor, Truly-in-the-Middle," he said gruffly. "But fair warning—the punishment will be worse next time if you lie to us again."

"I won't, I promise," I told him. "Thanks, Dad."

I couldn't believe my ears—I wasn't grounded anymore! I could hardly wait to get out of my shimmertail and join the Pumpkin Falls Private Eyes again.

CHAPTER 37

"Now *that* was awesome!" said Scooter, basking in the afterglow of a successful performance.

Jasmine nodded. "It's so different with a real audience."

My brother and friends were clustered around me, chattering gleefully as they waited to make their move. *Our* move now, since I was free to join them.

"Hey, guys, I've been thinking," said Lucas. "When we get to the island, I think one of us should take some rope and go to the tunnel by the boulder, just in case—"

Scooter's hand shot out, muffling him.

"Scooter!" I protested.

He jerked his chin toward something behind me. I whipped around to see Amanda Appleton standing there.

"Just in case what?" she said. Her eyes were hidden behind her sunglasses, but I knew they were focused on us with hawk-like intensity.

"Nothing," I told her, smiling sweetly. "We were just talking about the play."

"Of course." She smiled back equally sweetly and walked away.

I looked around wildly for my brother. "Hatcher! Diversion! Now! I think she overheard us."

"One diversion, coming right up," he said, pulling a bottle of Terminator hot sauce from his pocket. He grinned and waggled it at me.

I frowned. "What are you planning to do with that?"

"Spike the lemonade."

"*That's* your diversion? Hot sauce in the lemonade? Hatcher, what are you *thinking*? You can't do that! Remember Uncle Rooster's reaction? These are little kids we're talking about! Somebody could get hurt!"

My brother's face fell.

"You'll have to think of something else—and fast."

In the end, though, he didn't have to. Whether inspired by Frederic and Mabel's romance onstage, or by the sunset over the lake, or by something else entirely, Bud Jefferson chose that moment to drop to one knee and ask Lucas's mother to marry him.

Beside me, Lucas went rigid.

We couldn't hear Mrs. Winthrop's response from where we were, but it was obvious from the whopper of a kiss that Bud planted on her that she'd said yes.

REALLY TRULY

As everyone rushed to congratulate the happy couple, I scanned the crowd for Amanda Appleton, then turned to my brother and friends. "She's going for her kayak! Grab that wheelbarrow and stick me in it—there's not a moment to lose!"

They manhandled me in, shimmertail and all, and thirty seconds later I was jouncing down the beach as Calhoun trundled me off in hot pursuit.

Cha Cha trotted alongside me. "Where are we going?"

"Bud's canoe," I said. "He left it on the far side of the H dock."

When we reached Mr. Jefferson's boat, my brother and our friends ran over and started dragging it toward the water.

"Paddle as fast as you can for Cherry Island," I told them. "I don't know how the finders keepers law works, but my guess is whoever stakes their claim first wins. And she is not going to win!"

"What about you?" called Hatcher as he jumped in and grabbed a paddle.

I glanced back down the beach. Dr. Appleton was headed for the lake, kayak in tow. That gave me an idea. "As soon as I take this shimmertail off, I'll borrow one of Camp Lovejoy's kayaks," I called back. "You guys go on ahead."

"I'll stay behind with you, Truly," said Calhoun.

Giving the canoe a strong push, he launched my brother

and our friends into the water, then came over to where I was struggling to get out of the wheelbarrow.

"Help me out of this thing," I told him. "I've changed my mind—I don't have time to take this tail off. I'm going to have to swim for it."

He nodded. "I'll grab a kayak and follow you."

"Wait! Before you do, could you go tell my aunt True? We're going to need backup, and she'll know what to do."

"Sure." He leaned over to heft me out of the wheelbarrow. "Oof! Dude, you weigh a ton!"

"I'm wearing thirty pounds of shimmertail!"

"Really? I hadn't noticed," he gasped, staggering across the sand toward the lake, but he winked to show me he was only teasing.

Out on the lake, my brother and our friends were paddling furiously, as instructed, but Dr. Appleton was already rounding the H dock in pursuit.

"She's moving fast," I fretted. "They're never going to beat her to the island!"

"They might not, but you will," Calhoun told me. "You're the best swimmer I know, Truly."

He smiled at me, and I smiled back at him.

Now, I thought, remembering Mackenzie's advice.

Maybe Calhoun was thinking the same thing, because a moment later our noses bumped together.

REALLY TRULY

"Ouch!" I protested, rubbing mine.

"Sorry," he said. "I was just—"

"Yeah, me too."

We smiled at each other again, and then he dumped me into the lake.

CHAPTER 38

I was flying.

And it wasn't just the shimmertail. Calhoun had tried to kiss me!

I am Grania—hear me roar! I thought, slicing through the water. It was half a mile to Cherry Island from shore, roughly eight hundred meters. That was farther than I'd ever swum the butterfly stroke. Usually I swam butterfly as part of a relay, but it was my best stroke, and my fastest, and I needed every ounce of speed if I was going to reach shore first. I fell into the rhythm of it easily, grateful for the shimmertail, which propelled me faster with each thwack of its flukes than my own size-ten-and-a-half feet ever could.

Too bad Coach Maynard isn't here to clock my time, I thought, as I passed Bud Jefferson's canoe. Hatcher waved his paddle and gave a Texas-size whoop.

"Go, Truly!" shouted Scooter.

REALLY TRULY

I pushed on, sucking down air with each forward arc of my body. Thanks to countless hours spent in countless pools at countless swim team practices, my legs and arms knew exactly what to do. As the shimmertail propelled me up and out of the water again, I glanced quickly over my shoulder. Dr. Appleton's kayak was closing in fast. I couldn't see Calhoun. Had he alerted Aunt True? I hoped so.

Amanda Appleton and I were almost neck and neck by the time we reached the shore. I gave one last flying dolphin leap and flung myself onto the sand. "I claim this island and any treasure it may contain!" I managed to gasp.

If Dr. Appleton heard me, she didn't give any sign of it. She threw her paddle aside, scrambled out of her kayak, and crashed away through the undergrowth without a word to me.

What just happened? I thought as I lay there in the shallows like a beached whale, struggling to catch my breath. I pondered my next move. I desperately needed witnesses to my claim. Otherwise it would be her word against mine, and who would believe a kid like me over someone with a PhD?

I could see the canoe moving steadily toward the island, and I heard the thrum of Camp Lovejoy's ski boat in the distance. Calhoun had come through—help was on the way.

But I couldn't just sit here and wait.

It wouldn't be long before Amanda Appleton found the boulder, and with it, the entrance to the cave. I, however, had one last card to play: The underwater entrance. Dr. Appleton may have overheard us talking about the tunnel, but she didn't know about the underwater entrance yet. If I could find it first and get to the treasure, surely that would be all I needed to stake my claim?

When my heart had stopped racing and my breathing had returned mostly to normal, I pushed out into the water again and dove down, making a slow pass along the shore. I wished that I had my swim goggles. The sun was sinking lower in the sky, and the water was murky. Still, it was obvious there wasn't an opening anywhere.

I surfaced again, feeling frustrated. What was it that Nathaniel Daniel's last will and testament had said? *Where the eagle flies, there lies the prize. Where the eaglet sleeps, harken to the deep.* There was something else, too, though. Something I was forgetting. I racked my brain, trying to remember. Something about courting days, and—wait, that was it!—*the sunrise of our youth.*

I glanced behind me, where the sun was slowly sinking toward the horizon.

I was on the wrong side of the island! I was on the *west* side, and the entrance was on the *east*—the side where the sun rose!

The canoe bearing Hatcher and Scooter and Cha Cha and Jasmine was in clear view now. I waved my arms overhead to attract their attention, then thrust a finger in the air and motioned going over the island, hoping they'd get the

REALLY TRULY

message that I was heading to the opposite side.

Without waiting for a response, I slipped beneath the surface and circled the island as quietly as I could. There was no point alerting Dr. Appleton to my plans. When I reached the other side, I looked for the tallest tree, the one with the eagles' nest in it. It wasn't difficult to spot—one of the enormous birds was perched on its edge, watching me. Hopefully he didn't think I was dinner. I did not want to tangle with those talons.

I did another surface dive and this time almost immediately found a spot where the shore fell away into a sharp drop-off. *Bingo!* I thought, swimming down to the tangle of roots and vines at its base. Grabbing a handful, I peered into the murk. If there was an underwater entrance, it was horribly overgrown.

I surfaced again and swished my tail back and forth, sculling my arms and treading water like a mermaid the way Zadie had taught me. I was trying to decide what to do when I heard a loud shriek from the interior of the island: "GOTCHA!"

Dr. Appleton had found the tunnel that led to the cave!

That did it. My Lovejoy competitive genes kicked in with a vengeance. I took a deep breath and dove down again. When I reached the tangle of roots and vines this time, I grabbed them and pulled with all my might. At first they didn't budge, but as I kept pulling and tugging, bit by bit they shifted. Not much, but enough for me to at least poke my head through. I could see that this was definitely the entrance to the cave.

But I could also see that this was definitely too dangerous for me to try and explore by myself.

Unlike last time, I didn't have a headlamp, I didn't have a rope, and, most importantly, I didn't have backup. *Never swim alone,* Sirena had said, and deep down I knew she was right. Thinking about entering the cave on my own reminded me of how I felt about hot sauce—it just wasn't worth the risk.

Still, I consoled myself as I swam to the surface again for more air, Dr. Appleton would be finding the tunnel by the boulder a tight squeeze. And it wasn't like she was going to be able to lower herself into the hole in the ground without help.

That meant the score was even for now. We'd both hit a roadblock, and the deciding factor for who got to explore further was the finders keepers law. My best bet was to wait for the witnesses to arrive and stake my claim again in front of them.

There was still no sign of the boats, though. Had my signal not been clear? Was everyone still on the other side of the island looking for me? I weighed my options. While I was waiting I could at least explore a little more around the *outside* of the cave's entrance, couldn't I? There was no harm in that.

Slipping underwater again, I dove back down to the bottom, then swam back and forth in front of the opening, patting the sand beneath me with both hands. Nothing. All I managed to do was dislodge a layer of leaves and debris.

REALLY TRULY

I decided it was probably okay to poke my head through and take another look, which I did. There wasn't much light to see by, but what there was revealed a whole lot more nothing. Certainly nothing remotely resembling a treasure chest.

This time when I went to pull my head back out, though, my hair caught on one of the roots. I tugged at it impatiently. Still stuck. I twisted and turned, scratching my face in the process, but I couldn't break free.

Stronger measures were called for. Drawing my knees to my chest, I positioned my body as if preparing for a kick turn in the pool. Steeling myself for what I knew was coming, I thrust out with the shimmertail as hard as I could.

The pain was sharp. I'd yanked out what felt like a fistful of hair. I had to press my lips together hard not to cry out, which would only result in me gulping down water.

But my head was free!

Unfortunately, though, now my tail was not.

My flukes were wedged firmly into the tangle of roots. Taking off the shimmertail was out of the question. I didn't have time for that. And I was starting to grow short of air. Sirena had said that she used to be able to hold her breath for almost two minutes, back when she was a professional mermaid. But I was just an amateur, and a slightly panicked one at that.

I flailed around, grabbing for something—anything!—to help me escape. My fingers closed on an object lying nearby in the sand. It was round and flat and heavy. A rock. Clutching it, I hammered away at the roots and at my tail, but to no avail. I was really truly stuck.

I floated there for a moment, exhausted, feeling the downward drag of the heavy shimmertail. I wasn't sure that I had the strength to make it to the surface.

And then a hand appeared in front of me—a pale, skinny hand.

Lucas!

I grabbed him and held on for all I was worth. As he pulled, I mustered all of my remaining strength and yanked, too. Together we finally managed to free my flukes, although not without nearly shredding them.

And then the two of us floated up toward the air and the light and the sun.

EPILOGUE

The water-ski boat was waiting for us when we surfaced. The canoe was tied up behind it. As Artie Olsen and my father pulled me aboard, Bud Jefferson leaned over and plucked Lucas from the water as easily as if he were a fish.

"You had us worried went you went overboard there, son," Bud said, wrapping him up in a big towel and an even bigger bear hug. Lucas didn't resist, I noticed.

"Lucas saved my life!" I blurted, and everyone turned and looked at me.

"What on earth were you thinking, going down there alone?" my father thundered.

"Hatcher and R. J. told us everything," said my mother.

I could tell by the expressions on my parents' faces that I had given them a fright. I could imagine I was a sight to behold, as Grandma G would say, from the scratches on my face and the bald spot on my poor scalp, which was bleeding profusely, to the rips in the flukes on my shimmertail.

I knew they wanted explanations.

But first I had something I needed to say. "I claim this island and any treasure it may contain under the finders keepers law."

"What?" My father stared at me, puzzled.

"The finders keepers law," said Aunt True, throwing a towel around me. "It's a treasure hunter thing."

As if on cue, Amanda Appleton came crashing through the undergrowth just then, emerging breathless but triumphant. Cupping her hands around her mouth, she shouted, "I claim this island and any treasure it may contain under the finders keepers law!"

"Too late," Aunt True called back. "May the best man—or in this case, woman"—she pointed to me—"win, remember? She already claimed it! In front of"—she did a quick head count—"ten witnesses!"

We left Dr. Appleton standing there, open-mouthed, and headed back to shore.

"Hey, what's that?" asked Cha Cha. She pointed to my white-knuckled fist, pressed tight against my clamshell bra.

I was still clutching the rock I'd found at the bottom of the lake. "Just a rock," I told her, unclenching my fingers to reveal—something that wasn't a rock at all!

Everyone on the boat turned and looked at my outstretched palm. On it, a big, heavy coin caught the last rays of the setting sun, glinting a warm gold.

REALLY TRULY

...

Later, while my parents took me to get my scalp stitched up, Aunt True and Professor Rusty and Bud Jefferson took the coin back to Bud's shop, where Bud did a little research. It turned out I'd found not just any gold coin, but the unicorn of gold coins: an incredibly rare 1703 Queen Anne "Vigo" five guinea piece. Only twenty of them had been minted from gold the British seized in 1702 from treasure ships in Vigo Bay off northern Spain, and of those twenty, only fifteen had been known to survive—sixteen now—and only six had come up for sale in the last half a century.

"I don't want to get your hopes up," Bud told my parents. "But the last one that was auctioned sold for—well, a lot."

Our ancestor's shady past quickly became big news in Pumpkin Falls—and far beyond. DANDY DAN, THE PIRATE MAN! blared the *Pumpkin Falls Patriot-Bugle*'s lame front-page headline. Janet's article accompanying it was good, though, and so were her photos of the coin and of Nathaniel Daniel's portrait. The Pumpkin Falls Private Eyes got star treatment too, with a whole sidebar of our own. We were rapidly becoming hometown celebrities.

The Lovejoy College history department mounted an official exploration of the cave, hiring professional divers and an underwater camera crew. It turned out the coin I'd found was the last of the treasure. There was little else left, just a coil of rope and a few pieces of wood that proved something had been there. Still, it was enough to create plenty of excitement for historians, including Professor Rusty, who had plans to write a book about Nathaniel Daniel. He already had the title for it—*Dandy Dan: The Pirate of Pumpkin Falls.*

After the exploration crew finished, a metal gate was placed across both the underwater entrance to the cave and the one by the boulder, and there were NO TRESPASSING signs on Cherry Island now. The sheriff didn't want anyone else getting hurt.

It was Professor Rusty who solved the mystery of the vanished treasure. The clue was in Prudence Lovejoy's last will and testament, which none of us had thought to look at. She'd left her husband's gold eagle ring to their son, Obadiah, but there was nothing about "the sunrise of our youth" or "where the eagle flies, there lies the prize." It was just a bequest, plain and simple.

A little more digging revealed that Prudence had been just as civic-minded as her buccaneer husband. With the money that he'd left her, she'd helped found the town's hospital, the library, the first school, and even the Grange. She did it quietly, though, and didn't paste her name all over everything.

"It was like she wanted to give it all away," Rusty told us all at dinner one night.

"She probably did," said Aunt True. "They were ill-gotten gains, after all, and she must have known it. And I hope whatever was left when she was done funded a comfortable retirement."

"Except she missed one coin," I added.

Marketing genius that she was, my aunt made hay with that single gold coin, putting it on display at the bookshop "FOR ONE NIGHT ONLY!" She hired Officer Tanglewood to work security for us after his daytime shift, and she rented a pirate costume for my father to wear. He was used to her schemes by now, and gamely put on an eye patch and a bandana and his Captain Hook prosthetic arm and stood around saying "aaargh!" a lot and scowling at anyone who got too close to the glass case with my five guinea piece in it.

The customers loved it. They couldn't get enough of the fake gold coins that Aunt True had specially made for the event, and they scooped up the Terminator hot sauce with its skull and crossbones label, and all the pirate and mermaid books we put out on display.

Miss Marple got to wear a bandana and an eye patch too, and Aunt True had her "conduct" an interview with me for our online newsletter, which proved hugely popular and got picked up by news media around the world. So did Carson Dawson's segment with me on *Hello, Boston!*

Yes, I was on TV again, only this time not in my shimmertail. Bud and Elmer had managed to repair most of the tears in it, but I politely declined Mr. Dawson's request that I show it off. I did, however, recount my adventure as vividly as I could, and I squeezed in mentions of both our bookshop and *The Pirates of Penzance*. Aunt True—and Augustus Wilde—had taught me well.

All the publicity helped sell out our performances at the Grange and brought a flood of tourists to Pumpkin Falls, which made Ella Bellow and all the other businesses in town happy. Aunt True brainstormed with Bud Jefferson and helped him set up a display of "pirate treasure"—pieces of eight, and a gold doubloon, and whatever else he had that looked vaguely piratical. His sales were brisk too.

Bud and Lucas's mother still hadn't set a date yet, but odds on the General Store porch were running in favor of a Christmas wedding. Lucas wasn't exactly enthusiastic about the prospect, but he was spending more time with Bud these days, and the two of them had even gone fishing.

And there was a third proposal that summer too—right in our bookshop! Augustus Wilde swanned in on a scorcher of a day in August—"my namesake month!" he announced to no one in particular—practically hidden behind an armload of purple roses. Getting down on one creaky knee wasn't easy for him, but he managed. His proposal was appropriately flowery, and he even worked in the title of his latest book, *Forever Mine*, the one he'd been working on during our play rehearsals. Belinda nodded shyly, took his flowers, and gave him a kitten in return. Augustus quietly slipped it into his backpack when she wasn't looking.

REALLY TRULY

"We're planning to elope," Belinda confided later to Aunt True and me. "Too old for all that wedding stuff."

Thanks to a literal boatload of witnesses, my claim to the treasure held up in court under the finders keepers law. We were worried that maybe Amanda Appleton would try to contest it, but she didn't.

"Wisely so," my aunt said. "You don't mess with tall timber."

What Dr. Appleton did do was cash in on the publicity gold. She gave interviews that painted her own role in discovering Dandy Dan's secret as much larger than it actually had been, which sent *Saga of a Ship* skyrocketing to the top of the best-seller list.

I didn't mind, though. After all, without her book, I would never have heard of Dandy Dan. And her media blitz ended up benefiting us, too. The auction house estimated that my coin could fetch a sale price of more than a million dollars, thanks to all the hoopla in the press.

Which it did.

Even more boggling was the fact that the money was technically mine.

"You found it, Truly," my father told me. "It's yours. The best woman won, fair and square."

That was nonsense, of course. It was Lovejoy gold to begin with, and it would remain Lovejoy gold. My family would never have to worry about money again. Inspired by

Prudence Lovejoy's generosity—and Nathaniel-Daniel-looks-like-a-spaniel's, too—I did have a few requests, though. I talked it over with my parents, and they agreed that Cha Cha and Jasmine and Calhoun and Scooter and Lucas should each get a share for their help in unraveling the mystery. It would go into their college funds, which thrilled their parents. And I insisted on sending a check to Delphine as a thank-you for the shimmertail, and to Sirena as a thank-you for teaching me how to swim in it. They were both surprised and delighted by this gesture.

Finally, I also secretly funded the restoration of the Pumpkin Falls Grange. I knew Prudence would be pleased, since she'd founded it, and I wanted to do something "civick-minded" to honor her. Our town's history was important, and it was worth preserving. Ella Bellow could be a pain, but she was right about that. She probably guessed who was behind the donation, as I noticed that she was being nicer than usual to my family and me, but for once she didn't say anything.

As for *The Pirates of Penzance*, it was a big success. There was one final surprise on opening night, though. When the curtain went up and the overture started, the audience applauded at the sight of the Rockin' Mermaid Malt Shop, which the stage crew had stayed up late the night before finishing. My family and friends cheered as I was rolled onstage on top of the diner's counter. I hammed it up, leaning back on my elbows and waving my flukes in the air the way Zadie and

REALLY TRULY

Lenore had taught me and smiling a big Esther Williams smile. I knew the set looked great, from the black and white floor and fake tile to the shiny red vinyl on the stools and booths to the jukebox, vintage Coca Cola machine, and shelves filled with sundae dishes, milkshake glasses, and—

"Hey!" blurted Lucas. "Isn't that the missing trophy?"

Elmer Farnsworth had had it all along! He'd picked up the paper bag containing the silver pumpkin on race day, thinking it was junk, and stuck it in his truck, then got distracted and forgot about it. The bag wound up in one of the bins in his barn, and he'd gathered it up along with a bunch of other stuff while looking for props for our set. It was after midnight when he'd put it on the shelf next to the vintage toaster, and he was tired and hadn't been paying attention.

Thelma Farnsworth's face had flushed with embarrassment. "Can't you tell the difference between trash and treasure, Elmer? And don't tell me you didn't hear all the fuss about the trophy being missing!"

"ALL THE FUSS ABOUT KISSING?" shouted Elmer, looking perplexed.

Calhoun and I exchanged a smile at that. We still hadn't had the opportunity for our first kiss. We would, though. I was pretty sure of that.

Things were a whole lot quieter on the porch of the General Store after Thelma insisted that Elmer get hearing aids. Meanwhile, the trophy was delivered to the window of the Starlite Dance Studio, where it would stay on display until next Fourth of July.

My mother followed through on her promise of a mother-daughter day all to ourselves. Shortly before summer camp ended and my sisters were due to return home, she whisked me away on a surprise overnight trip to Boston. We stayed in a hotel overlooking the Public Garden, and we took a ride on the swan boats and went to tea at the Boston Public Library in Copley Square and got manicures and pedicures and facials—which I didn't think I'd like, but which I did, a lot—and we saw a movie and ordered room service and went shopping for new clothes.

"A girl can't start eighth grade without a new wardrobe, Little O," she told me.

Eighth grade! I still couldn't believe it. Only one more year until high school!

There was so much change ahead.

The biggest change of all was the wedding that our family had to look forward to. Aunt True asked me to be her chief bridesmaid, "because tall timber sticks together." Lauren was going to be a bridesmaid too, and Pippa couldn't wait to be the flower girl. My mother would be the matron of honor, and Miss Marple was going to be the ring bearer. Gramps and Lola would be coming home for the wedding too.

The date had been set for October, when all of New Hampshire's hills would be covered in a blaze of glory, as my

REALLY TRULY

aunt described it. Autumn was her favorite time of year.

And just like the seasons kept changing in Pumpkin Falls, things would keep changing for me, too. I understood that now. Because life was about change, just like Aunt True had said. There were surprises around every corner.

And that was really truly fine with me.

BLUEBERRY DONUT MUFFINS

1/3 c. vegetable oil
1/2 c. sugar
1 egg
1/2 c. milk
1-1/2 c. flour
2 tsp. baking powder
1/2 tsp. salt
1/4 tsp. nutmeg
1 c. fresh blueberries

Topping:
1/2 c. butter, melted
1/2 c. sugar
1-1/2 tsp. cinnamon

- Preheat oven to 400 degrees. Grease a muffin tin or line with paper cups.
- Cream oil, sugar, and egg. Mix dry ingredients together and add to creamed mixture alternately with milk. Gently fold in blueberries.
- Spoon batter into greased muffin tin and bake 20-25 minutes. Remove muffins immediately from pan, roll in melted butter, then in cinnamon-sugar mixture. Enjoy!

MISS MARPLE'S PICKS

Eloise by Kay Thompson and Hilary Knight
The Little Mermaid by Hans Christian Andersen
The Mermaid by Jan Brett
The Mermaid Handbook by Carolyn Turgeon
The Pirate Queen by Emily Arnold McCully
The Pirates of Penzance by W. S. Gilbert and Arthur Sullivan
The Tail of Emily Windsnap by Liz Kessler
Understood Betsy by Dorothy Canfield Fisher

Truly, Madly, Sheeply

ALSO BY HEATHER VOGEL FREDERICK

The Pumpkin Falls Mysteries
Absolutely Truly
Yours Truly
Really Truly

The Mother-Daughter Book Club
Mother-Daughter Book Club
Much Ado about Anne
Dear Pen Pal
Pies & Prejudice
Home for the Holidays
Wish You Were Eyre
Mother-Daughter Book Camp

The Spy Mice
The Black Paw
For Your Paws Only
Goldwhiskers

Once Upon a Toad

The Voyage of Patience Goodspeed
The Education of Patience Goodspeed

Truly, Madly, Sheeply

A Pumpkin Falls Mystery

HEATHER VOGEL FREDERICK

Simon & Schuster Books for Young Readers
NEW YORK • LONDON • TORONTO • SYDNEY • NEW DELHI

SIMON & SCHUSTER BOOKS FOR YOUNG READERS
An imprint of Simon & Schuster Children's Publishing Division
1230 Avenue of the Americas, New York, New York 10020
This book is a work of fiction. Any references to historical events, real people, or real places are used fictitiously. Other names, characters, places, and events are products of the author's imagination, and any resemblance to actual events or places or persons, living or dead, is entirely coincidental.
Text © 2023 by Heather Vogel Frederick
Jacket illustration © 2023 by Charles Santoso
Jacket design by Krista Vossen © 2023 by Simon & Schuster, Inc.
All rights reserved, including the right of reproduction in whole or in part in any form.
SIMON & SCHUSTER BOOKS FOR YOUNG READERS
and related marks are trademarks of Simon & Schuster, Inc.
For information about special discounts for bulk purchases, please contact Simon & Schuster Special Sales at 1-866-506-1949 or business@simonandschuster.com.
The Simon & Schuster Speakers Bureau can bring authors to your live event. For more information or to book an event, contact the Simon & Schuster Speakers Bureau at 1-866-248-3049 or visit our website at www.simonspeakers.com.
Interior design by Hilary Zarycky
The text for this book was set in Fournier.
Manufactured in the United States of America
0723 FFG
First Edition
2 4 6 8 10 9 7 5 3 1
Library of Congress Cataloging-in-Publication Data
Names: Frederick, Heather Vogel, author.
Title: Truly, madly, sheeply / Heather Vogel Frederick.
Description: First edition. | New York : Simon & Schuster Books for Young Readers, 2023. | Series: A Pumpkin Falls mystery | Audience: Ages 10 to 14. | Audience: Grades 4-6. | Summary: When someone keeps stealing Jack-o'-lanterns and a mysterious haunting begins at her Aunt and Uncle's old farm, Truly and the other Pumpkin Falls Private Eyes work to uncover the cause behind the fall shenanigans in their home town.
Identifiers: LCCN 2022026547 (print) | LCCN 2022026548 (ebook) | ISBN 9781534499683 (hardcover) | ISBN 9781534499706 (ebook)
Subjects: CYAC: Mystery and detective stories. | Lost and found possessions—Fiction. | Autumn—Fiction. | LCGFT: Detective and mystery fiction. | Novels.
Classification: LCC PZ7.F87217 Tr 2023 (print) | LCC PZ7.F87217 (ebook) | DDC [Fic]—dc23
LC record available at https://lccn.loc.gov/2022026547
LC ebook record available at https://lccn.loc.gov/2022026548.

*For Jamie and Elisabeth,
our family's newest little lambs—
and for all my new friends,
both two-legged and four,
at the real Liberty Hall Farm*

PROLOGUE

It's all Ella Bellow's fault, if you ask me, which nobody ever does.

If only she'd kept her famously big mouth shut, the fall of my eighth-grade year would have been a nice, fat helping of normal.

And here's the thing—I really *like* normal.

Unfortunately, my life has been anything but normal since my family moved last winter from Austin, Texas, to Pumpkin Falls, New Hampshire, and I accidentally became a middle school private eye. You wouldn't think all that much could happen in a town as tiny as ours, but somehow, I keep stumbling over mysteries that need to be solved.

Ella couldn't resist a juicy piece of gossip, though. Once she'd blabbed to my aunt that the Farnsworths were thinking of selling their dilapidated old farm, in the shake of a lamb's tail—literally, a lamb's tail—my life was turned upside down again.

This time around, instead of that nice, fat helping of normal I'd been looking forward to, regular stuff like school and swim team and hanging out with my friends and helping at our family's bookstore, I found myself knee-deep in sheep droppings in a possibly haunted barn, embarking on a life of crime. Well, okay, maybe not a life of *actual* crime, but how many eighth graders do you know who've had to learn how to pick a lock? I say "had to" because I didn't have a choice, really—not if I wanted to clear my brother's name and save our town's biggest festival of the year. The Halloween Pumpkin Toss may not sound like much to the average person, but here in Pumpkin Falls, it's like the Fourth of July and Christmas and your birthday all rolled into one.

"Sometimes, crazy is the best thing to do," my aunt True says, and I certainly did my fair share of crazy this time around. Of course, I had no idea that any of this was on the horizon back when my aunt first told us about the farm. All I'd been thinking about—all any of us Lovejoys had been thinking about—was the wedding.

CHAPTER 1

"Don't you think you're being a bit hasty?" said my father, reaching for the platter in the center of the kitchen table.

I watched as the fingers of his prosthetic hand deftly plucked a waffle from the pile and transferred it to his plate. My father had come a long way in the year since he'd lost his right arm to the war in Afghanistan. None of us gave his expertise with his titanium fingers a second thought now, including him.

"Hasty?" Aunt True frowned. "I've known Rusty since kindergarten!"

My father snorted. "I'm not talking about the *wedding*, True—I'm talking about the old Farnsworth place! What do you two know about farming?"

"Living on a farm has always been one of my fondest dreams," my aunt told him loftily. "Rusty's, too."

My father gave her a dubious look. "Since when?"

"Since I spent six weeks on a sheep farm in New Zealand," my aunt replied.

The titanium fingers, which had now latched onto the pitcher of maple syrup, froze. "That was two decades ago! You were on a high school exchange program!"

My aunt was silent, but only for a moment. "There was also my trip to Tibet."

"What happened in Tibet?" I asked, hoping for a story. Aunt True was a world traveler, and her adventures in remote corners of the world often sparked epic tales.

"I worked with yak herders" was all she said this time, though.

"What's a yak?" asked Pippa, my youngest sister.

"It's like a big, ugly, hairy cow," my middle sister, Lauren, told her.

Pippa scrunched her nose. "Maybe they should call it a yuck."

"Good one, Pipster!" My brother Hatcher slapped her a high five.

"Spending a few weeks with sheep, or with yak herders, or whatever other experience you think you've had, is a whole lot different from running a farm of your own," my father persisted. "And what about Rusty? He's spent most of his life shut up in a library!"

My dad had a point. Aunt True was always insisting that Erastus Peckinpaugh, her history-professor fiancé, had what she called "hidden depths." But he didn't exactly strike me—or anyone else in town, for that matter, judging from the talk I'd overheard at the general store—as farmer material. He must have kept that side of himself really well hidden.

"Libraries are fine places to learn a great many things," my aunt said stiffly.

My father snorted again, and this time, my mother stepped in.

"Perhaps it's time to mind your own business, J. T.," she told him. "Everyone's entitled to their dreams."

My father speared a piece of syrup-drenched waffle with his fork. "Fine. But everyone knows that place is a wreck. It was a wreck even back when we were kids!"

"I'll admit it needs work," allowed Aunt True. "That's why we can afford it."

"What it needs," my father declared, shoving the bite of waffle into his mouth, "is a bulldozer."

"Daddy's talking with his mouth full," Pippa observed, and my mother shushed her.

My father and his older sister had been going around and around like this ever since Aunt True had announced that she and Professor Rusty—soon to be Uncle Rusty after their wedding next weekend—had bought the old farm on the outskirts of town.

It was Ella Bellow, our town's retired postmistress turned knitting store owner, who broke the news that it was going up for sale. Ella considered herself in charge of gossip in Pumpkin Falls. I'd known something was up when I glanced out the window of our bookshop and saw her burst from the front door of A Stitch in Time and make a beeline across the street. Either her entire yarn supply was on fire, or Ella had news to share.

"True!" she'd called, barging in through the bookshop door. The bells attached to the top of it jangled vigorously, apparently as excited as she was. Miss Marple, my grandparents' golden retriever, who had been napping in her dog bed by the counter, lifted her head and woofed.

"My aunt's in the back office, Mrs. Bellow," I told her. I was killing time before my piano lesson, trying to come up with a concept for a special window display for the leaf peepers. "Leaf peepers" were what the locals called the hordes of tourists who descended on little towns all over New England every autumn, eager for a glimpse of our famous colorful fall foliage.

"True!" Ella called again, louder this time. "Have you heard?"

We were having a quiet afternoon, fortunately. There were only two customers in the store at the moment, neither of whom were local. If Ella had something embarrassing to share, at least they wouldn't know who she was talking about.

My aunt emerged from the back. "What's up, Ella? Is everything okay?"

Ella drew herself up to her full height, which was considerable. She was almost as tall as my aunt and me, and we both stood six feet in our socks. After a dramatic pause, she blurted, "The Farnsworths are selling up!"

Aunt True gave her a puzzled look. "What do you mean?"

"I just got off the phone with Thelma Farnsworth. She finally managed to talk Elmer into retirement. They're moving into town to live with Ethel and Ike."

Ethel was Thelma Farnsworth's sister. She was married to Elmer Farnsworth's brother, Ike. Ike and Ethel owned Pumpkin Falls's general store.

My aunt looked thoughtful. "Is that right?"

Thelma's been wanting to do this for a while now," Ella barreled on, "but you know how Elmer is when he digs his heels in."

Sadly, I did. Part of living in a small town was knowing exactly this kind of detail about, well, pretty much everybody. Elmer Farnsworth was famously stubborn.

"It was the mix-up with the pumpkin trophy that pushed Thelma over the edge," Ella continued. "She gave Elmer an ultimatum—he could move into town with her, or she'd go alone."

That mix-up had been a big part of my summer. The whole town had been in an uproar when the silver pumpkin trophy disappeared after the Fourth of July road race, and while everyone was relieved when it turned up safe and sound again, no one was happy with Elmer, who had inadvertently caused the commotion in the first place.

"They may already have a buyer, in fact. Apparently some developer has been sniffing around."

Aunt True snapped to attention. "What do you mean, developer?"

"Real estate," Ella replied, clearly pleased to have delivered such an item of interest. "He's looking for land to build a strip mall. That's prime property, right on the road into town."

"A *strip mall?*" My aunt stared at her, aghast. "But that would be a crime! That dairy farm has been in the Farnsworth family for generations! It's a local landmark!"

Ella nodded, trying unsuccessfully to arrange her face into a mournful expression. But she couldn't hide her smile. My aunt's gratifying reaction to her exclusive tidbit had clearly made her day. News delivered, Ella swiftly bid us goodbye. I watched as she trotted away down Main Street. Ella was more efficient than the Internet when it came to spreading gossip, and I gave it less than fifteen minutes before all of Pumpkin Falls knew about the Farnsworths' farm.

She was barely out of sight before Aunt True grabbed her jacket. "Truly, can you watch the store for me for a few minutes? I have an errand to run—I won't be long, I promise."

If Elmer Farnsworth was famously stubborn, my aunt was famously determined. The real estate developer didn't stand a chance once she'd made up her mind. There'd been a flurry of interest from other buyers as well, including Luke and Laura Mahoney of Mahoney's Antiques, the business next door to ours. The Mahoneys thought the property would be the perfect spot for expanding their business, and had hoped to turn the barn into a larger retail area for their store. And there was also a retired couple from New York City looking for a weekend home. But in the end, Aunt True and Professor Rusty convinced the Farnsworths to sell the farm to them instead, and now it was theirs.

Truth be told, I kind of agreed with my father. Aunt True had never mentioned anything to me before about wanting to own a farm. I gave her a sidelong glance. She was dressed in her usual part hippie, part parrot fashion: a shapeless, fuzzy lime-green sweater pulled haphazardly over camouflage leggings. Bright yellow clogs completed the outfit. Her hair was pulled up in a messy bun skewered with what looked like, and probably were, chopsticks. Chopsticks brought back from a trip to some obscure country I'd never heard of on the other side of the world, no doubt.

Was she farmer material? I took a bite of waffle and pondered this question.

My pondering was cut short by a loud honking outside as a rattletrap truck pulled into the driveway. Professor Rusty emerged from the driver's side, wearing overalls and a huge grin. Spotting my aunt through the kitchen window, he held up a set of keys and dangled them triumphantly.

Aunt True's face lit up. "Rusty got the keys to the farm!"

Darting out the back door, she launched herself at her fiancé. We were all right behind her.

"Congratulations, homeowners!" said my mother.

"Who wants a tour?" asked Professor Rusty.

Aunt True looked over at my parents. "Do we have time?"

"No," said my father, at the same time that my mother said, "Yes."

Gramps and Lola were flying in for the wedding from Africa, where they were stationed in the Peace Corps. We were skipping church to drive down to Logan Airport in Boston to meet their flight from Namibia. Lauren and Pippa had been busy for days with colored pens and glitter decorating welcome signs for us to hold up to greet them when they arrived.

"Oh, come on, J. T.," said my mother. "Stop being such a stick-in-the-mud. We can manage a quick tour and still make it to Boston in time."

We didn't even wait for my father to reply. Without another thought for our unfinished breakfast, my brothers and sisters and I all piled into our family's minivan. My mother slid into the driver's seat, then leaned out the window and smiled at my father. "Coming?"

"Do I have a choice?" he grumbled, but he gave her a reluctant smile in return. "Although I can't say I'm not curious to see what kind of a mess True's gotten herself into this time."

And with that we followed my aunt and almost-uncle's truck out of the driveway.

CHAPTER 2

My father was right about one thing. The farm did need a bulldozer. Or maybe dynamite.

"Wow, the farmhouse is so—it's so . . ." My mother groped for the right word. *"Quaint."*

"Does 'quaint' mean it's the perfect location for a horror movie?" Hatcher whispered to me as we stared at the property that our aunt and soon-to-be uncle were about to call home.

If the farmhouse's peeling paint and shabby exterior qualified as "quaint," the barn that loomed beside it was positively scary. I was usually a big fan of barns, ever since Lola had read *Charlotte's Web* to us when we were little. But Hatcher was right, this one definitely looked like horror-movie material. Its once-bright-red exterior had faded to the rusty color of an old scab, part of the roof had caved in, most of the windows were either cracked or broken, and the missing clapboards gave it a gap-toothed look, like Pippa back when her baby teeth had fallen out. On top of that, the entire structure was leaning at an alarming angle, as if it was planning to cut and run.

"Elmer and Thelma really let things go around here," said my father, shaking his head.

Aunt True was oblivious to our dismay. "Sure, it needs a little work, but look at that view! Could it be any more glorious?!"

She was right about that, at least. Situated just down the road from the Freeman family's farm, where my friend Franklin and his sister Annie and their parents lived, the Farnsworth place shared the same sweeping view of the Pumpkin River Valley. Even though peak color was still a week or two away, according to the weather reports—everybody got involved when leaf-peeping season rolled around, even the weather forecasters—the foliage was impressive, a bright patchwork of reds and oranges and yellows threaded with evergreens.

Technically, I guessed I qualified as a leaf peeper too. Before moving to New Hampshire last winter, we'd only ever visited Gramps and Lola during summer vacation and at Christmastime—never in the fall. I used to think the whole idea of leaf peeping was ridiculous, but as the colors had intensified over the past couple of weeks, I was beginning to understand what people got all excited about. It was pretty amazing.

"The house was built in 1779," Professor Rusty told us proudly. "It's one of the oldest in Pumpkin Falls."

"It looks like it, too," Hatcher said under his breath.

"Come see the barn and outbuildings, J.T.!" Professor Rusty charged down the driveway without waiting for a reply.

Lauren grabbed Pippa's hand and followed. "Let's go see the animals!"

My sister Lauren was a huge animal lover. Aside from Aunt True and Professor Rusty, she was the only one in the family who'd been enthusiastic about the whole farm idea from the start. The fact that it was located practically next door to her best friend, Annie Freeman, didn't hurt, either.

My oldest brother, Danny, loped off after them, while Hatcher and I followed our mother and aunt toward the house.

"Wait until you see inside, Dinah!" Aunt True enthused, fumbling with the keys to the front door. "It has an open hearth with the original beehive oven, and the most gorgeous wide-plank floors."

Given the farmhouse's dilapidated exterior, I was surprised at how inviting it was inside. It was shabby, for sure. The floors were worn from centuries of use, the wallpaper was peeling, and everything smelled faintly of woodsmoke. Other than that, though, it wasn't bad. No piles of dust, no cobwebs. October sunshine poured in through the front windows, lighting up the enormous brick fireplace in the living room—almost big enough to stand in—along with all the stuff that the Farnsworths had left behind.

"There are some valuable antiques here, True," said my

mother, scanning the room in surprise. "You should get Luke Mahoney out to appraise them for you. That clock on the mantel is a beauty, and I think this desk might be bird's-eye maple. And heaven knows what's in all those boxes!"

Aunt True nodded. "Thelma and Elmer don't have kids, and their nieces and nephews already took what they wanted. They were happy to leave us the rest."

I was sure they were—especially Thelma. She found Elmer's piles of junk exasperating. Elmer Farnsworth was a notorious hoarder, famous for picking through trash and surfing yard sales and junk shops. "One man's trash is another man's treasure" was his motto, but personally, most of his "treasures" always looked like trash to me.

The farmhouse was much smaller than Gramps and Lola's house over on Maple Street, where my family was living. Next to the living room was the dining room, and off that was a snug bookshelf-lined room that my aunt told us would be Professor Rusty's office.

"It's called a borning room," she said, opening the door to show it off. "It shares a wall with the fireplace and would have been the warmest room in the house back in the day. Babies were born in here, and if anyone wasn't feeling well, they would have slept in here, too."

We went upstairs next. There were three bedrooms, all with sloped ceilings under the eaves.

"Cozy," my mother pronounced.

TRULY, MADLY, SHEEPLY

"I'm going to check out the attic," Hatcher said, opening a narrow door at the end of the hallway. "Wanna come?"

I took one look at the steep, cobweb-covered stairway and shuddered. Spiders were at the very top of the list of things I was not good at. "Maybe another time."

Hatcher shrugged and disappeared. I followed my mother and aunt down the steep back stairs to the kitchen.

"Wow!" I said in surprise.

Aunt True beamed. "I know, right? I saved the best for last. I would have bought the house just for this alone."

The kitchen took up most of the back of the house. There was a huge deep sink with a window over it that looked out toward the barn, a breakfast nook, an enormous pantry, and an equally enormous old cast-iron stove.

"Thelma says it still works, and they used it from time to time just for fun, but there's a real stove, too," said my aunt, patting an appliance in an eye-watering shade of turquoise.

My mother eyed it dubiously. "You're probably going to want to replace that. It looks nearly as old as Elmer."

Aunt True nodded. "It's on our list."

The breakfast nook was lined with windows looking out over the valley. Taking a seat on one of its built-in benches, I gazed at the view across the sloping fields to the Pumpkin River far below. It gleamed in the distance like a slender silver ribbon.

Hatcher came clattering down the back stairs and I motioned him over.

"How's the attic?" I whispered as he slid in beside me.

"Total haunted house," he whispered back. "It's going to be a huge job to clear out all the stuff Elmer left behind. There's an antique mannequin that scared the socks off me!"

Aunt True crossed the room and knelt beside us. "Our property extends all the way down to the river. There's a path you can take through the woods to River Road." Resting her elbows on the windowsill, she surveyed her new kingdom and sighed happily. "This view! I don't think I'll ever want to leave the kitchen."

"That's good news for Rusty," said my father, as he and Danny and my almost-uncle came through the back door just then. "Maybe you'll finally learn how to cook."

My mother swatted him. "J. T.! Behave yourself!"

"What?" he replied, grinning.

"He's just kidding, Mom," added Danny. "Aunt True's a great cook . . . sometimes."

My mother gave my brother a swat as well. "I don't know what I'm going to do with you two."

"So what do you think of the house?" Professor Rusty looked at her, his expression hopeful.

"It's showing its age, for sure, but I think that you and True will be very happy here," my mother told him. "Give it a paint job inside and out—plus some updating and repairs—and I'm sure it will last another two hundred and fifty years."

"We can handle the updating," Aunt True said, which

probably wasn't true. I'd never even seen her screw in a lightbulb. And I was pretty sure her fiancé wasn't the handyman type, either.

"The barn, on the other hand, is a different story," said my dad. "It's a complete disaster."

Professor Rusty's hopeful expression faded. "J. T. is right, unfortunately."

"It isn't a do-it-yourself job, either," my father warned. "You'll need a professional crew. It's going to be expensive."

"Well, we have a head start on that," Aunt True told him, rising to her feet. "Mom and Dad called from the airport in Windhoek before they caught their flight last night. After looking at the photos of the farm that we sent, they decided that helping with the barn repairs would be the best wedding gift they could give us."

That gave me an idea. I turned to my parents. "Hey, how about we chip in too? From the Dandy Dan Fund, I mean."

"Dandy Dan" was the pirate nickname belonging to one of my ancestors. I'd found a gold coin this past summer that had belonged to him, and we'd sold it for a lot of money. "Could we? Please?"

"Technically, it's your money," my mother said slowly, her eyes sliding over to my father.

"Dad?" I begged. "I haven't gotten Aunt True and Professor Rusty a wedding present yet!"

"That's the college fund for you and your brothers and

sisters," Aunt True said sharply. "I wouldn't hear of it."

My father inhaled, held his breath for a long moment, then exhaled. "Actually, it's a good idea. I know I tease you a lot, True, and I'd be lying if I said I wasn't worried that this whole farm venture is going to be a disaster, but we all want to see you and Rusty succeed."

My mother slipped her arm through his good one, beaming up at him. "I agree." She turned to my aunt and Professor Rusty. "Nothing would make us happier than to help you two get off to a good start here at—what are you going to call this place, anyway?"

"How about *Bleak House?*" suggested Hatcher, who was reading Charles Dickens in his high school English class.

"Hatcher!" my mother scolded. "Honestly, you Lovejoy men have no manners at all!"

"I'm kidding!" my brother protested, smiling his big sunflower smile. Hatcher got away with murder, thanks to that sunny smile of his.

"We haven't decided what to call it yet," said Aunt True. "It needs something besides 'the old Farnsworth place.' Something with 'croft' in it, we think. 'Hillcroft Farm' has a nice ring to it, but we're still thinking about it."

"What's a croft?" I asked.

"It's the Scottish term for a small farm." Aunt True and her fiancé exchanged a glance and smiled. "By the way, we finally settled on our honeymoon plans."

This had been a topic of intense discussion for weeks now. Historian that he was, Professor Rusty had been angling for a spot with lots of museums, someplace like Williamsburg or Washington, D.C. Aunt True wanted more of a *destination*—Bali, Bora Bora, and Uzbekistan were her top three choices.

"We're going to Scotland!" my aunt announced.

"Why?" asked Hatcher, speaking for all of us.

"Sheep," she replied.

Seeing our puzzled faces, Professor Rusty added, "Some of the finest in the world can be found in Scotland, and we want to learn more about them."

Traveling to Scotland to research sheep didn't sound like much of a honeymoon to me, but what did I know?

"Rusty and I have decided that we want to raise sheep on our farm," Aunt True explained. "Just a small flock to start with."

We gaped at her. She might as well have announced that she and my soon-to-be uncle intended to raise a herd of pterodactyls.

"The knitting community is thriving worldwide," my aunt continued, "and knitters everywhere want hand-dyed wool from small-scale, independent sheep farmers. It's all Ella can talk about these days. I figure A Stitch in Time will be our first customer, and if all goes well, we'll expand throughout New England. Maybe set up a website and sell our products online, too."

"But you don't know anything—" My father coughed as my mother elbowed him. "Uh, I mean, I'm sure you two will be very happy raising . . . sheep."

Lauren and Pippa burst through the back door just then.

"Where are all the animals?" Lauren demanded. "I thought this was supposed to be a farm. All we found were some dumb chickens."

"The Farnsworths sold their cows, but they left us their hens as a housewarming gift," Aunt True told her. "We need to get things shipshape around here first before we become a real live farm. But I was just telling everyone that Rusty and I are planning to raise sheep."

Lauren's face fell. *"Sheep?"*

"Maybe a cow someday, too. We'll see. Or goats."

"No horses?"

Aunt True shook her head. "Probably not, honey."

Lauren gave her a sidelong glance. "You could have kittens." She'd been angling for a kitten for ages now, but my mother had put her foot down.

"I have to draw the line somewhere, Lauren," she kept telling her. "We have a dog, a hamster, and a rabbit. That's enough pets for any family!"

Aunt True smiled. "I'm not sure what Mephisto would say about that." Mephisto was her large black cat. He spent his days intimidating Miss Marple at the bookshop and his nights ruling the roost in my aunt's apartment above it.

Lauren gave her a rueful nod. She knew Mephisto as well as the rest of us did. I had a feeling he wasn't going to like living on a farm.

"I tell you what, though," my aunt continued. "Every barn needs a barn cat to chase away the rats and mice. Maybe you can be in charge of finding us one. Mephisto doesn't even need to know it's there. He isn't exactly outdoorsy, so I doubt he'll be spending any serious time in the barn."

Lauren brightened. "I'll ask Belinda! She can help me."

"Excellent plan!"

Belinda Winchester was an older lady who was part-owner of our bookshop. Or at least she used to be. She'd stepped in and saved the day last winter when it was looking like the store might have to close. We'd since paid her back with some of the Dandy Dan money, but Belinda still spent a good chunk of her time at the bookshop "volunteering," as she called it. The rest of her time was spent fostering kittens and finding homes for stray cats. Taking one of them for the farm would make her insanely happy, and it would be the best thank-you that Aunt True could ever give her.

"Can I look after the chickens while you're on your honeymoon?" asked Lauren. "I could ride my bike over before school."

"Sorry, kiddo—I already promised that job to your grandparents."

My mother frowned. "But I thought they were staying with us."

"Slight change of plans," my aunt told her. "They're going to house-sit—or is it farm-sit?—for us while we're in Scotland."

"Speaking of grandparents, we'd better get a move on if we want to get to Logan in time for their flight," said my father, glancing at his watch.

As we all headed back outside, something caught my eye in the nearby pumpkin field. It looked like an orange boulder. "What's that?"

"That," Aunt True replied, "is Elmer Farnsworth's prize pumpkin. We promised he could leave it here until the festival."

No one needed to ask which festival she was talking about. Competition for the biggest pumpkin award at the annual Halloween Pumpkin Toss was fierce in our town. We all trooped over for a closer inspection. By the looks of it, Elmer had a good chance of winning. His pumpkin was truly impressive. A sign had been stuck into the ground next to it. On it was scrawled: ELMER'S PROPERTY! KEEP AWAY!

"What's in that shed down there?" asked Danny, pointing to a small structure on the far edge of the field, close to the path through the woods that led down to the river. Like the old barn, the shed looked like it was on the verge of collapsing.

"We want to turn that into a sugar shack eventually," Professor Rusty replied, running a hand through his wild thatch of dark hair. "There's a stand of maple trees on the property we can tap for syrup. But we told Elmer he can keep it for now, until he finds a new place to store his antique truck and tractor collection."

As we made our way back across the pumpkin field toward the driveway, I thought about what Hatcher had said earlier. "Total haunted house," he'd called our aunt and almost-uncle's new home. Surely he was only joking. The farmhouse wasn't that bad. Old and shabby and in need of some work, as my mother had said, but hardly haunted. Plus, there weren't such things as haunted houses.

At least, I didn't think there were.

The barn, though, was another story entirely. It was enough to give anyone the creeps. I glanced over my shoulder. The shattered windows above its ramshackle door were like two blind eyes staring back at me.

The sun slipped behind a cloud just then, and a sudden gust of chilly wind swirled the leaves by my feet. I shivered and ran toward the minivan.

CHAPTER 3

It was surprising, the things you discovered about people you thought you knew. Like, for instance, the fact that Scooter Sanchez was an engineering genius.

If you'd asked me to predict my classmate's future last year when we first moved to Pumpkin Falls, I'd have voted for him for "Least Likely to Succeed." The only thing Scooter had seemed destined for was being a bully.

But here he was now, totally crushing our school's competition for best catapult. The winner would be entered in the annual Halloween Pumpkin Toss.

"Compared to that, ours looks like something Fred and Ginger made," whispered my friend Cha Cha Abramowitz, gazing enviously at Scooter's creation. Fred and Ginger were her family's cats, named after Fred Astaire and Ginger Rogers, two famous old-time Hollywood dancers. Which was totally fitting since the Abramowitzes owned the town dance studio.

TRULY, MADLY, SHEEPLY

Cha Cha and our friend Jasmine Sanchez and I gazed mournfully at the jumble of wooden bits that squatted on the table in front of us. I'd known about the Halloween Pumpkin Toss and the eighth-grade project forever. My brothers and sisters and I had grown up hearing Dad brag about building the winning catapult when he was in eighth grade, and every year Gramps and Lola sent us newspaper clippings about the festival. We'd even seen it covered on TV now and then by news programs looking for feel-good segments on small-town life. But nothing had prepared me for actually having to try to build a catapult of my own.

I glanced over at the contraption on the table to my left. It belonged to Lucas Winthrop and R. J. Calhoun, whose first name we'd learned last winter was Romeo. Not surprisingly, he hated being called that, much preferring R. J., or better yet, just Calhoun. Their catapult didn't look much better than ours. In fact, nobody's did. Scooter had the competition in the bag, and he knew it.

"If your brother's chest puffs out any farther, he's going to explode," I muttered to Jasmine, as her twin carried his catapult to the front of the classroom. Most designs, including ours, incorporated a large rubber band that worked like a slingshot. But Scooter had come up with a completely different design.

Jasmine sighed. "I should have said yes when he asked me to be his partner."

The corners of Cha Cha's mouth quirked up in a smile. "Poor baby, stuck with us losers."

While most of our classmates had chosen to team up, Scooter had decided to go it alone. I watched as he carefully placed his handiwork on the counter in front of Mr. Bigelow, our science teacher. It occurred to me that Scooter had grown over the summer. Most of the boys in my class had, as a matter of fact. Even scrawny Lucas was looking taller. Unfortunately for him, the added inches only made him look even skinnier, if that were possible.

Scooter, Franklin Freeman, and Calhoun were now almost eye to eye with me. Which was a relief. Being the tallest kid in every classroom at every school I'd attended over the past few years had been no fun at all. My mother kept telling me to just give it time, and that things would even out eventually. It was finally beginning to look like she was right.

"Don't worry, we'll make up some ground in the jack-o'-lantern design category," I assured my friends. Thanks to all the display windows I'd helped out with at our family's bookshop this past year, plus the set design work I'd done for a local theater production over the summer, I was feeling pretty confident. If we had no chance of a prize for best catapult, at least we'd have a shot at best jack-o'-lantern.

"Now THIS, my friends, THIS is something special!" said Mr. Bigelow, rubbing his hands together in enthusiasm. "What is it that you've named it, Scooter?"

"The Beast," Scooter replied without an ounce of embarrassment.

"Ah, yes. The Beast." Mr. Bigelow bounced up and down on the balls of his feet as he whipped out his measuring tape and measured Scooter's catapult. Unlike the boys in my class, Mr. Bigelow hadn't shot up since last year—he was still just as short and round as ever. And just as nice. He was pretty much everybody's favorite teacher at our school.

It still tickled me that our school only had one science teacher. Our entire school had less than a hundred students—kindergarten through eighth grade, all in one building. Hatcher said that it was like something out of *Little House on the Prairie*, and he was only partly joking.

We'd been back at school for over a month now and I still wasn't used to not having my brother around. Our town was so small it didn't even have its own high school. Instead, Hatcher got up extra early every morning and drove with Danny to the regional high school over in West Hartfield. I'd be joining the two of them next year, but meanwhile, I was stuck here with my sisters. I loved all of my siblings, but Hatcher and I were extra close. He'd always been my safety net, the buffer between me and the world, and I hadn't been able to break myself of the habit of looking for him in the hallways between classes. I kept expecting to see him and his sunflower grin appear around every corner, like the Cheshire cat in *Alice in Wonderland*. But he—and it—didn't.

As Mr. Bigelow measured and marveled and jotted down notes about Scooter's catapult, I slipped my hand into my pocket and slid my fingers over the smooth contours of the small wooden owl I'd tucked inside earlier this morning. It fit perfectly in the palm of my hand. I'd been carrying it around ever since Gramps and Lola gave it to me. They'd brought presents for all of us from Namibia, and mine couldn't have been more perfect. Owls were my favorite birds, and Gramps, who was a fellow birder, knew it. I loved everything about owls—the beautiful markings on their feathers, their big, luminous eyes, and especially the way they glided silently through the air. Pure magic.

"It's to commemorate spotting your first one," Gramps had said as I'd opened my present. I'd finally seen my first owl in the wild this past spring break, and he understood exactly how special that day had been.

It was really, really great having Gramps and Lola back home with us. We'd videoconferenced with them while they were away in Africa, of course, but nothing beat being together in person. We'd stayed up so late last night talking that both Pippa and Lauren had fallen asleep on the floor.

"Earth to Truly!"

I looked over at Cha Cha and Jasmine and gave them an apologetic smile. "Sorry. What did you say?"

"I said you'd better be right about us making up some ground in the design category, because otherwise we are totally sunk," said Jasmine. "Mr. Bigelow looks like he wants to marry that thing of my brother's."

"Gather round, class!" cried Mr. Bigelow. "I want to explain to you why this is special. A catapult—like the ones you all made, and be assured I do appreciate your valiant efforts—"

"In other words, *losers*!" whispered Cha Cha, making Jasmine and me giggle.

"—makes use of the tension or energy of a twisted rope or sling," Mr. Bigelow continued. "Remember David and Goliath? Of course, David wouldn't have used a rubber band in his slingshot. But the principle is the same." He turned back to Scooter. "What Mr. Sanchez has made isn't technically a catapult, it's a trebuchet." He picked up a piece of chalk and wrote the word on the blackboard. "That's a French word, pronounced *tray-boo-shay*."

Jasmine raised her hand.

"Yes, Ms. Sanchez?"

"If it's not a catapult, shouldn't it be disqualified?"

Scooter glared at her, but she ignored him.

Mr. Bigelow's rubbed his chin. "Fair question. However, I've examined the rule book, and while there are plenty of rules, as you know—there are height limits, and motorized parts aren't allowed, for instance—there's nothing that says a participant can't make a trebuchet. It's really only due to town tradition that most contestants have designed simple catapults for their pumpkin launchers."

Jasmine looked disappointed.

"What's a trebuchet?" asked Franklin.

"I thought you'd never ask!" Mr. Bigelow bounced again. "A trebuchet has a sling as well, but it makes use of the energy of a raised counterweight to launch it. The lever"—he pointed to the long, wooden arm-like thing that stuck out of the back of the Beast—"is weighted. Large rocks and boulders were often used in the Middle Ages, but I see that this one will rely on your own body weight, am I correct?"

Scooter nodded.

"Splendid. So you will press the lever down, and then when the weight is released, wham! The trebuchet's arm launches its payload into the air. Would you like to tell us where you got the idea for your design?"

Before Scooter could explain, though, there was a knock on the classroom door and Principal Burnside poked his head in. Our principal had red hair and a long, skinny neck and reminded me of a flamingo. Or a periscope. Or maybe both. *Flamingoscope?* I suppressed a smile at the mental image.

"Good morning, Mr. Bigelow," he said. "Mind if I interrupt for a moment?"

"Not at all—come in, come in."

Our principal entered the classroom, a dark-haired boy trailing behind him. "Class, I'd like you to meet Emilio Frangipani," he said. "Emilio is from Milan, Italy, and will be joining us for the school year while his mother is a guest professor in the art department at Lovejoy College."

Pumpkin Falls was tiny, but thanks to the presence of the college it had more than its fair share of international students and visiting scholars and other interesting people roaming around. Including my soon-to-be uncle and Calhoun's father, who was president of the college and a renowned Shakespearean scholar.

That was me last January, right after we moved to Pumpkin Falls, I thought, sizing up the new boy. He didn't look nearly as awkward as I'd felt on my first day, though. Emilio regarded us through eyes as cool and gray as a pigeon feather, his expression neutral. His dark hair was slicked back and he was dressed more formally than we all were, in neatly pressed khaki pants like the ones my father and brothers wore to church every Sunday, a white polo shirt, and a navy cardigan with some sort of emblem on the breast pocket. Instead of sneakers, he was wearing shiny brown loafers.

Out of the corner of my eye, I saw Scooter stir. *Uh-oh,* I thought, catching the look on his face as he spotted Emilio's shoes. Something told me the new boy had just landed squarely in my classmate's sights.

Which was not a good place to be. Not at all. Fitting in at Pumpkin Falls hadn't been easy for me in the beginning, thanks to a few Scooter-size bumps in the road.

"Welcome, welcome!" said Mr. Bigelow, shaking Emilio's hand with enthusiasm. "You're joining us on one of the most thrilling days of the year. We're just about to head to the covered bridge to practice launching our pumpkins!"

That probably wasn't a sentence that translated well into Italian, I thought, noting the blank look on Emilio's face. It was pretty unusual in English, too, come to think of it.

"Don't be shy!" said Mr. Bigelow, grasping Emilio's arm and towing him across the classroom toward all of us. "We're all friends here! First things first, I'll need to assign you to a team. Let's see, how about we put you over here with Lucas Winthrop and Romeo Calhoun."

Calhoun winced.

A flicker of interest appeared in Emilio's eyes. "Romeo?" he said. *"Parli Italiano?"*

"Um," said Calhoun.

Calhoun was smart, but I knew for a fact he did not *parli* anything but English. I, on the other hand, did—well, at least a few words and phrases, thanks to the fact that my family had lived in Germany while my father was in the army. We'd traveled all over Europe during those two years we'd been stationed near Wiesbaden, and my father had made us learn a little bit of the language in every country we visited.

I remembered only too well what a difference it had made when someone was nice to me when I first got to Pumpkin Falls. That someone had been Cha Cha, and we'd been friends ever since. I groped for the Italian words for "Hello" and "Welcome to Daniel Webster School."

"*Buongiorno!*" I blurted finally. "*Benvenuti a scuola Daniel Webster.*"

Emilio looked surprised. "*Buongiorno,*" he replied cautiously, inclining his head slightly, like royalty acknowledging a peasant. Then, as his eyes traveled from the top of my head down to my size ten-and-a-half feet, he added under his breath, "*la giraffa.*"

I stiffened. I didn't need to know Italian to translate that.

Neither did any of my classmates, including Scooter.

"What's the new kid's name again?" he asked loudly, scowling fiercely at Emilio.

Brace for impact, I thought.

Sure enough, Scooter fired right on cue. "Did you say 'Emily Fancypants'?"

"That's enough, Scooter," warned Mr. Bigelow.

"*Scooter?*" said Emilio Frangipani. He gave my classmate a withering look and continued in impeccable English, "I have a scooter at home in Italy. It lives in a shed behind our villa. Perhaps you belong in a shed too."

Scooter's face flushed. He opened his mouth and shut it again. For the first time since I'd known him, he was speechless.

Scooter Sanchez had just been out-Scootered.

CHAPTER 4

October in New Hampshire was pretty much perfect. Crisp sunny days, bluer-than-blue skies, trees aflame with color—I totally understood now why fall was my aunt's favorite season. And our field trip to the covered bridge really *would* have been perfect, except for one thing.

"I can't believe he called you that!" whispered Jasmine, giving Emilio a dark look. The new boy was oblivious, walking along next to Mr. Bigelow with his hands thrust into his pockets.

I lifted a shoulder. "It's okay."

It wasn't really, though. And my friends knew it. I'd gotten used to being tall, mostly, and to being teased about being tall, mostly. But "giraffe"? From a complete stranger I was only trying to be nice to?

"Okay, class, listen up!" Mr. Bigelow clapped his hands as we gathered on the sidewalk near the red covered bridge. The long wooden structure spanning the Pumpkin River was our town's top tourist attraction. It held a few memories for me, too, from providing the final clue for the very first mystery I'd helped solve last winter to my unexpected dramatic plunge from its railing into the icy water below. Just thinking about that still made me shiver.

"Is that waterfall not a stunner?" enthused our science teacher, pointing to the cliff over which our town's second-most famous tourist attraction tumbled and splashed. "Have you ever seen such a sight?"

Emilio shrugged. "We have waterfalls in Italy, too."

"Not like this one you don't," Mr. Bigelow replied cheerfully. "Look at those red maples framing it! Take a picture and send it to your mama. She'll be happy to know that you're already fitting in here at your new school."

"Fitting in here" my big foot, I thought bitterly, as Emilio did as he was told.

"Okay, people!" Mr. Bigelow continued. "Bring your catapults over here and line them up! Trebuchet, too!" He indicated the level spot on the grassy riverbank where the official pumpkin toss would take place three weeks from now. "You've got this week and next to fine-tune your entries, and then we'll vote on the winner to represent our school."

Everyone in my class—with the exception of Emilio, who had apparently decided that taking more pictures of the scenery was a good thing—turned to look at Scooter, who grinned. Unless The Beast was a complete dud as a launcher, I figured it was already a done deal as far as whose design would be chosen to represent Daniel Webster School.

That didn't mean Scooter would win the whole shebang, though, the way my dad had back in the day. The Beast would be up against stiff competition. First, anyone in town who wanted to cough up the entry fee was eligible to enter. Some people used the same catapult year after year, while others designed brand-new ones for each festival. Second, about ten years ago, Pumpkin Falls had started holding an annual lottery for a handful of spots reserved for out-of-towners. According to Ella Bellow, who of course had the inside track, the number of entries in the lottery had grown astronomically, the proceeds from which went to supporting the festival and other local events and projects.

"Our little town is on the radar screen!" she'd announced proudly to everyone within earshot the other day at the bookstore. "We keep raising the price of the lottery tickets every year, and every year we get more applicants."

For such a tiny town, Pumpkin Falls sure made the news a lot—we'd been featured in newspapers and magazines and on TV shows and podcasts and WeTube channels. Tourists loved visiting places steeped in tradition, and Pumpkin Falls was bursting at the seams with it. No tradition was more central to our town's history than the Halloween Pumpkin Toss.

The very first one was held the same year our town was

founded, back in 1769, by Nathaniel Daniel Lovejoy, my ancestor whose portrait hung in our living room at home. Nathaniel Daniel, whom my sister Pippa always referred to as "Nathaniel Daniel Looks Like a Spaniel," had named half of the stuff in town after himself: Lovejoy College, Lovejoy Mountain, Lake Lovejoy—the list went on and on. Sometimes it made living here a little embarrassing. The way the story went, the son of Nathaniel Daniel's next-door neighbor was a mischief-maker who got into trouble a lot. One time he was caught stealing pumpkins around town and pitching them into the river. The town council was all set to throw him in jail, when Nathaniel Daniel spoke up on his behalf. Maybe he saw a bit of himself in the boy, given his former life as a pirate. At any rate, in a now-famous speech—well, famous in Pumpkin Falls, anyway, where it was read aloud every year from the steps of the library on Halloween night, to kick off the Pumpkin Toss—my ancestor suggested that instead of punishing the boy, the town should put him to work planting new pumpkins to replace the ones he'd stolen. To seal the deal, he added a final flourish: "That he carve each into a jack-o'-lantern, to be carried forth by ye goode townsfolke to yon river on All Hallows Eve, hence to be tossed in order that evil spirits be cast forth and the town be preserved for another year."

It sounded to me like Nathaniel Daniel was making it up as he went along to try and help out his neighbor's kid, but his idea was a huge hit. It became an annual tradition and there's been a Halloween Pumpkin Toss here ever since. Over the years, the event kind of mushroomed to include the catapult contest, the jack-o'-lantern design contest, the biggest pumpkin contest, and so on. The celebration was a huge fundraiser for our town now as well as a tourist attraction.

"We put the fun in fundraiser!" was the event's unofficial motto, which I was pretty sure Nathaniel Daniel didn't make up. That sounded like the bright idea of some marketing whiz in the 1960s, not the 1760s.

"Hop to it, Ms. Lovejoy!" called Mr. Bigelow. "This is no time for daydreaming—we need ammunition!"

"Sorry!" I replied, grabbing the handle of the little red wagon we'd dragged along from school. Looking at it, it suddenly occurred to me that something similar could totally work for our bookshop display window. A classic red wagon piled with orange pumpkins—plus autumn-themed books, of course—could be a winner. Simple, but effective. I made a mental note to share the idea with Aunt True after school.

"Just use the small pumpkins today, people," our science teacher told us. "No point wasting the bigger ones just yet."

Mr. Bigelow had us line up our catapults and aim them directly at the waterfall. And then the fun began.

Well, fun for Scooter, anyway.

"Ready, aim—fire!" Mr. Bigelow called, as Jasmine and

Cha Cha held our catapult frame steady and I pulled back, back, back on the rubber sling—then let it go, firing off our first pumpkin. We watched as it gave a halfhearted lurch into the air and then fell directly onto the grass at our feet.

"Are you *kidding me*?" Cha Cha put her hands on her hips and glared at the pumpkin in disgust.

Jasmine reached out with her toe and prodded down the grassy slope and into the river.

"No cheating, Ms. Sanchez!" Mr. Bigelow's tone was severe, but he was smiling broadly, clearly enjoying the whole spectacle. "I saw that! Who's next?"

Franklin Freeman and Amy Nguyen's catapult performed only slightly better than ours. The pumpkin they fired actually made it into the river without any extra assistance, but it landed just off the riverbank and certainly nowhere near the waterfall, which was our target. Results from the next few catapults were about the same. Finally, it was Calhoun and Lucas's turn. And Emilio Frangipani's, too, since he was now part of their team. Not that he'd had anything at all to do with the design. He just stood to the side and watched, arms crossed and feigning disinterest. I could tell he was intrigued, though, because he kept sneaking shots of the proceedings with his cell phone. Probably texting them to all his friends in their villas back in Italy, I thought sourly, showing them what country bumpkins we were.

"Bravo, gentlemen!" cried Mr. Bigelow, pumping his fist

into the air as Calhoun and Lucas's pumpkin landed with a splash about a swimming pool's length from the base of the waterfall. "We have a contender!"

The final launch of the day was Scooter's.

He bustled about importantly, placing the pumpkin just so in the cradle on his trebuchet's wooden arm and making a big show of grunting loudly as he pressed down on the lever with all his might.

"Fire in the hole!" he hollered—and released it.

Jasmine watched open-mouthed as her twin's pumpkin sailed into the stratosphere and made a direct hit on the waterfall.

"Well done, Mr. Sanchez, well done!" cried Mr. Bigelow.

"I definitely should have said yes when he asked me to team up with him," his twin said, shaking her head and sending her dark hair rippling around her shoulders.

Scooter might have had hidden engineering talent, but his ego wasn't hidden one bit. "That's front-page news right there, folks!" he crowed. "My ticket to fame and fortune."

"The front page of the *Patriot-Bugle* hardly counts as fame," Jasmine scoffed. "Big deal."

Mr. Bigelow whipped out his tape measure. "Let's just double-check to be sure," he said, measuring Scooter's trebuchet one more time. "Hmmm, you've stretched it to the upper limit on size, young man, but it looks like it's still legal. Friends, unless one of you really steps up his or her game as you're fine-tuning your catapults this week, The Beast is the one to beat!"

Scooter swelled even larger with self-importance, if that were possible. "I probably should have called it 'The Truly,'" he remarked to no one in particular. "You know, because it's—"

"Tall?" I snapped. "Yes, I'm tall. We've established that."

"I'm just *joking*! I meant it as a compliment! You don't need to get all huffy about it."

"I'm not huffy! Just quit it with the stupid tall jokes already!"

Emilio watched this exchange in silence. A few minutes later, he came over to where I was restacking the pumpkins in the red cart for the trip back to school. He stood there for a moment watching me, then said abruptly, "My mother also is tall."

I glared at him. "Don't you start, too."

"My father's nickname for her is *la giraffa*."

I kept glaring. Was that supposed to be comforting?

"Also," he added, tipping his head to the side and giving me a faint smile, "giraffes are my favorite animal."

I stared at him as he turned and went back to join Lucas and Calhoun.

Had Emilio Frangipani just apologized?

Wait, was he *flirting* with me?

I had no idea.

Honestly, boys were above pumpkin-tossing on the list of things I wasn't good at.

CHAPTER 5

"Belinda!" called Aunt True. "Did you take Wally's head?"

I froze, then reminded myself that it was early, and the bookshop wouldn't open for several hours. Which was a good thing, because it meant there were no customers around to overhear my aunt's cringeworthy question. People thought our family was weird enough as it was.

I was rooting through the small cupboard under the counter of Cup and Chaucer, our store's mini café, for Aunt True's molasses ginger cookies. They were her new signature treat for the bookstore for fall and they were really good. I'd stopped by to grab one on my way to swim practice.

Belinda materialized from behind one of the shelves in the mystery section and pulled out an earbud. I could hear the faint strains of the Beach Boys' "Surfer Girl" from across the room. "What?"

"Did you take Wally's head?" my aunt repeated.

TRULY, MADLY, SHEEPLY

Wally was the scarecrow that my aunt and I had created a few weeks ago as a fall decoration. Propped up in a wooden rocking chair outside the bookshop's front door, he was dressed in a pair of overalls and an old flannel shirt belonging to Gramps—the Walter Lovejoy for whom Wally was named. I'd painted a grinning face on the pumpkin we'd used for his head, then we'd taped a pair of glasses to it and added a curly white wig and bushy eyebrows made of white yarn. Around his neck hung a sign that said: WELCOME TO OUR BOO-SHOP! Belinda placed a new selection of sale books in his arms every day.

"I thought you took it," said Belinda. "Couldn't imagine why."

Aunt True frowned. "Now why on earth would I do that?" She sighed. "It's probably just a prank. Happens every fall around here, thanks to those lunkhead fraternity students. Truly, do you have time to check the back alley?"

"Sure." I did as she asked, checking behind the pile of cardboard boxes awaiting recycling and poking around in the dumpster. I even checked behind Mahoney's Antiques and the Klip 'n' Kurl for good measure. But there was no sign of our scarecrow's head.

Back inside, I glanced at the clock and grabbed my duffel bag from the bench by the door. Coach Maynard was a stickler for being on time. "Gotta run!" I told my aunt. "I'll make another head for Wally after school if it hasn't turned up by then."

I made it to swim practice with a minute to spare, joining my teammates on the pool deck for warm-up stretches.

"Listen up, people!" said Coach Maynard. "We've got a big meet this weekend, and I expect you all to be in tip-top shape. No slacking. No stuffing your faces at parties. I'm looking at you, Truly Lovejoy." He sounded stern but winked to let me know he was teasing. Our meet was on Sunday, and most of Pumpkin Falls would be at Aunt True's wedding the day before, including Coach Maynard and his wife. Face-stuffing was pretty much guaranteed.

A short while later, as we were leaning on the edge of the pool taking a break from the punishing set of intervals we'd been given, I glanced over at Lucas. He yawned, and I saw that he had dark circles under his eyes. "Let me guess, fire drill?"

He nodded and yawned again.

Back when Lucas was a baby, some insurance agent did a number on his mother with a presentation that involved a battery-operated dollhouse. When he got to the part about fire insurance, he pressed a button and it lit up with fake flames. This totally terrified Mrs. Winthrop, who to be fair was pretty much totally terrified of everything. So much so that ever since Lucas could walk, she'd held regular fire drills like the ones we had at school. She sprang it on him randomly once a month at night. When Lucas heard the smoke detector go off, he had to get out of bed and head for the nearest exit. Then he had to wait in a safe place on the lawn in his pajamas until his mother called the all-clear. Everyone was hoping that Mrs. Winthrop would calm down a bit after she married Bud Jefferson, who owned the stamp and coin shop in town. But that wasn't going to happen until next spring, so Lucas had a lot more fire drills to look forward to until then.

"Somebody took Wally's head," I told him.

"The jack-o'-lantern at Lou's disappeared, too," he replied, not missing a beat. "I heard Lou complaining about it to my mother this morning."

"Aunt True thinks it's college kids."

"She's probably right. These dumb pranks happen every fall. Last year they put a live cow inside the general store."

I gaped at him. "Seriously?"

Lucas nodded again. "The Farnsworths were cleaning up cow patties for days."

"Ew." I'd lived in rural New Hampshire long enough now to know what a cow patty was. Definitely nothing a person would want to step in—especially not inside.

At school, our first class was Language Arts. I was heading to the classroom when I heard someone calling my name. Turning around, I saw Cha Cha hustling toward me. If you could call her graceful lope a hustle. It was more like watching a sandpiper scoot along the edge of the shore. Cha Cha was as tiny as I was tall.

"Wait up!" she called, linking her arm through mine.

Jasmine was right behind her. When we reached the doorway the three of us stopped in our tracks and stared at our teacher.

"Good morning to you!" Ms. Matthews announced, greeting us with a low bow. She was wearing a scraggly black wig, a black mustache, and a black cape.

"Is that a real stuffed crow on her shoulder?" Jasmine whispered as she and Cha Cha and I edged cautiously past her, just in case she'd lost her mind or something.

I shuddered. "I hope not."

"Happy Halloween!" Ms. Matthews continued as we all took our seats. "Well, almost Halloween. At any rate, this is the perfect time of year for us to get to know one of the literary greats—the master of mystery and the macabre!"

She motioned to Calhoun and Scooter, who'd been recruited to pass out paperback copies of a book called *Selected Tales and Poems of Edgar Allan Poe*. The cover looked familiar; I was pretty sure we carried it in the bookshop. On the front, a man was posed against a blue backdrop, looking mournfully back at me. He was dressed like our teacher, with longish dark hair, a droopy mustache, and a black cape. A bird was perched on his shoulder, too.

"Let's all open to the table of contents, shall we?" said Ms. Matthews.

The titles sounded intriguing enough: "The Telltale Heart," "The Pit and the Pendulum," "The Raven," "The

Premature Burial," "The Cask of Amontillado," "The Purloined Letter."

"What's 'purloined'?" asked Scooter, who may have been an engineering genius but was seriously lacking in the literary department. Books were not on his radar screen.

"Stolen," said Calhoun, before anyone else could answer. Ever since we'd started eighth grade, Calhoun had gotten bolder about letting people know how smart he was. Of course, it helped having a father who was a famous Shakespearean scholar. Calhoun knew a lot about literature.

"Very good, Romeo," said Ms. Matthews. "That's exactly right. 'The Purloined Letter' is a detective story. I think it's fair to say that Poe invented detective fiction. His work predates Sir Arthur Conan Doyle's Sherlock Holmes."

She asked us to divide ourselves into teams of two or three, and there was a scraping of chairs and scurrying of feet as we all rushed to be with our friends. I chose Cha Cha and Jasmine, of course. We looked over to see Emilio standing quietly by himself. He was wearing normal clothes today, at least, which was an improvement over yesterday's formal look.

"Ah, Emilio. How about we team you up with . . ." Ms. Matthews scanned the likely possibilities, grabbed a few arms and did a little rearranging of groups, then said, "Scooter Sanchez."

Scooter stiffened. So did Emilio. Neither made a move toward the other.

Uh-oh, I thought. Ms. Matthews had no idea what she was unleashing. At the very least, further hostile skirmishes. At the worst, all-out war.

Our teacher gave Emilio an encouraging nudge, but he didn't move. Across the room, Scooter was planted with his arms crossed.

"I trust you'll make our new student feel welcome, Scooter," Ms. Matthews said firmly.

Fat chance of that, I thought.

"How about I team up with Emilio?" offered Lucas, saving the day.

"That's very kind of you, Lucas," Ms. Matthews replied. "Scooter, you may remain partners with Romeo. Now, while I hope you'll take the opportunity to sample several of Mr. Poe's stories, we're going to be studying 'The Cask of Amontillado' together as a class. I'd like each team to prepare a presentation of some kind for us all. Creativity is highly encouraged. You'll be commenting on the story itself, of course, but I'd also like you to do some research and share information about Edgar Allan Poe himself. You may choose whatever format you'd like—perhaps a podcast or a short film, a poem or a piece of artwork. The sky's the limit! You can dress up"—she indicated her own bizarre costume—"use props, visuals, music, whatever you want. Based on the number of votes your presentation receives, your team may win a prize."

She crossed to the far side of the room, black cape flapping.

"Meanwhile, to get us in the mood, I thought we'd kick things off today by watching a WeTube video I found of a famous actor reading Poe's poem 'The Raven.'" She pointed a remote at the big flat-screen TV that hung from the ceiling. "I think you'll find it deliciously creepy."

Half an hour later, just as our discussion of the video ended, the bell rang and we all flooded out into the hall.

"*Quoth the Raven 'Nevermore!'*" Cha Cha intoned as we headed down the hall to math class. "That's pretty much how I feel about that stupid poem. I *nevermore* want to read it."

"Me neither," added Jasmine. "I sure hope the short stories are better."

"Plus, what's so creepy about a raven?" I complained. "They're playful and can mimic human speech and are super intelligent—right up there with chimps and dolphins."

"Well, aren't you a fountain of knowledge," said Cha Cha.

"*Scusi*, but what is 'creepy'?" asked Emilio.

I jumped. Turning around, I saw that he was right behind me. "Um, scary, but not super scary. More like spooky. You know, like when you get goose bumps."

He frowned, still puzzled.

"You know, like . . ." I rummaged for the word, wishing I knew more Italian than just "please," "thank you," and "Where's the bathroom?" Reaching into my backpack, I took out my cell phone and scrolled to the translator app. It had come in very handy the year we lived in Germany. Changing the setting to Italian, I pressed the mic and said "goose bumps."

"*Pelle d'oca,*" came the prompt reply.

Emilio's puzzled expression vanished. "Ah," he said, pinching his arm and smiling at me. "*Capisco.* I understand. You are correct, the poem was not very 'creepy.'"

"Somebody likes you," whispered Jasmine a few minutes later as we took our seats in math class.

I made a face. "I don't know about that."

"Well, I do," she said, and gave me an impish smile.

After school, on my way to the bookshop, I stopped by Lou's to grab Autumn Elixirs for my aunt and me. Despite the fact that we now had a fancy espresso machine at Cup and Chaucer, Aunt True still loved Lou's elixir teas the best. The winter one was her favorite, but the autumn one was good, too, a fragrant blend of ginger tea, hot apple cider, and a dash of pumpkin flavoring.

I could hear loud voices even before I opened the diner door. Ethel Farnsworth from the general store was standing by the cash register, complaining to Lou and everyone else within earshot that the jack-o'-lantern had disappeared from the store's porch.

"The nerve of those hooligans!" she said. "Last year that blasted cow and now this! It was there this morning when I arrived, but when I came out a little while ago to go to the post office, it was gone."

TRULY, MADLY, SHEEPLY

I delivered the news of the latest theft to Aunt True along with her Autumn Elixir. She'd already heard it from Ella Bellow, though, who was busy spreading the word about the rash of missing pumpkins through her invisible grapevine. The news was all over Pumpkin Falls by dinnertime.

By the following morning, it was all over the front page of the *Pumpkin Falls Patriot-Bugle*.

My dad sipped his coffee and smiled as he read the story. He loved this kind of thing. In fact, his favorite part of the paper was the police blotter, which he called a snapshot of small-town life. I, on the other hand, called it ridiculous. We had a police force of exactly one—Officer Tanglewood—and nothing ever happened in Pumpkin Falls anyway. Certainly nothing that qualified as newsworthy. Why bother reporting about nothing?

Still, I made sure to snap a photo of the blotter every week to send to my cousin Mackenzie, who loved it as much as my dad did. The town that time forgot! she'd always text back, right on cue.

Usually, the reports were pretty ordinary. Well, ordinary for Pumpkin Falls. Somebody turned in a lost pair of sunglasses. Someone else registered a complaint about the church choir being too loud. A prowler reported outside the Pumpkin Falls Bed & Breakfast turned out to be a raccoon rooting through the trash. My personal favorite? "A possibly injured woodchuck moved along after being poked with a stick."

Hatcher and I had laughed about that one for days.

Lauren was reading the comics, Danny and Hatcher were sharing the sports page, and my dad had the front section. Pippa was staring at the back of the cereal box. I snagged the pages with the want ads and this week's police blotter and scanned it while I ate my scrambled eggs. The string of jack-o'-lantern thefts were noted of course, and there was a complaint about bees escaping from a hive and wandering onto a neighboring property. I raised my eyebrows at that one. Officer Tanglewood was supposed to wrangle bees? He wasn't my favorite person in town, but that almost made me feel sorry for him. Finally, there was a report of a snapping turtle creating a traffic hazard near the intersection of Hill Street and the entrance to Lovejoy College. I stared at the newspaper. Seriously? A snapping turtle? What planet had I landed on? I took a picture of the column and texted it to Mackenzie along with a turtle emoji and one of a forehead smack.

"What's so funny, Daddy?" Pippa asked as my father chuckled.

He folded the newspaper and placed it on the table, tapping the giant front-page headline with his forefinger. My little sister laboriously read it out loud: "PURLOINED PUMPKINS PUZZLE PUMPKIN FALLS!" She looked up. "Why is that funny?"

"Because it's a tongue twister," said Lauren.

Pippa stuck out her tongue and tugged it, considering.

"Because it pretty much sums up our blip-on-a-radar-screen town," I added.

"What's a blip?" asked Pippa.

"Something the size of a peanut."

She frowned. "What does 'purloined' mean?"

"Stolen," I replied. My father lifted an eyebrow and gave me a nod of approval. I silently thanked Calhoun and my Language Arts class.

Pippa stared at the headline. Her blue eyes looked worried behind her pink sparkly glasses. "Maybe somebody just borrowed them."

Lauren made a dismissive noise. "That's dumb. Who'd borrow a pumpkin?"

My father pushed back from the table. "I hope the purloiners get the book thrown at them," he said. "These pranks need to stop."

"Yeah," Lauren agreed, taking a bite of cereal. "They'd better not try purloining our pumpkin." She and Pippa were proud as punch of the lopsided jack-o'-lantern they'd carved under my father's careful supervision.

"Nobody's purloining anything around here," said Lola, who came into the kitchen just then. "I'll sic Miss Marple on them!"

I tried to picture my grandparents' elderly golden retriever in hot pursuit of anything besides her next meal. It was impossible.

"Isn't that right, Miss Marple?" Lola cooed. "Ooh, how I've missed you!" She whisked a crust of toast off my dad's plate and held it out.

"Mother!" protested my father as Miss Marple gulped it down. "We're trying to put some manners on her!"

"Too late," said my grandmother, winking at my sisters and me. "Haven't you heard? You can't teach an old dog new tricks."

At school, the pumpkin thefts were all anyone could talk about. Everyone had a theory as to who was behind it.

It's probably the new kid," said Scooter. "It's too much of a coincidence—first he shows up, then pumpkins start disappearing?"

"Just because you don't like someone doesn't mean they're a criminal, Scooter," I replied. "Plus, why on earth would Emilio Frangipani steal pumpkins?"

"Why not?" Scooter retorted. "You can tell he thinks everything about this place is lame."

Including you, I thought, but wisely kept that to myself. No point throwing fuel on the fire. "Well, he's kind of right. I mean seriously, an annual Halloween Pumpkin Toss? You'd think our town was hosting a royal visit from the way we make such a fuss about it. Talk about bumpkin central."

"We're not bumpkins!" Scooter could get very defensive about Pumpkin Falls.

Lucas came charging into the cafeteria just then and made a beeline for our table. "My mom texted!" he said, breathless. "It's Cider Doughnut Day!"

I shot Scooter a look. "I rest my case."

When it came to Lou's cider doughnuts, though, I was as big a bumpkin as anyone else in town. Cider doughnuts cropped up all over New England this time of year, at farm stands and general stores and just about every supermarket from Maine to Massachusetts. But the ones at Lou's Diner were hands-down the best I'd ever had. Lou had been written up in newspapers and magazines, interviewed on TV, featured on food tours, and more. People came from all over for his cider doughnuts. Part of the magic was that he didn't make them all the time—only in the fall and only on one random day per week. He said he liked to build anticipation, like Christmas.

It worked.

The day crawled by. None of us could concentrate. Lucas got caught sketching a doughnut instead of an octagon in geometry. Jasmine made up a doughnut song and sang it softly under her breath in science class as we worked on our catapult. As for Edgar Allen Poe, how could I be expected to focus on "The Cask of Amontillado" when all I could think about was sinking my teeth into the crisp cinnamon-sugar outside and moist, nutmeg-and-apple-scented inside of the cider doughnut I knew was waiting for me? It was pure torture.

"Should we invite Emilio?" Cha Cha asked as the final

bell rang and my friends and I bolted down the hall and out the door. Our new classmate was standing a few steps below us, fiddling with his cell phone.

"Why?" said Scooter, his tone belligerent. "He's a jerk."

"He's not so bad," said Calhoun. "He had some really great ideas for increasing the thrust on the catapult that Lucas and I built."

Scooter just scowled.

"I'll ask him," I offered, surprising myself.

Equally surprising was the fact that Emilio turned me down. "I would love to try your cider doughnuts, but my father is on his way to pick me up. I have a piano lesson."

Emilio played the piano? "Who's your teacher?"

"Ms. Patel."

"She's my piano teacher too! She's really nice; you'll like her."

A low-slung sports car turned onto School Street and headed our way. Behind the wheel was a dark-haired man in stylish sunglasses. Emilio's father. He waved as he pulled up at the curb.

Emilio turned and smiled at me. "*Va bene*. That's good. That will be two people in this town I like." He got in the car with his father and they drove away.

I felt my face flush. It wasn't my imagination—or Jasmine's. Emilio was definitely flirting with me.

"Ready for a doughnut?" asked Calhoun, poking me in the back. I jumped, startled, and felt my face flush again. Had he overheard my conversation with Emilio? Calhoun wasn't my boyfriend, exactly, but I was pretty sure he liked me. And I was pretty sure that I liked him.

A few minutes later, cider doughnuts in hand—hands, really, as Lucas's mother had saved us each two—we all headed down the street to the bookshop.

"Yoo-hoo! Pumpkin Falls Private Eyes!" Ella Bellow hollered at us from across Main Street.

My friends and I all cringed. No one would ever accuse Ella of being subtle. She was standing on the front steps of A Stitch in Time, waving vigorously at us. We hurried across the street to join her.

"I'm mad as a hornet over these disappearing pumpkins," she snapped. "Our town has never seen the likes of it!"

"We didn't take the pumpkins, Mrs. Bellow," Cha Cha told her indignantly.

"I *know* that," said Ella. "But someone's been taking them, and I want to find out who. This is bad for our town and bad for business. Right before leaf-peeping weekend, too! I'm having a security camera installed tomorrow, but we need to get to the bottom of this now. I don't want to risk losing Woolly."

I glanced over at the rocking chair outside the door of her shop. Ella had brazenly copied Aunt True and me with her pumpkin-headed scarecrow. Only hers was a sheep, not a man meant to resemble my grandfather. Woolly was wearing a hand-knit sweater and clutching a pair of knitting needles in his paws. Or were they hooves? What did sheep have, anyway? His pumpkin head sported a painted-on black nose and Ella had knitted him a pair of floppy white ears.

"Woolly and Wally! Won't that be cute?" she'd burbled to my aunt and me last week when she'd unveiled him, trying to smooth over the fact that she'd copied us.

"I'm offering to pay for your services," Ella continued. "I'd like to hire you kids to catch this"—she paused for a moment, searching for the right description—"this pumpkin snatcher."

My friends and I looked at each other in amazement. A paying client? The Pumpkin Falls Private Eyes were coming up in the world!

CHAPTER 6

Aunt True raised an eyebrow as the six of us barged into the bookshop. "Where's the fire?"

"Nowhere," I told her. "Can we use the back office for a few minutes?"

"Sure. Your father went . . . He went . . ." She frowned. "Actually, I'm not sure where he went."

I frowned too. This had been happening a lot lately. Just a few days ago, I'd overheard my mother and Aunt True talking. They'd stopped the minute I walked into the kitchen, but not before I'd managed to hear the tail end of their conversation.

"That's the third time this month that J. T. has had to reschedule his physical therapy appointment!" my mother had said. "I don't know where he keeps disappearing to."

I didn't either, but I didn't have time to solve that particular mystery now. Not with the prospect of a paying job dangling out there. All thoughts of my father's whereabouts were swept away as my friends and I crammed into the small books-and-paper-filled room that served as the store's receiving area, bookkeeping headquarters, lunchroom, and general storage closet. I plunked myself down in the chair at my father's desk while my friends perched around me on piles of boxes full of books.

"This official meeting of the Pumpkin Falls Private Eyes will come to order!" I told them.

Before we could get down to business, though, the office door burst open. We all swiveled around, startled.

"Sorry I'm late," panted Lauren. "I just got your text!"

Last spring, we'd allowed my middle sister to join our group. She'd missed out on our case over the summer because of camp, and as a result she was raring to go.

"We're just getting started," I assured her. "You haven't missed a thing. Where's Pippa?"

Now that Lauren was in fifth grade, my parents had decided that she was old enough to babysit our little sister a couple of times a week after school. After we moved to Pumpkin Falls, our mother had gone back to college to get her teaching degree, and she had several late-afternoon classes. I helped out from time to time with Pippa, too, and so did Belinda, but my schedule was pretty busy this fall, what with working at the bookstore, swim team, and piano lessons. Plus of course now we had the wedding preparations, too.

"She's at the Abramowitzes," Lauren told me, glancing

over at Cha Cha. Pippa and Cha Cha's little brother were best friends. "She and Baxter are playing in their fort. They're coming over later for snacks."

Cha Cha's father had built Baxter a treehouse over the summer, and Pippa was madly in love with it. She'd been spending nearly all her free time hanging out up there.

"Speaking of snacks, where are ours?" demanded Scooter.

"Later," I told him. "We need to focus on"—my pen hovered over the pad of paper in front of me—"*the Case of the Purloined Pumpkins.*" My friends all groaned as I wrote the words at the top of the page with a flourish.

"What?" I grinned at them. "It has a nice ring to it, right? Plus, just think of how proud Ms. Matthews would be. You can't say we haven't learned something in school this week."

As always, I divided the page into two columns. At the top of one I wrote *What We Know* and at the top of the other, *What We Don't Know.*

"We know whose pumpkins have been stolen so far, right?" I said, and started writing furiously as my sister and my friends called out the names of the victims.

"We should interview everyone on the list," said Jasmine.

I nodded. "Absolutely. Anything they can remember—the time of day they discovered their pumpkin was missing, any little detail could help us at this point."

"I'll take Lou's," said Lucas. "I can ask my mother for details tonight at dinner."

On a second page I wrote *Lucas—Lou's*. "Who wants to take the general store?"

Calhoun's hand went up and the list of victims was quickly divided among the rest of us.

"Lauren and I will talk to Aunt True and Belinda again about Wally's head once we're done," I told my friends.

"Should we meet tomorrow after school to go over our findings?" asked Scooter.

I shook my head. "You guys can meet if you want, but this week is going to be tough for Lauren and me. I've got to finish our display window and we're helping my mom and Aunt True and Lola decorate the church, plus Friday night there's the wedding rehearsal and rehearsal dinner."

"How about we just meet at school during lunch?" Calhoun suggested.

"Yeah," said Cha Cha. "And we can always text each other if something comes up."

Before we could head out to grab our snacks from Cup and Chaucer, the door to the office burst open again.

"Lauren!" Pippa squealed. Cha Cha's little brother was right behind her. "Come and see!"

"See what?" Lauren asked.

"The surprise kitten!" blurted Baxter.

Pippa glared at her friend. "You weren't supposed to tell!"

Baxter's hand flew up to his mouth. "Sorry."

Lauren pushed past them both, her face alight. The rest of

us followed her out into the bookshop. Aunt True and Belinda were standing by the cash register with huge smiles on their faces.

"Where is it?" Lauren asked, breathless. "Baxter spilled the beans."

Belinda reached into the pocket of her purple overalls and pulled out a little scrap of orange and white fluff. She passed him to my sister.

"He's an early bridesmaid present," said Aunt True. "Our future barn cat."

I really hoped I wasn't going to get a kitten for my bridesmaid present. Cats were not my favorite, although I'd gotten used to Mephisto, more or less.

Aunt True spotted the expression on my face and grinned. "Don't worry, Truly. I have something completely different planned for you."

Pippa looked worried. "Is there a flower girl present?"

"Of course there is, sweetheart. But the kitten is just for Lauren, because she's wanted one for so long."

I couldn't remember the last time I'd seen Lauren look so happy. Maybe when we'd gotten Thumper, her bunny, or Nibbles, her hamster. The kitten was pretty cute, as far as kittens went, with its orange and white stripes, fat little exclamation point of a tail, and perfectly round eyes that stared at us in astonishment.

"He's going to have to live here in the bookshop until

the barn is rebuilt," said Aunt True. "In fact, he may end up being a bookstore kitten and not a barn kitten. We'll have to see which he prefers."

"What about Mephisto?" asked Lauren, looking around in concern.

Hearing his name, my aunt's cat came sauntering over. Mephisto didn't like anybody, really, except my aunt. He'd grown to tolerate Miss Marple, but he still teased her at every opportunity. Kittens, though—kittens were *w-a-y* up the list of things that Mephisto didn't tolerate, and Belinda always gave him a wide berth when she had any on her. Which was pretty much always.

Mephisto's green eyes narrowed to slits as he spotted the kitten in my sister's arms. The kitten looked on with interest as the big cat's black tail thrashed back and forth.

"Keep away!" warned Lauren, turning her back on Mephisto and clutching her furry bundle protectively.

Somehow, the tiger-striped kitten managed to wriggle out of her grasp. Before Lauren could stop him, he jumped to the floor and bounced, stiff-legged, closer to my aunt's cat. Instead of hissing and swatting, however, which was Mephisto's usual modus operandi—that was a detective term I'd learned that meant "method of doing something"—this time the big black cat stopped short. He blinked, then approached the kitten cautiously and sniffed it.

"He's going to eat it!" shrieked Pippa.

My aunt held up a finger. "Give him a moment."

Mephisto gave the kitten a tentative lick.

"He's tasting it!" wailed Pippa.

"Shhh," said my aunt. "Listen."

"Is he *purring*?" boomed Cha Cha, whose deep voice still surprised me sometimes.

It startled Mephisto, too, who hissed at her. As Lauren hovered protectively over her furry gift, the kitten rubbed up against the big black cat. Mephisto looked startled. He stared down at the little creature, hesitated, then lay down on his side and resumed his big, rumbling purr. Lauren's kitten immediately snuggled up next to him.

"I think we can safely say that Mephisto has finally met his match," said Belinda.

My aunt shook her head in astonishment. "Unbelievable! He's never done that before around another cat—or a dog. I guess there's a first time for everything."

"Does my kitten have to stay here? Can't I take him home?" Lauren asked. "Somebody needs to protect him, just in case."

As Scooter squatted down and reached out to pat the kitten, Mephisto's ears flattened against his head. He hissed again and swatted the offending hand away.

Aunt True laughed. "I don't think you need to worry, sweetie. It looks like Mephisto's got things covered in the protection department. Plus, I promised your mother I'd keep him either at the bookshop or out at the farm."

"You can't put him in the barn!" Lauren's face puckered with concern. "He's so little! What if he doesn't like it there?"

"Don't worry, we won't rush him. He can stay at the bookstore as long as he wants, and when he's bigger, if he doesn't like the barn, we'll figure something out."

"Can a bookstore have two cats?" asked Jasmine.

"Why not?" said Aunt True. "Double the fun! Plus, we already know how much our customers love kittens."

It was true. Belinda's steady stream of furry little charges were always a hit, especially at story time on Saturdays. She managed to unload a surprising number of them, too.

"We should call him Tiger!" said Pippa.

"That's dopey," Lauren scoffed, and Pippa's face fell.

"What Lauren means," Aunt True said quickly, setting out a plate of molasses ginger cookies, "is that Tiger is, well, a bit of an *obvious* name. Not a bad one, but perhaps Lauren is looking for something a bit more subtle."

"What's 'subtle'?" Pippa asked.

"Unexpected," said Calhoun, whipping out another word definition. "Under the radar."

"How about Pumpkin?" suggested Lucas. "Since it's almost Halloween and everything."

Lauren shook her head. "No."

"Marmalade?" I said.

"Muffin?" offered Lucas.

"Gingersnap would be cute," said Cha Cha, reaching for a cookie.

Our suggestions came thick and fast, but Lauren rejected them all just as swiftly.

"While you all are hashing out a name, who wants hot cider?" Aunt True crossed to the Cup and Chaucer counter. As we clustered around, Lauren's gaze fell on the tray of condiments beside the espresso machine. Her face lit up.

"I know!" she said. "I'll call him Half-and-Half. Since he's half orange and half white."

"Very clever," said Aunt True, nodding in approval.

"He can be 'Halfling' for short," Lauren added. "Like from *The Hobbit*."

"Cool!" said Scooter, who I knew for sure had never read any of the Tolkien books but who was a big fan of the *Lord of the Rings* movies.

Calhoun took off his baseball cap with a flourish and gave a low bow. "All hail Halfling and Mephisto, the bookstore cats!" he said in his best Shakespearean voice.

I smiled at him and he smiled back.

Behind us, the bells over the bookshop door jangled furiously. We turned to see Laura Mahoney from Mahoney's Antiques come barreling in. Ella Bellow was right behind her.

"My back was only turned for a moment," Mrs. Mahoney fumed. "Literally just a *moment*, I tell you! Someone stole our jack-o'-lantern, too!"

CHAPTER 7

"It's Abracadabra Day!"

The whispered words pierced my sound sleep and I sat bolt upright in bed, squealing like Pippa. I didn't care if I sounded like a little kid. In our family, Abracadabra Day was hands-down the best day of the year. When I opened my eyes, though, I was surprised to see Aunt True standing there instead of my mother and father.

"I must have been dreaming," I said, flopping back down again in disappointment. "I thought I heard someone say 'Abracadabra Day.'"

"That would be me." My aunt pulled the covers back and grabbed me by the feet, swinging my legs over the edge of the mattress. "I'm getting in on the action this year. Up and at 'em, sleepyhead—out of bed!"

I peered at my alarm clock in disbelief. "Are you *serious*?"

"Early bird catches the worm—and everything else we'll

be catching today. Meet me downstairs in the kitchen in five minutes."

I yawned. "Fine. What should I wear?"

"Layers," she told me. "Sturdy shoes. Bring a fleece. Maybe a down vest, too."

Confused, definitely not awake yet, but happy nonetheless—it was Abracadabra Day, after all!—I shuffled out of bed and across the hall to my bathroom. It was still dark outside. Chilly, too. October mornings in New Hampshire weren't quite winter-cold, at least according to my father, who refused to turn the heat on until November first on what he called "general principles," but they were cold enough. I headed downstairs past the portraits of my ancestors that lined the stairwell.

"Obadiah, Abigail, Jeremiah, Ruth," I whispered automatically, naming them. "Matthew, Truly, Charity, and Booth."

I could hear my father whistling in the kitchen. My father rarely whistled, even before Black Monday, as we called the day he lost his arm in the war. Only when something extra-specially good happened, like when he got promoted to lieutenant colonel, or when Danny won the state wrestling championship, or the day Pippa was born. As I came through the door, he passed me a bowl of oatmeal loaded with walnuts and sliced bananas and drizzled with maple syrup, exactly the way I liked it.

"What's going on?" I asked suspiciously.

"What's going on?" he echoed. "It's my favorite eighth-grade daughter's favorite Abracadabra Day breakfast, that's what's going on." He smiled at me and sloshed my oatmeal with milk. "And my sister is getting married this weekend, and it's a beautiful day in the neighborhood, right?"

Now my aunt was eyeing him with suspicion too. He was definitely acting weird. We didn't have time to think about it much, though, because just then there was a brief toot from a car horn outside.

"Rusty's here," said Aunt True. "Two minutes until lift-off. Eat up!"

I did as I was told. We Lovejoy kids always did as we were told on Abracadabra Day.

"Is Professor—I mean Almost-Uncle Rusty—coming with us?"

My aunt shook her head. "Nope. We're swapping cars. You'll see him later today, but for now it's just you and me, kiddo."

"Where are we going?"

She gave me a mysterious smile. "You'll see."

"What about swim team?"

"I cleared it with Coach Maynard," my father assured me, taking my empty bowl and handing me a blindfold. "Put this over your eyes."

I'd never been asked to wear a blindfold for Abracadabra

Day, but once again I did as I was told. My father checked to make sure it was tied securely, then took me by the hand and led me outside to Professor Rusty's new truck. Well, new old truck. He'd run out and bought it the day he'd heard that the Farnsworths were going to sell him their farm.

"Have fun, Truly-in-the-Middle," my father said, buckling my seat belt for me like I was five. He ruffled my hair and closed the door. I heard him whispering to my aunt and Professor Rusty, then my aunt got in and we were off.

We drove in silence for a while. My heart was pounding with excitement. If there were three better words in the English language than "It's Abracadabra Day!" I hadn't met them yet. Abracadabra Day was a longtime tradition in our family—or had been, before my father was wounded in Afghanistan. My mother had pressed pause on the tradition last year, while our family was in crisis mode and my father was in his silent-man phase. The idea was inspired by one of his favorite books growing up, *Mr. Mysterious & Company,* by an author named Sid Fleishman. In the book, the magician's kids got one day each year—Abracadabra Day—when they could pull pranks without getting punished. For us Lovejoys, there were no pranks involved, but instead we got to skip school and spend the whole day with one or both of our parents, doing something fun.

I was Pippa's age when we'd first started Abracadabra Days. Usually, they weren't anything all that over-the-top—we'd gone to water parks, for instance, and to the movies and museums and miniature golf and stuff like that. Lunch at a favorite restaurant was involved, and the day always ended with ice cream somewhere. It was the fact that we had our parents all to ourselves that made it so special. Growing up in a family with five kids, that was a treat all by itself.

When my father was stationed in Germany, we'd had some extra-cool Abracadabra Days. The first year, instead of separate outings, we did one together as a family. We left the base super early in the morning and took the train to Salzburg, Austria, where the movie *The Sound of Music* was filmed a zillion years ago. We all watched it every year with our mother on her birthday because it was her all-time favorite. As a surprise for her, my father had booked us on a tour of the familiar sites from the film. She still talked about that Abracadabra Day.

The second year we were living in Europe, my older brothers got to go to Disneyland Paris because my father had a conference nearby. Lucky dogs! I would have gone, too, except for the fact that I had a super-important swim meet. My consolation prize had been pretty good—my mother had taken me to watch the Olympic swim trials, which were held near the army base that year—but still, it wasn't Disneyland.

"Hang on!" said Aunt True as we made a sharp left turn onto what must have been a dirt road. I could hear the crunch of gravel and loose rocks under the tires as the truck lurched and bumped along. "I hope you don't mind me kidnapping you this year."

Mind? I thought. I got the day off from school, and she was asking me if I minded?

"Of course not," I told her. "But when can I know where we're going?"

"I guess you can take your bandanna off now."

We drove along a while farther in the dark, until the headlights illuminated a wooden sign up ahead: LOVEJOY MOUNTAIN TRAIL. Aunt True slowed down and pulled over to park.

My heart sank. Hatcher and Danny got to go to Disneyland Paris and my Abracadabra Day was *mountain climbing*? Hiking was way up on the list of things I wasn't good at, right alongside running and tennis and soccer and all the other sweaty sports that didn't involve being in the water.

"We're here!" Aunt True saw my expression and grinned. "Cheer up, Tall Timber. It's not the only thing on the menu today. It'll be fun, I promise. And totally worth it."

I sure hoped she was right. We got out of the truck, gathered our gear, and headed into the woods. It was still pitch-black outside, but Aunt True had brought headlamps so we could see where we were going. Even so, the trail was steep and I had to watch my step so that I didn't trip over any tree roots. It was a little eerie, too, being out in the wilderness in the dark with no one around for miles. I stuck close to my aunt and hoped there were no bears.

Lovejoy Mountain wasn't a real mountain—more of a

very large hill—but it was still a good hour to the top. The last bit was especially challenging and involved lots of clambering over big boulders.

"Mind the scree," Aunt True called back to me as I lost my footing and ended up on my hands and knees. She was panting, too. "The loose rocks on the ground. It's easy to slip and fall."

"Thanks for the warning," I muttered under my breath. Keeping low, I crab-scrabbled the final few yards to the top, where I collapsed in a heap on a smooth, broad expanse of granite.

"That wasn't so bad, was it?" said my aunt. I grunted in reply, and she laughed. "At least we made it in time for the show."

The show? That sounded intriguing. She patted the ledge beside her and I scooted over, dangling my legs over the edge like she was doing. I started to say something and she pressed a forefinger against my lips. "Shhhh. Just watch."

There weren't all that many things in this world that had the power to take my breath away. The first time one of the chickadees in Gramps and Lola's backyard landed on my bare palm last winter had done it. So had my first owl sighting. And now, I thought, as I watched the first faint glimmers of light reach over the horizon, I could add "dawn on a mountaintop" to the list.

We were high above the Pumpkin River Valley, and as the light grew stronger, the landscape began to swim into focus. The sun reached the treetops first, silhouetting the jagged firs against the pale gray sky. Bit by bit, like a watercolor being painted before my eyes, the full palette of a new day began to appear, from the dark green of the trees to the colorful leaves that splashed the valley with autumn's bright hues. Far below, a ribbon of early-morning mist hovered over the river.

"Now, *this* is October," Aunt True said with satisfaction, finally breaking the silence. She rummaged in her daypack, pulled out a thermos, and poured me a cup of steaming hot chocolate. "Just think, Truly! Lovejoys have lived here in this valley for two hundred and fifty years."

I thought of the portraits in our stairwell at home, generations of Lovejoy ancestors who had lived under the same roof as I did now. Had any of them ever climbed up here to watch the dawn?

"And before them, there were the Abenakis and other Native American tribes," Aunt True continued. "People have been enjoying this view for thousands and thousands of years."

We lapsed into silence again and sipped our cocoa. A light breeze stirred, bringing with it the sharp, clean scent of pines. A deep feeling of contentment settled over me.

"I'm getting married this weekend!" Aunt True said. "Can you believe it?"

I bumped my shoulder against hers. "Nope."

"I know, neither can I."

As often as she had assured me in recent months that things

wouldn't change, I knew that they would, of course. For one thing, a new uncle would soon be joining the ranks along with my mother's six brothers, my Gifford uncles from Texas. For another, there was the new sheep farm. The probably-not-but-maybe-possibly-haunted sheep farm.

"Mephisto's going to hate living on a farm," I said.

She pursed her lips, considering. "He is a bit of a city cat, but he's surprised us once already in recent days. Who knows? Maybe he'll like sheep."

I doubted that very much.

"I'm going to miss you when you're in Scotland," I said, and Aunt True slipped her arm around me and gave me a squeeze.

"I'm going to miss you, too. But not that much!" She winked. "It is my honeymoon, after all. And when Rusty and I come back, there will be a whole new chapter to look forward to!"

We'd had the mountaintop to ourselves this whole time, but now other hikers were beginning to appear. The trail was clearly a popular one, especially during leaf-peeping season. Aunt True stood up and stretched.

"Time for Abracadabra Day: Part Two," she said, extending her hand and pulling me to my feet. As we posed for a selfie, she gave me a sidelong glance. "Have you ever been sheep shopping?"

CHAPTER 8

I had not been sheep shopping, as it happened. Not once, not ever.

I couldn't say it was high up on the list of things I was eager to do, either. Especially not on my Abracadabra Day. But I loved my aunt, and she was obviously excited about the prospect.

Put your game face on, I told myself sternly. Aunt True had been right about the hike—it had been totally worth it for the view. Maybe this woolly shopping expedition wouldn't be as lame as it sounded.

Our first stop was Lou's, where Professor Rusty joined us for a hearty second breakfast. We chose seats at the counter so we could chat with Lou and Lucas's mother, who was working the early shift.

"Wait, your parents let you *skip school*?" Mrs. Winthrop said when I explained about Abracadabra Day.

"It's good for the soul to cut loose once in a while, Amelia," my aunt told her. "You should try it sometime."

Like that will ever happen, I thought. Mrs. Winthrop was allergic to breaking the rules.

My aunt and I filled everyone in on our predawn outing and showed them our pictures, which didn't even come close to capturing how beautiful sunrise on the mountaintop had been.

As I dove into one of the diner's enormous cheese omelets and signature cinnamon rolls, I was grateful I'd been sprung from swim practice. With everything I'd been shoveling into my stomach this morning, I would probably have sunk immediately to the bottom of the pool. The hike had made me hungry, though, and I ate every bite.

Lou came over to top up my aunt and almost-uncle's coffee and slid a mug of hot chocolate over to me. "On the house," he said with a smile.

"Thanks!" A double dose of cocoa never hurt anyone, I told myself. Plus, Abracadabra Day only came around once a year, right?

As I lifted the mug to my lips, a dark-haired young man with glasses who didn't look much older than Danny slid onto the stool next to me.

"Have you met our town's newest resident?" asked Lou. "He's taking over for Janet Foster at the *Patriot-Bugle*."

I'd heard that Janet was leaving to focus on her pet

photography business, and I'd heard that there was a new reporter in town, but our paths hadn't crossed yet. I glanced over at him curiously.

The newcomer stuck out his hand and I shook it. "Clark," he said. "Clark—"

"Kent?" asked Aunt True.

The reporter winced. He probably got that a lot.

"Sorry, I couldn't help it," said my aunt, not sorry at all by the looks of her smirk. She shook his hand, too.

"It's Barque, actually," the reporter told her, sliding a business card across the counter. I picked it up. Sure enough, his name was Clark Barque. Which was possibly even worse than Clark Kent, if you asked me, which nobody ever did.

"He's a Lovejoy College alum," Lou informed us. "Went on to journalism school in New York City, and now he's back and eager to make a name for himself. Only been on the job for a week."

The new reporter's phone number and email were printed at the bottom of his business card, along with the instruction: CALL/TEXT WITH NEWS TIPS. I hoped he was prepared for lots of possum sightings.

I passed the card to my aunt, who glanced at it and arched an eyebrow. "Welcome to Pumpkin Falls, Clark Barque."

Lou winked. "Don't worry, his *barque* is worse than his bite."

We all groaned. The new reporter blushed furiously. With a name like his, he was going to have to put his big boy pants on and deal with it, I thought. He was bound to get teased a lot, living in this town.

A news-free zone like Pumpkin Falls was also bound to be a disappointment. This place would be a tough assignment for a freshly hatched reporter who probably had big dreams of being a war correspondent. I smothered a smile, thinking of the police blotter.

Lou glanced up as another customer came in. He frowned. "Don't look now, but it's that real-estate developer."

I felt Aunt True stiffen beside me.

"The one who wanted to buy the Farnsworth place—I mean, our new farm?" whispered Professor Rusty.

"Mm-hmm," said Lou.

The developer—who was dressed kind of like Emilio on his first day of school, all shiny loafers and slicked-back hair—headed for the stool next to my soon-to-be uncle.

"Wesley Thrush of Digger and Thrush over in West Hartfield," he said to Professor Rusty, thrusting out his hand and giving him what he probably thought was a pleasant smile.

No one had ever looked less like a thrush to me. Thrushes were gentle, unassuming songbirds. Wesley Thrush's vibe was pure big bad wolf.

"Word on the street is you're Erastus Peckinpaugh," he said to Professor Rusty. "New owner of the old Farnsworth place. I hear you're getting hitched this weekend. Is this the lucky little lady?"

He couldn't have picked a worse thing to say to my aunt.

She stood up, which immediately established the fact that she was not little. Not at all. The real-estate developer's wolf grin faltered as she stalked over and leaned down, putting her face very close to his. "Let me make one thing entirely clear," Aunt True said. "The answer is no. No, we don't want to sell. No, we don't care what you're offering. No, you can't buy the farm. Not now, not ever."

Beside me, Clark Barque surreptitiously slipped a notebook out of his pocket, placed it on his lap under the counter, and started taking notes.

Wesley Thrush blinked. "Don't you want to help bring this town into the twenty-first century? That property is perfect! There's room for a supermarket, a pharmacy, a new restaurant—all the conveniences that you have to drive into West Hartfield for now."

"No," Aunt True repeated calmly, looking him square in the eye. "Not for any amount of money."

"Everyone has their price," the developer replied, but he didn't sound quite so sure of himself.

"Not this time," said Aunt True.

The real estate developer motioned to Lou to pour him some coffee as my aunt turned on her heel and walked out. Professor Rusty and I were right behind her.

"The nerve of him!" Aunt True exploded the minute we were outside. "He's so certain he can just buy people off!"

"He's all bluster," said Professor Rusty. "He can't force us to sell. Shake it off, True, and let's go have us some new farm fun."

He cranked up the radio as we drove out of town. Now that he was about to be a farmer, my soon-to-be uncle had not only purchased himself a pickup truck, but he'd also sprouted a sudden interest in country music. He settled on an oldies station, and the three of us sang along at the top of our lungs to Patsy Cline and Loretta Lynn and Hank Williams. I knew all the words, thanks to my Texas-born-and-raised mother.

We arrived at the sheep farm in much better spirits.

"Greetings and salutations!" said Aunt True, hopping out of the truck as a wiry man in well-worn jeans and a flannel shirt spotted us and came over. "Thank you for meeting us here this morning."

"Happy to help, True, happy to help," he replied.

"Truly, this is Albert Harrison. He's an old friend of your grandparents."

"Nice to meet you, Mr. Harrison," I said politely, shaking his hand.

He tipped his hat, revealing a thatch of thinning gray hair. "Call me Bert," he told me. "All my friends do."

I liked him right away. There was something about his alert brown eyes that reminded me of the barred owl I'd seen up close last spring. Aunt True explained that Bert was one of the most experienced sheep breeders in the Pumpkin

River Valley, if not all of New England. Ever since she and Professor Rusty had made the decision to raise sheep, he'd been patiently answering their questions and offering advice.

"Shall we head inside?" Bert gestured toward the barn at the far end of the field where we were parked. "Theresa is waiting for us."

Aunt True and Professor Rusty went on ahead, talking excitedly together as Bert and I followed them. I caught a few words here and there—"merino" and "Romney" and "Rhinebeck." They might as well have been speaking a foreign language.

"So, what do you know about sheep, Truly?" Bert asked, falling in beside me.

I shrugged. "Not much. They make yarn—uh, wool. I took a knitting class last spring break."

"That's a good place to start. Did you like it?"

I leveled a hand and waggled it back and forth. "So-so."

He laughed again. "Well, keep at it and you'll soon be a pro like my wife, Dot. She keeps me in socks and sweaters." He lifted the leg of one of his jeans to reveal a pair of sky blue socks with a circle of fat white sheep dancing around his ankle.

"Nice."

"Yup." He winked at me. "So's Dot. Now then," he continued, "let me tell you about sheep."

According to Bert, sheep were paragons of virtue in the animal kingdom. Hardy, low-maintenance, and eco-friendly, they were blessed with a strong herd instinct, he told me, and thus easily manageable. They thrived on grass, kept down weeds, and hardly ever caused damage to trees or vegetation, unlike goats, which he didn't seem as fond of.

"You won't see golf courses renting out herds of goats to keep their lawns trimmed," he said, nodding sagely. "But many do just that with a flock of sheep."

I learned that sheep dung (ew!) was a fabulous fertilizer, and that no part of a sheep went to waste—you could even use its milk to make yogurt and cheese. I couldn't imagine anyone actually milking a sheep, but apparently it was a thing.

"Double the calcium of cow's milk," Bert informed me, before turning his attention to wool. This really got him going. "No better fiber on the planet," he enthused. "It's second to none in terms of insulation. Hypoallergenic and biodegradable, it's both sustainable and renewable—you don't harm the sheep when you shear it. In fact, it's a kindness to the animal to do so. The fleece of an unshorn sheep will continue to grow until the weight of it becomes life-threatening. Plus," he finished triumphantly, "wool is naturally flame retardant, and did you know that it can help absorb toxins from your home?"

I did not. Nor did I particularly care, but of course I didn't say that.

"And on top of all that, sheep are friendly animals and make wonderful pets."

Oh boy, I thought. Lauren was going to be in heaven.

TRULY, MADLY, SHEEPLY

As we neared the barn, Professor Rusty pulled a card out of the pocket in the bib of his overalls and handed it over to Bert. "Just in case you need it for anything. A discount, maybe?"

"Well now, son, that's mighty fine, mighty fine indeed." Bert glanced down at the card with a quizzical expression on his face.

Aunt True gave her soon-to-be husband a squeeze. "Your enthusiasm is one of the things I love best about you, Rusty. Don't ever change."

Bert Harrison might have been the most knowledgeable sheep farmer in the Pumpkin River Valley, but my soon-to-be uncle was definitely the nerdiest. He didn't have a single sheep yet, but he was already a card-carrying member of the New Hampshire Sheep and Wool Growers Association.

My cell phone buzzed just then, and I slipped it out of the pocket of my jeans. It was Cha Cha.

WHERE ARE YOU? she'd texted. SICK DAY?

NOT EXACTLY, I texted back, adding a smiley face. WILL EXPLAIN LATER.

"Let me introduce you to my good friend Theresa Wallace," said Bert, as a cheerful looking woman in a hand-knit sweater emerged from the barn. "We call her the sheep whisperer. What Theresa doesn't know about sheep wouldn't fill the toe of a sock."

Professor Rusty pointed to a wooden plank hanging above

the barn door. On it was painted LIBERTY HALL FARM. "I like your sign," he said. "Very patriotic."

Theresa laughed. "That was actually my husband's idea. He and his brothers always loved visiting their grandparents, because they'd let them do whatever they wanted while they were there. Ice cream for breakfast? No problem! Ride their bikes in the house? Sure! 'It's liberty hall around here, kids,' their grandfather would tell them, meaning they had a free pass to do as they pleased."

"Hey! That's kind of like Abracadabra Day," I said, and then of course I had to explain all about Abracadabra Day.

"It sounds like our families would get along famously," said Theresa, smiling at me. She turned and gestured toward the barn. "So, would you like to pick out some sheep?"

We followed her inside, where she led us downstairs to a pen in the lower part of the barn.

"I drove by your new place the other day and checked out the pasturage," Bert said to Aunt True and Professor Rusty. "Sweet spread you've got there. If I were a decade or two younger, I'd have given you a run for your money. In fact, if you ever decide farming's not for you and you want to sell, keep me in mind."

Aunt True shook her head. "Two offers in one morning! Thanks, Bert, but no thanks. We'll be keeping the farm."

Bert nodded. "I'd do the same if I were in your shoes. At any rate, as I was saying, with the pasturage you've got available right now—you can always clear another meadow or two in the future—you don't want any more than, say, half a dozen ewes. We'll add a ram and call it a day."

The sheep spotted us and began milling around in excitement. I leaned against the wooden slats of the pen and watched as Theresa and Bert waded out into the flock and inspected them one by one. They both had an air of calm confidence that the sheep must have found reassuring, because they stopped their anxious bleating.

"Now, that is a handsome ram," Bert said approvingly, pointing to a large chocolate brown sheep in a separate pen. "He'll do just fine."

One by one, he made his selections for my aunt and almost-uncle's new flock, explaining his choices as he pointed out this one's strong points and that one's disposition.

"Excellent conformation on this ewe," he said, and seeing my puzzled expression, added, "strong back and neck, straight legs. See how she's shaped kind of like a big footstool? That's the sign of a good, healthy Romney sheep."

"You'll love Romneys," added Theresa. "They're easy keepers. Good mothers, too—calm and nurturing." She pointed to her sweater. "And you can't find a better fiber producer. The wool is excellent! Great stitch definition."

I figured she was talking about the cables and zigzags and other squiggles running up and down her sweater.

"They'll be ready for shearing by the end of the month,"

she told my aunt. "I'll put you in touch with a shearer. Romney's fleece grows half an inch a month and you need three inches to process it, so they'll need shearing twice a year."

Beside me, Aunt True was making notes. "And lambing?"

"Once a year, late winter. These girls were bred over the summer, so come February, you'll start seeing lambs."

"Just imagine, Rusty! Lambs of our own!" My aunt clutched her fiancé and they smiled at each other.

"We actually set up a 'lamb cam' every winter here at Liberty Hall. Folks from all over follow us on social media, and it's fun for them to watch the wee ones arrive."

I could practically see Aunt True's mental wheels turning. Her new farm definitely had a lamb cam in its future. Marketing whiz that she was, she wouldn't be able to resist that idea.

Sure enough, a moment later she said, "We could set one up now! That way we could keep an eye on our new flock while we're in Scotland."

Theresa coaxed the sheep she was holding over toward us. "Come on in," she said to me, holding the gate open. I stepped inside. "Now put your hands in and feel this fleece."

I thrust my fingers gingerly into the ewe's woolly back. To my surprise, my hands sank in almost to my wrists.

"Impressive, right?" said Theresa, grinning at the expression on my face. "With her fleece, she's close to two hundred and fifty pounds."

The wool was warm, and smelled—well, not unpleasant. Kind of barnlike. I wiggled my fingers and gave the ewe a tentative back rub, and she closed her eyes blissfully and leaned up against me. "She seems pretty friendly."

"Beatrice? Oh, very. I always say sheep are the best dogs you'll ever have. They're good companions, full of personality."

I moved one hand to tentatively stroke the sheep's head. "Hey, what's this metal tag in her ear?"

"That's a federal requirement," Bert explained. "It means she's been certified healthy by a vet. She's ready to go home with you. And so are these ladies." He pointed out five other ewes he'd selected and Theresa moved them, along with Beatrice, into a separate pen.

Our sheep shopping complete, Aunt True and Professor Rusty sealed the deal with Theresa while Bert attached the trailer he'd brought along to the back of Professor Rusty's pickup truck. I took a few pictures and Theresa gave us some final tips while she and Bert loaded the ewes inside.

"Now, always remember to gate check, and never forget that water is the most important nutrient," she said. "Call or text if you have any questions at all. You have my number, right?" Aunt True and Uncle Rusty nodded. Theresa looked over at me. "How about you?"

I shook my head, and she made me take out my cell phone and save her number, too.

Bert gave us a rueful grin and held up his battered flip

phone. "Sorry, I'm old-school. I don't do text messaging, and this thing is usually off. Landline is the best way to get ahold of me."

The ram was loaded last, protesting loudly as he was bundled into the back of the pickup truck. Once he was safely stowed, Professor Rusty put it in gear and slowly started out of the field where we were parked. Bert trotted along beside.

"I'll be over in the morning to pick up my trailer and see how you're getting on," he called to us loudly, trying to be heard over the clattering of unhappy hooves in the truck bed behind us. The ram was kicking up a fuss, clearly not pleased about being separated from the ewes in the trailer. He pressed his face to the window of the cab and baaed vigorously in protest.

"Theresa said she hadn't named him yet," Aunt True said as we pulled out onto the road. "But I would say he's definitely a Benedick." She smiled fondly at her soon-to-be husband. "To go with Beatrice."

I knew exactly where that name had come from. My aunt and Professor Rusty had been in Shakespeare's *Much Ado About Nothing* back in high school, as understudies for the two main characters, Beatrice and Benedick. The names had been clues from the very first mystery I'd helped solve in Pumpkin Falls.

"You're worse than Lauren," I told her. "You know she's going to make pets of them all, right?"

Aunt True sighed. "I've resigned myself to that fact. On the other hand, did you see how cute they are? I'll probably make pets of them too."

The cuteness factor had escaped me. I glanced back over my shoulder at Benedick, who was still peering through the window angrily at us. The horizontal pupils in his eyes were a little creepy. But then, I was much more of a fan of feathers than of fur. Wool. Whatever.

Now that Aunt True was a bona fide sheep farmer, though, was that was about to change?

CHAPTER 9

It turned out Aunt True had one final surprise up her sleeve. "Time for Abracadabra Day: Part Three!" she announced as we pulled into the driveway of the new farm a short while later.

My mother was standing by Aunt True's car, which she must have brought over from where we'd left it at Lou's. Spotting the trailer full of sheep, she smiled and gave us a big thumbs-up. "It was a success, then?"

Aunt True and Professor Rusty jumped out and started jabbering about their new flock and Bert Harrison and Theresa the sheep whisperer and the joys of farming while they unloaded a still-protesting Benedick and the ewes and guided them around the back of the barn to the lower level, where their pens were located. Theresa had told us that when a flock was first brought home, it was best to keep them penned up for a few days, to train them to know that this was home base.

"You gradually make their boundaries larger," she'd explained, "until they can graze freely in a fenced pasture."

I kept a safe distance during the proceedings, wondering what I'd gotten myself into. I'd agreed to stay out at the farm with Gramps and Lola for the "sheep-sitting gig," as Gramps was calling it, while my aunt and her new husband were away on their honeymoon. For me, Aunt True's new sheep-farming venture was kind of like swimming in a really cold lake. I had to dip my toe in first and get used to it bit by bit.

"Honey, have you seen the pitchfork?" Professor Rusty asked my aunt after Benedick was finally safely in his pen. "I'm sure I left it right here in the barn last night, after I finished spreading the hay for the sheep bedding."

"Straw," said Aunt True. "Hay is for eating, straw is for bedding, remember? And no, I haven't seen your pitchfork. It's probably with the wire clippers you misplaced yesterday, after you and Dad worked on repairing the fencing. Has Elmer been by to check on his pumpkin? Maybe he borrowed them."

"Ah," said Professor Rusty. "That's probably it."

"Unless"—my aunt's voice dropped to a low, spooky quaver—"we have a *boggart* on our hands!"

"What the heck is a 'boggart'?" I asked.

"A Scottish poltergeist of sorts," said Aunt True. "A mischievous household spirit. They're often blamed when things go missing, or get moved, or when the milk sours, or there are loud unexplained noises—that kind of thing."

"You mean like a ghost?" I squeaked.

"They're mythical, of course!" she quickly added. "There's no such thing. Rusty is so excited about the farm, it's all he can do to keep his head on straight. Right, Rusty?"

Her fiancé raised a hand. "Guilty as charged."

She gave him a kiss. "Give Elmer a call while we're gone, sweetheart. I'm sure you'll get everything sorted."

Professor Rusty waved as my aunt and my mother and I drove off. I turned and looked at the farm as it receded down the road behind us. Aunt True had said there were no such things as boggarts. What if there were, though?

Stop being an idiot, I told myself crossly. *What are you, five?*

Twenty minutes later, the three of us were seated at a table in the dining room of the Inn at Lovejoy Mountain, the most luxurious resort in the Pumpkin River Valley.

"Lunch and a view," sighed my mother. "It doesn't get much better than this." She gazed dreamily out over her salad to Lovejoy Mountain in the distance. It was hard to believe that I'd been on its peak just a few hours ago.

"Ha!" said Aunt True. "Just you wait."

Sure enough, after we finished our lunch, there was more.

"I have to spoil my maid of honor and chief bridesmaid," she told us as we were whisked down the hall to the spa.

A person could get used to being spoiled, I thought a little while later, wrapped in a fluffy white robe and glowing from my first-ever facial. Manicures and pedicures followed, and then it was time to relax on lounge chairs made of heated tile. They were grouped in a room the spa ladies called a "solarium," angled toward floor-to-ceiling windows that looked out onto the expansive lawn. At the far end stretched a stone wall, and hemmed in behind that was a maple grove, its trees aglow with shades of red and orange and yellow in the late-afternoon light. My mother sighed happily again as an attendant brought us crystal champagne flutes filled with sparkling apple cider.

"Now, *this*," she said. "It couldn't possibly get any better than this."

"Maybe, or maybe not," said Aunt True, raising her glass. "To us!"

"To us!" my mother and I echoed.

My cell phone buzzed and I pulled it discreetly from the pocket of my robe and glanced at the screen. The Pumpkin Falls Private Eyes had been hard at work. **LOU SAYS THE LAST TIME HE SAW HIS JACK-O'-LANTERN WAS YESTERDAY AT LUNCHTIME,** Lucas had texted to me and our friends. **IT DISAPPEARED SOMETIME BETWEEN LUNCH AND WHEN HE CLOSED FOR THE DAY.**

Lou's Diner was only open for breakfast and lunch, and usually closed shortly after school was over.

DITTO THE GENERAL STORE, added Calhoun. **THELMA SAW IT WHEN SHE CAME IN FOR THE MORNING, BUT IT HAD DISAPPEARED BY MIDAFTERNOON WHEN SHE WENT TO THE POST OFFICE.**

Scooter was the last to chime in. MRS. MAHONEY SAYS HERS DISAPPEARED BETWEEN THE TIME SHE WENT TO LOU'S FOR LUNCH AND CAME BACK AT 3 PM.

I slipped my phone back, mulling this information over. From the sounds of it, the pumpkins were disappearing in broad daylight. How was this possible in a town the size of ours, though? Hadn't anybody noticed?

My aunt rummaged in a tote bag she'd brought with her and pulled out two small, beautifully wrapped packages. She passed one each to my mother and me.

My mother opened hers first. Inside was a gold necklace in the shape of a maple leaf. Her initials—*DGL*, for Dinah Gifford Lovejoy—were etched on the front, and on the back were the words "Love always, True."

"True, you shouldn't have!" my mother protested.

"Yes, I should have," my aunt told her. "You're the sister I always wanted and am so glad I got." She reached out her hand and my mother took it and squeezed.

My aunt smiled at me as I unwrapped my present. "Sorry it's not a kitten."

"Oh darn," I replied. "And I was so hoping for one!" I caught my breath when I lifted the lid of the small box, revealing a beautiful silver and amethyst ring inside. It looked old.

It *was* old. Over a hundred and fifty years old, as a matter of fact.

"It belonged to our namesake," Aunt True told me. "The

original Truly Lovejoy. It's all we have left of her, really, aside from her portrait and her brooch and the diary you found last spring. Your grandparents gave it to me when I was about your age, and I've been waiting for the right moment to give it to you."

Angling the ring toward the light, I could just make out the faint inscription inside: *For Truly with love from Matthew, Christmas 1860.* Somehow I wasn't surprised to find that it fit me perfectly.

"Thank you so much, Aunt True!" I said, leaping up from my lounge chair and flinging my arms around her.

"You're so welcome, Tall Timber."

I lay back down again, admiring my ring. The three of us relaxed for a while on our lounge chairs, sipping cider and talking.

"I still can't believe you bought a farm, True," said my mother. "Of all the things to do!"

"I know!" my aunt replied, grinning. "It's crazy, isn't it? But sometimes, crazy is the best thing to do. Rusty and I are giddy. It's almost as fun as getting married."

"Nothing is as fun as getting married—to the right person, that is," my mother added.

My aunt laughed. "I said *almost.*"

"Will we still see you at the bookstore?" I asked. I'd had a full-on meltdown this past summer, worried that she might move away. Buying a farm meant my aunt was putting down roots, right? Which was a good thing. But still, was I going to see much of her now, with a new husband and all those sheep to take care of?

"Of course you're going to see me!" she said. "Every single day. Rusty and I can't make a living as full-time farmers. At least not yet. And we're not even sure we want to. Rusty loves teaching, so this may be more of a hobby farm; we'll have to see. For now, he'll keep his job at the college, and I'll keep my job at the bookshop. When your grandparents return from Africa for good, they may want to give us a hand at the store. If they do, perhaps then I'll step back to part-time and devote more time to the farm and our fiber business. Nothing's set in stone at this point."

I thought it over and decided I could live with that.

Aunt True sat up. "So, I have it on good authority that Abracadabra Day always ends with ice cream. Is that right?"

My mother nodded, her expression serious. "It's the Lovejoy law. Right, Truly?"

"Cross my heart and hope to fly!" I replied, trotting out my father's favorite expression from his days as an army pilot.

"Well, we certainly want to be law-abiding citizens," said my aunt. "Let's go, ladies!"

Mac's Maple was our family's favorite out-of-town ice cream destination. A short drive from Pumpkin Falls, it was at the end of a long dirt road in the middle of what felt like nowhere.

TRULY, MADLY, SHEEPLY

It had started out over half a century ago as a dairy farm—well, it still was a dairy farm—but they'd added a little store with all sorts of maple-themed stuff for sale and an ice cream stand where they made the most amazing maple creamees in the world. Maple creamees were a New England thing, and Mac's did them better than anyplace else. The waffle cones were homemade, and filled with fresh soft-serve maple ice cream made with milk from the farm's own cows and maple syrup from their own sugar shack. As if that wasn't enough, the whole thing was topped off with crumbled bits of homemade maple candy.

"I was wrong on both counts earlier," my mother said as she took her first bite and made swooning noises. "It doesn't get any better than *this*, right here, right now, does it?"

"Nope," agreed Aunt True, making swooning noises of her own. "It does not." She looked over at me and smiled. "I hope you've had a good Abracadabra Day!"

I nodded happily, licking a piece of maple sugar candy off my ice cream. I stretched out my hand and turned it this way and that, watching the late-afternoon sun sparkle on the original Truly's ring. Between Aunt True's gift, the dawn hike, the spa pampering, and the sheep shopping—where I'd learned more about sheep and wool than I'd ever in a million years thought I would—it certainly hadn't been the Abracadabra Day I was expecting.

But it was absolutely, truly, the best one I'd ever had.

CHAPTER 10

PUMPKIN FALLS PUMPKIN SNATCHER STRIKES AGAIN!

From Ella Bellow's lips to Clark Barque's ears, I thought, bending down to grab the pile of newspapers that were waiting on the sidewalk outside the bookshop. Judging by the blaring headline, our town's new reporter had been talking to Ella. Her nickname for the jack-o'-lantern thief appeared to have stuck.

This time around, he—or she, as we didn't really have a clue yet as to the thief's identity—had raided the library, nabbing a trio of pumpkins from the front steps. Mr. Henry, our town's children's librarian, had spent ages carving them to look like characters from some of his favorite books. There was one meant to be Wilbur from *Charlotte's Web,* and there was Aslan the lion from *The Lion, the Witch and the Wardrobe,* and he'd also carved what was supposed to be Hagrid from the Harry Potter books. Mr. Henry's version of Hagrid was totally different from the movie version, so there'd been some discussion around town about that. Mr. Henry argued that the characters we envision in our heads when we read a book always trump the ones in the movies, but not everyone agreed.

"Let me hold the door for you."

I looked up to see Luke Mahoney coming out of the bookshop. I smiled at him. "Thanks."

He smiled back, then strolled off toward his antiques store next door.

"It's just a crying shame," I heard Ella saying to my aunt and grandmother as I backed into the bookshop, my arms full of newspapers. Miss Marple woofed a greeting. "Mr. Henry worked so hard on them!"

I plunked the papers down with a thud in their usual spot at the end of the old church pew by the door that served as a bench. "I just heard the news," I said as they turned and looked at me. "All three of them? And Mr. Henry was so careful about bringing them inside every night to keep them safe! How could this have happened?"

"You tell us!" said Ella. "Any progress with the investigation? We need to bring this thief to justice."

I shook my head. "Nothing yet. We're working on it, though. I'll let you know the minute anyone has something to report." I bent down and scratched Miss Marple behind the ears. "What was Mr. Mahoney doing here so early?"

Aunt True flapped her hand. "Just a last-ditch effort to get us to sell him the farm."

"Are you going to?" I asked, straightening up again.

She snorted. "Not in a million years."

The door behind me jangled, and my mother came in with Belinda and Captain Romance, as Hatcher and I called Belinda's fiancé, Augustus Wilde. He was our town's most famous resident, a romance author who wrote novels under the pen name "Augusta Savage."

"Greetings and salutations!" said Aunt True.

"Where's J. T.?" My mother looked around. "He was supposed to meet me here."

Aunt True shrugged. "Maybe he stopped for breakfast at Lou's."

My mother held up a paper cup with LOU'S DINER printed on it. "Nope. We were just there."

There was an awkward silence. My father had disappeared again.

"Well now, I'm sure it's nothing to worry about, Dinah," said my grandmother. "He'll turn up."

My mother didn't look worried, though; she looked annoyed. The bookshop was closed today so that she and my aunt and Lola—plus Ella and Belinda and Augustus—could decorate it for the wedding reception tomorrow. Aunt True had her heart set on hosting the reception at our bookstore, and even though it was a holiday weekend and the leaf peepers and their wallets would be out in full force, the whole family had agreed to closing it to the public for the day. The idea sounded kind of weird to me—who had a wedding reception at a bookshop?—but that was Aunt True for you. My father was supposed to help move shelves and furniture to make room for all the tables.

It had been an all-hands-on-deck kind of week for the Lovejoys. Yesterday, after my Abracadabra Day outings, Professor Rusty and Gramps and my father and brothers had spent the evening moving extra beds and other furniture from our Maple Street house over to the new farm, so that Gramps and Lola could settle in there after the rehearsal dinner tonight. I was scheduled to join them tomorrow night after the wedding, and somewhere in between, the three of us were supposed to get a crash course on taking care of the sheep and chickens before my aunt and soon-to-be uncle left on their honeymoon.

This was not a good time for my father to disappear.

"Do you want me to speak to him, Dinah?" asked Lola.

My mother shook her head. "I'll talk to him tonight. We've got more pressing things to think about right now."

So did I. "See you all after school!" I called, grabbing my swim bag and heading back out the door. With the swim meet looming on Sunday, Coach Maynard had scheduled an extra practice this morning.

I jogged all the way to the pool, arriving just in time to run into Lucas in the lobby. I was surprised to see Emilio Frangipani with him.

"Emilio's on a swim team back in Italy," said Lucas. "Coach said he was welcome to join us."

I mustered a smile. "Great," I said, and loped off toward the locker room. I hoped this wouldn't be awkward. I couldn't afford to lose my focus, and being flirted with could definitely mess with a person's focus.

A further complication awaited me out on the pool deck.

"What are you doing here?" I asked Calhoun.

He shrugged. "Thought I'd give swim team a try."

"But the season's already started! Plus, I thought you played soccer?"

"Soccer practice is after school; swim team is before. My coaches said I can do both."

I digested this information.

Calhoun was looking at me intently. "You don't seem very happy to see me."

What was that supposed to mean? Why did he care if I was happy to see him? Did his sudden appearance have anything to do with the fact that he'd overheard Emilio flirting with me the other day?

Instead of replying, I dove into the pool. I was so not good at boys.

Swim practice ended up being the Emilio and Calhoun

show. I had no idea that Calhoun was so competitive. Coach put the two of them in adjacent lanes, and they wore themselves out trying to outswim each other.

"Where have you boys been all my life?" Coach Maynard crowed as we wrapped up our final set of freestyle sprints. "West Hartfield isn't going to know what hit them at this weekend's meet."

My times, on the other hand, were some of the worst I'd clocked in practice all season. At this rate, I'd come in last in every event I was entered in. I stumped off to the locker room in a foul mood. I couldn't believe that I'd allowed a couple of dumb boys to shatter my focus.

We only had a half day of school because of the holiday weekend. We worked on our catapults some more with Mr. Bigelow, and then watched Franklin Freeman and Amy Nguyen give their presentation on "The Cask of Amontillado" in Language Arts. Jasmine and Cha Cha and I still had a few days to practice for ours, which was a good thing, since I had my hands full with family stuff.

Franklin and Amy's idea was a clever one: Edgar Allan Poe being interviewed by a TV reporter. I listened as Amy grilled Franklin, who was dressed up as Poe in a black cape and droopy mustache, about his motivation for writing such a gruesome story.

I had a hard time concentrating, though. Between the abysmal swim practice, anticipation of tomorrow's wedding, the deepening mystery of my father's puzzling disappearances, and a nagging suspicion that my aunt's farm might be haunted—the farm I had volunteered to stay at for the next two weeks—I had a lot to think about. And that didn't even include catching the pumpkin snatcher!

"Can I go home with Baxter?" asked Pippa, tugging on my arm as she and Lauren and I headed downtown after school. "We want to play in our tree fort."

I turned to Lauren. "It's your call," I told her. "You're the babysitter."

"If it's okay with Mrs. Abramowitz . . ." Her voice trailed off. Lauren had gotten stuck with babysitting Pippa a lot lately, and I could tell she was getting sick of it and could use a break.

"I'm sure it's okay," said Cha Cha, but we stopped by the Starlite to check anyway.

"Of course you can come over, Pippa! In fact, I'm heading there right now, and I feel inspired to make brownies. How does that sound?" Mrs. Abramowitz looked over at Lauren and me and lowered her voice. "I know you all have loads of wedding preparations to juggle, so consider this my contribution."

"Thank you, ma'am!" Lauren and I chorused in the über-polite manner that our parents had drilled into us.

Baxter, whose backpack was nearly as big as he was, started jumping up and down, squealing with excitement, which set Pippa off, too. Relieved of our pesky younger siblings, my sister and my friends and I made our way toward Lou's. Lucas's mother had offered to treat us to lunch, but Main Street was jammed with tour buses and there was a line out the door at the diner. Even though the holiday weekend hadn't officially started yet, the leaf peepers were already swarming.

"Change of plans," I said. "How about lunch at our house?"

Lauren and I made grilled cheese sandwiches for everyone, then we all headed up to our usual meeting spot in Lola's studio over the garage. Now that my grandmother was back, she'd reclaimed it—well, sort of. She had another studio set up in one of the bedrooms out at the farm, too, and spent time at both of them, whenever she had a free moment.

"Your grandmother is a really good artist," said Lucas, wandering over to look at her latest work-in-progress. Somehow, Lola had found time to get started on a painting of the new farm. She was hoping to have it done by the time Aunt True and Professor Rusty got back from their honeymoon, to hang over their mantel as a surprise.

I nodded. "Yeah, I know."

I'd ended up borrowing one of Lola's fall landscapes for the bookshop display window, where I'd placed it on an easel behind the red wagon piled with pumpkins and autumn-themed books. The painting had attracted a lot of attention from customers and passersby, and we'd already had a few offers from people wanting to buy it. My grandmother wasn't sure she wanted to sell it, though. It was one of Gramps's favorites.

"So, does anyone have anything new to report?" I asked as we settled down to work. "We know that at least three of the jack-o'-lanterns disappeared in broad daylight, right?"

My friends all nodded.

"Make that four," said Jasmine. "I stopped by the library on my way to school, and Mr. Henry is pretty sure that the ones on the library steps were taken yesterday between lunch and when he went home for dinner."

"Any suspects?"

She shook her head.

Scooter raised his hand. "Ike Farnsworth swears he saw Reverend Quinn creeping around the general store the day their jack-o'-lantern disappeared."

I laughed out loud. "Seriously? What possible motive could our minister have for stealing a pumpkin?"

"I'm just repeating what I heard," Scooter said defensively.

"Scrabble," blurted Lucas. "The two of them play all the time at the diner. They're archrivals."

I shook my head in disbelief, but added Scrabble to the "Motive" column and Reverend Quinn to the column labeled "Suspects" anyway.

"I told my dad what was going on and he and the Dean of

Students held a meeting for the entire student body," Calhoun told us. "Anyone caught stealing pumpkins will be expelled. He said if it's college students playing a prank, that should take the wind out of their sails."

"Okay." I jotted that down, too. "Have any of the missing pumpkins been found? Have there been any smashed-pumpkin sightings?"

My sister and our friends all shook their heads.

"It's so weird!" Jasmine burst out. "Why would anyone want to steal jack-o'-lanterns? What the heck are they doing with them?"

"Maybe they want to make sure that theirs wins the design contest," said Lauren.

My sister had a point. I added "Eliminate the competition" to the Motive column. "Do we know who's entered into that contest? Besides everyone at school, of course."

"I can find out," said Jasmine. "My mother is one of the volunteer organizers."

"Maybe we should focus on whose jack-o'-lanterns *haven't* been stolen," Cha Cha suggested. "Unless the thief is really sneaky, they probably didn't steal their own pumpkin."

"Good point," I said, and made two more columns. Those who'd had jack-o'-lanterns stolen included Mahoney's Antiques, Lou's Diner, Mr. Henry at the library, the general store, the Klip 'n' Kurl, and our bookshop. Those who hadn't included Suds 'n' Duds, Bud Jefferson's stamp and coin shop, the post office, the Starlite dance studio, and Ella Bellow's yarn shop. I stared at the second column and chewed on the end of my pencil. None of them seemed like likely suspects.

"It's not my parents, that's for sure," said Cha Cha, and I crossed Starlite Dance Studio off the suspects list.

"It's probably just college students," Lucas said with a sigh. "All this work for nothing."

"It's weird, though—have you noticed that so far, they've only been taking pumpkins from businesses, not from people's homes?" said Calhoun.

"Yeah, that is weird," Cha Cha agreed.

I drew a big question mark and wrote this observation down beneath it.

"Maybe we should do another stakeout," Scooter suggested. "I can see if my dad will let us borrow his camera again." Mr. Sanchez's motion-activated camera had helped us solve a case last spring. The only problem was, Scooter hadn't actually asked permission to borrow it, which had gotten him grounded.

"Maybe," I replied. "I suppose you could ask. But meanwhile, let's just keep our eyes peeled and our ears to the ground. Lauren and I are going to be busy until the wedding is over. Maybe we can get together again Sunday after the swim meet?"

I carefully avoided looking at Calhoun. I was still kind of annoyed at him for showing up unexpectedly at the pool. On the other hand, if I was honest with myself, I was also a bit flattered—I was pretty sure that he'd come because of me.

After we finished our meeting, we headed back downtown. Annie Freeman spotted us as we crossed the village green and came running over. "I have a new dress for the wedding!" she announced breathlessly. "It's made of o-r-g-a-n-z-a and it's pink and f-l-o-u-n-c-y and wait until you see it—it's s-p-e-c-t-a-c-u-l-a-r!"

"I'm sure it is, Annie," I said. My classmate Franklin's sister was not only Lauren's best friend and a chatterbox, but also the reigning Grafton County junior spelling champion. She could spell as fast as she could talk.

She and Lauren ran off. The rest of my friends all peeled away to their various destinations and activities, and I continued on to the bookstore alone.

Things were looking very different than they had this morning. The freestanding bookshelves that were normally arranged throughout the store had all been pushed against walls, leaving a big open space in the middle that would serve as a dance floor. The reading nooks had vanished, their comfy armchairs temporarily banished to the basement. Long folding tables lined the edges of the room, covered with crisp white linen tablecloths and topped with piles of tiny orange pumpkins, greenery, and colorful paper autumn leaves as centerpieces. Garlands strung with more fake leaves hung from the tops of the bookshelves, crisscrossing the room.

"It's perfect," said Aunt True, surveying everything with satisfaction.

The wedding was scheduled for eleven tomorrow morning at our church, with an open house back here at the bookshop afterward. The wedding ceremony itself was small—just family and a few close friends—but pretty much everyone else in town was invited to the reception. It was going to be casual, because my aunt wasn't a formal person and because people would be busy with the holiday weekend and the leaf peepers. Aunt True and my mother had come up with the open-house idea so that those invited could stop by at any point during the workday to congratulate the new couple and grab a bite to eat.

I heard whistling and a moment later my father came through the back door.

"Where on earth have you been, J. T.?" snapped my mother. "You promised to give us a hand here today!"

"Did I?" he said absently. "Sorry. I had a thing."

Before she could press him further for an explanation, the bells on the bookshop door jangled and Professor Rusty burst in, his normally wild dark hair looking wilder than usual.

"I talked to Elmer, and he swears he didn't touch anything!" he announced to Aunt True, clearly agitated. "I found the pitchfork in the *pantry*, of all places, and the wire cutters were in one of the nests in the henhouse!"

"Well, Elmer is a bit forgetful these days," said my aunt. "I'll talk to Thelma about it."

TRULY, MADLY, SHEEPLY

Professor Rusty shook his head. "Maybe this whole farm thing is a bad idea. Maybe we really do have a boggart."

"Stop being a drama queen, Rusty!" said my aunt. "I was only joking about that. There's no such thing as boggarts. I'm sure there's a perfectly logical explanation."

Our town was full of mysteries and secrets all of a sudden. My father's unexplained disappearances. Vanishing jack-o'-lanterns. And now it seemed that Aunt True's new farm was keeping a secret, too. One that might mean it was haunted.

As much as I hoped that Pumpkin Falls Private Eyes would be able to catch the pumpkin snatcher and earn Ella's reward, I was hoping even more that my aunt and almost-uncle got to the bottom of the possible boggart situation. I did not relish the thought of spending two weeks in a house haunted by some mythical Scottish creature.

Not one bit.

CHAPTER 11

Aunt True's wedding day was perfect, until it wasn't.

The morning started off a little rocky, when Pippa got up on the wrong side of the bed and had one of her famous meltdowns. It began with a list of complaints and escalated from there: Her new haircut was too babyish. Danny hogged the last of the Rainbow Puffs at breakfast. Annie Freeman's dress was prettier than hers. Lauren got a kitten for a bridesmaid present, and she didn't.

"Your aunt gave you a lovely gift," my mother told her. "Just think! Horseback riding lessons!"

"But I wanted a PONY!" Pippa wailed. "Plus, it's NO FAIR that Truly got an Abracadabra Day and I DIDN'T!"

My mother sighed. There was no reasoning with Pippa when she was like this. "Yours is coming, sweetheart."

"WHEN?"

"You know I can't tell you that. It would ruin the surprise!"

"I don't WANT a surprise! I want Abracadabra Day RIGHT NOW!"

"Pipe down, young lady," my father said sternly, striding into the kitchen. "That's an order."

But even one of Lieutenant Colonel Jericho T. Lovejoy's orders wasn't enough to stifle Pippa. She continued to wail as my parents hustled her into the minivan, and she wailed all the way to the church. It wasn't until we were actually inside and getting ready to take our places that Belinda swooped in and saved the day.

"Here," she said, reaching into the purple purse that matched her dress and thrusting a furry white bundle at my little sister. "Have an emergency kitten."

Pippa opened her mouth to wail again in protest but Belinda held a finger to her lips. "Nope. Can't do that, honey. You'll scare Snowball."

Pippa hiccupped. "His name is Snowball?" She couldn't resist reaching out a finger and stroking the kitten's soft fur.

Belinda nodded. "Yes, and he's a special wedding-day surprise. See? He matches your aunt True's dress."

We all turned to see my aunt floating into the vestry. I'd already spotted the dress hanging in her closet, but this was the first time I'd actually seen her wearing it.

"Wow," breathed Lauren.

"Aunt True looks like a princess," whispered Pippa, awestruck.

"You look beautiful!" I blurted.

My aunt grinned. "Don't sound so surprised."

"The girls are right, True, you're positively radiant," said my mother, giving her a hug. "Rusty's not going to know what hit him."

Aunt True winked at us and twirled. "That's kind of the point of a wedding dress, right?"

I was really surprised that she'd chosen a traditional white dress. I guess I'd figured she'd show up in clogs and something multicolored from Peru or another one of her far-flung trips. But the wedding dress was all white lace and chiffon, and her usually messy hair had been carefully smoothed and arranged into a sophisticated updo, courtesy of team Klip 'n' Kurl. She was even wearing lipstick.

Pippa calmed down after that and was the perfect flower girl, walking sweetly down the aisle clutching her bouquet—and the white kitten. My father looked handsome in his dress uniform, my mother elegant in a dress the color of rich gold autumn leaves. Gramps and Lola held hands and cried. Reverend Quinn, who had baptized my aunt when she was a baby and watched her grow up, got teary-eyed too, as he read the wedding vows. Professor Rusty, who was wearing a kilt, probably in anticipation of his upcoming trip because he wasn't Scottish, actually blubbered. He didn't wait for the vows, either—he started bawling the minute he saw Aunt True. My mother was right about the dress.

TRULY, MADLY, SHEEPLY

To be honest, by the end we were all crying. I'd been to quite a few weddings before. With six uncles, it was kind of inevitable. But this one was the best.

I was pretty sure Augustus Wilde thought so, too, as I spotted him secretly taking notes in his pew at one point. Ideas for his next novel, probably. He'd come as Belinda's plus-one, a purple handkerchief peeking jauntily out of the breast pocket of his gray suit. He and Belinda were big into matching, and purple was their favorite color these days.

That was pretty much it for the wedding party—well, along with Professor Rusty's parents. Aunt True had been determined to keep the actual wedding ceremony small. In fact, she'd originally wanted to elope.

"It's so *personal*, sharing your wedding vows!" she'd told my mother. "It's private—I don't want the whole town listening in."

So they hadn't.

But they'd all been waiting outside the church, and they all let out a cheer as my brothers flung the doors open and the newly married couple appeared.

Rusty's parents had hired a bagpiper for the occasion as a surprise, and he piped us down the steps and onto the sidewalk, where a spontaneous reception line quickly formed.

"Mazel tov, True," said Mrs. Abramowitz, who was first in line. She gave my aunt a hug and hugged my new uncle, too. As the bridal couple made their way through all the well-wishers, my family and I followed them down Main Street to the bookstore, the piper leading the way. Tourists gaped. Cars pulled over to the curb and the passengers inside jumped out to take pictures of our impromptu parade. So did Clark Barque, which probably meant our family was destined to be splashed across the pages of the *Pumpkin Falls Patriot-Bugle* again. For once, I didn't care about being in the spotlight. It was my aunt's wedding day!

Inside Lovejoy's Books, we all raced into position. My mother had enlisted my father's help organizing everything, and he was running it like a military operation. Everyone had a post. Danny greeted guests at the door. Hatcher ushered them to the tables, already piled high with food thanks to the Lovejoy College catering crew. Augustus slipped behind the counter at Cup and Chaucer and began serving up hot beverages while Belinda manned the punch bowl next to him, ladling up cups of cold apple cider for Lauren and me to hand out. Gramps was in charge of the photographer and musician, while Lola and my mother were in charge of Aunt True and my new uncle, bringing them food and drinks and making sure they had everything they needed. Only Pippa didn't have a job. Out of the corner of my eye I saw her slipping in and out of the crowd, whispering and giggling with Baxter. There was no sign of Snowball, which meant Belinda must have whisked her "emergency kitten" to safety after the wedding.

"Here you go, sir," I said, passing a cup of cider to a man in a dark gray suit. "Fresh from Freeman Farm."

TRULY, MADLY, SHEEPLY

"Thanks, Truly."

I did a double-take, astonished to see that it was Lou from the diner. I'd never seen him without his white apron before.

He laughed at my expression. "I clean up pretty good." Turning to my aunt, who had come up behind us, he added, "But I would have been more than happy to help out with the catering, you know."

"No way were we going to stick you with that on my wedding day," Aunt True told him as he gave her a bear hug. "It's enough that you made our cake. Today you are an honored guest."

"An honored guest who might just have a surprise for you," Lou said, tapping a finger on the side of his nose. But no amount of wheedling on our part could get him to tell us what that might be. "You'll see soon enough," was all he'd say.

A little while later, I wandered over to one of the tables where Hatcher was taking a break by the shrimp platter.

"You might want to leave a few for the other guests," I told him, eyeing the pile of peelings on his plate.

"You snooze, you lose," he replied, giving me a shrimp-encrusted grin.

"Gross!"

"Hey, I didn't know they were going to be here," he said, plucking another shrimp from the platter and wagging it toward the entrance to the bookshop.

I turned to see Emilio and a couple who were clearly his

parents standing in the doorway. Danny greeted them as they entered, but then they hesitated, looking unsure of themselves.

"I should go say hello," I told Hatcher, but before I could, my new uncle spotted them and swooped in. He started chattering away to them in Italian.

"And I didn't know that Prof—I mean *Uncle* Rusty"—I was going to have to get used to saying that—"spoke Italian."

My brother nodded. "Yep. And French and German and Spanish, too. And a little Portuguese and Russian."

How did Hatcher know all this?

"True!" my new uncle called. "I want you to meet the Frangipanis!"

Aunt True and my mother and grandmother were seated at the table beside Hatcher and me, and Uncle Rusty towed Emilio and his parents in our direction. Curious, I edged a little closer. Emilio saw me and smiled. I smiled back.

"So, you are the artist?" Mrs. Frangipani said after Uncle Rusty introduced her to Lola. She had the same dark hair and eyes as Emilio, and her voice was brushed with the same light accent that his was. Emilio was right—she was tall. Almost as tall as Aunt True and me. *La giraffe.* "That is your painting in the window?"

Lola nodded.

"I like your work very much," Mrs. Frangipani said. "Do you have more paintings you could show me?"

Lola shrugged. "Sure, if you'd like."

Emilio's mother handed her a business card. "I'm teaching at the college this semester, but I have a gallery back in Milan."

As Hatcher ushered Emilio and his parents to the refreshments, my grandmother stared down at the business card. "Well, what do you know about that?"

"What I know about that is that my wife is an incredibly talented artist," said Gramps, coming over to join us and slipping his arm around her waist. "About time the world took notice."

"Indeed," said Calhoun's father, helping himself to some shrimp. "That's quite a compliment, Mrs. Lovejoy. Lena Frangipani is one of the most well-known art historians in Italy!"

"Well, what do you know about that?" my grandmother repeated, but I could tell she was pleased.

"Have you met my children?" Dr. Calhoun continued, waving them over. "Romeo! Juliet!"

There was a brief pause in the buzz of conversation in the bookshop as his voice boomed out. Calhoun and his sister's names still did that to people. It couldn't be easy, having a father who loved Shakespeare so much that he named you for his two most famous characters.

"Romeo, is it?" said Lola when they were introduced.

"He goes by R. J. mostly," I told her. "Or Calhoun."

She smiled. "I've heard good things about you from my granddaughter, R. J."

"Lola!" I protested.

Calhoun blushed furiously, but I could tell he was pleased to hear this.

Over at the Cup and Chaucer counter, Augustus Wilde tapped a glass loudly with a spoon. The bookshop fell silent again as my new uncle climbed up onto a chair beside him.

"True and I would like to propose a toast," he said, raising a cup of cider in the air. My aunt stood on the floor beside him, holding hers aloft too. "To all our family and friends here in Pumpkin Falls. It's each of you who makes this place so special, and it's thanks to each of you—and the Farnsworths, of course—that we're happy to be putting down roots at . . . Rivercroft Farm!"

They'd chosen a name! As the bookstore erupted in applause, I turned it over in my mind and decided I liked it. Plus, surely a place with a name as nice as "Rivercroft Farm" couldn't be haunted.

"And now," Uncle Rusty continued, "we'd like to introduce the Valley Fiddlers. It's time to get this party started!"

The trio of fiddlers struck up a tune, and everyone backed away toward the edges of the room. My new uncle led my aunt out into the middle of the bookshop floor for their official first dance. The lilting melody was vaguely familiar, something Scottish, I was pretty sure.

"Don't they make a lovely couple!" said my mother with a happy sigh as the two of them waltzed their way around the room.

"I've never seen True look more beautiful," Lola added.

Gramps nodded. "And Rusty doesn't look half bad in that fancy kilt."

"It's pretty cool," agreed Hatcher. "I wouldn't mind having one of those."

"You are *not* going to start wearing a kilt!" I sputtered.

He gave me a sidelong glance. "I shouldn't ask for one for Christmas, then?"

I punched his arm and he laughed.

Everyone clapped as the official first dance finished. Then the fiddlers swung into a rollicking tune and the contra dance began. The caller whom Uncle Rusty had hired told everyone to grab a partner and form a line.

Calhoun and I exchanged a glance. His face went beet red again. He opened his mouth, presumably to ask me to dance with him, but before he could, Emilio materialized at my elbow.

"Would you like to be my partner?" he asked me, bowing slightly. Somehow, he managed to make it look natural and not weird at all.

"Uh, sure, I guess." It would be rude to say no, right? Emilio took my hand and tugged me toward the line of people in the center of the room. I studiously avoided looking at Calhoun.

Contra dancing was kind of like square dancing, but a lot more fun. The music was lively and upbeat, and I'd never been whirled around so much in my life. I actually had to sit down at one point because I was so dizzy.

It wasn't as if Emilio was my only partner, either. Everybody pretty much danced with everybody else, as the lines we formed moved up and down and all around the bookshop. I danced with Calhoun, eventually, and with Lucas Winthrop and my brothers and Gramps, and with Uncle Rusty and Dr. Calhoun and Bud Jefferson and Lou.

"Have you seen your father?" asked my mother, breathless, as we were taking a break a while later.

"Um, no," I replied. "He was here earlier, though. I saw him twirling Belinda around."

My mother frowned. "He'd better not have disappeared again. Not on his sister's wedding day."

"He'll be back," said Danny, flopping down on the bench beside us. "I saw him drive off a few minutes ago. He said to tell you not to worry and that he wouldn't be gone too long."

My mother's forehead creased with concern. "What is the matter with that man! What on earth is he thinking, skiving off on True's big day?"

I didn't know what to say to that. Fortunately, I didn't have to say anything because there was a commotion over by the door just then. We looked over to see Lou trundling a cart into the bookshop.

"Oh my word!" said my mother, all thoughts of my father's whereabouts temporarily forgotten. "Is that—"

TRULY, MADLY, SHEEPLY

"Yes, ma'am," he said, smiling. "A doughnut pyramid."

Even better, it was a *cider* doughnut pyramid. So this was Lou's surprise!

"I took a chance with this instead of a traditional wedding cake. I wanted to make you something memorable, something that really said Pumpkin Falls," Lou explained to Aunt True and Uncle Rusty as everyone clustered around the towering three-foot-tall arrangement. Decorated with ribbons and flowers and a tiny bridal couple on top, it was a real show-stopper. "That plain-Jane cake you ordered just wasn't special enough for you."

"This is the best wedding cake *ever*!" said my delighted aunt.

"There's more, too," Lou added, gesturing outside to where the food truck from Mac's Maple was pulling up to the curb in front of the store.

I gasped. "No way!"

Who needed cake, when you could have cider doughnuts from Lou's and maple creamees from Mac's Maple instead?

While Aunt True and Uncle Rusty posed for photos by the doughnut pyramid, the rest of us stampeded for the door. Passing tourists, stunned by their luck, were swept up in the rush and treated to free ice cream. The bagpiper reappeared, joined by the fiddlers, who gave an impromptu concert on the sidewalk while we were all waiting in line. I'd never seen Main Street in such a festive mood.

Suddenly, there was a loud droning noise overhead.

"It's an air raid!" cried Lucas's mother, clutching him to her in a panic. "Duck!"

"Calm down, honey, it's just J.T.," said Bud Jefferson, slipping one of his bear-like arms around her.

Not all secrets were bad ones, as it turned out.

Above us, a bright red old-fashioned bi-plane dipped low and buzzed past. My mouth dropped open. Bud was right. My father was at the controls! He waggled the plane's wings and waved to us.

"THAT'S MY DADDY!" shrieked Pippa, hopping up and down in excitement.

"True! Rusty! Get out here on the double!" my mother called.

The plane circled back. A banner streamed out behind it, the lettering crystal clear against the blue sky: CONGRATULATIONS, TRUE AND RUSTY!

"Oh my goodness," said Aunt True, shading her eyes to look. "Rusty, do you see that?"

We all watched in astonishment as my father performed a series of stunts overhead, looping and rolling, dipping and diving.

"I can't believe it!" my mother kept repeating as she dabbed at her eyes with what looked like Augustus Wilde's purple handkerchief. "J. T. is *flying!*"

"So this is what he's been up to!" said my aunt. "I had no idea. Did you know, Mother?"

Lola shook her head.

"I did, but I was sworn to secrecy," Bud Jefferson confessed sheepishly. "Sorry, Dinah."

My mother patted his arm. "All is forgiven. I just can't believe J. T. is *flying* again! It's a miracle!"

The little airplane flew low over Main Street one more time, waggled its wings at us in farewell, then roared off in the direction of the small airfield on the outskirts of town.

Half an hour later, my father rejoined us.

"I'll never be cleared as a commercial pilot, but it turns out I can fly for fun," he told my mother, his face alight. "I'd been looking into the possibility for a while, and what with the wedding coming up, I thought it might be a nice surprise."

"You should have said something, J. T.!" my mother scolded, but she was smiling, too. "I was worried sick about you, the way you kept disappearing!"

"I didn't want to get anyone's hopes up," he explained. "It was hard enough keeping my own in check."

As the party was winding down, I wandered back into the bookshop's office to take a breather. I found my mother sitting there alone. She looked up as I opened the door and smiled when she saw me.

"Everything okay?" I asked.

She nodded. "Just counting my blessings."

My mother loved to count her blessings. I sat down on a carton of books beside her as she began ticking them off on her fingers.

"Our family, of course. Your father's recovery—he's *flying* again, Truly! In our wildest dreams, we couldn't have imagined that a year ago! Then there's True and Rusty's beautiful wedding. Plus, the bookshop is thriving and so are all my chicks." Putting her arm around me, she pulled me close with a happy sigh. "Including my Truly-in-the-Middle."

I thought about this for a minute. She was right. I *was* thriving. Even though I still felt a tug toward Texas from time to time, Pumpkin Falls was beginning to feel like home.

I put my head on her shoulder and we sat for a while without speaking.

"I suppose we're neglecting our guests," my mother said finally, standing up and pulling me to my feet. "Shall we head back out to join them?"

All of that was the perfect part of Aunt True's wedding day. What happened afterward was the not-so-perfect part.

Shortly before sunset, we said a noisy farewell to Aunt True and Uncle Rusty, pelting them with birdseed as they climbed into Aunt True's little car. Hatcher and Danny had snuck out earlier and painted JUST MARRIED on the rear window and tied a bunch of empty tin cans and old shoes to the rear bumper. People honked and whooped and cheered as they clanked away.

After they left, a few stragglers stayed to help us with

the cleanup. We were just about finished putting the bookshop back to rights when Ella Bellow stomped in, followed by Officer Tanglewood.

"Someone tried to steal Woolly!" Ella announced, glaring at us. "And my new surveillance camera caught the culprit in the act."

Officer Tanglewood stepped forward and placed a hand on Hatcher's shoulder. "Son, I'm going to have to bring you in for questioning."

We all turned and stared at my brother, aghast. Hatcher was the Pumpkin Falls pumpkin snatcher?

CHAPTER 12

None of us slept a wink that night.

I couldn't get the stricken look on Hatcher's face out of my mind. I'd tapped two fingers under my chin—our private shorthand for "Keep your chin up"—as Officer Tanglewood led him away, but he'd barely glanced at me. My brother looked like a prisoner already, I'd thought, my heart nearly tearing in two as I watched him slump out of the bookshop with Gramps and our father and Ella Bellow.

After they left for the police station, my mother and Lola hustled the rest of us home. Any remaining fairy dust from the wedding had completely vanished by this point, replaced by the stone-cold reality that Hatcher had been accused of being a thief. Hatcher! Of all people!

Pippa lurched into full siren mode again as soon as she buckled her seat belt. "What if he goes to JAIL?!" she wailed.

"That's not going to happen, honey," my grandmother assured her. "It's just a pumpkin."

"But Daddy said the people who took the pumpkins were PURLOINERS and they should have BOOKS thrown at them!"

"I'm sure it's just a mistake," said my mother soothingly. "Your father and Gramps will sort everything out."

But they didn't.

It was dark by the time they returned. Pippa was in bed asleep already, worn out from the excitement of the wedding and the arrest and her twin meltdowns. Danny and Lauren and I were sitting on the front stairs, waiting to talk to Hatcher, but he passed by us without a word, a grim look on his face.

"You kids leave your brother alone," our father told us. "It's been a long evening. Danny, you sleep in the guest room tonight." He made a shooing motion. "Off you go."

Instead, we just waited until all the grown-ups went into the kitchen, then snuck downstairs again to eavesdrop.

"Officer Tanglewood is being stubborn," we heard our father report. "He says videos don't lie."

"Hatcher insists he was just putting the pumpkin back," Gramps added. "The problem is, Ella doesn't believe him and she's planning to press charges."

"Over a *pumpkin*?" My mother's voice shot up an octave.

I heard my father sigh. "She says it's the principle of the

thing and that the culprit needs to be taught a lesson."

"Ella needs to get off her high horse," growled Gramps. "It was a silly prank, not a breach of national security."

"If Hatcher didn't do it, as he claims," our father continued, "we'll need to prove his innocence. I called Alberto and Maria Sanchez and they're going to help."

My siblings and I exchanged a glance. This wasn't a good sign. Things had to be serious if Dad was bringing in Sanchez & Sanchez, the law firm owned by Jasmine and Scooter's parents.

"What did they say?" Lola asked.

"Well, for starters, they got Hatcher released to my custody, but he has to be on his best behavior until the hearing. He can go to school, but he needs to come directly home afterward. No sports. No spending time at the bookshop. No socializing."

"Even with his siblings?" asked our mother.

"We'll figure that out tomorrow."

"What about the video?" asked Lola. "Surely that showed that he didn't do it."

"Officer Tanglewood reviewed it with us when the Sanchezes arrived," Gramps explained. "While there's some ambiguity—it was dusk and the front of the shop is partially in shadow—the part that is completely clear shows Hatcher holding the pumpkin."

"Holding it as in putting it back or holding it as in taking it?" our mother demanded.

Gramps cleared his throat. "That's the ambiguous part. The surveillance camera is motion-activated, and it must have malfunctioned because it only recorded some of what occurred, not all."

"Ella can't press charges on 'some, not all'!" our mother protested, her voice heading for the stratosphere again.

"It's okay, Dinah," our father reassured her. "I've known Ella my whole life. She'll come around."

"She'd better. If not, I'm going to make her life a misery."

My cell phone buzzed just then—and kept buzzing. As I scrambled to silence it, I heard a chair scrape on the floor of the kitchen.

Danny jerked his thumb over his shoulder. "Time to vamoose," he whispered, and the three of us quickly fled back upstairs.

Lauren followed me down the hall to my room and flung herself dramatically onto my bed. "What are we going to do?"

"The first thing I'm going to do is to answer these text messages," I told her, glancing down at my cell phone screen. A text thread was blowing up with messages from the other Pumpkin Falls Private Eyes wanting to know what was going on. Word had obviously gotten out about Hatcher. I'd known that it would—there was no way something like this could stay under wraps. Not in our town. And especially not with Ella Bellow in the middle of it.

I texted my friends back, explaining what had happened,

which of course triggered another flood of texts.

"What are they saying?" asked Lauren, crowding in to peer over my shoulder.

I shrugged. "Exactly what you and Danny and I did—that Hatcher is innocent, and that Ella Bellow is a major pill."

"What are we going to do?" my sister repeated.

I knew what I was going to do. I was going to figure out what happened. I didn't care what Ella's video showed—I believed Hatcher. My brother wasn't a thief. No way. If Hatcher said he'd been putting Woolly's pumpkin head back, then that's exactly what he'd been doing. Although I did wonder why he was putting it back, and where he'd found it. I needed to find a way to talk to him.

"We're going to figure out how to help Hatcher, of course," I told Lauren.

"What's the plan?"

I lifted a shoulder. "I'll come up with something."

But that was easier said than done. After Lauren left, I tried texting Hatcher. Still no reply, which meant my father—or worse, Officer Tanglewood—had probably confiscated his phone. I thought about sneaking upstairs to try to see him, but the door to the attic was directly across from my parents' bedroom, and I didn't want to risk getting caught. I'd have to wait until tomorrow.

Sleep was impossible. I tossed and turned for what felt like hours. I still couldn't believe Ella hadn't given my brother the

TRULY, MADLY, SHEEPLY

benefit of the doubt! I knew she was mad about the attempted theft of Woolly's head, but still—it wasn't fair.

As I finally drifted into a fitful slumber, one thing was crystal clear. I was facing the biggest case of my life: clearing my brother's name.

The question was, how?

CHAPTER 13

Thanks to all the drama after the wedding, Sunday's swim meet was a bust—for me, at least.

My teammates had fallen silent when I came out on the pool deck, a sure sign they'd all been talking about me.

"Tough time for your family right now," said Coach Maynard, patting me on the shoulder. "If you want to take a pass in any of your events—or all of them—I'll understand."

I shook my head. "I want to swim."

"Okay then, let's go get 'em!"

It was a shame, really, because this was the first time my grandparents had ever watched me compete in real life. They'd seen videos over the years, of course, but live swim meets were completely different. The atmosphere was electric, with everyone shouting and cheering for the competitors. I'd so wanted to shine for them! But my head and my heart were totally not in the game.

TRULY, MADLY, SHEEPLY

Race after race, my sleep-deprived self churned down the lane on autopilot. All I could think about was Hatcher. I needed to talk to him face-to-face. There'd been no sign of him this morning before I left for my meet, though, and he wasn't answering my calls or texts. I didn't know what was going on. And now that I was about to move out to the farm for two weeks, contacting him was going to be even more difficult.

I managed to take third in the 100-meter freestyle, but only because my stiffest competitor from West Hartfield was a no-show. If she'd been there as usual, I'd have been shut out entirely. Which was exactly what happened in the 100-meter butterfly, usually my best race. And my relay team tanked in the 400-meter medley, too, thanks to my underwhelming performance. My teammates tried really hard not to make me feel badly about it, but I could tell they were disappointed.

It was only thanks to Calhoun and Emilio and Lucas that our team managed a respectable overall score. Calhoun and Emilio's budding rivalry got them a few first- and second-place wins, but it was Lucas, surprisingly, who was the star of the meet. His spindly legs propelled him to several personal bests, along with a major upset in the 100-meter breaststroke when he beat West Hartfield's top male swimmer, who'd been favored to win. Mrs. Winthrop and Bud Jefferson had about blown the roof off cheering for him.

"Well done, Truly!" said my grandmother when I came

out of the locker room afterward. "What an exciting meet! I'm so glad we finally got a chance to watch you swim."

She put her arm around me, and I rested my head against her shoulder. Which wasn't easy, since I was nearly a foot taller than she was. "Thanks, Lola. I was pretty terrible, though."

"You looked like a star to me," she said firmly, steering me toward the door. "Your suitcase is in the car. After supper, we'll head out to the farm."

My family had planned to go out for pizza, because with all the hoopla of the wedding preparations no one particularly wanted to cook. Now, though, after what happened yesterday with Hatcher, that sounded like punishment. I could hardly stand the thought of food, let alone eating it in public. All of Pumpkin Falls would be watching us and whispering.

I put my game face on, though, since Pippa and Lauren were clearly excited about going out to eat. Pizza was their favorite thing in the whole world. Well, cheese pizza, anyway. Pippa didn't like toppings.

"*We're going to Tony's, to Tony's, to Tony's,*" she sang loudly from the back seat. I gritted my teeth as Lauren joined in. Fortunately, it wasn't a long drive to the pizzeria from the West Hartfield pool.

And in the end, my fears about being out in public were unfounded. There wasn't any actual whispering, just sympathetic glances. I spotted a few of my teammates, including Calhoun and his father, who both waved. Then, just as we took our seats around the biggest table, Emilio and his parents came in.

They headed for a booth near the door, but Gramps waved them over. "Pull up some chairs and join us," he said, smiling. As they did, I saw him discreetly elbow Lola as if to say, *Here's your ticket to fame and fortune.*

My grandmother was soon deep in conversation with Mrs. Frangipani about art. Emilio, who had squeezed his chair in between me and Lauren, politely put his napkin in his lap and turned to me.

"Good swim meet, *sí?*"

"For you, maybe," I said, giving him a sidelong glance. But I didn't want to be rude and burst his bubble, so I added a smile. Out of the corner of my eye I could see Calhoun watching us, so I smiled and waggled my fingers at him, too.

Mr. Frangipani was loud and funny and outgoing. Laughter bubbled up around our table as he teased my sisters and me, and even my parents and Gramps. He glanced over at Emilio at one point and winked at him. "Sports and pizza! My Emilio is a real American boy now!"

It was the first time I'd ever seen Emilio look embarrassed. Parents were the same everywhere, I guessed.

The pizza arrived and my mood lifted slightly as I snagged a piece. I was hungrier than I'd thought. Tony's made the best pizza in the Pumpkin River Valley. It was one of our family's favorite hangouts, but as I watched Emilio and his parents take their first bite, I wondered what they'd think of it. Italy was where pizza was born, after all.

"*Molto bene*," Mr. Frangipani said, trying not to sound surprised. "Very good!"

The pizzas disappeared quickly as the conversation flowed. Nobody mentioned Hatcher. Maybe the Frangipanis were the only people in Pumpkin Falls who hadn't heard about what happened, I thought. Or maybe they were just too polite to bring it up.

"So," said Emilio, taking a sip of root beer. "Did I hear your grandfather say that you are moving to a farm?"

"Well, not *moving* moving," I replied. "It's just temporary. My aunt and uncle bought a farm, and I'm going to help my grandparents take care of it while they're on their honeymoon."

"Ah, I see." Emilio took another sip. "Pigs? Horses? Cows?"

"Sheep."

"So I should call you *pastorella* now—shepherdess—instead of *la giraffa*?" He gave me a sly grin.

"No to both," I told him, but I smiled back.

Gramps and Lola and I were soon on our way to the farmhouse with a bag of leftover wedding doughnuts and Miss Marple. Now that my grandparents—her original owners—were back, Miss Marple had been in a dither trying to decide whom to follow around. I was her favorite Lovejoy when Gramps and Lola were away, but now her loyalties were clearly divided. Fortunately, with the three of us together for the next two weeks, she wouldn't have to choose.

"I'll put the kettle on," Lola said as we walked into the farmhouse kitchen. "I think we have time for peppermint tea and some gin rummy before bed."

"Sounds good," I told her. Gin rummy was Lola's favorite card game.

Gramps set our suitcases at the foot of the back stairs and turned to me. "Shall we make sure the animals are tucked up snug for the night? I haven't had a chance to set up the lamb cam yet—I'll do that tomorrow. I know True is worried about how they're settling in."

There was a bit of a commotion as we entered the barn and descended the rickety wooden stairs to the lower level where the sheep pens were. Miss Marple had followed us and the flock baaed anxiously, clustering together as far away as they could from the pen's wooden slats as she stuck her muzzle through and sniffed.

"Nothing to worry about, ladies," Gramps assured them. "Just a sheep in golden retriever's clothing."

I had to laugh at that. Gramps had a point. Big, fluffy, and friendly, golden retrievers were kind of the sheep of the dog world, I decided. Or were sheep the golden retrievers of the sheep world? I watched as Miss Marple cautiously inspected the barn's new inhabitants. Having determined that the sheep were neither snacks nor the enemy, she settled onto the barn floor and watched as we counted heads and did the gate check that Theresa the sheep whisperer had cautioned us never to neglect. Then we peeked into the chicken coop, too, where the chickens were clucking sleepily on their roosts.

"Good night, then, to all you woolly and feathered ladies!" said Gramps. "And to you too, Benedick," he added, with a bow toward the pen where the ram was glowering at us.

We went back upstairs, closed the main barn door tightly, and crossed the driveway to the house. At night, with the farmhouse's shabby exterior softened by the darkness and the lights inside glowing warmly, Aunt True's new home actually looked cozy and inviting. Definitely not haunted.

"Everything all buttoned up for the night?" asked Lola, who had set out mugs on the kitchen countertop.

"Snug as a bug in a rug," Gramps replied, eyeing the bag with the leftover cider doughnuts in it. "You know, dear, it's wasteful to let food get stale."

"Walt, those are for breakfast!" Lola scolded.

"They won't be as good tomorrow morning!" he protested, waggling his eyebrows at me as he reached for the bag. "It's clearly our duty to eat them."

My grandmother relented and put the doughnuts on a plate. I took my mug of tea and wandered into the living room, where a jumble of furniture from Rusty's apartment and Aunt True's apartment was piled haphazardly. Nothing was arranged properly yet, and there were boxes everywhere and no sign of my aunt's cool artwork on the walls—art she'd collected from her travels all over the world—but even so, it was beginning to look like a home.

Back in the kitchen, Gramps asked me what time I needed to be at swim practice in the morning.

"Uh, early—six thirty," I told him. With the season now well under way and more swim meets on the horizon, Coach Maynard was upping our practices to three a week. "Sorry."

"No need to apologize," he said. "I'm an early bird, as you know. We'll plan to leave at six fifteen. Your grandmother and I can have breakfast at Lou's before we head to the bookshop."

"Will the sheep be okay by themselves all day?"

Gramps nodded. "They should be fine. They need another day in the barn before we can let them out anyway."

The three of us settled in at the table in the breakfast nook, and after a few hands of gin rummy, it was time for bed. Miss Marple followed me upstairs, her toenails clicking against the hardwood floors. As she settled on the floor beside me, I found myself smiling. She'd made her choice—me! Even though I really wasn't a dog person, this made me happy. I'd gotten used to having Miss Marple around.

Thanks to the wedding and the swim meet taking up most of my weekend, I had some homework to catch up on. I climbed into bed and stayed up for a while working on the sketch for my team's jack-o'-lantern design and finishing "The Cask of Amontillado." I wasn't quite sure what the big deal was about Edgar Allan Poe. Ms. Matthews seemed to be a huge fan, but the short story wasn't all that scary, just a little claustrophobic, especially at the end, when the main character walled up his friend alive. That hit uncomfortably close to home after what happened to Lauren last spring break. I made a note to myself to keep it out of sight when she was around. Bookworm that she was, my sister couldn't resist anything in print.

Turning out the light, I slid down under the covers and closed my eyes. The minute she thought I was asleep, Miss Marple jumped up on the bed and curled up against my back. I pretended not to notice. This was the little game we played every night. Technically, she wasn't allowed on the furniture, but I didn't have the heart to shoo her off. Plus, her warm bulk was comforting.

Maybe staying here won't be so bad, I thought as I started to drift off to sleep.

Then I heard the noise.

CHAPTER 14

I sat bolt upright in bed, startling Miss Marple, who lifted her head and woofed sleepily.

Short and staccato, the noise had sounded like something between a shriek and a howl.

Had I dreamt it? I held my breath and listened intently. For several long seconds, all I heard was the wind in the trees and the ordinary kind of sounds that old houses make. That had taken some getting used to when we'd first moved into Gramps and Lola's house on Maple Street last winter. None of the base housing we'd lived in around the world was two hundred and fifty years old, and our house in Austin, Texas, the one we'd given up to move here, was practically brand-new. I'd never heard floorboards creak and groan in the middle of the night before or windows that rattled for no reason.

Just as I was starting to relax and think that maybe it was all in my imagination, the unearthly screech pierced the darkness again. I clutched Miss Marple, who leaned against me and whined.

Was it the boggart?

The sound stopped as abruptly as it had started, but not before I realized that it was coming from outside. That was some comfort, at least. If it was a boggart or a ghost, it wasn't lurking upstairs in the attic.

Where, then? The barn, maybe? Still clinging tightly to Miss Marple, I knelt on my bed and peered out the window. The barn was shrouded in darkness, but beyond it, at the far edge of the pumpkin field, I glimpsed a light bobbing in the blackness. A light that looked suspiciously like it might be coming from a flashlight.

Ghosts didn't carry flashlights.

Or did they?

The light bobbed away from the tumbledown shed where Elmer kept his antique truck collection and headed toward the trees at the edge of the field. I frowned. If it wasn't a ghost or a boggart, was it Elmer? But what would he be doing prowling around his old farm close to midnight? Could he be checking on his trucks? Or on his prize pumpkin? That didn't seem like a very Elmer thing to do. Plus, what was the deal with that awful shrieking sound?

There was only one way to find out.

I threw back the covers and started to pull some clothes on over my pajamas. "You can come too," I whispered to Miss

Marple, who started whining again the minute she saw me put my sneakers on. "But you have to be quiet."

Cracking open the bedroom door, I paused and listened, wondering if the horrid noise outside had woken Lola and Gramps. But the only sound coming from their room was the steady rumble of my grandfather's snores. Lola probably had her earplugs in. I hesitated for a moment, wondering if I should wake them. I was reluctant to disturb their sleep, though. They had to get up so early tomorrow to take me to swim practice. Surely this was something I could handle by myself. Well, not completely by myself, but with the aid of a furry companion?

"Miss Marple, girl detective!" I whispered. "Let's do this."

The two of us crept down the back stairs to the kitchen, where I grabbed my fleece jacket from its hook in the mudroom and quietly unlocked the back door. Holding tightly to Miss Marple's collar for moral support, I stepped out into the darkness.

It was cold. I pulled up the hood of my jacket, flicked on my cell phone's torch app, and started across the backyard. The barn loomed large and silent, and as we drew near, I tried not to look too closely at it. The off-kilter walls and gap-toothed windows gave me the creeps. All was quiet inside, at least. The sheep were dreaming their woolly dreams, oblivious as Miss Marple and I slipped by like a pair of ghosts.

Ghosts.

I shivered, my inner critic suddenly on high alert. *You probably shouldn't be doing this on your own*, it scolded. *You should have woken Gramps! This could be dangerous!* I glanced down at Miss Marple. She wouldn't be any help, if that were the case. She was too friendly to be much use as a watchdog. *And what if the someone with the flashlight isn't a someone at all, but a something . . .*

A cold frizzle of fear slithered down the back of my neck at this thought. *Don't be an idiot*, I told myself sternly. But I couldn't silence the *What if? What if? What if?* loop that raced through my mind as I picked my way across the pumpkin field.

I switched off my torch app as I neared the shed. Peering cautiously into the darkness, I looked for the light I'd seen bobbing about earlier. There was no sign of it now. The flashlight and its owner seemed to have vanished. Still, I didn't want any surprises in case I was wrong. I stood silently for a minute or so, watching and listening.

Nothing.

What if I'd dreamt the whole thing? The noise, the bobbing light, all of it? It was possible, right? A lot had happened over the past few days, and I couldn't deny that I was tired. Yes, I decided, that was probably it.

As I started to turn back toward the house, Miss Marple whined and tugged on her collar.

"What is it, girl?" I asked.

TRULY, MADLY, SHEEPLY

She tugged again, and I released her, watching as she trotted off toward the shed.

I followed, switching on my cell phone light again as she began sniffing around by the base of the door. I shone it in her direction. The beam revealed a clear line of footprints leading away toward the trees, and most likely to the trail Aunt True had told me about that led down to the river road.

"Aren't you the clever one!" I exclaimed. "Good girl!"

I hadn't dreamt it after all. Someone *had* been here, and that someone was definitely human. Unless ghosts and boggarts were carrying flashlights and wearing shoes these days. Was Elmer Farnsworth the mystery visitor after all?

Or was it someone else—the Pumpkin Falls pumpkin snatcher, perhaps? Not a single stolen pumpkin had turned up since they'd started disappearing all over town. Remote and unsupervised, this shed would be the perfect spot to stash them.

In fact, what if Elmer himself was the pumpkin snatcher? It made sense, kind of. Elmer loved picking up castoff items and random stuff. Plus, he was a bit forgetful these days. Was it possible that on one of his rambles around town, he'd seen a jack-o'-lantern and thought the owner had set it outside for the garbage collectors?

I could imagine it happening once, maybe. But multiple times?

That was a stretch.

Still, I thought, even if the possibility was a remote one, I should probably explore it. If Elmer really was the Pumpkin Falls pumpkin snatcher, I needed evidence. After my public humiliation last winter when I'd falsely accused Ella Bellow of stealing a rare first-edition copy of *Charlotte's Web* from our bookshop, and after mistaking marauding raccoons for Bigfoot this spring, I wasn't in a rush to make a fool of myself publicly again. This time, I needed unmistakable proof.

And proof meant I needed to get into the shed and see for myself what was inside.

Grabbing the wrought-iron handle, I gave the door a tug. It yielded slightly, and I cringed as the movement produced a mini version of the earsplitting shriek I'd heard earlier. There was one mystery solved, at least. Someone had definitely been here, and that someone had opened the shed door.

I, on the other hand, couldn't. It was locked tight as a drum, firmly latched with a big old-fashioned metal padlock.

Skirting the building, I stood on tiptoe and shone my cell phone light through one of the windows. The glass was smeared with what looked like and probably was decades of dirt and cobwebs, though, and I couldn't see a thing. I made my way around the entire shed, but the other windows were just as dirty. I spotted a small window way up by the peak of the roof that looked like it might be cracked open a bit, but there was no way to reach it.

If my admittedly preposterous theory was true, and there

really was a giant pile of stolen jack-o'-lanterns inside, I wasn't going to be able to confirm it tonight. I chewed my lip. Was there really no way in? Confirming it could help clear Hatcher's name, and I'd do anything to help my brother.

Should I break a window?

Out of the question—I could only imagine what my parents would have to say about that.

What other options did I have?

I eyed the padlock. It wasn't a combination lock like the one on my school locker or my locker at the pool. This one was old-school. Big, heavy, and equipped with a lock that needed a key.

Locks that needed keys could be picked, right?

In order to do that, though, a person would have to know how to pick a lock, which I didn't.

Could I learn? Maybe there were instructions online? Or maybe there was a book on the subject at the library—*Lock-picking for Beginners*, perhaps?

Mr. Henry had helped the Pumpkin Falls Private Eyes with a lot of things, but I couldn't picture myself asking his help finding a book like that. I had a feeling he'd draw the line at breaking and entering.

But would picking the lock on the shed really qualify as a crime? Technically, Rivercroft Farm belonged to Aunt True and Uncle Rusty now. Elmer was only borrowing the shed from them temporarily. Maybe I could argue that I was just checking on my aunt and new uncle's property.

I tried not to think about what Lieutenant Colonel Jericho T. Lovejoy would have to say about "technically." I knew exactly what I'd be risking if I decided to do this. But I also knew that if there was even the slightest chance that I could help Hatcher, I was going to take it.

The wind had picked up, and a chilly gust caught me full in the face. "It's wicked cold out here!" I said to Miss Marple. "Wicked" was New England slang for "very." We Lovejoys were discouraged from using slang—my mother loathed it—but sometimes it popped out.

The expression jogged my memory. I suddenly remembered a present that Danny had gotten last Christmas. Gramps and Lola always gave us books for Christmas, and they'd given Danny one called *Wicked Good Survival Skills*. I'd flipped through it briefly at the time. It was mostly skills that I was pretty sure I'd never need, like how to tie a bow tie, escape from an angry elephant, or throw my voice like a ventriloquist. But there'd been some useful information in it, too. Stuff like how to survive a riptide or light a fire without a match. Had there been a section on lock-picking? I racked my brain, trying to remember.

It was a long shot, but it was worth checking out before I did anything rash like smashing windows. I'd text Danny in the morning.

Miss Marple and I headed back to the farmhouse, deep

in thought. Well, one of us was deep in thought, at least. The other one was mostly sniffing for squirrels.

My deep thoughts kept leading me back to the uncomfortable conclusion that I was probably about to embark on a life of crime. There really wasn't any way around it. If I wanted to solve this case, I was going to have to learn how to pick a lock.

CHAPTER 15

"Truly!"

"Go away," I mumbled, pulling the pillow over my head. This was the second time in less than a week that I'd been awakened before dawn.

Someone whisked the pillow away. I cracked open an eyelid. It was Gramps.

"There's something you need to see," he said.

I grunted. "What?"

He gave me an encouraging pat. "Come on, sleepyhead. Get dressed and meet me in the kitchen."

Even Miss Marple didn't get up this early, I grumbled to myself as I reluctantly did as I was told. I left her on my bed, blissfully chasing squirrels in her sleep.

"It's barely five a.m., Gramps!" I protested, glancing at the clock on the kitchen wall. Another of the things Elmer and Thelma had left behind, it was one of those black-and-white cartoon cat models whose tail and eyes moved back and forth, ticking away the seconds. A "Kit-Cat Klock," Aunt True called it. "I could have slept for another hour!"

"This is worth getting up for, I promise. Follow me."

My fleece jacket was hanging on the hook in the mudroom where I'd left it last night. I slipped it on and followed my grandfather outside, yawning.

"Is it the sheep?" I asked, suddenly wide-awake as he led me toward the barn. It would be awful if Aunt True were to come home from her honeymoon and find that we hadn't taken proper care of her new flock. "Are they okay?"

"The sheep are fine," Gramps assured me. "I was up early and decided to go ahead and install the lamb cam. I checked in on them then."

When we reached the barn, he stopped so abruptly that I barely managed to avoid plowing into him. He pointed wordlessly upward and shone a flashlight at the window above the hayloft.

My mouth fell open. It wasn't a yawn this time. Not even close. This time, it was amazement as I spied a pair of heart-shaped white faces. "Barn owls!"

My grandfather nodded happily. "I think they're a mated pair. We had some at the house on Maple Street when I was growing up, but I've never seen any around Pumpkin Falls since. They rarely venture this far north anymore, from what I've read."

The owls watched us, their dark eyes gleaming. My grandfather and I stared back at them in silence. One of the things I loved best about Gramps was that he felt the same way I did about birds. He took my hand in his and squeezed. I squeezed back. I knew that his heart was beating just as fiercely as mine was right then. The two of us stood there for several long minutes, then Gramps murmured, "What a blessing for True and Rusty!"

"Really?" I whispered back.

He nodded.

"Why?"

"I've always felt that owls are good luck. Although I don't much believe in luck. Life is what you make of it, good and bad. But in my own experience, owls have always been a harbinger of good."

"What's a harbinger?"

"A sign of sorts. I met your grandmother the summer I added my first snowy owl to my life list, for instance."

Life lists were records that birders like Gramps and me kept, to keep track of the birds we spotted. Mine was barely two pages long. His filled an entire notebook.

"Your aunt was born the year I traveled to the Pacific Northwest and saw a spotted owl, and your father came along shortly after I spotted my first great gray. That was something." He was quiet for a moment, remembering. Then he gestured toward the two exquisitely beautiful creatures above us and continued, "Barn owls are considered the most romantic of owls. Probably because of those Valentine-shaped faces of theirs. It's a very sweet start to your aunt's marriage, to have these two choosing to nest here in their barn."

I knew a few other things about barn owls, too, thanks to the books that Gramps had given me over the years. I knew that they mated for life, and that a pair of them could catch more than two dozen mice a night, which had to be a good thing for a farm.

"And maybe," he added, glancing down at me, "they're harbingers of good for you, too."

"Me? Why?"

Gramps ruffled my hair. "Owls have an ability to see what others can't—and because of that they have long been a symbol of wisdom and intuition. As I recall, seeing clearly is something very much needed at your age."

He didn't know the half of it, I thought ruefully. From more boys in my life than I knew what to do with to the looming prospect of a life of crime, I had a lot I needed to think clearly about these days.

Sunrise at the farm wasn't anything like it had been on top of Mount Lovejoy, but it was still pretty spectacular. In the brief span of time that we'd been standing there watching the owls, the sky had begun to lighten and was now stained a deep pink. Fingers of gold reached toward us as the sun peeked over the far edge of the pumpkin field. The owls retreated inside, away from the light. I knew they'd spend the day sleeping, before emerging again after dark to go hunting.

Meanwhile, restless noises and scattered clucks and *baa*s from inside the barn told us that the sheep and chickens were awake.

"Sounds like our barn friends are ready for breakfast," said Gramps. "Since we're already up, I suppose we might as well take care of morning chores."

I followed him inside. It was a funny thing, but as much as I wasn't the world's biggest animal lover, aside from birds—and Miss Marple—I had always adored barns. I loved everything about them. I loved the way they looked like they *belonged*. Like they'd sprung up out of the ground and been there forever. I loved the soaring space inside that reminded me of church, and the way the dust motes danced in the light that filtered down through the high windows. I loved the creaking floorboards and the wooden beams worn by decades and sometimes centuries of use. Most especially, though, I loved the smell. And as rattletrap a barn as this one was, it was still full of the same perfect barn smell as any other barn I'd ever been in.

I'd felt this way ever since Lola read *Charlotte's Web* to me one summer when we'd visited Pumpkin Falls. It was her favorite book, and she was always quoting from it. One of the parts that she'd memorized was a description that the author, E. B. White, wrote about the barn that Wilbur the pig lived in.

I still remembered the last line: "It often had a sort of peaceful smell—as though nothing bad could happen ever again in the world."

Mr. White was exactly right, I thought, closing my eyes and inhaling deeply. It definitely was a peaceful smell. I also detected the fresh straw that Uncle Rusty had laid down in the sheep pens, and a pungent but not unpleasant mixture of chickens, fleece, and an unnamable something that was probably sheep poo. It didn't smell bad, though, just kind of earthy.

"So, let's see what we need to do." My grandfather headed downstairs to the sheep pens with me close on his heels. He fished his reading glasses out of his pocket, propped them on what he grandly referred to as "the Lovejoy proboscis"—the large and rather hawk-like nose that I saw echoed on my dad's face and which Hatcher was terrified he was going to end up with—and peered at the chalkboard that Uncle Rusty had put up on the wall by the gate.

At the top was written IN CASE OF EMERGENCY along with Theresa the sheep whisperer's cell phone number. Underneath was a list of the names of each sheep along with the tag number in their ear. Aunt True and Uncle Rusty had been busy before they left, naming their flock. Besides Beatrice and Benedick, there was what my aunt called her new husband's "Ladies of American History": Abigail, Martha, Harriet, Frances, and Sojourner—for Abigail Adams, Martha Washington, Harriet Tubman, Frances Scott Key, who wrote the "Star-Spangled

Banner," and Sojourner Truth, a famous African-American minister.

Grabbing my cell phone, I snapped photos of the names on the chalkboard and the sheep milling around in the pen and texted them to Mackenzie and Jasmine and Cha Cha: *Just hanging out in the barn with my new besties.*

Mackenzie wouldn't be up for ages—it was the middle of the night in Texas—but Jasmine and Cha Cha texted me right back.

HAHA!

SOUNDS LIKE ELLA BELLOW'S SENIOR SATURDAY KNITTING GROUP!

While Gramps served up breakfast—hay that he pitchforked into the metal baskets that hung around the edge of the pen at intervals—I grabbed two buckets and filled them with fresh water, which Theresa had told us was one of the major food groups for sheep. I took the first bucket inside the pen with the ewes, who were intent on their breakfast and ignored me. Benedick was giving me the evil eye, however, so I just lifted his bucket over the edge of the pen and placed it carefully on the ground.

When I was done, I leaned on the railing for a bit while Gramps and I watched the sheep eat.

"Look at them go!" said Gramps admiringly. "Busy making wool for knitters."

When they were done, he poured grain into the trough that ran around the base of the pen.

"All right then, ladies," Gramps told the ewes as they jostled each other to get at the treat. "I'll leave the barn doors open for you so you can peek outside at your new home. It's a beautiful morning! But you have to stay here in your pens for another day or so until you acclimate to your new surroundings. You too, Benedick." He glanced over at the ram, who was watching him with his odd, sideways eyes. If a sheep could glare, Benedick would be glaring. "You're not sure you like me being in here with your harem, do you?"

That would be a no, I thought, as the ram gave a sharp bleat in response. My grandfather chuckled and gave him some grain as well.

"Looks like True wanted to be sure we wouldn't forget," he said pointing to a big sign in capital letters that my aunt had posted above the bottom of the stairway. It read GATE CHECK!

I nodded. "Already done."

"Good. We don't want coyotes carrying off any of these lovely ladies. And gent."

"That's it?" I said as we headed back upstairs. "We don't have to muck out the pens?" I'd had friends back in Texas with horses and they were forever cleaning manure out of the stalls.

My grandfather shook his head. "Nope. Sheep are much lower maintenance than cows and horses. From what Bert said, with the deep bedding method they're using, Rusty and True will only have to clean out the pens a few times a year."

Gramps saw the horrified look on my face and laughed.

"Well, thank goodness sheep are different than people, right?"

Back inside, we hung up our jackets in the mudroom.

"Since someone so foolishly and shortsightedly talked us into finishing up the cider doughnuts last night," said Gramps, "how about pancakes for breakfast?"

I gave him an enthusiastic thumbs-up.

"Good. I'll whip up a batch while you get dressed."

Upstairs in my room, I slipped my cell phone out of my pocket and texted Danny: DO YOU STILL HAVE THAT BOOK GRAMPS GAVE YOU FOR CHRISTMAS?

WICKED GOOD SURVIVAL SKILLS?

YEAH.

CAN I BORROW IT?

MAY I AND YES.

I rolled my eyes. Since when had Danny turned into the grammar police?

CAN YOU SEND IT TO SCHOOL WITH LAUREN?

He sent me an okay fingers emoji. I thrust my cell phone back into my jeans pocket, grabbed my backpack and swim duffel, then headed downstairs to breakfast.

CHAPTER 16

Coach Maynard kept us later than usual at swim practice that morning with a punishing series of dry land strength-training exercises. "Just because you won a meet yesterday doesn't mean you'll win the next one," he told us. "No resting on your laurels around here."

"The only thing I want to rest on is a chair," grumbled Lucas when we finished the final set of squats.

"No kidding," I replied, wincing as I rose to my feet. "My glutes are on fire."

"Glutes?" asked Emilio, who was developing an inconvenient habit of materializing unannounced.

I felt my face go pink and sheepishly pointed to the spot in question.

He laughed. "Ah! *Didietro*. Si!" He stuck his backside out and waggled it, making us laugh.

Calhoun came over just then. He looked at the three of us. "What's so funny?"

I shook my head. "Nothing."

Behind Calhoun's back, Emilio waggled his rear at Lucas and me once more. I couldn't help it, I started laughing again. Calhoun rolled his eyes and stalked off toward the locker room.

"Wait!" I said, running after him. "It was just—"

He flapped his hand at me. "It's fine. It doesn't matter."

But it did. I watched the locker room door swing shut behind him. Why did things have to be so complicated, especially where boys were concerned? Gramps was right. I needed the wisdom of an owl to navigate life.

At school, we spent most of the morning at the covered bridge again, making final adjustments to our catapults and trying one more time to beat The Beast. As if that was going to happen. Finally, after an hour of humiliation, Mr. Bigelow put us out of our misery and declared Scooter the winner.

"You'll be representing Daniel Webster School two weeks from now at the Halloween Pumpkin Toss," he told him. "We expect you and The Beast to do us proud."

I stopped by my locker before lunch to check and see if Lauren had delivered the book from Danny. She had. I flipped through the pages on my way downstairs to the cafeteria. Yes! There was a section on lock-picking! I scanned it briefly, then stuffed the book into my back pocket.

At lunch, Scooter couldn't stop bragging about his contraption. I kept waiting for an opening in the conversation to tell my friends about what had happened last night and share my plan for breaking into the shed, but I couldn't get a word in edgewise. None of us could. Finally, I slid the book out of my pocket, held it up, and said in a loud voice, "DOES ANYONE WANT TO LEARN HOW TO PICK A LOCK?"

Unfortunately, I spoke just as Scooter finally paused long enough to take a bite of his tuna sandwich. As my words rang out through the lunchroom, everyone nearby—students, teachers, lunch ladies, and Principal Burnside—turned and stared at me. I clutched the book to my chest, mortified, and slunk down in my chair, wishing I were in a galaxy far, far away.

"What was that?" whispered Cha Cha.

"I think you heard me," I whispered back. "I think pretty much all of Pumpkin Falls heard me."

"Why would any of us want to learn how to pick a lock?" asked Jasmine.

"Because it's cool," said her twin, spraying her with tuna sandwich crumbs. Jasmine made an "ew" face and brushed them away.

The noise in the cafeteria quickly returned to its usual boisterous level and I leaned forward. "So here's the deal," I began, and explained—in a low voice this time—what had happened at the farm last night. Then I pointed out the pertinent section in Danny's book. "I've looked it over and it doesn't seem all that complicated."

"We definitely need to get inside that shed," said Calhoun.

Scooter nodded. "I'll bet you anything Elmer is the real pumpkin snatcher."

Emilio, who was sitting at a neighboring table talking to Franklin and Amy, must have overheard our excited chatter, because he kept glancing over at us.

"Keep it down," I told my friends, adding in a whisper, "If we go right after school today, we'll have the place to ourselves. Gramps and Lola will still be at the bookshop."

Cha Cha shook her head. "I can't. I promised my mom I'd help her teach a beginning ballroom class."

"Me neither," said Jasmine. "Dress fitting for my cousin's quinceañera. Can't you wait until tomorrow?"

"Guys, it's *Hatcher* we're talking about!" I protested. "This can't wait! He's in trouble, and the faster I can clear his name, the better."

One by one, my friends were forced to drop out. Scooter had a math tutoring session with my dad, who was running a thriving after-school business at the bookshop. Calhoun had soccer practice. Lucas was heading to the stamp shop, where he'd promised to help Bud Jefferson, his soon-to-be stepfather, with a reorganizing project.

"Plus, my mom would kill me if she found out I was learning to pick locks," Lucas added, which was probably true.

I knew Lauren was babysitting Pippa again, so that was that. I was on my own.

"Okay, fine," I said. "I'll let you all know how it goes."

Our last class of the day was Language Arts. We were just settling in to watch Scooter and Calhoun act out the final scene from "The Cask of Amontillado" when I caught a flash of something white outside. I glanced over at the window, frowned, then did a double take. Was that a *sheep* on the front lawn of our school?

It was! I gave a yelp and dashed over to take a closer look.

"Truly, could you please sit—"

"Ms. Matthews, I think that's one of our sheep!" I cried frantically. Chairs scraped against the floor around the room as my classmates all rushed over to join me. Ms. Matthews did, too.

"Oh no!" I said in dismay, counting frantically. It wasn't just one sheep—all six ewes had managed to escape! But how? I was sure that Gramps and I had double-checked the gates this morning!

Grabbing my cell phone, I called my grandfather.

"Hold the fort!" he said crisply when I'd filled him in. "Your dad and I will be right over."

"Sorry, ma'am, but I have to go," I told my teacher. "This is an emergency!" She nodded mutely and I ran out of the classroom and flew down the stairs two at a time. My entire class was right behind me.

Principal Burnside was already outside, making flapping motions with his hands and looking more like a flamingo than ever. "Shoo, sheep!" he called, as the flock eyed him—and the growing crowd—uneasily.

"Please don't," I said in a low voice. "You might spook them. Those are Aunt True's sheep! Gramps and Dad are on their way."

Mr. Burnside stopped mid-flap. "What should we do?"

"Um," I said. How should I know? *Think, Truly, think!* I racked my brain, trying to remember any instructions we'd been given about runaway sheep. Were there emergency maneuvers for rounding up strays? Grabbing my cell phone again, I quickly scrolled to Theresa the sheep whisperer's number, deliriously grateful that she'd made me save it.

HELP! My thumbs flew as I texted her, filling her in on the situation. I pressed send and prayed she'd answer.

She did!

STAY CALM OR THEY'LL RUN, she texted back.

I repeated her words to the crowd gathered around me. My cell phone buzzed again.

FORM A HUMAN CHAIN AND SURROUND THEM QUIETLY. REMEMBER THE GRAIN CAN? THEY'LL FOLLOW IT HOME.

I stared at my cell phone screen, flabbergasted. Grain can? Did she think I'd brought that to school with me?

"Cha Cha!" I called in a flash of inspiration. "Can you grab one of the maracas from the music room?"

"You bet." As she dashed off, I thought of one more thing that might help.

"Lucas!" I grabbed him by his skinny arm. "How fast can you get to the pool?" I told him what I wanted and he nodded and sped away as quickly as his equally skinny legs could carry him.

"Can you get the sixth and seventh graders down here?" I asked Mr. Burnside. "We're going to need more people for our human chain. I don't think anyone younger than that will be strong enough to hold on if the sheep make a run for it. Some of these ladies are pretty big."

"Done," he said, and sprinted back inside.

While my classmates clasped hands and spread out in a long line, I walked slowly toward Beatrice.

"Hey, girl," I said in a soft voice. "It's me, Truly. Remember the back rub?"

Beatrice eyed me skeptically and kept her distance.

Cha Cha reappeared with the maraca. I took it from her and stuck it in my back pocket. Mr. Burnside was right on her heels with the sixth and seventh graders. They joined my classmates, stretching out the human chain. Our teachers spaced themselves out along it like beads on a necklace.

"Hold tight, even if they make a run for it," I told everyone, keeping my voice low. "They won't bite or anything. Think of them like big dogs."

That's what Theresa the sheep whisperer had said, right? Sheep are the best dogs you'll ever have? I fervently hoped she was telling the truth.

In the distance, I could see Gramps and my father and what looked like half of Pumpkin Falls racing toward us down School Street. The ewes spotted them, too, and started milling around restlessly.

We couldn't wait. We needed to move now. I was worried the flock might bolt at any moment.

"Start circling around them—slowly, slowly. That's it! Mr. Burnside, you take one end of the chain that way and I'll take the other end this way. We'll meet on the other side of the sheep."

I grabbed the nearest hand and started moving to the right. The person I'd grabbed squeezed my hand and I looked over in surprise to see that it was Calhoun. He smiled at me, the first real smile I'd seen from him in a while. I smiled back.

Moving as quietly as I possibly could, I led my end of the human chain along the side of the school building, keeping close to the shrubs and trying not to spook the sheep. Mr. Burnside, meanwhile, headed in the opposite direction.

When we were fully stretched out, I motioned everyone to begin to curve around. By now, the ewes definitely knew something was up, and as we slowly encircled them they began bleating anxiously.

"Stay calm, girls," I said softly. "We're just trying to get you home." Letting go of Calhoun's hand, I motioned him to keep moving toward Mr. Burnside.

Gramps and my father had almost reached us. I held a finger to my lips and then used the military hand signals we'd learned as little kids to let my father know what I wanted his group to do. He nodded and signaled back with a thumbs-up, then swiftly whispered orders to the crowd behind him. They spread out, too, forming a human chain to match ours. I saw Lola take Belinda Winchester's hand, and Mr. Henry grabbed on to each of Cha Cha's parents. The Mahoneys from the antiques store joined hands with all four of the Farnsworths. The ladies from the Klip 'n' Kurl had even brought their clients, some of whom still had those weird foil wrappers in their hair that made ladies look like aliens. Reverend Quinn, Mrs. Winthrop, Bud Jefferson, and Lou, who was still wearing his white apron—practically everyone in town was there. Everyone except Ella Bellow, who was giving my family a wide berth these days.

Lucas returned just then, skidding to a stop in front of me. He held out one end of the rescue hook from the pool and I took it from him, nodding my thanks. It was the closest thing to a shepherd's crook that I'd been able to think of.

"Good thinking, Truly," my father said quietly as he

reached for Mr. Burnside. "Steady as she goes."

At the other end of the line, Gramps clamped onto Calhoun and the human chain finally closed, spread out in a large ring around the sheep. I exhaled a sigh of relief. If the sheep bolted now, we'd still have a chance of stopping them.

"Easy, ladies!" I said, stepping toward the center of the ring. I held the maraca up and shook it. "You know what this means! Grain! Treats!"

Just like big dogs, I told myself as the flock crowded around me. I could do dogs, right? I felt a sudden surge of panic as all that fleece closed in. *Deep breaths, Truly. Pretend they're Miss Marple!* Thank goodness there was no sign of Benedick. His gate must have held. All we needed right now was a big ram with a protective streak.

Using the makeshift shepherd's crook, I began to nudge the ewes off the school lawn and we started slowly up the street. I shook the maraca every few steps in encouragement.

Rivercroft Farm was only a mile from the center of town, but when that mile was taken at a snail's pace so as not to rattle a flock of sheep, it felt like an eternity. Every few blocks one of the ewes spooked and made a run for it, but the human chain held.

Word spread like wildfire, of course, and pretty soon the gawkers came out in droves. Clark Barque, the new reporter at the *Pumpkin Falls Patriot-Bugle,* ran alongside us, snapping photos with his camera.

Great, I thought, squirming inwardly as I recalled our

family reunion last summer and the embarrassing newspaper headlines that had followed. I just couldn't seem to manage to keep myself out of the newspaper these days.

Officer Tanglewood did his job for once, stopping traffic to keep the coast clear for us. The startled leaf peepers were getting more local color than they bargained for today. Everyone was taking photos. I could tell practically the exact moment the images hit social media, because all of a sudden college students flooded the streets, dashing out of their classes to see what all the fuss was about. People crowded onto the porch of the general store, craning to see the spectacle that was us. I spotted Calhoun's father and Emilio's parents and Coach Maynard. Reverend Quinn and his wife, too, along with the real estate developer, Wesley Thrush, and plenty of strangers.

Oh well, I thought, at least we'd saved the sheep. That made all the public humiliation worth it, right?

When we finally reached the farm, I ducked under Calhoun's arm and ran inside the barn, returning with a rope halter and the real grain can. I shook it hard.

"Snack time, ladies!" I called. As the sheep surged forward toward me, I slipped a rope halter over Beatrice, who as the biggest and bossiest of the ewes was the unofficial flock leader. Where she went, the rest would follow. At least I hoped they would.

I tugged her toward the rear of the barn, making encouraging sounds at the Ladies of American History.

Sure enough, they trotted obediently after Beatrice, and I led them all down around the back to the lower door, and from there straight into their pen. Gramps fastened the gate securely behind us.

"Well done, Truly-in-the-Middle," said my father, clapping me on the back. "I couldn't have done better myself."

I beamed. This was high praise, coming from him.

"You've got the makings of a natural shepherdess," added Gramps.

My smile faded and I made a face. Just the career path I never dreamed of.

A crowd gathered as the rest of the human chain joined us. Emilio came over with my friends to congratulate me.

"I've never seen anything like that at home in Milan," he said. "A sheep parade!"

"Uh, yeah, right," I replied, imagining more bumpkin reports filtering back to his friends in Milan.

We all hung out for a while, watching the flock munch on a late lunch of hay with a bit of grain for dessert. Gramps gave an impromptu lecture about sheep's stomachs and how, about an hour from now, they'd basically regurgitate or barf up their meal, which by then would be called "cud," and then they'd sit around chewing it over again to extract even more nutrients. This grossed everyone out except the boys, who shrieked and hooted in delight.

A short while later, a school bus rumbled into the driveway.

TRULY, MADLY, SHEEPLY

"Your ride back to town is here, folks!" Principal Burnside announced. "All aboard!"

My father turned to me as my classmates and friends from town dispersed. "Ready to go?"

I shook my head. "If it's okay with you, I think I'll stay here. Class was almost over anyway, and I've got some chores to do and I might take a nap. It's been a long day."

He nodded. "I'll let Gramps and Lola know."

"Oh, and can you please ask Cha Cha to get Lauren to drop my backpack at the bookstore after school? Gramps can bring it home to me tonight."

The bus pulled out of the driveway in a flurry of horn toots and jubilant shouts. Calhoun waved at me and so did Emilio. Clark Barque leaned out one of the windows and snapped a few final photos of the farm. The newspaper headline was practically writing itself: *Great Sheep Escape Has a Happy Ending!*

I gave a final wave and turned toward the house. It was time for Truly Lovejoy, private eye, to learn how to pick a lock.

CHAPTER 17

I was wrong about the headline. It was much worse.

"PUMPKIN FALLS HAS A NEW SUPERHERO!" yodeled Scooter, flapping the *Pumpkin Falls Patriot-Bugle* over his head and capering around our homeroom. "DARING YOUNG SHEPHERDESS SAVES THE DAY!"

"Shut up, Scooter," I told him.

He ignored me, of course. "Truly Drooly strikes again!"

I gave him a withering look as my classmates dissolved into laughter. He'd promised not to use Hatcher's horrid nickname for me, but Scooter could never resist being—well, Scooter.

As if the blaring headline wasn't bad enough, thanks to Clark Barque and his camera, my face was plastered all over the front page. The photograph was huge and showed me shaking a maraca in one hand and brandishing the rescue hook from the pool in the other. I looked like a demented Macy's Thanksgiving Day Parade balloon.

"We're laughing with you, not at you," said Calhoun, lying through his teeth. Beside him, Lucas tried and failed to stifle a giggle. "C'mon, can't you take a joke? It's not that bad. All's well that ends well, right?"

I glared at him in response. How dare he quote Shakespeare at me!

"Calhoun's right," said Jasmine. "Nice ink."

Emilio raised his eyebrows at this.

"You know, 'ink' as in the ink they use to print newspapers?" said Jasmine. "It's what reporters say to each other when someone writes a good story."

"Ah, *si*." Emilio nodded. "Yes, very good story. You are the town hero, Truly. Or perhaps I should say, superhero."

He smirked at me. I made a rude noise as my friends dissolved into laughter again.

Calhoun punched me lightly on the arm. "How'd it go with the lock-picking?"

"Wait, that I understand," said Emilio, whipping around and raising his eyebrows at me again. "You picked a lock?"

I opened my mouth, then shut it again. There was a price to be paid for humiliating me. "I'll tell you at lunchtime," I replied loftily. "Maybe."

"Okay, you guys want to hear about it?" I said later in the cafeteria, finally relenting. My friends nodded, all ears, except for Emilio, whose father had scooped him up for a dentist appointment. I began to relate yesterday afternoon's events.

After the bus had left, I'd gone into the house and changed into my barn clothes. Then I checked in on the sheep—all still present and accounted for, gates still firmly latched—and made a beeline across the pumpkin field for the shed.

The farm was deserted, of course, which in some ways was even creepier during the daytime. At least Gramps and Lola and Miss Marple had been there when I'd crept out of bed to investigate last night. Now, it was just me and a flock of sheep. Plus the chickens. None of whom were likely to be any help at all in protecting me from potential intruders. Or boggarts.

Benedick would, maybe. I briefly contemplated returning to the barn and seeing if I could get him to come along with me, but quickly abandoned the idea. Even though Theresa the sheep whisperer had said the ram was really just a "big love"—she'd used those exact words, "big love"—he looked like anything but to me. Plus, with my luck, he'd just run off, or trample me.

Put your big-girl pants on, Truly, I'd told myself. *Breathe in, breathe out.* I'd forced myself to swing my arms jauntily and admire the view. It was another beautiful October day. Elmer's prize pumpkin was practically glowing in the sun, which was warm enough that I barely needed my jacket. Over at the edge of the field, a breeze chased the brightly colored leaves on the trees. It was ridiculous to feel afraid.

Still, the quicker I got this over with, the quicker I could retreat to the house, or better yet, to the barn, where I could sit in safety with the sheep like Fern in *Charlotte's Web*. They'd do for company until my grandparents and Miss Marple got home.

When I reached the shed, I gave the door a tug—still locked, of course—then fished Danny's book out of my back pocket, where thankfully I'd stashed it after lunch. I propped it open next to the doorsill. Taking a pair of large paper clips I'd brought with me out of another pocket, I settled down to work.

For a while the only sound was the rustling of leaves in the trees overhead and my own quiet breathing. Lock-picking was fiddly work. Periodically, I'd refer to the instructions in the book, then squat back down again and peer at the padlock while I inserted the paper clips, twisting and turning them as instructed. The breeze blew my hair in my eyes, and I pushed it back. I hadn't concentrated so hard on something since I'd tried to learn to knit last spring break, and all that had gotten me was a misshapen pair of socks. I was hoping this would turn out better.

The minutes ticked by. Finally, after a number of false starts, there was a *click*.

"Hey!" I exclaimed, sitting back on my heels in surprise. I'd done it!

I rose to my feet and unclasped the padlock, then grabbed the door handle and gave it a tug, wincing as it made the same unearthly screech that had frightened me last night. The noise sent my heart racing again, even in broad daylight. I glanced over my shoulder, then told myself not to be silly. No one was watching me. There wasn't anyone around for miles.

At least I was pretty sure there wasn't anyone around.

Or any*thing*.

Firmly pushing thoughts of a possible boggart away, I opened the door wider and slipped into the shed. A dim light filtered through the dirt-smeared windows, and I had to wait for a moment or two for my eyes to adjust. Then I made the rounds, lifting the tarp on every single one of the antique vehicles crammed inside, looking for stolen goods. But there was no sign of a single pumpkin, missing or otherwise.

If the lock-picking had been a triumph, the end result was not. There was nothing, nada, zip. I'd come up completely empty-handed in the stolen jack-o'-lantern department.

"Back to the drawing board, I guess," I told my friends, who were leaning in around the lunchroom table listening to my report. Their glum expressions mirrored mine.

"I guess that rules out Elmer as a suspect," said Cha Cha.

"Yeah. Unless he's got another hidey-hole somewhere around town," I replied. "He'd find it pretty difficult to stash stolen pumpkins in his new apartment over the general store, though."

"Um," said Jasmine, slanting me a glance as she plucked a potato chip from her lunch bag, "are you one-hundred-percent sure that Hatcher didn't take them?"

"Of course I am!" I said hotly. "How could you even say that?"

"I know, I know." She waved her potato chip at me. "It's just—don't you think it's weird that no more jack-o'-lanterns have disappeared since Officer Tanglewood questioned him? If Hatcher's not the thief, the real one must be pretty smart. By not stealing any more pumpkins, he—or she—is making it look like your brother is guilty, *and* making it harder to prove that he's innocent."

Jasmine would make a good lawyer someday, I thought. Her parents would be proud. It was true, though. I'd thought the same thing myself. But I wasn't about to admit it.

The thing was, I really needed to talk to Hatcher.

CHAPTER 18

After school, I finally got my chance.

"I forgot the sheet music for my piano lesson," I told my father, stashing my backpack behind the bookshop's sales counter. "Gotta run home for a minute. I'll be right back."

He nodded absently, too busy helping Lola unload a shipment of books to pay close attention. Not that it would be awful if he knew my real reason for heading home. It wasn't as if Hatcher was off-limits or anything, or even officially grounded. My father—both my parents, and my grandparents, and all of us—were giving him the benefit of the doubt. "Innocent until proven guilty," as my mother put it. "And we know he's innocent."

I just didn't want to draw attention to our visit. Better to keep it off the radar.

I ran all the way home. The last time I'd run up Main Street was for the Four on the Fourth road race in July, and

TRULY, MADLY, SHEEPLY

I arrived sweaty and panting. My brother had better be home after all that.

"Hatcher!" I hollered as I burst through the front door.

My voice rang through an empty house. I knew my mother was in a class at the college, and I was pretty sure that Lauren and Pippa were down the street visiting Belinda Winchester, who was fostering a new batch of kittens. Danny was at his after-school job in West Hartfield, and Lauren had told me he had plans afterward with his girlfriend, who'd volunteered to drive him home. Gramps's old truck was in the driveway, the one my brothers were using while he and Lola were in Africa, which according to my calculations meant that Hatcher should be here.

I took the stairs two at a time, not even bothering to run through my usual singsong repetition of my ancestors' names as I passed their portraits. Dashing down the upstairs hall, I yanked open the door at the bottom of the attic stairs and poked my head in. "Hatcher!" I hollered again.

I heard a muffled grunt.

"Didn't you hear me calling you?" I demanded, pounding up the stairs. I skidded to a halt at the top. After we'd moved in last winter, my brothers had taken over the entire attic, and they used the large open space as a combination bedroom and gym. It smelled like a gym, too, I thought, wrinkling my nose. The center of the room was covered with mats for wrestling practice, and a jumble of free weights and jump ropes were scattered around like an obstacle course. Hatcher's bed was tucked under the eaves. He was lying on it with his earbuds in, listening to music and reading the graphic-novel version of *Redwall*. Comfort reading, apparently, as that had been one of his favorite series back in fourth and fifth grade.

"Hey," I said. "I was hoping you'd be here."

My brother propped himself up on his elbow and popped an earbud out. "Hey." The smile he gave me in return wasn't his usual broad sunflower smile. Halfhearted at best, it was gone almost as quickly as it appeared. Silence hung between us for a long moment.

"Um," I said finally, suddenly feeling awkward. "Can we talk?"

He lifted a shoulder. "About what?"

"About the missing jack-o'-lanterns, duh."

"What's the point?" My brother flopped back down again.

"The point is, you're being framed for something you didn't do! Don't you want me to help?"

"There's nothing you can do, Drooly. Ella's made her mind up; she has the video as evidence, and that's that."

I stared at him, frowning. This was totally unlike Hatcher. He was usually in the front line of battle when there was an injustice to be corrected. How could he be so resigned?

"Of course there's something we can do!" I insisted. "We can find out who really did it!"

He shook his head. "Not going to happen."

"What do you mean? Why not?"

He didn't reply, but just lifted a shoulder again. My eyes narrowed. Was he trying to protect someone?

I took a deep breath. "Can you at least tell me straight-up if you did it or not? I mean, I know you didn't, but . . ." My voice trailed off.

He gave me a look. One that said, *You of all people should know me better than that by now.* Then he put his earbud back in and turned his face to the wall.

I'd never known Hatcher not to want to talk to me. Something was wrong. *Very* wrong. "Hatcher, I—"

He made a show of picking up *Redwall* again, pointedly ignoring me. I'd been dismissed.

I opened my mouth to say something more, then closed it again. My brother could be stubborn as all get-out when his mind was made up, and he'd clearly made his mind up not to talk to me. Heaving a sigh, I retreated back down to the second floor, closing the attic door behind me. I leaned against it for a moment, unsure of what I should do. There had to be some way to get him to talk to me!

Not when he was like this, though.

I pondered our brief conversation as I walked back to the bookshop. Hatcher wasn't the pumpkin snatcher. I was certain of it, now more than ever.

But I was also certain—beyond a shadow of a doubt—that he was hiding something. The question, though, was what?

CHAPTER 19

"It's amazing how quickly you can get things done when you throw money at a problem," Gramps marveled as we watched a line of trucks pull into the driveway at Rivercroft Farm bright and early Thursday morning.

"No kidding," agreed my father, who'd driven up from town to help with the project launch.

Aunt True and Uncle Rusty knew about the wedding present that we were all giving them—money to help fix up the barn—but what they didn't know was that Gramps and my father had arranged for a construction crew to fast-track the work, so that we could surprise them with the completed repairs when they returned from Scotland.

My father and Gramps headed down to the barn to talk to the crew supervisor. I trailed along behind them, yawning. It was early—six a.m. But I had to get up anyway for morning chores, and I was curious to see our secret project get underway before swim practice.

Within minutes, a dozen men and women were unloading their trucks and piling the driveway and surrounding area high with timber and roof shingles and other materials.

"Got to make a mess to clean one up sometimes," said Lola, who'd come up behind me. She was still in her fleece bathrobe, but had exchanged slippers for barn boots. She tucked her arm through mine. "It'll be worth it in the end, though."

I listened as Gramps gave the crew careful instructions not to disturb the owls. "They won't bother you if you don't bother them," he said. "Just give them a wide berth."

The chickens, he told them, could fend for themselves and come and go as they pleased, but we'd transfer the sheep to the pasture during the hours they were here.

"They'll be out of harm's way," Gramps said a few minutes later, as the two of us led the ewes outside. "Don't want to rattle the flock."

Benedick was obstinate at first about leaving his pen—he could hear the pounding of the construction crew's footsteps upstairs and was apparently eager to keep a sharp eye on them—but we managed to coax him outside, too, with the help of the grain can.

"There you are, sir," said Gramps, closing the gate to the

smaller pasture next to the one where we'd stashed the ewes. "Front-row seat to all the proceedings."

"Do you really think the construction crew can finish before Aunt True and Uncle Rusty get back?" I asked a few minutes later over breakfast.

"If the good Lord's willing and the creek don't rise," my father replied, quoting one of his favorite Johnny Cash songs. "The weather's supposed to hold for the most part, which is one thing in their favor. We may get a day or two of rain, but other than that it's nothing but clear skies predicted through Halloween."

Aunt True and Uncle Rusty were due back a week from tomorrow, on Halloween morning, just in time for the town's mammoth celebration. From what I'd overheard Gramps and my father discussing down at the bookstore, I knew that in addition to the fleet of pickup trucks that now crowded the driveway, there'd be some big machinery arriving before long to help shore up the foundation and straighten the barn's structure. Beyond that there was the roof to replace, broken windows to repair, clapboards to mend, and paint to be applied. Plus probably a bazillion other invisible jobs once they got a close look inside. I didn't see how it could be done in a week.

It was hard to believe that Aunt True and Uncle Rusty were almost halfway through their honeymoon. Gramps and Lola and I had videoconferenced with them twice since they'd left last weekend—both times more because they wanted to hear all about their sheep. They'd been watching the lamb cam, of course, ever since Gramps got it set up, but they wanted details, and naturally we'd obliged them.

We'd heard about their stay in Edinburgh ("dreamy," according to my aunt) and their time in Glasgow ("impressive architecture and museums," said my new uncle). The more they talked about their trip, the more it made me want to travel to Scotland someday. I'd spent a fair amount of time abroad, thanks to my dad's overseas postings—more than most other kids my age, except for other army brats. We'd traveled all over France and Italy while we were stationed in Germany, and we'd visited London once, but we hadn't made it north to Scotland. Aunt True made it sound like a magical place.

The rest of their honeymoon was scheduled to be spent exploring the highlands as they made their way across the country to the Isle of Skye, stopping at sheep farms all along the way. From there they'd take a ferry to the Outer Hebrides, and specifically the island of Lewis and Harris, which had two names but was actually just one place. They were supposed to visit a crofting family there who were friends with one of my aunt's college roommates, where they'd stay in their holiday rental and pick up more tips about raising sheep.

During our last call, Gramps had confessed about the sheep escaping. I was pretty sure that half of Pumpkin Falls heard Aunt True's shriek all the way from Scotland.

"Dad!" she'd yelled. "You were supposed to make sure the gates were shut!"

"I did! Honestly, I did. Truly was there with me—we both double-checked."

I nodded vigorously.

"Who let them out, then?"

"It wasn't me," said Lola.

"We don't know," said Gramps. "We're still trying to get to the bottom of it. The lamb cam only showed the gate swinging open. Which I suppose might have happened on its own if the latch was loose."

"Boggart," muttered Uncle Rusty.

"There's no such thing as a boggart, Rusty," Aunt True said automatically. "Don't be a numpty."

"What's a numpty?" I asked.

"It's a Scottish expression we learned the other day," she told me. "It means a numbskull or nitwit. Someone who lacks common sense."

"Hey!" Uncle Rusty protested. "I have plenty of common sense!"

"Not if you believe in boggarts, you don't."

Numpty. I liked the sound of that one.

While there'd been no further sheep escapes, other worrisome things had been happening around the farm. On Monday evening, Lola had discovered salt in the sugar jar and sugar in the salt container. She'd blamed herself for the switch, but my grandmother was and always had been as sharp as a tack, so

I had a hard time believing that. When her paint brushes all disappeared on Tuesday, she chalked it up to absentmindedness, but was she really absentminded enough to stick them in one of Gramps's barn boots? That's where they'd turned up yesterday morning, along with Gramps's other barn boot that had gone missing from the mudroom two days ago. I'd stumbled over them in the middle of the driveway on my way to the barn for early morning chores. They were filled with water—and there hadn't been any rain all week.

None of us said anything on the video calls about these strange happenings. Nor did I bring up the light I'd seen outside, or the fact that a still-unidentified someone had been in the shed. No one needed to know about that, including Gramps and Lola. I didn't want anyone discovering that I'd picked the lock.

"I know we don't want to worry them on their honeymoon," Lola had said, "but I have to admit I'm beginning to wonder...."

"Now, sweetheart, True is right—there's no such thing as a boggart," Gramps told her firmly.

"I know, I know. But it sure seems that someone—or something—doesn't want us here."

"Don't worry," he assured her. "We'll get to the bottom of it."

I certainly hoped so. Because, like Lola, I was beginning to wonder too.

CHAPTER 20

It was Friday night before I saw Hatcher again. Our whole family had gathered at the bookstore to help with another of Aunt True's schemes for getting more customers in the door. This time it was something she'd launched last summer—a board-game night, or "Family Fun Friday!" as she called it.

Held once a month, the event wasn't just aimed at families. Aunt True wanted to cast a wider net, as she put it. Plastered across the posters and newspaper ads beneath the picture of Miss Marple with her paw on a Scrabble board was the tagline *Come one, come all—everyone is family here in Pumpkin Falls!*

As usual, my father had been skeptical about the idea, and as usual, my aunt had been right. The kickoff had been warmly received and was beginning to attract a loyal following. Actually, it was pretty fun, and none of us minded giving up an occasional Friday night to help out. Even Danny had rearranged his after-school job schedule to be available.

TRULY, MADLY, SHEEPLY

As word had gotten out in our community, reservations had increased and we were fully booked through November. People had to register ahead of time, so we knew how many tables to set up, although Aunt True left what she called "wiggle room" for a few walk-ins. There was no fee to play the games, but if you wanted snacks—and they were good ones—you had to show proof that at least one person in your family or your group had bought a book.

So far, it had worked like a charm.

"Your sister is a marketing whiz!" Lola marveled to my father as tonight's customers began streaming in.

"Mm-hmm," he replied. "I have to give her that." He turned to my mother. "What have you rustled up for snacks?" My mother and Lauren, who loved to bake, were in charge of food for the events.

"Since the theme tonight is classic board games, we thought we'd go with old-school snacks," she replied, proceeding to tick the items off on her fingers. "Homemade caramel popcorn and chocolate chip cookies, although I did add something special to the lineup—apple fritter cake. For the healthy eaters, there's the usual veggies and hummus, of course, along with sliced apples. Plus we're serving cold and hot apple cider, and Augustus is going to whip up salted caramel lattes for those who want one, but they'll cost a little extra."

"Your mother's apple fritter cake?" asked my father. She

nodded and he leaned down and kissed her cheek. "I married the right woman."

As he and my mother and Lola moved toward the door to begin greeting customers, I opened the cash register and got ready to start ringing up sales. Over at the Cup and Chaucer counter, Augustus, looking uncharacteristically casual in a purple fleece instead of his usual purple cape, was firing up the barista station while Hatcher set out paper cups for the apple cider.

Registration for tonight's event was our largest ever, and before long we were bursting at the seams. All of the Pumpkin Falls Private Eyes were here, along with their parents and siblings, and the Frangipanis had come, too. Emilio spotted me and waved. So did Calhoun. The realtor from West Hartfield who'd helped Aunt True and Uncle Rusty buy the farm had come along as well, with her family. She made a beeline for Gramps when she spotted him.

"If your daughter and her new husband ever want to sell, the retired couple from New York City are still interested in the property," I heard her tell him. "And please tell her they're willing to pay—a lot."

Gramps thanked her politely and told her he'd pass the message along.

Just as we'd done for Aunt True's wedding reception, we'd pushed the freestanding bookshelves against the walls, clearing the middle of the store. My father and brothers had set up large tables, each one devoted to a different board game. I heard Scooter groan when he learned there wouldn't be a table for Settlers of Catan or Ticket to Ride tonight, his favorites, but his mother shushed him. He opted for Monopoly instead and took a seat between Mr. Henry and Bud Jefferson. Elmer and Thelma Farnsworth chose that table, too, along with Emilio and his parents. They probably had Monopoly in Italy.

Not surprisingly, given the fact that he was such a Shakespeare fanatic, Dr. Calhoun went for Scrabble. A game was already underway at his table, where Lucas and his mother had settled in alongside Annie Freeman, the Mahoneys, Denise from the Klip 'n' Kurl, and a bunch of other people I didn't recognize. I could hear the click of tiles as Calhoun's father set them down on the board. "Knave!" he called. "Double letter score for the *K*."

Calhoun and his sister, Juliet, meanwhile, had joined the Clue table, where I spotted Coach Maynard and his wife next to Clark Barque and Ms. Matthews, my Language Arts teacher. She was the reporter's date for the evening, which felt really weird and embarrassing, because teachers weren't supposed to have lives outside of school.

The only person from our regular crowd that I didn't see was Ella Bellow, who, until the whole mess with Hatcher was cleared up, was *persona non grata* with our family. "An unwelcome person," Gramps had said, explaining the term. "She knows better than to come over here right now, so she's keeping a low profile."

From my vantage point at the sales counter, I could see a light on in her knitting store across the street. Being excluded from the fun must have been killing her. *Serves her right,* I thought, then smothered a grin as I imagined her squatting behind one of her yarn displays with a pair of binoculars, trying to lip-read. Family Fun Friday was the perfect opportunity to gather gossip.

"You have customers, Truly," my father called, crossing back toward the sales counter and nodding toward the children's area, where Jasmine and Cha Cha were waiting for me to help supervise Candyland and Sorry! "I'll take over here."

I'd been hoping to get a chance to talk with Hatcher before taking up my evening's duties, but it didn't look like that was going to happen. I glanced over to Cup and Chaucer and waggled my fingers, trying to catch his eye. Nothing. I couldn't tell if he was deliberately ignoring me or just didn't see me. I hoped it was the latter.

Augustus didn't respond, either. He was busy chatting up the realtor from West Hartfield. He was giving her what Hatcher called "the full Augustus"—leaning in close and turning up the wattage on his smile as he combed his fingers through his artfully long silver locks. The poor thing didn't stand a chance. I watched as Augustus came out from behind the counter and maneuvered his dazzled prey over to "Miss

Marple's Picks," the shelf of recommended books that had made my grandparents' golden retriever famous. Aunt True had hit a home run with that one, and Miss Marple's image, with a pair of reading glasses perched on the end of her long nose, graced our shop's bookmarks, newsletter, and website.

Augustus had been at his guerrilla marketing again, I noticed, sneaking his books from the romance section over to that prominent shelf. In no time at all he smooth-talked the realtor into buying his complete Heart's Ease trilogy, which he autographed for her on the spot with a flourish.

"To Doris Wheeler, with my heartfelt thanks," said Augustus, reading his own inscription aloud as he wrote. He signed each book with his pen name, "Augusta Savage," and handed the pile to her with a wink.

"We should hire Augustus," my father said, as we watched the realtor clutch her purchase and scurry back to her chair, breathless from her close encounter with a real-live celebrity.

"Why?" I replied. "He practically lives here anyway."

It was true. Wherever Belinda went, Augustus wasn't far behind. He still managed to churn out bestsellers, though, and I often saw him tucked into a corner of the bookstore, tapping away on his laptop while Belinda worked the cash register or straightened shelves in the mystery section, her favorite, or tried to foist a kitten off on an unsuspecting customer.

We weren't the only ones watching Augustus. "So when are you two going to tie the knot?" bellowed Elmer Farnsworth as I made my way to the children's area. He still had a tendency to talk loudly despite his new hearing aids.

Augustus grabbed Belinda around her ample waist and pulled her close. "None of your beeswax, Elmer!" he bellowed back, planting a smooch on his beloved's wrinkled cheek.

"Ew," Jasmine said under her breath.

"You have to admit it's kinda cute," whispered Cha Cha.

"No, I don't."

They grinned at each other.

"Thanks for helping out tonight," I said, sliding into an open seat. I glanced back at Elmer, wondering if maybe I could corner him later and ask a few questions about his shed. Like who else might have a key to it, for starters.

"You bet," boomed Cha Cha, reaching down and fishing Baxter out from underneath the table. "It's a nice break for my parents."

She nodded toward the Scrabble table. Mr. and Mrs. Abramowitz were sitting next to Lauren, who had joined her friend Annie Freeman.

"Yeah, and for Lauren too," I said virtuously. I'd volunteered for the kids' table duty to give her a break.

"Q-U-E-T-Z-A-L!" Annie shouted triumphantly, clacking down her tiles. "It's a bird—Truly showed me a picture of it in a book. Triple letter score for the *Q*, plus a double word score!"

I was pretty sure that Dr. Calhoun didn't stand a

chance against the reigning Grafton County Junior Spelling Champion.

Lauren saw me watching them and waved. I waved back, glad to see that she was enjoying herself. To be honest, my motive for volunteering tonight wasn't entirely unselfish. I'd come straight from doing my chores in the barn and figured it would be better if I stayed downwind.

"Sorry if I'm kind of smelly," I told my friends, explaining my predicament.

Cha Cha leaned over and gave me the sniff test. "Yep," she said. "You're ripe."

"Shhhh!" I whispered furiously, slanting a glance into the main room and hoping no one had heard her. Especially not Calhoun and Emilio. "You don't have to advertise it!"

Just as we'd finally gotten little bottoms into little chairs and settled into our first game of Candyland, Belinda came by with a basket of kittens.

"Hey!" Jasmine cried as all the kids jumped up to admire the furry visitors. "No fair!"

"Resistance is futile," I told her, quoting one of Hatcher's favorite lines from *Star Trek*.

As Belinda squatted down, bringing her basket level with the circle of small faces, I felt a tap on my shoulder. I looked up to see Emilio standing there with a paper cup in his hand.

"Salted caramel latte?" he asked. "Decaf, of course, since we have a swim meet tomorrow morning."

Jasmine nudged her knee against mine under the table and gave me a mischievous "I told you so" grin, her dark eyes gleaming.

Ignoring her, I took the cup. "Uh, sure. Thanks." Out of the corner of my eye I could see Calhoun watching us from where he was playing Clue. A moment later he pushed back from his chair and made a beeline for the snacks, then strolled over to join us.

"How about some caramel corn?" he asked, thrusting a plastic baggie full at me while simultaneously scowling at Emilio.

"Um," I said, giving them both a weak smile. It was undeniably flattering being fought over, but I had a major problem. I was pretty sure that the aroma I was giving off was more *Eau de Sheep* than *Eau de Please Be My Boyfriend*.

I was literally saved by the bell as my father rang the one on the sales counter and called, "Snack time!" I stood up abruptly as the board-game players stampeded toward the food.

"Thanks, guys, gotta go to work now!" The two of them watched, puzzled, as I scuttled past and headed over to join my father and Lola.

I could feel my cheeks burning as I busied myself setting out paper plates with slices of apple fritter cake on them. Mr. Henry was first in line, and his eyebrows shot up as he took a bite.

"I'm going to need this recipe," he mumbled with his mouth full.

"It's pretty great, right? It's my Grandma Gifford's." I jerked my thumb toward my mother, who was helping Hatcher hand out cups of cider. "She's the one to ask."

The bells over the front door jangled just then and I looked over to see Officer Tanglewood walk in.

And then the fireworks began.

"Here you go, Hank," said Lola, passing him a slice of apple cake.

"Oh, I couldn't," he protested, eyeing it greedily. "I just came by to check and make sure you weren't over your occupancy limit." He gave a nervous chuckle. "Town ordinances, you know."

Town ordinances, my big size-ten-and-a-half foot, I thought crossly as my grandmother ignored his protests and shoved a paper plate into his hand. The real reason Officer Tanglewood had stopped by was for the snacks, and everybody knew it. He was famous for timing his trips to the bookshop to coincide with whenever Aunt True pulled something fresh from the oven. He'd proven repeatedly that he'd be happy to eat us out of house and home—well, bookshop.

"Numpty," I said under my breath.

Mr. Henry looked over at me in surprise and then burst out laughing. "Where on earth did you learn that expression?

Oh wait, let me guess—your aunt is in Scotland on her honeymoon, right?"

I nodded.

"Well, it's a good one." He leaned closer and whispered. "And you're right—Hank can definitely be a numpty sometimes!"

Cha Cha and Jasmine had managed to pry our little charges away from Belinda's basket of kittens and were herding them toward the snacks. Pippa froze when she spotted the policeman.

"IS OFFICER TANGLEWOOD GOING TO ARREST HATCHER AGAIN?" she wailed.

"He didn't arrest him the first time," Lauren told her, exasperated. "He just questioned him."

Pippa's sobs escalated. "I DON'T WANT HATCHER TO GO TO JAIL!"

"Nobody's going to jail, sweetheart," my mother said, swooping in to try to soothe her.

The rest of the tables fell silent as my little sister's wails rocketed toward a full-blown meltdown. I saw Clark Barque reach into the pocket of his pants for his reporter's notebook. So did my father. He crossed to the Clue table and stared down at him, arms crossed. The reporter wilted under his stern gaze.

"Family matter," my father told him. "Not a word of this in the newspaper."

The reporter sheepishly slid his notebook back into his pocket. "No, sir."

TRULY, MADLY, SHEEPLY

Everybody fell in line when Lieutenant Colonel Jericho T. Lovejoy issued an order. Even the press.

Everybody except Pippa, that was. She was the only one of us Lovejoy kids who could get away without replying "Yes, sir" to our father's orders. It was the blond curls, Hatcher said. Resistance was futile.

My father turned to her. "Pipe down now, Pippa."

"I CAN'T PIPE DOWN!" she howled. And still wailing like a siren, she grabbed Baxter Abramowitz by the hand and ran out of the bookshop.

CHAPTER 21

My mother sighed. "Would you please go after her, Truly?"

"Sure." I trotted out the door after them. "Pippa!" I called, looking up and down Main Street.

There was no answer, and no sign of my little sister or Baxter. They'd vanished.

"Pippa!" I called again, frowning. The street was pretty much deserted. Very few businesses downtown besides ours were still open at this time of night. Even though I knew that Pumpkin Falls was one of the safest places on earth, it was still a little eerie and I felt a clutch of panic as I peered into the darkness. *Where was she?*

Then the door to A Stitch in Time flew open and Ella Bellow stuck her head out. "They went that way," she told me in a stage whisper, pointing toward the Starlite Dance Studio.

I opened my mouth and then closed it again. I couldn't do it—I couldn't bring myself to say thank you. Not after what she'd done to Hatcher. Fortunately, Ella didn't wait for me to say anything, but withdrew immediately back inside and closed the door.

Checking for cars, I crossed the street and approached the dance studio. The silver pumpkin trophy from last summer's road race gleamed under the light in the window, but other than that it, too, was dark. Which made total sense, since Cha Cha's parents were back at the bookshop playing board games.

Where else could Pippa and Baxter have gone? I hoped they hadn't run off toward the covered bridge. I knew from experience how dangerous that could be at night.

"Try the treehouse!" boomed Cha Cha behind me.

Her deep voice startled me, and I jumped. "Duh. Of course!"

It was just a few short blocks to the Abramowitzes' house. The two of us jogged along and I shivered, wishing I'd brought my jacket. October nights in New Hampshire were chilly.

When we reached Cha Cha's house, sure enough, there was a light coming from one of the trees in the backyard.

"Pippa!" I called, crossing to the base of it.

There was a squeak of dismay from above.

"DON'T COME UP!" Baxter hollered.

I ignored him and started climbing. Cha Cha was right behind me. Reaching the wooden platform that the treehouse was built on, I managed to squeeze myself through the hole that had been cut in it. Standing up, I immediately banged my head against the ceiling. "Ouch!" I said, wincing. Mr. Abramowitz had not designed the structure for a six-foot-tall eighth grader. Crouching down, I looked around. "Hey, it's pretty cool up here." Then I did a double-take. "Wait, is that Wally?"

Pippa was standing there clutching a jack-o'-lantern. And not just any jack-o'-lantern. It was unmistakably Wally, our missing bookstore scarecrow's pumpkin head.

"What's going on?" I demanded, as Cha Cha wriggled her way through the hole in the platform.

"Nothing," Pippa said miserably. I could tell she was on the verge of tears again.

"Pippa, I can *see* you. That's not nothing—that's Wally. Why is he up here?"

She and Baxter exchanged a glance. Neither of them said a word.

"Baxter," Cha Cha said firmly. "Out with it."

"We borrowed him," her little brother said in a small voice. "We wanted some company up here."

The light dawned on me. "And then you took Woolly too?"

They both nodded.

"Because Wally was lonely and needed a friend," my little sister confessed.

"I see," I said. "So when you 'borrowed' him, did Hatcher catch you?"

Pippa nodded. "We didn't mean to get him into trouble."

So my brother really *had* been putting Woolly back, just like he'd said! I knew it!

"What about the other pumpkins?" Cha Cha demanded.

Pippa and Baxter shook their heads. "That wasn't us," Baxter said. But his wobbly voice and the way his eyes slid over to my sister told me there was more to the story.

"Baxter," Cha Cha said again, "you need to tell us *everything*."

In reply, Pippa stepped over to the far side of the treehouse, where a white sheet was draped over something lumpy. Part of their fort, I'd figured.

Cha Cha and I gasped as Pippa twitched the sheet away. All of the missing jack-o'-lanterns were lined up beneath it on a makeshift bookshelf! Hagrid, Wilbur, Aslan, and more—they were all there, grinning at us.

"What the—?" I began.

"We didn't take them!" Pippa protested, and Baxter nodded vigorously in agreement.

"Who did, then?" demanded Cha Cha.

"It was our friends from school," her little brother replied.

"When we told them about Wally, they wanted him to have some company up here, too," Pippa explained.

"Wait, you're telling me that the infamous Pumpkin Falls pumpkin snatcher is actually a bunch of *first graders*?" My voice shot up an octave.

Beside me, Cha Cha broke out in a grin. "I can't wait to see Officer Tanglewood's face when we tell him. And Mackenzie's going to love this week's police blotter!"

Pippa turned as white as the sheet in her hand. "Don't tell Officer Tanglewood!" she begged.

I sighed. "Sweetie, we need to go back to the bookstore and clear this up right now. Hatcher's in a lot of trouble because of you."

The tears spilled over as my little sister started to cry. "I DON'T WANT HATCHER TO GO TO JAIL!"

I put my arm around her shoulders. "He's not going to jail, Pipster."

"I DON'T WANT TO GO TO JAIL, EITHER!"

Baxter looked like he might start crying, too, at this alarming thought.

"NOBODY is going to jail," I told them both. "I promise. Not you two, not Hatcher, not any of your friends. You kids just made a mistake, that's all. But the thing about mistakes is, you have to correct them. Just like when you're doing math problems. And that's what we're going to do right now."

I took Wally's jack-o'-lantern head from my little sister and then Cha Cha and I hustled them out of the treehouse, through the Abramowitzes' backyard, and back down Main Street to the bookshop. Game night was drawing to a close by now, but there were still far too many witnesses for my liking. I would have preferred what was coming to be family only, but there wasn't really any choice. It had to be done, for Hatcher's sake.

Everyone turned and stared as the four of us came through

the door. Cha Cha prodded Pippa and Baxter forward. I followed behind, Wally's head in hand.

"Wally!" cried Belinda, rushing over to us open-armed, as if welcoming a long-lost relative. She plucked the pumpkin from me joyfully. "You came home!"

"Um," I said, not sure how to respond.

Officer Tanglewood stared at us open-mouthed, which was particularly unattractive since he'd just taken a bite of apple fritter cake. His second piece, no doubt.

"You two are the thieves?" he said, staring at Pippa and Baxter in disbelief.

My little sister shook her head vigorously. "We didn't steal Wally, we just borrowed him."

"Then we thought he needed some company, so we tried to borrow Woolly, too," added Baxter, his voice barely a whisper. He was staring at his toes. "But Hatcher caught us."

I glanced over at my brother, who was watching the proceedings silently.

"There's more," said Cha Cha, and she poked her little brother, who reluctantly explained about the other jack-o'-lanterns.

Officer Tanglewood looked from Baxter to Pippa. He had an odd expression on his face, along with a smear of frosting. "I'd better go get Ella."

The two of them returned shortly. Ella had the grace to look embarrassed as the policeman explained the situation.

"You gonna have these two arrested along with the entire first-grade class, Ella?" asked Augustus Wilde.

"Well, uh, no," Ella said grudgingly, glancing down at the repentant duo. "I guess no harm has been done." She turned to my brother. "But why didn't you just tell us what happened?"

"I did, ma'am," said Hatcher. "I told you I was just trying to put Woolly back. You didn't believe me."

"But you didn't say that it was Pippa and Baxter who were the real thieves!" Catching sight of my father's expression, Ella hastily amended her words. "I mean, borrowers!"

"Mmmm," said Hatcher noncommittally.

I knew what that *mmmm* meant. It meant "No way was I going to throw my six-year-old sister under the bus." Lovejoys didn't rat each other out.

"And you didn't say a word about the other missing jack-o'-lanterns!" Ella added.

"I didn't know about them," Hatcher replied simply.

Ella raised a dark eyebrow. "I see. Well, I guess apologies are in order."

I noticed, however, that she didn't actually apologize.

To his credit, Hatcher was gracious about it. "Apology accepted, ma'am. It's not a big deal."

Yes it is, I thought. Would I have done the same thing, if I'd been the one to catch Pippa and Baxter in the act? Or would I have thrown them under the bus to save my own skin?

TRULY, MADLY, SHEEPLY

I was uncomfortably aware that the answer to that was probably the latter.

"Proud of you, son," said my father a little while later after Ella left and Officer Tanglewood went to call the rest of the first grader's parents. He clapped his good hand on my brother's back. "You handled that like a man."

Hatcher lifted a shoulder modestly, but I could tell he was pleased by the compliment.

The crowd thinned out quickly after that. Mr. Henry and Dr. Calhoun offered to help Cha Cha's father return the other jack o' lanterns to their rightful owners. Cha Cha's mother stayed to help with cleanup, and so did my friends.

Afterwards, my friends and I gathered by the Cup and Chaucer counter.

"There goes our reward," Scooter said glumly.

"You win some, you lose some," I said philosophically.

"At least the 'Case of the Purloined Pumpkins' has been solved," said Jasmine. She turned to Cha Cha and me. "And speaking of Edgar Allan Poe, should we practice this weekend for our presentation?"

We both nodded.

"How about after your swim meet tomorrow?" Jasmine suggested. "Maybe we could come out to the farm. You keep promising to show us around."

"Show you around where?" asked Emilio, drifting over to join us.

"Her aunt's new farm," said Cha Cha.

"Maybe we can have a sleepover?" I asked hopefully, glancing across the counter at Lola, who was putting the cider away.

My grandmother smiled and nodded. "Sure, why not?"

"Hey, what about us?" Scooter demanded. "We want to see the farm, too."

"Why don't you boys all come for brunch on Sunday?" my grandmother suggested. "I'll make waffles after church."

This met with an enthusiastic response, although it took a bit to explain "waffles" to Emilio.

Later, I lay in bed thinking back over the evening's unexpected events. Jasmine was right; at least the mystery of the pumpkin snatcher was solved. The boggart, however—or whoever was responsible for the shenanigans on the farm—was still on the loose.

This was definitely our toughest case yet!

CHAPTER 22

"So, are we ready for our dress rehearsal?" Cha Cha asked.

We were back on the farm after a successful swim meet. It had been a long afternoon, but definitely worth it. I'd finally gotten used to having Calhoun and Emilio as teammates, and between that and Hatcher now being off the hook for the pumpkin thefts, I'd swum well, coming in first in all three of my events. I even beat my own personal best time in the 100-meter butterfly.

"Ready as I'll ever be," I replied.

Cha Cha and Jasmine and I had decided to collaborate on a song-and-dance routine for our Language Arts project. Cha Cha had choreographed the dance, Jasmine was in charge of the lyrics, and I—well, I was pretty much just along for the ride. Dancing was not exactly my strong point—in fact, it was way up on the list of things I wasn't good at, although I was better at it than when I'd first moved to Pumpkin Falls, thanks to last winter's required cotillion classes. Unlike Jasmine, I wasn't great at writing lyrics, either, but it turned out I was pretty good at coming up with ideas. Like using the chorus to ABBA's "Mamma Mia" for the tune. It was one of my mom's favorite classic pop tunes, and its catchy beat made it perfect for shaping lyrics to.

So far, the presentations our classmates had come up with had all been pretty creative. Lucas and Emilio, who it turned out could draw almost as well as Lucas, which was not surprising considering Mrs. Frangipani's job, had created a huge poster-size mural of what they imagined the cellar looked like, with the bones in the walls and everything. It gave me the creeps just looking at it. And after being interrupted earlier in the week when the sheep escaped, Calhoun and Scooter had finally had a chance to present their final scene, the one where the main character walls up his friend, hamming it up for all they were worth.

The three of us ran through our presentation in my bedroom one more time, then we put on our black capes and droopy black mustaches and trooped downstairs. Gramps and Lola were waiting for us on the living room sofa. We lined up in front of them, bowing deeply.

"Presenting the Edgarettes!" Cha Cha announced. She placed her cell phone on the coffee table and tapped it to start the music. I watched her out of the corner of my eye, waiting for my cue to start dancing. And then we were off!

TRULY, MADLY, SHEEPLY

"Edgar Allan! There you go again.
Poe, Poe—how can we forgive you?
Edgar Allan! Does it show again?
Poe, Poe—how much we resent you.
Yes, we've read Amontillado,
Since Ms. Matthews said we had to.
Why, why did we ever give in?
Haven't slept a wink since then!
Just one book and I can hear a raven sing
One more book and I forget everything. . . .
Edgar Allan, we just want to know—
Why, why do you write such creepy stories?
Fortunato's double-crossed by his friend—
Who walls him up at the very end—
Edgar Allan, there you go again
Poe, Poe, with your crazy stories!"

The verses went on for a while, and by the time we all swooped down on one knee for the big finale, my grandparents were laughing so hard they were crying.

"I think, girls, that you have captured the essence of Edgar Allan Poe," said Gramps, wiping his eyes.

"Well done, you three!" Lola agreed. "If your teacher doesn't give you an A-plus for this, I'm going to march down to the school and give her a piece of my mind."

Gramps glanced at his watch. "Do you and your friends

want to visit the barn again before supper, Truly? I can do the final check on them later tonight."

"Sure."

"Lock everything up tight when you come in," he reminded me.

"Yes, sir." After the great sheep escape, there was no way I was going to forget that.

The construction crew had left a mess behind, and we picked our way around piles of lumber and sacks of concrete in the driveway on our way to the barn. They were making progress, though. The whole structure was straight again, thanks to the big machinery that had clanked down the driveway yesterday morning and tugged it back into place.

"It doesn't look like it's trying to run away anymore," I said.

"Huh?" Jasmine gave me a blank look.

"Nothing." Inside the barn, I flipped on the light and led my friends down the rickety wooden staircase to the sheep pens on the lower level.

"Can we see the owls, too?" asked Cha Cha.

I shook my head. "They're probably out hunting. We'll have better luck early tomorrow morning."

The sheep, who had quickly learned that footsteps usually meant food, heard us coming and welcomed us with eager *baa*s.

Jasmine wrinkled her nose. "It smells—"

TRULY, MADLY, SHEEPLY

"Like sheep?" I asked with a grin.

Jasmine nodded. "Yeah. It's not a bad smell, though."

We replenished the flock's water and gave them a little grain for a treat. Beatrice came over for a back rub, leaning against the slats of the pen.

"Try it," I encouraged my friends, plunging my hands into the ewe's thick fleece.

"Whoa!" said Cha Cha as she did the same. "It's really warm."

"Like a sweater with legs, right?" I teased. "Aren't you, Beatrice?"

The ewe gave us an encouraging bleat, and the three of us spent a few minutes working our fingers up and down her back. When she finally moved away, Jasmine rubbed her hands together and looked at me in surprise.

"My hands feel so soft!"

"That's the lanolin in the wool," I explained. "Aunt True says it's a natural oil, and she's planning to use it to make a line of Rivercroft Farm lotions and stuff."

"Your aunt sure has a lot of ideas," said Jasmine. "She's cool."

I pulled an old wooden dairy stool over for her to sit on, and scrounged a couple of five-gallon buckets for Cha Cha and me. We turned them over and sat down, too, and the three of us watched the sheep for a bit.

"Can you tell them apart?" asked Cha Cha.

"Mostly. Gramps has them all memorized. I know Beatrice, of course, and Benedick's a no-brainer."

Hearing his name, the ram butted his head against the side of his pen and *baa*ed loudly.

"I think he's feeling left out," said Cha Cha.

I explained about rams and why they had to be separated from the ewes.

"How come he doesn't have horns?" Jasmine asked. "I thought rams had horns."

I shrugged. "I guess some breeds do and some don't. These are Romneys." I pointed to a light-brown ewe at the edge of the flock. "That's Frances Scott Key. We call her Fanny. And that's Sojourner Truth, and I'm pretty sure that one over there is Harriet Tubman. The only two I still get mixed up are Martha Washington and Abigail Adams."

"It's peaceful down here, isn't it?" said Cha Cha, and I nodded. "I like it."

"Me too."

We watched the sheep in silence again. After a while, Jasmine whispered, "Do you think if we sat here long enough we'd understand what they were saying, the way Fern did in *Charlotte's Web*?"

I didn't want to admit I'd wondered that myself.

"It's funny, how the books you read when you're little stick with you," Cha Cha said.

I nodded. "Mr. Henry would be happy to hear you say that."

My stomach rumbled just then. "I don't know about you guys, but I'm hungry. I know what's on the menu for dinner, too—you're going to love it!"

We took turns making sure that the gates to the pens were closed tightly, along with all the doors, then went back to the house.

My grandmother had made "alien casserole," a Lovejoy family favorite. My mother had invented it to try to get Hatcher to eat when he was a picky toddler and only ever wanted hot dogs and applesauce. When she ran out of the elbow macaroni the recipe called for, she'd used pasta shaped like little flying saucers instead. Danny had been the one who named it "alien casserole." Hatcher was intrigued enough to try it, and that was that. A new family favorite was born.

"This is really good," said Jasmine, shoveling in another mouthful.

"Yep," I replied, holding my plate out for seconds. I'd snarfed my first serving down in nothing flat. When you grow up in a family with a lot of kids the way I had, it was hard not to eat like a vacuum cleaner. "You snooze, you lose" was the name of the game around our dinner table.

The casserole was kind of like fake lasagna, with all sorts of gooey cheese in it, along with finely chopped spinach and zucchini and other vegetables that my mother had wanted Hatcher to eat. There was Lola's famous homemade lemon ice cream for dessert, too, which was even better. Afterward,

Gramps built a fire in the big living-room fireplace and we all hung out in front of it, playing cards. Then my friends and I went upstairs to watch a movie before bed.

After we'd finished and turned off my laptop, I set up the rollaway cot that Gramps had brought in for me. The bedroom I was staying in had two twin beds, which I'd given to my friends. We turned the lights out and lay there in the dark, looking at the moon in the sky outside. It was about three-quarters round—"waxing gibbous," Gramps had called it—and would be full and fat by next weekend, just in time for Halloween.

"Emilio likes you," Jasmine said to me out of the blue.

I snorted.

"He does! And so does Calhoun." She gave a dramatic sigh. "You're so lucky! Franklin doesn't even know I'm alive."

"Of course he does," said Cha Cha.

"Well, yeah, he knows I'm *alive*—but you know what I mean."

We were quiet for a bit, then Jasmine continued, "How about you, Cha Cha? Is there anybody you like?"

"Mmmm, maybe. There's this guy at our synagogue who lives in West Hartfield. His name is Josh. I went to his bar mitzvah last year and we danced. But it's not like we live near each other or see each other much or anything. Plus, my mother says I'm too young to be thinking about boys."

"Mine, too," I told her, and stifled a laugh, thinking about my boy-crazy cousin Mackenzie. She'd been thinking about boys since forever.

Not me, though. This was all still new territory for me. I had a strong suspicion that Jasmine was right, and that Emilio liked me. He was certainly acting like he did. And I was pretty sure that Calhoun did, too, although he hadn't come out and said anything. But even if he did, what would I say back to him?

"Boys are so confusing!" I said, pulling the covers up under my chin. I could hear my friends nodding in the dark.

Miss Marple nosed her way into the room and sniffed around until she found me. I dangled my arm over the side of the cot and scratched behind her ears as she settled down on the rug. It would be a tight squeeze for the two of us tonight up here on the cot.

"I like this place," whispered Cha Cha.

"Yeah, I like it here, too," I whispered back.

It was true. I liked everything about the farm. The cozy house; the way the barn smelled; the incredible view. I had a feeling Aunt True and Uncle Rusty were going to be happy here.

Too bad I didn't feel the same way the next morning.

CHAPTER 23

"Gramps!" I pelted across the yard, calling for him at the top of my lungs. "Gramps! The sheep are gone!"

I'd woken up early—so early it was still dark outside—and when I couldn't get back to sleep, I'd headed to the barn to surprise Gramps and take care of the morning chores. That's when I discovered the flock was missing.

As in, *completely* gone. Nowhere to be seen. The barn was empty; the only sound the quiet clucking of sleepy hens.

It was as if the sheep had never been there at all.

I ran toward the house, my heart pounding as hard as if I'd just finished a 100-meter butterfly. "Gramps!" I called again.

The phone was ringing as I burst through the back door into the kitchen. My grandfather, wearing his pajamas and bathrobe, his white hair sticking up in spiky tufts like an owl's, emerged from the stairwell and crossed the room to get to it. The farmhouse had an old landline just like the one back at our house on Maple Street, but instead of being tucked in a closet under the stairs, it was hanging on the wall in the kitchen.

"Walt here," said my grandfather, answering its shrill ring. "Yep. Yep. I understand. We'll be right there." He hung up and turned to me. "That was Lou. He's getting ready to open up and says the sheep are loose down on Main Street."

I felt a surge of relief, quickly followed by a wave of indignation. "We locked the pens and the barn! Honest!"

Cha Cha and Jasmine, who had been awakened by the commotion, stumbled sleepily downstairs to join us. Lola was right behind them.

"She's right," said Cha Cha, her deep voice raspier than usual, thanks to the early hour. "We triple-checked."

Gramps nodded. "I know. I did the same when I did my final check on them. There's definitely something strange going on around here." Glancing over at Lola, he hurriedly added, "And no, it's not a boggart."

"What's a boggart?" asked Jasmine.

"A sort of mischievous Scottish house spirit or goblin," I told her. "Aunt True was the one who mentioned it—to tease Uncle Rusty, I think."

Jasmine's dark eyes widened. She reached over and clutched Cha Cha. "You mean this place is *haunted*?!"

"Now, girls! Don't get carried away," my grandfather told them. "Of course the farm isn't haunted. There's a perfectly logical explanation—we just haven't figured it out yet." He turned to me. "Truly, you and I will take the truck. Jasmine, Cha Cha, get dressed. You'll go in the car with Lola."

Gramps and I were downtown in five minutes flat, still in our pajamas and bathrobes. At least I'd had time to pull a fleece on, too, plus my barn boots. My parents and brothers arrived right after we did, followed by Augustus and Belinda, who had been called in like the cavalry. Lou was standing in front of the diner waiting for us, shaking a can filled with something noisy.

"Dried beans," he told us with a grin. "Almost as good as a maraca, right, Truly?"

The sheep were in a loose semicircle around him, awaiting their expected treat. All but Benedick, that was. He was still AWOL—military speak for "Absent Without Leave."

"He'll turn up," Gramps said, after we did the head count. "No way is he going to stray far from his harem."

I sure hoped so. Aunt True would never forgive us if something happened to her prize ram.

"At least we know what to do this time," I said, stepping in with the real grain can. It was funny, I thought as the sheep crowded around me, in just a week I'd gone from being borderline afraid of them to feeling much more confident. Maybe Gramps was right, and I was destined for a career as a shepherdess.

Where did that thought come from? I wondered, and pushed

it away. Slipping the rope halter I'd brought along over Beatrice, I pulled her close.

"Good girl," I said. "Stay calm now."

Lola's car pulled up and she and Cha Cha and Jasmine hopped out. My father and Gramps organized a human chain, and once again I found myself walking up Main Street at the head of a sheep parade.

Fortunately, it was still early, so we didn't have a huge audience this time. And no reporter to cover the spectacle, either. The dawn crew—what Lou called the regulars who arrived at the diner just as it opened—looked a bit startled as we passed the big plate glass window, but we just smiled and waved.

By the time we reached the farm, the construction workers were beginning to arrive. I led the ewes around their trucks toward the back pasture. I'd feed them outside this morning, to keep them safely out of the way.

"J. T., Augustus, how about the three of us head into town and look for Benedick?" Gramps suggested, after the flock was fed and safely penned up again.

"I just called Bud Jefferson," my father replied. "He's bringing Amelia's minivan to shuttle us all back." He turned to my brothers. "Danny, once we get back to town, you bring your grandmother's car here so she'll have a ride. Hatcher, you're in charge of getting your little sisters up and dressed. We'll meet you all at church."

"Mr. Lovejoy, Lieutenant Colonel Lovejoy, you need to see this," said the foreman from the construction crew, beckoning to Gramps and my father.

They started across the driveway toward the barn. The rest of us were right on their heels. The foreman led everyone inside, then pointed silently upward. *Oh no,* I thought, my heart skipping a beat. *Has something happened to the owls?*

But it wasn't the owls.

Beside me, my mother gasped.

The mannequin from the farmhouse attic was dangling from one of the wide beams. In its arms was clutched a crude sign with words scrawled on it in black paint: LEAVE NOW, BEFORE IT'S TOO LATE!

"Right," growled Gramps. "This has gone far enough. I'm calling the police."

"Take that thing down, boys," my father ordered Danny and Hatcher. "The rest of you, let's keep this under our hats for now. Not a word to True and Rusty! I don't want their honeymoon spoiled."

Cha Cha's green eyes were like saucers as we left the barn. Mine probably were, too. This was way different than finding salt in the sugar bowl. That seemed like a harmless prank by comparison. Whoever was responsible for this had deliberately broken into the farmhouse and gone up to the attic to get the mannequin. Had they come while Gramps and Lola and

TRULY, MADLY, SHEEPLY

I were away at school and the bookstore? Or had they crept upstairs while we were sleeping? I shivered at that thought.

"Do you think it's the boggart?" Jasmine whispered.

"I don't know," I whispered back. "But somebody—or something—really wants us Lovejoys off the farm."

CHAPTER 24

"I hope you're proud of yourself," Gramps scolded Benedick sternly. "Look at the mess you've made!"

My family was standing on the library steps, along with the entire congregation from our church next door. We'd been in the middle of the final hymn, with Ethel Farnsworth flailing away on the slightly out-of-tune piano, when Mrs. Winthrop had glanced out the window and spotted the big ram, setting off a stampede as everyone ran out to try to catch him.

Which we did, but we were too late for the massacre. Benedick had eaten Mr. Henry's jack-o'-lanterns.

My grandfather continued to scold, but the big ram, whose muzzle was smeared with pumpkin remains, failed to look the least bit ashamed.

"Honestly, the way you eat, I'd swear you were part pig," Gramps said, slipping the rope he'd grabbed from the truck around Benedick's neck.

TRULY, MADLY, SHEEPLY

It took some doing to pry the ram away from his jack-o'-lantern buffet—who knew that sheep were fond of pumpkins?—but Gramps and my father and brothers finally managed to wrestle him down off the steps and into the bed of the pickup truck.

We'd dropped Cha Cha off at her house before church, since the Abramowitzes attended synagogue on Saturdays. She showed up as the rest of the Pumpkin Falls Private Eyes and I were glumly regarding the remains of Wilbur, Aslan, and Hagrid.

"What the heck happened here?" she asked, and we filled her in.

"Who gets to tell Mr. Henry that his jack-o'-lanterns are gone again?" asked Calhoun. "Permanently, this time."

I sighed and raised my hand. "That would be me. Stupid Benedick belongs to my family, after all."

I snapped a photo of the crime scene and texted it to Mr. Henry. **SORRY! WILL BUY NEW PUMPKINS AND HELP YOU CARVE THEM.**

NOT TO WORRY, he texted right back. **SHEEP WILL BE SHEEP.**

There was a reason why Mr. Henry was everybody's favorite librarian.

Emilio and his parents, who worshipped at St. Anthony's in West Hartfield, drove up just then.

"*È successo qui?*" asked Mr. Frangipani, peering at us over his sunglasses. "What happened here?"

And we had to explain it all over again.

He and Emilio's mother offered to drive the boys to our waffle brunch out at the farm, since Lola's car was full with me and Cha Cha and Jasmine and Lauren and the truck was full with Gramps and a baleful Benedick. Driving slowly, so as not to rattle his woolly cargo any further, my grandfather started up the road out of town, the rest of us creeping along behind.

"*Oh, che bello*!" said Mrs. Frangipani as she stepped out of her car and caught sight of the view. "How beautiful!"

Lola nodded. "Isn't it lovely? Would you like a tour of the property?"

"Yes, please!"

As Emilio's parents and my grandmother headed toward the barn, my friends and I helped Gramps wrestle Benedick out of the truck and into the smaller pasture. The ewes rushed to the fence between them and bleated a welcome.

"'I am glad that all things sort so well,'" said Calhoun.

I gave him a sidelong glance. "Shakespeare?"

He grinned. "*Much Ado*. Act five, scene four."

Calhoun was definitely his father's son. I mimed gagging myself and he laughed.

We went down to the main field to inspect Elmer's giant pumpkin, and then Jasmine and Cha Cha and Lauren and I gave the boys a tour of the barn, from the hayloft to the ground level. We hung around for a while watching the workers, who were busy repairing the roof outside and shoring up some of the beams inside.

"That's where we found the mannequin this morning," I said, pointing to the big central one.

"It was scary," said Cha Cha.

Scooter made a disgusted noise. "I can't believe someone would do that to your family!"

"Someone . . ." His twin lowered her voice. ". . . Or some*thing*."

Scooter's eyes narrowed. "What do you mean, some*thing*?"

"It's nothing," I told him. "Just one of Aunt True's jokes." I explained to the boys about the boggart.

"So it's mythical?" Calhoun smirked. "Kind of like Bigfoot?"

We all started to laugh. All except Emilio, who looked puzzled.

"What is this 'Big Feet'?" he asked.

"*Foot*. It's Big*foot*. And it's an inside joke," I told him, not even sure where I'd start to try to fill him in on last spring break's adventure. "It's kind of hard to explain."

We met up with Emilio's parents and Lola again at the back door to the house.

Mr. Frangipani had stepped in some whitewash or concrete dust back in the barn and left a trail of footprints across the driveway. He glanced over his shoulder and frowned. "I must clean my toes before I go inside."

"*Feet*, Papa, not toes!" muttered Emilio, blushing furiously.

"*Si*, that is what I meant, 'feet.'" Smiling, Mr. Frangipani wiped his shoes vigorously on the mat and went inside.

My friends and I followed.

"Truly, how about you give everyone a house tour while your grandfather and I get the waffles going?" said my grandmother.

Doing my best to channel my mother and Aunt True, I led the group to the living room, pointing out the original wide-plank floors and the beehive oven tucked into the brick fireplace. "Back in the day, most of the cooking was done on the hearth," I explained. "But the oven would have been fired up once a week or so to bake the family's bread, rolls, pies, and baked beans."

"Kind of like brick-oven pizza?" asked Lucas.

"Yeah, I guess."

"Can you still use it?" asked Scooter, peering in curiously. "It would be awesome to try making pizza in it."

I shrugged. "I'm not sure. Maybe? This house is really old. It was built in the 1770s." My voice trailed off as I realized that this probably wasn't all that impressive to people who lived in a country that had stuff like the Colosseum and Pompeii. Italians were used to old.

But Emilio's mother made encouraging noises, so I continued my tour. Up next was the borning room that was going to be Professor Rusty's office, and then I showed them the upstairs. When we got to the bedroom that Lola had set up as her satellite studio, Mrs. Frangipani's face lit up.

My grandmother had been painting up a storm since she arrived home from Africa. Half a dozen canvases were set up around the room, all but one of them covered in bright, sun-soaked colors depicting scenes from the village in Namibia where she and Gramps were living.

"Are these for sale?" asked Emilio's mother, circling the room.

"Maybe? Well, not the one of the farm. That's a wedding present for my aunt. But I heard my grandmother and my aunt talking before she left, and it sounded like they were planning to display them in the bookshop. Lola is hoping to raise money for the school library that she and my grandfather are helping to build in Africa."

"I will buy them all," said Mrs. Frangipani. "They are exquisite."

We took the back stairs down to the kitchen, where Emilio's mother made a beeline for my grandmother. A few minutes later, they were shaking hands on the deal.

"You must stay for brunch," a beaming Lola told Emilio's parents.

"Are you sure?" Mrs. Frangipani asked.

"I made enough food for an army! That's an American saying," my grandmother quickly added, seeing the puzzled looks on the Frangipanis' faces. "It means yes, of course, we have plenty."

"*Grazie*," Emilio's mother replied. "We would love to join you."

Gramps and Calhoun brought in a folding table and chairs for the grown-ups, and my friends and Lauren and I crammed into the breakfast nook. Lola brought over platters piled high with sourdough waffles, scrambled eggs, and the general store's best chicken apple sausage, our family's favorite. There was butter and real maple syrup, too, of course.

"The maple syrup comes from the farm just down the road," Lola told the Frangipanis.

Emilio's father poured some on his spoon and took a taste. "This we do not make in Italy. I am liking the flavor very much."

Lola poured coffee for the grown-ups. For us, there was Gramps's special cocoa that he made with a dash of cinnamon in it, plus cinnamon sprinkled on the whipped cream.

"This view!" said Emilio's mother, sipping her coffee and gazing out the bank of windows behind the breakfast nook. "I would never leave this room."

"That's what my aunt says, too," I told her.

She turned to my grandmother. "When do the newlyweds return?"

"Saturday morning," Lola replied. "They're coming in on a red-eye in time for Halloween."

"And you are going to surprise them with the new barn, *sì?*" said Mr. Frangipani. "Will there be *una festa*, a party?"

"I hadn't considered that," said Lola. She turned to Gramps. "Should we have a party, Walt?"

Gramps scratched his head. "A barn-warming? Sounds like a plan to me. The repairs are on track to be completed in time." He smiled. "If we really want to heat things up, we could have a bonfire."

"A *Festa dei Falò!*" said Mrs. Frangipani. "In Italy we have many 'fire festivals.'"

"We can't have the party Saturday, though," said Lola. "True and Rusty will be jet-lagged!"

My grandfather made a dismissive noise. "They're young, they'll survive."

"But the day is already so jam-packed. The bookstore will be hopping, plus there's the Little Trick-or-Treaters' parade, and then the pumpkin toss. Don't you think it's too much?"

Scooter shook his head vigorously. "A party's a great idea, Mrs. Lovejoy. We can celebrate my win!"

My friends and I scoffed at his gloating, but he was probably right.

"Plus, the sheep shearer is scheduled to come that afternoon," my grandmother added.

Gramps flapped his hand. "The kids can squeeze in a nap

somewhere. We'll just make the whole day one big party! Belinda and Augustus can hold down the fort at the bookshop in the afternoon, or we can close early. We'll invite our guests here to watch the sheep shearing, then they can stay for supper and the bonfire."

"What about trick-or-treating?" Lauren sounded worried. "Will we have time for that?"

"We'll work that out, too," Gramps assured her. "Maybe I'll rent the school bus to take you kids into town."

"It all sounds *fantastico*!" said Mr. Frangipani.

"You and your family are invited, of course," my grandmother told him. "I'll have to call Dinah right away. And Lou—I'll bet he'd cater it for us." Lola looked around the kitchen at us all and beamed. "I guess that settles it. We're going to have ourselves a party!"

CHAPTER 25

"Missing boots found in the driveway filled with water," said Officer Tanglewood, scribbling in his notebook. "Pitchfork in the pantry. Salt in the sugar bowl, sugar in the salt shaker." He looked up, peering over his glasses at Gramps and Lola. "Got it."

It did sound kind of ridiculous, when everything was listed out like that. Still, I had to fight the urge to wipe the smirk off the policeman's face.

"Somebody let the sheep out," Gramps said stiffly, who clearly felt the same way. "Twice."

"Or maybe somebody forgot to close the gate," Officer Tanglewood countered, looking pointedly at me. "Twice."

I scowled at him. *Numpty.*

"Are you forgetting the mannequin, Hank?" said Lola, an unaccustomed dose of starch in her usually gentle voice.

Officer Tanglewood snapped to attention. "No, ma'am, I

haven't forgotten." He closed his notebook and slid it back into his pocket. "We will definitely look into this right away."

I wasn't sure who the "we" was. Officer Tanglewood was a police force of exactly one.

We were cleaning up from brunch when he'd arrived. Gramps had taken him down to the barn to show him the mannequin, and the policeman had talked to the construction crew, who confirmed they'd found it hanging from the beam earlier. He'd poked around for a bit there and in the attic and took some pictures, and then he'd interviewed Lola and Gramps and me. It was clear he didn't believe us about the strange goings-on, but it was also clear that we weren't making the mannequin up. There was a prowler loose on the farm, intent on trying to scare my family away.

I could tell that it was going to take more than our town's bumbling policeman to solve this mystery, though. It was going to take the Pumpkin Falls Private Eyes.

"Emergency meeting of the PFPE!" I called to my friends as I burst through the back door.

They were seated on the steps, waiting for me. All eyes slid over to Emilio.

Uh-oh, I thought. I'd completely forgotten about him.

"PFPE?" he said blankly.

"Um," I replied. "It's kind of a private club." Emilio's face instantly shuttered, and suddenly he was the same cool, remote boy I'd seen that first day in our science class. I quickly added, "But maybe you can be an honorary member this year, while you're here in Pumpkin Falls."

Scooter glared at me and drew a finger across his throat. I gave him a *What was I supposed to do?* look in return.

"PFPE stands for 'Pumpkin Falls Private Eyes,'" Lucas explained. "We solve mysteries."

"We're pretty good, too," added Jasmine. "Last summer we found pirate treasure."

Emilio shrugged, trying not to seem too interested. But I could tell that he was.

"Nobody's forcing you to join," Scooter said belligerently.

Ignoring him, Emilio inclined his head in what I now thought of as his regal nod. "I will join your club."

I glanced around, considering our options for a meeting place. The barn was definitely out—too many construction workers. The house was probably out, too. Through the window, I could see Lola standing at the sink, talking on the phone. She was probably discussing plans for the surprise party with my mother. I knew Gramps would either be stretched out on the living room sofa or upstairs in his bedroom. He looked forward to his Sunday afternoon nap all week. Although I wasn't sure how much napping he'd get done today, what with all the hammering in the barn.

"I have an idea," I said, and beckoning my friends to follow I headed across the pumpkin field toward the shed.

When we reached the padlocked door, Calhoun raised his eyebrows. "Are you going to pick the lock for us?"

"You know how to pick a lock?" Emilio looked impressed.

I reached into the pocket of my jeans and groped for the two large paperclips I'd used before, hoping I'd left them there. I had. I dangled them and grinned, then hesitated, glancing back at the house. Could Lola see us? What about Gramps? What if he'd woken up from his nap and decided to do some birdwatching? I was pretty sure he wouldn't be thrilled with the view through his binoculars if he spotted his granddaughter breaking and entering.

It was a risk I was willing to take. Crouching down by the padlock, I went to work.

I was self-conscious at first, with my friends watching so closely. I could feel Scooter's breath on my neck. Fortunately, things went more smoothly this time—always helpful when a person was showing off. After just a minute or two of fiddling, the padlock gave the click I was listening for. I tried not to look too pleased with myself as I opened the door—slowly, to avoid as much of the hair-raising noise as possible—and we all slipped inside.

My friends spent a few minutes lifting tarps and examining the antique vehicles underneath.

"*Un camion dei pompieri!*" exclaimed Emilio, delighted. "A fire truck!"

"Yeah, it's pretty cool," said Lucas. "Elmer always

leads the parade through town in it on the Fourth of July."

"Guys!" I said, beckoning them over. "Bring it in. We don't have much time." Gramps would be awake soon for sure, and he was scheduled to take everyone home. It would be bad news if we were caught coming out of the supposedly locked shed.

"We need to set a trap," I said as my friends gathered around me. "We need to catch this prowler—or this whatever-it-is—in the act."

"*Boggart*," whispered Jasmine in her scariest Edgar Allan Poe voice. Then of course we had to explain to Emilio what a boggart was.

"Ah, *un folletto*," he said, nodding. "My grandparents had one at their villa in the mountains."

That pretty much brought the conversation to a screeching halt. We stared at him. How could he be so matter-of-fact?

He shrugged and continued, "It was always switching the salt with the sugar. My *nonna* was so angry!"

I felt the hair on the back of my neck prickle. *No way!* Boggarts weren't real. Aunt True had said so. Plus, Lola was certain she'd been the one responsible for the mix-up in the kitchen, even though she'd made Officer Tanglewood add it to his list.

Could it be true, though?

What if it was? What if the prowler really was a boggart?

"Shut up, Emilio," said Scooter finally. "You're freaking everybody out."

Emilio lifted his hands and shrugged in the classic *Who knows?* gesture.

We managed to drag the conversation back to trap-setting and brainstormed for a while about strategies. Scooter was all for video surveillance, like we did last spring when the sap lines at our friend Franklin's farm were cut.

"I thought about that, but the problem is the construction crew," I told him. "Any video equipment we set up would be in their way. Plus, the lamb cam didn't do any good when the sheep escaped. Whoever the prowler is, they're crafty. He or she must have spotted the camera because all we saw on the video was the gate opening and the sheep rushing out."

"Definitely *un folletto*," muttered Emilio, which wasn't helpful. "They are clever creatures."

"How about a stakeout?" asked Scooter, who was still pushing this idea too.

"The thing is, it's risky," I told him. "The likelihood of us getting caught is pretty high. Plus it's a school week, and with swim practice and early morning chores here at the farm, I can't be staying up all night."

My friends nodded ruefully, conceding the point.

"Meanwhile, the clock is ticking," I added. Aunt True and Uncle Rusty would be home next Saturday, and I was determined to have this case cracked before then.

"What about suspects?" asked Lucas.

I ticked them off on my fingers. The Mahoneys, who had

made my aunt and uncle that last-ditch offer the day before their wedding. Bert Harrison, who loved the view and had also made an offer. Wesley Thrush, the real-estate developer, although none of us had seen him around Pumpkin Falls lately. And finally, the couple from New York whose names no one could remember, but who wanted a weekend getaway and had left their cards with Doris Wheeler, Augustus's starstruck realtor fan from West Hartfield. I reminded my friends that she'd brought it up again at Family Fun Friday.

"Do you really think it's one of them?" asked Cha Cha.

I shrugged. "Maybe? I don't know." I chewed my lip as I scanned the list again. Bert Harrison? Really? And the Mahoneys were our bookshop's neighbors and had always seemed really nice. Could they really be responsible for something as horrible as the threatening mannequin?

"It has to be a boggart," whispered Jasmine again.

We were quiet for a while. The wind had picked up and I could hear it whistling through the open window under the eaves. I thought about the mannequin with its threatening sign, and about the construction mess in and around the barn, and then about Mr. Frangipani wanting to clean off his "toes."

And just like that, the pieces slipped into place and I felt the same "snick" that I always did when I completed a Sudoku puzzle.

I knew exactly how we could trap our prowler—and find out if it was a boggart at the same time

CHAPTER 26

It rained for two days straight, a real nor'easter, which put a damper—literally—on our plans to set the trap. After Gramps had driven everyone home that afternoon, I'd gone up to my room to start my homework, and by dinnertime the rain had started in earnest. The wind was blowing like crazy, too, and just as we sat down to eat, the power went out.

"Good thing they built these old houses as solidly as they did," said Gramps, fishing a lantern and some candles out of the pantry. "This place has withstood many a storm over the past two hundred and fifty years. We'll be safe and sound here inside."

The power was back on by the time the construction crew arrived Monday morning, and work continued uninterrupted on the barn that day, despite the continuing deluge. The workers had finished the roof just in time, fortunately, and were able to concentrate their efforts inside out of the rain. Meanwhile, the

TRULY, MADLY, SHEEPLY

prowler was back with a vengeance, continuing to wreak havoc.

Tools disappeared, or showed up in odd places. Supplies went missing. Batteries were drained, cords hopelessly tangled, paint colors switched. The list went on and on.

The construction workers were getting spooked. "Nonsense," declared Gramps, when he heard that there was speculation the farm was cursed. He marched over to "have words," as he put it, with the foreman, and even called on Elmer to try to stop the rumor mill.

Despite his efforts, word quickly spread around town that the old Farnsworth place was haunted. Cursed, now that it had been sold out of the family. Zachariah Farnsworth, the story went, who settled the land and built the farmhouse back in 1770, wasn't happy. And now he'd come back to haunt the place.

Even after Elmer Farnsworth made a public pronouncement in Tuesday morning's issue of the *Pumpkin Falls Patriot-Bugle* that his family home wasn't now and never had been haunted, that didn't stop the story from spreading like wildfire. Once social media and the wire services got ahold of it, within hours the phone was ringing off the hook with reporters wanting a quote from Gramps or Lola.

"I happen to know that old Zachariah Farnsworth is slumbering peacefully in his coffin in the Pumpkin Falls graveyard," Gramps shouted into the phone after the third call during dinner Tuesday night. "And he hasn't set foot out of it since he landed there in 1810!"

He hung up the landline with a slam. Lola crossed the kitchen and patted his arm. "Now, Walt, I understand your frustration, but there's no point fretting about it or taking it out on others. It's just human nature to want to latch on to something like this. Plus, it's irresistible, right before Halloween. We'll get it sorted."

By Wednesday morning, the rain had slowed to a drizzle. While we were eating breakfast, Lou called to let Gramps and Lola know that Channel 5, who had been in touch with him earlier about doing a feature on his cider doughnuts, was asking if he might be able to put in a good word so they could interview our family.

"Apparently *Hello Boston!* is planning to cover the pumpkin toss and the other Halloween activities in town, and now they want to add a segment on a haunted farm," said Lola, settling back into the breakfast nook after she hung up.

"Oh, for Pete's sake," said Gramps. "As if we don't have enough to worry about, without some camera crew sniffing around." He threw down the *Pumpkin Falls Patriot-Bugle* in disgust. The headline blaring across the front page read: *The Haunting of Rivercroft Farm!*

I'd been focused on my oatmeal, but when I heard this news from Lola I sat up straight.

Hello Boston! was synonymous with its host, Carson Dawson. The numptiest of the numpties. We'd had a few run-ins this past year and I was not thrilled to hear that he was planning another trip to Pumpkin Falls.

"I can't believe he's coming here *again*!" I wailed a few minutes later to Aunt True, whose face loomed large on Lola's tablet screen. "I can't get away from him!"

We'd gotten a video call from the honeymooners close on the heels of the news about Channel 5. My aunt and new uncle were about to board the ferry for Lewis and Harris, the last island they were stopping at before heading home. After a brief chat with Lola and Gramps, I'd taken the tablet into Uncle Rusty's office-to-be in the borning room for a quick heart-to-heart with Aunt True.

She grinned at me across the miles. "Suck it up, Tall Timber. Find a way to turn it to your advantage. Maybe he'll want to visit the bookshop again—you know, check in on us and see our progress over the past year? That would be a nice little publicity boost." Seeing my expression, she laughed. "Don't worry, the cavalry is coming. We'll be home on Saturday."

That was three whole days away, though, and the PFPEs still had a prowler—or a boggart—to catch.

At least we had a plan for that. All the pieces were in place, everything had been set in motion, and now all we needed was for the rain to stop.

The school day dragged by. The only bright spot was our

Poe presentation, which just as Lola predicted had brought the house down. Our classmates gave us a standing ovation, and although I could tell Ms. Matthews was chagrined that we weren't as in love with Edgar and his work as she was, she said she had to give us full marks for creativity.

By lunchtime the drizzle finally started to let up, and by our last class of the day, it looked like it might be clearing. Sure enough, halfway through geometry I spotted a patch of blue sky out the classroom window.

When the bell rang, my friends and I all gathered on the front steps as we'd arranged.

"All systems go?" I asked them.

Everyone nodded.

"Are we going to synchronize our watches?" Emilio looked hopeful.

I shrugged. "Sure, why not?"

It wasn't as easy as it looked in the movies, though. Especially since Emilio and my sister Lauren, whom my parents said was still too young for a cell phone, were the only ones who were wearing watches, and synchronizing a cell phone was pointless since they were synchronized already. Finally, we gave up and agreed to stay in touch by text.

"I'll see you all tonight!" I grabbed my bike and headed off toward Main Street, waving to Lola as I passed the bookstore. She was adding more sale books to Wally the pumpkin-headed scarecrow's arms.

TRULY, MADLY, SHEEPLY

I sped on toward the farm. I wanted to check on the sheep before starting my shift at the store. Both Gramps and I were now completely paranoid about them escaping again and we checked on them multiple times a day, either in person or via the lamb cam. I was coasting down the driveway to the barn when I heard someone calling my name. I turned to see Lauren and Annie Freeman closing in on me.

"Didn't you hear us?" my sister said as they skidded their bikes to a stop. "We were right behind you!"

I frowned. "Where's Pippa?"

"It's Wednesday, remember? Camp Belinda."

That's what our family called Belinda's bouts of daycare. She was our pinch hitter when Lauren or my mom needed a break. Belinda was great with Pippa—and with Lauren, too, although Lauren would have balked at the idea of needing a babysitter. There were always kittens to play with at Belinda's house, of course, but beyond that she could also be counted on for baking and crafts and games. Plus, thirty years as a lunch lady had prepared her for dealing with any potential Pippa meltdowns. And it turned out that Augustus was pretty good with little kids, too. Glitter was his specialty, and Pippa adored glitter.

"I thought Gramps and Lola were going to bring you here with them after the bookshop closes?" I said to my sister. Part of our plan was for Lauren to have dinner out at the farm and spend the night, which hadn't been difficult to arrange since it was my last night here with Gramps and Lola. We were celebrating with one of my favorite desserts—my grandmother's homemade pumpkin cheesecake.

My sister shrugged. "I got invited to play at Annie's house. Don't worry—I let Lola know."

The two of them followed me down to the sheep pens, where we leaned up against the railing and watched the flock in companionable silence. Well, Lauren and I were silent. Annie was her usual chatty self.

"They're so a-d-o-r-a-b-l-e!" she burbled. "Except that one." She pointed to Benedick. "He doesn't look happy to see us."

I nodded. "Benedick can be a bit c-a-n-t-a-n-k-e-r-o-u-s." Two could play at this game.

Annie grinned at me. She'd changed her hairstyle this year, I noticed, going for a more grown-up look now that she was in fifth grade. The little braids she'd worn bobbing around on her head like antenna had given way to a more natural look. Smooth on the sides and back, her dark curls were pulled into an updo I'd heard her call a big puff. The explosion of exuberant curls on top suited Annie to a tee.

It still surprised me that she and Lauren were fifth graders. Next year when I started high school, Lauren would be starting middle school! Which at Daniel Webster School just meant moving up to the second floor, but still. She wasn't a baby anymore.

"I can't wait to watch the shearer," Lauren said. "Lola told me he's old-school and uses hand shears instead of electric ones."

"Yeah, she told me that, too."

"Are you going to try to knit something with the wool Aunt True is planning to have spun from all the fleeces?"

I lifted a shoulder. "Maybe. Knitting's okay but it's not really my thing. Mom will, for sure. I can just imagine the Christmas sweaters we'll get next year."

We grinned at each other. Our mother made themed Christmas sweaters for the whole family every year. We'd had Disney Christmas sweaters and snowflake Christmas sweaters and sweaters with skiers on them and Christmas trees on them and ornaments on them. Last year the theme had been Christmas angels, since our mother had told us we needed a lot of those in our lives after my father's accident in Afghanistan. Danny and Hatcher weren't wild about theirs and only wore them for our family photo and on Christmas Day and once to church, but they'd been Pippa and Lauren's favorites.

"And Aunt True told me that next spring, there'll be lambs!" Lauren said, looking at the flock.

I nodded.

"I can't wait to see them, can you?"

Surprisingly, I couldn't. To my embarrassment, I'd found myself checking the lamb cam several times a day—ours and Theresa the sheep whisperer's—and I'd even started following the #LambSpam hashtag on social media that Aunt True had showed me right before she left for Scotland. Shepherds from all over the world posted pictures of their sheep and lambs, who were incredibly cute.

All of this had me worried that maybe Gramps was right, and I was destined to become Pastorella the Daring Young Shepherdess. Beatrice came over for her back rub and I stroked her thoughtfully. I just didn't see "sheep farmer" in my future. Not that I'd given the future all that much thought. I had a vague idea about maybe being an ornithologist someday—someone who studied birds. But it was something I assumed I'd figure out when I got to college.

Lauren and I were both on pins and needles during dinner.

"You two have ants in your pants tonight," Lola commented.

"Just excited to be together," I told her, hoping my chirpy tone wasn't too over-the-top.

"For our 'sheepover'!" said Lauren.

"Plus, it's my last night at the farm," I added. It hardly seemed possible that I'd been here for nearly two weeks—the time had flown by.

We must have sounded convincing because our grandmother nodded and smiled. "It can't be a late one, though," she reminded us. "School night, after all."

"We'll turn out the lights early, I promise. Right after we do the final gate check."

"Are you sure you still want to do that?" asked Gramps.

Evening gate checks were usually his responsibility, but I'd offered to take it over for tonight.

I'd rehearsed my words carefully. "I just thought you could use a break from all the excitement," I told him. The press hadn't let up on their barrage of phone calls and emails, and he'd been fending them off all day. "Plus, Lauren wants to spend as much time with the sheep as possible while she's here."

Hearing her cue, Lauren nodded vigorously.

Gramps smiled at us. "That's fine, then, girls."

The minutes ticked by agonizingly slowly. I served myself up a second piece of pumpkin cheesecake and tried to focus on the geometry proofs that my math teacher had assigned. Surprisingly, given my history with math—I was famous in my family for once getting an F-plus—geometry was my favorite subject so far this year. Maybe it was because solving proofs reminded me a bit of sudoku. The process wasn't unlike solving mysteries, either, I thought as I made two columns beside the first problem. I labeled one "Statements" and the other "Reasons." Geometry was methodical and required logic and deductive reasoning, just like our work as private eyes did.

A while later, my sister stood up to stretch. "Just another hour to go," she whispered, glancing at the Kit-Cat Klock on the wall.

Finally, I couldn't stand it any longer. I slammed my math book shut and slid out of the breakfast nook, then poked my head in the living room.

Gramps glanced up from his book. "Heading out to the barn?"

I nodded.

"Take Miss Marple with you, would you? She could use a final potty break."

"You bet." I called to her, and she heaved herself reluctantly off the rug in front of the cheery blaze in the fireplace. "I might try to show Lauren the owls, too, if they're around."

"Mmmm," my grandfather murmured, already deep in his book again.

Lauren and I grabbed our jackets from the hooks in the mudroom, along with the backpacks we'd left there earlier. We headed outside with Miss Marple at our heels.

"T-minus five minutes and counting," my sister whispered, pointing to her watch.

We finished the final gate check in two minutes flat and raced back upstairs to the main floor of the barn. By the time we got outside, we could see lights approaching along the road. Our friends were on their way!

"Made it!" panted Cha Cha as she coasted into the driveway. "With a minute to spare."

Our friends switched off their bike lights quickly so as not to attract attention. I didn't think Gramps and Lola would be pleased to find us all out here. Not only was it a school night, but it was also after dark. We'd be in all sorts of trouble.

"Did anyone see you guys?" I asked. It was just a short

ride from town, but still, five kids on bikes at nine o'clock at night? That was sure to arouse suspicion.

"Not a soul," said Calhoun.

Sometimes, it paid to live in a small town. "Good. Let's get to work. You all know what to do."

Moving as silently as was humanly possible, my friends stashed their bikes out of sight behind Uncle Rusty's pickup truck and Elmer's old red tractor, which had come with the farm. Then we all took the bags of flour that we'd bought earlier at the general store out of our backpacks.

"Quietly, now," I whispered and we spread out around the barn, sprinkling a wide swath of flour along the foundation as we circled it. It wasn't exactly invisible, but thanks to the clouds overhead it wasn't illuminated by the moon, either.

"Now all we can do is hope the prowler shows up and walks through it," I whispered when we gathered back behind the tractor.

"Miss Marple just did," said Lauren, pointing to a line of paw prints that led from the barn to where our grandparents' dog was sitting in the middle of the driveway. She gave us her best golden-retriever smile.

"Great! That means it works."

The "trap" we'd set was a simple one, designed to capture any footprints that might lead us to the culprit. The plan was for me to set my alarm earlier than usual and slip out before

Gramps and Lola got up. If there was no sign of an intruder, Lauren and I would hose off as much of the flour as we could before the workers arrived and no one would be the wiser. Any residual flour would just look like concrete dust, the stuff that Mr. Frangipani had walked through and wiped off his feet before brunch.

On the other hand, if there were footprints, Lauren and I would take photos and measurements and alert the authorities. Well, authority—Officer Tanglewood.

"How will we know if a footprint is human or . . . ?" squeaked Lucas, his voice trailing off. Emilio's tale about the *folletto* must have gotten to him, because he was clearly spooked.

"The tracks that my *nonna* showed me, they were very small—like for *un bambino*, a child," Emilio said authoritatively. "Although sometimes they looked like tiny *zoccoli*." He frowned, searching for the English equivalent. "Hooves?"

Tiny *hooves?* I recoiled at the thought.

Jasmine and Cha Cha looked equally horrified. Lucas paled. Even Calhoun was aghast, clearly repelled by that mental image. Only my sister Lauren seemed unfazed. Knowing her, she was probably calculating ways she could keep a boggart for a pet.

Our work complete, my friends gathered up their backpacks and mounted their bicycles.

TRULY, MADLY, SHEEPLY

"Text us the minute you know anything!" Cha Cha whispered over her shoulder.

"I will," I replied, and waved as she and the others rode away.

The trap was set. There was nothing left to do but wait.

CHAPTER 27

I barely slept a wink that night.

Every hour or so I woke up, glanced at my alarm clock to check if it was time to get up, then peered out the window to see if I could spot anything. Which of course I couldn't, since there was no moon in the sky. Even the stars were obscured by the clouds.

Lauren, on the other hand, slept like a log. I hated to wake her when my alarm finally went off, but I knew she'd kill me if I didn't.

"Lauren!" I reached out and shook her by the shoulder. Nothing. I shook her again and she gave a muffled grunt. "Time to check on our trap!"

This got through. She opened an eyelid, took a moment to figure out where she was and why I was standing over her, then sat straight up. "I'm awake!"

I grinned. "Yeah, right. We've got half an hour before Gramps gets up. Let's go."

We pulled sweats on over our pajamas, then headed down the hall to the back stairs. Miss Marple followed us, toenails clicking.

Grabbing our jackets and barn boots from the mudroom, we stepped outside. A breeze had sprung up since I'd last checked the sky, because the clouds had blown away. It looked like it was going to be a beautiful, clear day. At four a.m. in October, it was still fully dark outside with no hint of dawn yet, but the stars were visible again, twinkling brightly overhead.

As we crossed the driveway to the barn, Lauren reached out and took my hand. For once, I didn't swat it away. I was as nervous as she was about what we might find. Human footprints? Little boggart ones? Or worse, tiny hoofmarks, like Emilio had described?

My heart was in my mouth as I switched on my torch app and pointed it at the ground around the base of the barn.

Nothing.

The swath of flour was still there, extending a couple of feet beyond the concrete foundation like a white moat. But that was all. There was no sign that someone had crossed it, no sign that it had been disturbed.

"Aww!" whispered Lauren, disappointed.

"Hang on," I told her. "We need to check the entire perimeter."

We made our way slowly around the building, stopping every few feet to sweep the ground ahead of us with my cell phone light. High above, a loud *hisssss* split the air, shattering the silence. Lauren clutched me and squealed.

"Calm down!" I whispered. "It's just the barn owls." I shone my light up to the eaves to show her, and we stood there for a moment, watching them watch us. Then we started our inspection again.

When we rounded the final corner of the barn, on the side farthest from the house, I stopped short. Up ahead, some flour was smeared into the grass. My heart racing, I moved closer, my heart racing, and zeroed in on it with my flashlight. "Gotcha!" I said with satisfaction.

A line of footprints led away from the side door of the barn toward the edge of the road.

Human footprints.

Big ones, too.

I hadn't realized that I'd been holding my breath. Beside me, Lauren exhaled as well.

"It's not a boggart," she said, a note of disappointment in her voice.

"Nope." I wasn't disappointed at all. A wave of relief washed over me, quickly followed by the sobering realization that the intruder was real, and had been here on my family's property in the last few hours, messing with our stuff in an attempt to try to intimidate us. I looked at the receding trail again and hoped whoever the footprints belonged to was really, truly gone, and not lurking about somewhere nearby.

Crouching down, I examined the clearest print. "Big feet," I said. I stood up again and placed my barn boot beside it. "Bigger than mine, even."

I took pictures of the footprint and measured it, whipping out the ruler I'd tucked into the pocket of my sweatpants. Lauren held it while I took photos from every possible angle.

I took a video, too, first pointing the camera at my sister and me and explaining what day and time it was, how we'd set the trap, then panning up to the road and back along the trail of prints, and ending at the side door of the barn.

"We should go inside and see what he—or she—has been up to," I said.

I didn't move, though. After the mannequin incident, I wasn't eager to see what new horrors might await.

"Maybe we should go get Gramps," said Lauren.

"Good idea." We headed back to the house.

"Would you look at that!" our grandfather said a short while later. He stared down at the trail of floury footprints, shaking his head in disgust. "Caught in the act."

Lola had come along, too, in response to our urgent knocking on their bedroom door. She glanced over at Lauren and me. "You two are pretty clever."

"It wasn't just us," I told her, and explained about the how the rest of the Pumpkin Falls Private Eyes were involved. Slipping my cell phone from my pocket, I added, "Which reminds me, I need to let everybody know it worked."

Within ten minutes, bicycles began pulling into the driveway. Our friends had been awake early, too, waiting for my text.

"I have to be back before my mother gets up," Lucas announced. "She'll panic if she finds me gone."

"We'll get you back in time," my grandfather assured him.

The last one to arrive was Emilio. He skidded to a stop and hopped eagerly off his bicycle. *"Un folletto?"*

I shook my head. "Human."

"Who do you think the footprint belongs to?" asked Jasmine.

"Hard to say. Someone not wearing barn or work boots, though, that's for sure. No tread on the bottom."

"Tread?" Emilio's forehead puckered and I turned up my foot to show him the sole of my barn boot.

"See those squiggly lines on the bottom? Treads."

He nodded, and we all stood looking at the floury prints.

"It looks like maybe dress shoes, or loafers," said Lola finally.

Loafers? Nobody in Pumpkin Falls wore loafers. Well, maybe on Sunday sometimes, and for weddings and stuff. The only other people I could recall wearing them were Mr. Frangipani—and Emilio, that first day of school.

My eyes slid over to my classmate's feet. He was wearing sneakers, like all my other friends were. Was Emilio our prowler?

He caught me looking at his shoes and made a big show

of sticking a foot out and planting it next to the floury print. It was nowhere near as big.

"My father wears the same size shoe as me," he said stiffly, and I reddened.

"Glad to know that, son," Gramps said calmly, patting his shoulder. "Not that either of you were ever under suspicion." He turned to my grandmother. "How about I go into the barn and see what mischief this wretched prowler of ours has been up to, while you take these kids back to the house for some cocoa. And maybe you could call—"

Before he could say who Lola was supposed to call, we all jumped. The same unearthly screech I'd heard last weekend in the middle of the night split the air.

"Good heavens, what was that?" asked Lola, pulling her bathrobe tighter around her.

"The boggart!" squealed Lucas and dove behind Gramps.

"It's the shed door!" I pointed across the field.

"Let's get him!" said Scooter, and he took off running.

CHAPTER 28

Scooter was fast, but my legs were longer. There was an advantage to still being the tallest person in my school. I caught up with him halfway across the pumpkin field.

"Hold on!" I panted, grabbing him by the arm. "You'll spook whoever it is and then we'll lose them."

Scooter slowed reluctantly to a halt. I shoved him down behind Elmer's giant pumpkin and we stayed crouched there, waiting for everyone else to catch up. Gramps and Lola trailed behind, bathrobes flapping.

"At least you don't have to pick the lock this time, Drooly," said Scooter in a low voice, jerking his chin toward the shed's open door.

"What was that?" asked Gramps, looking over at us sharply.

"Nothing, sir," I replied, giving Scooter the stink eye.

Through the dirt-encrusted windows, we could see a dim light bobbing around inside.

"Maybe it's not the prowler," whispered Lola. "Maybe it's Elmer, checking on his trucks."

"Only one way to find out," said Gramps grimly. "Stay here—you kids, too. I mean it. Don't anyone move an inch."

We nodded mutely and he strode away, crossing the rest of the field with Miss Marple at his heels. I could hear Calhoun beside me, breathing hard. I could hear all of us breathing. And then—

Miss Marple came running out of the shed, barking. We waited a few seconds, but my grandfather didn't reappear.

"Something's wrong!" I said, rising to my feet. "Something's happened to Gramps!"

This time it was me who took off running. I didn't care that he'd told me to stay put. Nobody messed with my grandfather.

I covered the rest of the ground in nothing flat and barreled into the shed—then stopped short. The others plowed into me, nearly knocking me over.

"*You're* the prowler?" I said in disbelief.

Clark Barque stood there, nervously pushing his glasses up the bridge of his nose.

"Those are *your* footprints out there? *You* hung that mannequin in the barn to try to frighten us into leaving the farm?"

Clark pushed his glasses up again. "Uh, I'm not sure what you're talking about."

Was he lying? I squatted down by his shoes and inspected

them. No visible flour. I pulled out my ruler and measured one of them. Too short.

"Hey!" he protested as I grabbed him by the toe and lifted his foot up. Ignoring him, I peered at the underside. So did my friends.

"Treads," said Emilio.

"Treads," I echoed, and stood up. "It wasn't him, Gramps. Not even if he changed shoes. His sneakers have treads on them, plus his feet are too small."

"My feet are not small!" the reporter protested. "And I don't know anything about a mannequin."

I crossed my arms and stared him down. So did Gramps and Lola and all my friends. After a moment or two, he sagged under our collective scrutiny.

"Okay, fine. It was me—but not the mannequin, or any of that other stuff! All I did was let the sheep out."

"*All* you did? ALL?!" Lola drew herself up to her full height, which hovered somewhere around my chin. "Do you have *any* idea how much trouble you've caused? And if you're not responsible for the—what did you call it in the paper yesterday? 'The Haunting of Rivercroft Farm'—who is?"

Gramps glared at Clark Barque as he shifted awkwardly from one foot to the other. "I don't know," he replied. "There was an unsigned note in my mailbox a week or so ago, along with a key to this shed, telling me that I'd be guaranteed a hot story if I'd just let the sheep out a few times. I was supposed to lock the ram in here, too, but, uh, that didn't go so well."

I smothered a grin. I could well imagine what Benedick thought of that idea.

The reporter held up the key. "I thought I'd try again one last time this morning."

Gramps plucked it from his hand and snorted. "And somehow you thought all of this was a good plan?"

The reporter shrugged. "It seemed harmless enough."

"Harmless? What you've done is despicable, young man! My daughter and her husband have a whole lot of hopes and dreams riding on that little flock of theirs. The sheep could have been injured—or worse."

Clark Barque's gaze dropped to the floor of the shed. "I didn't mean to hurt anyone."

"'Didn't mean to' might work for first graders who borrow pumpkins," snapped Gramps. "It's no excuse for a grown man."

The reporter reddened. "Please don't tell anyone! I'll lose my job!"

"You deserve to!"

Lola stepped forward and laid a hand on my grandfather's arm. "Walt, he's hardly older than Danny."

Gramps heaved a sigh. "What were you *thinking*, Clark?"

The reporter shook his head. "I was just—I was only

trying to—nothing happens around here!" he finally managed to blurt out. "I just wanted to have a good story to tell, that's all. And for a few days it seemed like I did. Especially after things went viral on social media and the wire services called and my coverage started getting picked up across the country—I guess it all kind of spiraled out of control."

"Kind of?" Gramps stared at him in disbelief. "If it's stories you want, son, just open your eyes and look around. How about Belinda Winchester, who's got a heart as big as all outdoors? Do you know how many kittens and cats she's rescued and found loving homes for over the years? Why don't you write a story about her? Or Mr. Henry? I have never seen such a devoted librarian. He goes above and beyond for this town every single day of the week. *There's* a story for you! You don't need to fabricate a mystery, or focus on doom-and-gloom for it to be news, young man. Didn't they teach you that in journalism school?"

I almost felt sorry for Clark Barque. He looked like he was going to cry.

"I've got one for you—how about a story about a pair of newlyweds who buy a dilapidated old farm in hopes of starting a new business in a tiny town?" Lola suggested, gesturing toward the house and barn.

"Or one about a retired couple going to Africa to volunteer for the Peace Corps?" I added, and she smiled at me.

TRULY, MADLY, SHEEPLY

One by one, we all offered up a story idea. My sister Lauren, ever the loyal friend, suggested the upcoming Grafton County Junior Spelling Championship. "You could interview Annie Freeman!"

Lucas piped up with the annual Pumpkin Falls Beautification Project. Jasmine noted that the covered bridge had an anniversary coming up.

"There's the Four on the Fourth road race, too!" said Scooter.

"And don't forget Cotillion," said Cha Cha. "My parents put a lot of time into running it every year."

Calhoun considered for a moment, then added, "The Polar Bear Plunge." His eyes slid over to mine, and he smiled. I flushed, remembering how he'd held on to my hand so tightly when I fell into the icy river last winter.

"I have one," said Emilio, not to be outdone. "A boy moves to a town far away from his home in Italy. He is lonely at first, but then he meets new friends who let him into their exclusive club."

By the time we were finished, the reporter had grabbed his notebook from his pocket and was scribbling like mad.

"And Pumpkin Falls isn't unique," Gramps concluded. "All across this great country of ours—all around this wonderful world of ours—there are stories like these. Stories worth telling. *Good* stories. Inspiring stories. You want to be a journalist, young man? Don't forget to tell these stories, too. Make your job count."

"I am so, so sorry," said Clark Barque, and I could tell he meant it.

"I can see that you are," said Lola. "Right, Walt? We all do chowder-headed things now and then."

Gramps sighed again. "I'll tell you what. I'm a firm believer in second chances, so I'll make you a deal. If you help us find the mysterious prowler who put you up to this, we'll overlook your involvement. You'll have to keep it quiet, though. Not a peep out of you, not a word, not a headline. Nothing that might scare him—or her—off. You keep the secret, and you help us catch him—or her—and we'll keep your secret, too." He glanced over at my friends and Lauren and me. "Right, kids?"

"Cross my heart and hope to fly," I promised, and my friends all promised, too.

My grandfather winked at the reporter. "Especially don't mention anything to Ella Bellow."

Clark Barque gave him a rueful smile. He may not have been in Pumpkin Falls long, but he'd been here long enough to know who was in charge of gossip in our tiny town. "Duly noted, sir."

Outside, the sky was beginning to lighten. Through the doorway I glimpsed blue sky overhead, and the sun reaching out toward the barn, which would be getting a new coat of red paint in a few hours. I was right; it was going to be a beautiful day.

"And now," Lola said, "while you and Walt lock up the shed, I think it's time for the rest of us to head back to the house for breakfast. We've all had enough excitement for one morning."

CHAPTER 29

"I think," said Gramps a little while later as we pulled up in front of the pool, "that we need one of Lou's best buttermilk doughnuts for breakfast dessert to celebrate this step of progress, don't you, Lauren? We are one step closer to catching this abominable prowler of ours."

Beside me, my sister bounced up and down on the seat and cheered.

"Hey! What about me?" Breakfast dessert was another cherished Lovejoy family tradition, and Lou's buttermilk doughnuts were almost as good as his cider ones.

Gramps glanced at me in the rearview mirror and smirked. "Don't worry, we'll eat a doughnut in your honor."

Lola caught sight of my expression and laughed. "He's kidding, sweetheart! We'll send one to school for you with Lauren."

After my friends had left earlier, while Lauren and I took

care of the sheep and I got ready for swim practice and school, Gramps had inspected the barn for anything that the prowler may have tampered with.

"Nothing," I reported to my friends when we gathered around one of the tables in the cafeteria at lunchtime. "Gramps says that with any luck, that's the last we'll see of him—or her."

Scooter nodded. "I'll bet our trap scared them off for good."

"Hopefully." I took my notebook out of my backpack, along with the doughnut Lauren had brought me. It was only slightly squashed, I was happy to see. "So," I continued, taking a bite. "What do we know now about the mystery prowler for sure?"

"We know that he or she is human," said Jasmine.

Human, I wrote in the "Facts" column

"They're not a boggart," said Emilio.

Not a boggart, I wrote beneath it.

"They have size-thirteen feet," said Calhoun.

Size thirteen feet, I added.

"That's big, right?" Lucas asked. "Bud wears size thirteen. I heard him tell my mother last time we went shoe shopping at the West Hartfield mall."

We all looked over at him.

"It's not Bud," he said defensively.

"Nobody said it was," I replied.

"But you're thinking it." He pointed to my pencil, which was hovering over the "Suspects" column.

"Lucas is right, Truly," said Cha Cha. "Bud has no motive at all, plus he's a super-nice guy."

"He's more than a nice guy, he's almost my stepdad," said Lucas, his voice rising. Lucas hadn't been keen on his mother dating Bud Jefferson initially, but they'd gotten closer over the past few months. I recognized the emotion in his voice. Lovejoys stuck together, too.

I blew out my breath. "Okay, I get it, you're right. It's not Bud. So, what else have we got?"

"Whoever it is probably wears loafers," said Lauren.

I wrote that down too.

The table went quiet as we gazed at my list. That was pretty much it.

"That's not much to go on," said Scooter.

"What do private eyes usually do now?" asked Emilio, frowning.

"Brainstorm," I told him, adding "Toss ideas around" in answer to his unasked question.

"We could keep an eye out for someone with flour on their shoes, I guess," said Jasmine.

I made a face. "They'll probably have cleaned it off by now."

"We could try to figure out who else in town wears size-thirteen shoes," said Lucas. "Librarians know everything—we could ask Mr. Henry."

"How about holding a contest for people with big feet?"

said Cha Cha. "We could advertise at the Starlite and offer free dance lessons to the winner."

"We only have the rest of today and tomorrow before my aunt and uncle get back from their honeymoon," I told her. "That's not enough time for a contest."

"Stakeout at the general store," suggested Scooter, who was clearly not going to let the whole stakeout idea go. "We could watch people's feet as they come and go."

None of these options sounded very practical. As the bell rang for our next class, we had to face the fact that we were stuck. We'd hit a dead end, and unless we had a breakthrough or got lucky, at this rate we might never know who was trying to scare my family off the farm.

CHAPTER 30

"Is that a fact?" Clark Barque lifted an eyebrow at me as Lauren and I walked past the *Pumpkin Falls Patriot-Bugle* on our way home from school later that day. He was standing on the sidewalk outside, talking to Luke Mahoney. "I will certainly consider a feature story on your business—I had no idea that antiques could be so exciting!"

As I glanced at the two of them, I noticed that the reporter had clasped his hands behind his back and was pointing frantically at the ground. I paused for a moment, frowning, then realized he wasn't indicating the sidewalk, but Mr. Mahoney's shoes.

He was wearing loafers!

Big ones, too.

I grabbed my sister by the arm. "Lauren!" I chirped loudly. "Stand right here by that cute pumpkin and I'll take your picture for Mackenzie!"

TRULY, MADLY, SHEEPLY

The *Pumpkin Falls Patriot-Bugle's* jack-o'-lantern was back on their doorstep, thanks to the repentant first graders from Daniel Webster School. And the trio of bats carved into it really *was* cute—but that wasn't what I was after.

Lauren gave me a puzzled look. I jerked my head toward Clark Barque and Mr. Mahoney, and recognition dawned as she saw the reporter pointing at the antiques dealer's shoes. She nodded and grinned for the camera.

"Perfect!" I chirped again as I snapped the photo of Luke Mahoney's loafers. "She's gonna love it."

But it wasn't my cousin I texted, it was my friends: **WE HAVE A LIVE ONE!**

Thanks to Clark Barque holding up his end of the bargain, it looked like we finally had ourselves a prime suspect. Maybe we could crack this case after all!

"Are you sure, Drooly?" asked Hatcher later that evening, after I'd brought him up to speed on the day's events. "Mr. Mahoney?"

The two of us were scrubbing the upstairs bathroom at the farmhouse. Lola wanted everything sparkling before Aunt True and Uncle Rusty returned from their honeymoon on Saturday morning, and the whole family was on work detail, cleaning. There'd be no time tomorrow evening, as my brothers had a big wrestling tournament. Like my earlier swim meet, it was the first one that Lola and Gramps would get to go to in person.

I frowned. "Am I sure? No. But he's the one who makes the most sense at this point, given the fact that he and Mrs. Mahoney really wanted to buy the farm—still want to buy the farm—and since his loafers look like they're the right size. If the shoe fits, right?"

My brother shrugged. "I guess."

Later, Elmer came by just as we were getting ready to head home.

"The gang's all here!" he hollered when he saw us. "That's good, because I need some help getting my pumpkin onto the trailer." He jerked his thumb at the ancient flatbed attached to his equally ancient truck.

"'Help' is the Lovejoy family's middle name," said Gramps, opening the fence to the pumpkin field with a flourish.

Elmer backed carefully across the grass to where his giant pumpkin bulged in the darkness. It took the combined efforts of my father, Gramps, Danny, Hatcher, and me to budge it.

"It's a whopper, Elmer," said my father, panting, as we struggled to roll it up the ramp. "Definitely a prizewinner, I'd say."

"Ayuh," Elmer agreed, which was New Hampshire–speak for "You bet." "I'm hoping she clocks in close to three hundred pounds. That'll show Jed, I reckon."

Jed Thornton was Elmer's archrival, from what Ella had told us. They vied for bragging rights for biggest pumpkin every year.

While the rest of my family was busy securing the

pumpkin to the trailer, I approached Elmer. I'd been waiting for an opening, and this was it. "I almost forgot," I said, handing him the key to the shed. "This belongs to you. Do you remember who might have given it to you?"

Elmer looked at it and frowned. I held my breath. Someone had given the key to Clark Barque, and if we could unmask that someone, we'd have our suspect fair and square—especially if they wore size-thirteen shoes, too.

Elmer rubbed his chin, then shrugged. "Not that I can think of. Well, besides the realtor, that is."

Doris Wheeler, the realtor from West Hartfield! Of course! She'd shown the farm to the retired couple from New York! I should have thought of her.

I stood there for a moment or two, thinking, as Elmer climbed into his truck, tootled his horn, and drove away. Could Doris Wheeler be our prowler? I remembered that she said the couple from New York was willing to pay a lot for the farm—could they have paid her to scare Aunt True and Uncle Rusty off? If so, though, what about the loafers? I hadn't paid any attention at all to her feet the last time I'd seen her, which was at Family Fun Friday at the bookshop, but I didn't recall her being all that tall. Was it possible she had feet bigger than mine? I glanced down ruefully at my size-ten-and-a-half sneakers.

"Penny for your thoughts," said Gramps, slipping his arm through mine.

"They're not worth half that. This dumb case has me tied up in knots, is all."

He laughed. "It's a puzzle, isn't it?" The two of us walked arm in arm back up through the field, closing the gate behind us. "I'm going to miss having my favorite mystery-solving bird watcher and sheep-sitter companion by my side."

"It's only for tonight and tomorrow night. You'll be back at the Maple Street house with us on Saturday, right?"

He nodded. "Indeed. The last thing the honeymooners need when they return is their parents underfoot."

We didn't get home until nearly nine o'clock. With all the excitement of the past few days I was feeling pretty worn-out, and I was looking forward to sleeping in my own bed again, as much as I'd enjoyed my stay at the farm. I was asleep practically before my head hit the pillow.

With no early morning farm chores to take care of, the extra hour of sleep on Friday morning was a luxury. I lay in bed for a while, looking forward to the kickoff of our town's Halloween activities, which would start with just a half day of school.

And with me getting my sisters ready and out the door!

I sprang out of bed. That was the whole reason for me coming home early from the farm! I was on tap as babysitter. My father had left at the crack of dawn to help Gramps and the construction crew finish up with the barn, and my mother was meeting Lola at the bookstore before her early class. Pumpkin

Falls would shortly be a madhouse, thanks to all the tourists expected to descend for the festivities.

Somehow I managed to get myself and my sisters up, showered, dressed, and fed—we only had time to slam-dunk bowls of cereal, but that's what Pippa and Lauren liked best anyway—and out the door in record time. We double-timed it down Maple Street to Hill Street and on into town, taking the shortcut across the village green by the bandstand and arriving at Daniel Webster School just as the bell rang. I slid into my seat in homeroom next to Cha Cha's, panting.

"Glad you could make it," she boomed, and held out her hand. "I hope you remembered to bring our design."

"You bet," I told her, pulling it out of my backpack and handing it over.

The next few hours passed agonizingly slowly. We were all eager to get our hands on our pumpkins. Finally, it was time to head to the gym, where the whole school spread out at the tables that had been set up for us to carve our pumpkins for the design contest.

"He's got a great face for a jack-o'-lantern," I said a little while later, standing back to admire my handiwork. We'd spent weeks perfecting our concepts, and now was the moment of truth.

"Kind of like a basset hound," rasped Cha Cha, and she and Jasmine and I all giggled because she was right.

"A basset hound with a mustache and droopy eyes," said Jasmine.

The design I'd come up with was like a two-sided coin, with Edgar on one side and his famous raven on the other. Arched above the raven was the word "NEVERMORE," which was proving more difficult to carve than I'd expected. It was precision work, and it was taking forever.

"We're definitely going to win," Cha Cha said confidently when I was finally done.

Jasmined nodded. "Good job, Truly."

I was cautiously optimistic. So far, though, in glancing around at the competition that lined the tables in the gym, I hadn't seen another design that seemed as creative as ours. Lauren and Annie's Hello Kitty was cuter than I'd thought it would be, but it wasn't a showstopper like ours. Lucas and Emilio's was probably our toughest competition—they were both decent artists—but I'd pick our Edgar over their Dracula any day. We'd definitely get points for originality, at the very least. Dracula was such a cliché, especially at Halloween.

Still, I wasn't counting any chickens before they hatched. Even if we won the all-school contest, like Scooter and his trebuchet, we'd be going up against the whole town tomorrow. I'd seen some pretty amazing jack-o'-lanterns around Pumpkin Falls, including Mr. Henry's Hagrid.

"I knew it!" crowed Cha Cha, when we returned from lunch to find a blue ribbon placed by our pumpkin.

TRULY, MADLY, SHEEPLY

Jasmine lowered her voice to a whisper. "It didn't hurt that Ms. Matthews was one of the judges."

Sure enough, our Language Arts teacher gave us a thumbs-up from across the cafeteria.

"Good job," Calhoun said. "You guys deserved to win."

I smiled at him. "Thanks."

Right on cue, Emilio materialized just then. "If I had to come in second, I'd rather be second to you than anyone else," he said gallantly, and Jasmine jabbed me in the ribs with her elbow.

"Truly's got two boyfriends, two boyfriends, two boyfriends," she singsonged to me in a whisper as we lined up by grade level with our jack-o'-lanterns. I shushed her as we all started off in a procession to the town hall, where the final judging would take place tomorrow morning.

After dropping our pumpkins off in their assigned spots, I said goodbye to my friends and jogged back to the bookshop to help with the crush of tourists. Lola and Belinda were on their own to deal with the holiday weekend shoppers, since my mother was in class and my father and Gramps were still out at the farm.

"Your lunch is in the office!" Lola called from the cash register as I came in. "Bagel sandwich from Lou's."

"Thanks!" I headed down the back hall. "Hey!" I said in surprise when I opened the office door and found my mother seated at the desk, eating a turkey bagel sandwich. "I thought you had classes all day."

"Just finished," she replied. "The afternoon ones were cancelled so that all the students could experience a 'venerable New England tradition,' as your friend R. J.'s father billed it."

"Venerable?"

"Old and respected." My mother patted the carton of books beside her, and I grabbed a bagel, too, and sat down.

"Well, I guess watching giant pumpkins being judged is educational," I said.

She laughed. "Bumpkin central?"

"If the shoe fits . . ."

She frowned. "Speaking of shoes, I noticed that Dr. Calhoun was wearing loafers today. You don't think . . ." Her voice trailed off.

"Calhoun's father?" I shook my head. "No way."

"It's just so strange. Who would want to do such a thing to True and Rusty? I just hope we've seen the last of him—or her." She smiled at me, changing the subject. "This is nice, having lunch with my favorite middle child."

"I'm your only middle child, Mom!"

Her smile broadened to a grin. "You're still my favorite. I've missed you these past two weeks. Did you have fun out at the farm with your grandparents?"

"You mean except for the part about being terrified it might be haunted?" I smiled back at her. "Yeah, it was fun."

After we finished eating, she stood up and held out her hand to me. "We'd better get back to work. There's a busload due any moment from some retirement community on Cape Cod."

Back out in the main sales area, I spotted Lauren and Pippa over in the children's section. They were eating their lunches and playing with Half-and-Half under Mephisto's watchful eye. Before I could go over to check on them, a bus pulled up in front of the bookstore.

"The Firwood folks are here!" Belinda called, and the next half hour was mayhem.

And then, in the middle of waiting on the flood of customers, Aunt True and Uncle Rusty walked in.

"Surprise!" cried Aunt True.

We all stared at her blankly.

"What are you doing here?" blurted my mother.

"In Pumpkin Falls, you mean?" my aunt replied archly. "I live here, Dinah, remember?"

"She's joking," said Uncle Rusty, giving his new wife a fond look. "We caught an earlier flight home. We missed you all—well, and the farm, too."

"And the sheep," added my father, who had come into the shop behind them. "Don't forget the sheep. That was all the two of them could talk about on the way home from Logan."

"You knew about this?" asked my mother.

My father grinned. "I'm getting pretty good at keeping secrets, right?"

We all abandoned our posts to rush over and hug Aunt

True and Uncle Rusty, and then everyone started talking at once. Finally, Lola held up a hand. "There'll be plenty of time for talk later. Let's get these customers taken care of so they can get back on their bus and go peep at more leaves or jack-o'-lanterns and giant pumpkins, or whatever they want to peep at."

Fifteen minutes later, customers dealt with, my father started to turn the OPEN sign on the door to CLOSED when Belinda stopped him.

"Augustus will be here any minute to help," she said, making shooing motions at us. "We'll watch the shop. You folks go get caught up and—well, you know." She gave us a broad wink. "Plenty of time for us to gawk later."

"Gawk at what?" asked Aunt True.

"The view, that's what," said Belinda. As my aunt and new uncle headed for the door, Belinda glanced over at my mother and me and mimed zipping her lips.

Once outside, we divided up between the minivan and Lola's little hatchback and caravanned out to the farm.

A few minutes later we pulled into the driveway. My aunt climbed out of the minivan and stared at the barn. For once, she was speechless.

"Are you *serious*?" said Uncle Rusty, who wasn't.

"Don't you like it?" Pippa's blue eyes were anxious behind her sparkly pink glasses.

Aunt True reached out and pulled her in for a hug. "No,

I don't like it one bit, Pipster," she replied, finally finding her voice. "I *LOVE* it!"

"The paint may still be wet," cautioned my father. "The crew just finished this morning."

"I don't know what to say," said Aunt True. "It's beautiful! I'm so happy I could cry."

And she did.

My aunt was right. The barn was absolutely, truly a beauty. It no longer leaned to one side but stood as straight as the day it was first built two hundred and fifty years ago. The new glass in the windows sparkled in the October sun. All the broken clapboards had been replaced, and there were no holes in the newly shingled roof.

"Where on earth did you find—" Aunt True pointed wordlessly to the brass windvane atop the roof, which sported the silhouette of a sheep.

Gramps put his arm around her and gave her a squeeze. "Nothing but the best for my only daughter. Bert Harrison brought it by yesterday. He said it was a 'farm-warming' gift. Oh, and by the way, he says his offer still stands if you ever want to sell."

Hatcher gave me a significant look. I mentally added Bert back to the list of suspects, although I couldn't picture him in loafers. But maybe his mild-mannered personality was only a cover. Maybe he was actually our Mr. Big, a supercrafty crook who had traded his barn boots for loafers to throw us off his trail.

"And that," Gramps continued, pointing to the smart new gilt-edged sign over the wide barn door, whose lettering spelled out RIVERCROFT FARM, "is from Theresa the sheep whisperer. She recalled how much you'd admired the one at Liberty Hall."

Aunt True just shook her head. "We can never thank you all enough! This is beyond our wildest dreams—and the best wedding gift ever, right, Rusty?"

"The best ever!" he echoed. "Can we look inside?"

The interior of the barn was equally shipshape. The walls had been given a new coat of whitewash, beams and broken floorboards had been repaired, the rickety treads on the staircase to the lower level had been replaced, and everything had been swept within an inch of its life. Tools hung tidily in their right places, and up above, bales of hay and straw were neatly stacked in the hayloft. It looked like a new barn. Well, a new *old* barn.

After they'd admired everything on the upper level, Aunt True and Uncle Rusty hurried downstairs to check on their flock.

"I'm home, babies!" my aunt cried. The sheep, ever hopeful of snacks, came rushing over to greet her. Even Benedick looked less baleful than usual.

Aunt True gave them all a grain treat, and the two of us gave Beatrice a back rub while we hung out by the pens for a bit, talking. Then Danny and Hatcher arrived in Gramps's old truck and there were more greetings and hugs all around.

"How about we head over to the house?" Gramps suggested to my aunt and uncle. "I seem to recall there's another surprise for you two."

He led the way, and it didn't take long for Aunt True to spot Lola's painting propped on the mantel.

"Mother!" she gasped. "Is this for us?"

Lola kissed her cheek. "It certainly is. It's not every day that my only daughter gets married."

The painting that she'd done for Aunt True and Uncle Rusty looked like an old-fashioned travel poster. The farmhouse and the red barn were in the foreground, while the background sloped away across green fields dotted with white sheep to the distant river. The white steeple of our church poked through trees decked out in full autumn glory, and above it all RIVERCROFT FARM was painted in stylized letters.

"You like it?" said Lola. "I wasn't sure you would. It's not my usual style, but I noticed all those vintage Scottish travel posters you've been collecting and thought I'd give it a go."

"This is an amazing gift, Mom," said my aunt, regarding it thoughtfully. "Two gifts, really—because it's given me an idea for branding our products. Can't you just see this image on a jam jar label?"

Oddly enough, I could. Of course, there were no jam jars yet, but that had never stopped Aunt True. I was guessing that by Christmas there would be a shelf at the bookshop devoted to products from Rivercroft Farm—jams, lotions, yarn, who knew what else—all sporting Lola's artwork on the label.

After that, we crammed into the kitchen, where we scrounged some cheese and crackers and apple cider and talked and laughed and listened to stories from the honeymooners' travels in Scotland.

"It was absolutely perfect," Aunt True said with a sigh, leaning her head on Uncle Rusty's shoulder.

He kissed the top of her head. "It was, indeed."

"I hate to break the mood, but there's something we haven't told you," said Gramps, and he explained about the prowler.

"We thought it was a boggart," I said sheepishly.

"And then we thought it was Clark Barque," said Lauren.

"The new reporter?" Aunt True looked surprised to hear this, and we explained about how we'd found him in the shed and how he was helping us track down the real suspect.

"Wait, now you think it might *Doris Wheeler?* The *realtor?* Or Luke Mahoney?" My aunt's eyebrows shot up even farther. "I don't know which is more preposterous."

"If the shoe fits," I told her, showing her the picture I'd taken earlier of Mr. Mahoney's large loafers.

"Whoever it is, he or she is still on the loose, unfortunately," said Lola. "But I think they know we're on to them, thanks to Truly and Lauren and their friends."

I let Lauren explain about our trap.

"Clever girls!" said Aunt True, giving us an admiring

look. "But someone's got another think coming if they think they can scare us away. Rusty and I don't rattle easily."

Her new husband reached over and gripped her hand. "We certainly don't, and we're not leaving this place. This is *home*."

"You're part of the family now, Rusty," said Gramps. "Lovejoys stick together, and we're all behind you one hundred percent."

My father glanced at his watch. "And speaking of sticking together, we'd better get a move on if we want to be on time for the wrestling tournament."

CHAPTER 31

For once, Mr. Henry wasn't much help.

"Loafers?" He glanced down at the red high-top sneakers which he wore pretty much every day, and frowned. "I don't pay much attention to fashion, I'm afraid, kids."

Officer Tanglewood had little more to offer, and the names he mentioned were already on our list of suspects.

"Reverend Quinn wears them on Sundays, I think," he said, scratching his head. "And mebbe some of those professor types up at the college."

The Pumpkin Falls Private Eyes were nothing if not thorough. I wanted to be absolutely sure of our prowler before we accused anyone of the crime, and we were up early on Saturday to cover as many bases as we could before the festivities started. But nobody had spotted anyone trailing flour in their wake; and everyone had found it too awkward to come right out and ask people what size shoe they wore. Everyone but Scooter, that was.

"Ike Farnsworth has big feet," he told us as we gathered on the library steps to go over our findings. "His wife told me he wears a thirteen."

"It doesn't make sense," I said. "Why would Elmer's brother try to scare our family off of his family's old farm?"

"Maybe he was mad at Elmer for selling?" said Cha Cha.

"Don't you think we'd have heard something if that was the case?" Secrets didn't keep in Pumpkin Falls.

Scooter lifted a shoulder. "I'm just telling you what Ethel told me. Ike wears a thirteen."

I sighed and added "Ike Farnsworth" to our list of suspects, then drummed my pencil on the pad of paper as I regarded the list doubtfully. We still hadn't been able to determine for sure who'd given Clark Barque the key to Elmer's shed. I'd gotten Augustus to call his realtor superfan in West Hartfield last night from the wrestling tournament. Doris was so flattered to hear from him—he told her that he liked to check up on his readers to make sure they were satisfied, which was a huge white lie but Augustus and I both agreed that the circumstances justified it—that she could barely stammer out a reply. I'd been counting on him catching her off guard, because I'd thought it was probably the easiest way to ensure she told the truth. She wouldn't have time to make up a lie.

"Oh, I gave the keys back ages ago," she'd said, when Augustus casually asked about them.

Was she lying? Had she taken a bribe from the couple

in New York? Was star-struck Doris Wheeler really Doris Wheeler-Dealer, criminal mastermind? And what about everyone else on our list? The motives were so thin they were practically see-through. The Mahoneys wanting to expand their antiques business and use the barn as a shop? Bert Harrison coveting the view? A real estate developer who seemed to have skipped town?

Maybe we'd never know who'd been trying to convince us that the farm was haunted.

Brushing off this gloomy thought, I followed my friends over to the village green to inspect the giant pumpkins. I was determined to enjoy the day. Or as much of it as I could while simultaneously trying to avoid the Channel 5 news crew. They'd been sorely disappointed to find that their big feature story had evaporated, since Aunt True had run them off the farm earlier this morning when they'd tried to interview her.

"Not haunted now, never has been, never will be," she'd told them, according to Gramps, who'd witnessed the encounter. I'd helped open up the bookshop earlier and he'd joined us after delivering some of my grandmother's homemade cinnamon rolls to the newlyweds. "You should have seen her, Lola!" he'd said with relish. "All fire and ice. 'And you can quote me on that,' she finished, and then she slammed the door in that fool Carson Dawson's grinning face."

"*Che zucche enormi!*" said Emilio as we wandered around the sprawling display on the village green, and I couldn't agree more. The giant pumpkins really were enormous—and amazing. I was happy to see that Elmer Farnsworth's bruiser had indeed beat his rival Jed Thornton's, but I'd have to congratulate him later. Elmer was proudly posing by it for the Channel 5 news crew and I didn't want to risk a run-in with Carson Dawson. Giving them a wide berth, my friends and I headed back to the library steps. We'd have the best view of the Little Trick-or-Treaters parade from there.

The group of costumed kids and their parents that had gathered to march around the green wasn't a large one, but it was enthusiastic. People had come from neighboring communities all around, and there were moms pushing strollers and dads dealing with overexcited toddlers, and a bunch of younger elementary kids parading solo, including Pippa and Baxter.

"Is that your little sister over there?" asked Emilio, pointing, and I nodded. "And her friend Buster?"

"Baxter."

"Ah, *si*. I like their costumes very much."

The two of them were dressed as matching salt and pepper shakers. It was Cha Cha's idea, and she and her mother had made the costumes. As we watched, they pretended to lean over and sprinkle themselves on one of the stroller's occupants. Predictably, the baby didn't want to be salted or peppered, and started to cry.

The town's brass band was seated in the white wooden

bandstand in the center of the green, and as they struck up the "This is Halloween" movie theme song, the parade began. We all whooped and cheered as the little kids circled around. The music had moved on to "Monster Mash" by the time the parade reached the library steps, and my friends and I and most of the onlookers started dancing. Mr. Henry, who was dressed up as Woody from *Toy Story* and had exchanged his red high-tops for cowboy boots, handed out prizes. All the little kids got one, of course—this wasn't a swim meet—and then he read a scary picture book aloud and passed out candy from a plastic orange pumpkin. After that, the participants raced off to the church basement with Reverend Quinn and his wife and the Farnsworth sisters for a grilled cheese lunch while the rest of us moved on to the town hall for the results of the jack-o'-lantern design contest.

I couldn't avoid the news crew there, unfortunately. I was stuck with Cha Cha and Jasmine behind the table where our entry was displayed. Emilio and Lucas were on our left with their Dracula pumpkin; Scooter and Calhoun were on our right. The elaborate spiderweb they'd carved on their jack-o'-lantern was pretty good but, like Dracula, kind of a Halloween cliché. I didn't see either one of them beating our Edgar Allan Poe and his raven.

"Do you think we have a chance at the prize?" whispered Jasmine.

Even split three ways, the one hundred dollars that would

go to the winner was nothing to sneeze at. I knew Jasmine was saving up for a fancy set of earbuds, and I had already mentally spent my share on a new book on owls that had just arrived at the bookshop.

"Maybe," I whispered back. "Hagrid is going to be hard to beat, though."

Ms. Matthews stopped in front of our table. After admiring all three of our entries, she leaned in toward Cha Cha and Jasmine and me. "Don't tell anyone, but I'm rooting for you girls!" she told us in a low voice.

"Too bad you aren't one of the judges," said Jasmine.

"Maybe you could give us extra credit," Cha Cha suggested, and Ms. Matthews laughed.

"Maybe I could! Not that you Edgarettes need it. That was quite the performance you gave our class the other day. I told Principal Burnside about it, and he thinks you should enter your act in the school talent show this year."

Unfortunately, the Channel 5 news crew chose that exact moment to cruise by. Carson Dawson swiveled in our direction.

"What's this about a talent show?" he asked, frowning at his program of events, which was printed up each year by the *Pumpkin Falls Patriot-Bugle* and distributed all around town.

Ms. Matthews flapped her hand. "It's just a school thing."

But the TV host was not to be deterred. "Tell me more— my viewers love small-town fare. A local talent show could be just the ticket." He glanced down at our jack-o'-lantern. "Edgar Allan Poe, eh? One of my favorites."

"Nevermore," whispered Cha Cha.

My stifled giggle caught Carson Dawson's attention and he looked up at me. "Say, I know you! You're that tall bookshop girl."

"Truly Gigantic," said Scooter under his breath, dredging up another old nickname I hated. I knew he was just trying to be funny, but I kicked him under the table anyway.

Aunt True had told me to try to turn any potential encounter with the TV host to my advantage. Not that she'd done the same this morning, from the sounds of it. More like burned her bridges entirely. Could I help mend them?

"That's right, Mr. Dawson," I said, giving him my smarmiest smile. "I'm Truly Lovejoy of Lovejoy's Books."

His smile faded. "Lovejoy? Oh yes. I had a, uh, chat with your aunt this morning."

In for a penny, in for a pound, I thought. I pointed across the hall, hoping he wouldn't notice the blatant attempt to deflect him away from talent shows and fire-and-ice aunts. "See that man over there? That's my dad. You interviewed him last winter, remember? The wounded warrior?"

My father loathed that term as much as I loathed Truly Gigantic, Drooly, *la giraffe*, and everything else my siblings and friends called me, but I knew it had a good chance of catching Carson Dawson's ear.

TRULY, MADLY, SHEEPLY

Which it did.

His face brightened. "I most certainly recall your brave father! Our ratings went through the roof for that segment."

"Maybe you could do a follow-up," I suggested slyly. "I'm sure he'd love to tell you all about what's happening at the bookshop these days, and about his progress. Did you know he's flying again?"

"Is that a fact?" A calculated expression crept across Carson Dawson's tanned, wrinkly face as he weighed potential viewer reaction to a follow-up story on a wounded vet versus one about a high school talent show.

"Nice save, Truly," said Jasmine, slapping me a high five as the host and his team scurried off toward my father. "I thought for a minute there the Edgarettes were going to have to sing and dance on TV."

According to the blurb in the program, it was tradition in Pumpkin Falls that the winner of the biggest pumpkin contest announced the winner of the jack-o'-lantern design contest. Sure enough, a few minutes later, I saw Elmer Farnsworth making his way to the podium, where he banged the gavel. A hush fell over the crowd.

"Ladeeeeez and gentlemen!" Elmer cried in a circus ringmaster voice, wringing the most out of his moment in the spotlight. "It is my great pleasure to announce that the winner"—he paused as one of the judges trotted over and thrust a piece of paper at him. Glancing down at it, he adjusted his glasses, then continued—"to announce that this year we actually have *two* winners. I've just been informed that there's a tie. The entries were simply too close to call."

Jasmine grabbed my hand and Cha Cha's and squeezed. I squeezed back.

"So this year's prize goes to . . ." Elmer let a few seconds tick by in an overly dramatic pause. "Mr. Henry's Hagrid . . . and Edgar Allan Poe, thanks to"—he peered at the paper again—"the Edgarettes?"

My family cheered wildly. So did Cha Cha's and Jasmine's.

"Good job, guys," said Scooter grudgingly.

Calhoun gave me a hug, which was unexpected. Not to be outdone, Emilio gave me one, too. I could feel my face flame.

"Truly has two boyfriends, two boyfriends, two boyfriends," Jasmine sang to me again as we went up to the podium to pose for pictures with Mr. Henry and our blue-ribbon pumpkins. Afterward, we collected our prize, my share of which was still enough to cover the bird book, I was pretty sure. Especially with the family discount.

And then it was time to head out to the farm. We had a surprise party to host!

CHAPTER 32

"I think I want to be a sheep shearer when I grow up," Lauren said dreamily, gazing at the freshly shorn flock. "Wasn't that *awesome?*"

"*Si*, awesome," echoed Emilio. "Lauren, you would be a very good *pastorella*, and a very good *tosatrice per pecore*, 'sheep shearer,' I am sure, just like your big sister."

I made a rude noise. The sheep shearing *had* been amazing, but that didn't mean I was ready to jump feet-first into a career in wool. I glanced across the barn to where Calhoun and Scooter were talking to the shearer. I could tell they'd enjoyed themselves, too. Everybody had. The barn was thronged with family and friends who'd come to watch as Beatrice, Benedick, and the Ladies of American History got their haircuts. Including Ella Bellow, who was back in my family's good graces, more or less, now that the pumpkin-snatching episode was behind us.

"Just here to check on my future sweaters!" she'd joked.

The shearer was old-school, just as Aunt True had told us he'd be. Instead of electric clippers, he used a giant pair of shears—a scissors-like tool that reminded me a bit of hedge clippers. The sheep had known something was up and were milling around nervously in the holding pen when he'd arrived. One by one they were brought out onto the main floor, where the shearer coaxed or wrestled them into a sitting position for the shearing. The poor sheep looked so surprised and ridiculous sitting there with their legs splayed out that Pippa and Baxter dissolved into gales of laughter.

"Will it hurt them?" Lauren asked anxiously.

"Not if it's done right," the shearer assured her.

As he got to work, I watched each sheep relax. The shearer had the same quiet, confident way about him that Bert Harrison and Theresa the sheep whisperer did, and I could see the animals respond to that.

We'd all watched with interest as he started snipping. First, he concentrated on the belly, then moved on to the haunches and sides and down to the "boots," the fluff of fleece that the Romney breed had around their lower legs.

"It's kind of like peeling an orange," Lauren said, watching the shears go around and around, the fleece peeling away in their wake.

I nodded, equally mesmerized.

When the shearer was done, the shorn sheep was led back

to the pen, looking oddly naked without its fleece, which now lay on the floor like a giant woolly blanket.

A blanket that needed a good wash.

"Don't worry," said Aunt True, when she saw my nose wrinkle. "It will go through quite a cleaning process before it's spun into yarn."

Benedick was up last. He made it abundantly clear that he was not interested in the whole event. It took Uncle Rusty and both of my brothers to wrestle him into place for the shearer. But finally, he, too, was shorn, and his fleece bundled into bags with the others to be taken to the woolen mill later for processing.

As my aunt and uncle led their flock out the door and around the back of the barn to their pen on the lower level, I grabbed a broom and started to help sweep up the main floor. We'd be needing it cleared out once the surprise party started.

Which would be anytime now.

Outside, Hatcher and Danny had placed the red tractor in the field and piled it high with pumpkins. It made a great backdrop for photos, and people were lining up for a turn. They were lining up for fresh homemade cider, too. Gramps had found an old cider press among Elmer's abandoned junk up in the hayloft and got it working, and he and Lauren and Annie had spent some time picking apples from the farm's small orchard to press.

"Macouns!" Gramps had crowed when he tasted one.

"They're the best for eating, and the best for pies and cider, too."

Aunt True and Uncle Rusty were still completely clueless about the coming festivities. They'd been told that we were all going back to the Maple Street house for dinner, where they'd hang out with Gramps and Lola and my parents until the Halloween pumpkin toss started.

"What's this?" said my aunt, when the van from Lou's Diner pulled in a few minutes later and Lou and his catering team hopped out.

"This," Lola told her, "is a barn-warming! Surprise!"

Danny and Hatcher set up folding tables and chairs in the barn while my father helped Lou fire up the grill. In short order, the catering team was cooking up burgers and hot dogs and setting out a buffet of Halloween-themed side dishes.

"Mm-mmm, sweet potato fries!" said Jasmine, looking over the generous spread hungrily. "And coleslaw served in mini pumpkins? Too cute."

"You're invited back for dessert around the bonfire after the pumpkin toss," my mother told the gathered guests. "Meanwhile, dig in!"

A little while later, as the meal was winding down, we heard honking and looked outside to see a school bus trundling down the driveway. True to his word, Gramps had hired a bus to take the trick-or-treaters downtown.

"Anyone else who wants to is welcome to ride along,"

TRULY, MADLY, SHEEPLY

Gramps announced to the adults. "Parking downtown will be a mob scene, so it might be easier. You'll be coming back here anyway after the pumpkin toss, and you can pick up your cars then."

"We'll open the bookstore just for you," my mother added. "There'll be hot beverages available, and you're welcome to hang out there with us while the trick-or-treaters make their rounds."

Hatcher and Danny had declared themselves too old for trick-or-treating, which was kind of cheating, since I knew they wouldn't think themselves too old to raid our candy haul after we'd gone to all the effort of collecting it. While they headed for their truck, the rest of us scrambled to get our costumes on and board the bus.

"That was, how do you say . . . a *blast*?" said Emilio, as my friends and I dashed back to the bus to dump off our collective haul of candy before heading to the village green. We'd cut it close; the pumpkin toss was about to start.

"*Si.*" I smile back at him from under my Edgarette wig. His Dracula fangs—we'd both dressed to match our jack-o'-lanterns—were kind of cute. "A blast for sure."

I grabbed a handful of candy and followed my friends over to the library. My new uncle was playing the role of Nathaniel Daniel Lovejoy this year, and he really threw himself into it as he read the famous proclamation from the library steps with gusto. He finished to thunderous applause.

"And now, I hereby declare this year's Halloween Pumpkin Toss . . . OPEN!" Uncle Rusty shouted, and there was a mad scramble as the gathered crowd surged toward the covered bridge, vying for the best viewpoint. I spotted Carson Dawson and his crew down by the riverbank near the wooden launch pad that had been set up, filming the parade of catapults that was heading their way. Scooter was proudly at the head of it, pulling The Beast in the red wagon from school.

"Go, Scooter!" cried Jasmine, who thought her brother was a pain most of the time—with good reason—but who was nevertheless a loyal twin.

My friends and I managed to maneuver through the crowd and wedge ourselves right up along the bridge's wooden railing. We were almost directly above the camera crew and had a great view.

I leaned on the railing and looked down. Below us, the river's dark water swirled and frothed as it rushed away from the waterfall and under the bridge. I shivered.

Calhoun, who was standing next to me, gave me a sympathetic glance from underneath the glossy black wig he was wearing, thanks to the college theater department's wardrobe collection. His father had talked Calhoun and his sister Juliet into dressing up as—*Romeo and Juliet*. I could tell Calhoun was regretting that decision. "Bad memories?"

I nodded and he bumped his shoulder against mine.

I smiled to myself. He hadn't reached for my hand and a shoulder bump certainly wasn't a kiss, but it was something.

Turning my gaze to the camera crew below, I stiffened. "Loafers!" I whispered to my friends. "Carson's wearing loafers!"

Cha Cha and Jasmine stared down, too.

"Yeah," boomed Cha Cha, "but look how tiny his feet are. If they were any smaller, they'd be hooves."

"Maybe he's a boggart," said Jasmine, and that set my friends and I all to laughing so hard that everyone around us turned and stared.

The covered bridge and the riverbank were jammed with onlookers. The crowd grew quiet as the first contestant stepped onto the launch pad. She took her time, lining up her catapult with the middle of the waterfall and setting her glowing jack-o'-lantern in the sling. Then she pulled the sling back, took aim, and fired.

A collective "Aaaahhhh!" went up from the onlookers, and I even heard a squeak of surprise from Carson Dawson below. A fiery pumpkin sailing through the air on Halloween Eve was quite a sight. No wonder our town forefathers were so enthusiastic about it.

The jack-o'-lantern landed in the water a considerable distance from the waterfall with a splash and an audible hiss as the candle inside was extinguished.

"Solid six!" cried one of the judges, who was standing in

a strategic spot on the opposite side of the riverbank. He held up a number painted on a white sign so everyone could see.

There were two dozen contestants, and it took some time to get through them all. Scooter, as youngest, was last. There were several strong entries, with two of them—scoring an eight and a nine, respectively—reaching the base of the waterfall, though neither touched it. Could Scooter beat either of those? He'd need a perfect score for a decisive victory, which meant actually hitting the waterfall.

"Stand back! Gimme some room!" Scooter said importantly when it was finally his turn.

"Let Ironman through!" someone in the crowd shouted. Scooter was dressed up as his favorite Marvel character.

"Is that thing legal?" yelled someone else.

"Already passed inspection," the head judge, who was standing by the launchpad.

Scooter swaggered onto the wooden platform, hefted his trebuchet from the red wagon, and set it into position.

"What is that contraption?" asked Carson Dawson, thrusting a mic in his face.

"It's a trebuchet," Scooter replied, grinning at the camera. "I call it 'The Beast.'"

He made a big show of drawing back the trebuchet's wooden arm and placing his jack-o'-lantern into the cradle just so. Then he pressed down on the lever with all his might.

"Fire in the hole!" he cried, and let it go.

TRULY, MADLY, SHEEPLY

The Beast's arm snapped upright, hurling the glowing orb up, up, up into the ink-black October sky.

"Dude, look at it fly!" cried one of the Channel 5 camera crew.

Scooter's jack-o'-lantern sailed closer and closer to the waterfall. I held my breath. On either side of me, my friends held their breath, too. Would it make it?

Scooter's pumpkin skimmed the top of the waterfall and then disappeared. A shout went up from the judge on the clifftop as it landed somewhere upstream.

Yes!

"That sucker's on its way to West Hartfield!" hollered someone in the crowd. There was a pause, and everyone peered at the top of the waterfall, waiting to see the score. Finally, a white sign appeared on the clifftop.

"Ten!" Carson Dawson hooted below us. "The Beast gets a perfect score!"

Scooter did a touchdown dance and mugged for the TV camera. People rushed over to congratulate him and he posed for pictures next to The Beast. The judges pinned a blue ribbon to it and handed over a pumpkin-shaped trophy and an envelope to Scooter—one hundred dollars that he didn't have to share with anyone else, the lucky dog.

"I'm going to be on the front page of the newspaper *and* on TV," Scooter bragged as we were getting back on the bus after all the excitement died down. Annoyingly enough, it was probably true.

"Are all towns in America this exciting?" asked Emilio, sliding into the seat beside me.

I glanced out the school-bus window at the village green, where Clark Barque was standing with his camera, trying to get a shot of the full moon behind the bandstand. Tomorrow, the giant pumpkins would be gone, the crowds would be gone, and our little town would be back to its usual assortment of Bumpkin Central police-blotter stuff—missing sunglasses and stray woodchucks and things that went bump in the night. I turned to Emilio and smiled.

"Nope," I said. "Just this one."

CHAPTER 33

By the time we got back to the farm, Hatcher and Danny and my father had the bonfire going, and the fiddlers that Gramps had hired for the party were setting up in the barn.

"Who's ready for a good time?" my mother called in her best Texas twang. She grabbed my father by his good hand and led him onto the barn floor, where they demonstrated the country line dance they were going to teach us.

"I had no idea my brother could dance like that," said Aunt True, watching in fascination as my parents hooked their thumbs through the belt loops in their jeans—one real thumb, and one titanium one in my father's case—and then grapevine, pivoted, rocked, and heel-toe-tapped their way through "Boot-Scootin' Boogie."

I nodded. "Yep. He and my mother used to go line-dancing all the time when they were at the University of Texas, from what they told us." My parents had met in college back in Austin.

Line-dancing beat the pants off any other kind of dancing, in my opinion. For one thing, a person didn't have to choose a partner. Which made it easier when a person wasn't sure who to choose.

When it was time for all of us to try it, I ended up dancing between Calhoun and Emilio, whose parents were in the line in front of us.

"Having fun, *Tesoro*?" Mrs. Frangipani called over her shoulder.

"*Si, Mamma*!" Emilio called back, and I could tell that he was.

We all were.

I looked around the barn. Cha Cha's parents knew the steps already, of course, but most of the rest of us were just bumbling along. No one cared, though. Everybody was smiling—Mr. Henry in his Woody costume; Principal Burnside, whose family of redheads were dressed in identical red T-shirts with the *Incredibles* logo on them but who still looked to me like a flock of flamingos; and Reverend Quinn and his wife, who were inexplicably dressed as a pair of camels. Finally, I realized they'd probably raided the Nativity costumes at church. Bud Jefferson, who hadn't dressed up, was lighter on his feet than I'd expected for such a big man, and beside him, Lucas's mother, who was wearing a fairy godmother getup, watched him in delight. Cha Cha and Jasmine, who like me were still wearing their Edgarette costumes, were dancing side by side and laughing their heads off. Behind them, Augustus and Belinda were "a sight to behold," as my Texas grandmother liked to say, dazzling in their matching purple-sequined cowboy shirts that Augustus had special ordered for the occasion.

We were right in the middle of "Should've Been a Cowboy" when there was a sound like a gunshot outside. Across the floor, I saw my father stiffen.

"Everybody down!" he shouted, as another rapid burst cracked through the air. "Now!"

We Lovejoys knew an order when we heard it, and so did everyone else. We all hit the floor, fiddlers included. My heart was pounding like crazy. Were we being ambushed?

Outside, there was a long whistle, followed by an explosion. And then the sky lit up—red, white, and blue, followed by a shower of sparkles.

Not gunfire. *Fireworks.*

"Someone threw fireworks on the bonfire!" Hatcher called.

The barn emptied as everyone ran outside to see. Which wasn't such a good idea, with all the whizzing and banging and sparks flying every which way from Sunday.

There were times I wouldn't trade having an ex-soldier for a father for anything. This was definitely one of them. In a flash, Mr. Military took charge, barking out orders.

"Call the fire department!" he told Lola, who nodded and ran toward the house. "Dad, you and Rusty stamp out any stray sparks inside the barn," he told Gramps and my new uncle. "The boys and I will take care of the outside."

Another explosion of fireworks set off a chorus of shrieks from all the little kids and my father shoved Pippa at Lauren. "Get your sister in the house. Augustus, Belinda, you round up the rest of the kids and follow. They'll be safe inside."

Lucas Winthrop's years of fire-drill training finally proved useful.

"Mr. Lovejoy, you should get all the grown-ups to safety, too, not just the little kids," he squeaked from inside his Headless Horseman costume. His mother had sewn it for him and the eyeholes weren't lined up properly, which made him look like a sinking ship as he cocked his head to try and peer out. "Someplace the fire can't reach. My mother always makes me wait for her under the apple tree in our front yard."

My father clapped him on the shoulder. "Good thinking, Lucas. Dinah, why don't you lead our guests to shelter by the vegetable garden behind the house?" My mother nodded and ran off, too. "Hatcher, Danny, you come with me. We need to round up the garden hoses, pronto."

If it wasn't so scary, it would have been exciting. It was like the Fourth of July had gone crazy. Fireworks were cracking and fizzing as they flew overhead, spiraling left, right, up, down, and all over. The air was filed with smoke and sparks.

Aunt True grabbed my arm. "The sheep!"

We darted back inside the barn and ran toward the stairs,

taking them two at a time. As we passed the chicken coop, Aunt True flung open the door and the hens came flapping out in a rush, squawking indignantly as they fluttered outside and away from the deafening noise.

The ewes were clustered in a terrified huddle in the far corner of their pen, bleating pitifully.

"Poor babies!" cried Aunt True. "Don't worry, we'll get you to safety."

There was no way the sheep would hear the grain can over all the commotion, though, I realized. We'd just have to drag them outside. I grabbed two rope halters and gave one to Aunt True.

"Get Beatrice and the rest will follow!" I told her, shouting to be heard over the barrage of firecrackers. "I'll get Benedick!"

She nodded and slipped through the gate to gather the ewes while I turned and crossed to Benedick's pen.

"A love," Theresa the sheep whisperer had called him. "Like a big dog."

He didn't look like either one at the moment, glaring at me from the far corner of his pen. He looked like—well, he looked like trouble.

"Benedick," I said quietly but firmly, channeling the shearer, and Bert Harrison, and Theresa the sheep whisperer. "We need to get you outside, where you'll be safe in case the barn catches fire."

Taking a deep breath, I opened the gate and advanced on him, rope halter in hand. I kept up a steady murmur of encouragement as I drew closer. I could see that he was trembling. The commotion had gotten to him, too. He eyed me with that sideways look of his but let me slip the halter over his head.

"Come on now, boy," I said, and tugged. He took a step forward. "That's it."

Inch by inch, I pulled him toward the door that led outside from the barn's lower level. Just as we reached it, there was another staccato burst of fireworks overhead. Spooked, the big ram exploded into motion, charging past me at top speed. Somehow, I managed to hold onto the halter, and he dragged me behind him like a water-skier in the wake of a boat.

"Stop!" I shouted. "Benedick, stop!"

He ignored me, of course, but my friends heard me. In a flash they appeared around the side of the barn. Calhoun took one look and grabbed Cha Cha by the hand. She grabbed Jasmine, who grabbed Lucas, who grabbed Scooter, who grabbed Emilio. They were forming a human chain!

Benedick was charging straight for them.

"Steady!" shouted Calhoun.

It was like watching a game of "Red Rover." Benedick flung himself at their outstretched arms, but they didn't let go of one another and he didn't break through. As he backed away and gathered his strength for a second attempt, Aunt True came up behind me and pulled me to my feet.

"Don't give up now, Tall Timber," she said, and somehow managed to slip the second halter over Benedick as he rushed past.

We tugged with all our might on the double halter, and the human chain held firm again. My friends herded the big ram back toward us and Aunt True and I managed to manhandle him into the pasture. We closed the gate firmly behind him.

"He'll be safe out here," Aunt True said, leaning against the fence to catch her breath. "They all will." She looked up as another round of fireworks sent a shower of emerald green sparks through the air. "We'd better go see what else we can do to help."

"The roof!" shouted Ella Bellow as we rounded the corner of the barn.

I looked up to see that several firecrackers had landed on its newly shingled surface. They lay there, smoldering, and as we all watched in horror, puffs of smoke appeared followed by little licks of orange flame.

"If the roof goes and the fire reaches the hayloft, we lose the barn," said my father grimly. "Hatcher! Danny! Where are those hoses?"

Danny, who was standing by the faucet near the barn door, gave him a thumbs up. "All connected!" he shouted back. But when he reached down to turn on the water, the spigot handle came off in his hand. He turned around and held it up, shaking his head.

My father never swore in front of us kids. He did when he saw that spigot handle, though. "Sabotage," he growled.

"*Il folletto*," whispered Emilio. "The boggart."

So that was what the prowler had been up to, the night we set the trap! This was all his—or her—doing. We'd been sabotaged!

"Bucket brigade!" called my father, and he and my brothers and Gramps and Uncle Rusty raced off to gather containers from the house and the barn.

I stared up at the roof, aghast. Were my aunt's dreams about to go up in smoke?

In the distance I could hear the sound of a siren. Lola must have gotten through to the Pumpkin Falls fire department. Help was on the way!

The only problem was, it would take them a while to get here, and we didn't have time to wait. We needed help *right now*.

The wail of the siren gave me an idea.

A crazy idea.

What was it that Aunt True had told me back on Abracadabra Day?

Sometimes, crazy was the best thing to do.

I turned and ran to go find Elmer Farnsworth.

CHAPTER 34

"Elmer! Is there water in your fire truck in the shed?"

"What?" He looked at me in a daze. I'd found him behind the house by the vegetable garden, where my mother had ushered our guests to safety. I repeated my question, louder this time to be heard over the explosions from the bonfire behind us.

"Maybe?" he said. "I can't remember if I emptied it after the Fourth of July parade."

It was a long shot, then—but still worth a try.

Elmer clutched my arm, suddenly catching my drift. "I don't have the key to the shed with me!"

"Leave that to me. How about the ignition key for the fire truck?"

He shook his head. "It doesn't have one. Just press the button on the dashboard. Oh, and it's a stick shift."

"Got it." I flung myself down the path through the

pumpkin field. "PFPEs!" I hollered at the top of my lungs, hoping they'd hear me. "*Please please please* let there be water in the tank," I muttered to myself, my Edgarette cape flapping and swirling around me as I ran.

I heard shouts behind me and glanced over my shoulder to see my friends racing to catch up. The barn was silhouetted against the glow of the bonfire, as were the outlines of their costumes, and with the fireworks still going off overhead, it made for an eerie backdrop.

When I reached the shed door, I found it padlocked, of course. I leaned against it for a few seconds to catch my breath.

"Calhoun, you'll have to drive," I told him as my friends arrived.

"Drive what?"

"Elmer's fire truck. It's a stick shift."

"Me?" He shook his head. "I don't know how to drive stick."

"Seriously?" I gaped at him, then turned to Scooter, who also shook his head. So did Cha Cha and Jasmine. I didn't even bother asking Lucas. His mother barely let him ride a bicycle.

"I can drive a stick shift," said Emilio.

Of course he could.

"Perfect. Let me just get this door open, then you can take it from there. Shine your lights over here for me, guys?" I reached under my Edgarette robe and thrust my hand into the pocket of my jeans, only to pull out—my little wooden owl from Africa? I stared at it, aghast. The big paper clips were in my *other* jeans.

Think, Truly, think!

"The window up by the roof is open a crack," I said, pointing up at it. "One of us can climb through."

In reply, my friends all looked at me.

"No way." I shook my head.

"You're the tallest," Cha Cha pointed out. "I'd never be able to reach."

"She is right," said Emilio. "This is a job for *la giraffe.*"

"I'll give you a boost," Calhoun coaxed, bending over and intertwining his fingers for me to step on. He gave me an encouraging smile. "You can do this, Truly. On the count of three."

As Calhoun flung me upward, I reached with all my might. My fingertips grazed the windowsill, but I wasn't close enough to grab it.

"Again," I said. "Higher." He flung me skyward again. "Got it!"

I dangled for a moment. "Some help, please?"

Below me, there was a scramble as Calhoun knelt down and Scooter climbed onto his back.

"Oof," said Calhoun. "Dude, how much Halloween candy did you eat?"

With Scooter standing on Calhoun, I was able to brace

my foot on his shoulder and push on the window. It yielded with a screeching protest. "I'm going in!" I called down to my friends, and managed to wriggle myself up until my top half was balanced on the windowsill.

I shone my cell phone torch around the rafters. There was a ladder leaning up against the far wall that shouldn't be too hard to reach, if I could crawl across the wide beam almost directly under me. A wide beam covered with —

"Are you *laughing*?" Jasmine called up to me, incredulous.

Did all roads in Pumpkin Falls lead to pigeon poo for me? It was only fitting, I supposed as I finally managed to get ahold of myself and wriggle the rest of me through the window. My adventures as a private eye had begun with pigeon poo, up in the steeple of the First Parish Church last winter, and now they'd brought me back to pigeon poo tonight, here in Elmer's shed.

A few moments later I jumped down from the ladder, landing on the floor with a soft thud. A quick scan with my torch identified Elmer's fire truck, which was the largest vehicle in the shed.

"Does it have water in it?" called Lucas, as he heard me pull back the tarp.

"How should I know?" I called back. "I'm going for it anyway."

"How are you going to get out?" Calhoun's voice was muffled by the shed's walls. "The door is still locked."

I hadn't thought of that. In the distance I could hear the

shouts of my family and our friends up by the bonfire. I could hear the siren, too, but it was still a ways off. "Watch me!"

Climbing into the driver's seat, I flashed my cell phone light around, looking for the button on the dashboard Elmer had mentioned. A frantic rustling told me that mice—or worse, rats—had made themselves a cozy little nest somewhere beneath me, but I couldn't think about that now.

There! I found the button and pressed it. Nothing. Pressed it again. Still nothing. "Anybody have an idea how this thing starts?"

"You need to step on the clutch," Emilio called back.

"What's a clutch?"

"Look for the *pedale*—the pedal—on the floor between the brake and the gas. You have to push it to change gears, too."

"Got it!" I pushed hard with my foot—thank goodness, *la giraffe* had long legs as well as big feet—and pressed the button again. This time, the engine roared to life.

"Out of the way, guys!" I shouted in warning, and released the clutch as I pressed down on the gas pedal with all my might. The fire truck leaped forward and crashed against the shed door.

Not hard enough to break through, though.

"Again!" hollered Calhoun.

I fumbled with the stick shift and threw it into reverse, then pushed down on the gas pedal again. This time there was just a horrible grinding sound.

"Clutch!" Emilio shouted. "Let it up *lentamente*—slowly—when you press the gas!"

I followed his instructions, just giving it a little gas this time. The fire truck inched backwards. I kept going until it bumped up against the antique tractor behind me, then stepped on the brake, this time keeping my foot on the clutch as I put it back in drive.

"Watch out!" I warned my friends again.

I floored it.

This time, the fire truck burst through the padlocked door, and I emerged to a chorus of whoops from my friends.

"Do you want to drive?" I asked Emilio as he and my friends all clambered aboard.

He shook his head and slid into the passenger seat beside me. "Why? You're doing fine."

"Don't say I didn't warn you," I told him, lurching forward as I pressed down on the gas and clumsily released the clutch again.

Calhoun, who was standing on the running board beside me, grabbed the door handle and held on for dear life as we bumped our way forward. I drove uphill through the field as fast as I could, dodging pumpkins all the way.

"Does this thing have a siren?" shouted Scooter from somewhere behind me.

"No idea!" I shouted back.

"Wait, there's a bell!"

TRULY, MADLY, SHEEPLY

I let out a groan. Scooter and bells were a bad mix. The last one he'd rung had been the Paul Revere bell in our church downtown, and I'd been deaf for days. I hunched my shoulders, bracing myself.

Scooter grabbed the rope and tugged on it for all he was worth. I winced at the explosion of clanging, but since I couldn't let go of the steering wheel to cover my ears, I just gritted my teeth and drove faster.

The bell had alerted the crowd by the vegetable garden and someone opened the gate in the fence for us. People scattered as the antique fire truck came flying through. I aimed for somewhere between the barn and the bonfire, stepping on the brake as we drew close.

Nothing happened. We were still barreling forward toward the flames.

"Clutch! Clutch!" Emilio yelled at me.

"Sorry!" I shoved my foot against the clutch, then the brake, and we finally came to a grinding halt.

"Turn on the pump!" I called to Scooter as I threw the gear into park. I left the engine running, though, as I had a hunch that it was needed for the pump to work.

"How?" Scooter asked.

"You're the engineering genius, Mr. Eighth-Grade Pumpkin-Toss Wonder of the World," snapped Jasmine. "You figure it out."

Elmer Farnsworth, who was surprisingly spry for an older

gentleman, trotted over from his safe vantage point in the vegetable garden to help. "See that lever that says 'On'?" he told Scooter. "Ayuh, that's the one. Flip it."

My father and brothers were beside us now, too, and at Elmer's direction they lugged the canvas hose out of its storage box in the back, attached it to the pump, and waited.

And waited some more.

"Give her a minute!" Elmer said. "She's an old girl—1921 American LaFrance—but she's reliable. If there's any water left in the tank, that is."

Seconds ticked by. Finally, a dribble of water appeared from the end of the firehose. The dribble quickly turned into a stream, and then a deluge.

"Stand back!" my father ordered. He shoved the canvas hose under his arm and clamped down on the brass hose-tip with his titanium fingers. With his good hand, he aimed at the blazing roof and focused on getting the fire under control as we all cheered him on.

By the time the Pumpkin Falls fire truck pulled into the driveway a couple of minutes later, the flames on the roof had been extinguished and the bonfire was just a hissing pile of smoldering embers. The firefighters—Officer Tanglewood's twin brothers, Otis and Paul—looked crestfallen at having missed the action, but also relieved. Nobody liked to see a house burn down. Or a barn.

I paced around the driveway, struggling to catch my

breath. My father came over and draped his good arm around my shoulder.

"Good work, Truly-in-the-Middle," he said, pulling me in close for a hug. "How did I ever get such a brave, smart daughter?"

"I'm a Lovejoy, remember?" I replied. "You always tell us we can do anything!"

He laughed and hugged me again. "We certainly can."

CHAPTER 35

I was helping Aunt True put the sheep back inside for the night when a flash of movement caught my eye. I looked over to see someone wearing a dark hooded robe detach themselves from the crowd and start to slip around the far side of the barn. I frowned, trying to recall who'd been wearing a Grim Reaper costume. Mr. Mahoney, maybe?

"Hey!" I called out, but the hooded figure just picked up their pace.

As they passed the remains of the bonfire, I saw the reflection of the embers on the shoes beneath the dark robe.

Loafers.

"BOGGART!" I yelled at the top of my lungs.

I had to hand it to my family and friends, they instantly got it. As I took off running, the Pumpkin Falls Private Eyes were close on my heels. And so were Gramps and Aunt True and Uncle Rusty and my father and brothers.

TRULY, MADLY, SHEEPLY

The person in the hooded robe was fast, though, and had a head start. They cleared the barn and sprinted for the row of parked cars.

"I think it's Mr. Mahoney!" I shouted. "He's getting away!"

"Not if I have anything to say about it!" Scooter replied, swerving back toward the barn. "He hasn't met The Beast!"

It was our only hope of catching him, unless my father and the rest of my family could stop him in time. My friends and I didn't hesitate. We turned and followed Scooter. We'd had one long-shot win tonight—could we have two?

Scooter whipped off his Ironman helmet and grabbed The Beast from the back of his parents' SUV, where he'd stashed it after the pumpkin toss. Wheeling it into position in the middle of the driveway, he held out his hand. "Ammo," he ordered, sounding like my father.

If there was one thing we had no shortage of at Rivercroft Farm, it was pumpkins. My friends and I lined up like a bucket brigade and started handing them to Scooter. There was no showmanship this time; he was all business. Down went the trebuchet's wooden arm, plunk went the pumpkin into position, down went the lever, and *zing* went the pumpkin as Scooter released it through the air.

The first two missed our mystery prowler entirely, one landing way too far ahead, the other way too far behind and just managing to avoid Hatcher.

"He's almost at his car!" cried Lucas, hopping up and down as he tried to peer through the eyeholes of his costume.

The third pumpkin landed close enough that the figure in the dark robe swerved, but he managed to dodge it just in time. He opened the door to his car and got in. It was a light-colored SUV, just like the one that the Mahoneys drove.

"It's definitely Mr. Mahoney," I said. We heard the roar of the engine as it came to life.

"Fourth one's the charm," said Scooter.

I certainly hoped so. I passed him another pumpkin, and he plopped it into place. He glanced up, eyes narrowed as he adjusted The Beast's trajectory, and let fly.

It was like the riverbank all over again.

Up, up, up went the pumpkin, arcing high over Uncle Rusty's truck and Lola's hatchback and our minivan and all the other cars that were parked beyond the barn—and then landed with a loud SPLAT squarely on the windshield of the fleeing car, spewing pumpkin guts from one side of the glass to the other.

The driver was blinded.

"Yes!" I shouted as the car screeched to a halt at the entrance to the driveway.

My dad and brothers and grandfather and uncle raced over to surround it. Officer Tanglewood, Bud Jefferson, Mr. Henry, and Lou were right behind them—and so were we.

"Come out of the car now with your hands up!" shouted

TRULY, MADLY, SHEEPLY

Officer Tanglewood, probably for the first time ever in his entire career in Pumpkin Falls.

There was a moment's hesitation, and then the car door slowly opened. The person in the hooded robe stepped out, arms in the air.

Aunt True marched over and yanked down the hood. We all stared, open-mouthed. It wasn't Luke Mahoney at all—it was Wesley Thrush, the real-estate developer from West Hartfield!

"Say, that's the feller I gave my keys to," Elmer Farnsworth announced. "Shame on you, you rascal!"

Elmer had said *realtor*, but he meant *real-estate developer*. Why hadn't I thought of that? I could have saved us all this trouble!

You don't mess with Texas, and you don't mess with Lovejoys, either. Especially not with three wrestlers in the family. Wesley tried to make a run for it, but my dad tackled him, and Danny and Hatcher had him pinned in a hold in nothing flat.

Officer Tanglewood read the real-estate developer his rights and shoehorned him into the back of his police car. I gave him a long, hard look as he passed me. There was only one thing to say to a man like Wesley Thrush at a time like this.

"Numpty."

EPILOGUE

In the end, Aunt True and Uncle Rusty didn't press charges beyond criminal trespassing, although Gramps had urged them to charge the real-estate developer with attempted arson. He was hopping mad over the whole thing.

"He ought to be taught a lesson," he'd insisted. "He broke into your house, for Pete's sake! And trying to run you off your property like that—he nearly burned the whole place down."

"I know, Dad. We thought long and hard about it, but Rusty and I have better things to focus on right now besides taking someone to court for some long, drawn-out trial," Aunt True told him. "We have a farm to run and a fixer-upper to fix up and a new business to launch—our Rivercroft Farm products. Plus, we might have something else up our sleeves," she added mysteriously, with a wink at her new husband.

Gramps got even, though, when he called in a favor with

Clark Barque and made sure that the story was covered in great detail.

"That skunk will have a hard time drumming up business in the Pumpkin River Valley after this, that's for sure," said Gramps with satisfaction, after the article ran.

Given that half the town had witnessed his attempts at intimidation, Wesley Thrush was quickly convicted of the misdemeanor trespassing charge. The judge slapped him with a hefty fine and one hundred hours of community service. Officer Tanglewood wasn't such a numpty after all, as it turned out, because he was the one who suggested that there was plenty of opportunity for Wesley to help out down at the sewage treatment plant.

The real-estate developer moved away to Palm Springs shortly after that.

In the end I decided to tell my father about my new lock-picking skills. To my surprise, I wasn't grounded for life—although I had to promise to give up my budding life of crime.

"I understand why you did it," my father told me. "You were protecting your family. And while I don't approve, sometimes it's okay to bend the rules a little."

I gaped at him. Was this Mr. Military talking about relaxing the rules? Life here in Pumpkin Falls really had changed him!

"But not often," he added, which sounded more like him. "Hardly ever, in fact."

The barn itself came through none the worse for wear besides the damaged roof and some scorched paint nearest where the bonfire had been. Both were covered by insurance and soon repaired.

The barn owls hadn't been scared off, either, I was thrilled to learn. Aunt True and Uncle Rusty were enchanted with them, and named them Thelma and Elmer in honor of the farm's previous owners.

Things settled down after that, and we all resumed our regular routines. The sheep were thriving, and Lauren and I rode our bikes out often to visit them when the weather was nice. Beatrice still liked her back rubs, and her fleece was beginning to grow out again. Next spring, there would be lambs.

Aunt True and Uncle Rusty worked at their jobs at the college and the bookshop during the day, and devoted their evenings and weekends to fixing up their new house. We all pitched in to help them, too. Slowly but surely, the diamond in the rough was turning into a beautiful home, just like my mother had predicted.

One afternoon in late November, I was at the bookshop after school with my mother and Aunt True when a delivery truck pulled up.

"It's here!" Aunt True called in excitement when she spotted the label on the half-dozen large boxes that the driver wheeled inside.

"What's here?" asked my mother.

TRULY, MADLY, SHEEPLY

"Come and see."

We scurried over to join her as she grabbed a pair of scissors and opened the first box. A riot of colors spilled out.

"Your new wool!" my mother cried, and Aunt True nodded happily.

The fleece she'd shipped off after the shearing had returned spun into wool—luxuriously soft wool whose shades reminded me of the farm and our beautiful valley. There was the blue of the river, and the green of the pastures, and there was barn red, pumpkin orange, and the soft whites and browns of the sheep themselves.

My gaze settled on a particular shade of blue that reminded me of the paint called "Mermaid" that I'd chosen for the walls of my bedroom back in Texas, a shade that Lola had recently helped me apply to the walls of my bedroom here in Pumpkin Falls.

I reached for it, but before I could grab it Aunt True swooped in and plucked it from the pile. "Ha! I knew you wouldn't be able to resist that one," she said. "Hang on a sec, I'll be right back."

As she ducked back into the office, I glanced over at my mother. I could tell she knew what was up by the way she was smiling at me.

Aunt True returned a moment or two later and handed the skein to me.

"The labels came in!" I said in delight, looking at the tag she'd tied to the blue wool.

She nodded. "Yesterday. But I wanted to wait to show you until the yarn arrived."

The label on the tag was a miniature version of Lola's painting, the one hanging over the mantel in the living room at Rivercroft Farm. There was the familiar red barn, the field dotted with sheep that stretched down to the river, the church steeple; the farmhouse. And of course, the name of the farm arching over all of it.

"Your mother and I gave that wool a special name," said Aunt True.

I hazarded a guess. "Mermaid?"

"Look and see."

I flipped the tag. On the back was printed not MERMAID, however, but TRULY, MADLY, SHEEPLY. I gave my aunt a questioning look.

"It's a bit of a play on words, but we named it in honor of you, Tall Timber," she told me. "As a thank-you for saving the barn. Don't think we haven't noticed the way that everything you've thrown yourself into, you're truly, madly, deeply all-in—friendships, family, your work here at the bookshop, swim team, solving mysteries, everything. You put your whole heart into all of it! Your mother and I think that you're a remarkable young woman, Truly Lovejoy."

My mother's eyes were misty. "Hear, hear!"

"Thanks," I whispered, glad there were no customers around to see me tearing up, too. I gave them both a hug. "I love it."

TRULY, MADLY, SHEEPLY

"I have plans to teach you how to knit a hat with that," my mother added, and laughed when she saw the expression on my face.

The three of us spent the next hour labeling all the skeins and placing samples on the new Rivercroft Farms products display shelf.

"Ella will grumble about competition when she sees it, but she doesn't have a leg to stand on after what she did to Hatcher, and she knows it," said my aunt. "I'll let her stew for a while as punishment, then I'll explain that they're just display samples. I promised she could be the exclusive distributor until I get my website up and running, and I'm planning to send customers across the street to her shop to make their purchases."

"That's very generous, True," my mother told her.

"I keep my promises," my aunt said.

Emilio's mother kept her promise, too, and bought all of Lola's paintings for her gallery. "You have many Italian fans now, Mrs. Lovejoy," she told her. "You must come to Milan sometime—I will host a show in your honor."

I still had an Italian fan, too—Emilio. I'd confided to my mother and Aunt True about my "two-boyfriends problem," as Jasmine called it. Well, potential boyfriends. Emilio flirted with me a lot and Calhoun had been extra nice lately. That counted, right?

My mother told me I didn't need to decide between them because I was too young to be thinking about boys.

Aunt True laughed when she heard that. "Have you completely forgotten what it's like to be thirteen, Dinah?" She turned to me. "Listen to your heart, Tall Timber. It will never steer you wrong."

I liked her advice better, and I was listening with all my might.

Autumn flew by. Gramps and Lola stayed for Thanksgiving, but by early December, it was almost time for them to go back to Africa. I was going to miss them terribly, but we knew they'd be home again—permanently, this time—when their tour of duty with the Peace Corps was over.

"You can come live with Rusty and me, of course," Aunt True told them one Saturday afternoon when we were all at the farm, helping them strip the wallpaper from one of the upstairs bedrooms.

"Not on your life," said Lola. "That would cramp your style big-time." I saw her exchange a glance with my grandfather, and it occurred to me that maybe she meant it would cramp their style. "How about we take over the apartment above the bookstore instead?"

My aunt stared at her, open-mouthed. "It's the size of a walnut shell, Mother! You can't be serious."

"Never been more serious in my life," my grandmother replied.

"But where will you put all your stuff?"

TRULY, MADLY, SHEEPLY

"Your father and I have been talking it over, and at our stage of life, we don't want to have to look after a lot of 'stuff' anymore. Houses, furniture, all of it. We feel even more strongly about this after spending time in Namibia. Life is about experiences and spending time with the people you love, not about things. We've spent the last year living in two rooms and we've never been happier." She smiled at my grandfather. "Isn't that right, Walt?"

Gramps reached for her hand and lifted it to his lips, gallantly kissing her paint-spattered knuckles. "Absolutely. The apartment will suit us just fine. Living above the shop! What could be more romantic? It will be like we're newlyweds all over again."

Pumpkin Falls wasn't finished with newlyweds, as it turned out. Right before my grandparents were due to fly back to Africa, Belinda and Augustus eloped to Las Vegas.

"Nothing beats Vegas, baby!" said Augustus, when they walked into the bookshop for the huge party we threw for them on the evening they returned. "Chapel of Love!"

Lou made the wedding cake, complete with purple frosting. Hatcher and Danny were the DJs and played all of Belinda's favorites—Elvis, the Beach Boys, the Beatles. Belinda gave out kittens as party favors.

"At this rate, we'll be renting the bookshop out regularly as a wedding venue," my father grumbled as he ladled out punch. It was purple, too.

"Now there's an idea," said Aunt True, her eyes lighting up, and he groaned.

Augustus breezed by just then for a refill.

"So where will you two lovebirds be living?" asked Gramps.

Augustus had a sprawling supermodern house on the ridge near Lovejoy Mountain. Belinda had a Victorian at the end of our street.

"We're combining our households," said Augustus, taking a sip of punch. The stain it left on his lips matched his purple cape. "I'm selling my house and plan to build a writing studio out in Belinda's backyard." He leaned in close and gave us a wink, then whispered, "Kitten-free."

Not for long, I thought, knowing Belinda.

There was one more piece of good news that evening.

"We were going to wait a bit to tell everyone," Aunt True announced, after the party had wound down and only our family and a handful of close friends were left. "But we decided there's no time like the present. Rusty and I are expecting a baby!"

"A honeymoon baby," said Uncle Rusty, oversharing. "Skye if it's a girl, Lewis if it's a boy. In honor of our trip to Scotland."

We all crowded around to hug and congratulate them.

"I hope it's a boy," said Lou, wringing my uncle's hand. "I can pretend he's my namesake."

TRULY, MADLY, SHEEPLY

I glanced down at the amethyst ring on my hand that had belonged to my own namesake, the original Truly. Somehow I had a feeling she'd be thrilled with this news. Another Lovejoy would soon be joining our family and carrying on our family traditions.

Maybe Aunt True and I could even introduce him or her to Abracadabra Day.

I couldn't believe how much things had changed in the past year. My dad's injury and recovery. Trading our old life in Texas for a new one here in New Hampshire. All the new friends I'd made and new adventures I'd had.

Pumpkin Falls would never have been my first choice as a place to live.

But now?

Now, I wouldn't trade it for anything.

MISS MARPLE'S PICKS

Alice in Wonderland by Lewis Carroll
Charlotte's Web by E. B. White
Harry Potter and the Sorcerer's Stone by J. K. Rowling
Mr. Mysterious & Company by Sid Fleischman
Much Ado About Nothing by William Shakespeare
Redwall by Brian Jacques
"The Cask of Amontillado" by Edgar Allan Poe
The Lion, the Witch and the Wardrobe by C. S. Lewis
The Lord of the Rings by J. R. R. Tolkien

GRANDMA GIFFORD'S APPLE FRITTER CAKE

Filling:

- 1/2 c. dark brown sugar, packed
- 1 tsp. apple pie spice*
- 1/4 tsp. nutmeg (freshly grated, if possible)
- 1 tsp. all-purpose flour
- 1 tsp. boiled cider**
- 3-1/2–4 c. peeled and chopped apples

Cake:

- 2-1/4 c. all-purpose flour
- 2-1/2 tsp. baking powder
- 3/4 c. sugar
- 1 tsp. salt
- 1/4 tsp. apple pie spice
- 12 T. unsalted butter, at room temperature
- 3 large eggs, at room temperature
- 2 tsp. vanilla
- 1 T. boiled cider**
- 3/4 c. buttermilk

Glaze:

    3/4 c. confectioner's sugar, or amount needed to achieve desired consistency
    2 T. milk
    1/2 tsp. vanilla

- Preheat oven to 350 degrees. Grease an 8" square cake pan.

- Filling: Peel and dice the apples; set aside. Combine brown sugar, apple pie spice, nutmeg, and teaspoon of flour in a medium bowl and set aside.

- Cake: In a large bowl, combine flour, baking powder, sugar, salt, and nutmeg. Add butter and mix. Beat in eggs one at a time. Add vanilla and buttermilk and mix briefly, until all ingredients liquids are absorbed.

- Assemble the filling by adding apples and boiled cider to the brown sugar ingredients previously set aside. Stir. Assemble cake by spreading half the batter into prepared pan, then top it with half of the filling. Add another layer of cake batter, and top with the rest of the filling.

- Bake for about an hour, until a knife inserted into the cake comes out clean. Let it cool for about thirty minutes before glazing.

- Glaze: Combine ingredients to desired thickness, and either drizzle over the cake or frost it.

Enjoy!

*If you don't have apple pie spice, you can make your own by combining 3 T. of cinnamon with 2 tsp. each of ground nutmeg and allspice. If you want to get fancy, you can also add a bit of ginger and cardamom.

*You can buy boiled cider at specialty shops, but it's easy to make your own too. Just simmer real apple cider (not apple juice) until it thickens to the consistency of honey. This can take a while—you'll have to be patient! And in a pinch you can substitute regular apple cider for boiled cider in this recipe. But boiled cider is yummier.